An Alien Landscape

■ EUAN MCALLEN ■

authorHOUSE®

AuthorHouse™ UK Ltd.
500 Avebury Boulevard
Central Milton Keynes, MK9 2BE
www.authorhouse.co.uk
Phone: 08001974150

First published by AuthorHouse 3/6/2009

ISBN: 978-1-4389-5245-1 (sc)

Printed in the United States of America
Bloomington, Indiana

This book is printed on acid-free paper.

Chapter One

Log Entry

I have arrived. This is my first log entry.

I have landed on a male of the species and have taken appropriate steps to remain attached to suitable parts of its brain. It suspects nothing. I have made a fleeting examination of the subject and can report the following:

a) The male is currently highly charged.

b) The emotions are mixed and reflect a confused, possibly aggressive state of mind. That said boredom is a major constituent.

c) Physically it is in good health and its core components are attached to a strong resilient frame.

d) With reference to point a) the body temperature seems unusually high, and some unnatural substances have infiltrated the system. This state of affairs may be linked to the communal drinking ritual in which the subject is presently engaged. I will investigate.

The subject is currently located in a public meeting place. I have yet to see its private dwelling. On first impressions this establishment is quite remarkable: the species – of which I think there are only the two sexes – is tightly packed together, in an atmosphere heavily polluted with waste material, and a temperature profile inconsistent with my earlier measurements. Despite this the communication flows are extraordinary. They are all intense, and operate at a furious pace, and there are so many that they constantly crash into each other. This causes many to terminate abruptly and others to start up instantly, possibly to take their place intentionally. Truly this place is highly charged.

In the main this crowd shares one common characteristic: all are greatly excited; all are highly emotive. The exceptions to this may be worth exploring further.

This is not what I expected. A very peculiar place. But it is only the start.

✦ ✦ ✦

Clarence did a double take. "Where's that Fiona woman gone?"

The man who had been speaking loudly and with self-induced passion stopped abruptly. "What do you mean where's 'that Fiona' gone?"

Clarence was forced to beg. "Well where is she?"

"Ladies. Where d'you think?" complained Harold. "Have you been listening to a word I've been saying?"

"Yes."

"What did I just say then?"

"Something about stupid exams for seven year olds" replied Clarence, sure of himself.

"No, after that."

The other drinkers sensed another fallout between Clarence and Harold. One coughed. Another stared at her glass, and scratched. She could not cope with violence on any level. Her father was a priest and her mother had a nasty temper.

Clarence glanced down at his watch. He had had enough for one week. "Sorry I have to go."

With that he emptied his glass of beer and stood up, and swayed, and nearly choked on cigarette smoke. He wanted to fart – but wrong place. He enjoyed farting in bed, just to annoy Tracey. It was his way of addressing the balance. Give it up he told himself. Battle did not take place and Ramsey, the PE teacher was disappointed.

Outside the pub Clarence began to chant.

'I will not drink tonight. I will not drink. I have no need for more drink.'

Enough said. He headed off home.

Unfortunately his bus stop stood within sight of his local off-licence, and he had to walk past it. He stopped: there was no beer in the flat, and probably no food. No matter. He glanced through the window and past the stacks of sale price beer and on towards the girl serving. She had served him many times before – at least three times. Now it was time to flirt, presume a connection. Perhaps she lived locally. He was still good looking. And he had a brain. It was time to buy some beer.

He entered the premises like a surgeon – the chief surgeon – going into the operating theatre, else the prime minister entering Parliament: either way as the centre of attention. She didn't look up. No matter.

He perused the bottles of red wine – French and Italian shelves only – and engineered the impression that he was making a considered choice. He knew how to act. It was part of his job, a necessity. The girl looked up once then, totally disinterested, returned to the headline story of her local newspaper.

Clarence didn't pick out a bottle. He was not much of a wine drinker. For him the concept was largely ceremonial: take it to dinner parties; keep

Tracey happy. Instead he satisfied his thirst with an eight pack of Belgian lager and for experimental reasons two bottles of real 'real ale' – the type given crazy names.

The girl served him with more than a flicker of recognition – but not much more – and did not bother to raise a smile. She shrugged off his attempt at light conversation. It was late. She was tired. He was a prat.

'Sod you then' he told himself and instead turned his attention to the packets of cigarettes on display. 'I must give it up' he told himself. 'I must give it up.'

Sod it. "And a packet of Benson And Hedges" he barked.

He threw a packet of 20 filter tip into the ring with a pompous packet of crisps and waited for his change while the girl in turn avoided looking him in the eye. He didn't say please. He didn't say thank you. She didn't say good evening. She didn't say good night. Their relationship had crashed before it had even left the garage.

Things continued to go down hill. When he got home he had to have a kebab after his first beer even though he was not drunk. The crisps, exotically name but much the same as always, were to blame. They had woken up his stomach and now it clamoured for food.

The kebab was the easy way out. It required only a phone call – local rates – and as near as damn it the exact fee as the man who dropped it off never ever had the correct change. Exact change was a constant battle: Clarence was fed up with being taken for a ride.

The second beer was as good as the first. The stuff on TV was crap. The kebab was spot on, a joyous event, and he had paid to within 10p of the bill. As expected the man could not give him 10p in change. The meat was lovely and greasy, the lettuce cool and crisp, and the chilli sauce was rocket fuel - the evening's challenge. The TV continued to belt out crap into his face but Clarence did not, dared not, switch it off. The silence would be deafening. He was stuck to it like a fly stuck to flypaper. Snuggled up deep within the recess of his armchair, and clutching a beer to his bosom, Clarence rocked in the cradle as the late night, third rate magazine show rolled over him.

With the TV on and a beer in his hand and a kebab down his throat Clarence managed to keep life at bay: Tracey and work in particular. It was a good feeling. It was a noble cause. He asked for nothing and he had nothing to give. The equation was solved. Some might call it give and take. He switched channels and found a film involving sex just starting. And the lodger was nowhere to be seen. Now he was in paradise.

Saturday.

No alarm call, just a creeping realisation that he was more awake than asleep. But it was a tenuous definition 'awake' and defining the difference with respect to 'asleep' could baffle the best. Sunlight streaming in through the window demanded that Clarence 'awake'. It dragged him screaming from his bed.

His head really really hurt. It thumped to a rhythm not of his making. It depressed the human spirit. Clarence had been here before. He knew the score. He knew he should have drunk lots of water before crashing into bed but the little bit of his brain which could have prompted the rest of it to take preventative measures just couldn't be arsed.

He navigated his way slowly to the bathroom. The bathroom was the pits. It was a man's bathroom, and had been for far too long. Only extreme circumstances would force any civilized woman to use it. Most of the time Tracey was a civilized woman and had been forced to use it on many occasions. She refused to clean it. So he didn't bother. Let the lodger do his dirty work.

A pile of dirty washing awaited him: being a week's worth topped up by a bank holiday it had reached critical mass. The underpants and the socks were the worse culprits. The offences they were committing, in real time, with regards to the environment, human suffering, and abuse of human rights many might argue demanded a full scale investigation and subsequent criminal charges under international law.

Within a few feet of said pile the laws of human decency were being twisted and skewed in much the same way that gravity is distorted by a heavy mass. Approach the pile of dirty washing - 'pile of crap' some might say – and time slowed. Clarence stepped over it, trying not to give a toss, and failing. (Deep down he knew he had to give a toss as he was running out of clothes.)

He splashed lukewarm water on his face. Good start. He began to brush his teeth but immediately gave up. The sensation of toothbrush scraping against teeth and gums combined with the taste of the paste proved too much to bear. No go straight to the coffee, the fountain of all wisdom.

Backing out of the bathroom in an orderly retreat he picked his dressing gown up off the floor and slipped it on. He felt better for it, like a knight 'suited up'. He headed for the kitchen, slowly, with stealth, as if it wasn't his kitchen in his flat. (It was and it was.)

The kitchen was also a dumping ground: a council skip for organic waste material clinging to crockery, cooking utensils, and other items of food transportation. Here cells divided and mutated and multiplied with evil intent. They took no prisoners. You entered the kitchen at your peril. Those of a sensitive disposition, or suffering health problems were strongly advised to keep out.

There was an ancient frying pan, possibly iron age, which, never having been properly washed and scrubbed, contained a deep pool of congealed fat – fat produced by bacon and the worse kind of sausages. It belonged in a museum, behind barbed wire, or in a hospital isolation ward, or in a maximum security prison, or in Hell.

Clarence would never wash it up now. It was beyond redemption, and the volume of washing up liquid required made such a task economically unviable. One day he would throw it away. Unfortunately it had been a 'flat warming' present from his mother and that day would never come.

As if in sympathy with the bathroom, or collusion, there was a pile of dirty plates, one for every day of the week, and more. Clarence ignored it all and looked for a clean mug. Bingo! He found his favourite: the chipped mug he had adopted at uni. They had been through a lot together his bruised brain boasted.

The mug required hot water. Clarence filled the kettle and switched it on. The mug of coffee required just that: coffee. He went to the cupboard in which it normally lived. It wasn't there. Someone had moved it again. Probably Tracey. He found it in the bread bin. Bread bin? Why put it in the bread bin?

Then there was the question of sugar. He was trying to give up sugar but sugar was staring him in the face. He would have sugar in his coffee. He had earned it.

Somehow the components all came together and on time, and a hot mug of coffee with sugar no milk was born. Clarence returned to the living room. It was his favourite place. Here he felt in command. Here were his books and CD's. He slumped into his leather armchair and stared out of the window. He switched off.

A few minutes passed. Clarence opened his eyes. He was back in the real world. The view from the window had not changed. Time was flowing again at its normal fixed pace of one second per second. He had a wonderful view. It was a busy street: lots to see; much to comment upon; and you were never noticed. Clarence was now the secret observer: watching all; deliberating; passing judgement. He sucked enjoyment from watching those who did not know they were being watched. It was one of his greatest kicks. And it didn't cost a penny.

Against his will Clarence was forced to close his eyes. A struggle of will ensued. Clarence opened his eyes. They were still there, still working. He stared out at the world at his feet. He scratched his balls. They were still there, still willing to perform. He picked his nose. He gave up again and closed his eyes again. Time slowed. Reality checked. Dreams, released, circulated, wishing to complete while the hurt inside his head continued. But no regrets. No disaster.

Clarence opened his eyes. The dirty laundry vaguely pierced his consciousness and drew his attention before it was drawn to greater things: to a good looking woman across the street. She had just come into view and was walking very fast, like there was no tomorrow. A fitness fanatic concluded Clarence. Club member. Back to the laundry: Clarence couldn't understand why he always let it become a liability. Why let the pile grow unchecked? He had to get his washing into the machine pronto, and get it dry by Monday. Back to the fitness fanatic. She had stopped to answer her mobile. Boyfriend checking up?

Clarence managed to down more coffee before again, without warning, his eyes slammed shut. A small dog pulling its old lady along by its lead joined the cast. It was being followed by a young man in a baseball cap. He was catching them up fast. Clarence reawoke, his ability to stay awake for serious lengths of time marginally improved. But it would win him no medals.

He stared out at the world. The little dog was the other side of the young woman. The young woman shouted down the phone.

"Well kick him up the arse."

The old lady stopped suddenly and turned. "What did you say?"

The dog, already on his way to Mandaley, was yanked backed on the lead and almost garrotted. He had been her pride and joy ever since her husband had inconveniently fallen asleep in the bath and died on her. His suit was still at the dry cleaners. She had refused to pay the bill.

The young woman turned and spat back her reply. "What do you mean 'what did I say'?"

The old woman delivered her words of conversation as if addressing someone who had not passed the eleven plus and was never going to. "Did you say kick him up the you know what?"

The young woman was confused. "Up the arse? Yes. Where else would you kick him?"

The old lady drew her rusty old sword. "Why kick him? He hasn't done anything wrong."

Her victim developed a sneer around the nostril region. "How the hell do you know!"

Baseball cap man cut in. "That's right you tell her. You tell her."

He had caught them up and heard everything and he was pissing himself.

The woman challenged him with her special look. The man continued to grin. The old lady glared at them both. Kids should show more respect. Husbands should die sooner.

The two pound coin hit the ground hard.

"I was on my mobile," the woman explained. She raised it high for the jury to see.

The old lady grunted and carried on walking, overtaking her dog who was seriously considering having a crap. He never got the chance. He was dragged away.

"Do you live round here?" baseball cap man enquired.

"Fuck off," replied the woman.

Fair enough. And so he did, with grace, crossing the road to avoid the deaf old maid with the pooch. Clarence wanted to take notes.

Coffee finished Clarence decided to shake himself awake with a hot shower. It proved to be a satisfying experience. Dry and fully dressed he felt like a civilized man. He sat on the bed. He laid back on the bed. He nodded off. He woke up, a changed man.

Foods levels having reached critical Clarence vowed to visit the local supermarket. He was reassured by an army of memory cells that it was only a short walk away. He would allow his legs to take the chance. He pulled back the front door and stepped outside into fresh air. The sun was smiling. Super clean, high specification cars were gleaming, begging to be driven at speed, and forever depreciating. As city sights go it was almost beautiful.

Clarence began to walk, his headache teasing. He found the supermarket where it had always been, on the side of the road, just downstream of a big plastic rubbish bin which was the exclusive preserve of external dog shit. Poetic symmetry? thought Clarence. No, he replied.

The deputy manager stuck on duty behind the spirits counter made a vague gesture of recognition. Clarence ignored him. He had it firmly stuck in his mind that the man was gay – a conclusion drawn from evidence collected over previous encounters. Clarence had nothing against gay men, he just didn't want to make their acquaintance. Shagging women was his thing. And getting pissed, before or afterwards, or both.

The supermarket was a confusing place. There was food everywhere, of all types. Every time it left Clarence bewildered, and unable to focus. To think about what food to buy meant having to think about how to cook it. Easy or hard? Easy cooking normally involved food, usually pre-prepared, which was easy to cook or heat up, and so was probably not that healthy. Healthy food involved fresh food: lots of different types of fresh food which had to be brought together in a way that, when served up, was edible. Decisions decisions decisions. And Tracey, the current woman of importance in his life, wasn't there to offer advice, or cook it.

Energy reserves plummeting Clarence rapidly tired as he wandered up and down the aisles. The head began to hurt more and soon he was shopping in a daze. At times he even nodded off despite being still awake.

The fish counter was in sight. Clarence strode over to it, masterfully.

His favourite mantra resurfaced: 'I'm no sad bachelor. I can cook'. He could tidy up. He could smile at babies. They could smile back. He could use a Hoover. And to balance the score: he was a happy man in charge of his own destiny. He could keep the lid on a pack of wild, mixed up schoolboys with nothing more than power of presence and personality. He could drink. He could smoke. He could make mad passionate love to beautiful women (if given the chance). He could shag other women and make them feel good. He could tell his mum and dad to let it be. He could tell his sister to shut up. But she never would.

Behind the fish counter stood a fresh faced pretty young thing. Clarence had never seen her before. New Saturday help perhaps. She beamed with customer care and attention, and in order to stay sane nurtured her sarcasm.

Though I have never met you, and though we have never exchanged a single word, my only purpose in life, my only raison d'etre, my only sense of fulfilment comes from serving you, making you happy with some purchase of fresh fish, or crab, or some other dead creature dredged from the depths of the sea by a crusty sailor bearing a large mortgage and a bitter revulsion towards holiday homes and government departments and all things EEC.

Clarence stared down in amazement at all the wonderful shapes and colours on display. It could have been in a trendy 'modern art' exhibition. It wasn't but it still felt good to look at. Out of the blue, as if breaking free from imprisonment by the baggage of accumulated prejudices, the clear thought struck him, like the tip of a spear, that this was what great painters lived and breathed for. Picasso suddenly made total sense and Clarence was very jealous.

Finally the pretty young thing caved in and spoke first. Her voice was soft, low-key. It was the voice of an angel. Clarence looked up and the silly part of him, the uncontrollable youth still alive inside, went doo-lally. The opposite part of him, the older part still at the controls, said give it a rest. There's Tracey you bastard.

"Can I help?"

"Just looking," Clarence replied, and turned to go.

But no! No! No! No pizza today or tomorrow! Pull back from the edge of total corruption. Say no to bloody useful convenience food. How you eat is how you live. Or something like that. Clarence told himself all this in seconds. He pulled back and looked down at the offers on show from the oceans of the world. He pointed indiscriminately, then looked back up at the girl for inspiration. She was ever so sweet, like a chocolate bar. He wanted to lick her. She could bear his children if only she'd let him. The old man tut-tutting away inside kicked the youth back down.

Clarence looked back down at the object which had caught his attention. "How do I cook that?"

She probably had a boyfriend the youth remarked, now a sore loser – beautiful but empty-headed. The old man said shut it.

The pretty young thing didn't look down. She stared him straight in the face, as she had been trained to, to focus the customer on the question.

"Cook what?"

"That pink thing there," Clarence replied. Then he noticed the little plastic notice board shouting out its name and price. "I mean the tuna steak."

She shrugged. "The easiest thing is stick it under the grill."

"Ah," replied Clarence, like a professor having received an above average answer from a favourite female student.

Grill it. Easy. But then the follow up. He would have to cook something to go with it. Salad? No salad was too cold, too complicated. Mashed potato? He loathed mash potato. Incorrect: he loathed making it. He hated powdered mash and he wasn't prepared to bugger around with real potatoes. Leave all that to Tracey. Tracey! Perhaps she would invite him round tonight and cook. Perhaps he could hold on 'till then.

No! shouted his stomach. No way. Food. Food. Food. Get me food. Something to fry. I need grease. Bacon. Clarence was hit by the word 'bacon'. The very sound of the word had a poetic weight which exceeded 'tuna steak' by half.

The old man wanted to head to the bacon counter but the youth, now recovered, wanted to talk to the girl more. Clarence smiled, intentionally bashful.

"How on earth do I cook that?" he exclaimed, pointing at a whole lobster.

The youth had her in the palm of his hand. Don't be so stupid commented the old man over his shoulder. He had seen it all before, and more. Clarence was being steered in so many different directions by unknown forces that it began to hurt his head. But he soldiered on. Man that he was.

Pretty young thing spoke. "You just boil it I believe." It was still the voice of an angel totally committed to the concept of customer care.

A year or two later pretty young thing would be offered a job and a fast-track career by the supermarket chain. She would politely decline, and lie to her girlfriends over a drink that she had told them to piss off. But that would be then and this was now.

Clarence went for the sympathy vote. "For how long?"

Pretty young thing shrugged again. "Twenty minutes?"

"Sounds good."

Why are you telling me this she thought. Just bloody buy something or piss off.

Clarence stood silent in open contemplation while the pretty young thing stood desperate for another member of Joe public to approach so she could serve them and ignore him. She was saved by a lady, the wrong side of middle-aged, who conducted her two business transactions with focus and speed. She fussed only slightly over the required weight.

Clarence was pushed to one side and left far behind. He gave up, tired out. He headed for the shelves where the sealed packets of bacon sat. Salvation. No fear of headache. Bacon equalled fried food. Fried food would settle the stomach. Back to the same old buying habits: bacon, eggs, baked beans. He toyed slightly with the idea of buying fresh vegetables. 'God meant his children to eat vegetables' said the cynic in Clarence. But Clarence did not believe in god, so no fresh vegetables. As a compromise he chucked a tin of spinach into the basket, then a second. He had discovered spinach. Finally bread. He always had to have bread, and always stick shaped. Milk followed. Finally a four pack. On his way to the checkout he grabbed some detergent, just in case.

Applying strict mathematical analysis of queue length versus goods piled up versus outstanding baskets versus trolleys versus speed of cashier versus age of customers he found the queue with the shortest escape time. As always it was the shortest queue. There he queued patiently and studied those around him.

The woman in front waiting behind a man looked glum, impatient: so close yet so far to go; and a mother to feed. The man in her way radiated the body language of a man who didn't give a damn any more. Where he was, where he had been, where he was going, what he would be eating next: none of these questions mattered now. His arms were folded to death and his eyes ached as they fixed on nothing. He didn't want to be in this place Clarence surmised. Clarence wondered if he was dead.

In another queue an old woman, next to be served, pushed her purse out in front her, more than ready to pay. She knew exactly what loose change she carried about her person. In the war she had worked the land she often boasted.

There was a young mother, with a big baby in a basket. She was in love with its little face. It spoke no words but communication was total. Clarence wanted his child to be like that. But he didn't want to change nappies.

Home.

Peace and Quiet it said on the label.

School papers to mark. Sod them.

Clarence settled down, fighting the urge to open a can. He closed his eyes and nodded off. Dream world returned for awhile. He opened his eyes, a new man, like last time. The word 'dedication' was drummed home inside his head. He found a pile of student papers and stared at them. Interesting. The phone rang. It was Tracey. Had he ordered the euros? Clarence panicked. No memories. He played it safe.

"Yes."

Tracey carried on talking without coming up for air and his eyes began to glaze over. This was a woman speaking he reminded himself. Men and women: they were different. Another 'yes' was required somewhere about now.

"Yes."

Satisfied Tracey ended the conversation and put the phone down. Also satisfied, Clarence fell asleep in the armchair.

Log Entry

My host is called Clarence. Its dwelling is of limited size and suffers a high degree of disorder. The treatment and disposal of organic waste appears, at first sight, to be a problem – though I must be careful not to jump to conclusions. There is however an issue of hygiene. It appears to live alone and have no mate.

The subject purchases food from a large distribution centre and though this is presumably a regular event in its domestic routine I notice it suffers a substantial degree of anxiety and indecision leading up to the event. This emotional state intensifies during the act of food selection then suddenly evaporates at point of purchase. This I find strange as the species is a sophisticated member of the planet's indigenous animal kingdom and as such a natural hunter-gatherer. It may be that there is some hidden danger associated with these places – I must follow up. That said it must also be noted that the actual point of purchase affects the species in different ways. I observed many different emotional states among the crowd: impatience; disinterest; keenness; compliance; resignation; wishful thinking; total apathy. I suspect that as a general rule, queuing is something these animals detest – a perfect example of emotion overwhelming logic as the concept of queuing provides for fairness and order.

Younger females attract the attention of my host and stimulate various areas of its brain. I presume this is because it has no mate. However it is odd that this contact, however fleeting and unproductive, appears to bring these parts of the brain into conflict. At such moments I am unsure if I should intervene, or by how much. I will need to investigate further the moral framework which drives this beast – being the superior, thinking creature on this planet I assume it has one.

Judging by the variety and volume of food on offer in these places I assume self-regulation of food intake must be a constant pre-occupation when quality food, conveniently packaged, is widely available without restriction. Neither is cost an issue as the price range of any one specific product is substantial. This presumably is to cater for those who wish to pay more than necessary – and be seen to be paying more I suspect, judging by the signals I picked up at the point of payment. The preservation and continuance of self-esteem and the constant need to foster feelings of superiority are natural consequences of a survival strategy in a socially and technologically advanced society.

One object in the home dominates: the television set, also known as the 'box'. This is a device which receives colour pictures and sound transmitted as radio waves – rather backward by our standards but adequate for the job. It has pride of place this 'box' as when my host turns it on it becomes almost mesmerised. Selective areas of the brain are focused upon the images which stream out of it – but at a cost as many other parts of the brain shut down.

The device can switch wavelength at the touch of a button convenient located on a remote control device, and so pick up any number of parallel transmissions, each supplying a continuous stream of broadcasts. My host does not have to leave his chair.

The news and education programs are relatively easy to identify: they have a distinct style of delivery – they talk 'into your face'. It is as if the presenter knows you are present and engages on a one to one basis. My host tends to avoid these.

Other programs are designed to entertain through a mix of fact and fiction. Separating fact from fiction is no easy thing – at times impossible. Some are clearly reporting the recreational activities of the society at large - sport in particular – and often in real time. Others are obviously pure fantasy, science fiction being the easiest to spot. There are however a number which are extremely difficult to categorize. For example my host sat and watched a program which simply showed a number of apparently very ordinary people sitting in a room talking at random about nothing of any consequence. After a few minutes I noticed that he was torn between watching this and switching it off, or over.

At one point I took control (partially to relieve my host of his stress) and wandered through the transmission channels at random. The quality varied and on the whole was poor. This surprises me. If these devices are widespread, and the audiences large, I would have expected something much better, especially as this is an advanced civilization. That said it could be that some of the programs are specially designed to send its audience to sleep, to help them stop thinking so to speak. A useful alternative to drugs I suppose and an approach worth exploring back home.

As I said there are many channels dedicated solely to sporting events: the competitive spirit has seemingly never diminished during the evolution of this species – quite the contrary it appears to have intensified. This beast, being perfectly designed for balanced manoeuvrability, loves to run and jump and hit fast moving objects either directly by use of its key appendages (two hands at the end of two arms and two feet at the end of two legs) or via a tool specifically designed to improve the speed and accuracy of the 'hit'.

Competitive games operate to a strict set of rules and are designed both around one to one confrontations and team engagements. The crowds these events attract are massive, as is the passion they generate. Team rivalry is reflected in the makeup of the crowd. Some of these sports are ruthlessly executed by the players, as the need to win at any cost is paramount. Perhaps these events are an emotional substitute for war.

I notice in the game of 'football' (a mainstream sport which attracts the largest and most vocal crowds) that a good haircut is a prerequisite for successful players – the two seem to go together.

Log Entry

As my host could not keep awake in the afternoon I decided to visit the commercial centre then make a more extended sweep of the local area.

Frequently I passed by individuals walking and simultaneously talking or shouting into a small handheld communication device. They were engaged in conversation with some other person presumably equally equipped. I could not help but overhear some conversations. One was an intimate exchange (conducted at my end by a female) on the status of an emotionally intense relationship with a third party male. Issues requiring urgent address and resolution was the subject of another, this time heated and threatening exchange. One young man's conversation was unfocused, lacking in substance, yet despite that highly charged and energised. Humans definitely need to talk a lot. Is it a biological necessity that the vocal equipment be constantly exercised? If it lies unused for long periods does it cease to function or become unreliable?

I came upon (and not for the first time) a mature man linked by a long length of metal chain to a small four-legged creature. The two moved along at speed, as one, in an almost symbiotic relationship. The pace was set by the small creature, in a display of fierce concentration and determination to reach some predetermined destination. This was in contrast to the man who showed little or no enthusiasm for wherever they were headed. It could be that he was being forced against his will to participate – though this does not stand up to argument as he could break the connection any time he wished.

I interrupted the man and requested from him - as politely as possible - information about the creature: name, evolutionary background, number of breeds etc. He immediately declined and moved on in a hurry, with a sudden onset of anxiety. The impatience of the creature and its hostility towards me may have had something to do with this. Later I tapped into my host's vast reservoir of trapped memories to learn that this four legged creature was a 'dog'.

The trading centre, local to my host's place of residence is large and purpose-built: designed to concentrate in one place an enormous range of goods and services for the purposes of public acquisition. As such the centre attracts a large crowd. All manner of people can be seen moving through this place: young, old, tall, short, fat, slim. Many different ethnic groups converge and interact. Social barriers and distinctions are non-existent. Is such a state of affairs peculiar just to these places? Negotiating one's way around is sometimes a challenge as people move at different speeds, coalesce into larger bodies, and are generally not alert to the movements of others around them. Again the activity of constant talking takes highest priority. At every turn there are invitations, sometimes subliminal, urging the audience to buy their particular product or service, and nobody else's, else suffer the consequences (of some danger undefined).

The number of variations available for any one specific item is remarkable, perhaps overwhelming. Factors for this include colour, texture and pattern, functional scope, quality of build materials, age (sometimes the lack of age is considered detrimental), and perhaps, surprisingly, nothing more than origin and name of manufacturer. With so much choice the process of decision-making must be a long arduous process with a significant chance of error. Some establishments I noticed left the customer looking tired, miserable, dissatisfied. Others left them just confused. To aid in the process of decision making many individuals were on hand, some freely making suggestive prompts, others handing out leaflets to all those who passed by.

Humans of intermediate physical development between post puberty and fully mature adulthood are recognised as a special case in this society, and given the label 'teenager'. The fast body changes on-going in this age group can result in temporary mental deficiencies, temporary facial disfigurement, loss of communication skills (perhaps temporary, perhaps permanent) both within and outside their group, and perhaps above all a sudden and strong disengagement with, and aversion to, social values and constraints which have been imposed upon them up to this point. To be specific this means a disassociation from, and confrontation with, their parents. This is unique behaviour which I have never previously observed.

I saw them gathered in small groups. They were openly hostile if I approached and tried to engage in dialogue. Either they talk very little, and only when pushed, or they talk incessantly, without interruption. There is no middle ground. The language they use is highly specialized: though disjointed and unstructured it manages to communicate with maximum effect and deliver immediate emotional feedback.

Their style of dress varies but is always distinctive: a conscious effort I believe to distinguish themselves from the other age groups. This is not behaviour unique to them. The top end of the age range also distinguish themselves with a dress code which is purposely low-key, near monochrome, and designed to deflect interest.

When these 'teenagers' huddle together two extremes of behaviour become apparent. Either their nervous systems become highly charged and a high state of agitation takes over or they become over-relaxed and suffer low-energy levels such that they physically and mentally stagnate, unable or unwilling to pro-actively engage with others within the group. It appears that they have hit an age when they suddenly stop thinking and get bored easily, or frustrated over the tiniest thing - and so quickly.

Like others beyond their age group they also engage in one-to-one communication via handheld radio transmission devices, else listen intently to the output of one-way only devices. In both cases there is a high level of concentration and a ferocity I have not yet observed outside their age range.

Along with dress wear, hair management is also a pre-occupation, and a distinct feature of this age group. Again the approach is one of two extremes:

1) do nothing, let the hair follow its natural course and flourish accordingly
2) apply features of colour and shape which are eye-catching: sometimes as one unified composition; other times in fragmented component parts designed to clash

The middle range age – those bearing the full burden of family responsibility and the first signs of the aging process - appear to be the most bewildered, the most engaged in the search for the basic provisions required for survival. They are always the most tired, the least relaxed, the ones with the fullest agenda but the least amount of time in which to action it. Their ability to cope is stretched to the limit where continuous stewardship of their small, pre-pubescent offspring is required. In family units of two parents (one per sex) and two plus offspring tensions between adults are particularly high. Personal engagement is often vitriolic, ill-tempered, unfocused and illogical else subdued, unexpressive, detached and pessimistic as if neither party has any desire to be where they are or do what they are doing. Their search for goods and services which meet their needs at an acceptable cost is a fraught drawn out affair.

I noticed a recurring activity amongst a small percentage of the population, especially amongst those concentrated together in places which catered for the public consumption of liquids. It consisted of burning a tube filled with some combustible material and inhaling the smoke into (I presume) that part of the body designed for breathing in air. The smoke was then discharged via the breathing tubes associated with the face. The reason for participating in this is unclear. It may be a communal activity - some kind of group therapy – or it may simply bring health benefits.

I came across a large strip of open, undeveloped land – land left in the main to natural growth. In it individuals, couples and family units passed time by pursuing various activities, most of them without any obvious purpose or end-product. For example a small male would kick a small spherical object towards its male parent with its foot who would then kick it back, with his foot. This continued ad infinitum.

Another small child spent a torturous time negotiating its way up a structure consisting of nothing more than interlocking poles while its parent looked on bored. Once it reached the top it looked around then realised the only thing to do was to go back down the way it had come up.

While watching the very young at play I was fascinated in how like and unlike adults they could be depending upon circumstance and stimulation. In their interactions they display all the core human traits seen in adults – envy, anger, self-interest, competitiveness – but without the additional masking or self-consciousness brought on in adults by social awareness or the wish for social inclusion.

My observations had to stop when I was approached by a man and a woman in a high state of anxiety. They were very aggressive and threatened violence. They ordered me in no uncertain terms to stop looking at their children. I smiled and introduced myself as 'Clarence' but to no avail. Again I was told to 'piss off'. This is a popular expression.

The competitive spirit I saw evident in the young I also saw in equal measure in a group of grown men: specifically two groups, each group dressed in a distinct uniform. It was this game of 'football' again. Between them they kicked the same spherical object around and fought for its possession within the confines of a marked out piece of ground, rectangular shaped. It was a fierce encounter: the purpose being to place the object between two markers laid out on the ground at either end of this rectangle. It was a highly charged affair and there were many loud verbal exchanges both within and between the two groups. Emotions ran high, producing extreme outbursts of behaviour including disbelief, anger, disappointment, despair and occasional elation. No women were involved. This was a male-only, ritualistic pastime.

By chance I discovered a fascinating construction: a large repository of reference information stored within a purpose-built, public access facility. The volume and variety of this recorded material (predominantly printed) – gathered together I presume at great expense - can only mean one thing: a strong desire by the populous to gain greater knowledge and understanding of the world around them, to expand their conscious intellectual boundaries. When I entered I discovered few people inside. This could be because most people were busy in the trading centre.

While there - wandering around and looking dare I say lost - I attracted the attention of another man equally engaged in some kind of research. He was very helpful, very sociable, very talkative.

I explained my wish to better understand the physical world and cultural society in which he lived and this generated in him a warmth and a desire, equally strong, to help me in my mission. His energy and enthusiasm were boundless and he holds strong views on many subjects. He knows a lot about this world and is enthusiastic to share these views. His conversation, though overextended at times, proved very instructive - even if much of what he said was nothing more than opinion. He even gave up much of his own valuable time to give me a guided tour so to speak of the complex and how it operated.

He is a few years older then my host, five perhaps ten years, and keen to learn everything about him. I obliged him with a number of personal, almost intimate details, in particular describing my job and living arrangements. His name is 'John' and we agreed to meet here again. I am sure his friendship will prove to be of great benefit.

Late in the evening my host again kept falling asleep so I decided to take control for another extended period and revisit the commercial centre.

The public places suffer from the same lack of cleanliness as the private places. In particular the pedestrian walkways are strewn with litter and foul animal deposits. I will have to tread carefully. Traffic – both human and vehicular – is light at the end of the day. The lack of crowds and vehicles appears to remove inhibitions of individuals. Generally they are noisy and proned to random, unprompted outbursts of behaviour.

One encounter with two females was rather unnerving. They were walking towards me – rather one was staggering and being held up by the other. They had decorative paint on their faces and wore flamboyant clothes, as if determined to advertise their presence. This may have been in order to attract the attentions of the opposite sex. Seeing that one was in difficulty I offered to lend a hand – one of Clarence's obviously. I received aggressive responses from them both and was told to 'piss off'. To 'piss off' is a colloquial expression meaning to 'please go away', or 'don't interfere'.

After the females I encountered two interesting males. One was fully grown, approximately the same age as my host Clarence. The other was much younger: a youth still maturing into manhood.

I came across the youth while he was engaged in decorating the outside wall of a building. He was adding colour and vitality to what was otherwise a grey drab and uninspiring piece of architecture. I approached, fascinated by his act of artistic expression and the technique he was employing to translate that into some tangible lasting piece of work. It was a pleasure to see the joy on his face as he engaged all his senses in intense artistic expression. Using just three colours he was building a complex mural. The mural was some kind of declaration that a philosophy for life should be built around 'love', not 'hate', and that this philosophy should be 'sucked on'. He was so preoccupied that it some time before he registered my presence. When he did finally realise I was standing behind him he stopped, seriously confused by my interest and physical inactivity. I tried to appear relaxed, disengaged.

I noticed that his general dress code was scruffy, his hair greasy, unwashed and that there was dirt under his fingernails. He also suffered from some facial disorder which left him covered in spots and tiny tuffs of bristle. The females on this planet appear to manage their appearance whereas males deny it.

Digging deep into my host's repository I tried to signal reassurance and calm through the appropriate use of hand gestures and facial expressions. But nothing worked and I was perceived as a threat.

When he finally did speak his tone was aggressive and I struggled to understand his language. It did not match that used by Clarence. Diversity in dialects is possible here even over very small distances. I decided not to linger. It was a shame that he did not wish to talk.

Passing a public lavatory invoked a strong negative reaction within Clarence, and the clear instruction never to enter under any circumstance. Whilst studying this phenomena I was approached by a young fit man. He was wearing a tight black jacket made from polished dead animal skin. He was friendly and keen to make conversation. He was intrigued as to why I was afraid to enter the men's toilettes. I suppressed Clarence's rapidly surfacing reservations towards talking to strange men late at night and proceeded to make conversation.

The man invited me for a drink. For some reason he felt compelled to tell me that he wasn't 'married'. (To be 'married' is to be in a formal, recognised union with another.) I obliged, and found myself in a place where the drug alcohol is served.

His emotional state suggested sexual overtures. This was a revelation. I had assumed up to this point that sexual engagements occurred only between opposite sexes. Sex is a more complicated affair than I had previously thought.

I asked him to explain the full picture re sexual activity within the species, and whether reproduction was always the objective. But he became pensive, embarrassed, and suddenly less communicative. His body language changed suddenly and suggested in no uncertain terms that he wished to extricate himself from the situation. I asked him specifically how men performed the act of sex seeing as they were not obviously designed for such a coupling. His face dropped and emotionally he became seriously disturbed. When I asked if men could reproduce he laughed nervously, no longer sure of himself. He looked at his watch and made an excuse to leave. I asked if he would like to meet up again but he hurried away without answering. Shame.

When I got up to leave I notice that people sitting at the next table were staring at me with a mixture of alarm and disbelief on their faces.

Back home I encountered another young man going about his business. He looked very worn out. He registered my presence and spoke a few words but I thought it best not to engage in conversation. This did not seem to concern him. I have yet to determine the relationship between my host and this other male.

Chapter Two

With relish Tim dumped down the next two pints of beer and collapsed joylessly back into his chair. He noted a look of concern on his friend's face. Clarence did not look a happy bunny – which after two pints was strange. It probably had something to do with women. Probably Tracey. Perhaps he was getting too little sex. Perhaps he wasn't giving enough of it. Perhaps she was back to breaking his balls, like in the early days.

"She giving you a hard time again?"

Clarence didn't flinch. He continued to outstare the pint which stood before him. It demanded to be drunk, like its mate.

"That man over there keeps staring at me."

Tim began to do the twist.

"No don't look at him! Stay as you are."

Despite being the type who hated taking orders Tim restrained himself.

"Perhaps he fancies you you gorgeous thing."

"Don't, it's not funny."

"Perhaps he's one of your ex-pupils?"

"He's too old stupid."

"Well go and tell him to fuck off then."

"I can't. He might be a nutter."

Tim began to lose patience. "Well let me go and tell him to fuck off."

Clarence raised a hand, as if to hold back the tide or ward off drunken spirits.

"No leave things be. I'll ignore him."

"Good idea," said Tim and with that compromise in the air they continued to drink on into the night.

The pub was awash with the racket of multiple conversations, mostly incoherent but never lacking in passion or froth. Where Tim and Clarence sat however there was a hole – a whole lot of deathly silence. Halfway through his drink Tim gave up and demanded attention, enthusiasm – anything, even if it was faked. It was like being married, only less stressful.

"For fuck's sake Clarence talk to me. That's why we're here for Christ's sake."

Clarence looked up from his prized possession but refused to make eye contact. Meanwhile the new nutter in his life had left.

Tim was his best friend but still Clarence did not want to admit to fear or confusion. It was an ego thing: egos had to be carefully nurtured and protected, like babies – but unlike babies they did not grow up. At best they became spotty, fraught teenagers. They stuck to you as you stuck to them and neither could - or would – let go.

At that point Mr Sad and his new woman sauntered past. He smiled at Tim in acknowledgement and anticipation. Tim smiled back and raised his glass.

"Arsehole," he said under his breath. "Sad's just walked in with a new girlfriend."

Clarence took note. This time she was actually good looking, and young. Mr Sad had finally pulled it off. Clarence wanted take the piss and shake the man's hand. Perhaps not. But had he slept with her yet?

"Wonder if he's shagged her yet?" The question had to be asked. It was his duty.

"Bet you no. They're both too excited. Too much talking: they've only just met. First night out I'm sure." Tim knew his stuff.

Clarence prodded. "Go on, ask."

"You go. He won't hit you you're a teacher."

"Fuck off."

Having slagged off an associate pub regular the troublesome pair returned to downing beer. Another week of work beckoned and neither could face it – despite the fact that Tim made a ton of money for just sitting on his arse in front of a big screen watching numbers change from blue to red to blue again.

Clarence caught his mate off guard when he answered the much earlier question. "It's been a weird weekend."

"Weird? What do you mean 'weird'? Michael Jackson weird? Or just Ian Duncan Smith?"

"I'm serious. Just weird."

Tim put his glass down on his virtual beer mat and slipped on his mask of fake concern. "I'm all ears my dear."

"Just tiredness I suppose. That sense of missing out on bits of your life."

Tim was far from sympathetic. "I have no idea what on earth you're talking about."

"Neither do I. Forget it," replied Clarence, and waved him off.

Tim forgot it. Clarence didn't.

"Tell me when you're knackered, pissed off, do you feel like time passes you by without you even noticing?"

"Like when you're sleepwalking?"

"Yes."

"No."

"No?"

Tim sensed a state of panic rearing up inside his best mate so he changed his answer. "Well yes, I suppose so. Don't we all?"

"I don't mean the odd five minutes of daydreaming but large chunks, whole hours."

Tim's left nostril and upper left side of his lip raised themselves in parody of a full sneer. His face wanted to shake Clarence off. "No. Not whole hours – not unless I'm asleep at night, or shagging the wife."

Tim paused for laughs but received none. "Are you OK?" he asked.

Clarence retreated back into the comfort zone of small talk. "Yeah fine. Just under the weather. Job's getting me down as usual."

"Well do something else."

"Like what?"

"Be a plumber. We need more plumbers. I need a fucking plumber."

"Piss off. I've got brains and a university degree."

"What's that got to do with anything? I'm brainless and left school with one A Level and I'm earning tonnes more than you."

"All right all right." Clarence was being to hurt so he changed the subject. "How's your job going?"

"My job? Same old recycled shit. The market goes up. The market comes down. It fucks you up. It spins you around. The screens go blue. More fool you. The screens go red. You're left for dead."

"Very poetic."

"I know. Made it up during lunch."

Clarence began to rotate the glass in his hand. It had reached the infamous halfway point. Half full to some. Half empty to others. Not that he gave a toss either way.

Tim suddenly thought of something smart to say, so he said it, boldly. "It was probably just total boredom interacting with a Friday night hangover: a cosmic conjunction stupefying your brain."

"Forget it."

Far away across the floor a gang of girls dug into their second round of drinks with the ebullience of a rugby team celebrating an assault and a result. For a laugh they had all agreed to each carry a pair of knickers in their handbags or about their person – knickers to wave at any desperate stupid men who bored them silly. Some knickers were dirty, unclean. A sign of the times.

In another corner a young man and woman huddled together and struggled to think of something fresh to say to each other. They had been dating for a whole month now and it was beginning to hurt. He wanted to be with his mates. She wanted to be with her sisters. They were both made for wanting.

Then came the next outburst from Clarence. "And then there was the library."

"What do you mean 'the library'?"

Clarence confessed. "I woke up in it."

"Woke up? Meaning you fell asleep there? That's not exactly news. Libraries do that to you. They did it to me as I remember."

"No that's the thing: I never remember going into the place. I just woke up in it. Like when you wake up still pissed in a strange house after the party."

Tim was stumped. He had no answer.

Clarence continued. "I was holding a book."

Tim could not help but take the piss. The temptation was too much. "A teacher holding a book. In a library. Whatever next."

"A book on natural history?" Clarence clenched his face muscles. "Something isn't right. And Tracey's starting to seriously piss me off."

"Tell me about it." Tim was being rhetorical but Clarence took it as a prompt to talk on.

"She says I'm a liar and a lazy layabout."

"Well you are – and layabouts are, by definition, lazy."

Clarence sneered. "I'll shut up if you want me to."

"No no go on. I'm listening. Serious."

"She said I said I'd got the money when I said I hadn't got it yet."

Tim winced. He wanted Clarence to draw a flow diagram. "What money?"

"Holiday money."

"Oh that. Send us a dirty postcard when you're sober, or email it." Tim felt a headache coming on: better to let the sad bastard talk it all out as quickly as possible so they could carry on drinking.

"She said I forgot to come over last night, that she rang three times but I was out. And I said I was in all evening. She had cooked something. She called me a liar." Clarence was in full flow and regressing back into a small poxy boy – but a small poxy boy who needed women for sex.

Tim came to the rescue. "You were in. I rang to ask if you wanted to go down the pub but you said you wanted to stay in and 'examine the television'. 'Examine the television': your words not mine."

"I don't remember that?" Clarence was well confused now.

"You sounded a bit off, sort of detached, like my dad. And you said you wanted to go for a walk of all things. I thought you were just being a sarcastic bastard."

"A walk? Round here?"

"I may have misheard you – perhaps you said 'wank'. That would make more sense – especially if you were having problems with your woman."

Clarence turned the tables. His manhood was under attack. Tim was pushing his luck. "So how's it going with you and Sam these days?"

Tim ducked the question with all the speed and skill of a Sunday cricketer who didn't want to be hit on the head by a high velocity cricket ball. Cricket balls were lethal things in the wrong hands (especially foreign, ex-British Empire).

"We get by, most days."

Hearing a familiar sound Tim looked across the room and pretended to be gob smacked. "Fuck it there's some loose women over there!"

The women giggled and sniggered loudly. Simultaneously their attention spans and imagination focused on their next object of interest. Tim tried his best to catch an eye. It would take time but Tim was a patient man. His job had taught him patience when it came to placing bets. Clarence played along. He was open to offers, above board and below decks.

For awhile they went unseen then one of the girls cottoned on and nudged a friend in the ribs. They conspired, though no words passed between them. Tim took it as a sign of weakness, an invitation to dance, a measure of their vulnerability. In reality the girls were mocking the sad boys in the ring, the bad dogs in the kennel, two prats even; and for a laugh reinforcing their stereotypes. They were wicked.

There was the precipitation of energized body language in the air, along with the smell of sweet and sour sexual politics. For Tim eye contact created a tenuous link which grew in substance and strength each time it repeated itself. In turn his target knew exactly what impact she was making. She led him on, on towards the big black hole she had dug. Despite the brilliant sunshine it lay hidden in the shadows. Tim, agitated, began to fidget, not knowing if to make the next move – the next move currently undefined, the first move presumed to have occurred. Clarence looked on with envy at the source of Tim's entertainment and cold sweat. Tracey was slipping onto the back page.

What the hell you only live once.

Eureka! Tim spotted an opening. 'His' girl had emptied her glass. He took a deep breath, uncrossed his legs, scratched himself silly, stood up, and ambled towards her - like a friendly waiter who wanted to extract a large tip. She counted down the seconds and threw him an engaging smile. It signalled both encouragement and weary anticipation in equal measures.

"You need a drink?" asked Tim.

"I need a drink," she replied automatically, trying hard not to piss take.

"Can I get you a drink?"

"If you like. A glass – a large glass mind you - of cabernet sauvignon." She did not compromise when it came to free drinks.

"And one for your friend?" Tim was forced to put the question. The friend was staring him in the face.

"Kim, the man's offering to buy a round. What will you have?"

"Vodka and mango juice," replied Girl Number Two (Kim).

Girl Number One (name unknown) swung back on to Tim and Tim smiled.

"No problem," he replied.

Feeling on top of something Tim marched to the bar, forced himself into a small parking space and switched to plead mode as he tried to catch the attention of a sweat encrusted barman. They were all young, steak fed Australians. And they all looked like fashion models, perfectly tanned. The bastards. On his return he exercised his right to sit himself down next to Girl Number One. Reluctantly Girl Number One gave him enough space to do just that.

"Mind if my friend joins us?" he asked, chest puffed out inside his head.

Girl Number One shrugged. "Sure if it makes you feel happy."

Her response was underwhelming but Tim didn't care and Clarence didn't know. He was called over and what little conversation Tim managed to generate immediately began to drag like Christmas lunch with the in-laws. It was painful to listen to and painful to behold. The girls made the boys do all the work. They just wanted to drink for free. Girl Number Two remembered her knickers but decided that the jury was still out. Timing was everything.

Soon the other girls homed in, nosy and noisy, like pigeons on the lookout for food. One asked Tim what he did. He said he was a dealer in the Gold Market. She was sort of impressed, but only just. She turned on Clarence and asked what he did. Before he could open his mouth Tim cut in, saying that his mate was a teacher at a comprehensive.

The girls were impressed. This guy was the clever type. Was the pay crap though? asked one of them. A flat 'yes' was the answer but Clarence did go on to say that he did it for the pleasure, because he believed in what he did: filling the heads and hearts of the nation's youth with knowledge and motivation, excitement and anticipation. As usual Clarence was lying out of his arse but it sounded beautiful. Tim had heard that drivel a thousand times before and each time it never failed to make him want to vomit. He had yet to match it for brilliance.

Clarence began to talk loose talk. Girl Number One led him on. Despite his best interruptions Tim was forced to take the backseat as Clarence got carried away. Tim wanted to get carried away. Tracey was dismissed. Clarence felt he was on to something. Tim thought hard, cracked a really good joke, then a second, and managed to get all bar one of the girls to laugh.

All of a sudden, in full swing, two of the girls got up and made lame apologies: they were leaving. That left Girl Number One and Girl Number Two. Perfect. Tim's eyes began to mist over. His groin area was fully alert to the situation developing. He could smell the body language. He was on to something with Girl Number Two. Likewise Clarence was impressed with the course of events. He still couldn't quite believe that they were pulling something off. He wanted to pinch himself – or Girl Number One.

The girls played it for all it was worth. They were hungry. They wanted food. They had both male tongues hanging out in anticipation. Tim asked if they lived locally. Girl Number One was evasive. She answered 'possibly'.

Then out of the blue two 'real blokes' appeared on the set. Like angels they were; only more aggressive, less forgiving, more prone to violence. Like the girls they were young and fit, poorly paid, still living at home, and looking more than slightly agitated.

"Sorry but better you two go now: our boyfriends are here," said Girl Number One. "Nice knowing you," she lied.

An angry Tim tried to smile - nearly cracking open his face in the process - and got up to slip away. Clarence followed on close behind, doing his best to preserve his dignity. Bastards.

❋   ❋   ❋

Clarence pounded on the door, waiting for Tracey to answer. This she did, knowing full well who was on the other side.

"It's me," he announced.

"It's you," she replied. Tracey paused. This was becoming a well-worn out ritual. "You remembered this time – and on time."

Her statement of fact chilled the air between them. It was Hitler versus Stalin. Alien versus Predator. Baddiel versus Newman.

Clarence revealed a bottle of something or other and a four pack to warm it back up again. Tracey took possession of the wine in silence and placed it on the table, dead centre. The bolognaise was bubbling away, literally. Heat turned the water into steam. The steam escaped. Time to do the pasta. She disappeared into the kitchen and Clarence slumped into her favourite armchair, a beer in his hand, the rest hopefully in the fridge. He turned on and tuned into the TV with the remote control. The pull-ring landed neatly in the waste paper basket. Clarence had always been a good shot when it came to throwing things away.

The TV sucked: she only had the four channels to choose from but Clarence soldiered on. Tracey did likewise, his beers taking up her fridge space.

'I'll open the bottle, pour, and do the black pepper bit' he promised himself.

With dinner ready to be served up Tracey spoke, and in reply Clarence offered to pour her a glass of wine. She accepted. It would get him out of her chair. She even went so far as to turn the volume down on the television.

"How was your day then?" Tracey asked, sniffing the air then her glass of wine.

"Usual. What's for dinner?" Clarence knew the answer.

"Usual: bolognaise."

They seemed to be back on normal speaking terms he concluded – hastily some might say.

Tracey cut to the chase. "So you didn't get any money?"

"No." Subject closed as far as he was concerned.

"Good cos I got some today. Will you cover me for half?"

"Of course. Don't I always?"

No she thought. "And those travel forms I keep telling you about? You didn't get them?"

"No. Sorry."

"Well get them tomorrow will you? Post Office like I said."

"Sure."

Tracey had drawn another line in the sand and Clarence dare not cross it this time. The holiday was again proving tiresome and it hadn't even started yet. Clarence wanted to eat, drink, and watch TV. Then he wanted to shag.

Business done Tracey returned to her kitchen to serve up. After a few minutes of inconsequential activity spent forgiving himself Clarence followed her and offered to help in anyway he could. The choices were limited. He was told to get the plates then grate cheese into the small bowl she pushed in front of him as she spoke. They ricocheted around her small flat like loose cannon balls: never quite colliding; the occasional bump but never a spark. Afterwards, using his own initiative, he put the salt and pepper out and poured himself a glass of wine. Best be seen drinking with her, he concluded. Look sociable.

They sat and ate and sipped. Clarence told his girlfriend how good the food was and his girlfriend thanked him. Pure poetry.

"How's school?" asked Tracey.

Whenever she said that Clarence felt like he was fourteen again and she was mother. There was a difference though: with Tracey he could be honest.

"The usual crap."

Clarence grabbed more cheese like there was no tomorrow.

"Did you get your promotion?"

"Don't know. Jury's still out. He won't say for ages." Clarence sucked on his spaghetti as he picked his next words. "I don't expect to get it. He knows my heart's not in it, not any of it."

Tracey twisted spaghetti neatly up into a ball around her fork. The fork she then held to attention before devouring it. As a teacher her man was becoming less and less impressive as the weeks and months went by. Change the subject – first one last throw.

"Jane's decided to do teacher training at last."

"Tell her don't bother. It's too much hassle these days. All paperwork no job satisfaction and the pay's crap."

Unmoved yet again by his mantra, Tracey spelt out the words 'you tell her' in her head, in capital letters. She began to look moody, illegitimate. In return Clarence began to come over all shy. It was the 'small boy meets bigger girl with the larger bike' routine taking hold.

"I don't understand. You don't like it. You call them all morons. Why don't you pack it in and do something else. Cheer us both up."

"Like what? Be a lumberjack? And anyway I'm too old to change my spots now." Clarence slurped his pasta again. "I've been thinking about it."

"Thinking about what?" Tracey rotated her fork in her spoon again.

"About what you said."

"What did I say?"

"You know. Living arrangements? Cutting down on overheads? Save the money for . . . whatever."

"Oh that."

Clarence cut to the chase. "Well I'm interested if you are."

The words 'now you're interested' popped into Tracey's head. As did the word 'fuck'. She went for the balls, both cooked and uncooked, both on the plate and down the trousers.

"Why the change of heart?"

"I don't know." Clarence flustered. He hated it when she asked awkward questions just for the sake of an answer.

"I won't be the dishwasher you know."

"We'll buy one." Sorted.

"And don't expect me to be the one who always fills the washing machine."

"Understood." As if.

Tracey began to panic. She could let him further in or wriggle out and shut the door (preferably not in his face – best leave no bad feelings). Indecision time.

"I'll think about it."

Think about it?

"Think about it?"

"What's there to think about? It was your idea?" The words crawled out of his throat.

'For fuck's sake' he wanted to add but a day at school had curtailed his habit of using the 'F' word.

Tracey was under attack. So she turned aggressive. She gripped her knife like a sword and pointed it skyward. Clarence held his pointing forwards like a flick knife. Standoff.

It was a scene from Fawlty Towers except he wasn't tall or funny or a hotel manager; and she wasn't middle-aged or overemphasized as an aloof, overdecorated, middle-England middle-class, bored wife (although she would dominate at times); and it wasn't set in a West Country seaside hotel in the Seventies. Nor was there a Spanish waiter in the kitchen.

Tracey avoided eye to eye contact. She looked down at her dinner, then her tablecloth. Finally she was sure she hated it. Mother had given it to her as a flat warming present, along with a toaster. That had long since been replaced. Father had given her money – less imaginative but far more useful.

Clarence tried to make eye contact. Tracey knew what 'Transparent Clarence' - as her sister Jane called him - was up to, and wasn't having any of it.

"Don't look at me like that."

"Like what?"

"I can change my mind if I want."

"You've changed your mind now? You wanted me to think about it!"

"Well I've thought about it now." Which strictly speaking was true.

"And you've changed your mind?"

Tracey looked up and glared into his face. 'Yes' she growled then looked back down.

'Fuck you then' was his coded response.

'I can do better' was hers.

Somehow dinner was not quite the same after that. All breadsticks demolished, the suddenly distraught lovers settled down in front of the telly, to watch a video and avoid having to talk to each other. Clarence had his beer. Tracey had her wine. They each had a cigarette. Clarence sprawled out alone on the sofa. (Tracey having grabbed back her armchair.) At some point he stopped wanting to watch TV and switched to thoughts of sex instead. The two said nothing. Instead the actors did all the talking.

As the film drew to a close (boy and girl reconcile their differences and live happily ever after - her aging parents rediscover new purpose and energy as they enter their third age - America invades Vietnam) Clarence did his best to make amends for whatever it was that might need mending, or amending. He apologized for sounding sharp and being critical. He respected her decision.

'He wants sex tonight' thought Tracey. 'And I think so could I'. A wincey-teeny tiny bit of her (but growing all the time) was glad the holiday was only to last seven days – six and a bit if you stripped away travelling time.

As usual Clarence farted. Third time that day. Tracey took no notice. Better out here than in there, in between her bed sheets.

Bed: that bastion of hopeless, unrequited love; that place where boys enter and leave as men, and women leave them to it. Bed: that place where you can scoff food while watching TV (in bed) – a bit like a living room. Bed: begins with a 'b' like 'bugger', 'bollocks', 'bullshit', 'blimey', 'bloke', 'blowjob', 'bullet', 'bombshell', 'bastard', 'boogie', 'banal', 'burdensome', 'bother', 'bothersome', 'bemused', 'blinkered', 'burp', 'bin liner' (strictly two words), and 'Bamby'. Bed: that place where you are forced to sleep (sometimes with someone else – in which case a good night's sleep is far from guaranteed). Bed: the heart of a home and its bowel movements. Bed: the place where the best and worse decisions in life are made.

Tracey was first to get to the bathroom. Clarence was not far behind. He wanted to shag. She squeezed the toothpaste from the bottom. He squeezed it anywhere. She put the toilet seat down. He forgot. She put the soap back in its dish. He didn't even consider such things. Soap. Soap dish. For her it was a simple enough connection which didn't require much in the way of deep thought.

She had her own electric toothbrush which only once did he dare to use. He was required to bring his own, else suffer. She squeezed her flannel tight until it was barely damp and folded it up neatly, with a mixture of affection and attitude. He would leave it sitting 'scrunched', still substantially soaked.

When he shaved in the mornings he would leave a fine trail of atomised hair clippings along the sides of the basin just begging to be wiped away. When she shaved it was a discreet affair with no signs left behind that the home improvements had ever taken place. When she got out of the bath she hosed it down meticulously with the shower attachment. When he got out of the bath he had to be reminded to do likewise.

Her last conscious thought on leaving her bathroom was to consider applying air freshener according to need. His last thought on leaving her bathroom, conscious or otherwise, was to weigh up the probability of getting a leg over that night.

As was the norm, Clarence fell into bed from the right hand side. Tracey followed suit from the left hand side. There was scope for variation: sometimes he fell in first; sometimes she fell in first. Sometimes – rarely - they fell in together then bickered about who had to get out again to turn the light off. During late autumn this could escalate into a major issue as she only switched the hall storage heater on when the cold truly arrived. Tracey saved her pennies. Clarence spent his pounds.

As was the norm Clarence would attempt to make conversation - 'how was your day' etc. Nine times out of ten he would fail. She was too tired or bored or he was too tiring or too boring. Small talk over, Clarence would make little, discreet overtures: a gentle sweep through her hair with his fingers (hopefully clean under the fingernails her response); a sly, soft hug perhaps; a cheeky squeeze of her upper arm; a grip of her waist as the final wake up call. That done, Clarence would follow through with a large, no nonsense, no holds barred, declaration of intent – the invitation to do the business inferred and self-evident. At that point her mind had to be made up, else confusion and dejection might ensue.

Tonight there was no small talk, and the bedroom light was still on. Tracey switched on her table lamp.

"I was in first: you going to switch it off?"

No response.

"I said are you going to switch the light off?"

Still no response. Clarence was staring up with blank expression at the ceiling. It was one of those rare moments when she had caught him in deep thought. That aside, 'tosser' thought Tracey, and under protest she pulled herself out of her warm bed. Crossing the room she hesitated before switching the light off. Her man was still deep in mental gloom or serious thought. The holiday was going to take its toll.

'Why do I need a man?' she asked herself.

'Because I'm buggered without one' her other half replied.

'And why this one in particular?' she argued.

'Because nothing better's come along, yet,' she answered.

'Do I want to make love tonight?' she wondered.

'Probably. It has been five nights.' she concluded.

Back in bed, Tracey decided to leave the lamp on for the time being. Perhaps he was planning to say something. Wakey wakey! Let's talk. Let's do it. Let's fall in love.

Still no reaction. Clarence was dead meat – nervous dead meat.

Tracey leaned over and dumped a question straight in his face. "Are you OK? Do you want to tell me something?"

Clarence twitched. He blinked. He tried to smile. He moved his head and tried to look her directly in the face, in that place where her eyes sat. He failed miserably. Routine went out of the window: this time she put her arm around his waist and squeezed him tight. Clarence began to tremble.

Blimey! thought Tracey. I've got a virgin in the bed tonight, else a schoolboy.

And suddenly, quite bizarrely, she found it exciting. She was in control. She was in charge, like the train driver. She could make all the moves. Had she really pissed him off earlier so badly? That was it: he was knee deep in a sulk of massive proportions. Why couldn't menfolk take rebuffs and rebukes from their womenfolk on the chin, like men rather than boys?

She stroked his hair away from his forehead. He still had a good head of hair Tracey reminded herself. She ran her left hand around and around, over and over his rib cage and stomach. As stomachs went for men of his age it was in good shape, better than average. It was not yet a beer gut, though the signs were there. She slipped her left leg over the top of his left and left it there. No harm done.

'Fuck this let's make love!' she screamed behind his back.

Clarence awoke with a primitive, almost bestial ferocity that hadn't manifested itself in ages – not since they had first jumped into bed and he had ripped away her best silk underwear. At last. A response!

He ran his hands over all regions of her body, and back again, and back again for a second look. All places were visited and revisited, and slowly, with gratitude and appreciation. All methods of titillation were applied and he kissed her all over. He found her love button and pressed it hard, several times. Foreplay was fucking marvellous and force-fed. The moments were captured in time, like mouthfuls of chocolate, fruit and nut.

And it goes without saying that Tracey loved every microsecond of it. Worth saying anyway. And he didn't say a single damn word – which was fine by her. She was in a Bond movie, with Sean, the first and only Bond.

Revved up and rearing to go Clarence fell on to his woman from the heavens and forced her legs apart, caveman style. And she loved it. He pushed and pulled and gripped and fingered and rearranged her hair in all directions to within the absolute limits of tolerance. And she loved it. He travelled down her throat with his tongue, taking notes on the way, and she loved it. And he didn't say 'I really love you' once. And she loved it.

With a spare index finger he drew invisible lines across her skin, mainly from top to bottom down her body towards the area of her reproductive machinery. And god how she loved it. She was at boiling point. With gratitude she wrapped herself around his trunk and fully engaged in the act of sexual intercourse. Pure pleasure and physical exertion remained balanced in equal portions. The whole was submerged in a torrent of heightened passion and extreme emotional outburst. Tracey was sixteen again. Clarence was, whatever. Tracey would sleep easy tonight, like a baby. And when he rolled off, she did. He didn't even spoil it by saying goodnight and giving her a peck on the cheek. Perhaps the holiday was going to be a good one. Roll on holiday.

⚜ ⚜ ⚜

Log Entry

This is now my sixth day (local measure of time, day equals one rotation of planet). The environment is becoming less confusing, though the dominant species is not. With practice I have learnt to make my requisitions of the host's functions less disruptive, more transparent. I can observe without taking total control, but with limited engagement. However there will be times – for the purposes of research - when I must completely dictate his actions. I hope to minimize this.

I am still confident that my host suspects nothing. It has been my good fortune to discover that he occupies his time (attitude suggests this is a contractual exchange of goods and services and not a recreational activity) educating the younger members of his society. They vary widely in size and weight though their body language and attitude (sex specific) are a more constant feature. Mentally, they are not necessarily less developed: some are; some are not. Either way they do not appear interested in fully engaging their brains. The girls seem to spend a lot of time watching the boys. Most boys barely notice this. Those that do pretend not to.

Technically speaking, his profession is that of 'teacher', but I have yet to see him perform adequately as such - i.e. impart knowledge, wisdom and understanding to stimulate creative expression or logical analysis. His attempts to do this in his specialist field are interesting to say the least. They vary from bouts of focused enthusiasm; through polite, formulaic execution; into bloody-minded perseverance; then finally tired fatalism.

He does not seem to care. Nor does his captive audience. Time and energy is wasted on both sides.

His engagement with his pupils is heavily ritualised and strictly formal, despite appearances to the contrary. He talks. They listen or try to listen or pretend to listen. He tells them things they don't need to know or want to know. He instructs them to turn to a specific 'page' in a 'book' (an ancient storage device for printed language and images) and read on. They read in silence while he wanders around the room, trying not to look bored as he checks for non-compliance. He asks questions. Some try to answer. Some ask questions. He tries to answer. A fair exchange but a strange system.

The agenda is inflexible, repetitive, and makes no allowances for their emotional states. Some students I noticed were totally preoccupied with their personal relationships with members of the opposite sex. Others were generating feelings of animosity towards their parents. Others were simply trying to stay awake. The remainder were mostly – extremely even – bored out of their senses. Only one male pupil I noticed was taking a strong active interest in what my host had to say. Upon closer examination of his mental state I realized that it was in fact an intended deception - a bit of fun to be enjoyed by others in the room.

The quality of their learning materials, the furniture, and teaching aids (black painted board and white chalk deposits in a technologically advanced civilization?) is poor. I guess that the transfer of knowledge, understanding, and thinking skills is not a high priority in this part of the world. Entertainment appears to dominate instead. But it is early days. I must not jump to conclusions.

Young females appear to be more receptive to new input, more flexible in nature, more willing to listen and observe. Perhaps females manage most things and men are tolerated for the purposes of reproduction and as a physical resource. In evolutionary terms though neither can survive without the other.

At midday feeding time my host socializes with fellow teachers. They fall into two groups. The first talk in depth about their work, both in the personal and professional sense. The other, smaller group say little and contribute nothing to debates. They just watched the first group and are easily bored. My host belongs to this group. It suits his temperament.

One young female teacher seems to affect the pattern of behaviour in the men, and in particular my host. In her immediate vicinity a muddled set of emotions are generated, sometimes in parallel, sometimes in series.

These emotions and associated thoughts they spark are in conflict. There is sexual attraction competing with a strange disquiet – fear almost – guilt and naked envy. Lust and envy dominate. The guilt presumably stems from the fact that he already harbours feelings of attraction towards another female. To date he has made a point of avoiding her. When they have spoken his conversation has been guarded, though sincere – almost nervous at times. Hers has been inviting, else perfunctory.

Another observation worth noting is the method by which my host journeys from his home to his place of work. He does this by 'car'. A car is a machine powered by hydrocarbon fuel, designed to transport small groups of people across land in absolute comfort. It does not fly. It does not float. It is not fully automated and cannot be pre-programmed. Though intended to carry him at high speed along a purpose-built network of lanes, this rarely happens in practice.

The irony is that just about everyone owns such a device (they come in all shapes and sizes, subject to some basis design constraints and themes) and so freedom of movement is limited, and progress is slow - very slow at times, if not completely curtailed. Often my host has to stop and wait for alternative flows to proceed according to system controls and legal deterrents.

Disputes between pilots over space, priority and manoeuvrability can become quite aggressive. Over time such behaviour has developed a whole new language of facial expressions, a language designed to clearly communicate from a distance a whole multitude of opinions, emotions and reactions: exasperation, disbelief, confusion, impatience; assertiveness, aggression, stubbornness; disenchantment, disengagement, disinterest, vagueness; and occasionally self-importance, aloofness, disingenuous politeness.

Rarely does sitting in a car make these people happy – even when they are travelling at high speed with their in-built, full surround, sound systems delivering high quality music, chat, news etc at high volume. Couples or groups travelling together rarely talk to each other. The alternatives I suppose must be far worse, else non-existent in places. Strange that such a sophisticated society has not developed a more imaginative, more efficient transportation system.

My host arrives at his destination tired and in a foul mood. Sometimes he fails to shake it off - worse still fails to mask this emotional state from those around him – especially his students.

The human body is a fragile, complex thing and highly sensitive to its surroundings. It can switch from feeling too cold to too hot in an instant. It's surface sweats a mixture of water and salt compounds. Excretion of waste products appears to be a very private and primitive affair. It is not a refined process by any means. The equipment used to channel away waste is standardized, though quality and upkeep varies according to location, age, and ownership.

The process of excretion is performed sitting, and can take any length of time. The ease of ejection of solids is a direct consequence of the nature of the food consumed, and when. The time is rarely wasted. It is an opportunity for creative thinking and general reflection. The process is definitely a private affair.

The rooms in which excretion is performed are clearly designed to accommodate one single person at a time. In addition to this the sexes are separated in public places. Excretion may be accompanied by the release of toxic gases before, after, or during the event – a by-product produced by the digestive juices when breaking down food stuffs. As such a tell-tale smell nearly always marks the occasion. These releases of gas, sudden and unscheduled, are known as 'farts'. Some cause major disruption. Most are barely noticed.

I have discovered that one should resist releasing toxic gas in public, even when there is no accompanying odour. The noise is not welcomed. It interrupts trains of thought. The mechanism for preventing this bodily function to occur deludes me. There may not be one.

To repeat, the species has two distinct sexes. I presume that at a very early stage natural evolution upon this planet (a planet I note which holds a large moon in orbit) caused a physical separation of the reproductive mechanism and the creation of two distinct components. Reproduction can only occur if one male connects its sexual organ with that of a female, and transfers an adequate supply of sperm into the body where eggs are waiting to be fertilised. In other combinations it is pointless exercise but still pursued for pleasure. The dynamics of this need further examination.

I have experienced the act of sexual intercourse with a female. It was quite an event: emotionally and physically a highly charged encounter. The impact upon the nervous system was mind-blowing – literally, I nearly disengaged in fright – especially at the end: the end being that point at which the male delivers a concentrated juice of reproductive cells at high speed into the female body - it being suitably engaged to maximise the chance of successful fertilisation. A lot of energy, physical and emotional, is released in the process by both parties. A very inefficient process, but exciting to participate in. The activity must be a popular pastime.

I found it difficult to make observations during the act. Its duration was short. The physical interaction was driven in the main by automatic responses on both sides. Conscious thought other than wild imagination was barely present. To engage him with maximum impact and vitality I simply removed my host's inhibitions along with previous memories of the same. It was then a case of 'being along for the ride'.

The female body (this one in particular) is so different from the male. I was totally unprepared for it. It is much more than just a case of different reproductive organs and distribution of body fats. The emotional and psychological landscapes also differ. Despite having different starting points and objectives the act of sexual intercourse appears to operate satisfactorily for both sides. Bear in mind though that they are probably both old hands at it, experienced performers. For others it may be a more traumatic experience, perhaps an anti-climax. Perhaps male and female parts do not always interlock to perfection. And at which point in the life cycle does one or the other cease the activity? Is it by mutual agreement? Is there a preset timetable? Do they keep going and only give up when the body gives in? What if one body wants to stop while the other wants to keep going? How often to partners change? Are mechanical devices used as substitutes for the failure of human equipment? Is sexual intercourse obligatory or just according to need or status? So many questions. More research is required.

Chapter Three

Clarence sat staring at his pint and swore. He was cursed, of that he felt sure. Strange fragmented images - for some reason these included the contents of old books - circulated around and around inside his head. Along with the mysterious lapses in consciousness it was no circus. He needed that bloody holiday, with or without Tracey. He had to recharge his flat battery of a brain. He needed his sanity back. The only bit of sunshine was that Tracey had the hots for him again.

As if struck by a dark premonition Clarence looked up. A man had just walked in. It was a face with which he felt strangely familiar, and it scared him. And then it dawned on him. It was the nutter from Sunday night. Shit. With lightening speed Clarence switched to scrutinizing the depths of his beer. Not much luck there. Out of the corner of his eye he saw that he had been spotted. The nutter was steering towards him. The nutter was smiling. Oh Christ. Clarence, gripping his pint for all its worth, clenched his spare fist.

The nutter stood over him, beaming broadly, holding back something wishing to burst out.

"Hello," he said. The greeting was almost a whisper, as if subversive.

Worse still his voice was silky smooth, suggestive, inviting – and it scared the remaining shit out of Clarence. In response he adopted his most aggressive, dismissive expression and stared up, doing his utmost to look put out, perplexed.

"Hello what?" he replied sharply, daring the other man to take up the challenge.

It was a good performance. The whole 'defence through attack' strategy worked a treat. His enemy was left disorientated. All the man could say was sorry. So he said it.

"Sorry."

But Clarence was already out of his chair and gone. He had been saved by the bell. Tim and Sam had just wandered in. They both looked knackered – by each other. Tim looked especially wound up. Sam looked especially fed up. Hard day at the office thought Clarence.

He grabbed their attention as he grabbed a new table. Sam issued instructions and husband was sent on a mission to the bar. Clarence did his best not to acknowledge the fact that the nutter come stalker was still watching him. The agony lasted only ten seconds though before the nutter gave up and went to the bar. With poetic irony he ended up standing next to Tim as he waited to be served. He would wait only a short time before having a change of heart and leaving the premises, thoughts of human nature weighing heavily on his mind.

Sam, typically switched on to what was happening around her, was keen to discover who the new friend was. Straight away her radar had picked up the signs that something was wrong. Clarence was looking worn out, hung up and hung out to dry. She sat down opposite him, fingered her wedding ring, and stated the obvious.

"You look like shit."

"Thanks."

"Bad week?"

"Pretty much."

"Is that why we're here?"

"Probably."

"Oh well you'll be lying comatose on a beach soon."

"Wonderful."

Enough said. Sam waited for her drink to arrive. She had had a busy day at the bank holding the back office together with little more than a fierce voice, deaf ears and, with regards to higher ranking management, the threat of mutually assured destruction. Husband had been punching screens all day and shouting down the phone. He had yet to come back down to earth. Clarence glanced at the nutter twice, whilst pretending not to. This did not fool Sam. When her drink was delivered she snatched it up, not bothering to say thank you.

"I'm going outside for a smoke," announced Tim, in a voice which sounded a little too grandiose for the occasion. He didn't wait for a reaction. He just went.

"He's off to sulk," explained Sam, not in the least bit put out.

"You two been arguing?"

"Yeah."

"What about?"

"Babies again."

Babies: a subject which Clarence declined to comment upon. He couldn't understand all the fuss.

Sam took up the baton and charged. "So what's wrong with you then?" she demanded to know.

Clarence had known Sam long enough to know she did actually have a caring side. She just brought it out for special occasions. She wouldn't accept bullshit and he had to tell someone. He couldn't – wouldn't – dare not - tell Tracey.

"Blackouts," replied Clarence. He spoke softly, his backbone broken; like a small boy who had experienced his first bad day ever but had never been warned that such a thing would happen to him in the due course of staying alive. "And things," he added.

Sam slipped into mother mode – no irony intended.

"Have you seen the doctor?"

"No."

"Why ever not? That's what he's there for you silly boy."

Perhaps it was matron mode.

"I don't want to be prodded and poked. I don't want to be certified. Not yet anyway. I think I just need a rest."

"So what happens exactly? These blackout things?"

"Don't know. There's never any warning. No pattern. No after affects. I'm fine – before and after."

"How long do they last?"

"Anything. Seconds. Minutes. An hour?"

Sam felt an urge to grasp his hand and hold it tight to an intimate part of her body. The feeling was mutual: Clarence wanted Sam to take his hand in hers. She was his secret big sister. His real sister was nothing on her - and she was younger so she could never be a big sister. As kids she had hung around him far too much, and that had irritated. Things really went down hill the day she stopped doing what he told her to do. It had been like that ever since, more or less.

Clarence presented more evidence. "Max says I stare up at the ceiling, just staring, saying nothing."

"Max?"

"My new lodger."

"Oh him. And who was that other man? That wasn't Max I take it."

A long miserable pause followed as Clarence tried to bluff it out. "What other man?"

"You know who I mean." Sam thumbed a lift. "That man who was watching you like you had just refused to marry him."

Clarence worked hard to come up with a safe, smart answer - so hard in fact that Tim reappeared before he could even start to think. Put on the defensive, he came over all sheepish.

"No one. He's just been bugging me. Some bloke who thinks he knows me."

Tim cut in. "Your boyfriend again? Have you told Tracey? You've got to choose: it's one or the other."

"Piss off."

No one laughed and no one spoke. Silence descended. It was a funeral. Clarence wanted to talk to Sam, but not while Tim was in earshot. Sam wanted Clarence to talk to her, but not while her husband was around. Tim wanted to be part of the conversation, but there wasn't one to be part of. He held his grievance in as long as possible then erupted.

"So are we here to drink and talk or what?"

"We are drinking," responded Sam.

"OK so let's talk."

"What do you want to talk about?" she asked, curious.

"I don't know."

Clarence kept his head down.

"Babies?"

Tim glared at his wife. She had crossed the line. She was taking the piss in front of his oldest friend and throwing their dirty washing out onto the street for all to smell. He snapped – having been trading all day and making bugger all except losses. Gold sucked.

"I'll see you later. I'm off home."

Sam watched her other half scuttle off and Clarence tried not to notice the 'situation'. In unspoken agreement they settled down into an innocent liaison and started chatting again. Sam, having no qualms, took a sudden interest in Tracey.

"Tracey? Hot and cold," admitted Clarence. "Currently hot thank God."

He turned the tables: like for like; an eye for an eye. "How are things between you and Tim?"

"We get by, most days."

As a night out this night didn't rate in the top ten percent.

✦ ✦ ✦

Friday lunchtime: school. Teachers and pupils alike conducted themselves with almost total freedom of thought and expression, but little in the way of common cause. Clarence could be seen marching down a corridor with a look of earnest concentration on his face, the look of someone with a mission. Pupils got out of his way fast.

Suddenly he did a right-hand turn and disappeared into the computer room. For Fiona this was a stroke of good fortune. She was running out of breath. She had been trailing him up the stairs and down the long corridor, trying to catch him up without bumping into pupils or having to shout out his name. She did not want to lose dignity or decorum, as shouting was not something she practised if she could help it. She had spoken his name loudly but to no avail. Clarence was half deaf today.

Fiona stuck her head around the door. Clarence was standing motionless and looking blankly at the row of screens and keyboards. His arms were folded, tightly, as if under orders to prevent his ribs unravelling. Some computers were switched off. Some had irritating little corporate logos bouncing off the sides of the screen as they did their bit to screen save. Some had sneakily put themselves on standby and awaited the call to arms: a tap on the keyboard; a nudge of the mouse; a bump in the night. The poor man looked lost.

"Forgotten your password?" asked Fiona. Her mood was cheerful.

Caught off guard Clarence turned suddenly and froze. Now he stared blankly into her eyes, as if to register the presence of someone unwelcomed or unexpected. Fiona gave him the benefit of the doubt and pushed on.

"I've got your adjustable thingy in the car."

Clarence looked down at the floor, then around as if searching for a place to rest and set up tent. His arms tightened their grip, if such a thing were possible.

The poor boy is shy she figured. Strange for a grown man who could stand at the front of a class. Then she made a leap of logic (or faith). It was her. He fancied her!

"It did the trick. Just like you said."

Still no response. Worse still he was sweating, shaking even? Fiona peered intently and focused in on his outline. Yes Clarence the geography teacher was shaking – ever so slightly it had to be said but shaking nevertheless.

She smiled and persevered. The man would have to speak sometime. "Shall I go and get it?" she asked.

Judging by the look on his face she had saddled him with a dilemma, which for a simple question was in turn confusing for her. Clarence released himself from his self-imposed arm lock, swept his hair aside and scratched his head.

Fiona could see he was thinking really hard now. It made him look rather cute. And he didn't seem to be shaking so much.

"These are all computers?" Clarence asked.

Fiona couldn't tell if he was being silly, rhetorical or judgemental with regard to modern teaching methods. Judging by their previous conversation the latter was possible. Either way she didn't answer. She had an adjustable spanner sitting on her front passenger seat wrapped up in a plastic bag. She didn't want to drive it all the way home again. Now that would be silly.

"Why aren't they doing anything?"

"What?" Fiona was stumped.

Clarence leaned forward and ran his fingers across the nearest keyboard. Right on cue the screen burst back into life.

Clarence pointed. "What's that?"

Fiona drew closer in until she could see over his shoulder.

"Google," she replied.

"Google? Strange name. What is it?"

"It's a search engine."

"Search engine?" Clarence leant in closer until his face was almost touching the screen. "What's it searching?"

Now it was Fiona's turn to fold her arms. "Nothing at the moment."

"What about when it's switched on then?"

Now Fiona was beyond stumped, if there was such a place. Was he thick or what? Or was geography such a backwater that he never used a computer let alone the web? She suffered a temporary time shift and answered his question like an easily bored teenager – a teenager who hated having her style cramped by too many questions.

"The internet of course."

"The internet?" Now Clarence looked like he was taking mental notes.

"Yes the internet. You know. The web - the world wide web."

"World wide?"

Fiona could see she had started something. Clarence was thinking really hard – so hard even she was hurting.

"Will you show me?"

"Show you?"

Clarence looked her straight in the eye. "Please?"

His request sat begging: it was dipped in syrup and was being served with clotted cream. Clarence had that look of someone hanging by a thread in a life or death situation: like halfway up a mountain on the end of a dodgy rope, or stuck on a lavatory seat having run out of paper. Fiona could not refused.

"Very well. Here."

She reached for the keyboard, intending to type, then hesitated. "What do you want to search on?"

"Search on?"

"Give me a subject. Any bit of text – text linked to something you're looking for."

"Humanity."

"Humanity? Nothing more specific?"

"No. Humanity."

"Very well. Humanity."

Search word entered, Fiona struck the enter key, and with all the fire and speed the broadband connection could muster a network request - deconstructed into a string of 0's and 1's - knocked at the door of the infinitely all powerful entity which was Google. The results were thrown back down the wire with all the faked enthusiasm of a thoroughly disengaged royal head of state waving to a small crowd of well-wishers while in a hurry to escape back indoors out of the rain and knock back a stiff drink or two.

"There you are, hundreds of thousands of pages."

"A page being?"

"Just about anything. Text, pictures, links - files on someone's web site. All you have to do now is trawl through it all to find anything useful."

"I think I understand."

Fiona looked at Clarence. She was slightly disappointed.

"It's not really that difficult you know. Anyway we just typed in one word. Be more specific and you'll get less back."

"Thanks I'll remember that."

Growing tired Fiona was in need of a change of subject.

"Your comment about kids culture yesterday. I've been thinking. I agree that they end up as 'manipulated consumers' to use your words, and all look the same – especially in those baggage jeans – but that's to miss the point."

No response, just that blank look again.

"I mean it's literally the thought that counts: the fact that they show that spark of rebellious thought, if not original creativity. Yes they may get gobbled up in some corporate marketing ploy but don't we all? And don't we all move on sooner or later?"

Now she heard herself sounding too serious, so another change of subject was required.

"And as for Oasis, I still think their second album is better. Not as raw as the first but the songs are more varied, put together better - more style. The first is good but the tracks sound a bit samey, almost the same bass line thumping away."

Still no response. Was she really talking out of her arse? Time to sign off.

"Well like you I didn't buy anymore of their stuff."

Fiona looked at her watch. The end of lunchtime was closing in fast.

"Look I'll go and get that spanner thing," she said, wishing for a way out.

"Yes thank you."

A response!

"No problem," Fiona replied, and then was gone – almost bumping into Ramsey the PE teacher on her way out of the room.

Ramsey was lounging at the door, peering in but not stepping in, on the edge of the conversation but not part of the conversation. Had he gone into acting he would have been perfect for the part of bouncer, fixer, undercover agent or doormat. Fiona made the point of not speaking to him.

His eye set on Clarence, Ramsey spoke, like a police interrogation officer in one of his happy moods. "Oh yes very smooth you devious little sod."

✦　✦　✦

It was not a happy pub that suffered an above average proportion of teachers for custom. It was a sight for sore eyes. There were only four teachers left out of the original seven who had met up for a after work drink: two men and two women; Clarence and Ramsey, Fiona and Jane. The symbolism – if there was any – was wasted.

Clarence thought the remaining circle had a certain symmetry. Ramsey (all round plastic action man with jointed arms and legs which could change position) thought nothing of it. He did not think as a rule. He just shouted or blew his whistle or chased after women. Often he would be doing any two of these three things at the same time.

They were into their third drink and they had run out of conversation, interesting or otherwise. In desperation they had talked about reality programmes, and had ended up agreeing – openly anyway – that the stuff represented the very worse of cheap, pointless, brainless TV entertainment, even those which included so called celebrities. Suffice it to say that they had all watched a full episode or two.

Fiona had already been interrogated about her first week in her new job. Reflections and conclusions were shortcoming. She had given safe, bland, uncontroversial answers, wishing not to make enemies, wishing not to talk the school down. In one of his rare moments of insight Clarence had seen through it and had assumed, wrongly, that deep down Fiona, like him, didn't give a toss. She did give a toss, a big one.

Ramsey as usual had been blunt and pointless, like a worn out pencil stabbing at the paper. It went something like this, Ramsey sounding like a magistrate:

"So Fiona what do you think of the little bastards after one week?" asked

"I hardly think it's right to be calling them little bastards," she retorted.

Jane cut in. "Quite right. They are young minds." She never missed an opportunity to face up to Ramsey.

"I wouldn't go that far," added Clarence.

Ramsey fought back with distinction. "Clarence says all our pupils are mindless morons."

Clarence responded with ease. "No I didn't."

"Yes you did."

"I said some of our pupils were morons. And I didn't use the word mindless. You did, just then. Morons are by definition mindless."

Jane snatched a laugh and Fiona tried to look ill-amused, and failed. Ramsey looked stumped by a difficult exam question.

The rivalry and underlying tensions which existed between Ramsey and Clarence were beginning to reveal themselves – much to the chagrin of the ladies present, and not before time. Even more embarrassing (but only to Fiona) was Ramsey's feeble attempt to chat up Fiona. It was like watching a hungry man trying to unwrap a crème egg whilst wearing a pair of thick gardening gloves: he ignored all feedback and was too stupid – too proud - to call it a day.

Jane, a previous target and long time observer, had come to the conclusion that Ramsey applied just one simple test in his search for a woman. *Is it female and is it breathing?* If the answer was yes to both questions the follow-up was *can she cook?*

Ramsey fired a shot at the enemy. (His guard was already up: Fiona had unexpectedly come to the defence of Clarence when earlier the lads had started to pull his leg in both directions.) "And how's your love life these days Clarence? Still going with that Tracey woman?"

He turned on Fiona. "Tracey is his girlfriend by the way."

"I know," replied Fiona, matter-of-factly.

Ramsey twitched. Clarence had told Fiona about his girlfriend. His model of how the universe operated with regards to members of the opposite sex did not allow for this.

Clarence went further. "We're just about holding it together if you must know."

Unconsciously he was looking for sympathy from the women around the table.

Ramsey, outflanked, fell silent. It would not last: sooner or later he would raise the subject of fitness and healthy living versus idleness and over-indulgence. And he did. Jane and Clarence took it in their stride. Fiona, new to the torture, tried her best to appear interested.

"Look at that my boy." Ramsey patted his stomach. "All muscle. No fat."

Clarence did a good impersonation of a small child being presented with the most cuddly teddy bear in the known universe. "It's beautiful. Can I kiss it?"

Fiona laughed and almost wet herself. Jane was too tired to even just laugh. She did however share the sentiment with a broad grin. Ramsey, confused, was stumped for a riposte. He had never been able to handle sarcasm. Footballs and cricket balls yes. Sarcasm no.

"No," he replied.

Clarence patted his own stomach. "Mine's a bit fatty nowadays. It's slipped a tad – but still kissable."

From then on the evening really began to drag. Ramsey sat cloaked in one of his moods and watched Clarence and Fiona converse, else the girl behind the bar, his eyes roving and recording. Clarence and Fiona talked while Jane listened and tried to keep awake until finally, when it dawned on her that she had to crash out, she got up and made her apologies. That was all Fiona needed to hear. She likewise grabbed her bag for the off.

'The girls are leaving. The boys are left', thought Ramsey, still entertaining the notion that he 'had a chance' with Fiona. If he had a chance with Fiona then IDS had a chance of a comeback with the Tory party.

Clarence pulled himself to his feet and drained his glass in one smooth, intentionally theatrical, action. Ramsey was baffled.

"Where you going?"

With the passion and delight that can only come from two men competing for the same woman Clarence stuck in the knife. "I'm with Fiona."

"You're what?" Ramsey recoiled as if he had been slapped in the face, which he had.

Clarence smiled and casually twisted his blade. "We're sharing a taxi. Fiona only lives a few miles from me."

And with that Clarence, Fiona and Jane spoke in turn, as if from the same script.

"Goodnight Ramsey," said Jane.

"Goodnight Ramsey," said Fiona.

"Goodnight Ramsey," said Clarence.

- the same two words, said three extremely different ways. Such is the richness of the English language.

⟡ ⟡ ⟡

Clarence and Fiona sat in the back of a fast moving but otherwise fairly decrepit taxi and stared out of their respective windows into the night. The odours which radiated from the backseat did so as waves and particles, and in a way which defied the laws of quantum physics. They could tell a thousand tales, and did, without any prompting. Clarence was quite happy with this arrangement as the view of dark, drab suburban streets did not require much in the way of reaction. Fiona was not so enamoured. She turned back in and started to talk. The taxi driver sampled the airwaves across his selection of preset FM stations before settling on the one which, in his opinion, passed as vaguely entertaining – i.e. something from the Seventies.

"I get the impression you and Ramsey don't hit it off?" said Fiona.

No response.

Fiona decided not to push it. Instead she reengaged with the view out of her window. It was for the want of something to look at. The taxi driver, assuming his passengers had fallen out, smiled to himself – his world view that the human life experience was total bullshit again reinforced.

When they arrived at her flat Fiona fished around inside her handbag for her purse. She thanked Clarence for the pleasure of his company. Still no response. Rude bugger aren't you thought the driver.

"I'd get yourself another boyfriend my dear if I was you," he suggested to the nice young lady as she passed him some money. "One that speaks."

The plastic dog which sat on the rear shelf nodded in agreement.

Fiona remonstrated. "He's not my boyfriend."

But the driver wasn't listening. He was too busy rubbing the grubby banknote between the thumb and first finger of his left hand and sniffing the air as if taking a measured, timely sample in the name of scientific research.

"This is only half," he declared.

"He's paying the other half," she responded.

"The bloke who's not your boyfriend?"

"Yes."

The driver turned on Clarence. "Where is it then buster?"

Still no response.

"Well?"

Still no response.

The taxi driver became angry. Fiona, seeing trouble not very far ahead, plunged back into her handbag. "Here. Here's the other half."

Now no longer fed up but extremely concerned Fiona handed over another ten pound note. No change was expected and none was given.

She touched Clarence lightly on the shoulder. "Are you feeling OK?"

Still no response and still Clarence stared out of his window – his view now taken up by a large red pillar box. The taxi driver was far less forgiving, though still more forgiving than his wife.

"Will you get him out of my cab." He was by nature, very territorial.

Fiona pushed Clarence again, harder this time. "Come on. Come with me. You're not feeling very well."

Still no response.

By now the taxi driver had had enough. He didn't need late night shit. He lifted himself out of his seat – hitting the tarmac with a vengeance – and wobbled with great effort around to the other side of the car. There he yanked open the passenger door and leant on it, peering in like a boiler inspector who was behind schedule. Though he was a big man and took no exercise he could move quickly when he wanted to traverse small amounts of space.

"Right you. Out and hop it. I don't have time for this."

Strictly speaking he had all the time in the world until his next booking.

Fiona tried one more time to avoid a situation. She took Clarence's hand and squeezed it between hers, before rubbing it, her mothering instinct fully engaged. And it worked! Clarence awoke from his trance. He looked up at the man who took no prisoners and smiled. Encouraged, he posed a question.

"Am I right in saying that you drive people around in this machine all day long as a means of earning your living?"

The taxi driver sneered. "And what of it? What the fuck are you talking about anyway? Look, out, now."

Unperturbed, Clarence added insult to injury. "Do you get enough exercise? You look very overweight for your age."

"That's it. Piss off now before I smack you one."

Fiona began to panic. "Please Clarence. Come on now let's go. You need to lie down."

She threw in the offer of a mug of hot chocolate as an added incentive. "I'll make you some hot chocolate, in a mug."

She dashed round to the other side of the car and placed herself strategically between the two men: one about to take up arms; the other about to get his face rearranged.

"I'll take care of him now," she pleaded. "He's just had a little too much to drink."

"I want him gone."

Fiona took Clarence's arm and levered him out. "Come on you."

He surprised her by not offering any resistance. Although he smelt and acted drunk he was meek and cooperative. She had expected some resistance, some grunting, but he was all smiles.

As he walked away from the car Clarence turned and threw the taxi driver one last question. "Do you feel satisfied with life? It must bore you terribly just driving around and around?"

The taxi driver slumped back into his seat and assumed the position. "Go screw yourself," he shouted. Thrashing his engine hard he sped off into the night, making lots of noise but with no idea of where he was headed.

Fiona climbed the steps to her front door and Clarence followed. He stood subdued, like a wet blanket, as Fiona fumbled for her latch key.

"I think I upset that man," he suggested cautiously, as if loathed to admit that he did not honestly know.

"I think you did," replied Fiona, her words weighed down with sarcasm.

Once inside the machine Clarence stood sheepishly in the middle of Fiona's living room, and like a lemon - if a lemon flavoured sheep were possible. He looked for all the world (and more) like a man about to have his backside probed as part of a thorough medical examination. Fiona, unsure what to do or say, did nothing and said nothing until she remembered the hot chocolate.

"Hot chocolate?"

"Hot chocolate?"

"Yes would you like some hot chocolate? Or coffee, hot coffee?"

Clarence pondered the choices for what seemed an eternity before replying. "Yes."

Fiona's journey towards the kitchen was interrupted by the shrill sound of her telephone erupting into life with something important to be said. She answered it without taking her eye off Clarence. He had not moved from his spot on the carpet.

"Yes? Hello. Oh it's you. No I'm fine. . . Honest." Fiona spoke in convenient half-truths. "No honest I'm fine. . . Did you? That's interesting. . . Me? . . . No."

Fiona made battle with the male voice on the other end of the phone. Once, not so long ago, they had had something, something shared, something bordering on beautiful, something worth pursuing down the corridor of time. Now they had shite, and it hung around, like a bad smell in the kitchen. And only she recognised it for what it was.

"The job? Too early to say really, but so far so good."

And still Fiona watched her guest. And still he hadn't moved. He looked like he was examining the ceiling. Perhaps he was into DIY in a deep way. Fiona returned to her painful conversation.

"What? So what? . . . So what about it? What exactly are you trying to say? . . . No not that. Not that again. Look we've been through all this. . . Yes we have. No yes we have. . . We have. . . We've been through it all before and I'm done with going over it all over again. . . No I'm not taking the piss. . . No I don't hate you. Honest. . . Well you'll just have to believe me. You've got no choice in the matter. . . Why? You know why. . . No. Forget it. . . No. . . I don't care if you've changed. I've also changed. That's the whole point. So we can't get back to where we were. . . No we can't. Trust me. . . Fine, that's your problem, not mine. . . No enough. Let's call it quits. Quits. That's a good word. . . I think that's quite enough now."

Fiona was suddenly struck by a thought. "Hey how did you get my new number? . . . Did she now. Great." She came up for air. "Well anyway that's enough now. Goodbye. . . Yes and good luck. Goodbye. . . Yes and goodbye. . . You too. Bye."

Fiona replaced the phone gently, despite wishing to smash it, closed her eyes and inhaled deeply, as if drawing on a cigarette. The man's timing, as ever, was excellent. She turned on Clarence.

"Sorry about that." She didn't mean it.

"Why are you sorry?" enquired Clarence.

"Well you know, you shouldn't have to hear stuff like that."

"I disagree. It was good for me."

"Good for you?"

"Well, whatever." Clarence backed away, and returned to the spot on the ceiling which had proved to be so fascinating.

Fiona became unnerved. When she spoke it was in the manner of a stressed out NHS patient. "What is it? Damp?"

Clarence was baffled. "Damp?"

"Damp patch. You know. You're the bloke aren't you?"

Clarence continued to stare up, so making Fiona ever more anxious.

"Tell me. What is it? Is there a leak?"

"No. Nothing I assure you. So just calm down."

Fiona hated being told to calm down. Had Clarence been her boyfriend (now ex-) she would probably have torn into him.

Clarence spoke again. "I take it he can't let go of you?" he asked.

Fiona was taken aback by the sudden shift of gear. She stalled momentarily, her recovery being sharp and decisive, much like an advisor to No. Ten Downing Street. She knew she was intelligent, and assumed, by job inclination that Clarence was the same. On that basis she gave him permission at the back of her mind to put such a weighty question. Once permission was given another two seconds passed before her mouth opened and sounds came out.

"Correct. Though I think he's finally got the point."

"That's good. It must be difficult to untangle yourself."

"It certainly is."

"Are they all like that?"

Fiona frowned. "They?"

"They. Men. Men in general. Not yours in particular."

"Thanks." The wheels inside Fiona's brain began to spin at high speed. She could feel a headache coming on. "In general? I don't know. Depends what you mean by 'that'".

"Good point."

Fiona didn't think so. Her reply seem to throw Clarence into a trance. She could almost see him thinking aloud, and it began to hurt. When Clarence did finally speak it was a great relief, like discovering that the clapped out old family estate had passed its MOT for another year.

"Unable to accept rejection?" he offered.

Fiona raised her eyebrows then lowered them again. It was one operation smoothly executed. She had been forced to consider. "I don't think so. Some are. Some aren't. Some don't give a toss."

"Fifty fifty?"

Fiona sat down. "Who knows. I wouldn't presume to be able to get inside the mind of a man."

Despite the offer, and the secret pleading, to take the other chair Clarence stood standing, much like a museum attendant.

"I'm trying," he said. "It seems to me that men – fully grown - feel lacking in credibility if they don't have a woman within reach to call their own and protect from dangers undeclared."

Fiona couldn't help but correct him. "That's not quite true."

"Really?"

"Well yes. Surely it's only true surely for men who like women."

"Meaning?"

Fiona stared up, as if at a child, a child who had attended all the classes and had completed all the homework, and who up to this point had never been considered an idiot by the teacher.

"Well some men only have relationships with other men don't they."

Clarence fell back into silence. Fiona could tell he was him thinking hard again. Then the penny dropped.

"Oh of course. You mean homosexuality," he exclaimed.

"Well done."

By now Fiona was annoyed – annoyed that she was sounding heavily sarcastic and uncaring – and equally annoyed that this Clarence kept coming up with interesting but sometimes irritating things to say. She was tired and she wanted to go to bed.

Clarence, oblivious to all of this, hit Fiona between the eyes with another big question.

"What made you decide it wasn't right – that he wasn't right for you?"

Before Fiona could answer – or be sure she was prepared to answer – Clarence had a follow-up question. "Was the sex good?"

Fiona crossed her legs. (She wanted to cross his.) "That was fine thank you very much."

"That's OK then."

Credit where credit's due she thought.

"Did he try to trap you with time?"

"Trap me with time?"

"He wanted his time to be your time?"

Fiona sized up the man who had cemented himself to her carpet, impressed but at the same time slightly scared by the overwhelming validity of his statement. She thought hard about the meaning behind the words, and was struck dumb by what she was thinking. It was awhile before she could bring herself to answer.

"You're right. I've never thought of it like that before. A lot of it is to do with time."

Clarence folded his arms and marched on through the mud which was the battlefield of human interaction.

"And did he feed off your moods?"

"Feed off my moods?" Fiona was gripped. It was turning – it had turned – into a very strange encounter.

"When you felt down, fed up, it gave him the reason – excuse perhaps – to feel strong and to act strong, so reinforcing his own perception of what it is to be a man in relation to a woman. Perhaps in such situations he came across as false, so making you feel used, or betrayed with regard to the contract of trust you had subconsciously written."

Fiona fell back before the onslaught of the analysis.

"Er yes. I suppose so. That's very good. I can't argue with that. Certainly can't." She couldn't and she didn't want to. Had he been a psychiatrist before taking up teaching? For a geography teacher he seemed to know a lot.

And still Clarence pushed on, despite an exhausted Fiona. "Did he demand space on his own terms?"

At this point in time Fiona suffered a surge of guilt. It came in a wave which washed over her. But Clarence had her in his grip and so she answered the question as best she could.

"We both demanded space," she mumbled, almost afraid she could be overheard by her ex-. He was many miles away, lying in bed watching soft porn on the telly.

"On your own terms?"

"Probably."

Then the wave collapsed, and no trace of guilt was left behind.

Clarence appeared satisfied. Fiona, desperately needing to laugh, laughed.

"I wish you would sit down," she said, this time openly pleading for him to stop towering over her.

But again a shift in conversation: Clarence had an announcement to make. "I need to go to the toilet, urgently I think."

"Understood." She pointed. "Just through there."

Clarence headed off in the direction indicated and Fiona waited, and waited, and waited, and wondered what he would come out with next. She waited and carried on waiting. She waited a reasonable length of time and then began to fidget and count the seconds – seconds which had already accumulated into minutes. She waited an additional length of time which rapidly changed from less than reasonable to a little unreasonable, then finally into totally unreasonable. It was inevitable. She began to worry about the state of her bathroom.

Fiona leapt up and like the cleaning maid impatient to enter the hotel room. She moved up to within an inch of the bathroom door. She listened out intently for the familiar sounds but she heard no sounds, familiar or otherwise. She examined her fingernails. Beneath they were clean. She adjusted her underwear. She examined the hall carpet at her feet. It was well worn – worn out in places. She looked at the cheap print hanging on the wall. She could see why it had been left behind by the previous owner. It would have to go, along with the bright orange, slightly radioactive lampshade.

It was her flat she reminded herself, and tapped with authority on the door which separated man from beast, husband from wife, Romeo from Juliet.

"Are you alright in there?" She spoke softly yet firmly.

"I'm fine. Thanks for asking." Clarence sounded cheerful, almost elated.

"It's just that you've been a very long time." She hated to imagine what he was up to. He wasn't being sick thank God.

"Coming out now."

And true to his word the door opened.

"Is everything OK?"

"Everything's fine."

"Would you like that cup of coffee now?" Fiona had forgotten about the hot chocolate.

"Hot?"

"Of course?" How else?

"Yes please."

"Well go and sit down and I'll go and make it."

Fiona bit her lip. She was not happy. She had just done a very good impression of her own mother.

Clarence did as he was told and slumped into the sofa. There he became as quiet as a church mouse, the really quiet kind. Fiona, satisfied that all was back under control, disappeared into the kitchen. She reappeared leaning against the frame of the living room door. The sound of the kettle heading towards boiling point could be heard in the background. She had a look on her face of renewed focus, energy and determination. Things were out of balance and she demanded that balance return.

"Now it's your turn. Tell me about you and this Tracey. You mentioned something earlier about it just holding up - holding together?"

Gracefully Clarence interlocked his hands, leant forward and placed them neatly between his knees, like a suspect awaiting interrogation, or a convict on death row, or a monk about to be promoted, else a philosopher, ancient yet fully functioning and deeply self-absorbed by a large question of his own making.

"Yes 'holding it together' is an apt description. It is a tenuous link. Each subconsciously afraid to break it, let it snap: to let go might be to drift, without direction or purpose or any chance of reaching the shore where survival is guaranteed - guaranteed in the emotional sense. The other human being is the anchor, the resting berth. To make things worse each side is unsure as to how they ended up like this. After all it did start so well.

And it's not a simple matter of just boredom taking hold. Boredom makes it easy to let go, to turn away, to lose all interest and association."

Clarence, eyes down while speaking, now looked up and examined the face of his female host, satisfied that he had given a full and accurate answer.

"Does that answer your question?"

Fiona wanted to gulp, but couldn't. "Yes, pretty much. I'll go and make the coffee. Instant for now I'm afraid. Sugar?"

"Hang on." Clarence thought hard for a second or two, the alcohol as always getting in the way. "Yes please. Just the one teaspoon measure. Preferably brown but that's not important."

Fiona took a deep breath, retreated, and made said coffee. She felt that she was caught up in a piece of theatre. This man had many sides to him, and hidden depths to boot: from the mundane, through the mindful, to the mysterious. She hated to admit it but she was looking forward to more of the same – more of the same but preferably with all the rough edges removed.

When Fiona returned clutching two hot mugs however she found the man crashed out on her sofa. Fast asleep he was, dead as a dodo. Reconciled to such events Fiona drank one coffee and poured the other down the sink. She turned off the living room light, made a fleeting visit to the bathroom, reassured herself that it was still a civilized place, and crept into bed. All was in order. Surprisingly she slept well that night. And her favourite teddy bear received a long hard hug.

※　※　※

Log Entry

This female Fiona is having quite an unsettling affect on my host Clarence. It disturbs me. In her physical presence the quantity of explosive, unfocused mental energy generated is alarming. It has no place to go. At one point I almost decided to abandon him for another host, one much older perhaps, or much younger, one where there is no sexual drive to produce chaos in the mind – but that would be to invalidate the project brief.

All that said, I have learnt to contain him in such situations. Just as I have learnt to contain him under the influence of the drug alcohol he readily swallows in the name of entertainment and hospitality. However to continually suppress his natural urges may lead to a far greater calamity. I therefore tread carefully.

Just as very positive emotions are generated by this female, so very negative emotions are generated by another colleague, this time a male of similar age. The outbursts of body language on both sides suggests that there is mutual animosity tempered by common history and shared values. But as nothing is said the evidence is inconclusive.

Some cultural aspects of this society are now beginning to make sense. Information weighs heavily in many minds – the need for it, the need to be close to it, the need to be in control of, and ironically the fear of not understanding it. In this corner of the planet it is easily accessible, dangerously so. Interactive screen/keyboard/pointer combinations are a popular – and I suspect universal – device for delivering visual and audio information at high speed from many disparate, unconnected sources.

Although the visual presentation is sophisticated and well laid out, the method of interaction between audience and the supplier (probably a machine most of the time) is not so, confined as it is to a reliance upon certain physical extremities of the human body. By this I mean the hands. Humans have two, and they are the only tools (and weapons?) available with which to manipulate the physical world around them. They have two feet on the end of two legs which together operate to provide the means of motion (traditionally horizontal).

Some of this information is of a dubious nature: its accuracy is suspect; the motives of its authors a cause for concern. I notice that some of the pupils at my host's teaching establishment seem to spend long periods of time staring at these screens, digesting vast amounts of information I presume, but for what purpose I know not. They do not appear to end up better informed. I tried to question two of them while they were engaged in this activity but met with resistance and, how shall I put it, 'polite hostility'. I suspect – judging by their change in attitude when forced to terminate the activity of concentrated information seeking – that the affect on their brains is akin to that of alcohol, this popular and universal drug. That is to say that the mind is raised to a new level of excitement and expectation, hysteria almost, (for what, enlightenment?) only to suffer a relapse and minor depression.

It is becoming apparent to me that humans have a close association with one other particular animal, the dog. There are many varieties of dog and they form close attachments, partnerships even, with humans in many areas: leisure pursuits, wealth creation activities, entertainment, and last but not least basic self-survival. The connection goes back a long way in time.

For many, dogs give strong emotional support while asking nothing in return. As a last resort they are the trigger for necessary emotional release.

Sometimes they are the first resort, taking priority over relationships with other humans. Some humans even talk to their dogs in a way which is intimate and guarded. I am not sure if there are some highly intelligent breeds which understand human language – unlikely as they are not physically equipped to respond in kind. The best they can do is bark.

Humans also have an attraction towards other, smaller, four-legged creatures: cats. Cats, like dogs, play a large part in the lives of humans. Note however that the two species are not only physically dissimilar but also completely different in temperament and character. Yet both are domesticated and heavily reliant upon a symbiotic relationship with man.

There is a preoccupation in the culture with these 'cars' (personal motorised transportation devices) which exceeds all reasonable relevance to need and purpose. The technology contained in some of these machines appears excessive and an extravagant waste of time and material wealth. To what end? Just to get from point A to point B in the quickest time, at maximum convenience and without social interaction of any kind?

In this part of the planet cars hold a strong position in the human psyche. Via the television set in particular humans are constantly bombarded with announcements from manufacturers that their model serves some highly critical, life-enhancing function, alongside seductive invitations to buy their latest, state-of-the-art model, and only theirs. The manufacturers appear desperate to sell large volumes.

Visual stimulation rules. Everybody it seems watches the television screen at some point in the day, and mainly in the comfort of their own home. Why? As I have said before the quality of the material is very suspect at times. In this social climate there appears to be a never-ending, almost anguished need for constant, real time reports on all activities around the world, both close to home and far away. Via the television a multitude of combined picture and sound communication channels feed this habit on a continuous basis. The supply is inexhaustible and non-stop, but also repetitive. Sound only channels are also provided in abundance via devices known as 'radios'. These are small and very portable, portable to the point that they can be carried easily about the person.

Chapter Four

Saturday. Midday. The doorbell rang and Tracey was forced to answer it. Clarence was in the shower, scrubbing himself down, removing dirt, checking for lumps.

A young woman was standing at the door. Tracey made her nervous by staying silent, having decided not to speak first. Instead she calculated probable age difference and noted the lady's dress sense. She was not impressed. In her opinion it left a lot to be desired.

The woman spoke. She did not sound nervous. "Is Clarence at home?"

"Yes."

From Fiona's perspective the air between them had frozen but she prepared to chop her way through it.

"Can I speak to him?"

"No."

"Why not?"

"He's in the shower."

"Oh."

"Why do you want to speak to him?"

"I've got his mobile phone," replied Fiona. As to prove the point she pulled it out of her handbag.

Now Tracey was genuinely suspicious. "And why have you got his mobile?"

"He dropped it down the back of the sofa."

"Did he now?"

I don't need this thought Fiona. "He kipped down on my sofa last night."

"Did he indeed."

Fiona thrust it out in front of her. "Here."

Tracey plucked it from her hand. "Thank you," she said through gritted teeth.

"It was half buried in the sofa."

But Tracey wasn't listening. She was impatient to close the door. "Well if that's all I'll be getting on."

Fiona threw one final hook into the water. "Is he OK?"

"What do you mean?" Now Tracey was weighed down by deep suspicion. She could not move from the spot.

"He was talking in his sleep."

"Was he?"

"Has he ever done that before?"

"No."

"Sure?"

"Yes I'm sure. I would know."

"Sorry."

Tracey tried a second time. "Well if that's all then."

"Yes. Sorry to bother you."

"No bother."

The lies came thick and fast on both sides.

"Give him my regards."

"I will."

Fiona stepped back and Tracey closed the door in her face, just managing to not to slam it. When Clarence appeared out of the shower she waved his mobile at him.

"Remember this?"

Clarence shrugged. He knew she knew it was his and he knew she knew he knew. "That's my mobile. So what?"

"A lady just handed it in at the door."

"A lady?"

"Said you dropped it down the back of her sofa."

"Oh Fiona." Clarence smiled but to ill affect. In fact it just made things worse. He gripped his towel around his waist more tightly.

"Who's Fiona?"

"A teacher at my school."

"What were you doing down the back of her sofa?" Tracey stalked her prey as it moved around the living room. Her joke didn't sound funny.

Clarence decided to stand his ground. "I was sleeping on her sofa."

He could tell by the look on his woman's face that further explanation was required.

"I couldn't get home last night. I was too drunk to get a taxi. We had all been down the pub celebrating her first week in her new job."

"So you just slept on her sofa."

"Exactly so."

Tracey examined her man as he clutched his bath towel tightly around his waist. Body language said guilty.

"Stop looking at me like that."

"Like what?"

"You know."

"So you didn't sleep with her."

Clarence was buggered if he was going to apologize. He hadn't done anything.

"Correct. Anyway why would she want to sleep with an old git like me?"

Self-depreciation seemed to be his only way out. And it worked. Tracey relaxed.

"OK. Go and get dressed."

Clarence did as he was told – in these situations he always did. Feeling his sap rising he made his exit in haste and got into clothes while Tracey toyed briefly with the idea of tidying his flat. He was slightly pissed off with Tracey because she hadn't invited Fiona in, not appreciating that this would have been totally unworkable. Tracey was greatly pissed off with Clarence because he never tidied his flat, even when he knew she would be round.

✦ ✦ ✦

Saturday night, TV and lager cans were a potent combination when left to set in the hands of men. Clarence and Max were no exception. One sat slouched in a rotting old armchair. The other sprawled across the sofa, equally rotting. Just lads. No women. Paradise.

The TV spoke volumes but two men alone, slightly drunk, spoke volumes more. For every action, event, statement of fact, opinion on the box each defended their own opinion. For every action there was reaction. Sometimes they agreed with each other. Sometimes they didn't. Sport scored the fastest reaction time and most emotional response, followed by the news, then some stupid talk show which could only attract those guests desperate for media attention or with something to flog. Clarence looked at his watch. It was still there. He stubbed out his cigarette. He was trying to cut down and surprisingly he felt as if he was succeeding.

"Where the hell is she?"

Max didn't turn but kept on staring at the screen, lest something interesting popped up. "Who?"

"My other half."

"You going out tonight?"

"Suppose to be."

Forced to move himself, Clarence slid off the sofa, managed to stand up – legs lacking blood – and shuffled off to his bedroom, there to make a phone call. Max continued his viewing undisrupted – even when the call was terminated by the sound of the phone being slammed down. Only when Clarence reappeared and slumped back into position did Max register interest.

Clarence spoke, holding a grudge. "She's not coming round tonight."

"Your Tracey woman?"

"She's in one of her moods. Doesn't want to go out."

"Women are like that. I should know. I've got three sisters back in Dublin."

"You poor bastard."

Max suddenly became defensive. "It's not that bad. A large family is better than no family."

"Whatever."

The talk hit a cul-de-sac and the two returned to the box, each feeling that they had missed something vitally important. But of course they hadn't and in time it drizzled out. Lager finished, Max got up.

"If you're interested I'm going down the pub."

"Sure."

"Then the nightclub."

"Nightclub?"

"That one behind the shopping centre."

"Can I come?"

Despite being the older Clarence spoke like a younger brother, daring to ask permission. It was an unintended lapse in self-worth and dignity. He looked lost, abandoned. Max looked on, faintly curious.

"Of course. It's a free country."

Clarence scrambled to his feet, grabbed his wallet, and followed his lodger to the front door. Then just as he was about to shut it he remembered something important.

"Fuck. Hang on."

He ran back inside and made a quick phone call. He apologized to Tim on the other end, saying they couldn't make the curry.

"Tracy isn't feeling well and I don't feel like going out without her."

Tim could smell the prize bullshit down the other end of the land line but made no protest. Instead he said have a good time.

The pair set off. Two blokes, one unattached, one attached but open to offers, both able to hold their beer, one more than the other, one still able to dance to a beat.

�֎ ✦ ✦

In the pub Clarence was on familiar territory and felt at house: just the two of them, foot up on the foot rest, elbows on counter, watching the skirt go by or stop. Nightclub: not so.

Clarence stood rooted to a spot in the dark, and did his best to look like he was enjoying himself as a continuous thump thump thump of a bass line did strange things to his internal organs and made his joints tingle, as if out of spite. Clarence was not a happy man. He was not in his natural habitat, unlike Max who seemed to be thriving in a place where normal rules of behaviour and communication did not apply. If there was body language Clarence couldn't read it. It may as well have been Latin, or Croatian.

Clarence looked around at the well-dressed young, lean heaving bodies. Some of the boys wore as much makeup as the girls. Nobody talked sense. People just screamed at each other. The flashing lights of the disco made him feel dizzy. Clarence did his best to hold back the dread that he was becoming middle-aged.

Across the dance floor a particularly drunk lad, depressingly thin, fit and good-looking, dropped his trousers and waved his prize willy affectionately at the women he was dancing with. He meant so harm. He was proud of his willy. It was his heritage. They laughed then clapped and whistled and waved back. He didn't know them and they didn't know him. More than satisfied he yanked his trousers up and returned to the beat. Clarence was gob smacked. The guy hadn't even introduced himself. Then with creeping fatalism it dawned on him that he couldn't remember when he had last been in a nightclub. I am getting too old for this he thought and, as if in a dream, found himself semi-collapsed outside the men's room, barely able to stand but glad to have escaped the worse of the racket. He was an alien on an alien planet.

Clarence stood with his back to the wall and soaked up the near return to sanity in a nearly normal environment of light and sound. The beat of a drum machine still penetrated his body. It came up through the floorboards. There was no escape. You were expected to enjoy yourself at any cost. Even if it meant you lost your hearing for a week. And the price of a small bottle of continental lager still rankled. It hadn't bothered Max though – which rankled just as much. Clarence felt sick. And his own sweat, now freezing cold, was torture from Hell.

A teenage girl, returning from a loo visit, stopped a second and stared.

"What?" snapped Clarence.

"Are you alright?" she enquired.

"I'm fine." Clarence felt like giving her some homework.

"There's some chairs down there."

"I can stand thank you."

She shrugged and moved on. Tosser.

Clarence continued to watch the world go by until some other young woman, barely out of her teens – perhaps still in them – also stopped and began to talk to him. His eyes glazed over. He assumed that he was being chatted up. And why not? He was still in his thirties.

The illusion was shattered when she asked why he was looking so miserable and why he didn't cheer up and have some fun. Chill out. Let loose.

'Fuck off' thought Clarence. He didn't like being patronised by someone almost half his age.

For something to say, and to change the sad subject, Clarence asked what she did. She stared back, grimaced, looked put out, then laughed.

"I shag blokes. What do you do?"

Clarence made the mistake of answering proudly with the truth, boasting even.

"I'm a teacher," he said and smiled. She didn't.

"Geography," he added, as if that made a difference.

Her eyes glazed over. She took a step back. Her eyes skimmed across his surface area from top to toe as if searching for an explanation, else a deficiency. She half-smiled and detached herself quickly, excuse being the reappearance of her mate from the ladies. The night was young and they didn't have mortgages, kids or husbands. Clarence wanted to shout after her 'well fuck you', but didn't. Instead he headed back outside for real air. There, his sweat turning to ice and freezing his body, he persuaded himself to head home. He had had enough and Max had left him stranded a good hour earlier.

Clarence got about halfway before he succumbed to a council bench. It looked disgusting, and it was disgusting, but his legs were knackered, like the rest of him. He sat down, feeling miserable, pissed off with everything and everybody and his current mental state of health. When he was in a bad mood he hated being in a bad mood, which only prolonged the condition.

A smelly, scruffy old man walked up holding a plastic shopping bag. It looked like he had just been shopping. Great thing these 24 hour supermarkets. Clarence looked at the bag. He has a good idea what the shopping was. The old man looked at Clarence looking at his bag, looked at his bag and wrapped the handles tighter up in his fingers. His plastic bag and its contents were precious to him.

Clarence became worried when he realised the old sod was about to engage in conversation. Be polite? Ignore him? Tell him to clear off? Clarence was determined not to be budged.

The old man grinned as if he had encountered an old friend from way back.

"You're sitting in my favourite spot," he said.

Clarence stared up. "What?"

"Only joking."

The old man sat down at the far end of the bench, far enough away not to alarm the punter. I was here first thought Clarence. I'm not moving for anyone.

The old man spoke. He couldn't resist a chat. "You look like shit."

"Thanks."

Satisfied that he had made a poignant point, the old man began drinking from a can. Clarence watched him, growing jealous by the second. Finally he couldn't resist.

"Can I buy one off you?"

The old man froze and looked hard at him back down the length of his can. It could have been a let point in a tennis match. Then he looked at his plastic bag.

"How much?" he asked suspiciously.

"You tell me" answered Clarence.

"Two quid?"

"Fair enough."

Clarence was handed a can. He opened it and began to drink. Rightly or wrongly his fellow drinker now felt a sense of bonding. It was not to be. Now Clarence had a drink he just wanted to finish it and go home. He was feeling sleepy and cold.

"So how did you get so fucked up?" asked the old man. "I've got my excuse."

Clarence stared backed. He wanted to slap the fellow down but he was a geography teacher and geography teachers didn't do such things – at least not in this country. He could never escape that fact. It clung to him and mocked him like a 50 yards swimming certificate. Swim 51 yards and he might drown. Perhaps he could teach the guy geography until he pleaded with him to stop.

"You're hardly one to talk."

"True."

Having stated the obvious both fell into a welcomed silence and watched the nightlife drift pass; some it of loud, some of it loony, some of it still lonely; some of it falling over but getting up again. Most of it was not a pretty sight, but there were exceptions, all of them female and very young, probably under age.

The tramp decided to speak. "I was in the Falklands."

"Fuck off."

✦ ✦ ✦

Clarence was dragged from a bad dream by a loud fart. He sat up. Blackouts and now this? He pulled himself out of bed, not wishing to but knowing he had to. He walked to the bathroom feeling less than one hundred percent. Funny smell on the way? A Tim special?

Bladder emptied (for now) he made for the kitchen. On his way he heard a noise of someone breathing heavily. There was someone asleep on his sofa. Max?

No not Max but some scrawny ugly little man. He could have been 40 but he looked 60. Clarence froze. He was only dressed in his bed shorts and felt naked. His mental faculties were two paces ahead of him but he was catching up fast. It was the fucking tramp dossing down in his fucking flat.

The old man opened an eye and smiled at him like an old friend. He sat up, scratched his itchy beard, threw back his greasy hair, and grinned. All was good in the world. Clarence smelt something nasty penetrate his nose. He took a step back and nearly fainted, but recovered enough to flee back into his bedroom, kicking the door shut behind him.

He sat on the edge of his bed, head thumping, but little in the way of useful thoughts generated. He dressed in double quick time and re-emerged, scared but pretending to be belligerent. The alien was still there, waiting to be served.

"Any chance of breakfast?"

Clarence, far removed from any comfort zone, dried up and answered yes. "I'll cook it now."

"Fry up?"

"Whatever." The man might turn violent if he didn't get what he wanted. So just feed him quick. And get him out.

"Thanks. Can I use the bathroom?"

"Yes." Clarence bit his tongue. Bad mistake – but dare he say no?

Twenty minutes later, fry up fried, Clarence stood back as the slightly cleaner man gorged himself on the contents of a large grill pan and a tin of baked beans (in tomato sauce). It was as if he hadn't eaten for a week, which he probably hadn't.

In broken phrases and with a high degree of repetition, the tramp continued to pour gratitude and affection over him. Clarence watched the food vanish off the plate, afraid to take his eye off the ball lest it smack him in the face. Thank God the man could eat and talk quickly at the same time. Clarence pleaded for Max to appear but Max was in a far far away place, beneath a duvet with a woman and a hangover brewing.

The tramp suddenly paused. "What you said last night. I was thinking."

Clarence didn't want him to be thinking. He wanted him to be eating. "Look I do have to be somewhere, like now."

"People like you put my faith back in human nature."

"Do we." Clarence stared down at the plate. He would have to pick it up to wash it. "Have you finished yet. I have to get on. Things to do."

The tramp tucked back in, scraping up every vestige of available food matter as if it were his last supper. "Almost."

He emptied his mug in one long gratifying swig and slammed it down, as if to make a point. "Can I have some more coffee?"

But too late, Clarence had rediscovered his backbone. "No. I'm late."

"Fair enough."

Plate wiped clean, the tramp was escorted to the front door with declared haste. There, as Clarence tried to shut the door, the tramp was determined to have the last word.

"I want to thank you – and not just for the food."

"Thank me?"

"For taking an interest."

"Right."

"It's nice when someone takes an interest."

"Sure. Look I've got to go."

"Understood."

With that the tramp let go and Clarence was free. Clarence watched him walk down the street from his window, just to be sure the man did as promised.

✦ ✦ ✦

Sam sat up in bed, delicately poised, buttressed against both cushions with her mug of coffee within reach: paper supplements dumped in her lap, and a ballpoint clasped in her hand. A collection of numbers fought for supremacy and order inside her head like it was the most important thing in the world at that very point in time – which it was.

She had the whole double bed to herself. No radio TV or DVD playing. No mobile within earshot. It was 'quality time'. It was her Sunday morning renaissance. It was the dead zone. And then the front doorbell went and spoiled it all.

Sam did not take it well. "For Christ's sake.'

Husbands were awkward things sometimes, and they timed it to perfection. Just as she had systematically barricaded herself into a corner she was now expected to graciously unravel herself and attend to his needs again. Why didn't he use his sodding key? She did a double take. He had forgotten his key. Again.

Before moving she carefully annotated a square within a grid with two numbers – two very tiny numbers tucked away in the corner, taking up no space - and laid her problem to rest. She found her slippers and after much frustration found her feet the right way round in her slippers. The hard bit done, she made for the front door, at a crawl and still gripping her supplement, unwilling to become detached from her problem lest she lose the plot. Also it was a useful flag of protest, a clear indication that she had been disturbed.

Sam opened the door and looked out. Somewhat put out, Sam stared ahead into what was a ghastly sight of a man. That said, on a Sunday morning she never looked too good herself.

Clarence said nothing. He was too distracted by the sight of this woman first thing out of bed. It was at odds with his regular image of a well-polished, well-presented female corporate missile.

"Clarence?"

"Can I come in?"

"It's a bit early. Can't it wait?" She sounded like a gruff gym teacher.

"No it can't. Sorry."

The man was not kidding. He sounded like he really meant it.

"Why didn't you phone?"

"Sorry. It was a bit spontaneous like."

Sam relented. She could do nothing else.

"You better come in," she said, matter of fact.

Clarence did as instructed and stood in the middle of the room, limp, lost, like a boy on his first day at cubs. Sam began to worry. This was not her Clarence by any stretch of the imagination. She waited for him to speak, or at least join a few words together, but he didn't say a word. Instead he acted like he had never seen her front room before. Which was very strange.

"You want a drink?"

"Yes please."

"Coffee?"

"No. I mean yes."

"Sit down." It was an order. Sam didn't know why but a Clarence standing felt peculiar. He ignored her.

"Did you see Tim?"

"I saw his car."

"Did he see you?"

"Dunno."

Sam retreated to the kitchen and while making fresh coffee decided to make toast. An onset of nerves was clawing at her stomach. She reappeared with a stack of buttered half slices. She always cut her slices in half. It was a habit which had been drummed into her from an early age. There was no alternative. Tim called it 'fussing'.

Clarence had finally sat down, hands folded, perched over his own legs. He looked like he was waiting for a train, desperate to get up and be taken somewhere, anywhere. Sam handed him the impromptu breakfast. He took it without ceremony and without thanks.

"Hang on." Sam turned and went back for hers.

When she returned with her own mug and mouth full of toast she sat down opposite her little lost boy and looked on, interested. Clarence chewed away like a child who wasn't sure if he liked toast or not.

"Well speak to me. You look like shit."

"Do I?"

"Yes take it from me you do."

"One sugar in this?"

"Of course one sugar. How long have I been making you coffee?"

Clarence carried on munching in the gloom. Sam knew she had her work cut out and to make things worse was itching for a shower.

"Is it me or is this more than a social call?"

Clarence looked around the room in circles. He had seen it many times before but somehow felt required to look around it again, just in case something had changed. Sam watched him like a hawk, a sparrow-hawk. The long pause became an interlude.

Sam broke the impasse. "I'm going to have to pop to the loo. Back in a minute."

"Right you are."

"Don't go away."

No answer she noted.

On return from taking her promised piss and adapting her hair Sam decided to take command. It was like being at work, only without the forms. She sat down next to the problem, the 'person problem'.

"OK. Come on. Tell me, what's up? There's something your dying to get off your chest."

She had a twelve year old on her hands and he wasn't playing ball.

Clarence looked across, wishing to say something, while wishing to avoid eye-contact. He only managed to achieve the one.

Sam pushed on. "Come on silly. Speak to me. You still having these blackouts?"

"Yes."

"Has the doctor given you anything? Sent you to see anyone?"

"No."

"Silly. Are they getting worse?"

Clarence looked vacant. "Depends what you mean by worse."

"Well I don't know. Longer?"

"Some must be but I don't remember."

"Well more of them?"

"I think so. Not sure. I'm not exactly counting."

Well that was a start thought Sam. "Well what do you want me to do about it."

"Nothing."

"Well why are you here then?"

Clarence stared into the depths of the repeating carpet pattern and finally made the confession he had been burdened with all morning. He stopped chewing on his toast.

"I woke up with a man in my room – in my living room."

Sam's eyes darted here and there, away from Clarence, searching for somewhere less hazardous to settle. Her mouth felt like solid concrete, and dry to the bone. Her ability to think or react had been crushed by the impact of a large fully-loaded delivery truck.

"He was on my sofa."

Sam asked the only question she could think off. "Someone I know?"

"No."

"Friend? Teacher?"

"No."

Growing rapidly impatient for a quick answer Sam became sarcastic. "Long lost cousin?"

"No."

The word 'no' was beginning to bore. "Well give me a clue."

"Just someone."

"Anyone?"

"Just someone."

Clarence finally laid his cards on the table. "He was a tramp."

Now Sam was impressed. "A tramp?"

"That's what I said."

Sam was afraid to let her imagination run away with her so assumed the only alternative scenario. "That's very commendable of you. Were his clothes clean? I mean did he mess up the sofa?"

"It wasn't like that."

"What the sofa?"

"No it."

"Meaning what?"

"I wasn't doing him a favour."

"Wasn't you?"

"No."

"Well what were you doing?"

"I don't know. I have no idea." Clarence struggled on with a heavy heart. "I don't know why he was there."

Sam suddenly jumped one step ahead. "You mean he had broken in!"

"No. Nothing like that." Clarence stared down at his feet. "I remember talking to him the night before."

"About what?"

"Nothing in particular. I brought a can of beer off him."

"So you invited him home?"

"No - at least I don't remember. I just remember a few words, enough to get a drink."

"You had one of your blackouts?"

"Must of done.'

"So you're not gay then."

"No!" Stung, Clarence dropped his toast.

"Leave it," Sam instructed firmly.

Clarence still had something to say. "He was friendly towards me, like he knew me."

Suddenly there was a big black hole in his lap, one threatening to swallow him up if he leant forward anymore or gave anymore away. Sam saw the pain on his face and was suddenly struck by the need to do something about it. She edged ever so closer and accidentally left bits of her dressing gown behind. In the confusion large areas of her thighs were exposed. Clarence noticed this, and felt it. He had seen her legs a hundred thousand times before. He had seen her in a bikini, pissed. They had swum in the sea together. But now suddenly for the first time in a long long time it felt very very different. Some law was being broken.

Sam took his hands in hers and immediately they began to tremble. The poor man was really suffering.

Clarence saw a woman's bosom within close range and freely available, no strings attached. He leant across and parked his face in her nice warm pounding breast. It was a wonderful place to be right now. It was the only place to be right now. Sam didn't say a word – an act which Clarence fully appreciated. Clarence didn't say a word – an act which Sam ignored.

Together, without realising it, they both listened to the tick tick ticking of the clock on the mantle piece. Just as Sam began to stroke his hair and vaguely consider the consequences there was a rattle at the door. A key was being turned impatiently and with unnecessary vigour.

Clarence sprang back into his previous position and Sam jumped up.

"Shit," she exclaimed.

Clarence followed her up. "I better go."

The two headed towards the front door on the ground floor and intercepted Tim on the stairs.

"Oh hiya," said Tim.

"What are you doing here?" asked Sam.

"Forgot something."

Tim put the same question to Clarence and at the same time gave his best mate a 'best mate' type squeeze - the type that doesn't raise eyebrows on a Friday night in the pub with the lads. No response. Clarence pushed on past in a hurry.

"Sod you then."

"Bye. Got to rush."

"Hang on."

"No got to rush. Really. Family stuff. Lunch."

Tim screwed up his nose. "It's way off lunch time."

"True." Clarence stalled while opening the door. Then he thought of an answer. "I had promised to get over early."

"Fair enough. Bye."

"Bye."

"Bye."

Sam watched the car drive away while her husband thumped his way upstairs to the bedroom. When Tim came back down stairs he was struck by a thought.

"What was he doing here anyway?"

"Blackouts are getting him down," explained Sam. "He needed someone to talk to."

The answer satisfied.

✦ ✦ ✦

Clarence drew up at his parents house. He had been driving around, killing time, enjoying the delights of an anaemic M25 on a Sunday morning, while at the same time holding at arms length all uncomfortable thoughts, fears and memories. Worse of all he was scared to think of Sam: she gave him an erection. He spotted his brother-in-law's car parked a bit further down the street so drove on and parked behind it.

Clarence rang the doorbell. His mother's voice boomed out from the kitchen with distinction.

"It's open!"

He pushed on it. It was, as she said. He peered inside. The usual smells were coming from the kitchen. He heard his sister's voice compete with his mother's for dominance when it came to the subject of kitchens, and how to get something edible onto the table quickly. Neither sounded like they were winning the argument and neither sounded like they were prepared to admit defeat: stalemate of the frenzied kind.

Next step. He ventured inside. He found Desmond sitting in the living room, head wrapped around a Sunday paper supplement.

"Hallo Des."

Desmond hated being called 'Des' and Clarence knew it. Desmond looked up.

"Hi Clarence," he replied, and returned to his paper. He pretended to be reading something interesting. As usual the two had nothing to say to each other. Clarence, for something better to do, headed towards the women in motion. He stood at the kitchen door and watched mother and sister firing on all cylinders. Their deadline was approaching. It was a place where the men were not wanted.

Mother turned and stopped stirring the gravy. She stepped forward and grabbed her son and gave him a big squeeze. She looked into his eyes as if performing a medical check-up and frowned.

"Are you getting enough sleep?"

"I'm fine mum."

She wasn't convinced, but let go of him anyway.

"When's lunch ready?" he asked.

"About twenty minutes."

Margaret cut in. "About now mum. Five minutes."

"Yes about now."

"Where's dad?"

"In his shed probably."

"And what's for lunch?"

"Roast."

"Roast what?"

"So many questions. Turkey. Roast turkey."

His mother turned her back on her son and continued to stir. "Speaking of which can you go and find your father."

"Sure."

As Clarence turned to leave he caught his sister's eye and felt obliged to counter the threat. "What's the matter with you?"

"Nothing." She returned to her cooking duties.

"How are things?" He asked the question automatically. It was ritual.

"Oh fine. As they should be."

She was willing to expand on the statement but the microwave went ping! Duty called and Clarence was saved.

Clarence found his dad in the shed. On the way across the back lawn he almost got hit by one of his nephews. There were two of them, and they were twins. Everything they did together was amplified, especially noise and trouble. The twins were physically joined and encumbered by an invisible length of chain. It was made of strongest metal and forever tugged on each other. It gave them strength but reigned them in. And they were forever tripping over it. Clarence had lost count of the number of times he had vowed to strangle them.

The radio was on, the same old radio, the same old channel. Dad was listening to classical and his head was swaying up and down by a few degrees. Clarence felt guilty over disturbing him, and slightly sad that he could never bring himself to join in.

"Dad."

Dad turned. "Hallo son."

"What are you doing?"

"Just tidying up."

"Screwdriver set?"

"That's right."

"Lunch is ready."

"Coming."

Clarence paused and watched his father intently. It was a familiar sight. Then he let it go and left the old man to it.

He didn't feel like going back inside just yet, so walked aimlessly around the back garden – and it was an enormous garden, too much for his aging parents – until the continuing noise of the twins squabbling drove him to the front garden. There he found a temporary peace and solitude until he was shouted back inside by Desmond.

The men folk were gathered at the table and marking out their territory. The women ricocheted between dining room and kitchen, like waiters on acid. God help anybody who got in their way.

Somehow it all came together, like a party conference. Upon instruction Dad brought in the roast on the tray. The twins sat and bickered. Desmond stretched his arms, kneaded his shoulder muscles and tried not to think of work the next day. It was looming on the horizon. He had folder his newspaper and placed it at his feet, having found something interesting to read.

Finally mother and daughter sat down, almost at the exact same time. Mother looked at her husband and son. Daughter looked at her own children who quickly declared a truce and became silent. They were starving and keen for the grand occasion to begin.

Clarence sat, prepared to go through the motions. He was too tired to eat. His brain said time to eat but his soul had no appetite. The bowls of vegetables, gravy, and other various accompaniments circulated around the table in time honoured tradition. Dad stood up at his end of the table and sharpened his two weapons before attacking the dead, unhappily deceased bird.

Clarence had seen it all before, so many times before that he was soon stiff with boredom. Boredom was one of his major hates. The devil inside him equated family lunch to a funeral – which was a bit unfair as at funerals no one had to do the washing up, and silence was expected. Here you had to talk to earn your meal.

Clarence watched his father laboriously and meticulously cut slices of meat from the joint. It was like watching surgery.

'Christ that's me in thirty years, less even, twenty-five - twenty if I'm unlucky' he thought. Secretly he measured the size of his stomach with a hand under the table.

Clarence would normally have piled his plate up high, to the limits of endurance, but today he was surprisingly self-restrained. He picked out just enough potato and veg to make it look like he was in on the party. Before he could give instruction Dad dumped a load of white breast on his plate, far more than he knew he could manage. But there was no point in trying to give any back.

He didn't even bother to pour Mum's gravy over proceedings, and as they all tucked she spotted something wasn't quite right. She cut through the conversation which was on-going between her husband and Desmond – a conversation about trains versus planes – and proceeded to interrogate her son, her only son.

"Clarence what's the matter? You not hungry?"

"No I'm fine mum."

"Well why aren't you eating?"

"I will. Just give me time."

"There's not much on your plate."

"I had a big breakfast."

His mother wasn't convinced. Things didn't add up. "You love roast turkey. You know you do."

"I know I do."

She returned to her own meal, still dissatisfied, and checked a roast potato before popping it in her mouth. She sat and chewed and swallowed and vaguely joined in the conversation while all the time keeping a sharp eye on her son. He said nothing, made no contribution to the fragmented, constantly shifting talk. Finally, perplexed, she returned to the problem of flesh and blood which was bugging her. Her son was still not eating.

"You're still not eating."

"Yes I am."

"You're just picking at it."

"Mum. Please." Clarence recognised the early onslaught of a large thumping headache. But she wouldn't be stopped.

"You know you don't look at all well."

"Mum I'm fine."

"No you're not."

Clarence looked around the table, luckily he was not the centre of attention. Dad and Desmond were talking the usual drivel about things inconsequential and sister Margaret was force feeding her kids like they hadn't eaten for 24 hours. He pushed a piece of meat into his mouth and smiled at his mother as if to prove that she was talking bollocks.

"Happy?"

"Don't talk with your mouth full."

"I'll talk how I like."

Margaret stormed in. "Clarence!"

Clarence turned. "What."

She glared back, saying nothing.

The twins found something to argue about and rushed into another argument with total commitment.

"Will you two stop it!" she snapped.

Mother picked up the line of questioning again. "Clarence why are you so touchy today?"

"I'm not touchy."

She ignored his remonstration. "You know you're looking rather scruffy."

"Thanks."

"You should look after yourself better."

"I do."

Margaret cut in. "No you don't."

Clarence turned on his sister. "Yes I do."

Mother took control again. "How are things with Tracey."

"She's fine."

"I haven't seen her recently."

"She's been busy. She's always busy. Busy. Busy. Busy."

"Meaning?"

"Meaning what?"

"Clarence you know what I mean." Mother noted it when her son – the clever one in the family – played word games with her.

Clarence shrugged her aside. He demolished a potato instead. He had to admit he did love mum's roast potatoes. He felt it coming. He knew it was coming. The big question was on its way. He forced himself to down some cabbage and waited for the big one.

"Are you two planning to settle down yet?" she asked.

Clarence closed his eyes and thought of Fiona, then he thought of Sam. Then he thought of the nasty little smelly tramp crashed out on his sofa.

His mother repeated herself. "Are you two planning to settle down?"

Clarence kept his eyes closed and just concentrated on Sam's broad bosom, though Fiona did creep into the equation. She was part of it now.

"Clarence our mother is talking to you." Margaret sounded aggrieved, though she had no right to be. Clarence wanted to smack her.

"I know. I can hear her."

"Well answer her."

Clarence threw his sister a sharp look and tried to shut her up with force of personality. "No we are not planning on settling down. We have no plans for anything."

"So no plans to get married."

"No plans to get married." Clarence replayed the same old mantra.

Dad suddenly cut in. "Time doesn't stand still Clarence."

Nice one dad, thought Clarence. He stared into his plate, one from the best set. The day was just getting worse and worse.

Mother changed the subject but not the tone of voice. "Tell us about the holiday."

"It's just a holiday mum."

"Well tell me about it anyway."

"What's there to tell. You jump on a plane. You get off a plane – when it lands. You lie on a beach. You get pissed. You sleep it off. You get pissed again. You fly home. Simple!"

Margaret slammed down her knife and fork. Clarence knew from painful experience that she was angry and looked away, well away. He fell on one of the twins instead.

"Why is he staring at me like that?"

"Because you look awful."

This was worse than Christmas. All in all a bad day.

Margaret did everybody a favour and changed the subject, back to the twins; and how well they were doing at school; and how many friends they had made; and how they were each developing their own distinct personality. Desmond joined in and Clarence was completely side-lined.

In one sense he was extremely grateful. He was being left alone. In another he was totally fed up with one of the possibly most boring subjects on the planet: the progress of Tarquin and Jeremy through life and how well they were growing into 'fully rounded human beings' – to quote his sister. He drifted off, and dreamt of sex with Fiona then Tracey, only to be jolted back into reality by a stern look of reproach from his sister.

"What?"

"Are you just going to sit there and say nothing?"

"What am I expected to say?"

"You could at least pretend to take an interest."

"In what?"

That was too much. Margaret began to fume. Dad and Desmond said nothing but dug into the pudding. Mother watched her children throw stones. She had experienced it so many times before it was not a news worthy event. She thought about the washing up ahead instead. The task would need volunteers. She did not believe in dishwashers.

Clarence didn't care a hoot. He was suddenly feeling very bloody-minded and spoke accordingly. "In your wonderful children?"

He saw his sister trying not to explode and thought it rather funny, a scream in fact. Unfortunately it was too much, more than enough to bring husband Desmond into the fray.

"You haven't got any kids Clarence."

A totally spurious observation, thought Clarence. "I know."

"Well when you do you'll be unashamedly proud of them. Just like us."

But I won't shove them in other people's faces thought Clarence. "Will I."

"Yes you will."

"I'll bear that in mind."

Dad suddenly jumped up. He had had enough. "Right that's enough all. Lunch is finished. Time to clean up."

Permission granted, lunch was terminated and the family scattered.

Clarence sought refuge outside but his sister found him and trapped him by the goldfish pond.

"What's got into you?"

"I don't know what do you mean."

"Is she giving you a bad time?"

"What?"

"Is that Tracey giving you a bad time?"

"No. 'That Tracey' isn't giving me a bad time."

"Well whatever. Stop taking it out on us."

"Leave me alone."

"Don't be so rude to mother."

"I wasn't."

Margaret stared back and stared him down into submission. Clarence looked at the clouds in the sky. They looked pretty boring but at least they were far away and harmless. Margaret moved on to another subject. This time one close to her heart.

"Did you get the presents?"

"Presents?"

"Did you get the presents?" she repeated, as if to someone hard of hearing.

"Yes," replied Clarence.

His sister looked him in the eye, demanding nothing less than the truth.

"No you haven't."

Clarence looked to the floor. "No I haven't."

"And you'll not have time to get them now before going on holiday."

"No."

"Desmond will have to struggle like anything to get them in time."

Clarence hung his head in shame. Then suddenly he brightened up. He had a great idea. He reached for his wallet. "Look here's £20, get them book vouchers."

Margaret looked back at her infidel brother in disbelief. "You gave them that last year. They're sick of bloody book vouchers. We stopped years ago. It's computer games now and you promised to get some."

"Sorry."

"You haven't got a clue."

"I said sorry."

"So you should be." Margaret switched into mother mode. "I really don't know what's got into you. God knows how Tracey puts up with it."

Clarence remembered back to the times when he was a kid and he had often wanted to fell his sister for always being so bloody right, or just irritating.

With most things off her chest for now his sister drifted away and left him in relative peace to count his few remaining blessings. He sat down on the wooden garden bench and stared into the pond. He couldn't see any fish. He hadn't seen any fish for ages. Perhaps they were all dead. The twins came out, licking their lips. The noise level went up. The pair began kicking a football around. Clarence did his utmost to ignore the commotion. Then Desmond came out. Clarence fiddled with his hair, realising for the first time that day that he hadn't combed it, or brushed his teeth for that matter. He watched his brother-in-law kick the ball about. Such was the man's feeble athleticism and attempts to control the ball that Clarence was drawn to indulge his truly wicked side. 'I may not be wonderfully, happily married with perfect kids and a nice piece of property but at least I can play a decent game of football.'

Tarquin ran up, panting, out of breath but feeling all the better for it.

"Will you play?"

Clarence folded his arms. "No."

"Please we need four."

"No."

Tarquin looked back at his brother, heartbroken. Jeremy ran up and stood by his brother. Equally out of breath he said nothing but just stared at the enemy. Clarence looked them both up and down. Whenever the twins stood side by side it made him feel funny.

Tarquin tried again. "Please play."

He repeated himself. "No."

Then their dad strode up and added his weight to the psychological warfare. The earlier insult had been stacked away with all the others in the cellar. "Come on Clarence. We can have two aside. A proper match."

A switch flipped within Clarence and suddenly he couldn't resist the opportunity to let of steam and demonstrate how useless Desmond was at anything when he was not behind a desk filling in his spreadsheets.

The four played football. It started innocently enough, boyishly enough. It was all good wholesome fun. Then the sweat began to flow and the body temperatures rose and the need to get the ball passed the improvised goalposts made of jumpers and pot plants became all devouring.

Suddenly it became deadly serious when Desmond scored a goal. Jeremy scorned pity on his brother Tarquin and Tarquin promised retaliation. Clarence likewise was determined not to let Desmond win the day with nothing more than luck and a complete lack of skill. It was one of those days when he felt the need to be seen winning. He fought back hard, with such force that Desmond stepped to one side, fearful of getting seriously bruised, and allowed him to score. An even score line did nothing to calm things down. Clarence and nephew Tarquin were equally determined to win. A draw would not do. It all became very physical until Desmond threatened to walk off unless Clarence calmed down.

Clarence put the ball away to win the match then did exactly as requested. Unfortunately in doing so he knocked over a large pot plant. Some of its soil fell into the crystal clear waters of the pond. Clarence sat down. He knew what he had done wrong.

"Oh fuck."

Desmond sat down next to him and contemplated the damage done. "She'll have you for that."

"Tell me about it."

The twins carried on kicking the ball about aimlessly, watched by their father and uncle.

"When are you back from holiday?"

"19th."

"Can I ask a favour."

Clarence gave no reply. He wanted to say no but etiquette dictated he couldn't. Perhaps if he stayed silent long enough the favour would go away.

"I need to dump an old sofa."

Clarence thought of Sam. "When?"

"Well anytime really, after you're back. But preferably before the 29th."

Clarence wanted to say bugger off but knew he was in debit when it came to family favours. He had no choice.

"Yeah OK."

Desmond was so well-organised. Clarence still couldn't work out why his little sister had married him.

Business completed, Desmond retreated back indoors. Left alone, Clarence sank into a stupor and watched each minute pass on his watch, waiting and waiting for enough time to pass before he could make tracks without resentment issuing forth from the nearest, dearest and fearless.

His mother meanwhile watched from the window as she dried cutlery, and considered.

✦ ✦ ✦

Log Entry

Very late in the day my host visited a building, one purpose-built for recreation and social interaction, though at some cost to health. Those present were nearly all younger than my host and congregated in a large dark room, in tightly packed groups. There they jumped up and down and made lots of noise. Some of them fell over – but still got up looking happy and acting joyful in the extreme.

The room was lit by a system of bright flashing lights. The premeditated synchronised performance of noise and colour was hypnotic, addictive, consisting as it did of subtle interwoven threads of both repeating and non-repeating patterns. Narrative was added as a discrete layer, sometimes shadowing and complementing the basic sound patterns, other times working in opposition for stark contrast. Some of it was hardly distinguishable from random noise, yet still it appeared to satisfy a craving inside the human head. That said my host was highly disorientated at times, and lacking confidence.

The audience was fuelled by large oral injections of alcohol. Some cast aside all inhibitions. One male, distinct from the crowd, was on hand to shout out instructions, repeatedly. It appeared he was in sole charge of the sound delivery system.

People in the mid to high end of the age range were not present. This was possibly due to the obvious health risks associated with such places and such behaviour.

A close encounter between my host and another male member of the population reveals the fact that the social scale is wide and social differences extreme. He had no assets to speak of, no ties to community, no family, yet on balance he was happy with his situation and held a positive outlook. He has a few friends, all in a similar situation.

His clothes lacked the usual coordination I have come to expect and the body smell was excessive. He was not affected by the rules of fashion as far as I could ascertain. His appearance I learnt was not purposely constructed but the result of a lack of financial funds and access to washing facilities.

He had a weather-beaten look, looked undernourished and was far from physically energetic. That aside he was mentally active and responsive when spoken to. His expression was continuous, unremitting and behind it there was intense mental concentration. It suggested an invisible barrier, a line across which no one dare pass.

He held many views and had experienced much: having encountered visits by other extraterrestrial space vehicles, acts of magic (a force in which the laws of physics are violated), and time travel. I wanted to explore these subjects further but the conversation became predominantly one-way and wishful thinking on his part dominated.

At one point I enquired about his upbringing and education. At which point he became subdued and seemed wanting to cry. I ceased questioning. However leaving was difficult, in fact impossible as he had become greatly attached to my presence and did not want me to go. So, wishing to avoid physical conflict, I allowed him to accompany me.

I have encountered my host's immediate biological relations for the first time. He has two biological parents and they have one other offspring, female. Upon entering their home he immediately became tense, defensive, subversive even, as if to join with them was to join in battle.

The mother takes great interest in the health of her children. The father does not. When questioned over his state of health my host lied.

For family, the act of consuming food is a highly ritualised affair. Routine dominated at the dining table. They presumably share a vast wealth of common experiences but had little to say to each other. There was no substantive talk.

The females dominated proceedings. They organised and coordinated while the men hung around awaiting orders. The mother directed many of the father's movements. At times he seemed incapable of making his own decisions. Likewise the daughter directed her mate and her offspring with diligence and haste, as if required by social convention. Only my host Clarence, appeared to exercise total freedom, though he exercised it with caution.

There is a strong bond between mother and daughter. The older generation say little to each other but understand each other well. This may be due to increased powers of telepathy as the human brain matures or the fact that over many years they can interpret each other's body language and mood extremely well.

Criticism between siblings engages strong emotional undercurrents and causes strong backlash. There is obvious rivalry, cloaked in guarded, polite conversation and an interest in the other's welfare.

Some friction had occurred between my host and John in an accidental encounter but John took it well. John takes great interest in my well-being and is a great source of knowledge and experience on many subjects. The feeling of empathy is strong, and at times there is a degree of intimacy bordering on the sexual. I have been invited back to his home for food. I am not sure whether to accept as an extended period of control along with logistics may cause difficulties.

There is a growing conflict in the mind of my host. It concerns the two females Tracey and Fiona. Now he cannot think of one without immediately thinking of the other, and making comparisons. There is no sense of guilt as far as I can determine, but if he tries to disengage one from his thoughts he fails, and becomes frustrated. This is bizarre: he shares a long history of sexual encounter with the one called Tracey, but when he thinks of sex his mind jumps to Fiona – or sometimes an old friend, also female.

Chapter Five

Monday was not a good day for Clarence. He was back at work and hating it. Things started badly. He did not perform well in the classroom. To be precise he did not perform. And his pupils noticed a difference.

Clarence tried to stare down the troublemakers and prowlers in his class of sixth formers but with little success. They were not a pretty sight, not by any stretch of the imagination. Acne and greasy hair ruled. And though he had once suffered the same experience he had no sympathy, shared no empathy. Hormone infestations were no excuse in his book. There was one exception but Clarence knew better than to feast his eyes on her, he might get arrested.

He was bored stiff and they were bored rigid. Plate tectonics and continental drift had ceased to appeal, along with rock weathering and the hydrological cycle. He was extremely tired and felt no compunction to drone on and on. Despite going to bed early he had woken up feeling shattered. He was bored stupid by the sound of his own voice pumping out the same old crap year on year. And at the end of the day what possible use would it be to them – to anybody? Why not teach them plumbing or bricklaying? Or how to service a car? Or how to simple argue a point of view coherently. Exam results that's why, he replied, and the university treadmill. Everyone must tuck away a university degree.

Then Clarence made the fatal mistake: he let his mind wander too far off the beaten track and now he was stuck in limbo land. He had lost his train of thought, completely, or perhaps the train had left him behind. The class knew it and he knew they knew it. He turned his attention to the clock and watched the minute hand twitch once every 60 seconds. Was each minute taking longer than the last to complete? It certainly felt like it.

Silence consumed.

The class became restless and began to stir with unease. A teacher not teaching and acting strangely was not something they were geared up to handle. Some stared out of the window and visualized the act of sex. Others worried about their looks. Others itched to switch on their mobile phones and start text messaging. A few who desperately needed sleep tried not to fall asleep. One failed. Another farted but this time no one laughed.

Clarence thumbed a lift towards the overhead screen, determined to break the impasse and recover his credibility. He wanted to be seen to be acting cool. "Are any of you really interested in any of this?"

No response. His pupils thought it was a trick question. Glances were exchanged but nothing was said.

"Come on someone must have a view."

Still nothing. They could not be so easily trapped.

"Not even one of you?" Clarence became belligerent. "Doesn't any of you have an opinion on anything?"

Enough was enough.

One boy - severely put out and pissed off - called out. "Yes!"

"Which is?"

"I not saying." His protest made, the pupil imploded and retreated.

Clarence gave up the ghost and lapsed back into silence, observing with irony that his class gave him their full attention when he stood motionless saying nothing than when he talked on and on. It was agony for all: an agony which endured until end of lesson.

The bell rang and Clarence never felt happier. The bell rang and the class never felt more pissed off about their education.

Things improved only ever so slightly at lunchtime. Canteen tray in hand and the brutal aroma of overcooked carrots worming its way up his nose and threatening to make him faint, Clarence entered the zone unofficially cordoned off for staff use only. It was an unspoken rule that pupils did not cross the line and disturb staff during lunch.

He spotted a spare place opposite Fiona, and went for it, like a dog after the rabbit. He needed cheering up and she was the one to do it. As luck would have it he was beaten to it by a faster, more agile PE teacher. Forced to make do with a place two seats away he listened in with open contempt as Pansy Ramsey attempted to chat the new girl up. It reassured him to see that Fiona wasn't the remotest bit interested. Ramsey droned on, oblivious to his continued lack of success. Clarence and Fiona exchanged glances and shared the joke. It was a sweet victory for Clarence and he recovered his appetite for school food. Why don't they ever cook a hot curry he asked himself.

Things got a lot better in the afternoon. In fact things got out of hand. In the staff rest room, enjoying the free period, Clarence sat and sipped his very instant coffee and nibbled a piece of dodgy shortbread and counted the hours of torture left in the day, all the time trying not to look downcast and knackered.

Then Fiona enter the room and immediately he perked up. She clutched a pink folder stuffed full of A4 close to her heart. 'Commitment' observed Clarence. I like that in a woman.

She continued to hold his attention as she drew tea from the tea pot: the one tea pot which had been in continuous service since as far back as Clarence could remember. Meticulously she examined the notice board. It had nothing to say. Clarence made a wish. The wish was granted. The woman saw him.

Fiona smiled. She approached. She even sat down next to him. She sipped her tea. And during all this time Clarence fought a running battle for control of all working parts of his body. He won, and his confidence grew. He was back in charge.

If Fiona was expecting him to speak first she was going to be disappointed. Clarence kept his mouth shut. It was the safest option. He could tell she wanted to say something important, and was impressed by his own sudden intuition. Someone had to speak first so she took the plunge. Clutching her mug of tea she asked him how he was. This was no small talk or idle chit-chat. She was seriously interested. Even so Clarence gave the usual bland mechanical answer one gave when one wanted to give nothing away. He was not prepared to lower his guard. She stuck at it.

"You know you don't look too well."

"Don't I?"

"Are you eating well?"

"Yes." Why do they always ask that?

"Have you been sleeping OK?"

"Yes." She was beginning to annoy.

"I was thinking about what you said in the morning. It was thoughtful, very supportive."

Clarence grinned sheepishly. Now he wanted her to leave him alone. Confusion was breaking out, like spots.

"What did I say?"

"You know."

"No I don't."

"You do, you're teasing." Fiona swept the room to check nobody was listening in. "That I have a strong nurturing instinct, that I have deep concern for the well-being of others, that I'm perceptive even."

Internally Clarence exercised contortions. Had too much beer really make him say all that?

"And?"

"Well it was very nice of you to say those things. I needed cheering up." Fiona paused, then confessed. "I needed the company."

Clarence bluffed it. "Glad to be of help."

The contortions ceased and some switches in the fuse box flicked to the 'on' position. A light went from red to amber.

"Yes what with the new job and flat it's all been a rather tiring, stressful. I'm feeling a bit empty at the moment."

Fiona stopped. She had said more than enough. She waited for a response, a follow-on but none was forthcoming. Clarence had nothing to say. She decided to make an exit before embarrassing herself further.

"Well I'd better get back," she lied.

Clarence looked up at the clock. They still had another 15 minutes of freedom to enjoy before being thrown back to the lions. He watched her rush to leave the room, dumping her unfinished mug of tea on the way, and tried hard to recall what exactly he had said to her that night he had crashed out in her flat. No such luck. He remembered swaying from side to side in the back of a taxi and waking up the next morning but that was it. That aside, the fact that she thought so highly of him gave him a very good feeling. Although he was seated he stood proud. Pity he didn't have the same effect on Tracey these days.

He watched the door close behind Fiona and he couldn't bear it. He felt left behind. His new teddy bear had been snatched away. He jumped up and followed in her footsteps. As Sod's Law would have it Harold got in his way, wishing to start or restart an argument. He had a point to make about something and was determined to make it.

Irritated, Clarence went through the motions of looking attentive and responsive. He must have said something controversial in an earlier life. He agreed as quickly as he could with whatever was being said – all the while keeping an eye on the door – nodded enthusiastically, and managed to escape in double quick time. Harold was left surprised to have had it so easy his way. Clarence was normally an argumentative little sod, which was why he put up with him.

Clarence fell into the corridor just in time to see his game turn the corner into the west wing. Walking at speed – running would make him look an idiot and make him a hypocrite - he caught her up. Fiona had stopped to exchange words with a boy. Out of breath he tapped her on the shoulder. The contact sent electricity through his body: his nervous system quivered and shivered to the core. Clarence never thought a simple tap on the shoulder – or anywhere for that matter - could have such an affect. And it had nothing to do with sex, or being drunk. Fuck Tracey.

Startled, Fiona dropped her folder. Its contents split out across the floor. She stooped to retrieve the sheets of paper. Some found liftoff and glided away. Clarence stooped to join her at ground zero, apologizing on the way. The boy, wishing to impress her, scurried after them. When he returned with his catch it was snatched from his hand by Clarence, and he was sent on his way, with not so much as a thank you, more a 'leave her to me'.

Between them they retrieved the entire contents of the folder, helped along by another boy who had picked up the few on his way. Such was his respect for the new, good-looking female teacher. The fact that he was undergoing transformation into a 6 cylinder, fuel injected sex machine had nothing to do with it.

Fiona came back up satisfied and composed, her dignity intact. Clarence came back up smiling, and feeling silly, so silly in fact that he tried to do a silly thing on the way up. He tried to kiss her.

He missed, badly: timing was not his strong point and they bumped heads. Stunned, Fiona staggered back, her head held in her hand. The word 'clumsy' did not do Clarence justice.

"Sorry," said Clarence. It was all he could think of to say.

"No matter." Fiona waved him away. "It was an accident."

Rubbing her head, she turned to go, then had to think hard to remember where she was going before the mid-air collision. Ladies. That was it. She was on her way to the Ladies. She took off, at speed.

The boy laughed. He had one hell of a good story to tell. Clarence gave him the dirtiest look he had in his teaching portfolio but to no avail. The boy was not to be so easily intimidated. He knew his rights.

Fiona turned another corner. This time Clarence panicked, though he had no reason to. She was heading towards a dead end. His blood up, he ran after her, turned the same corner, and almost crashed into her. Fiona had stopped outside the Ladies, her path blocked. Another woman was on her way out.

Now or never. The choice, made mutually exclusive for no reason except male preconditioning, thumped inside his head and pushed aside all other options. Her path clear, his woman was about to go through a door, into a place which for Clarence was as dark as the dark side of the moon. Now.

Clarence tapped Fiona on the shoulder again - this time it was more of a prod and almost hurt. Without waiting for a response, or time to think, he followed through. She turned, alarmed. He grabbed her around the waist - that lovely slim, diet conscious waist – and pulled her in up close, and without hesitation or deviation or waiting for permission he kissed her firmly on the lips. She tasted good.

Fiona, awestruck and trembling at the knees, fell back. Likewise her mouth fell open and hung limp where it had fallen. She forgot to close it for quite some time. She didn't protest but neither did she write him a thank you note.

Clarence began to shrivel up, like a piece of fresh fruit in the strong midday sun, only quicker. Deep down he was stripped of all energy, all ego and all coherent thought. Sweat dripped from his forehead and he didn't feel good about himself. Without a cause to fight for or a reason to remain he mumbled a vague apology and hurried off back the way he had come. He had no idea where he was going.

Fiona sought shelter on the toilet. For a little while she remained a little bit shocked, a little bit stunned but also she was a little bit impressed, a little bit flattered, a little bit satisfied – a little bit self-satisfied even. Knickers down around her ankles she contemplated the mysteries of the male psyche.

✤   ✤   ✤

Clarence sat at his kitchen table and stared out of the window. He was holding onto a packet of cigarettes but he felt no need to light up. There was no view to speak of and the radio was playing only because he couldn't be bothered to get up and switch it off. The most annoying, dumb adverts were playing but he was past caring. He heard the front door open then slam shut. Mad Max was home. There was the sound of a heavy bag hitting the floor, followed by limited, almost polite swearing and coughing.

Max marched into the kitchen, hungry and thirsty, his muscles aching; and feeling homesick. He did a double take when he saw Clarence sitting in the corner, shell like and looking sorry for himself. He said hello. He got no reply. Fair enough, this is England. He put the kettle on and began preparing his meal. Easy: beans on toast again, perhaps a raw carrot for afters. His mother had always told him to eat well if he wanted to drink well, as well.

"Cup of tea?" he suggested.

Still no reply.

"I said cup of tea?" With repetition his Irish accent was harsher, more demanding, and less willing to be ignored.

Clarence twitched. "No thanks." He continued to stare out of the window.

Beans finally on toast and tea secured, Max sat down opposite his flatmate, blocking his line of vision. Clarence looked down at the beans with envy. The toast was burnt he noted. The beans were lacking brown sauce.

Max, sensing the man was not in a talkative mood, got stuck in. Clarence watched, as if afraid he would miss out on something vitally important. He tracked the journey of the fork through the air each time it when to deposit its next load into the yawning mouth. Max, eyes down, knew he was under close examination, and he didn't like it. He became quickly narked. Table manners were everything. Finally he snapped and threw down his knife. The fork he used to stab the air.

"Look is something up or what?"

Clarence snapped to attention and his brain clicked into place, ready to receive. "What?"

"I said is something up or what?"

"What?"

"Or what? There's something on your mind. It takes no fucking genius to work that one out. Excuse my language." When sober Max was always polite.

Max carried on chewing and waited for a fresh expression to appear on the face of one lonely looking man. The cup of tea was pushed aside for something stronger: Max retrieved two bottles of Guinness from the fridge. He placed them on the table, side by side, rescued the bottle opener from the sink (why it was there he didn't know), and opened one. In all this time Clarence was still considering the question. It wasn't a difficult question but his brain was ticking slowly. Max was puzzled as to why he was taking so long to come up with an answer. A simple yes or no would suffice.

Max opened the other bottle and pushed it closer to Clarence. "Here drink this. You need it."

Tentatively Clarence reached out and grasped the bottle for all its worth. He studied the label – as if it was a bottle of wine – then began to sip – as if it was a glass of wine. There was a look of pure joy on his face. It was as if it was his first ever taste of alcohol. In contrast Max threw his back.

"Now tell me about it."

Clarence told him.

"I did a stupid thing today. I've been doing a lot of stupid things recently."

"Like what."

"I kissed a girl today."

"And what's wrong with that?"

"I shouldn't have kissed her."

"She gave permission?"

"No I can't say she did."

"She wasn't your girlfriend?"

"No. She certainly wasn't my girlfriend."

Max recalled his youth back in Ireland. "That's tricky. Where did you kiss her?"

"On the lips."

"I mean 'where', where did you kiss her?"

"At work, outside the ladies' toilets."

"When you say 'a girl' do you mean a real girl or a women, a teacher like you?"

"A teacher like me."

Max drew a heavy sigh of relief. "Thank God for that."

Clarence looked up sharply. "What d'you mean?"

"I mean had she been a pupil you would be in serious shit right now."

"Yeah, I see what you mean."

"I fucking hope so."

Simultaneously and spontaneously the two men put a break on the talking and gave their full, undiluted attention to the act of absorbing alcohol. Max finished his bottle first and started on his second.

"So what you going to do about it?"

"Do about it?"

"You've got a girlfriend already. If this is a serious kiss you've got to give one up. If it isn't then no problem. Is it a serious kiss?"

"It's a serious kiss." Clarence spoke under his breath, as if worried a third party might be listening in, with a tape recorder.

"So you've got to give one up. Get one out of your system."

"Give one up?" Clarence sat on the last remark. "Suppose so."

"Suppose nothing. You've got to sort it out else it will drive you bonkers, round the bend."

I'm already round the bend thought Clarence.

"Well?" In his customary, Irish way Max turned his head to one side slightly, while keeping his eyes fixed on the same spot. "Well?"

"I don't know."

Max made a suggestion. "Dump the girlfriend."

"I don't want to dump her." That was a lie – quickly corrected. "We're going on holiday together. It's all booked up and everything."

"Dump her when you get back."

"Possibly."

Max sought clarification. "So you don't want to dump her?"

"I don't know. I don't think I should go out with a teacher at the same school – that complicates things. And anyway I just kissed her for Christ's sake."

"You told me it was a serious kiss."

"Well it was."

Wishing now to wind things up, Max put forward the obvious alternative. "Well apologize to her, make it up, get back on an even keel. You've got to work with this woman. You see her every bloody day of the week."

"Yes make it up."

"I mean like a proper apology. Else it will always be there, hanging over both of you, getting in the way of things."

"Yes a proper apology."

"Do you know where she lives?"

"Where she lives? Yes. I know where she lives. Not to far away."

Max slammed down his bottle, jolting Clarence further back into mainstream reality. "Excellent!"

"What?"

"Go and apologize right now. Do it NOW before she has the time to make a judgement - and before you lose the bottle."

"Now? No I can't."

"Yes you can. Do it right now. While the whole thing is fresh. The longer you leave it the heavier it becomes. You can't leave fruit to rot."

'You can't leave fruit to rot' thought Clarence. What the fuck does that mean? He still needed convincing, but he was more than halfway there.

"She'll respect you for it."

"Will she?"

"Certainly. And it sets you up beautifully if you decide to dump the girlfriend after the holiday."

"True."

"Do it."

Clarence nodded. He was sold on the strength of his lodger's logic. Mad Max was starting to turn into a real mate. Do it right away. It would be good to see her again. Perhaps he'll catch her off guard. Perhaps just coming out of the shower: answering the door in her dressing gown perhaps. Just one more bottle of beer first. Perhaps two. Perhaps.

✦ ✦ ✦

Clarence drove to Fiona's place and parked discreetly way down the street. He sat in the car, tuned into Radio Two, and planned what exactly it was he was going to say. His plan didn't come to much. It boiled down to 'sorry', that useful but overused and overstretched word. Still it was the perfect excuse to see her again. It was amazing how 3 bottles of beer could rebuild a man's confidence and sense of worth in such a short space of time.

He got out of his car and walked, with slightly dazed expression, and ended up standing at her front door. There his nerves began to fray at the edges. If he had been wearing a cap it would have been ripped from the top of his head and squeezed tightly in both hands. If he had been holding a newspaper it would have been twisted up and made unreadable. He reached inside his shirt and scratched his chest, reminding himself that he had a good hairy chest – hairs to be proud of, and no grey villains. Strictly speaking she didn't live in a flat but in a ground floor maisonette. He had been here before but he could only remember coming out, not going in.

Clarence counted to three, then again, then on to ten; then rang the bell. No answer. Fine. She was out. Pity. Some other time perhaps. He turned to go, but the sound of door opening scuppered his change of plan.

Fiona stood on a hairy, hostile doormat, holding a sealed packet of dry spaghetti sticks.

"Clarence?" Her surprise quickly deflated into contained, perhaps constrained expectation of some grand gesture.

"Hallo Fiona." Clarence looked at the spaghetti. Many of the sticks had snapped. "I've caught you at a bad time."

She corrected him. "No you haven't."

"You're cooking your dinner. I'll come back some other time."

"No. Honest it's OK."

Fiona noticed Clarence was keeping his hands firmly tucked away in his trouser pockets. Give him a conker tied to a length of string and a school cap and the scene would be complete.

"What do you want?"

Crunch point.

"What do I want?" Clarence wasn't hard of hearing, he was simply repeating the question to himself in a different context and to a deeper level of significance.

Fiona waited, but she could only wait so long. "Well what do you want. I am in the middle of cooking."

Clarence spat it out. "I want to come in."

"What?"

"I mean I want to come in and apologize."

"Can't you do it here?"

"No not really."

Fiona, soft at heart like jelly and ice cream decided to take the risk. "OK come on."

Delighted, Clarence followed her in. Fiona led him down a short hallway, a door on either side, and on into her living room. She sat down in her usual chair and gestured Clarence towards the sofa opposite. Clarence looked at the sofa. He remembered waking up on said sofa and feeling bloody awful.

Conscious that she clutching sticks of spaghetti Fiona felt silly. "Well?"

She sounded annoyed. It was unintentional: she wasn't so much annoyed as impatient to get the silly incident out of the way. Men would be boys and boys would be boys. She had learnt that long ago during teacher training. She waited for the apology. She didn't mind what shape it came in just as long as it was short and sincere, and not too embarrassing.

Clarence sat rubbing his hands together in his lap - examining the walls of the room as if he had never sat alone with a girl before. Fiona had a small boy on her hands, one well under the weather. She remembered the sweet, dear things he had said to her, about her, and made a spur decision. She would invite him to stay for dinner. She had pasta aplenty – she was holding the stuff – and enough topping to go round. She just didn't have any wine. Dinner with wine? What am I thinking off she asked herself.

Still silence from the man on her sofa.

"Well. Speak to me. Please?"

Clarence found the first word of the first sentence he wanted to articulate impossible to construct. The bits were stuck in his throat. Everything else was backed up behind it.

"Look if you want to say sorry just say sorry. It's enough. We all lose our heads every once and awhile. We're only human."

"I've been losing mine a lot recently."

"Sorry?"

"Nothing. Just going through a bad patch." Clarence folded his arms and sat back, less nervous, more exhausted.

Fiona took in the familiar image of male vulnerability and her warm side began to shine through again. The boy needed feeding, mothering perhaps. The conversation restarted on a different note. Apologies were forgotten.

"Have you eaten tonight?"

"No."

"Are you intending to eat tonight?"

"Hadn't really thought about it."

"Did you eat a proper meal yesterday?"

"Sort of. My mum's Sunday lunch. But I didn't have much of appetite."

"Would you like to stay for dinner?"

"Would I like to stay for dinner?"

Clarence repeated the question inside his head. It sounded like a great idea, like the opening title of some great classic pop song.

"Sure. If it's convenient. I don't want to put you out."

"You won't put me out."

Clarence beamed. He liked the sound of her riposte. Fiona could relax: Clarence was smiling.

"There's just one condition though," she added.

"Condition?" Clarence didn't like the sound of that word.

"We need a bottle of wine."

"Oh right. I'll pop out and get one right now." He stood up. "Red?"

"Red. It's quorn with spaghetti - bolognaise."

Deja vu slammed into him like a delivery truck.

"I guessed that," he said, wishing to demonstrate that he knew something about cooking, and all that stuff.

Fiona finally admitted something to herself. She had enjoyed the kiss. Shame though that it hadn't been in the best of places. Chris could finally go to hell (and not come back).

Clarence moved swiftly to the front door and Fiona had to pursue him to keep up. At the door he stopped abruptly and turned to speak, right in her face. He felt good about himself and wanted to say something.

"Look I really am sorry about this afternoon."

"Honest, don't bother yourself anymore."

"I embarrassed you. I think I upset you."

"No you didn't – well yes you did – but I got over it."

Peace made, Clarence was a happy teenager again and Fiona was his sweet new thing.

"Get the wine," she commanded.

"Get the wine," he echoed, and left to do exactly that.

Fiona closed the door behind him. Clarence ran to his car. Fiona dashed back to the kitchen. Each was in a rush of their own making. Each wanted to be busy.

Clarence drove to the off-licence – his off-licence. Fiona put the spaghetti in to boil then did a very naughty thing and sanctioned a night of extremes. She paid a quick visit to her bedroom for a safety check. She checked for dirty knickers on the floor and other items of dumped clothing, dirty or otherwise, and quickly gave it the once over. There was a half full mug of old cold tea on her bedside table. The tea was topped by a nasty looking layer of something which had been born out of spoiled milk. Delicately she picked up the mug, carried it out to the kitchen, and poured the diseased liquid down the sink, following it with a long flush of hot water. The mug she would wash some other time, or throw it away.

I can always back out she told herself. I can always back out, at any time. What am I thinking of? she asked herself. What am I thinking of. She tried to calm herself. She failed. Luckily she had her cooking into which to direct all her nervous energy.

She hadn't had sex for three months.

She reminded herself of the salient facts. You've just untangled yourself from one relationship. Give it a break. You need a break from men. And she dismissed them all.

And still she hadn't had sex for three months.

She caught her breath. The bolognaise needed stirring and the cheese needed grating and the table needed laying, for two: two, back to laying for two.

Clarence bounded into his familiar off-licence, feeling happy and acting happy. The girl he had adopted as his own was on duty. He grabbed an inexpensive bottle of red wine from Australia and approached. He grinned. She kept her head down.

He spoke. "Evening."

He was determined to prove to the young lassie – lassie? Wasn't that the name of a dog? – that he could be a bubbly, exited and excitable young man, not a miserable old sod. (He guessed that in her world men fell into only these 2 categories, and he wasn't far from the truth.)

She didn't answer. She just papered over the bottle, registered the financial transaction, took his ten pound note and picked out his change. As she counted it out she finally felt compelled to pass comment. She couldn't avoid the happy face any longer.

"You're looking very cheerful tonight, for a change."

The second half of her statement was purposely loaded and intended to bite. But Clarence wasn't bitten and fought back. Sod you then he thought. I'm just trying to be nice.

He dropped his change into a jacket pocket and bounded out. The girl returned to her magazine, one all about celebrity news and fashion and how to make it as a model; and how to accidentally convince yourself that an ordinary life spent doing ordinary things was not a life worth living. She would continue to spend most of the evening leaning on the counter, except when it hurt or she was disturbed by customers

The door blew open again and Clarence blasted back in, in even more of a hurry second time round. He grabbed 2 bottles of beer between the fingers of one free hand. The label was evocative of South West England, and villages which had been in existence since Anglo-Saxon times; and farmers with 2 heads or 12 fingers, and 10 siblings who all looked identical. He slammed the bottles down on the counter, disturbing the peace.

"And those." He didn't say please. In the space of thirty seconds he had got over the wench.

"You want them in a bag?" she was forced to ask.

"Yes."

She put them in a bag and registered the financial transaction. Clarence gave her a two pound and a one pound coin. She picked out his change, a little bronze, almost not worth the bother, and dropped it into the palm of his outstretched hand. There was no love loss.

And he was gone.

The girl picked up her magazine again, and continued to read all about the science of face packs.

Meanwhile Fiona had laid the table; grated some aging cheddar; checked her hair; stuffed all her dirty clothes into the laundry basket; cut up a beef tomato and cucumber, and neatly lined up the slices on a small plate which she placed in the middle of the table. She had not wasted a second: she had also fixed herself up with a bra; changed into a fresh pair of knickers; reapplied deodorant; emptied the kitchen bin; set the video; washed up and dried two wine glasses; and advised herself to calm down, slow down, back off or back away.

Clarence returned: ready to eat, ready to drink, ready for anything.

"That smells great," he declared, wishing to warm things up.

"Thanks," replied Fiona. He had said the right thing and she fully appreciated it.

Clarence pulled the wine out of the plastic bag and placed it on the table. Then he pulled out a bottle of beer.

"Do you drink the bottled stuff?"

Fiona became unstuck. "No. Just wine thanks. I'll get the corkscrew - and a bottle opener."

While the cook was in the kitchen Clarence stared longingly at the TV screen.

"Do you mind if I switch on the telly?" he shouted. "I just want to see the football score on ITV."

"OK!" She gave permission, not realizing she was now driven to please him.

"Do you mind if I smoke?" he shouted next.

"Yes!" she shouted back. She had her limits.

Fair enough: he was trying to give up anyway.

Fiona returned with bottle opener and corkscrew. Clarence opened his beer and began to drink, watching Fiona as she opened the wine before returning to the screen. She hurried back into the kitchen. He waited for the score to flash up.

The food was served up.

Clarence switched to his place at the table and watched a mountain of pasta land on his plate. The score was still nil-nil. Fiona handed him a large wooden ladle.

"Here, help yourself to the sauce."

Clarence did as instructed. The lumps of something vegetarian came in a thick red tomato sauce. Fiona switched off her television set with the remote control. Football. That was not a plus in her book. She sat down and helped herself to what was left. There wasn't much. Clarence took some cheese. Fiona followed suit. Clarence grabbed the pepper pot and twisted, furiously. He liked his pepper. Fiona copied him, with less violence. She poured out the wine as Clarence hastily disposed of his first beer. She timed the moment then made contact: glass on glass. Chink.

"Cheers."

"Cheers."

And the two got stuck in.

It had to be said that by now Fiona was as equally famished as her guest, and wished that she hadn't given him so much of the pasta. No matter. She could cut more bread later. It was granary bread.

She watched Clarence eat. He said nothing but made a lot of noise. Like most men of his age (and younger) (and older) he ate as if in a hurry to be somewhere else, somewhere more important. He slurped his spaghetti. She looked on with an air of familiar resignation and remote female grace. She studied him, curious. Whatever was there – and she was sure there was something there – she was struggling to find it again.

The wine gave her mental strength and impetus. She had him in her sights. She decided to have a go and try to dissect him. It was a fair exchange: she had fed him, now he had to talk. Clarence carried on eating and slurping, eyes down. When he looked up it was to reach for his glass. To be fair he did remember to pay her another cooking compliment.

"Nice."

"Thanks."

Clarence yawned. The wine on top of all the beer that night was taking its toll. "Excuse me. Long day."

"Tell me about it. All the days are long."

"They certainly are."

Fiona produced a broad smile. She had made contact. She jumped in. Life was too short.

"Tell me about Tracey again. Tell me about you and Tracey." There was urgency in her voice.

Clarence looked up. She demanded to know. The woman opposite who had just cooked him this wonderful meal was asking questions about his Tracey. He didn't know what to say. He didn't feel compromised, he just didn't know what to say.

Immediately Fiona knew she had said the wrong thing, or said it at the wrong time. "You don't mind me asking do you?"

"No."

Which meant yes.

"You said so much last time."

"Did I?"

Now the man was playing games with her and Fiona didn't like that.

"Yes. Yes you did." Fiona thought of her one encounter with the woman in his life. It still rankled.

Clarence turned to his glass of wine for help, swivelled it, and emptied it in one fell swoop.

"Top up?" he asked before refilling it.

He was ready to pour forth but Fiona guarded her glass with her glass. "No. Thanks. I'm fine for the moment."

She waited and waited then decided on one last push. "Things aren't going well are they. That's what you said."

"Did I? I don't remember."

"You don't remember?"

Clarence parked his knife and fork on his plate, picked up his glass, and leaned back in his chair, looking anything but relaxed. He looked like someone about to make a confession: stiff, with a plank stuff down his back.

"Not a word."

"You don't remember? Not a single word?"

"Nothing."

Clarence avoided eye contact. Fiona took this to be a bad sign. She was mystified. He had been so eloquent, so analytical, so sharp and precise, and so sober.

"You don't remember anything from that night?"

"I remember sitting in the taxi. I remember you giving me a cup of coffee in the morning – fresh wasn't it?"

"No. I normally do fresh but I only had instant."

"I was on your sofa."

Clarence reached out towards the bowl of cheese and scooped up most of the remains into his mouth. Fiona had hoped to use it on toast the next day. Clarence decided to lay his cards on the table. He didn't want her to think he was an idiot when drunk - or sober.

"I've been having these blackouts you see. And lack of sleep. Yes lack of sleep."

He finally looked his hostess in the face. He had her full attention. Worry and alarm were written across her face. It was a sweet thing to see and it cheered him up. He was headed in the right direction. For an instant he thought of Sam. Good old Sam. He felt an erection coming on.

Fiona wanted to share his moment of misery, and wanted to be seen to be sharing his moment of misery. "I knew something was wrong. I could tell."

Encouraged by this vote of confidence Clarence continued. "And these vague memories."

"Vague?"

"I have these vague memories of things happening which can only be recent yet they seem so far away, like childhood memories, like your first day at school, or your first kiss with a girl, or first day at school – teaching I mean. You know what I mean?"

"I know what you mean."

Fiona finished her wine. Now she needed a refill. She reached out for the bottle but Clarence was there first and obliged. A true gentleman she thought. No mistakes tonight thought Clarence.

"How long do these blackouts last?" she asked.

"Most of them seem very short. Perhaps only minutes. A few are longer, much longer. Perhaps an hour or more if I'm unlucky. But then that's only the ones I remember. There may be others."

"Others?"

"I don't always know if I've had one – just the sense that I can't explain where the time has gone."

"We all have a bit of that don't we?"

"Possibly. But we always know where we've just been don't we? What we've just done?"

Fiona couldn't argue with that.

"And I don't sleep well at night. I always wake up feeling really shattered, knackered."

"Give me one of these vague memories."

"Reading lots of books really fast."

"What's wrong with that?"

"I don't read lots of books. And if I do read a book I read it slowly. I'm not a fast reader. I'm not a book person. What with books at school all day I'm sick of books at home."

Books aside – and she could see his point - Fiona was impressed, and felt honoured: the poor man was holding nothing back. Clarence was nothing like Chris - now ex-Chris. She reached forward and took his hand in hers. It was sweating. She pulled it towards her, across the table, accidentally pushing the fork off his plate on the way. Her grip was tight, unyielding and Clarence was happy to be reeled in, thrilled in fact. His erection rediscovered its mission and soared. This time he was not thinking of Sam.

Suddenly everything went up a gear, out of second and into third. And it was only a 4 speed gearbox. Fiona placed her both hands around his one. She wouldn't let go now. Clarence waited for her to say the next thing, not daring to open his mouth in case he said the wrong thing. She said nothing. She just stared into his eyes – as if counting them, or checking they worked – and gave him that long hard look of weary commiserations mixed up with compassion, passion and personal desolation.

Something told them both – a little whisper in each ear perhaps – to get up and go crash out on the sofa. This they did, breaking physical contact for the shortest amount of time required. On the way inhibitions were dumped by both consenting parties, along with all sense of guilt: guilt from Clarence in that he had a girlfriend; guilt from Fiona in that Clarence had a girlfriend.

Unusually in such situations, the woman made the first move. She stroked his hair. It wasn't beautiful hair and it needed washing but it was sound enough. She glanced down, whereupon her eyes were fixed in place. She could see an erection. She was impressed. That was all Clarence needed to know. The signal couldn't be clearer. He grabbed her. She tried to grab him but he had the upper hand and he applied it with imagination, determination and gusto. They snogged, furiously, as if making up for lost time, or living on borrowed time: either way time was the enemy. They fondled: Clarence playing the lead part. They withdrew all sense of decorum. Each made both bodies tingle with expectation and each was extremely grateful.

In all this Fiona still managed to do some thinking. She thought about Tracey and she remembered being insulted by Tracey and a sparkling, shiny new thought crossed her mind: I will have him. I'll make better use of him than you.

She hadn't had sex for three months.

Decision made, Fiona led the way to the bedroom. It was a stone's throw away. A stone was thrown. It produced ripples. She hadn't had sex for three months.

Clarence was in heaven, or somewhere close. It was beautiful. She was beautiful. Her underwear was so sexy. She was so slim. It was like driving a brand new car – a sports car – on an open road, in sunshine, with no destination in mind and all the time in the word to kill. He ripped her knickers off. She loved it. He almost pushed her off the bed. She didn't mind. Far from it. She hadn't had sex for three months.

Yes she was a brand new car, a small piece of his brain declared – a small piece lodged somewhere at the rear, out of sight. She was a fresh body, in mint condition, perfectly sculptured, lovely finish, and no emotional baggage (yet) and no expectations, reasonable or otherwise (yet).

As he moved in and moved things on and made all the natural movements associated with the ride towards orgasm, Clarence decided that Tracey was fat - at least too fat for him. Fiona was small and slim, which made him feel big and tall. For now his problems were reduced to a minor inconvenience. It was just him and her in bed, making love. Turn the engine over and rev it up.

Afterwards he laid flat out, stretched out, shagged out. He had time to think. He wanted a cigarette. A fresh start perhaps? Perhaps. But there was still that holiday to endure. It was not so much a holiday now, more an extended test of self-control under pain.

At this point Clarence noted, Tracey would roll over and go to sleep (or him). Fiona however continued to cling to him. She's a mermaid and I'm the rock he fancied. He could almost see it for real. Very real in fact: he suddenly felt like a large cold solid lump. He pulled her in close and rubbed the palm of his hand across all accessible surface areas to pull himself back to reality. He left little of it unexplored. He was charting her territory and she loved every bit of it. He had beautiful hands and buried somewhere deep within a beautiful soul. The hands in fact were quite ordinary – it was just that Chris did mountaineering.

Clarence looked forward to first light. I'll make love to her again then she can cook me breakfast. Should be able to. Does she do fry ups? Shit: got to go home first then get to school. Shit. School. Don't kiss her at school again whatever you do. Tracey elbowed her way back into his thoughts and with her came a little idle sentimentality, like a poodle on a lead: it had once been this good between him and her. But somewhere along the way they had lost it – or thrown it away – and hadn't noticed. Clarence rolled over. Tough luck Tracey. You had your chance.

✦ ✦ ✦

It was the night before the holiday and in a hidden corner of a pub nothing stirred, not even a mouse. Even the cigarette smoke was lazy. Clarence and Tracey sat, and drank, and smoked and killed time, and sowed seeds. Taken as a whole, the combined activity was something they enjoyed doing together, even though it kept them apart. It was a shared addiction: nothing to do with romance, more the act of best mates. Little was said. They were waiting for Sam and Tim to turn up, both relying on their appearance to inject a little pace.

If they did talk they talked about fresh items of news, their few common friends, the latest films out, family hassles, but not the holiday – not now all arrangements had been settled – and certainly not about themselves, as a couple. If they did talk about themselves it was as individuals. The writing was on the wall but it was a high wall and neither was looking up so high.

The conversation was pushed back and forth across the table as each found it inedible, hard to swallow. Clarence pushed brittle words out of his mouth, in the game of avoiding saying anything of substance or which might hurt. At one point Tracey brought her sister into the conversation, and her sister's aspiration to go into teaching. Again Clarence rubbished the idea. It made for depressing listening.

They were both impatient for the other couple to appear: so Clarence could talk to Tim; so Tracey could talk to Sam. Clarence knew Tim very well. They were best mates from way back: the perfect male talking companions. Tracey had only met Sam through Clarence so didn't know her that well: the perfect female talking companions.

Suddenly Clarence had an apparition and the shock propelled him back into the land of the living. Only it wasn't. It was real flesh and blood.

"Shit."

"What?"

"Here comes that fucking manhole cover again."

"What man?"

"That one over there. The one who looks like a middle-aged scout master."

Clarence leant back as far as the furniture would allow to conceal himself behind Tracey's bulk. She in turn felt put out by the developing pantomime.

"Perhaps he's touting for boys."

"This is no joke. He's been stalking me."

"You know him?"

"Of course I don't know him! I don't want to know him!"

Clarence held his breath and Tracey took in a long deep one, via her filter tip. She had never seen him look so scared and she was beginning to find it slightly amusing. The man was cutting a path through the undergrowth of drinkers and skirting table edges as he prowled. Then just as he ran out of space and seemed about to leave by the rear door he glanced sideways, spotted Clarence and let loose a broad inviting smile. He set his sights, and steered towards his intended target like a well-designed torpedo.

Clarence gulped and gripped his chair, and drew heavily on his dying cigarette. Tracey looked at the man, looked at Clarence then looked back at the man again. He seemed harmless enough. Dress was proper, conventional, cheap, naff. Stomach was expanding. Hair was receding. Small triangular beard looked quaint, slightly ridiculous, out of place. Yes he did resemble a scoutmaster, or a comic book Austrian.

As the man closed in he focused on Clarence, and slowed. The closer he drew, the slower he became: the mathematics behind his stride meant that he was in danger of never arriving. With this in mind Clarence relaxed a little, just a little. The man looked like he had – or was – having serious doubts about his original intentions. Clarence prayed that they didn't include him.

Then suddenly the man plucked up courage and turned up the speed. He halted in front of them, holding tightly in one hand what was a box or a book inside a brown paper bag. He looked out of place in the smokers' retreat and his body language declared that a fact. He continued to outstare Clarence. It was a one-sided contest: Clarence made no attempt to stare back. The table top had been his favourite view all evening and it was more so now. Staring at the table meant you could avoid having to speak. So thought Clarence.

Tracey could sense that the man was pissed off about something and, being an expert in office politics, kept her mouth shut. He would have to speak first. She knew Clarence was not about to open his mouth unless pushed, probably by her.

The man made the usual movements with his mouth and jaw. Their muscles were working overtime at a furious rate to express frustration.

"So here you are. Talk about having to track you down. Are you avoiding me or what?" The man looked flustered. He was angry. And he had trouble containing himself. He was being messed around. He was being discarded. "Are you in a foul mood again? Playing hard to get?"

The man stopped to take breath then continued. "Are you not speaking to me? This is getting like good cop bad cop."

Sentiments expressed, the man folded his arms and nearly dropped his book. He recovered and tried to pretend that the slip up had never happened.

Tracey spoke on behalf of her now timid boyfriend. "Who are you?"

"You – he knows who I am."

Allegations: Clarence was finally forced to break his vow of silence. "No I don't."

"So I don't know who you are or where you live? Is that it?"

Clarence gave a most emphatic, poisoned reply. "Yes." His mouth did not move, his tongue only slightly, but the word managed to slip out.

The man looked at the woman, hoping to extract some sense out of her.

"How can we help you exactly?" asked Tracey, hand on gun holster.

The man glanced down at his brown paper package. It had seemed like a good idea at the time.

Tracey continued. "Look why don't you sit down. You're making me nervous standing to attention like that. It's very confrontational."

Clarence stared at his girlfriend. His eyes nearly popped out. But he knew better than to cross her in tense situations. And this situation was tense.

Her friendly gesture and tone lowered the man's defences.

"OK."

And he sat, legs crossed, hands holding package tightly in his lap, frowning. It was like he was waiting to see the doctor for a full check-up or a jab to avoid catching some exotic disease in some exotic country on some exotic holiday. Tracey wasn't prepared to put up with it. His demeanour was making things worse.

"Clarence go get him a drink."

Clarence nearly fell out of his chair. "What!"

"Go get the man a drink," she repeated, without dropping her sights from the stranger who sat rigid at their table, like a monk at a loss to explain why he had been caught reading Playboy.

"What do you drink?"

"I don't drink."

"You must drink something." Tracey suddenly sounded severe. It was not an acceptable answer.

"Coke – no orange juice and lemonade."

"Clarence go get him an orange juice - "

Clarence interrupted. "I heard."

Tracey pretended he hadn't. " – and lemonade. And then we can sort this misunderstanding out."

Clarence was very hacked off, but that aside did as he was told. The fact that Tracey had given away his name hadn't helped matters. While he was away at the bar, pushing to the front and vying for service, Tracey and the stranger observed each other, saying nothing.

Tracey wanted to know what was going down. Her Clarence denied all knowledge of this man but the man's behaviour spoke volumes. He had been expecting to make an intimate connection with her bloke and was extremely frustrated when it was not forth coming. Intimate? Just how intimate? Initially she had sat him down for a joke, a bit of a laugh, to wind up Clarence; but now she was operating on a much more serious level. Her claws were out and they were sharp.

She reached into her pocket and felt her packet of cigarettes. "Smoke?"

"No."

The answer didn't come as a surprise. He certainly hadn't just wandered in for a drink and a fag in the smoking zone.

"What's in the bag?"

"Bag?"

"Paper bag. You're holding a paper bag."

The man looked down but wouldn't answer.

"What's your name by the way?"

"John. My name is John," he replied, as if being questioned by a hard, no nonsense, crusty detective in an unpleasant, smelly room at the back of a run down police station.

"What's in the bag John."

John rebelled. He wasn't prepared to be pushed around. He wanted back his self-respect. "And what's your name?"

"Tracey," she replied. "And what's my boyfriend's name?"

"Boyfriend?" John had the wind knocked out of his sails.

"Yes boyfriend." She repeated herself as if speaking to a five year old.

"Clarence. His name is Clarence."

"Full name?" She demanded to know.

"Clarence Kennan."

"And where does he live?"

"16A Appleby Road."

Correct each time. This 'John' was for real thought Tracey. So what the hell was going on. And why was Clarence denying everything. Then the obvious but highly incredible, highly improbable, answer smacked her right between the eyes. She blinked, twice.

No. No way. She knew a gay man when she met one – even a closet gay desperate to hold it all in. Clarence was definitely not gay. No. Never. Not in a thousand years. She simply wouldn't have it. Slept with a gay man? No way. There had to be a more sinister explanation - she hoped - she begged. (Please God.)

"Again what's in the bag John?"

"A book."

"For Clarence?"

"Yes for Clarence." John sounded bitchy.

"May I ask what kind of book?" She hoped it wasn't pictures of naked men.

"No. It's a present, a surprise."

"Fair enough." Tracey decided not to push it. She liked surprises.

The conversation collapsed and the two combatants waited for Clarence to reappear. He duly did, almost dropping the drink he had been forced to buy into the lap of its intended recipient as he attempted to slam it down with high theatre. He crashed back into his seat and for the first time seriously studied the face of the man who was causing him serious grief.

"Why didn't you tell me you had a girlfriend?"

"What?"

"Why didn't you tell me you had a girlfriend?"

"Get out of here."

John looked Clarence in the eye, wishing him to prove that he really meant what he had just said. Nothing.

Tracey took control again. "John has a present for you."

Against his will Clarence registered the name. "I don't want a present."

"It's a book. That's right isn't it? John."

"That's correct." John pushed it across the table. "I thought you would find it useful." It was now a peace offering.

"Why?"

"Why?" John frowned. He was puzzled. "Well because of what we talked about?"

Tracey speculated. A book on male sexuality? Or something about football?

If Clarence's ears could have physically pricked up they would have. They didn't, but still he looked like someone who had just been switched on, disturbed out of a day dream. Clarence wrapped both hands tightly around his pint and clung on.

"And what exactly did we talk about?"

"Is this some kind of game you're playing with me?"

"No game. Tell me what did we talk about?"

Tracey suddenly leaned forward and pushed in. "Hang on a second how did you know we were here tonight?"

John gave his answer to Clarence. "I spoke to the man at your flat. He told me you were here. You didn't tell me you were living with another man."

Tracey settled back and Clarence gave her a funny look, possibly one of exasperation.

He put the question again. "What did we talk about?" He almost screamed.

"All sorts of things," replied John quietly.

It was now John's turn to study faces and he studied the face of the man who had so unexpectedly entered his life, to cause confusion. Did he really have such a bad memory? Or was it just highly selective? Was he schizophrenic?

Clarence grew more impatient, more aggressive, less afraid.

"Like what exactly?"

Tracey studied them both, like a doctor of medicine. She didn't want things turning ugly. John looked at the woman more than once. The act was so deliberate and inviting that Clarence was driven to do the same. Tracey grew alarmed. Had she really slept with a gay man without realising it? Was she that stupid?

"Earth's resources and how fast they are being used up, and who by, and the like."

"Like what?" exclaimed Clarence.

"And oil: the whole picture; the politics and the economy of oil."

"Oil?" Why the fuck would I want to talk about oil Clarence asked himself. "So what's this book for?"

"Further reading. It's a very good book – written by an American – on the history of the American economy, especially with respect to globalisation, the growth of the large corporations, and impact on natural resources – social hierarchies even." John ran out of breath.

For a moment Clarence felt as though he was back in class, but this time sitting behind a desk and trying to understand the lesson. Tracey wanted to burst out laughing: this was surreal, Comedy Store. With difficulty she managed to contain herself: Clarence might fly off the handle and she didn't want that, not the night before the holiday.

Clarence didn't touch the book. He stared at it - glared at it even - like it was some contaminated object. It suddenly took on a life of its own, a purpose, some status in the world of living conscious human beings. It contained some important, life or death, message. John concluded that Clarence was afraid to pick it up, let alone read its pages.

"I take it you're not interested in it then."

"Too right I'm not."

Despondent, John pulled it back to his end of the table. On its way it soaked up some spilt beer. John noted the accident and was annoyed. It was a brand new book. Even paperbacks were not cheap these days.

Clarence reconnected with his glass, trying not speculate on events. Tracey continued to worry if something gay, closet-based, was going on here. Talk about economies, oil and the USA just didn't fit the bill. Both she and John waited for Clarence to speak.

Clarence twitched. "Where? Where did we talk?"

"In the library of course."

Of course thought Clarence. In the library.

"Our local library?"

"Yes our local."

"What was I doing in there?"

"Doing? Reading books of course. And very fast if I may say so."

"Very fast?"

"Very fast. I was impressed – and you convinced me you were taking it all in."

Clarence went silent again and Tracey took up the cause.

"And what else did the two of you get up to?"

John was starting to dislike this woman. She was as hard as nails, more possibly. Sod her. He wouldn't be intimidated. Why did Clarence put up with it?

"If you must know lady we spoke about relationships."

Tracey froze. Her worse nightmare was becoming real. It was baring yellow teeth and threatening to bite. It had bad breath.

"Relationships?" She struggled to enunciate the word. It came out as a messy string of sounds.

"Relationships?" repeated Clarence. He blurted the word out. He had not yet put it into any context.

"In its widest context," added John. He did not wish to initiate controversy or engage in confrontation, especially so late at night. He was tired.

Tracey spoke, with thunder. "Tell me."

John looked at Clarence: possibly for help, possibly for inspiration. Clarence looked away - the same nightmare was looming up in front of him – and was ecstatic to see Sam and Tim moving through the crowd towards him, especially Sam.

"You'll have to go. Leave us. Now."

"What?"

"Go. Right now. You can't stay."

John got the message and stood up. He was glad to go now. "When will I see you again?"

Clarence glared up. He wanted to punch the guy. "Don't push it."

The volley of concentrated anger drenched John. From the top down it left him feeling weak and betrayed. He didn't finish his drink.

Sam and Tim both watched him leave.

"Who was that?" Sam asked as matter of routine, though she had other things dwelling on her mind, like a man she had growing feelings for but who wasn't her husband.

"No one," said Clarence.

"No one," said Tracey, as if to confirm that the answer was the correct one.

✦ ✦ ✦

Log Entry

With regard to the female Fiona I decided at one point to release Clarence from the self-imposed constraint which was in danger of making him explode. The end result was sex, more sex. Sex here occurs at regular intervals. The partner can be changed with ease. When authority, commitment and involvement is applied in equal measures by both sides it is a great success and provides, for both parties, a great release of tension, a sense of solidarity. Both are left feeling very positive about themselves.

Chapter Six

Wednesday began as a busy busy day. Max was busy getting ready for work. Clarence was busy getting ready before the taxi turned up to take him and Tracey to the airport. He was almost packed. There were just the least obvious things left to think about, which was hard. Tracey was ready and waiting, waiting in bed: her stuff done she had rolled over and gone back to sleep when Clarence had disturbed her hours earlier.

Clarence gave instructions to his lodger on how to look after the flat, and phone numbers to call if problems arose. It's only for one sodding week thought Max. As a favour – and to demonstrate that he could cope – Max volunteered to put the rubbish out. Relieved of that duty Clarence went and pulled Tracey out of bed. Max filled a black plastic bag and pushed past Tracey as she pushed past him on the way to the bathroom. Joylessly she pushed herself under the hot shower. She had drunk less alcohol than Clarence but had suffered the fallout by a far greater margin.

Max opened the front door, took a step out into the sunshine, then quickly took a step back. The man he had spoken to the previous night was still there, standing on almost the same spot. The man looked unsettled, apprehensive, just as he had the like night before. He was scratching his beard. Max had to recover his sense of time.

"You again."

"Is Clarence in?"

Less impatient this time, thought Max.

"Clarence there's a man at the door!" he shouted.

Clarence raised his head. He was tinkering around with bits and bobs.

"Tell him he's early!" Clarence shouted back.

"You're early."

John became confused.

"He doesn't understand! I don't think he's your taxi!"

"Quite right," added John.

Clarence changed tone. "Ask him his name!"

"What's your name." Max turned the question into a statement. He was not happy being someone's doorman.

"John."

"He says his name is John!"

Brilliant thought Clarence, and he appeared at the door like a shot, clutching a mix of items: walkman, two tapes and a baseball cap.

"What do you want?"

John looked at the two men, dividing his time in equal measure, and wishing to be left alone with Clarence. Max took the hint.

"I'll leave you two to it then."

"No stay where you are," said Clarence.

It was a firm order and Max raised his eyebrows. It was his only act of protest.

Clarence repeated the question, more viciously this time. "I said what do you want?"

"I wanted to catch you before you went off to work."

"What do you want? It's a simple question."

"Can we talk?"

"No we can't 'talk'."

"Why not?"

Unexpectedly for John the answer Clarence gave was very reasonable. "Because I'm extremely busy that's why. I'm off on holiday any moment now."

"He is," added Max, as if the man on the doorstep didn't believe a word of it.

John came out with it. "I wanted to apologize."

"Apology accepted. Now fuck off."

"No really. I really want to apologize."

"No. Max shut the door." There's no insulting this man thought Clarence.

"Fair enough," said Max and he closed the door. He saw himself drifting into the plot of some TV soap. He wasn't sure if he wanted to stay with it or get out.

Just as it clicked shut Clarence jumped forward and ripped it open again. Max moved aside quickly to avoid his toes being crushed.

"No wait. Come in. I'll give you five minutes."

"To apologize?" asked John.

"No I want to ask you a question."

Clarence led John The Baptist into his living room and dumped the items he had gathered up – and managed not to drop – in the nearest chair. He pointed.

"Stand there." Clarence was back at school.

John stood 'there'.

"Now tell me. What did you mean by 'relationships'?"

"Pardon?"

"You heard me. You said we discussed 'relationships'. What do you mean. Tell me."

"We talked about relationships, in their broadest context."

"What does that mean?" The words love, soul, spirit and sex entered Clarence's head and connected up in ways which terrified him.

"You asked me about the various permutations of human relationships." John paused, not sure whether to continue. The look the man's face said no. He did anyway. "And I explained. I explained them all."

"Them all?"

Next door, in the kitchen, Max stopped what he was doing (which wasn't much) and stored away the last statement which the man called 'John' had made. This was far from a normal conversation, even for London. Not for one moment did Max believe his name was John.

John didn't say anymore. He waited for Clarence to speak but Clarence had nothing to say. He had heard the shower being switched off, as had Max. Two out of the three men held their breath. Tracey stepped out.

"Make me coffee and toast please!" she shouted.

"You've got to go now," whispered Clarence.

He tried to steer and push John towards the front door, but as he was not prepared to lay a finger on the man this proved difficult. Instead he had to coax him, as if dealing with a possibly mad, definitely diseased stray dog who had wandered in.

"Understood," replied John sympathetically.

He left without further fuss, much to the relief of Clarence. Clarence watched him head off through the window, just to make sure he didn't turn round and come back. John had no intention of hanging around. He sauntered off. He had his dignity back.

"Toast please. And coffee!" shouted Tracey again. "I'm on holiday!"

"Understood!" shouted Clarence.

Feeling gracious Max slipped two slices of bread in the toaster and pushed down the lever. Then he topped up the kettle, having just boiled it for himself. He was starting to wonder about this place. No matter. He'd be back home in Dublin in three months – unless of course the building contract was extended.

Clarence took over and made the coffee and toast, just the way Tracey always wanted it.

Tracey got dressed and did her hair.

Clarence finished off his packing.

Max left for work.

The taxi arrived, only ten minutes late.

And the holiday began, in earnest.

✦ ✦ ✦

Tracey and Clarence killed time on the beach. They laid side by side on raffia mats provided by the hotel, at no extra charge: it was all included in the cost. One mat had a disagreeable stain which Clarence endeavoured not to make skin contact with: Tracey had had it first, but then she swapped it, and now he had it. They had got up early, devoured breakfast, and recced a good spot. 'We've beaten the Germans' Clarence had joked. 'Don't embarrass me' Tracey had replied, joke demolished.

Their lack of dexterity and food management at the buffet bar had advertised to all that they were newcomers. By late morning the no man's land around them had filled up and now choked in places with human bodies, but they were past caring: worn out and washed away by the heat of the sun they were.

Clarence still clung to yesterday's newspaper he had bought at the airport. He spent time reading about things which didn't normally interest him in the slightest. Tracey had her book. She read two chapters before giving up. It had became just too hot to concentrate the mind.

The flight over had not been a barrel of laughs. Tracey had continued to badger Clarence about the mysterious John and his last cryptic comment. Clarence had kept repeating himself until blue in the face. He did not know this F'ing John and had no F'ing recollections of ever meeting the guy. He was a fantasist, unhinged, Clarence had decided. The notion that John could be linked in any way to his blackouts, Clarence was not yet prepared to entertain. But it would only be a matter of time. Tracey only let it go when she noticed that people were watching them.

Things had not improved upon arrival at the hotel. Their room had not been up to spec. After a long drawn out - bordering on furious - conversation with an assistant hotel manager Tracey finally secured a swap for something better and which met the terms of the contract. So pissed off were they with the first day, and so knackered, that they went to bed early and relatively sober, both wishing to start the next day on a fresh note. Hence early to rise and early down to the beach. John was definitely not for discussion during the entire holiday. Clarence would not have it.

They took in the new, and discussed. They took in the temperature of the sea, and discussed. They took in the clean state of the beach, and admired. They covered themselves in suntan lotion, and fell asleep.

Tracey woke up first. Still too tired to read she sat up and observed the antics of other holidaymakers: some close by, some in the distance; some young, some old; some families, some couples. She wondered if she was missing out on anything. Not yet she told herself, not yet. She laid down again – it was the least tiring position to sustain – and turned her addled, heavy head to one side. She spied on Clarence. He was doing a very good impersonation of a fried corpse, laid out for inspection by loved ones and friends. His mouth was open.

He stirred. Tracey rolled her head back to the skyward position. She heard him sit up, and felt sand hit her arm. It stuck to the suntan lotion. The fierce dazzle of the sun – despite sunglasses – disappeared as he leant over her. She felt his breath on her face. She heard him sniff. This was no different from being in bed with him. He got up and walked off. She watched him go. Why he had bothered to check if she was asleep she couldn't fathom. Perhaps he had wanted to kiss her then changed his mind. The holiday might still restore the romance yet.

Clarence wandered along the beach, stopping to take in the crowd, much to the irritation of some. He stopped by an incomplete, multiple sandcastle construction. It was being built with great passion by a father and son team. Words were spoken but Tracey could only see gestures and the less subtle facial expressions. Clarence offered to help. The help was declined. Clarence moved on.

Tracey saw him chat with an old couple. They talked for what seemed ages. Then he broke off, walked straight into the sea and stood stock-still when the water reached his knees. He stretched both arms and neck up as high as they could go, and pointed towards the sun with both index fingers. God I hope he hasn't discovered religion thought Tracey.

When he returned, dripping, he slumped down, immediately closed his eyes, and fell asleep. Tracey had to endure the snoring again: an all too familiar sound. Then, barely a minute later, he man woke up again, sat up, and looked around like a stiff man bored stiff. This time he jumped up and marched straight down to the shore. He kicked the sand around as if looking for trouble then kicked the waves and look even more bored. Tracey continued to observe. Her bloke was turning back into a stranger before her eyes. Nothing seemed to ignite him until five women, all in their twenties, ran onto the beach and laid out their few possessions to form a make-do net line. Clarence was drawn to them, like a hungry dog to a bowl of pedigree dog food. He watched from the sidelines: like a kid on the outside looking in he was eager to join in. And his patience paid off. They were five. He made it six. He was allowed to join the party.

Tracey was glad to see him having fun - and being fun - at last. He was excited. He was engaged. He was happy. He was too happy. She felt stung, left behind, left out; and the girls were all good-looking, and younger than her, and their bikinis covered less buttock area. It was a crime.

⸙ ⸙ ⸙

The two went sightseeing. They got on some bus and got off in the centre of some town as instructed by some woman at hotel reception. She had given them a map, the type designed for tourists. The streets were marked with places to go and things to see but it wasn't written in English - which makes it an adventure Tracey had said. Clarence wasn't convinced but he went along. He had to go along. He had no real choice in the matter.

Tracey wanted to see things, anything. Clarence didn't want to see anything. She asked him if he had any preference. Clarence didn't care. Preferences? Who gives a toss? 'You're choice darling' were his exact words.

They plodded around. They looked around. They were hassled by street sellers. They got hot. They brought bottles of mineral water. They stared into shop windows. 'Just like home' one knackered Clarence remarked privately.

They discovered the cool shade of trees set in some municipal gardens. There they sat and watched a fountain do what it did: continuously eject water at high speed. They finished their bottles of water – now warm water – and Clarence demanded a real drink. So, after watching ducks in the pool do the things only ducks do, they headed off to find a bar. Clarence was happy when he grasped a drink in his hand. All he needed now was the BBC and a kebab, or crisps. Tracey studied the map and found a museum. She had to visit it, having come all this way. Lunch could wait.

"If we eat lunch now we're be too tired to do anything."

"That's the whole point of eating on holiday," moaned Clarence but Tracey won and they headed off.

"Look, the museum. Let's have a look around."

"Why? And anyway look we have to pay."

· 122 ·

"Because we're on holiday that's why."

"Why stare at things we'll forget all about one hour later?"

"It's culture. Foreign culture. Something different from all the stuff back home."

"It's a set up. They just throw together any old crap for the tourists. I bet it's not cheap."

Tracey did the calculation and was forced to admit that this time he was right.

"Let's go and eat, or back to the beach, or another drink somewhere - somewhere with a better view this time, not the bloody main road."

"You just want to drink yourself silly all the time," she complained

"I'm on holiday. It's my right."

"There's more to life than getting drunk."

"Who said I want to get drunk? Semi-drunk will do me."

Tracey gave up. "OK. Let's check a few more shops – just in case we see something we like – then call it a day. Back to the beach."

"Something we like?"

"OK I like. I'd like to buy something summery, something distinctive for back home."

They trudged on, like automatons, like soldiers on dawn patrol. But there was no enemy, just the joke of tourist ambition meets summer heat. Tracey, the stronger of the two, took point. Clarence was tied to a long piece of rope, and it she pulled him along. Tracey was on a mission to save money while at the same time spend it. The sun beat down. The prices confused. Tracey was tempted into one fashion shop but complications arose as the girl didn't speak English. Bruised, Tracey called it a day. This made Clarence very smug, and she knew it. They sat and drank beer and waited for the bus back to the hotel. Back to the beach. Back to sleeping in the sun and back to barely talking to each other. Tracey decided to get rat-arsed that night. The hotel had organised a disco.

✦ ✦ ✦

Evening: Tracey bided her time in their room, harbouring that sinking feeling; Clarence was elsewhere, probably drinking. There was this disco and Tracey was determined to enjoy herself. She dressed herself up, put on make-up, and stepped out. The disco was not packed but it looked promising. Most of mainland Europe it seemed was represented: from Germany down to Spain; from Spain across to Croatia; from Croatia up to Poland. Clarence was dug in for the long haul at the bar with other UK nationals. Tracey decided to give him one last chance to make her feel good. Like a foreign virus she approached the circle of men and infected the male banter with her female presence.

Clarence raised his glass and using its sign language offered to get her a drink. She would be easier to handle with a drink in her hand.

Tracey refused. "Let's dance first. I want to dance."

Clarence had a get out clause. "I'm still drinking."

"Finish it later."

The man from Norwich stuck his oar in. "I think your wife wants to dance."

Clarence and Tracey spoke as one.

"She's not my wife."

"I'm not his wife."

"You going to dance?"

"I don't want to dance."

She tugged at his sleeve. "Come on dance."

"I don't want to dance."

"Would you dance with John?"

"Leave it." Clarence wasn't yet drunk enough to say fuck off to his girlfriend, and she wasn't drunk yet to take it on the chin. "I need another drink. You know I hate dancing when I'm sober."

Tracey conceded the point: he was telling the truth. "OK. Get me a glass of wine then, red."

Clarence did as instructed and returned to the safety zone of 'blokes chatting and talking bollocks'. Tracey stood outside the circle and was ignored. Where are the women folk she asked herself.

Sod this thought Tracey after five minutes. This is boring the tits off me. She put down her drink and buggered off to the dance floor. There was a sufficient crowd to camouflage one person dancing alone. She went through the motions of moving to the beat, her heart not really in it. Then it changed for the better: a well-groomed Italian, roughly her age, asked her for a dance in broken English. She remembered him talking to her at the swimming pool. She accepted. He would do for now. He tried to converse further, but the more he spoke the less she understood. Like last time she just smiled at the right moments and this kept him satisfied. After awhile she noticed Clarence watching her. He had stopped talking with his new mates and was now just standing like a wet blanket, lager and cigarette in hand. The music paused to switch tracks. This was his chance to cut in. He didn't, so she carried on dancing, and flirting. She had been starved of fun and was making up for lost time.

When she next looked across the floor Clarence was sitting down and staring into his glass. Point made. She peeled off from the Italian and grooved opposite empty space. Clarence had an open invitation to join her. He didn't.

The space was filled by another Mediterranean man, this one younger and a better dancer than the one before. Tracey felt smug: she could still pull the younger man. The John Travolta wannabe grabbed her around the waist. Perfect timing. She scanned the horizon for Clarence. He was nowhere to be seen. That's it she thought, sod you. Dance and get drunk. Roll on the flight home.

Later, much later in the night – after midnight to be precise – a sunburnt Clarence did hit the dance floor. Like a man possessed he leapt around and twice fell over, but Tracey was not there to witness it.

✦ ✦ ✦

One knackered Clarence was forced awake by the light of a bright morning sun. It pierced his eyelids and boiled his cheeks like cuts of ham. He threw back the bed sheet. He was baking. Suddenly he bolted upright in a state of high anxiety, as if someone had shoved a red hot poker up his arse. This was not his bedroom. The bed was pointing the wrong way, else the walls and windows had moved. The balcony had been removed. That was not Tracey's underwear on the chair but those were his underpants on the floor.

He crept into the bathroom to take the first triumphant piss of the day. Take a piss and get out quick he told himself. This he did, looking and feeling like shit in his crumpled clothes – clothes which smelt of beer and fags. On the way, and for no discernible reason, he noted the room number. It meant nothing to him. Watching his back he made his way back to his room.

The room was locked. Shit, Tracey would be at breakfast. He swallowed the deep lump in his throat and headed down to the dining area. On his way he tried to comb his hair with his fingers. It was a sad sight to see.

Dining room. Funny smells. Families with kids and loud babies. Hell. Clarence looked around. Tracey was sat next to some daft old bat, doing her best to avoid conversation. He walked towards her: head thumping with fear of painful retribution. He knew he couldn't invent some neat explanation. His legs wobbled. He was weak at both knees. He was a stretcher case.

The daft old bat - well perhaps not so old Clarence admitted – looked up and gave him that knowing look. She was genuinely pleased to see him. The look of recognition on her face unnerved him, to extremes. Worse still hers was not the face of a complete stranger. Had they met a long time ago? Was she from England? Then the implication struck him like a dead fish in the face. He almost fainted.

Tracey turned: he had ho choice but to walk on into the abyss. He ignored the face which terrorized him the most and locked in on the other. The middle-aged, not so daft old bat immediately realised her mistake and immediately switched her attentions elsewhere. Such were holiday encounters.

Tracey almost recoiled at his appearance. She too had a look of guilt on her face. Each struggled to speak, let alone start a coherent sentence. They called it quits.

✦ ✦ ✦

Log Entry

Human beings have perfected a means of rapid movement through their atmosphere, against the gravitational pull, using a rudimentary means of gas propulsion applied to a rather peculiar transportation system: a system which involves squeezing as many of their number as possible into a flying machine which as first sight appears designed for comfort. But there is barely room for them to stretch their limbs. Seating arrangements appear specifically designed to prevent adhoc socialising or sexual intercourse. The sexes however are not separated.

Using this method a massive amount of planning, organisation and sheer hard work goes into continuously concentrating large numbers of humans into groups before dispersing them at high speed through the atmosphere to various points on the globe. Once onboard (the process of embarkation is lengthy, slow, and mentally tortuous) the rules of engagement are strictly enforced: you sit where you are told to sit; you strap yourself down prior to acceleration and deceleration; you eat what you are given. Food packaging is light and tight, reflecting the fact that space and weight are key factors which must be strictly costed and controlled.

This ancient method of 'flying through air' can seriously batter the senses. I noticed that the female companion (the one I experienced sexual intercourse with) looked pale and withdrawn during most of the journey. She never spoke to my host unless circumstances dictated. He in return made no attempt to speak to her. This arrangement suited both sides it seems. I had to hold on for dear life when my host was subjected to the intense acceleration. Strapping yourself to a big chemical rocket may be a rather out-dated way in which to manipulate the space-time continuum but it sure is fun.

My host Clarence has travelled to some place very hot and very different from his home environment. It is located next to a large body of contaminated liquid they call 'saltwater':-

The typical hydrogen-oxygen combination which floods this planet for the most part exists in liquid form on the surface. In the colder polar regions it is solid. Traces of it can be found in the atmosphere as both gas and liquid. This liquid, 'water', covering the majority of the planet surface is contaminated with sodium chloride (amongst other things) – a substance which is not toxic to humans in small quantities, and in fact forms part of their diet. This is 'salt'. Hence 'saltwater', the liquid which defines the boundaries of the land masses.

While here my host does little other than eat and drink, swim and sleep. In the evenings recklessly consumes large measures of his favourite drug, alcohol, until he falls over or falls asleep. This activity runs through his head both as a pleasure and a conflict. When pushed he will partake in physical sports.

Like many of those around him, he spends a large proportion of the daylight hours laid flat out on the stretch of land immediately adjacent to the saltwater. It's surface is an accumulation of tiny granules of eroded rock: they are continually deposited there by natural tidal action. Most of the time he is asleep - at best semi-conscious – the result of alcohol abuse the previous night. Such behaviour is not peculiar to him. Quite the opposite in fact. It appears to be obligatory among the men, and some of the women. There are many in the same shattered state scattered along this thin strip of semi-permanent, shifting land. Like Clarence they wear clothes which do just the minimum required to conceal their sexual organs from public view. Most females also make the point of covering their nipples. Some do not. Coverage is vaguely related to body age. The younger they are, the less they cover their bodies.

I presume popularity of this location is due to the fact that it is adjacent to this large body of cool circulating saltwater: allowing humans to jump in and lower their body temperature after lengthy periods spent exposed to a very hot sun. It produces a great feeling of rapture and security when one submerges one's overheated body in it. Get hot. Cool off. Exercise.

Sleep. Eat and drink. Sleep. Maintaining these cycles of imbalance are an intrinsic part of the overall experience.

Key to all this is this strip of land, the 'beach'. The beach is the place to be. Young children enjoy it the most: just running, jumping, shouting, plotting, making up games. Inventing games is a skill children seem to be born with. But the rules do not stay constant and they will argue over their interpretation. They huddle and plot and investigate things together very well. This is in contrast to their parents who keep to themselves.

This behaviour of simply lying around in the sun and doing nothing is widespread. Why then they travel vast distances to do this I do not know understand. It may be instinctive. It may be seasonal. It may be a legal requirement, a requirement to relax and do nothing every once and awhile. Who knows. Is there no space close to home where these people can lie flat out under the sun wearing minimal clothing?

Those that do make the effort to do something look lost. They walk around without direction or purpose: too much time on their hands - no way to fill it except to do what they did the day before.

In an attempt to prevent the skin burning visitors rub various oils and creams over their bodies. They do not always succeed. Some suffer serious sunburn. Others turn deep shades of brown and suffer premature aging.

There is a preoccupation among many of the mature males and their offspring to fashion large quantities of the rock deposits into complex structures. They do this using simple colourful tools made of low grade carbon polymers. This task can take up a good part of the day, and can involve whole family units, or at least its male component. Upon completion they usually destroy the structures they have created in a state of frenzied hysteria, removing all signs that they ever existed. It is as if they wish for no one to recognise their work. Strange.

Again an observation which keeps reinforcing itself: even here, in unfamiliar territory, in a far away land, females love to talk amongst themselves; men do not.

This place contains a great multi-cultural mix, as demonstrated by the many different languages I hear spoken, and the subtle differences in body language. I have noticed that in the building where my host is lodging there is a growing tendency for these different groups to coalesce at feeding times.

In addition to natural saltwater an artificially created body of purified water is also a magnet, especially for the young. They love jumping into it, thrashing around, and making lots of noise. In contrast the older generations prefer lying at its perimeter for long periods, some deep in thought, perhaps meditating. Securing the best place is a priority for some. They arrive early to ensure success.

I may have blundered in allowing an unknown, older female to apprehend my host and persuade him to partake in sexual intercourse. I lowered his defences to allow the release of a dangerous level of stress. I believe it has caused a great emotional rift between him and his companion; and has placed him in a permanent, heightened state of embarrassment, though little in the way of guilt it seems. Performing the act of sex with someone other than your current partner companion appears to be socially unacceptable.

Interestingly the other woman approached him much later after the event. However the harsh words he expressed immediately curtailed any further involvement. She has not been seen since.

I presume my host and his companion will travel home together. In which case will they exchange words on the journey or ignore each other? Relationships between opposite sexes on this planet are fragile, complicated affairs. They can snap easily. Strange for such a determined, forthright, and dare I say confrontational species? In all aspects it dominates this planet and all its species, totally, to a degree which raises concerns over evolutionary balance and long term integration.

Chapter Seven

Clarence took a day off work and spent it, in the main, drinking. He drank to get over the shock, insult and humiliation of having been dumped, by a woman. It was a minor disaster amplified by the fact that he had wanted get in first with the axe. And now he couldn't, which really pissed him off. So from lunchtime onwards he sat in the pub and drank until bored by the company – retired or retro - then continued the activity at home, there bored by some weird black and white 50's film. He watched the clock for the time when Fiona would be home from school. He would phone her up. She would cheer him up. They would make love. But she didn't. And they didn't. He only got as far as a phone call, and not one of his best.

She apologized and was very sorry, but she didn't want to see him that evening. She didn't want to complicate things she explained calmly, and with an astonishing sense of calm assurance considering she had a drunk breathing down the phone. 'Let's keep things on an even keel and put our one moment of passion behind us' were her words. She didn't want to compromise her teaching she said. And she hoped he was better soon. Compromise what? had been his stark reaction: a reaction which she did not understand. He tried repeating his request in a louder voice and with more manly rigour in the hope that she would break or bend, but she didn't.

After that the drinking continued with extra vigour and vengeance well into the evening, until he fell asleep in front of the TV. Max dutifully turned it off when he came in from work. Being in charge for a week had made him quite house proud. He had discovered that it didn't hurt to wash up and clean up and load the washing machine just like his sisters.

Clarence stirred one hour later and left the flat. He had a long walk ahead of him, and though he was very wobbly on his feet he managed to make it intact to John's house, to take up the offer of free food. John was so pleased to see a happy looking Clarence on his doorstep that he almost hugged him.

"May I come in? I think I'm having a bad day."

A bad day? thought John. He's hiding it well.

"Have you been drinking?"

"Yes. Alcohol. It's an addiction."

Despite the strong smell of the stuff on his breath Clarence sounded coherent.

John stroked his beard and considered the weight of the opportunity. "Come in then."

He led Clarence into the living room and sat him down.

"You said I could come round for dinner."

"Did I? Yes I did." John would have preferred advance warning but he decided to forgive him. What the hell, you're only young once. (John was 45.) And he said he was having a bad day.

With no notice it was a case of a takeaway – Chinese takeaway – delivered free within a 3 mile radius. Today it was Good Cop Clarence John noted and together as they sat on the couch, John having rearranged the cushions to suit.

John had to take charge. Clarence it seemed had come over all shy. He needed prompting. "You said you were having a bad day?"

"Yes I did."

John flooded the room with Debussy and soft illumination from wall lights. He broke out the wine. In for a penny in for a pound.

"The relationship with my female companion has been terminated abruptly."

"Has it?"

"Yes. It has."

"So what happened exactly?" And why are you sharing this with me? John hoped it was for all the right reasons.

"For some reason – though she never stated it as a fact – my friendship with you was a contributory factor."

"Was it."

"Yes. It was. And with respect to our friendship I must apologize for those instances of disengagement and denial."

Clarence spoke like a solicitor, so John replied like one. "Apology accepted."

"It will happen again. There's nothing I can do about it."

"Meaning what?"

"Meaning it's another me, another part of me."

That explained everything and nothing.

"Perhaps you should see someone?"

"Someone?"

John choose his next words carefully, wishing not to offend, or rock his boat now it had set sail. He didn't want his sailor jumping ship.

"Someone who can help with these things, these . . . problems of the mind shall we say. A specialist."

Clarence shook his head. "No need for that. It's not a problem of mental health." He sounded very sure of himself. "You live alone?"

"I do yes."

"Are you in a relationship with a female?"

"No. No relationship with a female." John tiptoed through the words.

"Is that normal?"

John squirmed, crossed his legs then lashed out. "Depends what you mean by normal doesn't it."

"I don't know, that's why I'm asking you."

John saw rough seas ahead. "So what went wrong?"

"Can't quite put my finger on it."

John stroked his beard again. "Try," he said firmly.

"So many things. The interactions seemed to conceal hidden agendas, more on an emotional wavelength that factual. Women appear to have more than one agenda at any one time, sometimes conflicting. And if you try to satisfy them all they denounce you as ambiguous, uncommitted. If you stick rigidly to the one then you're told you're unresponsive, got a one track mind. All the time they judge you by some emotional history rather than hard facts."

"Well that's women for you."

"Other than the physical love making – you know the sexual intercourse thing – nothing else seems to work, or have purpose."

John saw his chance. "I agree. They fascinate me but they cause so many hang-ups, so many silly little problems, and for what? Just a bit of sex now and then? A convenient way to reach orgasm? Followed by what? The washing up?"

"Yes. Well put."

"They're not the easiest creatures to understand."

"But are we?"

"I think so." His reply was instant: John saw it no other way.

"They expect a certain emotional response to a question – giving the correct answer is secondary – one which fits their current emotional state, regardless of yours. Sometimes they don't even bother putting the question and just expect the emotional response out of the blue. Why is that?"

John thought it was his turn to speak. He was wrong. The pause was not for him.

"And they don't always express what they feel. They guard it, store it up. And when they do let it out it comes out like an explosion: and they are caught off guard, and they hate that, so they take it out on you. Why is that?"

"Beats me. Venus and Mars I suppose. Or is it the other way round?"

"You're talking about the planets? Second and fourth from the sun."

"Yes?"

"But how could two distinct halves of the human race have evolved on different planets?"

John laughed, took Clarence by the hand and gripped it tightly. He liked a man who could make him laugh. "I'm talking about the book silly billy."

"Sorry. I got confused."

Clarence sounded downhearted so John took the other hand and squeezed them both in his. No resistance was detected. He wanted to cry. Clarence, sensing an imminent emotional collapse and wishing not to be held responsible, told him not to.

"You mustn't drink so much Clarence. You mustn't let it drive you to drink." With gravity in his voice John held back his tears.

"It?"

"Whatever it is within you that is responsible for your doubt and despair. Women are not the only thing in life you know."

"Oh believe me I know that. Tell me about it."

Now John was confused but saved by the doorbell. The food had arrived, and just in the nick of time.

"Come on let's eat," croaked John. Together they stood up, still holding hands.

John led the way to the door, forgetting to let go of his new sometimes wayward friend. The man delivering the food - funnily enough Chinese, second generation - made no comment.

The conversation was hung on a coat peg and the food was consumed. Dishes were washed, dried, and stacked away: their leisure points earned, John allowed himself to switch on the television. Watching the evening news was in his blood. And it was his job: he was a research assistant with a popular newspaper. People like him and the journalists they supported made events current, issues mainstream, and celebrity trivia trustworthy titillation.

The two watched the news unfold like a happy couple. With women out of the way they settled down on the couch and talked, at length: the topic of conversation jumping from one subject to the next. John loved it. And when it came to the state of the environment John couldn't be stopped. And they continued to consume wine long into the night, though it was only John who got drunk. Clarence had started out drunk.

❉ ❉ ❉

Clarence awoke with a stinging hangover. Nothing unusual in that. Mentally he had to crawl on all fours away from the unconscious state and on towards semi-consciousness: from there it was a hard climb up some steep steps to full consciousness. He opened his eyes, one at a time, and stared at the ceiling. Something was not right. The ceiling pattern had changed over night. And something was not right beneath him. The mattress felt lumpy. It was poking him in the back. And the bed sheets had a peculiar smell. He assumed it was the smell of unwashed sheets. In fact it was the reverse: it was the smell of crisp, clean, fresh – sanitised almost – linen. Then the view of a room which was not his room closed in from the sides and completed the construction of his new nightmare.

The thought of another one-night stand with a complete stranger yanked him up into the upright position. He had fallen asleep drunk and woken up where? In whose bedroom? And what had he done in between? Fragments of his dream world were still floating around inside his head. They collided and bounced off the walls of his head like plastic balls in a lottery: giving clues and immediately snatching them away again; to leave a trail of stale question marks. And for some reason that John the nutter occurred in lots of them. And he was smiling, and the words 'wake up Clarence I've got to go to work' hung around, long after the ground on which they sat had shifted. Clarence put it down to invention, or Tracey. Yes, blame her for his misery.

Clarence felt below: he was in his underpants. He looked around: his clothes were neatly folded over the back of a chair. He never folded his clothes. As a rule he just dumped them in thin air and let gravity do the rest. Someone had folded his clothes. A woman's touch? He struggled in vain to place the room but to no avail. It was alien.

His body jerked: sounds of movement had startled him. Somebody was slowly climbing stairs. He froze rigid, frozen by fear of the unknown; like a patient in hospital – private hospital, own room – who had been resuscitated, brought back from the edge of eternal darkness, knowing he had been somewhere awful, and knowing he still had somewhere awful

· 134 ·

to go: heart bypass operation perhaps; or surgery for a brain tumour; else testicular cancer, or a large hospital bill for those aspects of care not covered by the health plan. Whatever it was it was not going to be nice.

The door opened slowly, as if for maximum theatrical affect. Clarence was half expecting Peter Cushing to walk in: the butler with a bolt through his neck. He pulled the sheets up around his neck, swallowed hard – which he found hard to do - and waited, eyes nailed to the scene unfolding. He wanted to leap up and run away but his legs would not flex, his muscles would not work. He drew his knees up to his chin and shrivelled up. He was fourteen again and in danger of being caught masturbating by one of his parents. Despite that Clarence still wanted mummy.

It was that man John again, trying to steady a breakfast tray. It was loaded with a pot of coffee and toast lined up in a cute little stainless steel rack. It was breakfast in bed and it was heading right his way. What had he done to earn himself breakfast in bed?

John smiled. "You're awake at last."

Clarence didn't answer. As John approached he shrank back even more, back into the smallest, tightest space possible. And John kept coming, creeping forward, eyes down, carefully balancing his tray. He parked it by the side of the bed – at which point he realised something was very wrong. His heart fell and his mouth fell open. Clarence looked traumatized. John stepped back, folder his arms, and leant against a wall for support. He was going weak at the knees. Bad Cop Clarence was back with a vengeance. He shook his head.

"No. No. No not again. Not in my house."

Clarence, still buggered for words, voice box incapacitated, withdrew in the opposite direction, slipping off the bed and barely managing to land on his feet. Like opposing magnets the two maintained as much distance between them as was possible within the boundaries of the room. Clarence, sheet ripped from the bed and wrapped around him, grabbed at his clothes then, once he had them back in his possession, froze. He wanted to put them on but didn't dare reveal himself. He stood in limbo. John got the message and left the room, feeling insulted.

"If you don't want the coffee and toast I'll have it," he said on his way out, spitting out each word. 'Waste not want not' his dad had told him, and still told him to this day.

Clarence tumbled into his clothes, falling over twice. Ready to go over the top he pulled open the door inch by inch, breath by breath. It was not Psycho but neither was it Willy Wonka And The Chocolate Factory. No sign of John. He crept downstairs. He heard sounds in the kitchen. He saw the front door and ran for it, like a boy fleeing the farmer's field – the farmer being the ugly old bastard type who shot anything that moved and then stuck it in a casserole.

Outside the sun was shining, not that Clarence was in any state of mind to appreciate the weather. He didn't recognise the street so chose a direction at random and started to walk away, as quick as his legs would allow. Then he slowed. Then he stopped, in a state of total anguish. A question of faith reared up inside him. It had to be answered. Had he been a C of E parish priest the bishop would have escorted down to the nearest pub and got bought him a drink. He had to talk to the devil. He could not walk away from it. He was attached to a long length of elastic and it was stretched to the limit. It would stretch no more. Now it yanked him back.

The momentum which had propelled him out the door had now diminished to zero. He did a 180 degree turn, and began walking again. The momentum gathered again and his speed increased. He came bursting in on John who, for what it was worth, raised his teaspoon. It was his only defensive weapon. He held a tight grip on the kitchen counter with his other hand.

"Leave me alone. I'm not worth it."

"I'm not going to harm you. I just want to know." Clarence held back. He could not complete the question.

"Know? Know what?"

"I just want to know." Clarence took a deep breath and clamped his lower lip between his teeth. He could not bring himself to say the words.

"Well? Know what?" John lowered his teaspoon but still clung to the counter.

"Did I – did you and I - " but Clarence could not complete.

"Did you and I what?"

The kettle blew its top and switched itself off. Clarence looked at it. John looked at it. The kettle had the stage. Finally it came out.

"Did you and I do things, together?"

"Do things together?" mimicked John. He was determined to hear Clarence say it.

"Did you and I have sex? Sex of some kind?"

John examined the poor excuse of a man standing before him – up and down a number of times as if sizing up the sale of the damage – before answering. It was as if he was searching for redeeming features, and finding none, not even one small one. His eyes wandered around the kitchen as he struggled to compose himself for the answer which would, in no uncertain terms, conveyed the feeling of insult and injury.

"No sir for the record we did not have sex. None was offered and none was given." John did not mince his words. He was not one for one-night stands.

"Then why did I wake up in your bed?"

"You did not wake up in my bed. You woke up in my spare bed, in my spare bedroom."

Clarence grabbed the next question on his list and threw it in John's face. "What was I doing here?"

"Visiting. You visited me last night, and you stayed the night."

"Drunk? Was I drunk?"

"I'm not sure. You didn't act drunk but you smelt drunk and you looked unsteady at times."

"And what did we do? What did we get up to?"

"We 'got up to' nothing. We had dinner. We talked. We watched television a bit. We had a good time."

"We talked? Like last time?"

"Yes we talked, just like last time." John moved towards the kitchen table. "Look do you mind if I sit down – if we sit down. This is tiring me out."

John sat down. Clarence followed. John spoke first.

"Look I don't pretend for one moment to understand what's going on here but I really do think you need help. Serious help. You understand?"

Wounded by a bullet of unsavoury truth, Clarence lost the will to carry on the fight. He stared down at the table - pine, second hand. He had nothing to say, which for John was unacceptable.

"Look at me Clarence. Look me in the eye."

Clarence looked up: he was back in detention.

"You've got a problem and you need help. Real help. Am I getting through here?"

The small boy nodded, against his will. When he did speak John heard the soft, crumbling voice of a broken man.

"Can I have that coffee."

"Yes of course." John jumped up and placed a hand on Clarence's shoulder. "Wait here. Don't move."

In a full about turn, Clarence now had no intention of going anywhere. He had lost the energy and the will, and all sense of direction.

John returned with the tray. The toast was stone cold but the coffee was still hot. He filled the cup. "Drink it quick. It's not piping hot. Sugar?"

"Yes. No. Yes." Clarence shook his head. "I can't remember."

John gave it to him black, no sugar. Clarence sipped it.

"I can put it in the microwave if you like."

"No it's fine. Thanks." The word 'thanks' crawled out from the gut and left a nasty stain in his mouth.

Clarence carried on sipping and shifting the thoughts inside his head, trying to lay them to rest in some neat little pattern: one which, if one stood back, would make some sense – a bit like a DIY garden patio, or a self-assessment tax form.

John, concluding he had a dumb animal on his hands, returned to making his own breakfast: tea and his own hot toast, possibly cereal if he had time.

"What did we talk about this time?"

"Women."

Clarence looked up surprised. "Women?" Somehow that was the least expected answer.

"Yes women. You're having women problems right now – or were having."

Women problems: an undeniable truth; and that very fact made it an unexpected source of relief. Clarence worked his knackered, gnarled brain to its limit to try and fill in the one enormous blank which again had invaded his life and his sanity. He failed, and for all his efforts was rewarded with an even heavier headache. He put his head in his hands. It thumped away.

"I need to lie down."

"No not here." John was adamant. "I need to get to work. Sorry but I do need to get to work."

"No of course not here. I didn't mean here." Clarence lifted himself up and with no more ado headed for the door. John followed behind, chaperoning him, to make sure that this time he did leave.

Just before they broke contact Clarence turned and humbled himself. "Can we talk some more, another time, later perhaps?"

"Sure. Another time but not today."

Taking pity on the crushed soul, John suddenly had a thought, the gracious, caring kind. "Here wait a mo."

He rushed off, to reappear in no time holding a scrap of paper. On it was a man's name and a long telephone number.

"This man is a friend of mine. I'll call him. Ask him to expect your call."

Clarence took it between finger and thumb, holding it at a distance like it was something he had pulled out of the kitchen sink plughole: an old piece of cabbage perhaps, or a slice of onion. He wasn't impressed, or grateful, or sold on the idea but he took it anyway. Best not to hurt the man's feelings. Defiance returned to bolster the spirit. He was just having these bloody blackouts. No need to panic. And no need to share it.

"I'll think about it."

"You do that – and my number is on the back, the one in blue."

"The one in blue."

Clarence began to walk away but after a few paces he stopped, leaving John looking worried. "Which way back into town?"

A simple question. John was relieved. "As you are. To the end of the street then a left. Keep going. You'll hit the station road."

Clarence stuck his hands in his pockets and began the long march home. He didn't say thanks.

He walked back through the centre of town, passing the library on his way. He stopped and took it in, craving for some untapped memory to spring forth and bite him on the bum. No such luck. Nothing resonated. It was just a building like any other. He could not remember having ever entered it. He tried an experiment. He went inside. He found nothing but books on bookshelves and a few, mainly old people shuffling up and down aisles or sitting at tables. Clarence was never comfortable around old people. They were a constant reminder that even when you were old and decrepit, and all your friends and family could be dead, you still had to soldier on: eat, drink, shit and sleep, for tomorrow you will have to do it all over again.

The place had all the ambience of a doctor's waiting room – One Flew Over The Cuckoo's Nest but without the jokes, not even the subtext. Clarence reversed quickly, and was gone. He never looked back.

✦ ✦ ✦

Back home.

Clarence did not want to be back home. He had a big black cloud hanging over him and he wanted a drink, but he did not allow himself a drink. He was resolute in his determination to remain sober. So boredom set in. He made himself a bacon sandwich but the pleasure of eating it was short-lived. He switched on the television, flicked through the channels and turned it off again. End to end the whole operation took less than two minutes. He fielded a phone call from the Head's secretary and promised on oath to be back in class next week. He was feeling a lot better he lied – some bug from abroad had upset his stomach.

He pulled the scrap of paper from his pocket. He wanted to tear it up but he could not bring himself to tear it up. He put it out of harm's way instead. He wasn't mad he shouted out inside his head. Just going through a bad patch. Put aside the blackouts and he was perfectly sane. There are lots of crazy people in this crazy world he argued – some of them taught at his school – but he was not one of them. Not yet anyway.

The physical dimensions of the flat oppressed and compressed him until he became depressed. He hated having to admit it but he was feeling vulnerable, fragile. He had to get out, see someone, anyone. The gang were all at work: desperate, he rang his mother. He meandered around his wallpaper pattern as he waited for someone to pick up the phone. Dad never answered the phone these days it seemed. Mum was quicker, lighter on her feet, and in charge – and still she took ten minutes.

"Mum. It's me. Your son."

"Clarence!" Pause. "Shouldn't you be at school?" Mum made it sound like he was playing truant – which of course he was.

"Off sick. Can I come over?"

Mother was confused. "Come over? It's not Sunday?"

"Yes Mum I know it's not Sunday. No reason not to come over though. No?"

"Well. . ." Mother stumbled. She was confused. This was not routine.

"You say you never see enough of me."

"Yes OK. But don't wake your father. He's asleep: we have to go out at Two."

"Understood."

Clarence drove to his parents with extreme care and subdued speed: like someone keen not to draw the attention of the police. He found his mother busy. She was fiddling and fussing and furiously attending to the needs of a family house: except that it had ceased to be a family house years ago. Now it was just a large house in which two retired people rattled around and sometimes rattled each other. The front door was flung open by a woman on speed.

"Wipe your shoes before you come in," shouted Mum over her shoulder. Before Clarence had time to reply she was already gone.

Clarence complied and stood awaiting instructions to be moved on as his mother attended to those tasks she was determined to complete. Items of clothing had to be put away, out of sight. Objects around the house had to be repositioned. Even the floor mats had to be realigned. He made no attempt to catch her up. He made no attempt to do anything.

Finally she slowed, slipped into neutral, put on the handbrake and took in the picture of her son. He was a wilting figure propped up against the wall in her hallway. He looked bad. Mother drew in close. He was cornered, no room for escape.

"You don't look too good you know." She stroked his hair back into what she considered to be its correct position. Clarence didn't try to stop her this time.

"Is this another hangover?"

Clarence didn't bother to answer. She already knew the answer so there was no point in lying. On top of that she had the habit of asking a question then moving on before she had heard the answer, let alone digest it. Today was not one of those days.

"It is isn't it."

"Just a little one."

"Did you get drunk with Tracey last night?"

"No."

So another night out 'binging with the lads', or whatever the expression was these days, thought Mother. She dragged her child into the living room.

"How is it with you and Tracey? I haven't seen her for ages."

"She's busy these days. What with her promotion."

"She got promoted. Why didn't you tell me!"

Clarence shrugged. "You didn't ask. Anyway it's not a big deal: she put in the extra hours above and beyond the call of duty and they changed her label. She didn't mention any extra money – at least not to me."

Mother sensed something was wrong. There was distance in his statement. "How was the holiday?"

"Holiday was fine."

"Just fine?"

"Good. It was good. Just what the doctor ordered."

Mother was not convinced. He lacked conviction. "And now you're off work sick?"

"That's right."

"But you were still able to go out drinking last night?"

"Mother please."

"Was there any romance?"

"Last night? No!"

"On holiday."

"Oh. A little. On and off."

Now Mother was thoroughly unconvinced: but she knew her place as an aging mother with an aging son so she held back from a fully armoured assault. That said, she could not resist a volley of criticism. "That's your problem. No sensitivity. No wish to pursue the emotions. That's why they always leave you in the end."

"Who said she'd left me!"

"No one. Calm down. It was just a passing comment."

Mother moved on to her second most important son-related topic: his eating habits. "When did you last eat?"

Clarence had her there. "This morning actually."

"A proper meal?"

"A bacon sandwich."

"When did you last eat a proper meal?"

"Last night apparently."

"Apparently? What's that suppose to mean?" Now Mother was irritated. She could only take jokes in straight lines – assuming it was a joke.

"Nothing."

Mother gave up. "Come on I'll make you something."

"A bacon sandwich?"

"If I must."

In the kitchen Clarence watched the bacon being grilled: ready to step in and rescue it if necessary. He tried to think of something positive to say as he chewed his food. The grease and fat went down a treat. Mum looked on, arms folded.

"We have to go out soon. I'll have to wake your father up in a minute."

"Don't let me stop you."

"Are you coming round for lunch on Sunday? We haven't seen you for two weeks."

"Two weeks is not a long time Mum." Clarence counted. "And it hasn't been two weeks."

"It is for us."

"Whatever."

Clarence felt himself draining of energy. He had a 'sicky' to enjoy but recoiled from the thought of so much free time on his hands. Then a thought struck: a comforting thought; a comforting thought which became wishful thinking; wishful thinking which demanded urgent attention.

"Mum have you still got my lego?"

Mum stopped leafing through her mental task list and looked up from the kitchen floor. It was more than dirty. "Lego? You mean the same lego you had as a child?"

"The same."

"What on earth do you want that for?"

"To fill in time. A bit of fun."

Mum raised her eyebrows. "I'll have to look."

Conscious of time, Mother tut-tutted and set of in a hurry, dragging her son along through the undergrowth of her memory map as she roamed the house searching out the places where she would have stored such a thing. No luck. Then, just as she was about to send her son up into the loft, she remembered.

"Silly me. I don't keep your lego anymore."

"You didn't throw it out did you?"

"No I gave it to your sister, for the twins, years ago."

"You never told me."

"You never asked?"

"That was my lego not hers."

"Clarence you're 35 years old."

"She'll only throw it away." Suddenly regaining control of his lego from his sister was a vital mission. "I'll have to go and get it. See you Mum."

Fired up, Clarence raced for the door, his mother happy to see him on his way in double quick time. Father had to be woken up. Mother waved at her son and her son waved back as he climbed into his car.

"Aren't you going to phone first! Margaret may not be in!" she shouted.

"On my mobile! In the car!"

She gave up and closed the door. She knew he wouldn't. Time to get Father out of bed.

❋ ❋ ❋

Clarence did not phone his sister. He decided to pounce instead. More fun that way: and fun was something he needed today, even if it was at someone else's expense. The Sister was in. The Sister was wearing rubber gloves and that look that betrayed annoyance at having been pulled away from something very important by someone who should have known better.

Clarence cracked a sour smile. "Hello."

"What are you doing here? What's happened?" His sister was flustered.

"Nothing's happened. Just thought I'd pop over and say hello."

"Say hello? What for? Use the phone? That's what it's for." She could not have been more dismissive.

Clarence grabbed at a straw. "And help Desmond with his sofa thing."

None of this was making sense to Margaret but all she had to fall back on were the standard rules of engagement. "You better come in."

"Thanks."

Clarence came in, in much the same way as the man from the gas board comes in to read the meter. "You look busy."

"I look busy because I am busy. I'm always busy. You know that."

Inwardly Clarence sighed. "Just making conversation."

"Well don't."

"Fair enough."

Margaret stormed on back into the garden. She was repotting plants and felt no reason to stop. In her mind this was not a visit but an interruption: he was just her brother so no favours or time out were due.

Bending down, she repeated the question. She wanted a better answer. "So what are you doing here?"

"Just wanted to say hello. See how you were getting on?"

Margaret stared up. Her brother was talking nonsense. And he looked like shit. She didn't trust him.

She had ceased to trust him on important matters from about the age of seven when she had discovered that her older brother told lies and was nasty. (She had to wait another seven years before she got the upper hand: specifically she blocked all access routes to her gorgeous looking mates with in-depth descriptions of his personal habits and moral code.)

· 144 ·

Clarence knew it sounded like a big out and out lie but on this occasion he did actually mean it. "Honest."

"You look like shit."

"I know."

"You've just come back from holiday and still you look like shit."

"OK. You've made your point."

The words were like a red rag to a bull. This was her house. She would make as many points as she wanted to. "Come on, cut the crap. Why are you really here? I can't stop by the way. I'm halfway through transplanting then I've got to get dinner on."

"Don't let me stop you."

"Don't worry I won't," she retorted.

Discouraged, Clarence sat down on the wooden bench close by. He pretended to take an interest in what she was doing – something to do with reorganising pots, plants, and dirt. Gardening was something about which he was totally clueless: so as for 'repotting', if Nature never did it why did it have to be done? He assumed position and very soon was miles away, trying to remember good times.

Digging dirt, Margaret waited in vain for an explanation. "Talk to me. What is this all about?"

She glanced across at her brother. He was hiding something. He had lost something: some kid had stolen his football cards, or his action man, or his girlfriend.

"She's dumped you hasn't she."

Clarence gave his sister that particular look a brother gives his sister when he is forced to concede her the point, and bow to her display of superior female intuition.

"Yes." Having crawled up his throat the word shot out of his mouth. He felt naked.

In return Margaret jumped at the chance to play the big sister for a change. After giving a new home to one of her prized plants she sat down next to her brother and pulled off her rubber gloves like a satisfied surgeon, post op. He had taken this one hard it seemed: which in itself was an improvement, a positive step change. Normally such an occurrence was cause for no more than a disgruntled shrug. Like a bus the next one would be along soon.

"Did you love her?"

"Love her?" Clarence found the question distasteful, naive even. "No I didn't love her. We just had a thing going, like you normally do."

'Like you normally do.' That's your big problem big brother thought little sister. "So what's the big deal then?"

She stood up, impatient to get on, driven to cook healthy family meals seven days a week – and then she did a double take. Clarence was staring up hard at her, face stiff. He looked like he had been knocked on the head, slightly dazed. She was going to ask him about the holiday but thought better of it.

"Clarence I haven't got time for this. If you've got something to say. Say it now."

"Have you got my lego?"

"Have I got your lego?"

"Mum says you've got my lego."

"I've probably got it then. But why do you want that? I mean, lego?"

"Just a bit of fun, innocent fun. Time filler. You know the sort of thing."

Margaret didn't know. She racked her brains. Yes the twins had played with lego but that was years ago.

"It could be anywhere. It probably got chucked out or passed on." Margaret didn't want to start a lengthy house search – more to the point she didn't have time. "Yes I'm sure I threw it out. It's gone," she lied. She waited for the backlash but none came; just an anticlimax, no accusation.

Clarence imploded. "Fair enough."

"Can I go now?"

"Sure."

"I don't mean to be rude but I've to get on - dinner to cook."

"Can I help?" He spoke in a quiet voice, and with unusual humility. Margaret could not work it out.

"You want to help me cook dinner?"

"Yes please. If that's OK."

If that's OK? This was not her brother talking. Margaret sensed a mystery and decided to let him stay.

"OK. But promise to be nice to Desmond. He'll be tired after work – and don't call him Des. You promise?"

"I promise."

Margaret nearly wagged a finger. She pointed it instead. "I mean it. I really mean it. Meal time is important for us. I don't want you messing it up."

"I promise."

Clarence gave no resistance. It was a mystery. They went inside.

Clarence looked around: the kitchen was clean and tidy, sterile by his standards. He was struck by the smell of cooking. "What's that smell?"

"I'm baking bread."

"Where?" The oven wasn't on.

"In my new machine. It makes bread."

"What for?"

"What for? What do you mean what for? To eat, that's what for."

Margaret pondered her options. Men in kitchens had to be given something simple to do. Dirty potatoes struck the right chord.

"You can wash and cut the potatoes."

"Roast?"

"Roast? Mid week? No these are for mash."

"Mash? Why not just open a packet?"

"I don't do packets."

Margaret pushed her brother aside – like Desmond he was getting in the way - and headed for the vegetable rack. She held up a bag of potatoes.

"Do half of these," she barked. "In there."

A subdued Clarence was handed a small scrubbing brush and left to stand over the sink in the utility room. When the potatoes were done he could be given carrots to rub down. Clarence was satisfied. He had a sense of purpose, a feeling that he was making some important contribution.

Margaret on the other hand suddenly found herself with a little spare time. She returned to her plants. Her delightful monsters were due home any moment – and that 'any moment' later the twins catapulted in, demanding recognition, gratitude and results. Finding Clarence scrubbing away at vegetables like a prisoner of war caught them off guard. Initial reaction was 'something's up', so they hung about, just long enough to confirm that nothing was up. Bored, and each rewarded with a large slice of yesterday's bread, toasted and buttered, they raced upstairs and on into their private world of recirculating daydreams: daydreams punctured and revitalised by a constant injection of spontaneous thought and immediate experience. Parents were not welcomed in this place, and certainly not other adults – uncle Clarence included, as he discovered when later he tried to join in. Clarence was not good with children if he could not dictate terms. And these children had never been good with Clarence, and they dictated the terms.

Upon completion of his duties Clarence was rewarded with a mug of tea - nothing else, not even warm chat. He was left to his own devices, to fill time as best he could with what little he had. The rejection only reinforced the lack of connection. He could have been staff.

Forced to wait for his supper, he was reduced to filling in time by reading a newspaper he normally considered not fit for consumption. The newspaper was a reminder of why he struggled to get on with the in-law. Worse still he was forced to listen to his sister's tirades as she prepared dinner. As she spoke she kept glancing at the clock, revising her husband's position in time and space, confident that he had caught the same train today as he had caught the day before, and the day before that, and so on. She maintained absolute faith in the train company's ability to keep to its schedule, but blew a gasket when it didn't.

Desmond worked fixed hours, and was a commuter, from birth. It was in the blood. As such he was confined to a unique model of space-time geometry by rules Albert Einstein could never have formulated, even if he had taken cocaine at university and listened to Pink Floyd. Desmond arrived home on time and in rhythm, stepping indoors as if stepping out of the rain. He slammed down his briefcase, dismissing the burden with contempt but never giving it up, and with both hands free to perform a body search stormed into the kitchen. In a flash he grabbed his wife around the waist and started to lick the back of her neck. He could taste the salt. She tasted good.

"Yummy," he declared. Against type his wife began to squirm and struggle to free herself. "Fancy a fight dear?"

"Clarence is here."

Desmond withdrew, fingers burnt. "Where?" He looked around. "Oh there."

"Hallo Des," said Clarence " - sorry Desmond."

"Clarence. Hallo."

Desmond was even more surprised than his sons – the apples of his eyes even though he had only been hungry for the one when the fruit basket was within reach – to see a downtrodden, glum looking brother-in-law sitting clutching a mug. He smelt something rotten in the air but did not pass comment. He was too tired. He picked up where he had left off. He was determined to subject his wife to his customary back home hug.

It didn't last. He was being watched and was being made to feel a prat. He excused himself to wash, reclothe, recover and reconstruct. Much like the twins he sought privacy and evasion.

Rejuvenated by a hot shower and the removal of the suit, Desmond came back downstairs to play the host. Clarence was where he had left him. He took pity and offered him a drink, the stiff kind. Clarence considered the offer, remembered his resolution, discarded it, and accepted with gratitude.

"So what brings you round our neck of the woods? And during the week?"

"He's staying for dinner by the way," explained Margaret in a tired voice.

Desmond took it on the chin. "Right."

Same expressions thought Clarence. The curse of couples. They congeal into one lump. Best make the effort though. "If that's OK?"

"Sure. Why shouldn't it be. Assuming we have enough food dear?"

"We have enough."

"Right." Desmond took it on the chin a second time.

When dinner struck, the family collapsed inwards and the conversation expanded outwards. The dinner table was the black hole. Clarence, a neutral observer, sat on the edge and did his best to avoid being sucked into the event horizon.

As they talked, and squabbled, and overreacted, and confided, and compared notes, and fought for recognition, and bargained, and bonded, so Clarence fell into a kind of trance. He would only resurface later when the little horrors fled the table for pastures new and the conversation slowed to a crawl, and regained some degree of adult literacy.

The mashed potato was the set piece. The twins were served fish fingers and worldly wisdom. Margaret served her husband and herself juicy swordfish steaks. Clarence received fish fingers.

"Sorry but you were unplanned," she explained.

"No problem," he replied.

The twins found the incident extremely funny and made no secret of the fact. They ate at twice the speed of their nearest competitors and were gone at the first opportunity. Three adults were left to pick up the pieces, and ferment.

"Do you want coffee? Or a brandy? "Or both?"

Too many choices for Clarence. "Whatever. No. Brandy. No both. Yes both please."

"What happened to that promotion you were talking about weeks ago?" asked Desmond.

"False alarm."

Desmond saw an opening. "You don't look disappointed."

"I didn't really want it. More responsibility."

"That's not the impression you gave us at the time."

"Wasn't it? Wrong impression then."

Desmond refused to be intimidated in his own house. "You hold a very important position but you don't seem to take it seriously. What you do or say, how you act affects those young minds."

Clarence gave his sister's husband a weary look. He really was starting to sound just like her. It would only be a short matter of time before they started wearing identical t-shirts.

"No it doesn't. Those minds were affected years ago. From the first day they were dumped in front of the TV or computer screen to shut them up. I'm just a diversion from their mobile phones, TV and internet." Clarence stopped for breath, sensing danger. "Lets talk about something else."

Desmond wanted to talk about government education reforms and league tables but Clarence wouldn't participate. He talked about the recent friendly with Argentina instead. The chat remained pleasant, and polite, until Margaret, perhaps mischievously, dropped Tracey into the waning conversation. Desmond saw his chance.

"I'm not surprised."

"Meaning what?"

"Well you know."

"No I don't. Why don't you tell me."

Margaret came to the rescue of her man and turned on her brother. Her loyalties were clearly defined. "You always end up taking them for granted."

"No I don't."

"Yes you do. Worse still you take them for granted in public."

"You're talking rubbish."

"When – if - you bring them round to Mum's you treat them like an appendage."

"Bollocks."

"Please don't say that in this house."

"What? Bollocks?"

"Yes." Desmond ignored the challenge by looking far off into the distance. He got as far as the fridge freezer.

Margaret came to her husband's rescue again. "You love their bodies Clarence but not their minds, not their souls. I'm a woman. I know these things."

"So why the split then?" asked Desmond.

"We grew tired of each other."

"We?"

"Yes. We." Clarence wanted to spell it out.

"Not she of you then?"

"No."

The boys were back in the playground.

"But she dumped you Margaret said."

"One of us had to do it. I was going to do it but she got in first."

"A bit like a race."

"If you like."

Margaret decided to sum up. "Unless you change your ways things will never change. They'll come and go with less frequency and you will get older and older and more desperate."

"I'm not desperate. Who said I was desperate? What is this? Get Clarence hour?"

"Just trying to help. Brother."

"I don't want – don't need your help. Sister."

"You need to settle down Clarence. Get real. Get married!"

Marriage. The subject came round like clockwork. "Please let's not start on that one again."

"It's what you need."

"Like a hole in the head."

"You're so dismissive."

Clarence fought back. "Look at you two."

"Meaning what exactly?"

"Nothing."

Desmond began to boil. "You meant something else you wouldn't have said it."

"Well . . .' Clarence struggled to come up with some constructive comment. "What I mean is . . ."

"Yes?"

Husband and wife waited on tender hooks, both ready to lay in, one fist each.

"You two are locked together all the time. Like your twins." Clarence almost said 'those fucking twins'.

"And? Even it that's true. So what. What's your point?"

"Can you still say you're individuals? That you exist in your own right? Do you still do things totally separate? Without explanation or warning or apology?"

"Yes we do! Don't we dear."

"Yes. When Desmond is at work and the boys are at school I'm all by myself – doing my own thing. I can do anything I like."

"Like what? Housework?"

"Housework has to be done smart arse. And anyway I do other things: yoga; books. I read books."

Clarence didn't want a fight. "I'll give you that one." He turned on the husband, the weaker link. "And what about you?"

"I row. Weekends."

"And Margaret knows where and when you row every weekend?"

"Of course. She has to. She has to drop me off and pick me up."

"Do either of you ever do something without telling the other?"

Husband and wife glanced at each other.

"We have no secrets, no place for secrets," she said.

"That's the secret – and joy – of a happy marriage," he said.

"Really." Clarence was not convinced.

"You can't stay single and lonely forever Clarence."

"Why not? And why does being single equate to being lonely?"

"OK alone then. And what are you going to do when you grow old?"

"Grow old? So that's what it's all about. Growing old."

"Yes, in some respects, growing old."

"I'll do what I like. Probably die."

"You'll need somebody."

"So it's about needing, not loving? You 'need' each other for fear of old age? Is that it?"

"No that's not it."

"You're just being cynical Clarence."

"Or to the point."

"We got married because we fell in love."

"That's handy – what with needing someone to look after you when you're old and decrepit."

The courtroom fell silent. The jury was out but the prosecution knew they had the case in the bag. The defendant even acted guilty. The judge didn't care either way: just as long as due process was followed and his golf was on.

Desmond stood up, for no reason other than to pick up two dinner plates. He looked fierce. "And it beats living alone in some dingy squalid flat that's never been decorated in years."

"What's wrong with my flat?"

"It's disgusting Clarence. That's why we never visit. Clean the place up."

Clarence looked at his sister and saw his mother, as she had been when he was a boy. God help Des.

"I've got better things to do with my time than spend it on housework."

"Like what exactly Clarence? Like what?"

Sister had him. Clarence was trapped by his own rhetoric. Desmond struck the death blow.

"You see. Snob. Just looks down his nose at everything ordinary. It's simply not good enough for him. What hobbies do you have Clarence?"

"I play squash. Once, twice a week. Most weeks. Football. Some weeks."

"Anything else? Theatre? Books? Clubs?"

"I don't have time for anything else. I'm a teacher remember?"

"And I'm not which makes you a superman is that it?"

"I didn't say that."

"You're a snob Clarence. An intellectual snob and you don't even use it. Just because you teach you think that puts you on some higher plane - don't have to try as hard as the rest of us."

"Yes and a slob in all other respects. Snob and slob."

"Snob and slob."

Clarence had had enough. "I think I better go. I've outstayed my welcome."

"Probably best."

Clarence left, feeling mauled and mutilated. The gems of truth which had stuck made him itch and scratch so badly that on his way home he took a detour, via a pub, and ended up in the vicinity of Fiona's front door, pacing up and down with no idea why he was there. He knew he needed to be handled with care by a woman – a woman who was not a blood relation and so, by extension, might be available for sex – but that was about it.

He held a bottle of cheap red wine in one hand, having stopped off at his off-licence; flying in and flying out without checking his change.

The girl who had been, if only fleetingly, the girl of his dreams was not registered. Surprisingly this rather put her out. She threw him a line on his way out but got no response.

"Nice tan! Been somewhere nice?!"

In his other hand he held a captive kebab. It was dead and chewed up. He held it like his old teddy bear from childhood. A front door opened – not Fiona's - and a middle-aged, plump but well-presented woman peered out. She looked interested in what Clarence was up to and when she spoke it was with punch. She was divorced, bitterly.

"What are you doing young man?" She equated the kebab in his hand to a loaded revolver. Perhaps he intended to rob a bank.

Clarence gave an answer which was very direct and very precise. "I'm walking down the pavement, in a straight line, pausing; then walking back along it back to the same spot. Then repeating the whole exercise."

The woman ignored the insult as best she could.

"Why?"

"Why? That's a good question." Clarence paused for deep thought. The woman wanted to smack him with her black leather handbag.

"Insecurity and a loss of direction generate the desire - the need - to perform and repeat some simple but compelling task to cope with and desensitize the flow of time."

Down the street a band of teenagers turned the corner and stumbled on towards their goal: a pub or party which would let them in. The woman, who was creeping towards 'stuck up little old lady' caricature, was on the verge of an explosion. Disrespect was the one thing she would not tolerate, which was why all members of her family, near and far, kept their distance. Only her poodle truly loved her. But he knew no better.

Somewhere a light came on and Fiona appeared in her doorway, just in the nick of time. Behind her stood a girlfriend who looked more than ready for a fight.

"It's OK Mrs Fox I know him. I'll take care of it."

Mrs Fox huffed and puffed and blew herself back indoors to her sleeping poodle and letter writing. She did not like this new girl on the block. This girl attracted the wrong kind of people. The gang grew louder, more intrusive, less benign. Clarence froze on the spot and waited to be addressed, eyes blinking furiously. Fiona looked nervously at the bottle of wine in one hand and the remains of the kebab in the other. The bottle was unopened, the implications of which made her more nervous. The bottle had to be drunk.

Nothing was said and Clarence began to sway. He shifted his weight from one foot to the other to maintain balance.

"What do you want?" Fiona finally asked.

"Just to apologize."

"Have you been drinking?"

"Yes but not intensely. I'm not drunk." And as if to prove the point Clarence did an impersonation of a ballet dancer and tried to stand on the toes of one foot. Fiona's friend laughed. She was impressed, as was Fiona. Satisfied, Clarence returned to a more conventional standing position.

"I just wanted to apologize for shouting down the phone at you. Hassling you. Questioning your right to judge a situation. I was drunk at the time. I am sorry. Honest I am sorry."

Clarence sounded sincere – for an incident which in Fiona's mind barely rated as significant. It was a sad fact that she had reached that point in life where she took such behaviour in men for granted. A little guilt swept over her and made her blush. Her friend waited with bated breath to see what would happen next.

Fiona looked at the bottle of wine again and, knowing she had backup, made an impulsive decision. A good bottle of wine should never be wasted. It would split nicely between three. Two glasses each would not hurt.

"Look you can come in but you can't stay over. Cathy is staying the night. She has the spare bed."

Clarence examined her face as if it was a crossword puzzle, then declined.

"Sorry I'm too tired. It's been a long and stressful day. It's imperative that I get to bed early and sleep. Sleep sleep sleep. My body needs a good long sleep."

The reply went down like a lead balloon. Silence descended, again like a lead balloon. It took a third party to break it: as the gang of hell raisers closed in they took in the scene and lapped it up.

"Give us a drink!" the tallest one shouted. He was the unelected leader of the pack, reason being he came up with the most creative ideas for rebelling against every aspect of life.

"Here take the whole bottle!" shouted Clarence.

The young man, now holding a whole bottle of wine, struggled to find a voice. He mumbled a word of thanks and passed it over to his nearest mate. He in turn read the label and pretended to know something about wine in order to impress the others.

With no more ado Clarence walked off. Fiona watched him go while her friend watched her for signs of reaction. There were none. It was all held in and pent up. The lads, reengaged with their crusade for party and girls, crossed the road and carried on.

✦　✦　✦

Log Entry

A second rejection by a female, despite her insistence, was not taken at face value. Instead it was regarded as a signal, a challenge for my host. I decided to intervene to pre-empt a worsening of the situation.

Put under severe pressure through change of circumstance, my host turns heavily both to the mind drug alcohol and old memories. These are precious, fleeting memories captured in the distant past. They provide temporary refuge though nothing in the way of problem resolution. Nor do they appear to hold any relevance with regard to current concerns. Yet I cannot believe they are totally random in nature.

In times of extreme stress my host turns to family for comfort and support. These interactions are peculiar: consisting of faked interest or extreme interest but not reasonable interest; competitive engagement or defensive engagement but not constructive engagement; critical or biased observation, rarely factual observation. Differences in lifestyle are a key point of friction. Blood relationships do not necessarily rouse loyalty, warmth or understanding. The opposite is equally possible.

Chapter Eight

It was Saturday and the Twins' birthday party still had a good head of steam. Margaret answered the door, head swollen by the noise of it all, expecting no more guests. She looked down. Clarence sat on her doorstep, morose, keen to get away but equally determined to see it through. He had arrived with a begging bowl which needed filling with good cheer. Clarence gripped his one present to his side. It was his entrance ticket. He could not be refused. It was a great big heavy book, an atlas of world history, big enough for two in his opinion. Clarence felt he had made a discerning choice and wanted the credit. Margaret was not happy and stood in his way.

Determined to be let in he forced himself to apologize to his sister for his rudeness at their previous encounter - or at least go through the motions. He even asked her to tell Desmond that he was sorry.

"You can tell him yourself, here he is," she replied.

"Tell me what?" enquired Desmond. Desmond viewed his appearance with suspicion.

"He wants to apologize for his behaviour the other night." Margaret rubbed salt into the wound. "Don't you Clarence?"

"Yes I do." The words dropped out of his mouth, driven by nothing more than gravity.

Clarence apologized a second time then tried to hand over his one present. Desmond thanked him but refused it, requesting instead that he go give it to the twins personally, warning him that he might have to explain why only the one.

'I can cope with that' thought Clarence.

Despite misgivings Margaret was forced to let him pass. As she did so she gave him one instruction. Behave!

Clarence sniffed the air. It smelt of cake and warm bread, burgers and burnt bacon, ham and cheap cheese. Margaret smelt booze on his breath, which reinforced her decision that the event would remain alcohol-free. This was a children's party and children did not drink alcohol, so neither should the adults. Nailed to the floor by his mother, who was put out to see the state he was in, Clarence had to suffer a lecture on healthy living. He was driven into a corner and remained there – a stale sandwich providing small relief - behind the barricades until she grew bored of raising a son and switched her attention to the next generation down the line. His present had already become a discarded item. The twins had not been impressed, but had been forced to thank him by their father.

Young bodies sweated as some battled for superiority, some just for recognition. All were growing with undue haste into something far more dangerous and far less discriminating. The underage crowd had already splintered into smaller fragments: one self-help (all girls bar one – he would grow up to be a doctor); one planning rebellion; one demanding official recognition and presuming to be in charge (led by the twins); one – just one – bored and already wanting to go home.

Clarence drifted around in the kitchen, sipped flat coke, and tried to make conversation with some of the adults who had decided to stay the full course and share the experience with their offspring, despite the fact their offspring did their best to avoid them. They languished, the one exception being Mary, an old friend of his sister's who had popped up on the edge of Clarence's radar screen a few times in the past. She spoke with enthusiasm for such events, seeing them as important for the development of social skills and networking. So she had read all the books Clarence noted, and she was going to seed.

Clarence decided enough was enough. Was it him or was the noise getting louder? Sod the consequences: he wanted alcohol, and he suspected so did a few others. Alcohol or he would leave. When Desmond drifted in, almost catatonic, he hassled him for a real drink. Desmond, secretly sympathetic, caved in and retrieved some bottles of beer from a place whose location he refused to divulge. Like soldiers between battles they drank them in the back garden. Their previous animosities were temporarily forgotten: after all they were family. Clarence drank at double speed and pushed for a second. The golden rule already confused, Desmond could not refuse. It could not last.

In time the two were discovered by the wolf pack combination of wife/sister and mother-in-law/mother. The trial was executed at speed, the verdict never in question. Although the defence did not contest the sentence was severe: Desmond received the harsher sentence as he should have known better. He would sleep in the spare room that night. Nothing less was expected of Clarence. Margaret made it clear that she would not speak to him for the rest of the day, and hinted that he should leave early. Clarence kept his mouth shut. It was a light sentence.

Clarence wandered from conversation to conversation, avoiding children wherever possible. Then he went into a daze and a haze descended.

He was next seen by his sister sitting on the floor deep in conversation with his nephews, all three surrounded by a few hangers-on. The twins had already confessed that their dad farted a lot, and nearly always loudly once a day; and that he picked his nose when he thought nobody was watching - just like them. Clarence also discovered that 'Mum talks too much at Dad and Dad gets annoyed and walks away but she carries on talking as if nothing has happened'.

Clarence told them to be more understanding. "Your mother was a rebel once, just like you; a teenage tearaway who smoked in secret, got drunk. She even had a crush on another girl. Nothing serious. At least I don't think so. Hard to remember."

Their eyes widened and their tongues almost fell out. At which point Tarquin pointed at his brother whereupon Jeremy shoved him aside, whereupon Tarquin pushed back, at which point Clarence physically intervened and somehow calmed them back down. The conversation continued. Mary's son William, having watched from a distance, drew in close. Up to now he had been happy to not join in with anything. Now he was sure he was missing out on something good.

When Mary saw her son burst out laughing she too wanted to join in. She took Margaret aside and remarked that Clarence must be a good listener.

"Your children are so animated. The sign of a good teacher."

Margaret was suspicious. "My brother a good teacher?" She could barely string the words together without choking.

Mary inched towards him until she was within sentence striking distance and waited to catch his attention. When the kids lost interest and the gathering dissolved to go hook new thrills, she spoke. "Hello Clarence."

"Hallo there."

"Still teaching I understand. It shows."

"Does it?" Clarence considered long and hard. "I don't think so." He looked around. "Which one is yours?"

"William." Mary pointed. "Over there with Tarquin – or is it Jeremy? I can never tell."

"William. Yes he was listening in all the time. He likes to listen but doesn't like to join in. Yet he hates to miss out on anything as far as I can see, which may leave him in a state of continuous tension within himself."

"Really? You can tell all that?"

"I think so, yes."

Clarence could not stop asking questions about Mary and her son, and Mary was happy to oblige. When Mary revealed that she was a single mother, that there was no father, Clarence's interest leapt. Like a native who had seen the sea for the first time, he ran down to the shore and threw stones. To be the centre of interest spurred Mary on. Today was turning out to be a good day. She was a big hardboiled egg and he snacked on her and she didn't mind it one bit.

There was a big oak tree in his sister's garden and it had bugged Clarence for years. It had been grown wild from birth and resembled more a bush than a tree. Clarence had a long held grudge against the twins: they had climbed it many times and he hadn't. Driven by a dark horse he jumped up, determined to put the matter to rest.

The twins watched him climb, fascinated: their uncle didn't do things like this. William was standing just behind them, and again felt he was missing out on something. He tried to climb up, but failed and had to ask Clarence for help. Clarence duly obliged. Once up he was not impressed: the view was so-so, rooftops, nothing special. TV was better. There was only one thing two people could do when stuck up a tree with nothing to look at, and that was talk.

Clarence took great interest in William's previous tree-climbing exploits and his friendship with the twins; and William warmed to the fact that everything he had to say was being listened to intently. William shared his schoolboy jokes and classroom gossip and made Clarence laugh. When his mother appeared William managed to smile down at her and mean it. She waved. Her son waved back: a rarity. Clarence also waved. Mary was impressed. Then she went and spoilt it all. Time to go home.

"I'm sorry but we have to go William," she said.

William stayed put.

"Off you go," insisted Clarence. "You can't stay here all day and we've done talking for now."

His presence no longer welcomed, William climbed down, but only after flashing a look of betrayal past Clarence.

Mary watched her son descend then run off indoors. Clarence stayed put. Margaret wandered up and stood alongside Mary, viewing her brother's behaviour with suspicion. Mary felt compelled to thank the man.

"Thank you, for cheering him up – even if I did spoil it."

"No problem. He wanted to be cheered up. He was waiting to be cheered up."

"Waiting?"

"Waiting."

Surgically she removed her son from the battle zone and led him away, promising to make up for it. She was left feeling invigorated. She threw Clarence – who was watching her with interest - a last line.

"Hope we meet again sometime." It was the broadest of hints.

Clarence smiled and turned his attention back to the sight of suburban rooftops and gardens.

At the door, while waiting for William who was now using the toilet as delaying tactics, Mary again turned to Margaret.

"Your brother can be very sweet sometimes, very innocent, and certainly engaging with the youngsters, even my difficult one. I can see why he took up teaching."

"Can he? Can you?" Margaret stumbled over her words. She was still dealing with an image of her self-interested, self-contained, cynic of a brother stuck up a tree, and looking like he was enjoying it. When she returned to the kitchen window she saw he was still where she had left him, up the tree, still acting a prat. Desmond had more style she decided.

When he came back down Clarence settled back into idle chat with his nephews again – though this time the truth was diluted by mischievous invention: the twins told a few porkies; one being that their parents wanted a divorce as each thought the other was dull and boring.

Dialogue was abruptly halted when Margaret saw him pass them cigarettes. They had each requested one, each promising not to smoke it until they were 18 years old. Just as Tarquin stuck his in his mouth and started to chew Margaret descended and exploded, followed by a more controlled but no less bitter outburst from her husband. Now they had the perfect excuse to expel the troublemaker from the house. Mother was so embarrassed that she pretended not to see him go.

＊ ＊ ＊

Clarence could not face going straight home. He headed for the one reliable source of comfort and companionship, his best 'best mate'. Upon arrival he deliberated, being in two minds over whether to knock or retreat back to that safe, uncomplicated place. Right now he was the ultimate miserable sod. He had just been kicked out of his sister's house for what he didn't know. Another blackout: that fact he swallowed like a mouthful of sour milk accidentally swigged from the wrong bottle. He pretended not to care any more and rang the doorbell. Inside Sam was peeled away from her ironing with mixed feelings.

She opened the door, acknowledged his presence, and made one long grand tour of his face. What displeasure he had caused evaporated in an instant when she realised the state he was in. She invited him in.

"Hallo you."

"Hallo me."

"No Tim?"

"No just me."

The talk stalled as the memory of the previous encounter rallied to the cause on both sides.

Clarence pushed his aside. "Is it OK? I've just had a shitty afternoon."

Sam applied logic and deconstructed hers. They were friends and things like that happened between friends. Emotional feedback could not always be tamed.

"Sure. Come on."

Clarence followed her into the kitchen, dog-like. The ironing board was out and crumpled shirts sat stacked, demanding to have their creases removed. One was halfway there.

Sam lifted the iron, disengaged her brain, and resumed position: right sleeve. "I must finish these."

"Your shirts?"

"No I've done mine. I usually just do mine."

Clarence sat down. "Where is he?"

"In a hotel bar somewhere in Berkshire getting drunk, hand round some young woman's waist pretending to still be twenty-five while I do his ironing." She could not have made her sentiments clearer.

"Meaning?"

A crease stuck in her mind. Sam attacked the shirt and ironed it out.

"Meaning he's been playing golf all day." The iron sizzled as she hit the steam button. "He was on a course last week and <u>suddenly</u> decided to stay on for the golf."

Clarence cast his mind back to such previous events. For Tim it was a growing perk of the job. "Funny that. Tim always does courses in a hotel next door to a golf course."

"And the course always finishes a day early but they book an extra night."

"So his room is free tonight?"

"Of course."

"Meanwhile I'm teaching my balls off for bugger all."

"Teaching your balls off?"

"Well perhaps not – but for bugger all that's for sure."

"Get out then. Do something else." Shirt done, Sam paused and stood the iron on end.

"Like what? And anyway I've got to get back to normal first." With that admission he suddenly deflated.

Sam slipped the shirt onto a hanger and did up the top button but one. That was her system and she made no apologies for it. Three more shirts to go, and she was counting all the way. "Still suffering those things?"

"Yeap. Like today was a good example."

"What happened today?"

"Turned up at my nephews' birthday party – for want of something better to do – had a drink or two, nothing much, wasn't drunk – went blank and the next thing I know I'm being chucked out of the house for some misdemeanour."

"What exactly?"

"Don't know. But they were pissed off about it. Another fucking blackout – it's worse than being pissed out of your brain all the time."

Sam remembered the opened wine bottle. "There's some wine over there if you want it."

Clarence got up and made haste. "Thanks."

"And refill me."

"Sure."

Drinks fulfilled, Sam carried on ironing and Clarence carried on watching. He had arrived fed up, miserable and feathers ruffled, but the act of watching a woman do her ironing had a calming affect. When there was no alternative except to watch someone iron, the human emotional drive was forced to switch down a gear or two, or three, until neutralized. Watching an iron iron was like watching paint dry. Doing the ironing was presumably like stirring the paint. If you were an ironing board salesman you probably took drugs in private to keep your sanity – drugs provided discreetly by your boss, similarly addicted. Another shirt was hung up: two to go.

"How's work?"

"Same old shit. And school?"

"Same old shit."

"And how's your lodger?"

"Max? He's fine. No problem. When he's not working he's down the pub."

"Just like you then."

"What do you mean!"

"Good company?"

"Definitely."

"Have you eaten?" asked Sam.

Clarence answered automatically, saying no even if the true answer was yes.

"No."

"Hungry?"

"Yes."

"I was going to do myself an omelette but we can order curry."

"Sounds good."

"You pay for that and I'll provide the beer."

"Sounds good."

"And the sofa is yours for the night – but no throwing up."

"Understood."

Shirts done, Sam collapsed her ironing board and returned to a pressing concern. "Those blackouts, are they getting worse?"

"Worse as in more?"

"I suppose so."

"No not really. But then I only notice the big ones, like today: lumps missing in my life which I have to work around."

"And you don't have any side affects, no warning, nothing?"

Clarence stepped back as Sam squeezed pass holding a still very hot iron out in front of her. "None at all: not before, not after. No warning they just fucking happen."

"You must see someone. Promise me you'll see someone."

"I will. I promise. I've got a name now."

"Is he good?"

"I don't know. I'll have to see. But he was recommended."

"By your doctor?"

"Not exactly."

"What do you mean not exactly?"

"He's a friend of that guy you met – in the pub? You remember?"

"Vaguely."

"Well it's some mate of his – but a pro, qualified or something."

Sam threw him a look of half-hearted acceptance. It sounded a bit too apologetic, a bit too lame. Still he was old enough to look after himself. "Let's order that curry."

That they did, and waited, Clarence drinking beer and Sam drinking wine then beer when her bottle ran out, the two in mutual embrace: she pulled his leg and he offered the other.

Clarence hovered as Sam produced plates from an overhead cupboard, his assistance not required.

"I thought Tim had gone off golf."

"He had. But not if it means missing out on a night out with the boys."

Next Sam produced some spoons and Clarence leaned up against the kitchen door. "I get the impression you're extremely pissed off with him."

"Pissed off because of the sudden notice, yes you could say that. He only told me today. But he was playing yesterday. Yesterday afternoon."

"Meaning?"

"He could have told me yesterday of course."

"But you know what he's like: that would be the obvious thing to do."

"Really."

Trays, plates and spoons ready, Sam slowed and in unconscious mimicry, leaned against the same wall. It was if they were holding it up, like St. John's Ambulance on callout.

Clarence continued his defence of his best friend with limited material. "He's always been one of the lads. You know that. I know that."

Sam found a reason to smile for the first time in many hours. "Yes maybe your right."

"He's always been a tosspot."

"Don't over do it."

"Remember that time with the car hire? Spain? He spent ages fighting his way through the documentation in some penny-pinching argument about the final bill. Even I was embarrassed."

Sam rubbed her nose and stalked the kitchen floor in circles, like a trapped, starving cat who could not open the fridge. "What happened with Tracey?"

"To be honest I haven't the faintest. I didn't think things were that bad."

"Did it get nasty?"

"Oh yes very nasty but only at the very end." The image of waking up inside someone else's room pricked his conscious, but it soon passed.

"Funny. On holiday you're normally having a good time: relaxing, dancing, boozing and all that. A stress free zone."

Clarence chewed over her comment, being reminded of the holiday began to take its toll. He went quiet. The doorbell struck a chord and the food arrived, delivered by a cheeky, cheerful Indian man who spoke with a rough South London accent and who wore a red sweatshirt stained with cooking oil explosions. He was happy. He and his father were making a fortune in the takeaway business.

Portions divided up, they steered their plates into the living room. Sam turned on the TV while Clarence scratched his bum. It was American indoor wrestling, or to be more precise, one big comedy where high camp knew no limits. They watched with token interest as two swollen animals, overfed, over exercised and overheated, and hyped up by a wooden script, tore into each other with high theatre. The language sounded like dogshit - if dogshit could talk.

Clarence remonstrated. "We're not going to watch this are we?"

"It's a laugh."

"It's stupid, pointless."

"You're just jealous."

"Of what? Two lumps of sterile meat?"

"Eat your dinner and shut up."

Clarence did as instructed, and together they shovelled up their food while holding current preoccupations at bay. Despite its scripted intention to do the opposite the wrestling quickly dulled the senses. Soon even Sam gave up on it.

"What's the point. We don't care who wins."

And with that she switched channels, over and over and over again until she found a film. She took the plates back into the kitchen and returned with two more beers, tossing one over to Clarence as one throws a dog a bone. Clarence reacted in kind.

Like a couple of teenagers – boy and girl but still 'mates' – they sat up close and watched TV while passing comment on the crap film and the crap world at large. These two were the kind of teenagers for whom sex, too little or too much, had yet to complicate their lives.

It was some superhero fantasy. It sported the latest digital special effects which, like a retired major driving a Jag, pushed everything else aside. Boredom set in and Clarence switched back to real life for diversion.

Real life explosions could generate shock waves which crippled the nervous system. Never ending explosions on the telly soon lost all impact.

"So everything's OK between you two?"

Sam pulled her legs in and retracted into a ball of contained vulnerability on her patch of the couch. It was a uniquely female posture designed to put men off guard. Clarence calculated that a change of subject was required.

"Have you got any chocolate?"

"Shelf above the cupboard with the coffee and tea."

Clarence lifted himself, got the circulation going, and went scavenging. He returned loaded with chocolate and crisps and a sense of temporary satisfaction. Everything was OK in the world for a time. He waved the packets of crisps. He was the hunter-gatherer again.

"I found these as well. Is that OK?"

"There'll be none left for Tim."

"That's all right then."

The pair settled back into the televisual netherworld and munched and crunched, intoxicated by the act of slumming it just like teenagers who had nothing to apologize for. They did their best to make sense of the film.

The film did not inspire loyalty. It demanded patience. Clarence had it. Sam did not. She was drawn to conversation just as Clarence was getting his teeth into the storyline and the characters.

"You must see someone – your doctor," she insisted.

Clarence shook her off. "I will. I will."

She wanted to grab his arm. "Promise me!"

"I will. I promise."

The urgency in his voice convinced her that this time he meant it. But he may have been faking it.

"How are your parents?"

"Tottering along. The usual clockworks."

Sam slapped him across the knee. "Don't say such a thing." She was suddenly 10 years older, he 20 years younger. It was a major time slip and all it took was a few words.

"Sorry. Didn't mean it in a nasty way."

"You'll miss them when they're gone."

"So everybody keeps telling me."

Wishing to laugh, but being unable to, she moved on. "I can't understand how you blew it with Tracey."

"She became a headache. I become a headache."

"And you spent all that money on that holiday."

"Money I haven't got."

"Because you're a downtrodden teacher."

"Correct."

Clarence was suddenly gripped by the film. "Hang on that's just stupid. He's just spent the last three hours beating the shit out of the bad guys, and running up and down skyscrapers. He comes home, dinner is on the table, and he suddenly gets all romantic with a woman. I'd be completed knackered."

"But you're not a superhero."

"But he's got no special physical powers like Superman. He's just very fit. And what about that frozen guy. What happens if he suddenly wants to go to the toilet."

"Relax it's just a film. Watch it don't mark it."

"How come she has a bat suit waiting for her which fits her perfectly? And Robin's suit just changed colour. It had red in it. Then black and grey. Now it's back to red again. And how can anyone not know that the two are Batman and Robin? Those masks hide bugger all."

His grievances registered, Clarence reached forward and snatched at another piece of chocolate. He conjured up an image of Tim, drunk, trying to remain standing and talking total bollocks. He wished he was there, with the boys.

"I wonder if he's fallen over yet."

"Who?"

"Tim of course."

"Oh him."

"What's that suppose to mean. 'Oh him'?"

Sam glared into the TV screen and held herself in check.

"He's really pissed you off this time hasn't he?"

"Don't remind me."

Clarence looked across the couch and noted the contained anger escaping its box. He couldn't resist indulging his curiosity. "What's the latest on babies?"

Sam didn't care to answer. She jumped up and went into the kitchen.

"Sorry didn't mean to pry!" shouted Clarence.

She returned with a packet of cheese biscuits. "It's not that."

"Are you two still OK?"

No reply. No reply at all. Clarence was left waiting. Suddenly he felt shamed and scoffed the last of the chocolate. Sam watched it slip away. She would not share her cheese biscuits.

"He just takes me for granted these days. At times I'm the furniture."

That's Tim thought Clarence. I expect nothing less. "Ikea?"

"And I take him for granted," she added, ignoring Clarence's special brand of acerbic wit.

Clarence stopped moving the melted chocolate around inside his mouth and fixed his sights on his best friend's wife. She was suddenly looking very fragile, worn out by the act of staying alive. She ripped open the packet of biscuits. She had purchased them a week earlier as an antidote to fresh fruit enforcement and now they were ripe for devouring.

"How desperate is he for his baby?"

"As desperate as ever."

"And you refuse to budge?"

"Of course. I have my rights. I've always made that clear. Right from the beginning he knew what he was getting into."

Clarence looked away. Tim probably hadn't. Sam had always come across as the dominant one, the one with the sharper mind and tougher job. Mechanically she began to slip biscuits into her mouth, one after another at speed. They were light tiny things so it was not such a daring feat of human digestion, aside from the salt.

Clarence didn't want to take sides, but felt compelled to cheer her up by downgrading his oldest friend. "Look Tim was born an arsehole – as I probably was. He's always been to lazy to change into anything else. I should know."

His words did not help. Saltwater welled up in her eyes. She placed the biscuits in her lap, unable to chew. Only with great difficulty did she manage to swallow the remains lurking in her mouth.

"He just wants to be one of the boys these days and I'm not one of the boys."

"You're one of the girls. Who in their right mind would want you to be one of the boys."

She lost her grip and the biscuits rolled on to the carpet. Clarence lunged down to grab them before they scattered. He captured the packet intact and placed it back in her lap where they belonged. Up close the smell of her breath and the brief collision of fingers invoked nostalgia on both sides for something which had never happened.

Suddenly Sam was no longer Tim's Sam but someone sexually alluring, devouring, intoxicating. Suddenly Clarence was no longer Clarence the Cynic but a source of refuge, and a strong pair of arms. Sam wiped the remaining chocolate spread from his lips and brushed his hair back into place. The display of neat affection overwhelmed him and his brain gave up the fight: the body demanded more, something seriously physical. Like lightening – like a lion - it closed the gap and sunk its teeth into her neck. She did not withdraw to a safe distance. Nor did she protest. Instead she clutched at her familiar object and held on for dear life. Actions turned to sex. Their thoughts had to catch up. Words were obsolete. They made love starting on the couch and ending up on the carpet. It was a small journey and the film went on. In other parts of the country people simply switched over, or switched off and went to bed, or logged on to the internet.

Afterwards, passion and energy spent, the two combatants sat in stunned silence, film still labouring towards its contrived punch line. Clarence could muster only one thing to say, so he said it.

"I'd better go."

It was a good suggestion.

"Probably best."

It was the best reply.

He left at speed, and never saw the film's punch line. Sam, dazed, did, and didn't give a damn about the ending. She now had more important things on her mind.

❋ ❋ ❋

Clarence spent Sunday in a stupor, self-inflicted; doing nothing until it hurt. He moped around, almost bumping into Max as he contemplated the mysterious world inhabited by those 'half crazy' people whose ranks he had now joined. Clarence refused to be crazy. He refused to give in, crack up, concede defeat to some unknown enemy. Worse still blackouts and his secret, inexplicable parallel life now took second place to a greater catastrophe. He had made love to his best friend's woman. And he had enjoyed it. It had felt so good. Collapsed in her arms would have been a great time to die. And he felt like dying.

He ambled around the flat, sometimes muttering to himself while waves of glee sometimes desperation sometimes consternation sometimes despondency rolled across his face. Max saw most of it and said nothing. Don't get involved with the English was his motto. He was stuck in a TV sitcom, the kind which received low ratings. But Max needed a place to stay so he held on. The price was right.

Clarence received a number of phone calls during the day. The first was from his mother. She wanted to know where he was. He was late for lunch. He should be with her and Father; eating, enjoying her cooking. He took a battering when he announced he had no intention of turning up, despite his only, feeble excuse being that he was 'feeling under the weather'.

After that he left all incoming calls to Max. This pissed Max off extremely but he had no choice: can't fall out with the landlord. Tim called. He wanted to go for a drink but Clarence wasn't in - whereabouts unknown. He called a second time, reason being he still wanted that drink. Max promised to pass on the message when he saw him. Where was the guy? No idea. Any idea when he would be back? No idea. Max was great at stone-walling. He was made to promise that he would pass on an important message to Clarence. Tim had to see him ASAP. On hearing that Clarence retreated to his room and sank into the mattress, wishing to drown.

Later Clarence did creep out for a walk but crept back in much the same state as he had left, only more tired. He had walked far, in a big circular motion, stopping only to sit and chat with some old people staked out on a park bench. His eagerness to listen to whatever they had to say had impressed them and proved to be such a stimulus that they talked and talked and talked; regaining lost years and nearly talking themselves to death. When he abruptly stood up and walked off they noted the lack of manners and immediately disassociated themselves. The encounter had mutated into some bizarre copy of a dating agency for lonely, bored OAPs who fancied their chances with the younger generation.

Clarence tried to pick up the pieces and put them back together but he could never get them off the floor. He wanted his Lego back. That had always fitted together nicely. Even his sister rang to harangue. Unlike Tim, Max could not fend her off. She cut right through his talk and demanded her brother be brought to the phone. She had to pass on an invitation from Mary, to join them at the Zoo on Wednesday. Clarence said impossible. He couldn't get a day off at such short notice. What Clarence didn't say was that he didn't want to go. She said fine by her but she had to ask: Mary had insisted. Get it? She hinted. Clarence got it. He sank back into the furniture, this time the sofa.

By close of day Max would take pity and drag Clarence off down the pub before he became mummified. There they would sip beer, avoid talk, and watch the TV, or watch the girls watching the TV. It would be a harmonious balance of sorts and calm Clarence; returning him, if only temporarily, to a sense of normality. But then thoughts of Monday would loom up large and he would find it difficult to swallow.

✦ ✦ ✦

Monday. School canteen. Clarence tackled his lunch slowly, feeling like shit and feeling like he was swallowing the stuff. The morning lessons had been like a lobotomy, undertaken without anaesthetic, and with an unforgiving audience standing in the wings with menaces. Like a gathering of righteous bishops or a platoon of soldiers the pupils had scored him as he stumbled around the coursework. He felt time was running out. Time to be a plumber? His heart had rarely been in it and now his head was definitely not in it. He felt himself slipping downhill fast. He tried to make sense of the gaps, the smelly tramp, John. John! John's bed!

He had been approached by an earnest looking pupil between classes. Hormones rampant and excited, the boy had an answer. Clarence had no clue as to the question. He listened patiently, attention faked, not caring to question the answer which tumbled out of a crowded, rotating head. He chewed over the answer as he chewed on his food. We are both mixed up he concluded - that conclusion was temporary light relief. The answer sounded good so he assumed it must had been a good question. He just wished he knew what it was so he could use it again. Meanwhile Sam haunted him while Tim hunted him. Together they were Jeykil and Hyde.

A shadow descended. Clarence looked up. Fiona was bearing down on him like a hospital consultant. She wanted a word and before he could decide a course of action she had sat herself down opposite and was breaking bread. The word was a long time coming and Clarence could not wait. He got in first, deciding to cut to the chase.

"Me and Tracey have split. I don't see her anymore and she doesn't see me."

Fiona noted the clarifications. She felt male rejection banging on her door and wasn't sure whether to open it. As a compromise she opened a window. "Not a good holiday I take it."

"No not a good holiday. A bad one even."

Clarence stabbed a chip. It broke in half on the way to his mouth. He didn't care. One half fell back on to his plate. The other fell into his lap. Still he didn't care. He needed feeding and Fiona wanted to feed him but knew, deep down, that it would not stop there. More would be demanded and she would crumble. Fiona didn't want to hear anymore details regarding the break-up but Clarence was determined to milk it.

"She decided to cut and run. No warning. Just a cold clinical execution of an escape plan. I tried my best to make it work but she was having none of it."

Fiona forgot to start eating. She felt tangled up and knew it was her own fault. She should have walked away. She wanted to raise him up but didn't want to have to hold him. Bearing a guilt complex for the state he was in was hard enough. As for her original reason to sit down at his table, that was now an abandoned impulse. Finally she remembered she had a plate of food in front of her and gave it her full attention. Eating gave her the perfect excuse not to say anything. She offered Clarence some of her chips then fell silent. To a make a point Clarence declined.

Fiona looked up from her green peas, having concluded that they were never ever any bother to anyone. They were being watched.

"Clarence we're being looked at," she whispered.

Clarence remained head down. "No I'm being looked at."

"No we both are," she insisted, still whispering.

"Well go and sit somewhere else then," he whispered back, his act of mimicry cutting her open.

She sunk back, hurting, and felt the weight of her knife and fork. They were heavy. He had sounded just like Chris – in total contrast to the Clarence she had first met. It was as if, over time, men simplified back to their basic core components. First Chris. Now Clarence.

She glanced sideways, across the tables. Two girls were watching her. Now she knew she was in deep trouble. She wanted to get up and walk away but was driven by honour to remain. Moreover to do that would be seen as an act of weakness.

She was saved by a rambling Ramsey. He blew in and sat down, determined to rattle the box. She could see it on his face. Clarence didn't as he was staring down into his fish and chips and wondering why he was bothering to eat. He needed a drink. He needed to hide down the pub. But lunchtime drinking was strictly banned.

Ramsey was there to break things up, not realising that there was nothing to break. His attacking manoeuvres would be wasted and he would run out of petrol.

He let loose his opening salvo. "You look terrible."

"Tell me something I don't know."

No points scored.

Ramsey switched to the long game. "How was the holiday?"

"Fine. Just fine."

Ramsey sensed weakness. "Just fine? No better than that? What with being on holiday with your girlfriend Tracey?" He stressed the name for Fiona's benefit but as usual found no target.

"No it wasn't better than that." Clarence looked up and stared into Ramsey's face, almost spitting out his next reply. "OK?"

Ramsey stalled. "OK. Don't get all nasty."

"I'm not getting nasty. I'm defending myself against an outbreak of nastiness."

Fiona liked the sound of that. It was almost her old Clarence.

Like a sewage pump Ramsey began to pump blood as Clarence stared him down into the ground. Take no prisoners. Fiona decided it was time to leave. Grievances might surface and she didn't want to be present. They never did. As she left, her meal unfinished, the Head circumnavigated his way onto the scene; weaving in and out of tables and chairs, on his way avoiding all eye contact with staff. Pupils tracked him as he flew overhead. Everybody knew their place when he was in the room, staff and pupils alike. Year 18 was no demarcation line.

He looked down at Ramsey, wondering why; and Ramsey withered, wondering why me.

"Will you excuse us," said the Head softly, each word pronounced with severe persuasion and reshaped into sharpened steel.

"Certainly." Ramsey melted away without a word of thanks.

The Head leaned on the table with his hands, looked Clarence squarely in the face, waited for him to stop picking at his food, and said seven simple but cataclysmic words. The ground shattered.

"Will you see me in my office."

Clarence did not reply but waited for the follow on.

"After lunch, before classes."

"Certainly."

Unlike his colleagues in the room Clarence knew the worst case scenario would be the scenario. He had it coming. He just had to keep his mouth shut and not make matters worse. Give nothing away. His calculating mind took up the baton: put it down to stress; the stress of a sudden broken relationship; a relationship which had offered so much; a relationship which seemed destined to go all the way. Clarence looked down at the last few chips and peas. He had hoped to get married, settle down and have kids, but it wasn't to be. No, don't over do it. Only if he asks.

Clarence glanced up. The head had slipped away. He never hung around: back to his current spreadsheet and his on-going analysis of expenditure versus budget for the current financial year.

❖ ❖ ❖

Log Entry

My host has performed the act of sexual intercourse with another female, this time under conditions different from those in place before. On both sides the wish to execute and complete in the quickest time possible was the overriding factor. The emotional state of each was one of disconnection from the physical act, distaste almost; each disowning their sexual desire almost as a perversion, and yet succumbing to its demands. High levels of stress were released on both sides, and as such this may have been the unconscious justification for proceeding with the act of sex.

Each performed as if for the last time, and with the fear of being discovered by a third party hanging over them. Afterwards there was barely any open recognition of what had passed, and no celebration. Reflection upon the event was private and hidden. They did not share thoughts in any way although these thoughts were intense and concerned the other. They went their separate ways immediately.

The act of lovemaking does not always bring pleasure and fulfilment it appears. Depending upon the relationship between the participants it can create its own uniquely peculiar set of social problems and emotional disturbances, even if executed efficiently and with physical dexterity.

In the case of my host this meant strong feelings of guilt and self-disgust, disorientation even. So strong were they that I have decided to remove all memory of the incident, as to leave it be would make his life intolerable and may negate my research. Removal is best done when he is asleep.

I have discovered that humans are capable of 'lying', i.e. not reporting absolute reality when it is possible within their knowledge base. A lie can take many forms and varies in scope and depth. At the bottom end of the scale there are those which deviate only slightly from absolute truth. Sometimes they can be considered a good thing if they serve a useful purpose: to avoid embarrassment or misdirected obligation being forced upon another, affected party. Sometimes their purpose is to make that other party feel good, that other party often being a child. Sometimes they are self-serving or self-promoting, and rarely a cause of harm to others. Here it is usually a case of **boosting** confidence, and promoting a sense of worth.

As one progresses up the scale lies build in complexity, impact and lifespan. Divergence from the truth increases and the reasons for lying become more and more driven by the desire to gain advantage – or reduce it in others - avoid responsibility, reinvent for prestige; or simply avoid confrontation or an uncomfortable, inconvenient truth.

Some lies start as mistakes, as sudden lapses of concentration or willpower. They may have short lives. They may not. The benefits they bring may prove so irresistible that the originator finds it impossible to make a retraction and set the record straight. So they continue along the same path, deviating more and more from the reality which surrounds them, until breaking point is reached and the whole structure collapses in on itself. Its social fallout more often than not results in real lasting damage.

Some lies are meticulously planned from the outset; and are executed with such commitment that reality itself is distorted: distorted to such a degree that the lie itself gains an element of truth; and as it goes on, generates truth upon truth, despite there being at its core an untruth. In the most extreme cases the lie becomes the new truth, and the truth which was becomes fiction. This phenomena is prevalent in the world of politics, large commercial organisations, and religions. Its victims are rarely those responsible for initiating or propagating the lie.

Some lies are not even recognised as such. In the mind of the originator reality is a relative construct, or undefined; to be manipulated and reconfigured according to current need or pain. For these perpetrators there is no such thing as absolute truth, only absolute opinion, and justifiable means to an end. Even when the lie is exposed and stripped bare of all credibility, they do not concede ground. Instead they retreat, behind psychological barriers of reinvention or denial, only to reappear when their definition of reality is no longer under attack and the source of their distress has departed. This can be seen in religious movements.

Some lies are small insignificant outbursts, the result of thoughtless action or reaction and an inability to recognise the truth for what it is. In the main they are of no consequence: triggers being the discussion of looks and fashion, family, personal health, happiness and hygiene.

Sometimes a lie can be justified: when the truth is too much to bear, it is considered wise to withhold it, perhaps forever.

Truth, at first sight a clear, absolute certainty, does have its complications.

Chapter Nine

Log Entry

My host, after some emotional deliberation and suddenly with much time to spare, accepted an invitation, earlier rejected, to visit a place where animals are held captive, primarily for the purpose of public display. Here animals - other than humans - are imprisoned indefinitely, their freedom of movement severely restricted, in order to be stared at by humans in the name of entertainment, and to a lesser extent education. The environment is artificial, the experience minimal and transitory for adults, though more extended for children. The crowd I encountered jostled at times for maximum advantage: some fathers of small children being the worst offenders.

My host found himself chaperoning the children when the mothers peeled off to talk at length in private; occasionally resetting their sights on their children, or on my host; taking a reading of body language and then letting go. When I exercised full control I had to give the children my constant attention – my reward for taking total interest in everything they said and did, even if it was at times meaningless. The mothers were more than happy for this state of affairs to continue.

Some in the crowd were transfixed, as if expecting an outburst or performance of some kind. Initial studies suggest such things are rare. Some animals stared back with an intensity equal to that of their audience, as if equally transfixed. Others did their best not to be distracted by the crowd which gathered around them. Some simply looked on bored, or too lazy to react; perhaps mildly amused. Some looked exhausted or sick. Some were simply depressed by the thought that their lives no longer had meaning. They were totally disconnected from their natural world.

Their natural instincts to stalk, graze, roam, feed, hunt and kill are suppressed by captivity and a regime where food is delivered to schedule and without failure. For many it is a lonely, singular life and the scenery is unchanging. Those which live in groups are both blessed and cursed in equal measure: they have company but it never changes. If they do not mix well there is nowhere to escape to. For some, the more sophisticated, the psychological pain is immense.

For those whose freedom of movement is severely restricted there is no escape from the constant flow and infringement of human traffic. They must endure a ceaseless barrage of noise and enticement from those who gather to stare, point, scream and shout, and generally make loud but inconsequential observations like 'look he's eating something' (even when 'he' is a she). If they show interest it merely encourages such behaviour. Some have learnt to switch off and pretend it isn't happening. Others simply lie around and sleep a lot. A few dream. A few have nightmares.

Humans require close emotional contact with the rest of the animal kingdom despite their carnivorous nature and sometimes savage treatment of them in the name of gratuitous entertainment. The second-hand experience via audio-visual transmissions is not enough. Humans have a strong urge to get up close: some wishing - expecting even - to take something away from the encounter; a few to see what all the fuss is all about. Perhaps they need to smell them – they are certainly not allowed to touch them. In one particular encounter I sensed each side contemplating the freedom of the other.

Living conditions for inmates varies from the barely adequate to the luxurious. For those used to a hard life in the wild where your next meal may be your last and comfort is a rare commodity, it is a twisted form of paradise. But there is a price to pay. And for some the price has been too high. They have been driven to madness. They stare with glazed expression, as if artificially suppressed by drugs, into any available empty space, else eat and sleep. That is the sum total of their existence. For the less sensitive, more primitive creatures, life is bearable: their artificial, restrictive environment registers only minor inconvenience and imposes limited deviation from their normal mental and physical states. Their bio-rhythms appear unaffected. The emotional framework is so basic as to remain in balance.

The effect of incarceration is, at the very least, to subject those more complex creatures to a constant, unremitting feeling of total boredom and dejection, and resignation to a fate they cannot comprehend. To make matters worse they are the main centres of attention.

One in particular, a large male gorilla (a species sharing common ancestry with humans) suffers badly from his life of total repetition, and an audience which has no comprehension of what he is going through as a wild animal unable to act wild. He would love to roam and chase females (the sex thing again) but he cannot roam; he cannot chase. He has forgotten or never experienced what it is like to rampage through a jungle and claim his territory – his private kingdom where anything and everything is his for the taking. He, like his human equivalent, has a large ego which must be exercised. Now it has all but shrivelled up. Only a half-hearted grunt remains, and even that is only released on special occasions. Most of the time he just stares forlornly through the bars of his cage – to proud to move – at the human faces which stare back at him, not realising of course that he is encouraging them. Some observe him with awe and are overwhelmed by his visual majesty. Some are barely impressed. Some simply giggle when he does make a sudden movement (and not just the children).

I took a break from my young companions, gave him my full attention, and waited. At first the gorilla ignored me. Then he registered my presence, and then he really saw me – saw me as something fresh and exciting to his eye and in his mind. The eyes projected a sense of something akin to humanity, intuition, hurt and soulful neglect. They judged. They waited. They expected.

I encouraged him to make emotional contact. He was both suspicious and intrigued – a reaction I find typical in humans with regard to something new. He shuffled across the floor of his cage and pulled himself up close to the bars, determined to examine my adopted face in detail. Out of the corner of my eye I noticed the fatherless child was watching us both intently. We were something of a curiosity. I reached out.

A gorilla's mind is complex: though not as complex as a human's it is nonetheless full of emotions – the emotions of aggression, compassion, fear, pride, passion; and is highly attuned to the input it receives from all the senses. Love in its highest, most spiritual sense is however missing – as it is missing in many humans I have noticed. This omission is balanced by a lack of hate. He sees the world in terms of simple truths, where cause and effect never confuse; where the passage of time is not a preoccupation. When he is hungry he eats. When he is tired he sleeps. When he is unhappy, angry, fearful, or wanting to impress a female he makes loud noises and theatrical movements. The similarities with the male human were immediately obvious and I realised they are close cousins in the evolutionary tree. The gorilla is more honest in his emotional dialogue. An outburst generates no internal consequences. He does not understand the concept of holding a grudge.

Next I reached out with a hand, stretching one finger to the limit. He responded in kind, hesitantly at first then with more confidence as he decided I was a friend. We touched at the fingertips. It made him happy.

Creatures of all shapes, sizes, and design inhabit this planet. Evolution has filled every physical niche with an abundance and variety of life – life able to harness the most sparse, inaccessible natural resources, and prosper. Some have the ability of flight and utilise otherwise inaccessible places to their advantage. Some dwell in freshwater, some in saltwater. Some have developed a dual existence both on land and in water, where each environment performs some critical function in the life cycle. Some jump. Some hop. Some crawl. Some run. Some walk. Only humans appear to walk upright and with good posture.

Some, especially the big carnivores, move with a grace and precision which reveals their sense of total self-confidence. These animals appear to fear nothing: accidents and disease are the accepted risk and old age is a bonus to be relished. The big carnivores have no natural enemies. Their only unnatural enemy are humans.

Some creatures live for hours, some for months or years. Some outlive humans, all other things being equal, which they are not. The variety of physical shape is astounding. Yet similarities and themes are evident across the whole spectrum of evolution. Extensions for manipulation and movement appear only to exist in multiples of 2: 2, 4, 6, 8 etc; never odd numbers greater than 1. Some are waterproof. Some are protected from cold by an outer layer of insulation which can sometimes end up as portable cladding for humans. Some discard their exterior layer on a regular basis as a mechanism for internal growth. Some have calcium deposits at their core: dense, hard structures build up over time. Some live inside these structures. Two eyes are the norm. Some barely have substance or register a presence. They get trodden on by humans and other larger creatures, and are squashed out of existence. Others dwarf humans, and in that sense gain their respect.

Some creatures inhabit the coldest regions of the planet, some the hottest. Humans have conquered nearly all regions of the planet by the application of their technology or natural resources at various levels of sophistication. They have reached the stage in their evolution where the select few now live in total comfort, without risk, and with a continuous supply of food to hand: food gathered together from many different places around the globe. They eat at anytime it suits them. Some do this to extremes, usually to the detriment of their health. Other life forms are farmed for consumption and suffer badly when cost and speed of delivery to the human mouth is critical. Humans rarely eat other humans. And if they do, I have yet to come across evidence of humans farming other humans. Their attitudes towards personal rights and freedom, along with social and cultural conventions do not permit such activities.

Some creatures live in isolation, only coming together for the purposes of sexual reproduction. Some live in pairs or family units. Some live in large groups of multiple families: there being safety in numbers. They can defend against enemies who would otherwise, on a 1:1 basis, be a danger.

Humans encompass the whole spectrum: living alone, as pairs, in family units (large and small); and even in extended self-sufficient communities tied together by common purpose, heritage and belief. Such communities are the exception, not the norm, but robust and with long histories of endurance against external pressures. Humans, in the course of their lives, sometimes split away from one arrangement (or dismantle it totally) and reconfigure into something new. Many attempt to live as one half of a permanent coupling for their entire adult life, but with mixed results. Culture, environment and family history affect the probability of long term success.

✦ ✦ ✦

Mary cooked herself into oblivion as a response to her son throwing a tantrum. He would not come out of his room or turn the music down. Many miles away, behind the wheel of his car Clarence focused on finding his way to her house. He had no wish to meet her yet he was driven to arrive. He had been instructed to be kind and soft to the touch by a sister who enjoyed organising the lives of others. She had passed on the invitation to dine and he had found himself unable to refuse, though refusal had been his intention.

The doorbell rang and Mary tried one more time to coax her son out into the daylight of social interaction. She insisted then pleaded, but the response was always the same: leave me alone, you're not wanted. Emotionally she was drained of energy. She did a final check in the mirror, taped her strongest smile across her face and opened the door. The man who stood before her looked slightly confused, guarded, dispossessed even, but his face changed in an instance to that of someone who was extremely pleased to be in her company. She held her breath but he did not speak so she was driven to speak first. Flustered by the fact that she was unable to command her growing son, and unwilling to admit it to anybody – even herself - she welcomed Clarence into her home like someone trying to bury bad news.

"Hallo Clarence." Mary sounded bashful, besotted even, even though she wasn't. It was nerves, refusing to calm down.

Clarence smiled broadly as if expecting a handout of sweets, and still he said nothing.

"Come in, please," she said, and waved him on through. She sounded upbeat, slightly artificial, and she knew it. Can do better. Clarence did as instructed, still saying nothing.

Mary said the only thing she could think off. "I'll tell William you're here." Even as she spoke she knew she was asking for trouble.

The sign on William's door – built up from separate pieces at different times – stated categorically 'Do not disturb! Ever! Never! Understood?'. The pounding baseline of his music dissolved the sound of her knocking. No reply.

She tried and failed to persuade him to come out. The effect was the opposite in fact. He was more dug in, more entrenched. To leave his bedroom was to abandon his private, safe haven and compromise his independence.

Mary issued a tired apology. "I am sorry about this."

Clarence, hands clasped together like a parish priest invited round for tea and biscuits, finally spoke. "No matter. I did not come to meet William. I came to meet his mother."

As a compliment it went down a treat, and Mary could only blush. As a diversion Mary knocked on her son's door again, this time with much greater force, and raised her voice against her will.

"William! Come on. Enough!" She was not by nature someone who shouted but her son was changing her nature.

A voice of variable pitch shouted back. "What!"

"Clarence is here! Come and say hello!" She turned. "Do you mind saying hello?"

Clarence, a million miles away, was caught off guard. "Do what?"

"Say hello?"

"No. No, not at all. I'm looking forward to talking to him."

"Hello!" the voice screamed back, business done.

For Mary this was not enough. "Turn the music off, come out and say hello properly!"

"Why!"

"Because it's the polite thing to do! And because I say so!"

Mary stood back, wanting something to happen, like the bedroom door being opened slowly and her son sticking his head out. But nothing happened.

Mary began to melt away. "I am sorry about this. He'll be OK in awhile, sometime, hopefully when food is on the table."

Clarence smiled and took stock. Her son had to be tempted out. Perhaps the solution was to tempt something in, perhaps himself. "Here let me try."

Clarence positioned himself up against the door; as if listening for signs of life; as if about to knock on the Headmaster's door. He knocked only once, but it was a sharp, stinging assault by one knuckle. It rang out and caught attention on both sides. Less was more.

"William."

"What?" The voice was quieter, driven back down by the sound of a deeper voice.

"I still have to answer your question about the incident with the gorilla. Remember? At the zoo?"

"I remember. I'm not stupid." A pause. "What question?"

"You asked why we touched fingers."

Slowly the door edged back and William stared out, his face disingenuously looking intrigued. He looked weighed down by all the cares of the world, frustrated that everything had to point at him. He was the burnt out medieval monk, on guard at the main gate while the peasants were in turmoil. He looked at his mum's new friend and wondered what all the fuss was. It was that Clarence: that crazy man who went up trees and made faces at gorillas. He could still see them eye-balling each other. Only the iron bars had kept them from hugging.

"Why did you stare at that gorilla like that?"

"Like what?"

"Like you were looking for a fight. Like you knew him."

"I was engaging his senses."

"Right," replied William, unconvinced.

"And we made friends – hence we made physical contact."

"The sign said do not touch – and anyway how can you make friends with a gorilla?" argue William.

"Easy. He needed something and I had it to give."

Baffled but impressed, Mary offered Clarence a drink. He declined. Unimpressed, William returned his computer screen and, point made, lowered his music. He had recently converted his mum to broadband through emotional blackmail and now he had some catching up to do.

Normally William guarded his bedroom retreat with attitude but this time he forgot to shut the door. After a quick smash and grab in a game of web based medieval combat he paused, hit 'save', and turned. Clarence stood in the doorway, looking like a lemon. Mother was back in the kitchen, the place where she kept her supply of aspirin. He could hear her on the move and making a clatter. Things were on the boil.

Clarence was determined to talk about the gorilla. "It's a great blow to their ego you know."

"What is?"

"Being held in captivity, for the foreseeable future, for the rest of your life."

"It's a zoo."

"For us maybe. For him it's living torture."

As always William found himself on the defensive, and having to attack. "He's treated OK isn't he? They feed him don't they? The guy never goes hungry."

"But imagine the sheer boredom, the lack of stimulation. Nothing to do day in, day out. Nothing new to see. No friends."

"Tell me about it."

"Tell you about what?"

"Nothing." And with that William returned to his screen, but conscious of the fact that this Clarence had not gone away his performance went downhill.

He gave it a half a minute or so then turned to face the intruder again. This time the man was leaning against the door, looking around, as if for something to do or something mislaid. William scored the clothes as stupid, and dismissed the scuffed shoes and stubble as showing off. William, his own senses heightened like a predatory beast, immediately sensed disorientation, weakness even, in the other. He broke off from his game again and pounced.

"You've come to eat with me and my mum?"

"I believe so."

William chewed over the answer then spat it out, all flavour extracted from the simple answer.

"Are you going to keep seeing her?"

"I don't know."

William was stumped. It was a boy's answer. He began to scratch himself violently. He wanted to return to his game but while the plank stood there such a thing was not on. He felt a headache coming on. His body language, though scrambled for much of the time, clearly communicated his distaste.

Clarence stepped halfway back into the hall: one foot in William's room, one foot out of it; unsure where to be. William turned his back on him again and played havoc with his mouse. In a far away place a male of similar age, also plugged into the web, reengaged a reinvigorated enemy. They would become friends and share moments but they would never meet.

Clarence finally spoke. "Can I make a request?"

"What request is that?"

"Can I see a boy's room?"

"What?"

"I'd like to see a boy's room if that's permissible."

William jumped up, closed the gap, and stood on guard for some con. "You must have seen one before?"

"Not in any true sense – only vague recollections."

"When you was a boy?"

"That's right."

"But you're a teacher mum says."

"Teachers don't teach inside boys' rooms. And I don't have children."

What the hell thought William. The act of giving a favour felt good and more importantly gave him the upper hand. He backed off, inch by inch, and Clarence took up the slack until he was finally in the room. William jumped onto his bed and watched as Clarence stood rigid in the centre of his room. His eyes wandered around the scene of chaos: some controlled, most unintentional; all the subject of devotion.

The room smelt of decaying food and dirty clothes. Objects with no obvious connection sat stacked up in piles; possibly awaiting disposal, dismemberment or reclassification. The wallpaper had virtually disappeared beneath an extra organic layer of posters - some purchased, some handmade – magazine cut-outs and paper scribblings.

Like his mother William was driven to speak first. "Well?"

"Well what?"

"Well what's happening. You keep looking around at everything."

"There's a lot of stuff here."

"It's all my stuff – so don't touch."

"Absolutely not. I appreciate this is all highly personal."

"Do what?"

"Your life is in this room, in this place." Clarence pointed at the door. "Not out there. In here I suspect you feel at your best, always on top: the king; in charge."

William looked his mum's new man up and down as if he was being drawn into a conspiracy by someone who made both no sense and total sense at the same time. He recalled the party: Tarq and Jerry had been on to something weird all right.

"Am I right?" asked Clarence.

William gave no answer. He didn't like others knowing too much about him, especially adults, especially his mum – except on his terms. So he always kept his guard up and his head down. He refused to answer.

Clarence let go of the question and instead focused on the monitor which took pride of place on a table saturated with all manner of miscellaneous objects: some fun, some serious, some reactionary; some swapped, some broken. It could have been a council tip for the under 16's.

"What's this?" he asked, crouching down.

"A game," replied William, just managing to avoid adding the word 'stupid'.

"How is it modelled?"

"Modelled?"

"How does it work?"

William shrugged. "I don't know. Move things around. Pick things. You shoot. You fight. Who cares how it works. It works."

"How do you win?"

William spoke up. This was one he could answer. "You grab the most land, build the biggest army. Destroy all others."

"For what point?"

"I just said: you have to grab – "

"No I mean what's the point? Why bother? It's just a game of chance encased within a set of rules supplemented by visual interaction."

William looked down at the carpet, blown off course by the weird question. "I don't know. Someone has to. Anyway it's fun."

"Good point. Fun. The opportunity for fun should never be neglected, especially if the activity is at no cost to anybody else."

William found himself agreeing without knowing why. It was the strangest sensation: agreeing with an adult about something deep.

"I notice you scribble a lot."

William became defensive again. "So?"

"Do you like scribbling?"

"Suppose so. Never thought about it."

"Do you think when scribbling?"

"About what?"

"About anything?"

William rolled his eyes around the room – his room – and began to scratch and twitch again. "Don't think so. Maybe. Don't know."

"More like meditation?"

"More what?"

"Mind drifting, in and out of things; things recent and things still lying around but which you can't put down?"

William began to tug at his clothes and the scratching stopped. He hedged his bets. "Possibly."

Clarence suddenly shifted up a gear. "The world out there must seem overwhelming at times, intrusive?"

William wavered between agreement and denial, concern and indifference.

"Are you ready to explode but feel compelled to hold yourself in?"

William drew his duvet closer in until the two became entangled. It was food for thought even if he did have a small stomach, limited appetite, and an unsophisticated palette.

Clarence smiled. "Don't worry I'm not expecting an answer."

"I can answer if I want to," retorted William, but at that moment his mum stuck her head around the door and spoiled things.

"Dinner's ready you two."

She sounded happy, sweet. She was the satisfied housewife, determined that they should eat together and on time. In her mind they were a threesome, if only temporarily. William immediately noticed the change and was not pleased.

"I must apologize for my son's room. I keep trying to get him to clear it up – or let me clear it up."

Clarence took up her call. He cranked himself up into the upright position and dutifully followed her out. William did not. Mary did not care to take up the challenge but left her child to stew. For her this was normality. Hunger would drive him out, to the place at the table where there were chips to be had.

Clarence sat where instructed and Mary transferred cooked food from kitchen to dining room with all the speed of a hospital nurse attending the wounded. A minute or two later William appeared and slipped into his usual place. This time he had been driven out not by hunger but by the need to keep tabs on this man who his mother was prepared to feed with such unbridled enthusiasm.

Both man and boy awaited instructions to feed. Mary had a full audience and enjoyed playing mother to the full. Suddenly she no longer considered herself overweight. Not that she was.

It was a special dinner tonight William noted. Everything was laid out to a fashion. There were extra knives and spoons. This man Clarence – stupid name – was getting his mum to do things that she never did for him. The observation stabbed its way into his consciousness and left a small but festering wound.

He sat perched at the table and monitored events on the front line. Nothing happened. There was no eye contact. There was no talk. Clarence sliced up his lamb into smaller, same size pieces and dissected his vegetables before committing. William watched him do it, and more. Clarence knew he was being watched and William knew that. Mary watched her son watching her guest like a hawk and suffered as a result. In the end it became painful for all. William did the one thing he was learning to do in life: he took charge of the conversation. "Do you like my mum's cooking?"

"Yes. Very good. I like the lamb."

The answer sounded as wooden as wooden could be.

"We've got desert afterwards right mum?"

"That's right." Mary smiled. Her son was sounding positive, wholesome, on the edge of full blown manhood with maturity to boot. He would make it.

"Lovely," added Clarence for affect.

They continued to eat, William at speed. Clarence, stumbling again, thanked her for all the effort she had put in. In return Mary thanked him for the thanks. William secretly groaned under the weight of pleasantries and twisted his legs around each other. That aside, during the course of the meal Clarence never spoke unless spoken to, which for William was a bonus. Mary put it down to shyness. William was just glad the man was not trying to chat his mum up. The fact that the two struggled to talk meant that she would probably not invite him around again, which was another bonus.

William suddenly chuckled out loud and Mary turned on him: she watched him stuff his face with ice cream and was about to admonish him but then saw Clarence do much the same, but at half the speed. William saw his chance and decided to not hang around. He had more important things to do, like chase dreams or reinforce his grievances; or just sit and wait for things to unfold. Clarence watched him go, his expression tinged with regret. Mary took note. She had lots of notes now.

The adults retired to the sofa, a big sofa which placed space between the adults. A coffee table on wheels was rolled into place. On it Mary placed a pot of coffee, cups and the like; and sat back to await events, how ever they unfolded – much like her son next door.

The photographs lined up along the mantelpiece caught Clarence's attention. Each was carefully positioned to receive an equal cut of the advertising space. Some were in colour. Some were in black and white. Some were large. Some were small. Some were framed. Some, the really old ones, held together by a whisker.

Two were extremely faded and gave a tantalising view of a world which had once existed but now barely left an echo or trace: an alien world in which people, for their main entertainment, loitered without intent in the streets; standing or sitting for hours on end to watch the world go by while understanding little of it; an alien world in which, to be at your best you had to be dressed in your best and that best had to be 'the Sunday best'; an alien world in which you believed without question whatever the man who dressed better, spoke better and ate better than you had to say to you; a not so alien world in which if you did not like someone you punched him, and if he was down kicked him, and if he was a threat killed him, and if you were weak raped his woman, and if you were ambitious appropriated his land; an alien world in which news from afar never ceased to disturb and dislodge, and recent homespun history was revered and preferred as the only acceptable excuse for the present.

Clarence examined the set of pictures in depth while coffee was poured.

"You like my pictures?" asked Mary.

"I'm fascinated. Can you tell me about them?"

"Which ones?"

"All of them."

"All of them?"

"All of them. Please? I'm dying to know."

Mary handed him a cup of coffee and a mint to boot. The mint slipped down his throat in two broken parts. On its way it was overtaken by a swig of coffee. The coffee burnt his throat and he nearly choked.

Mary looked up and inspected her collection of family photographs. She was pleased with what she saw. She stretched out her arm and pointed. "That's William aged ten, then five or seven – not sure – then again at three; then one; then a day or two after he was born."

"How old is he now?"

"Thirteen."

"You adore him?"

"Adore him? Yes of course I adore him. He's the only thing I've got."

"The only thing?"

"The only thing." Her voice dropped and took on greater intensity: her reaction to the sudden shift in gear. "It was a disastrous relationship - worse than a one-night stand."

"Meaning?"

Mary stared into her cup, unsure whether to elaborate – as if she had any choice in the matter. "They say a one night-stand is short and sharp. You blink. It's gone. No emotional baggage before or after. This dragged on and on, and drained my spirit." Mary was bursting to breath out. She had been holding her breath for years. "William was never planned but he made me very happy the moment he arrived – just in time as they say."

She stopped herself. Back to the photographs. "That's me and my sister. Celebrating O and A levels if I remember. The one in the middle was her boyfriend at the time: her first I think. Mum didn't like him, and said I couldn't have one for another couple of years." Mary pointed. "Next to that is the four of us on holiday."

"The four being?"

"Me, sister, mum and dad. We were digging sandcastles with dad's help." She smiled. "Dad always had to help. He was the expert. He knew how things were done."

"Your father was an expert on building castles out of sand?"

Mary put her hand up to her mouth to stop herself laughing. She choked instead. "No silly."

"So he was lying?"

"No he wasn't lying. I was being sarcastic, or something. Silly."

"What did you do with the sand?"

"What do you mean?"

"After you built these constructions, these sandcastles."

"Knocked them down of course - or left them for the sea to wash away." Mary smiled belatedly at her dinner date. He was starting to tire.

Satisfied, Clarence moved on. "And that one?"

"Oh that's my grandmother and mother. I think mother was in her early twenties – just before she met dad anyway."

"That's an old car?"

"That's my granddad's, an old 50's model – though it wasn't old then of course. She grew to love that car my mother, especially after she passed her test. She did most of the driving in their later years."

"What's that?"

"An ice cream van." Mary cast Clarence a sideways look. It had sounded like a serious question. "You've seen an ice cream van before?"

"Probably. I can't remember. They were for transporting ice cream?"

"Yes."

"To sell?"

"To sell, yes." This time Mary looked Clarence straight in the eye, her inherent shyness long since derailed. "Stop winding me up. You're as bad as William."

She fell back on the coffee and offered him a refill. Clarence declined. Instead he marched on.

"Why is this one black and white?"

"Old. Just very old. My grandmother's family: the first shot of her with her fiancé, my grandfather of course."

"Why are they all standing to attention?"

"It was formal pose. Hence suits and best dresses."

"You hold a strong attachment to these images?"

"It's family. Don't you have lots of pictures of family?"

Clarence shook his head. "No I don't think I do. But then I'm the child not the parent."

With that the conversation collapsed. Mary was looking tired and Clarence, recognising that fact, said nothing. When it did restart it was in fits and starts, and for little duration, and the passing of time began to grind on the soul.

They did manage to talk about one more subject and this closed proceedings on a positive note. The subject was art and the trigger was a poster of a famous painting by Van Gogh: one of his many sunflowers. Mary found herself talking at length with passion about a subject which excited her. She found Clarence attentive and eager to learn more about the subject, in all directions. He declared total ignorance, and a wish to change. They agreed to follow up, and when Mary closed the front door she was on a high. Getting old was suddenly on hold.

❖ ❖ ❖

Log Entry

I have made contact with a cat: the small, domesticated variety. This has been difficult as the cat and my host share a history of mutual suspicion and animosity. Its fur is unusually clean and sterile, manicured even. It lives locally and does not wander far. My host does not take to cats in general, though I can find no solid reason for this: he has no bad memories of cats. It appears to be just a position he has taken over the years – preferring dogs on principle – and this position has become fossilized in his mind so as to now generate strong, negative, sometimes aggressive reactions whenever a cat gets too close. That said, this particular cat is connected with a specific female who generates emotions of disinterest and disquiet within him.

I have watched it wander up and down the street, and through gardens, occasionally depositing excrement and then examining it – for what I don't know. Perhaps it is a consistency check. It has a certain style, an arrogance of ownership almost for its 'territorial patch', and holds itself in the highest esteem. It is always on guard. I say 'it'. I should say 'she'.

The emotional responses of a domesticated cat – not wild yet sharing many characteristics and impulses of the larger wild species – have proved difficult to engage with. Manipulation is all but impossible as they are raw, extremely focused, and unyielding unless persuaded by opportunity for advantage or immediate gratification. This particular cat is a very confident, very focused creature.

Though she does not have to hunt for food she still conducts herself like a hunter, ready to pounce even when there is no obvious target. The similarities with its truly wild cousins are striking - but to be expected? She is a pet and has been all her life. There is almost a memory of evolutionary inheritance at work here.

At the invitation of a new acquaintance I visited the centre of a city today: a city being a vast area of concentrated human habitation, supporting human intercourse across the full commercial and social spectrum. The city centre is the ultimate focus of the city community, and beyond. Everything is here: all commercial and social activity; along with government institutions; and the deep mark of history, engrained in the infrastructure.

All space is utilised so human density is high, so much so that personal space is at times compromised and emotional stress is prevalent. People move about with an expression that varies from detachment through resignation, to outright despondency in the worse case. There is rarely a positive outlook. This is strange, considering that there is a desire to congregate here. Some look lost, confused. I suspect these cases are visitors passing through and lacking local knowledge.

Twice a day there is a dense, fast moving flux of people: they enter the city centre in the morning; they depart it in the evening. In places this causes overcrowding and increases the emotional stress. All races, cultures, trademarks and personal lifestyles are represented; likewise the emotional spectrum.

Along the edges of roads reserved primarily for motorised traffic, a little space is set aside for those moving on foot. Some walk close behind another in front, step for step, as if to a beat, as if along invisible lines laid down for the very purpose of steering the crowd. In places these walkways are so crowded as to force people off and into the road, there to compete for space with all manner of vehicles and risk collision.

The roads are heavily congested with vehicles on the move or at rest. Each one fights for space, to move forward, to reach its destination. Any disruption to the flow is met with frustration, anger, or resentment that vehicles elsewhere are moving at greater speed. The vehicles vary enormously in size and shape. Some are designed to carry exclusive people, some to carry goods. Some have as little as 2 wheels, some have 6, 8 even. The biggest of these are two storey buses, designed to carry large numbers of people along pre-designated routes – the passenger makes a financial contribution even though they have no direct control or influence over where and when they operate. This is just one mode of public transport and like all the others it is never free of charge. With regard to private transport the costs both to the passenger and to society at large are more obscurely defined. To complicate matters further there is a competitive tension between those who self-propel on simple two wheel frames and those who drive motorised transport.

Those on foot have authorised places at which to cross these crowded, busy roads. If they cross at other points, they do so at their peril, and with a lack of sympathy from drivers – hostility even. Controlling, containing and streaming all this movement of humans and machines are signs and signals: signs and signals everywhere, at every turn; instructing on the what, where, when, and how. Nothing is left to chance, memory or education. And core to the act of signalling are three precisely manufactured sources of light: red, orange and green. These three colours dictate rights of way, and indirectly the passage of time.

All exterior surfaces are polluted, even the air. I could taste it, smell it, see it above me, and hear it - it being noise pollution. Silence is unknown here. There is only a continuous stream of noise, from all directions and different sources; always in conflict; never harmonious; rarely intended.

A system of connected tubes deep below the surface transport large numbers of humans around the city at high speed in purpose built machines which run on tracks. Seating capacity is maximised. Comfort is a secondary consideration, as is hygiene. Their design is similar to those which travel above ground. During the twice daily mass movements demand peaks and personal space is extremely limited. As with the act of walking, strangers do not converse in these confined places unless placed under pressure to respond to a direct question. To reach the embarkation points you descend from the surface by standing on moving steps. Sitting down is not permitted and retaining your balance is crucial.

Buildings stand tightly packed and without a coherent strategy with regards to design, style, function or access. Some are short but wide. Others are slim but tall. Some are extremely tall and tower over all others in the immediate vicinity. Some are very old and highly decorative, both with regards to interior and exterior. Many are covered in the emissions of animals, principally those which fly. Floor space must be a highly prized asset as the younger the building, the greater its height.

Very old buildings stand in isolated pockets or as part of larger groups such that their resonance and power to charm is magnified, and not diluted by the surrounding younger constructions. The larger and older the building, the greater the prestige of its occupants or function, the head of state being the prime example.

In the land of my host, the head of state is female, despite the dominance of the male sex. Her large, lavish property occupies an extensive, prime piece of the city centre. It dominates all that surrounds it and is a magnate for crowds. They gather at its outer boundaries and stare. (I am reminded of scenes at the zoo.) It is not enough to see it in picture, they are compelled to witness it in the flesh, and capture its image as proof.

One old building we visited had no other purpose as far as I could see other than to store and display a variety of objects not suited for placement elsewhere. This unnatural place was their natural home. The objects varied wildly: in size and shape; in construction and materials; in colour and texture. Some were solid objects which could be completely circumnavigated and viewed from all directions. Others were flat panels fixed vertically to walls, with surfaces intentionally decorated with a wide variety of colours and patterns; some representing objects found in real life, some definitely not.

Access to these objects is allowed at fixed, pre-determined times. When people enter the building to view them, there is a distinct psychological shift. In some it is substantial, in others only slight. The sound level drops dramatically and the state of self-consciousness is amplified.

These objects bewilder, excite, impress, hypnotise even. They rarely bore. Only a few human reactions are negative or hostile. I suspect this location is critical for there to be any acknowledgement, let alone a reaction. Place them elsewhere, worse still in isolation, and they might not even be noticed.

This psychological shift I observed in the female friend. She would stand at length in front of a hanging panel and stare, without comment, at a colourful, partial representation of some, slightly skewed, landscape or seascape. When she did ask my host for his reaction I decided to protect his interests and react with an equal measure of intoxication: deep satisfaction mixed in with admiration and awe.

Her feelings towards him on this day of city exploration were very positive, overwhelming at times, but never demanding or judgemental. The absence of a fully-functioning female relationship is a sense of grievance for my host, and a distraction, though not a loss. I feel it is my duty to ensure that her feelings are reciprocated with like for like, whenever they can be identified and isolated within his inner being. With regards to relationships with females (and I presume males) the most positive, most noble attributes of my host deserve recognition and reward.

Chapter Ten

Log Entry

I and the cat met again this morning. She has definitely taken a liking to me, and expects favours. Suspicion has now been totally removed and she is friendly, inquisitive. My gifts of odd scraps of flesh taken from dead creatures may have helped in this. She has even invited herself into the living quarters of my host. She appears interested in how my host lives and conducts himself, and watches him – I should say me I suppose at such times - intently. Smells also fascinate, especially the unfamiliar ones. I managed one time to force the body of my host to pass wind (the fart). She definitely took note. At such times I dare not release my host from total control as the consequences of him discovering this animal in his home could lead to confrontation and undesirable consequences.

✦ ✦ ✦

Clarence answered the doorbell, shaken from his chair, having lapsed into deep sleep after another bad night's sleep and dreams of fiction which felt like borrowed memories. It was the woman from two doors down, the one who sometimes dressed like a knitwear catalogue. She stood stiff, which in turn made Clarence stand stiff. They both stood uneasy, yet dignified, and determined to see it through. They could have been diplomats. He had only his dressing gown on and felt exposed. She was looking for her cat and likewise felt exposed. She mumbled something and Clarence was jerked back into reality, and the hard work of human contact.

"What?"

"I said have you seen Judy?"

"Judy? I don't know a Judy. Who's Judy?" Clarence wanted to fall asleep again.

"She's my cat."

"Your cat's called Judy? That long haired one?" Clarence managed not to say 'that long haired thing?'.

"That's her. Judy."

It seemed a stupid name for a cat but Clarence decided not to follow that one up.

"Sorry. Can't help."

"Sorry to bother you then. It's just that I saw you stroking her yesterday – and the day before that." She looked around his waist. Clarence pulled his dressing gown closer in until it was tight all round.

"Judy!" she exclaimed.

The woman knelt down, just as a long haired cat, purring, appeared out of nowhere and rubbed itself around and about the lower half of Clarence. Then, as she held out her hands, Judy discarded Clarence for her mistress – her source of food and shelter, and constant emotional dialogue.

Clarence was perplexed, then fatalistic. He looked up to the ceiling then down to the floor, then fleetingly into his neighbour's face, then eyes down.

"Look, honest, I didn't know she was in here. Honest. I didn't know. Honest." He sounded terrible. He looked terrible; and he knew it.

In return she gave him a funny look, took Judy up in her arms and hugged her closely, as if on a rescue mission. Judy took purring to new heights. She was about to explode.

"Are you OK Judy?" asked her mistress.

No reply.

"Is she OK?" asked Clarence, faking concern and goodwill.

His neighbour looked Judy in the face, square on, and stroked her across the top and down the back of her head. "She looks fine, happy."

"Good."

Clarence hunted around for an explanation or an excuse. He found both close to hand. "Look I must apologize. I think my lodger let her in this morning before he went off to work. He's from Ireland – has lots of dogs and cats back home – lives on a farm. I think he misses having a cat around."

She accepted his explanation graciously, looked him up and down, and sensed something was wrong, way off balance. The man looked exhausted, like someone who was not sleeping well, if at all. His karma was knackered. He had spots. His hair was greasy. He had not shaved.

"You're not at work – I saw you wandering down the street yesterday lunchtime."

"Not at work, no. On sick leave if you must know."

Shit. He didn't know why but he wished he had not shared that piece of information with this woman. She was the clinging type. Give her the chance and she would cling, like Clingfilm, or worse.

"You teach don't you?"

"Yes. How did you know that?"

"You told me once, ages ago, when you were drunk. I had just moved in? You tried to chat me up? Remember?"

"No, sorry." He did remember but didn't want to admit it. He sensed it would be a grave mistake.

"You don't remember?" she asked, sounding like the crown prosecution.

"No. Sorry. But then I was drunk."

He waited for her to let go, and go, but she did not let go. He didn't want to insult her but it was coming to that. The weight of her dress sense began to bear down on him and he was not impressed. Then the penny dropped: the jumper was homemade, and smelt of cat; else she smelt of cat, her cat Judy. What would she call a goldfish? Nigel?

"You're on sick leave?"

"Sick leave that's right."

Judy began to fight the clutches of her mistress. She had been squeezed enough for the time being. Refusing to be pacified she finally won her freedom and was allowed to fall to the ground. She straightened up and wandered off, dignity regained, senses on alert.

"I must admit you do look under the weather – if you don't mind me saying so."

"Tell me about it. Sorry I meant that in a nice way. Thanks. Thanks for your concern."

Absorbing this admission she suddenly came over all intense and interested in his welfare. All men needed looking after. It was written so, somewhere.

"My name's Rebecca by the way." Rebecca held out her hand and smiled. "Just in case you'd forgotten."

"Hello Rebecca."

Clarence was forced to take it and shake it. It was limp, slightly sweaty. The handshake was weary on both sides. Pause. Then it dawned on him that he was expected to introduce himself: a self-inflicted form of 'name and shame'.

"Clarence."

"Clarence." Rebecca thought back, hard. "That's right, I remember now. Clarence. Geography wasn't it? Or rather isn't it?"

"That's right."

"Like teaching geography?"

"Love it."

Rebecca analysed him, head to foot, and Clarence felt her grip. He tried to break free but felt unable to slam the door in her face.

"Are you eating well?"

Clarence was flippant. "As well as can be expected."

"Can you cook?"

"Yes I can cook. When I want to." He tried to sound upbeat. "Which isn't often." His attempt at humour was lost on Rebecca.

"You should cook more often: fresh food, fruit and veg – boring but good for you. None of that ready made stuff – overpriced and too much salt and preservatives and God knows what."

"Thanks for the tip. I'll bear it in mind." The sarcasm also went over her head and crashed landed on the pavement. He almost had another Ramsey on his hands. That made this encounter just a teeny little bit enjoyable.

The phone rang and his heart missed a beat. Salvation. Clarence was saved.

"Sorry I have to go."

"Sure don't mind me. I'll see you around."

"Certainly. Now we know each other, again."

Again Clarence heard himself say too much and wanted to bite his tongue off. But he needed his tongue: without it he could not articulate, let alone say the right thing. As he went to close the door Judy sprang forward and tried to dart inside.

"No no Judy leave the man alone," pleaded Rebecca passionately. She caught hold of Judy and gathered her up in her arms again. "Silly."

Yes silly, thought Clarence. Get lost. Both of you.

"Bye."

"Bye."

The door closed.

Clarence picked up the phone. It was his sister. She was blowing hot air.

"Is that you Clarence!" she bellowed.

"Yes of course it's me," he replied quietly.

She defended herself. "It could be your lodger, that Irish one."

"In which case I would have an Irish accent – and anyway you know my voice."

Margaret had no answer to that. She backed off slightly. "How are you?"

"I'm fine."

"You're off work: sick leave I understand?"

"That's right. Who told you?" He had purposely not told her, not anyone.

"Mary told me. She tells me everything."

Clarence threw the last remark aside. It sounded to much like a bluff.

"What's wrong with you?"

"Nothing."

"Nothing? It can't be nothing. What's wrong with you? Tell me." She battered her brother with words.

Christ she was starting to sound like their mother, with teeth.

"Just been under the weather – need a break."

Clarence held his breath. That had generated a long pause. She was thinking hard. He could hear her breathing down the phone. He almost believed he could smell her – either that or he could still smell her next door and that cat. Judy? What sort of name was that for a cat? Perhaps she was a Judy Garland fan? Or was it Julie Garland?

"Mary called me."

"Did she. Did she?"

"She did. She had another great time apparently. She 'looks forward to seeing you again'. Her words not mine. Can't quite believe it myself. And she keeps saying you're shy. You? Shy? Anyway it makes her feel good."

Clarence kept his thoughts to himself. "Does she."

"She does. Though why she can't tell you herself."

"Perhaps she's shy?"

"She is."

"Well that's settled then."

"What?"

"Nothing."

In an instant Margaret changed the subject. She had no more interest in Mary's interest in her brother. As far as she was concerned her long time friend was suddenly a bad judge of character. Best keep out of things and stay neutral was her strategy. Though if Mary asked if she thought Clarence would make a good husband and father to her son, she would have to be honest and say 'no way', better that than a future disaster. That said, a married Clarence might be completely different from the bachelor boy Clarence, and hence could only better. He needed to be reined in.

Mentally Margaret had to shake herself free and get a grip. She was drifting off her agenda, the one she had cemented before picking up the phone.

"Look I want a word with you."

Clarence cringed, and held the phone at arm's length, but only for two seconds, no more. He knew he couldn't avoid her music. It was heavy metal without rhythm or words. "What?"

"I don't want you talking to my children. At least not without getting my permission first – and with me present, or Desmond. Understood?"

"Understood." Clarence didn't understand but didn't want to know more, or argue with her. Today she was firing on all cylinders.

"I don't want you filling their heads with rubbish. Understood?"

"Sure. Understood."

"I tell my children what they need to know, what I want them to know – not you. Understood?"

"Yes understood." Understood. Understood. Understood.

"Especially with regard to my life. Understood?"

"Yes I understand I understand."

"I don't think you do. But I can only hope." The second sentence was spat out like a piece of gristle.

Clarence knew from bitter experience that it was best to remain docile in such situations. Though this was the worse, mainly because he didn't have a clue.

"Don't ever tell them I used to get drunk all the time in my teens."

"I won't." Clarence didn't know he had but he knew the situation was hopeless. He put it all down to his one big problem. It was all dirty washing. Put it in the washing machine. Then find a way to turn it on. Then step back and watch, perhaps cry.

There was another long pause, during which Clarence prayed that this be the end of the eruption. But he was wrong. God did not believe in half truths or half measures. It was all or nothing and damn the consequences.

"And one more thing brother Clarence." This sentence had pins sticking out of it which made it hard to swallow.

And the phrase 'Brother Clarence' - rarely used - meant it had something to do with Mother and Father.

"What's that."

"Don't ever talk back at Mother like that again. Don't confuse her or compromise me."

"Like what?"

"You know exactly what I'm talking about." The word 'exactly' allowed no room for negotiation.

She stumbled over her next words, words of denouncement and disbelief combined into one. It was Nuremberg, without the accents or military escort.

"Why? Why did you do it?"

"Do what?"

"Don't play games with me."

"I'm not. Do what?"

"Tell her."

"Tell her what? Tell me for God's sake."

"Tell her about – you know – me at university."

"What about you at university?"

"Me and that Jane."

"Jane? Oh that. I didn't tell her a thing."

"Don't insult me. Of course you bloody well told her! She told me you bloody well told her!"

"Look if I did I honestly am sorry. I don't remember things easily these days. Blackouts or something."

"You're just making this up now. You little worm."

"Honest I've been having these lapses of memory and control. Ask Sam."

"Sam?"

"Tim's wife."

"Oh that Sam."

"She'll confirm it – these blackouts." At least he hoped so.

Margaret drew breath. She was not finished yet. One last salvo to come:

"This is revenge isn't it?"

"Revenge?"

"For the party."

"No. No revenge." Clarence gave up. "Sorry but I've had enough. I'm on sick leave. Goodbye."

And with that defiant demonstration of self-worth Clarence slammed the phone down, feeling good with himself that he had cut his sister off. Let her boil and bubble. He had his own problems, and they were building into a funeral pyre. His thoughts turned to Mary. It had been weird enough going over for dinner but why the trip up to London and back? And why no memories of anything substantial? Why no rhyme or reason? Why no self-control? And to make matters worse he knew he would have to go and apologize to Mother for something he could not remember saying.

✦ ✦ ✦

Adequately dressed but semi-comatose, Clarence headed into town on a food finding mission. Now he was missing his school dinners he had to cook for himself much more often; which meant spending more time in the kitchen; which sooner or later meant having to wash up. He could only get so much out of Max. He would have to do half, perhaps more seeing as Max lived on Cornish pasties most of the time.

Back in his favourite supermarket – favourite by lack of real economic choice – Clarence floated up and down the aisles, looking for ideas, avoiding trolleys. He found the pizzas and the ready meals, stacked in their usual place. Best idea yet. Same idea.

"Hallo Clarence," said a soft female voice from behind.

The sound entered his head like a piece of shrapnel and his heart missed a beat – one of many missed that day. It was a fresh yet familiar voice. Clarence turned, expecting to see Tracey. But no it was her with the cat. Punch and Judy.

"Hallo." He fought a losing battle to recall her name.

"Buying for one?"

"Yes. Buying for one as they say – the sad bachelor." He cringed at having said sad. He wasn't sad yet, just half demoralised – flattened by events beyond his control or understanding.

"Same here. Makes things difficult at times."

"Does it?"

"Fixed volumes – not designed for single people."

"No. Never." Clarence didn't have a clue what the woman was talking about, but at least she was dressed normally.

Rebecca looked at the cheap pizza he was hanging on to: some very 'unItalian' concoction involving curried chicken. She truly felt sorry for him, and him a teacher, an intellectual.

"You're not going to eat that are you?"

Clarence looked down at the offending item, examining it for flaws. He found none.

"Well yes?" he replied, looking for some trap.

"Cheap and nasty, and no good for you." Rebecca wanted to say her piece.

Clarence made a confession, too tired to fight his corner. "It's all I know."

"You need a good balance diet to stay healthy you know. Eat nothing but bad food and you end up feeling bad both inside and out." Rebecca had said her piece.

Clarence said nothing. She pushed on, undeterred, or possibly encouraged. "Have you looked at yourself in the mirror recently?"

"Yes I look like shit."

"Yes, not exactly the words I would have used." She restarted. "Do you like lentils?"

"Don't know. Probably not." Little boy lost was back.

"Look let me suggest something. A little presumptuous I know but why don't you let me take you round this place: show you the good stuff; show you how to cook it."

She expected to receive a dismissive 'no' but unexpectedly the 'no' turned out to be a 'yes', Clarence having felt he could do with a laugh. She led the way, preaching goodness and good sense, and Clarence ended up amongst other things buying spring greens and a big 'oily fish' which he could stick under the grill. There were no crisps, no pizzas, no readymade meals. He did manage to hold onto the bacon, and a porkpie for afters.

They ended up at the checkout together, Clarence unable to shake her off but still slightly amused inside that he had managed to wind her up without her realising it: a soft touch – shame about the dress code and the cat called Judy. Despite the fact that she was beginning to seriously bore him, as they left the supermarket a strange sense of shame rose up inside him and threatened to engulf. He was driven to make amends quick.

"Here let's swap. I'll carry yours. You carry mine."

"Thanks," exclaimed Rebecca, genuinely touched.

She gave him her two bags. He gave her his one heavy one. He began to follow her along the pavement, always slightly behind, as if afraid to be associated with her, still trying to work out why he had made the offer and had to walk all the way home with her. He passed a familiar scruffy face. It was the tramp who had invaded his flat, now selling some magazine and after his cash. Clarence tried not to be recognised. He failed. The tramp moved towards him, calling out with a voice which sounded scratched and torn.

Clarence speeded up. The tramp speeded up and easily caught him up. Rebecca stopped and turned. Clarence jumped in quick and demanded that he be sold a magazine. The tramp complied. Clarence walked on, in front this time, hoping that he had shaken the man off. But he hadn't. The tramp desperately wanted to talk, and was addressing him like an old friend, which was the last thing he was.

Clarence had to deal with it. He halted suddenly and Rebecca almost crashed into him. His shopping was beginning to hurt her wrist so she swapped hands. Now it could hurt the other.

"Look will you excuse me. Him and me have some unfinished business."

"Sure." Rebecca walked on a little before stopping at a polite distance to watch what was going on.

Clarence pulled a note from his wallet, checking carefully that it was not in fact two stuck together. It was a big brown note. He spoke in hushed tones. The tramp came over all serious, grave and respectful. Then the tramp took the note and walked off, in a lighter mood. Clarence walked on – marched on - and caught Rebecca up in no time.

"You gave him ten pounds."

"Yes I keep giving him money but he's starting to take advantage of me."

"Often the way. But still what do you do? You can't stop be generous."

Clarence had no comment to make.

As they reached home, and their respective front doors, Rebecca felt the only natural – and in this case charitable – thing to do was to invite Clarence in for a decent meal. Let him experience some real home cooking, her home cooking.

"I'll show you how to really cook," she boasted.

Again he surprised her by accepting the offer, not knowing he rarely turned down a free meal. Even though there was a definite lack of enthusiasm in his voice she did detect a strong sense of gratitude. Shyness? Or a very lonely man? A very lonely man she decided, perched on the edge of some cliff and, God forbid, waiting to fall. Suddenly Rebecca felt it was her job to pull him back from the edge and put him to rights – ignoring the fact that she was completely unqualified to do such a thing.

Great, thought Clarence. No cooking. No washing up. Just a snack will get me through dinner. Porkpie perhaps. Just hope the cat's not there. The bad news was the cat was there. More bad news was he had to eat something made with lentils and broccoli, and other green stuff, and cheese. That said, it tasted better than it looked. The same could not be said for her flat. Clarence couldn't put his finger on it but it didn't appeal to his senses: a bit too 'fluffy', 'in your face'; too overcrowded with knickknacks, jars of things undefined; and books books books everywhere; and posters on yoga and spiritual healing; and beads and baubles, and things hanging from the ceiling; and candles candles candles everywhere.

He threw his food down quickly, declined the green tea – and all the others - and hastily excused himself. On the way out he passed Judy. She tried to rub herself up against his leg but missed. Another time another place she promised.

Back home Clarence took one look in the kitchen, saw the dirty plates and their ilk piled up, and thought 'sod it'. Call the lodger's bluff and see if he does it – or even just some of it: his and a little bit extra would be fine. Clarence went back into the living room and put on a DVD. Time flies when you're enjoying yourself he thought, almost eloquently, but not when you're not.

※ ※ ※

Max thundered in, dumped his tool bag and slipped under the shower to scrub away the day's dirt, dirty talk, and the day's complaints. Dried and casually dressed he lurched into the living room, where he found one sorry looking Clarence staring at a half-eaten bacon sandwich, contemplating the universe, or lacking the stomach for food.

It looked like a good bacon sandwich: the substantial kind; the kind gorged upon ravenously; the kind which left no trace of its existence behind. Straight away Max knew something was up. He wanted out but he had to get past Clarence to the kitchen.

"Hiya."

"Alright Max."

"Yeah fine. Knackered but fine."

"Busy day then."

"Busy day. I'm making coffee. Want one?"

"Yeah why not."

Max stormed the kitchen – only to find every space covered in crap. Clarence hadn't been to work but with all that spare time he still couldn't be arsed to clear up. Max struggled to find two clean mugs. In the end he did, and was forced to make two coffees, and worse still share time with one dodgy looking Clarence.

Clarence reached for the sandwich and examined it. He didn't care to eat it but neither did he put it down. He just noted that it was stone cold, with no visible fat. Finally he tried to put it in his mouth but could not muster the willpower or energy. He put it back on the plate. There it would stay, abandoned and rejected.

"Look, mind if I turn the telly on?" Max needed the company.

"No go ahead."

Max went ahead and from that point on allowed himself to be sucked into the day's news. He still couldn't get use to the fact that the news seemed different here from that which he got back home in Dublin. He glanced across at Clarence a few times. The man was not drinking his coffee. So why had he asked for the bloody thing?

"Look, you're having all this time off and it's not doing much good is it? What exactly is the beef?"

Clarence stared at the screen awhile longer before condescending to answer. "Women are pissing me off."

"What? Women are pissing you off? So what?" Max didn't get it.

Another bomb in central Baghdad had exploded, killing twelve, injuring many. No Americans harmed so no American presidents alarmed.

"That's right. Pissing me off."

More unexpected Taleban resistance in Afghanistan.

"I don't know if I'm coming or going," concluded Clarence.

"Meaning what exactly?"

"Meaning I don't know."

Something about a lack of a Nato response.

"You must know something. It's your problem."

"There's two of them – possibly three."

"Three women? Three women what? You're shagging three women? I don't believe you."

Not enough troops in Afghanistan.

"No I'm not shagging three women. I'm not shagging any of them thank you very much."

Something about a democrat after sex with boys.

"I don't understand. What exactly is the problem then?"

Now Max was desperate for his own bacon sandwich, but not from that kitchen.

"The problem is . . ." Clarence leaned back and looked up at the ceiling as if it were heaven, then fell back down to earth. " . . .I don't know."

North Korea promise to explode atomic bomb. South Korea takes it as a threat.

Max heard himself repeat himself. "You must know something, if only a little."

"I do, sort of. I fancy one woman. She fancies me. We slept together once. It was great. Now she won't admit it."

"That you slept together?"

"No, that she fancies me."

No more spare space in prisons.

"Perhaps there's someone else?"

"Doubt it. No, she's above that sort of thing. I'm sure of it. It's got something to do with work. I'm pretty sure that's it."

"Why what does she do?"

"She's a teacher."

"Like you?"

"Like me – at my school."

"Ah. That could have something to do with it I guess." That left two. Get it over with thought Max, then piss off. "And what about the other two?" he asked.

The pound was down against the dollar, up against the euro.

"One of them fancies me a bit. I don't know what's going on. I've known her a long time and now she fancies me I think, over her husband. And I've been having these blackouts."

"Blackouts?" Max wanted out. Get the man to a doctor.

"Total blackouts. Or – and this is the funny bit – something else: not a blackout as such but something else."

"Sorry but I'm fucking confused."

"I'm awake, but not in control. You know what I mean?"

"No."

Dodgy payments to the Irish Prime Minister. Max missed that one completely.

"I can see what I doing, but I don't know why I'm doing it, why I'm saying it. I'm not in charge. I'm just along for the ride."

"Why don't you go and see somebody?"

"No way. They may lock me up."

"I see." Max didn't. "And what about this other woman? Number three?"

"Number three? Don't know. I just seem to keep seeing her. Socialising. She likes me. She definitely fancies me."

"You fancy her?"

"Are you kidding? She's older than me. And she's got a kid, a teenage kid. She's a single mum. Probably desperate. Old friend of my sister's."

"So you've known her a long time as well?"

"I've known <u>of her</u> a long time – not quite the same thing."

"So why do you keep seeing her?"

"I don't know! That's what I keep telling you."

Fair enough.

"So you don't like her then?"

Clarence looked troubled. "No I didn't say I don't like her: just, don't fancy her."

"And you're not seeing that Tracey anymore?"

"That's right. She and me called it quits."

"So you're not getting any then?"

"No."

"And you want some?"

"Yes – oh and to make matters worse I allowed a neighbour to cook me lunch today. I was too friendly."

"A woman I take it."

Clarence looked up, spotting the sarcasm. "Yes. A woman – the kind who doesn't have a bloke and wants one I think."

"So what's the fucking problem. You've got two to choose from."

"Two?"

"Woman at work – just convince her it can work – or this neighbour of yours."

Clarence looked up at his lodger, as if the man hadn't understood a single word he had said.

"I don't think it's that simple."

"Well I think it is. Just choose or give the whole thing up – and if you can't do any of that, well <u>make sure</u> you act honourably to them all."

"Act 'honourably'. I'll try to remember that." The sarcasm rebounded.

Finally the national weather report for the next three days. Much as before.

"What are you doing tonight?" asked Clarence.

"Why?"

"Just wondered if you fancied a pint."

"Can't. Not tonight. Going out."

"Drinking?"

"And clubbing."

"Can I come."

"Difficult. There's four of us you see: two blokes and two girls if you see what I mean."

Clarence took the hint. He didn't want to fight. "Fair enough."

Max untied himself and was gone in an instant. Clarence was left alone. He picked up the phone and rang his best friend Tim. Sam, his best friend's wife, answered.

"Hallo it's Clarence." Clarence did his best to sound cheerful, or at least normal.

"Clarence." It was not a greeting but a statement of fact, delivered with distrust.

What no hallo? Sam sounded a bit like his sister. "Can I speak to Tim?" asked Clarence.

There was a pause. Now Clarence felt he was speaking to his sister. No hot air blowing yet, even so something was not right. He became more insistent. "I do need to speak to Tim."

"I don't think that's a good idea."

Clarence felt a cold shoulder barge into his. He tried to push it aside. "And why not?"

Another pause. "Because he's not in."

"Not in. Fair enough." Somehow Clarence could not bring himself to believe her, but he could hardly call her a liar.

"How are things? Are you holding it together?" asked Sam.

"Surviving – but I need to talk to Tim."

"Well you can't – as I said he's not here."

Now Clarence definitely did not believe her. She far too insistent in stating the fact. He had never known her lie before but there was always a first time for anything.

"Any regrets?" she asked.

Strange question thought Clarence so give a safe answer. "Regrets? No. No regrets."

"So you're still happy, despite it all."

Clarence lied. "Just about. I have to be don't I, to survive."

Another pause, broken by a reinvigorated Sam sounding very upbeat. "Sorry I must dash now. See you soon. Bye!"

Before Clarence could prolong the encounter the line went dead. Now Clarence saw the barefaced lie: Tim was at home and she wouldn't let him talk to him – Tim, his best friend. He needed a drink or two. He checked the fridge for signs of life but it was bare – plenty of wholesome, fresh food but no alcohol. That Rebecca had forced him to think just of food. He looked around. There was nothing to drink in the kitchen. So off to the off-licence, to make polite, slightly intimate, slightly intrusive conversation with his favourite serving girl. Suddenly she was a girl of his dreams again, perhaps even in with a chance.

She was where he expected her to be, and waiting for him he declared, to nobody. Nothing had changed, except the special offers in the window. She saw him looking in – 'him' not realising for one moment that she could see him clearly. She watched him warily as he shuffled in and scanned the various labels of English beer. Their prices were immaterial. He was single, unattached: money was no problem. In her opinion he looked like something off the street. The tan had faded and he had let basic standards of presentation slip. Were it highlighted she could not now deny the fact that the two now had a connection. His presence now made an impact and grabbed her attention. He was no longer a minor irritation or a boring repetition but a major irritant and distraction.

Deciding not to go home Clarence picked up a six pack instead: bottles needed bottle openers. While he was thinking of something smart to say another male blew in and was at the counter before Clarence could blink. He held back, wanting her all to himself.

The other man brought some cigarettes and a bottle of whisky as an afterthought, revealing her name in conversation when he paid. Clarence was all ears: these two knew each other! But no matter, he knew her name now. As the man made to leave Clarence rushed forward to take his place at the head of a queue which did not exist. He suddenly had something to say.

"This is probably a silly question Sally but do you sell bottle openers?"

The man, hand on door handle, held back. He didn't like the look of this low-life who was addressing his friend by her first name. He could see she didn't take kindly to the infringement of her privacy.

Sally remained calm: sell him something and he'll be gone. "Funnily enough we do."

"You do?" Clarence was caught out. He looked at his six pack. "Hang on a mo then I want to change this for some decent beer."

Sally took it all on the chin. He was a harmless twit.

Her mate gestured. "Everything OK Sally?"

"Fine Frank. No problem." Sally smiled reassuringly and Frank went on his way.

Clarence discarded the six pack – dumping it back in totally the wrong place - and picked out some bottles of English beer instead: each one claiming to be different from its rivals; each one of different strength. He now planned to spend the evening 'British beer tasting'. He returned to the counter, this time to definitely make a purchase, and a good impression.

"And how are you tonight Sally?" he asked, cheerfully, like a recently promoted bank manager.

"I'm fine. How are you? You're the one with the problem," she replied dispassionately.

Clarence was gob smacked. The girl had no cause except to be nice to him: after all he was the customer; he had never been nasty to her; he had never let her down.

"What d'you mean?"

"Look at you. You're a mess." She described him as if she had a passing interest.

Clarence, alarmed by her brutal honesty, immediately shut the conversation down. "Look just let me buy my booze and I'll be on my way."

"Are you sure that's a good idea?" The girl raised her eyebrows and gave him a junior version of an old, black and white Margaret Rutherford look.

"Yes I'm sure, quite sure. Let me pay." As he spoke he produced a piece of plastic.

"OK." End of the matter as far as she was concerned.

Clarence watched the pin machine process his card. The machine, connected to some vast financial network of computers and numbers, temporarily took centre stage. Both Clarence and the girl of some of his dreams waited. It blinked. It beckoned. Clarence punched in his four digit pin number - finding it surprisingly easy to recall - and as he did so he suddenly felt the urge to stand up for himself. This he did in the strangest way: he told the girl Sally that he and his girlfriend had split.

"You've split, you and your girlfriend," she replied. Her anticlimax - visible as well as audible - felled him. He was flattened.

"That's right," he whimpered, stuffing knocked out. Now he wished he hadn't said it. It had made him sound like a dick.

"I'm very happy for you."

At least she knows how to be sarcastic thought Clarence. Business done, he left quickly – but not before having the last word at the door.

"I'm not an alcoholic you know. I just need a drink. Going through a tough time right now."

"So am I but I'm not bragging about it."

On that note of disenchantment Clarence was gone, serving girl Sally having had the last word. Well there was always next time – if there was a next time. He saw no reason why not.

Clarence had only one place he wanted to go right now. So he went there, and damn the consequences. The walk would do him good. It didn't. He arrived knackered, at Fiona's front door - less five yards. This distance he maintained. He did not want to knock. He did not want to be discovered. Neither did he want to retrace his steps and end up back home. He was stuck in no-man's-land. The timing felt right: he opened his first bottle of beer and noted the label, then looked around. Lights were on: she was in. He began to drink. The beer tasted good, as beer should. He wanted to sit down but felt required to remain standing. If he sat down he might be mistaken for a tramp.

He thought of Fiona inside, perhaps marking papers or checking her syllabus; perhaps watching TV; perhaps on the phone to a dodgy ex-boyfriend; perhaps naked and rifling through her knicker draw, having just stepped out of the bath. Perhaps she was just lying around, completely exhausted after a day spent teaching 'that which cannot be taught' to those who did not want to be taught. He asked himself why they were not together, a couple, an item, in love even. He had been great in bed. She had been great in bed. He demanded an answer: he did not like being messed around. None was forthcoming.

He became angry, but the anger was contained deep within that interior part of him which controlled the exterior part of him without ever being recognised or rewarded for all its hard work. Anger had come into existence but it was being strangled at birth. He wanted to become really angry. He had earned it. It was his right. He wanted to fly into a rage, but nothing was forthcoming. A volcano within wanted to explode but it was capped, sealed; its force overpowered, neutralized. He wanted to bang on the door, announce his arrival, and if necessary drag her out, and snog her. It boiled down to a sexy snog but he couldn't raise the adrenalin. He could not convince himself that he really meant such violent, crude thoughts. He was as flat as a pancake, and without sugar. He wanted to shout out her name. He couldn't. He found himself wanting.

He tried to think harder to force himself to shout out. But still he remained unconvinced that that was what he really wanted to do. So he tried even harder, even harder to convince himself. One half of his mind was fighting the other. But it was not left versus right. It was top versus bottom, high versus low, young versus old.

Finally he made it. He broke himself. He knew he wanted to shout out at the top of his voice: call out her name and either persuade her that he was hers for the taking else embarrass her and have done with it. He became angry. He couldn't shout out. He wanted to shout out. He was still holding himself back. Finally something clicked and he exploded.

"Fiona!"

The word exploded and, point made, Clarence collapsed back into indecision and inactivity , this time harbouring an inferiority complex, if only temporarily. He was a spent force.

A door opened. The lady 'from next door' stuck her head out. She recognised Clarence. Clarence recognised her. She was not one to mess with. She told him in no uncertain terms to clear off. Clarence was more than happy to. He had said his piece. He had made his point, some point; and he knew that tonight he was not at his best, so probably best not to be seen by those who mattered: best call on Fiona another time. Fiona meanwhile had not the faintest clue what was going on. She was elsewhere and had left the lights on for security.

✢ ✢ ✢

John blew out of the train station, dodging other commuters as he did so. Although it was not into fresh air, it felt like such. He was no longer a commuter but a human being. With renewed energy and a sense of recovered dignity he walked home. A day in the office had left him shattered and the time spent on the train home had left him shaken, rattled and hungry. Moreover the unprofessional attitudes of work colleagues had dented his faith in fair play and the human spirit. Newspaper publishing was a rough tough business.

As his house came in to view he increased his speed. But it didn't last: he slowed; then stopped. Someone was camped out on his doorstep. A tramp? A meter reader? Parcel Express? Then the head lifted. It was Clarence, and he was holding a bottle. That could spell trouble.

John took a deep breath, reminded himself of his high moral principles, and made contact. "Hello Clarence."

Clarence looked up, startled and surprised, as if the last man he expected to see right there and then was the man whose house he was sitting in front of. John was wearing a look worn by exhausted nurses or pissed off prison wardens. "Hello."

John folded his arms and examined the carcass which laid slumped at his door in detail, from head to foot, looking for redeeming features. "How many of those have you drunk?"

"Just my second. This is just my second."

"Promise?"

"Promise."

John look him straight in the eye for any sign of a lie. Clarence appeared to be telling the truth. "How long have you been sitting here?"

Clarence looked around, as if for a clock. "Not long. Twenty minutes?"

"I suppose you want to come in?"

"Yes please. If that's OK?"

John struggled with himself to say no. He lost. "I suppose so. Just as long as you promise to behave yourself."

"I promise."

Not drunk, but like a drunk, Clarence negotiated his way into the upright standing position and watched John turned his latchkey, as if expecting some party trick or deceit. He followed him inside, much like a tired old dog, obedient but disinterested. John sat his patient down on the couch, out of harms way and examined him for signs of damage or improvement.

"So why are you here exactly?"

"I don't know."

"You don't know. Well that's a start."

"To chat I suppose."

"Chat? Chat about what?"

"I don't know."

"Well why you think about what you want to chat about I'll go and make myself a cup of tea. I'm gasping. I take it you're happy with that beer?"

Clarence looked down at the bottle he gripped so tightly, as if having to remind himself that he was still in possession of it. "Yes don't worry about me. I'm fine."

For John, the words 'I'm fine' had a hollow ring and failed the truth test. He left Clarence to his own devices and sought escape in his kitchen. As he made his cup of tea he considered his position; and concluded, in an instant, that the 'Clarence problem' was his problem. He could not refuse to be a friend and support in time of need.

Armed with his cup of tea John sat himself down next to the man who never ceased to confound him with his erratic behaviour, memory lapses and scruffy dress sense. The shirt (grey shirt?) was missing a button and as usual the shoes were in need of a long overdue polish. One of these days, swore John, I'll take his damn shoes and give them a damn good polish. They deserve to shine.

"So everything's fine is it?"

Clarence chewed on the question. He could not swallow it. Neither could he spit it out. All he could do was turn it over and over between his teeth, like a piece of tasteless chewing gum, and try not to choke. "Not exactly, no."

"Anything in particular? Anything I should know about?" John spoke softly and trod carefully whilst observing closely the man who now considered him some kind of ally.

Clarence looked away, to guard against accidental intimacy. "I seem to be upsetting a lot of people around me."

"Really." For John that announcement was not news.

"And I seem to be getting involved with people – women – women I don't want to get involved with."

"Is that so." It was the problem with women. It was always the problem with women. John crossed his legs and reached out to take Clarence by the hand, perhaps even to remove the bottle from his clenched fist. But Clarence avoided all physical contact.

John stood up and scratched his beard. It needed trimming. He was tired and lacking in patience so he came straight to the point. "Look. Have you seen my friend yet?"

"What friend?"

"I gave you his number remember?"

Clarence thought hard, until it hurt. Yes, he remembered a piece of paper. "Oh him. Yes I remember."

"Did you keep the piece of paper? The piece of paper with his number on?"

"Yes I've got it somewhere. Haven't throw it away. Honest."

John suspected he probably had, judging by the tone of his voice. "So you haven't seen him yet," he concluded.

"No."

"And you've lost his number?"

"Probably."

"Hang on." John left the room and returned with a small shiny business card. He handed it to Clarence. "Here. And don't lose this one."

Clarence turned it over and read the small print. "This guy's a psychiatrist!"

John clapped. "Well done!"

"I not seeing no fucking psychiatrist. No way." Clarence growled through his teeth and was barely coherent.

John was not put off. "That was a double negative."

"What?"

"Nothing. Look. Please. Go and see him will you? I really think you should see him. He can really help." For added measure John threw in a warning, intending to scare. "Before it's too late. Your behaviour is no way normal Clarence. If you don't do something about it you'll crack."

"I'm not mental."

"I didn't say you were. Please. I beg you. Do it for me."

John sat back down and looked deeply into the eyes of his messed up, mixed up, part-time soulmate; but Clarence turned away. He could not bare to make contact. John studied Clarence: there was a glimmer of hope that his message was getting through. Clarence was definitely in thought mode.

"Do it for me."

Do it for you? Why should I do it for you? thought Clarence. Then there was a bang on the door and he jumped up and out of his skin, as if it was the police, or Tracey. He stood up like a lemon, with no idea where to run to - or if to run for that matter.

John followed him up much more slowly; calmly, with grace and composure. That will be George in a mood he thought. When in one of his moods or having a panic attack George always banged on the door rather than use the doorbell. He left Clarence to stew and went to answer the summons.

As he much expected it was George, and George was desperate, determined to gain admittance. He was in a flap and loaded down with something to say. His double chin quivered with the nervous energy which was backing up as it waited to be directed out of his mouth. He held a handkerchief up to his runny nose. Both were wet and full of snot. This was always a bad sign. John guessed it had something to do with Toby.

"Johnny darling thank goodness you're home. I thought you might be still stuck on a train." George blew his nose.

"What is it George?" John spoke without a hint of emotion to avoid stoking the hysteria.

George stalled. Johnny still stood in his way. He had not let him in. "Can't I come in?"

"You know it's really not a good time right now."

"Why what have I done?" George was indignant.

"You? You've done nothing."

"So why can't I come in? Would you turn away your oldest, dearest friend?"

John considered his situation. He had two dysfunctional and fragile friends on his hands. If he was forced to choose he had to admit that George probably had the greater claim on his time than Clarence, the new boy on the block. George had come far, at speed, judging by the heavy perspiration. His shirt was hanging out – his pink shirt – and he was biting his fingernails. Another bad sign. What the hell: let George in and watch the two crash into each other. It might be fun and he could do with a laugh. And even if it wasn't fun, it would take his mind off work and those young brainless Turks.

"Of course not. Come in."

John stood back, arms wide open. George ignored the invitation to hug and barged his way past, heading for the couch. He was stopped smartly in his tracks by a fierce looking fellow who looked anything but harmless, and who had stolen his place. He recoiled at the sight of so much potential aggravation.

"Oh hello."

For his part Clarence was confronted by the sight of a man who was overweight, sweating, wearing baggy trousers; and who was flaunting a pink shirt, Austin Powers style. Clarence took an instant dislike to him. He tried to reply with a simple 'hello' but could not bring himself to even do that. Somehow he wasn't surprised that his host kept such friends.

John caught them up and George turned towards him. "Sorry I'm interrupting something." Now he sounded offended.

"No you're not. George this is Clarence. Clarence this is George."

"Hello," said George a second time, this time hoping for a response. Still he didn't get one. He just got a blank expression of puzzlement. "So you're that Clarence fellow." He spoke as if to condemn the man before the trial had started.

"Meaning?"

"Meaning nothing I'm sure." George turned to his Johnny for reassurance. His Johnny had none to give - and had he had any he still would have lacked the energy to dispense it.

George was put out. He wanted Johnny all to himself but instead had to share him with a man holding a bottle of beer like a football supporter – the kind of people he did not care to mix with. He liked rough but they were a little too rough for his liking, and rarely educated – his ability to stereotype knew no limits. The fact that dear Johnny had one trapped in his living room was very worrying. With the man's eyes fixed on him as if looking for a fight, George felt vulnerable. His energy began to drain away. He was in danger of fainting. He fell back on Johnny.

"Can we go next door?" he asked.

John did not deliberate. He knew his George too well. "Certainly. Clarence sorry about this but will you excuse us a moment."

Clarence raised his bottle, as if to make a toast, too disinterested to reply. John reclaimed his cup of tea. Back in the safety of the kitchen John offered to make his friend one while his friend presumed, as always, to rearrange the contents of his kitchen.

"No. No tea. I'm off tea now." George was adamant.

He's off tea again thought John. "Coffee then?"

"No. I'll just have a mineral water."

John looked in the fridge. "It will have to be tap water."

"Orange juice?"

"Yes I can do you orange juice."

Orange juice it was. John filled a glass and lowered one stressed out George into a chair. He pushed the glass slowly across the table with care and attention: George could not control his arms and elbows. As it came into reach George grabbed it with both hands and clutched it tightly whilst making painstaking efforts to control his breathing.

"So what's wrong George. Tell me. Tell your Johnny."

George wanted to burst into tears but was inhibited by the thought of the awful man inhabiting the next room. He examined his handkerchief in his hand. It still had a use. "Oh you know, the usual thing."

"Toby?"

"Yes Toby."

Just the mention of his name was enough to antagonise, and prompted George to feel sick. For John it was a simple matter of changing the fuse, again.

"What's he done this time."

George swivelled his glass and stared into the depths of the orange liquid which promised vitamin C and good skin complexion. He pursed his lips and sucked in air through his front teeth. "Got any nibbles, crisps? Biscuits?"

"Hang on." John retrieved two packets of crisps from storage – his last two – and dumped them unceremoniously in front of George; as if to emphasize the point that maybe, just maybe, George was starting to take him for granted. Then he remembered his other problem holed up next door.

"Clarence do you want any crisps?" he shouted.

"Yes!" Came the clear-cut reply.

"Stay there. Don't move."

John snatched back one of the packets and took it next door. George checked the remaining packet. It was cheese and onion. He loathed any cheese which wasn't soft and blue and he loathed raw onion. The combined smell was unbearable. He picked up the offending packet and rushed after his Johnny. He interrupted the man Clarence just as he was about to rip open the other packet.

"And we swap?"

"What have you got?"

"Cheese and onion."

Clarence examined his. "No."

"No?"

"No."

George looked to John for help. He demanded a recount. John shook him off with raised eyebrows.

"Not my problem. I've just got back from work. I'm tired and I want my cup of tea." And with that he withdrew back into the kitchen to microwave his cup of tea, and to treat himself to a biscuit or two: chocolate digestive. George pursued him all the way. That man Clarence seriously scared him.

George whispered into John's ear. "So that's Clarence?"

"Yes that's Clarence." John spoke back at the microwave.

"Is he always like this?"

"Yes – well no. That's being a bit unfair. He does have his moods swings, but on the other hand his company can be pure joy at times, invigorating even." John gave his friend an accusatory glance. "A bit like you were sometimes." It was a sharp reminder of a failed affair.

George was in no fit state to identify either compliments or complaints. It went over his head. "I don't know what you see in him."

"I don't."

"Don't what?"

"I don't see anything in him. If I did I don't anymore."

George took his friend's hand and squeezed it. Suddenly the tables had turned and Johnny boy was the one in distress - crying out for help he was. Together they watched the seconds count down on the microwave control panel. Finally it went ping and the tea was hot again – far too hot to drink. John slipped his hand free from George's wet grip and made a point of wiping it dry with a clean tea towel. Now the tea towel had to go straight back into the washing machine. He dare not dry cutlery with it.

Toby. I'd rather talk about Toby thought John. "So what's up with you and Toby? Have you had another quarrel?"

George rested his elbow on the microwave, hand on chin. The dislocated layer of fat was not a pretty sight. John tried not to stare. George had not always been this fat. Once, a long time ago now it seemed, he had been gorgeous.

"Yes I suppose you could call it that. Another quarrel."

"A row this time?"

"No not a row this time, just a spat."

"Well that's an improvement," commented John, not knowing how a spat compared with a row in George's volatile, now emotionally over-charged life.

George rubbed his nose then wiped it across the back of his hand. It continued to discharge, aggravated by the change in temperature from one room to the next, and from outdoors to indoors. Noses hated climate change and never stood up the opportunity to protest. "Yes I suppose it is."

"What was it about this time." John was dying not to know.

"He's let me down again. He makes promises then breaks them. He just doesn't care about the things which are important to me."

"Let you down again? I can't believe that. Not after the last dressing down you gave him."

"Toby hasn't printed off my leaflets."

"Oh please come on. There's plenty of time." John's patience was wearing dangerously thin.

"That may well be but you know what he's like. If he hasn't done it by now he never will."

"Look send me the file."

"Send you the file?"

"By Email. You know Email? You can send me an Email over the Internet. Send me one with the file attached: the file, the document, the picture file whatever it is and I'll find a way of doing a print run."

"Are you sure?"

"Don't start. Of course I'm sure. I work for a newspaper don't I? Printing is what we do."

"Of course. Sorry." Reassured and stripped of something to anguish over George calmed down and sat down.

John made to join him but before he could George leapt back up again, all of a sudden feeling happier, more energetic; so much so that this Clarence chap next door ceased to scare him. Quite the opposite in fact. George was nosey by nature and wanted to know more about Johnny's 'new friend', as Johnny had previously referred to him.

"Come on. It's rude of us to stay in here while your friend is sitting all alone in there." George tugged at Johnny's arm, which John didn't like but didn't challenge, and grabbed the packet of chocolate digestives.

"Quite right too," replied John.

Clarence was on the verge of leaving when the two men re-entered the room. The sight of fat, fancy-free George standing side-by-side next to John; almost holding on to him, and staring like a tourist at the zoo – the zoo, Clarence tried not to think of the day at the zoo – was unsettling. They both looked down on him as if he was in need of medical attention or spiritual healing, or both. And they stood very close together: a bit too cosy; a bit too intimate for his liking. It did not bode well. George moved forward, leant over, and hung over him, as if to check his hair for nits. He held before him a packet of biscuits, opened at one end. Clarence leaned right back, until blocked by the back of the couch.

"Is there a problem?" he cried.

"No problem. You're Johnny's new friend I understand." George was gloating as if he and Johnny shared a secret at the expense of new boy Clarence.

Clarence did not take kindly to the term 'new friend', or even just 'friend' but to refute it would be to invalidate his excuse for being there.

"That's right," he replied.

George continued to offer Clarence a biscuit; pushing one almost half out of the packet with his thumb until it balanced precariously, waiting to be accepted or rejected, but ready to topple. "Have a biscuit."

"I don't want a biscuit."

"They're chocolate digestives."

"I don't want a biscuit." Clarence waved it away.

George pushed the packet even closer, until it was almost under his nose. "Go on. You know you want to."

"No! I know I don't want to!"

The exposed biscuit fell out, hit Clarence on the knee and bounced off.

"Oh dear. Sorry. My fault." George went to brush the crumbs off the trouser leg but he was pushed away with menaces.

"Don't touch me."

"Sorry I'm sure. Just trying to help."

"Well don't."

George turned to John, as if to ask 'why?' but John just smiled and tried not to get involved. He still had to drink his cup of tea. It weighed heavily on his mind now, much more than the broken hearts and heads of men.

"Mentioned next Saturday to him?" asked George.

"No. Can't say that I have."

"What about next Saturday?" said Clarence, miffed. There was something in the fat man's manner which made him take exception to being by-passed in conversation. "And will you please not stand so close," he added, again with menaces.

George, stung, took a step back. "There's a big protest rally planned in London. Coming? Everybody's going to be there."

"A protest about what?"

"Against the G8."

"And why should I protest against the G8?"

George gave Clarence a sideways look of incomprehension, as if he was from another planet. "Where have you been?" George turned on John again. "Johnny?"

John shrugged him off, as it to say 'Don't look at me. You started it.'

Clarence meanwhile was slipping into a foul mood: having two gay men stand over him like guards was beginning to more than irritate. "Will you please sit down. Even if it's just one of you."

"Sorry yes." John sat down, knowing George would not.

George remained standing, hands in pockets. "So are you coming?"

"No."

"Why not."

"Because I don't want to."

"That's no reason."

"I think it is."

"Come on you must have a better reason than that." With Johnny present George felt some measure of protection, and with that the courage to say things to this man he would otherwise not dare to say.

"Because quite frankly I don't want to march up and down like a tosser, shouting at the top of my voice, and looking like a prat." Clarence had seen his chance to flatten, crush even, this fat lump of lard; and had taken it. "I'd rather watch the football on TV. In fact I will watch the football on TV."

George felt crudely, perhaps cruelly insulted. He drew breath like an asthmatic. With no room for argument he turned his venom on Johnny. How could Johnny let such a thug into his life? He put his hands on his waistline and threw Johnny a look of total disgust, and total disbelief. John winced. Now he was being hounded, and in his own home.

George tried one last thing. "Will you at least sign the partition?"

"No."

"Why not?"

"Because I have no beef with the G8."

"Even though they've done nothing to curb global warming, help fight third world poverty, or remove unfair trade barriers which distort the world economy?"

"Even that."

George shook his head. "I don't know how you live with yourself."

"Neither do I."

"Sarcasm is the lowest form of wit."

Clarence looked up accusingly. "Who said I was being sarcastic?"

"You've got a real attitude problem you know that don't you?" George had run out of steam. He began to wind down.

Clarence stared back: a verbal fist fight with this fat slob was something he could take great pleasure in. It wasn't so much that the guy was gay – John was gay but it didn't bother him, not now anyway – it was the fact that the guy was in his face, and presumed some kind of moral high ground.

"Have I now."

George collapsed into a spare chair, the one furthest away from the source of his discomfort. He could not believe Johnny claimed this moron as a friend. Where had he found him? In the gutter? John meanwhile started to count down the minutes – seconds even – waiting with a growing sense of 'friend fatigue' for them both to go. The second hand on the wall clock seemed to be moving at a snail's pace.

"Don't you care that the world is going to the dogs?"

Oh dear thought John. George is beginning a rant. We could be here all night if we're not careful.

Clarence considered the question carefully. It carried with it an element of accusation, and emotional frustration really intended for a much wider audience.

"Tell me about it."

You may be dismissive, thought George, but I won't let go that easily. "Tell you about what?"

"The world is going to the dogs: a figure of speech I take it?"

George fell flat, into stony silence. He was not prepared to rise to the bait of more infantile sarcasm.

Clarence persisted. He got up and took the chair opposite George, much to George's disquiet. Only a table separated them, and a vase of flowers, and the packet of biscuits.

"In line with economic growth the population of the planet is increasing I understand."

"Correct. And what about it?"

"Is this growth planned, controlled?"

"Economic growth?"

"No, population growth."

"Population growth? Controlled? Who by?"

"Anybody. Are there limits set on growth?"

George shook his head. "No don't be silly."

John cut in. "it's a fair question: targets possibly. In some countries they try to persuade people to have larger families don't they? And in China it's the other way round I believe."

"Reason being?"

"Keep the economy going I suppose and to avoid starvation."

George interjected. "Expand it more like. Feed the beast."

"It's not just about the economy George. You need young people to look after the old people."

"It's a conveyor belt?" asked Clarence.

"Sort of. Yes I suppose you could call it that."

"But if it's not in balance how does it continue to operate?"

"It obviously doesn't."

"George you said feed the beast? You regard the economy as a single entity? To be a distinct entity does it not need to exist in its own right?"

"Meaning?"

"Well take away human beings and it does not exist."

"Well OK it's not an entity in the strict sense of the word. But while we exist it exists."

"It's a product of our daily activity and continued existence?"

"Yes I suppose so."

"It reflects our patterns of behaviour?"

"More than that sweetheart it dictates them. It determines how and what we eat and drink, and how much we have to work to earn the right to eat and drink and keep a roof over our heads."

"And have sex?"

George hesitated. "I'm not sure about that."

"Sex is the one activity which is not controlled, dictated?"

"Definitely not. It's always been free and fun, no matter how poor you are."

"Or rich!" added John in jest.

"Or rich," echoed George.

"Once he or she comes into existence he, or she, needs to eat and drink, and after developing a fully functioning reproductive system perform sex on a regular basis?"

"Yes I suppose that's pretty much it, if you strip it back down to the bare essentials – that plus a roof over your head."

John was not satisfied. "No it's more than that. If it was just that we'd still be living in caves."

"In caves?"

"Still living in the stone age. No we need much more than that. And because we do – we did - we progressed, we evolved."

"Towards what?"

George took up the baton. "Towards what we are today."

"Which is?"

"I don't know. You tell me. You keep asking the questions."

"Well in this part of the world I would argue a highly charged individual, motivated entirely towards self-preservation - by which I include immediate family – and consumed with a passion for collecting objects."

George and John chewed over his assessment. This was the Clarence John liked.

Clarence pushed on. "So you are sold things you don't need to buy?"

"Yes."

"So why don't you just not buy them?"

"Some of us do, just not enough."

"Is the majority easily manipulated?"

George felt a speech rising from his gut. "Yes I would say so. Those with more money want something better, more expensive than those with less, and so on up the line, until you meet those at the top who have got so much money they don't know what to do with it. They just sit on it and watch it grow - at the expense of everybody else I might add. Meanwhile those at the bottom struggle to stay alive for another twenty-four hours."

"Perhaps some people like money more than others."

"Perhaps some people do. That thought had never occurred to me before." With that reply George gave Clarence his most killing look. But it went unnoticed.

"How does it operate this beast?"

"It locks you in."

Clarence and George faced each other across the table, locked in combat.

"Into what?"

"Into rules, mindsets. It fools you into thinking you can't do without; manipulates you into thinking you must have this, have that, eat this eat that. They dictate what we put in our stomachs."

"Who dictates what we put in our stomachs?"

"The big supermarket chains, the multinationals."

"Can't we refuse to put it in our stomachs?"

"It's not as simple as that."

"Why not?"

"We don't always have the choice."

"I've seen lots of choice. Food everywhere."

George became yet more agitated. "But you're missing the point. It's all controlled. It's one big monopoly. They force down the price of food. They provide the cheapest and it's all the same."

"Cheap food? Is that why there are so many overweight people in this country?"

"Yes."

"Can't you take the food off the shelves? Is not price inversely related to availability? People will eat less and control their weight?"

"That's silly. That could never work."

"Why not?"

"You have to have plenty of food around: you have to have choice."

"But you just said you have no choice, and it's too cheap."

George scratched his head of hair furiously. "It's just not as simple as that – and you're putting words in my mouth. We live in a free market economy."

"The beast?"

"Yes the beast."

Again John saw his chance to jump in with a contribution. "It makes things too cheap in one place, at the expense of someone in some other place. It distorts the market."

"Everything becomes throwaway. Nothing is properly costed. We're digging a big hole in the ground and simultaneously have no idea where to dump the mess it creates."

"And where is this hole? How large is it?"

"It's everywhere. How large? Depends how you measure it."

"Is it thousands and thousands of cubic metres?"

"What? No. I was speaking metaphorically."

Clarence nodded, absorbing the remark slowly. "And this hole bothers you?"

"Of course it bothers me."

"Passionately?"

"Yes passionately," replied George, with passion.

"And me," added John, coolly.

"Can you not refuse to follow these rules?"

"We can and we do. Hence Saturday. But we're a minority. Most people just stick to the status quo. It's the most comfortable position."

"And the safest option."

"Yes as Johnny says, the safest option."

"Tell me about this protest." Clarence sounded firm.

"Why should I tell you anything? You obviously don't give a damn." George spoke in a hurry. He sounded hurt.

"Please. Tell me. I am interested, sincerely interested."

"It's in London."

"Central London?"

"Yes central London. Where else?"

"And how many people will be protesting."

"Thousands. No tens of thousands. Perhaps even hundreds of thousands."

I don't think so, thought John.

"And how will they protest? All in the same way, at the same time? Or individually, each according to their own, and within the context of their own standpoint?"

"You've lost me. It's a protest march." The man was a buffoon concluded George.

"So you all march from some place to some place else?"

George didn't particularly like the wording but had to admit that that was pretty much it – except for the speeches. "And don't forget the speeches: we get to hear some top speakers, some big names."

"Are the places significant? Do they add weight to the argument?"

"No they don't add weight of course not. But they're significant in the practical sense. And people know where they are. They're meeting points."

"But why the marching? Why not stay in the same place and focus your energies elsewhere?"

"We march to demonstrate, draw attention, create news. That's what it's all about: create news." George was getting louder. John was getting worried.

"So by marching you mean you'll be making lots of noise? And this noise adds weight to the argument?"

"Yes. Of course yes. That's the whole point of a protest isn't it?" George turned on John again. "Johnny help me out of this will you. Your so called friend is starting to really get on my tits."

John intervened. "Clarence give it a rest will you. He's not used to you like I am."

"Sorry I'm just trying to understand the concept, the point of it all."

"The point of it all? I've already explained. It's to wake up the G8. Kick 'em up the backside. The G8. Get it? It's not a difficult 'concept'." George banged the table. He was beginning to lose it. John had to get one of them out quickly, preferably both.

Clarence continued unruffled. "This G8. Am I right in saying it's an economic forum for governments who manage highly developed economies?"

George clapped. "Well done."

"I sense you don't hold it in high regard."

"You sense correctly. It's nothing more than a horse-trading club for old boys."

"It trades horses?"

John tried to bottle his laugh but failed. One guffaw escaped. Clarence smiled in return. George looked at them both in turn. Now he was the centre of the joke and on the outside of some new secret. This could not be allowed to continue.

"By your silence I take it it does not trade horses." Clarence moved on to another question. "There's a lot of passion in your voice, sometimes vitriolic passion. Why is that so?"

George was the nosey one, and didn't like it when others turned the tables on him. "I'm a passionate man. I feel strongly about things. Isn't that right Johnny?"

"It certainly is George. You're a very passionate man. As is Toby."

"Leave Toby out of this."

"Sorry."

"Who's Toby?" asked Clarence.

George glared back. "None of your business," he snapped. But he could not resist the chance to boast. "My friend. My boyfriend."

"Your boyfriend?"

"Yes my boyfriend. Why is that a problem?"

"No. No problem. Is it a sexual relationship?"

"Well what do you think?"

"I assume yes."

George clapped again. "Well done again."

"Do you enjoy it? Despite the biological irregularity? The mismatch of body parts?"

George turned bright red, flaming red. He sprang up suddenly, almost jack-knifing and overturning his chair in the process. He trembled violently, barely containing himself.

"You seem to be very emotionally charged right now," noted Clarence.

"Do I. Do I indeed."

"Is there anything you don't feel strongly about?"

"I'm sorry Johnny but I've had just about enough of this for one night. Possibly for ever."

"I'm sorry George. Clarence apologize. Apologize now."

"Sorry I don't understand. Apologize for what?"

"You're rudeness. You can't just talk to people like that."

Clarence stood up and took a step towards George. It was meant as an act of reconciliation. George took one step back and held up his hands to ward of attack.

"I do apologize. I didn't realise I was being rude. I was just trying to get an answer to a question."

"Well you were and I've had enough. I'm sorry Johnny, I'm tired and I have to go."

"Very well. I'll see you out."

"Can I come on the protest match?"

George did a double take with his double chin. "What?"

"I'd like to join you. Saturday you said?"

George was suspicious. "Why do you want to come now?"

"I want to see a mass of people protest, vent their anger. Crowd behaviour fascinates me."

"You want to see a load of people vent their anger? Johnny what the hell is he on about?"

"Don't ask me I don't know. I'm tired. I think you should both go. Please. It's been a long day."

The strength of feeling in John's voice left no room for doubt, and George and Clarence moved promptly towards the front door, George keeping his distance at all times.

Clarence still sought an answer. "And can I come?"

George left it to John to answer.

"Yes you can come. Just behave yourself. Now please, both of you, go. I've got a headache coming on."

Outside Clarence tried to shake George's hand and say goodbye, and wish him well. But George wasn't having any of it, and made off in a flash as if he had a train to catch, shouting goodbye to John over his shoulder. He had no train to catch, only a bus or taxi. Clarence said goodbye to John instead and shook his hand, to death. John shook it back, just as vigorously, glad to be rid of him. One last thing caught his mind as Clarence peeled off.

"Remember what I told you!"

"About what?"

"Call my friend. Go and see him. I beg you."

"I will. I promise I will."

And still John did not believe him. He went back inside and put his cup of tea back in the microwave. When it was hot again he took a sip. It tasted rank.

✦ ✦ ✦

Clarence sat on his bed, near naked, and continued to drink beer, like it was going out of fashion. He thought of Fiona, then Mary, then fleetingly Sam – unsure if there, there was anything really wrong - then that Rebecca, then that bloody cat. Then he started from the top again and finally settled on Mary. Mary he could do something about. With Mary he knew what his problem was: too much over-familiarization; too much socialising. Just cut her off without cutting her up: just one swing of the sword.

He thought about what he would say, and how to say it. Come straight to the point. Be unemotional. Be polite but be firm.

Bollocks, he thought. I'm thinking total bollocks. She would start crying and he would feel like shit and that son of hers would curse him for the rest of his life, perhaps even beat him up when he turned eighteen. No play it gentle. Be humble. Be considerate. Be . . . be something nice.

Bollocks he didn't know how to do that either. Just tell her he was not worthy of her. Tell her he was an arsehole and leave it at that.

Still extremely frustrated Clarence drifted off to sleep, aided by beer; expecting to have a bad dream, and almost looking forward to it. Unexpectedly he had a very good one. It was in sharp focus, and precise. It took him by surprise.

He found himself making love to Tracey for the first time again, and then Fiona, and then again Tracey – again for the first time. It wore him out. Next he was back at school: and this time a teenage rebel. It was sports day and he was doing the one hundred yards dash, and he was out in front, miles out in front: so far out in front that he could not see or hear any other runners. He was playing conkers, and winning. He was invincible. He was running for the number 159 bus. He was late but he didn't care. He caught it: jumping on and then holding on by wrapping himself around the white plastic pole. And he avoided paying for a penny by looking cool. He was invisible. And still all the sixth form girls were looking at him, with respect, grand respect. And they all wanted to be shagged by him.

It was snowing, heavily. There was a snowman, grinning, with a stupid carrot for a nose. He kicked it over. Margaret had made it. He was storming his way through a field of wild flowers, falling over and picking himself up again without a care in the world. Margaret he noticed was in front of him and skipping just like a girl. He tried to catch her up to push her over but despite his far greater speed – he stormed like a bloke whereas she skipped like a girl – he could never quite catch her up. The sky was brilliant blue and the sun was honey roast – and now Margaret was not yet born. There was a heavenly choir of angels floating above his head. They were singing an old Police single, Walking on The Moon. He was eating an enormous triple-decker beef burger. Next he was spitting it out. He was drowning in a vat of beer. Next he was throwing up.

He woke up. He felt sick. He went to the bathroom and tried to throw up. But he wasn't so sick. He crawled back into bed. He fell fast asleep. There were no more dreams.

Chapter Eleven

Log Entry

I accepted an invitation to dine with a female who lives close by and who is the owner of the cat. She is known to my host. Her desire to take him under her stewardship was evident. She has a mothering instinct amplified by a lack of children.

My presence in her home provoked much physical and nervous energy. The female was desperate to please and gave me her full and undivided attention whenever possible: cat or cooking being the only distractions. She talked incessantly at the cat, and to it; even though it never did, and never can talk back. Despite this apparent lack of communication they display a strong bond of companionship and understanding. The cat-human relationship is quite unique on this planet, and subtly different from the dog-human relationship, its nearest competitor for the attentions of humans. It is as if cats are regarded as equals, and dogs just acquaintances, the two being thrown together with common cause.

During cooking duties (the subject of food acquisition and preparation being close to her heart) she turned to her cat for advice, clarification and even permission to act. The cat never provided any of these, yet she was satisfied.

Her face was decorated with coloured substances, designed to highlight key features, namely mouth and eyes. Perhaps it was to impress. She flaunted her sexuality with a dress code which revealed more than it concealed. Yet never once did she make sexual overtures or invite such behaviour. The slightest hint of intimacy appeared to trigger a state nervous withdrawal, short-lived but nevertheless intense.

The constant attention I gave her cat – in return for that which it gave me - while waiting for the food to be served impressed her no end. It conveyed emotional warmth and sensitivity: in her mind prized assets. This took great effort on my part as I had to contain my host's deeply held aversion towards cats, and this cat in particular. I had to suppress fierce, reactionary tendencies: to run home, or kick it; or kick it and run home.

Her cooked food included no dead animals. It was all vegetables: cooked in interesting, complicated ways; and presented with a degree of flamboyance. She had gone to great effort to make a lasting impression.

And compared with my host's cooking abilities, it was far superior. I told her so and this went down very well.

From the first moment I could tell that the female was eager to please, and to be taken seriously; yet at the same time in denial of this – a lack of confidence combined with confusion on her part. It left her in a perpetual state of tension. She only really relaxed once she delivered the meal to the table and began to drink alcohol. In the course of the evening she consumed a large quantity of the drug and it went to her head, there to excite and cause trouble.

Conversation was difficult as it was mainly one-way: I quickly realised that I was there to listen. She has a compulsion to share and prescribe her deeply held beliefs and fixations – her condemnation of human behaviour towards this planet being chief among them. She fears for the state of the planet, and the declining spiritual strength and integrity of humanity as a whole; as if her own immediate well-being and future prosperity – I suspect spiritual rather than materialistic – is at risk. The fact that I listened and absorbed, without interruption or disagreement, fuelled her enthusiasm for my company. My lack of a sexual motivation in my pursuit of friendship added to her pleasure and the opportunity for bonding. I got the impression that I had broken a long episode of isolation, possibly self-imposed.

The actions of her fellow human beings, with regard to the environment in particular, makes her angry; and the 'demise of the spiritual age' (her words) she treats as a personal attack. She talked at length about the subject. 'We are driven by the most base instincts, to get and gain at any cost. We're dumbing down. It's like a return to the dark ages.' (Her words.) Its restoration is a personal crusade. She refuses to succumb to the materialism of the modern age. That said, her main living room was packed full of objects and artefacts, most of them highly decorated and most of them redundant in the functional sense.

The female asked me if I attended church service, regularly or otherwise. I replied that I had no recollections, recent or otherwise: it was possible but as I could not recall any occurrences it was improbable. This answer, though met with puzzlement, satisfied in the sense that it answered the question, but dissatisfied in that it was not the preferred one. She urged me to join her at her 'Church'. A Church in its fullest sense is an organisation of people sharing a common belief and agenda, centrally administered and directed. I promised to take it under consideration. She made me swear an oath. I advised that as I (i.e. my host) did not believe in anything any oath would be worthless. Still she demanded I swear an oath.

She asked me what I felt in my heart. I described in detail that it was that of an isolated individual languishing in a routine which had no end in sight, no resolution; no agenda, no purpose, no design; no commitment and no prosperity other than financial. The word 'isolated' triggered a strong emotional outburst and empathy with the plight of my host. It brought tears to her eyes. She hugged her pet closely, so closely that it cried out in pain until she relaxed her grip. Even then it was not satisfied and leapt away to recover in private. I may have over stated the gravity of his situation. And I believe my residence may be making things worse.

Intrigued I persuaded her, through keen interest and coercion, to reveal more of her life; in depth, and with regard to the past which had shaped her into what she is now: isolated and possibly self-contained, but embittered by the actions of total strangers. Unlike the man John she does not appear to have a correct perspective on the issues current in her society.

With excess alcohol having a strong influence, encouraging her to open up and reveal inner truths, she admitted that she was lonely and suffered bouts of depression – a mental state in which the human brain's ability to function at speed and react to external stimuli is severely reduced, so weakening the entire conscious state and hence general well-being. Isolation she admitted was a state of being she knew well, having suffered bullying at school for her refusal to 'be part of the gang' (her words) and always arguing with the group consensus.

Bullying is an activity performed by two or more people upon one other single individual, or less frequently a number smaller than their own; often with the intent of enforcing certain behaviour or loyalties by the use of physical violence, or the threat of it. Sometimes there is no intent: it is simply performed for the challenge and pleasure of subjugating others. This in itself is understandable considering the evolutionary history of the species. It has always been very competitive and very unforgiving, hence the divergence of prosperity and influence across the planet. This activity starts very early in life and only tails off somewhere around the mid to late life period, when the incentives for bullying fail to materialize. Bullying which continues into later life tends to be subtle, sophisticated and less obvious to third parties: the activities of politics, sports and business management being prime arenas for such behaviour. Even then it causes no long-lasting emotional damage, only immediate pain and gain.

Like John's friend George, the female holds a passion for protesting and questioning. Unlike George she seems to keep it all bottled up, bringing it out only on special occasions such as when she has a guest (like me) who is willing to witness her outbursts. Then and there I decided to invite her along to the Saturday protest rally. She accepted at once, and subjected me to an extended emotional outburst.

She tried to kiss my host on the cheek, but I did not allow it: it would have been unfair to my host, considering the other complications and commitments in his life, to allow such intimacy to progress. She found this rejection bizarre but accepted my explanation that it was too soon for such intimate contact, and respected it. It increased our sense of bonding, and in her I suspect a sense of brooding.

The female holds a deep fascination with the local star systems. She believes, absolutely, that these distant objects define human nature and hence influence human activity for the entire lifespan, from birth through to death – their paths across the sky being the driving factor. She believes this as an undeniable truth, despite the lack of a proven mechanism for cause and affect; or any hard evidence of any kind. The moon is held in similar regard. This I can accept as having some element of truth; more so in the distant, pre-scientific past when superstition and ignorance of the physical world ruled supreme. The sight of a large alien body in the night sky could well have influenced immediate behaviour and decision making on a regular basis. But like the stars it could not have materially altered actual mental architecture and processes. My muted responses fuelled her determination to express herself. I did not argue with anything she had to say but neither did I endorse. This spurred her on.

She is adamant, despite my insistence to the contrary, that aliens have landed in transportation craft, many times; and continue to do so. I agreed that aliens must exist but denied their haphazard interference in the affairs of humans at any level of interaction: local, national, or international. She claims to be able to point to evidence of landing sites and has promised to show me one such site. It is located deep in the countryside, some distance away, and can only be reached by motorised transport. She promises me it will be worth the effort. Perhaps the quarantine has been lifted.

At one point in proceedings, late into the evening and at a point when her energy and focus for socializing were beginning to weaken, she begged knowledge of my host's birthday, and birthplace. At first I presumed that this was fact gathering in relation to the possibilities of reproduction, perhaps combined with a formal partnership of some kind. It was in fact to exercise the subject of star sign theory and character definition.

She told me, with total conviction and a sense of satisfaction, that yet again she had been proved right: that 'I was a typical Pisces'. She stated that my host was a dreamy romantic and affectionate – his secret – with her cat being a prime example of male emotion hidden away, and only brought out when it was thought no one was watching. I decided best not to tell her that he hated cats, both in principle and in practice.

She asked if he was an 'honest character'. I did some research, deep into his large store of memories (some still there despite attempts to discard them) and struggled to reach a sound, secure conclusion. There were many memories – held against his will because they were linked to guilt, the guilt of dishonesty – but the circumstances were minor and limited; short-lived, trivial even. And they were not the result of intended dishonesty or deception.

There were a few significant cases which could be classified as major, and which were intentional acts of dishonesty. However only one of these had caused immediate real damage and had any lasting significance.

In the final analysis I decided: yes he was, on balance, honest; and told her so. This greatly pleased her, especially as it was delivered with significant delay and obvious intensity of thought. This woman appeared to be both emotionally and sexually attracted towards males who thought a lot.

Finally she asked him if he exaggerated. I thought and searched hard, and on balance decided: no. Only under certain conditions of self-protection and survival did he succumb to that action. However as that condition is universal throughout the species – especially within the males – that is proof of nothing. She was very satisfied, and we parted company on strong, friendly terms. She was downhearted that I did not attempt a kiss on her set of lips with my host's equivalent set.

✦ ✦ ✦

Day after day the homework stared up from the page, and bit. Today was like no other in that respect. It dominated and demanded his cooperation, grudging or otherwise. It was a tug of war, a battle for resolution. He nearly always gave it. It was the way things were, and always had been. It was always questions, stupid questions and stupid pictures; and they had to be answered. It was always, annoyingly, a reminder of the classroom, and its rules. It could not be ignored or thrown into the bin liner. It could not be set on fire or buried in the ground. But it could not be finished, so William stared at it until his head hurt, and still it did not go away. He had even switched off the telly but it made no material difference. It remained off because he was too lazy to switch it back on. A feeling came. He played with himself, and it went away. It would come back.

The doorbell sounded. That would be mum, late. He waited for the door to open and for her to appear, asking questions and checking the scene out. It didn't. She didn't. He frowned. He stood up - with a fresh grievance else one reconstituted – and stared ahead. The front door would have to be opened. The doorbell rang again. It sounded heavy. Cautiously he moved towards it, all while his suspicions mounting and his wish to not to have to open it gaining strength. There was a refusal in the air but he had to open it. It was the rules.

It was that man Clarence standing outside. The man was back again. He just wouldn't go away. He looked out of place, like a new boy in the playground. He looked down but didn't speak. Perhaps he was unable to speak. A strange thing for an adult to be unable to do: speak. As adults went he looked a sorry sight and for the first time William felt his equal. Furthermore he sensed that he had the upper hand. He played it.

"What do you want?" The words erupted like machine gun fire but Clarence took it on the chin.

"I popped round to see your mother. She's expecting me. Is she in?"

"Is she in?" echoed William.

"Is she in?" repeated Clarence for clarification.

"No," stated William.

"No?" asked Clarence.

"No," repeated William again, for clarification.

Clarence was thrown: his route was blocked; his journey had stalled. It was possibly cancelled before it had even started. William waited for him to say the next something. It seemed to take an age: William wanted to shut the door in the man's face. When Clarence finally did speak it was to ask the next obvious, logical question.

"Any idea when she'll be back?"

William thought of the time. He still had it inside his head. "Should have been now."

"Can I wait?"

"Sure." It seemed a silly question. The answer would always be 'sure' thought William.

Clarence rocked on the heels of his feet, nervous, tense; like a pop star killing time at the side of the stage or a gardener displaying his best vegetable. When he finally spoke it was as if against his will.

"Can I come in? Can I wait inside?"

William deliberated. He had the power to choose. He had a request. He was in charge. He played for time just to see the reaction. It would be fun. The man Clarence was well narked.

"Well can I?"

William gave way. "I suppose so."

He stood back and monitored the man as he entered. Every step was logged. Every movement was measured and noted, as if the man had the capacity to cause trouble or take power.

With excess nervous energy Clarence looked around for some corner of the room into which to deposit himself, preferably with his back to the wall. He spotted a chair in a suitable place and adopted it, claiming it as his own.

William watched him. Had he been his mother, or anybody else for that matter, the man would have asked for permission to sit – and waited until it was given. Instead he had taken the liberty. William closed the door, returned to the table, sat down and stared into the page. It had not changed. He picked up his pen, as if to demonstrate that he really took the whole subject – and the whole subject of homework – seriously. He knew the man Clarence was watching him. Vectors. It was a puzzle which involved vectors.

Clarence said nothing. He knew kids of William's age too well. Best keep away, at arm's length, head down. At this point in time he was not teacher, he was just another ordinary human being.

He looked around the room. It vaguely reminded him of something: he didn't know what. He tried, in vain, to conjure up something inside his head to say: something nice and quick and simple to express. But it kept unravelling, like a football match, before he could store it away for safe keeping. He managed to construct an open but never made it to the middle. It got lost and he got nowhere.

He took a chance and looked across at the teenager. The boy had his head down. He was deep in concentration. His hands were moving. They were folding paper. Then his head rose, and with it his hands. They were holding a paper aeroplane, or rather an imitation of a good paper aeroplane.

The boy threw it, with attitude. It crashed and sank without trace, somewhere in the vicinity of Clarence. There were no passengers. There were no survivors. There was no blame. There were no insurance payouts. There was no enquiry. Clarence leaned over and picked it up. He scrutinized it. It was overloaded at the front and the wings were too small in relation to the main fuselage. And one wing had a crease in it. It was shoddy work.

Clarence threw it back, just to confirm that he was right. It failed again. It could never fly. William slipped out of his chair and picked it up, saying nothing.

"The wings are too small," declared Clarence as William recovered his place behind the table. He spoke with an intended air of authority.

William had no idea what the man in his mum's room was talking about. It was just another paper aeroplane.

Clarence stood up, goaded on by the lack of response. "Here let me show you."

William looked up as Clarence approached the table. Concerned, he clung on to his pen and book, drawing them in close, as if they were prized assets to be protected. He did not like the book but it was his and nobody else's.

Clarence pointed to the spare pad of A4. "Can I take a piece?"

William didn't care. "Sure."

With a fresh, undisturbed and unfolded piece of paper Clarence began to build his perfect paper aeroplane. He thought he had an interested audience but he didn't. William looked away whenever possible, just to make the point that he was not the least bit interested. But there was no escaping the man. Clarence did not care either way. The challenge of making a paper aeroplane which could really fly had grabbed his full attention – and thankfully it filled the barren wasteland of under-utilised time.

It had been a very long time since he had last made a paper aeroplane. He had probably done one in the classroom while the pupils were heads down, all groaning inside, like him. He could not remember. Whatever: he found it all very easy to do. It came naturally. It made sense. It added up.

Great big wings he gave it, and little in the way of body. He folded down the edge of the wings, giving them fins with which to further trap the swell of whatever it was that pushed it up and along. He flew it. It flew, like the wind. It found the wind. It created its own wind. It flew around and around in a big circle, going nowhere but with cause. The big circle got smaller, by degrees, until a random current threw it off in a totally new direction and it slammed into the back of a chair.

In a few seconds Clarence went from looking aggrieved – as if he had suffered some massive, tragic loss – to looking satisfied: job done; point made; honour intact; ego lifted. He stood proud.

"That's how it's done."

"Is it?"

Clarence looked into the face of the boy William but William pretended not to be seen.

"Did you see?"

"No."

"Do you want me to do it again?"

"No."

Clarence woke up and immediately took the point. He decided to make the effort to remain completely detached. But he was still a teacher and he could not ignore homework.

"How's the homework?"

"Alright."

"Easy?"

"No."

"Hard?"

"No."

"Fair enough."

Clarence sat back down. He knew when he was not wanted, and when not to tangle with teenagers. They were out to get you, like no other creature on Earth. They were like no other creatures on Earth. But he could not deny the fact that he had once been one.

William suddenly spoke. "What did you do in London?"

"What d'you mean?"

"Your day out with my mum. What did you do?"

Clarence grew alarmed. He wanted to stand up but felt strapped to the chair. The boy was placing electrodes on him; and he looked like the kind of guy who would have no compunction about switching on something evil to wreak him.

"You just said it. We went to London."

William looked on, scornful. Inside he was looking for a fight. He was not satisfied by the answer. The man was taking the piss.

"All day?"

"Yes all day."

"Mum said you went to see art stuff in a gallery."

Ah that explains it, thought Clarence. Bloody oil paintings in my head, all that traipsing around, swollen ankles.

No reply but William pushed on. He refused to be beaten into submission by silence from this man. "Which gallery? A famous one?"

Clarence searched the wallpaper, looking for inspiration in the pattern. There was none: just the same pattern, repeating itself. But then that was what patterns did, most of the time.

"I can't quite remember."

Clarence suddenly grabbed the makings of a better answer from a response his father had once given under similar hard questioning. It had usefully stuck in his mind ever since. William stared back, aggrieved, demanding something much better. Clarence was not intimidated. He could take on a crowd of these any day.

Clarence spoke when he had it. "I can't quite remember because I'm getting on a bit these days. Slowing down. Head can't always trap the detail."

Clarence laughed inside. It was a great piece of face-saving bullshit. Then he was slightly scared. He had just sounded like his father.

Clarence faked it further. "It was that big new one."

William sniffed the air for bad smells. "What did you do afterwards?"

"Afterwards?"

Clarence thought hard. Think of something obvious, safe, normal; and hope it never comes up in conversation again. He looked at William looking at him and he smelt trouble. The boy was looking for something: a mistake; a contradiction; deception possibly. Then he reminded himself that it didn't matter. He was cutting loose and about to go on his merry way - or at least his troubled way.

"Usual thing. Food and drink. A coffee. A train home."

A train home: Clarence was sure about that. Even the food rang a vague bell.

"What did you talk about?"

"Talk about?"

"Did you talk about me?"

"No. Definitely not."

William hesitated. He wanted to shout 'why not?'.

Clarence saw his chance. "We talked about art, pictures. Boring stuff. Nothing that would have interested you."

William relaxed a little. That made sense. But still he didn't trust the man. Clarence in turn relaxed a lot. He had beaten the teenager back down and was still in one piece. He thought again about what he was going to say, but he was none the wiser. He was groping in the dark. He could not string coherent words together. So he gave that up and concentrated on trying to remain relaxed, at peace. That in itself was a colossal challenge as it never came to him these days.

William continued to watch him, looking up occasionally while hugging his homework and doing nothing about it. Clarence continued to look William back down when he was staring at him too much. Somehow the two of them managed to maintain a balance and air of accommodation despite a total lack of understanding or empathy, and with no game plan. They occupied the same restricted space like two king lions at the waterhole: each refusing to leave; neither willing to give ground; neither wishing to be there; each thirsty for life.

There was a noise at the door. A key rattled and turned in a lock. William jumped up, excited and equally rattled, almost crazy with anticipation. Clarence stood up and began to sweat.

Mary dutifully dragged herself into the room clutching tightly the shopping bags which weighed her down. Both William and Clarence – suddenly both men - locked in on the bags. Like wolves in competition they scented a kill, a prize. They both went for the bags. Mary was not surprised to see her son. She was surprised to see Clarence. Then just as suddenly the surprise evaporated: she remembered that she was late and he was expected.

Mary felt something wicked stir between her legs. Something she had not felt in a long time. Her sexual urge had returned with a vengeance and it demanded compensation if not action. She didn't know whether to celebrate, cry or cringe. She threw it off and it ended up on the back burner. She had tea to make, and quick. The issues of food and cups of tea were far more important.

William got to the bags first and pinched one. That left one. Clarence, the timid one, offered to take it out of her hand, and put it where directed. In the kitchen he presumed. William was already in there.

He reached out. "Can I help you with that?"

"Thank you." Mary handed it over, glad to be shot of it, relief dripping from her aching arm. "Sorry I'm late. I meant to be back a good hour ago."

"No problem. I haven't been here that long."

"Did William make you a drink?"

"No." As he spoke Clarence felt like an informer.

"I'll make a cup of tea." Mary spoke with comfort, regard and efficiency; all typical of a hardworking mother. As a hardworking mother she knew of no other way.

"Thanks." Clarence spoke with minimum fuss and bother.

"Do you like muffins?"

"Muffins?" Clarence thought about the word. "They're like buns but bread?" He thought a little bit more. "No. More like flat rolls?"

Mary smiled. "That's right." She turned towards the kitchen. "William can you put the kettle on!"

She looked back down at the plastic bag. Clarence had the handles wrapped around his wrist as if his life depended on it. "Can I take that?"

Clarence also looked down at the bag. He didn't like plastic shopping bags. They reminded him of supermarkets and having to go out shopping.

"Yes, thanks," he replied, and handed it over, glad to let it go.

"Look sit down and I'll bring some tea and muffins out. Jam? Marmalade? Marmite?"

Marmite sounded like the correct choice so Clarence choose that. "Marmite please."

Satisfied, Mary followed her son into her kitchen which sat in her house and together they unpacked the groceries, and put them away in their allotted places.

Clarence sat back down and tried not to eavesdrop, tried not to get involved. He wanted to say something – he had something to say – and he wanted to get out.

There were noises: the sound of complaining being foremost. Clarence vaguely picked up some remark relating to cereal and the wrong type, then something in a similar vein about the yoghurts: flavours and size. He looked around the room again. He knew the wallpaper off by heart now. And the carpet was nice, if carpets were your thing, he thought to himself with brutal comedy. One third kept telling him to leave – ordering him almost. One third told him he had to stay and see it through. The remaining third was standing back, smoking a cigarette, and wondering what exactly to say and how to say it; and whether this was still a good time to say it, and whether there was any good time to say it.

Clarence heard more excited conversation. The boy was excited, and the mother was driven to loud replies, rebukes even. There was the sound of crashing cutlery and a whistle blowing. Mary popped her head around the door and asked in a cheerful voice if he took sugar. She apologized for not remembering. Clarence bolted upright and answered the question like a rabbit caught in headlights or a boy caught on the hop, despite having done nothing to be ashamed of. In time she returned with a tray of tea and toasted muffins; her son in tow, watching the lie of the land and looking put out, insulted by the situation.

Dutifully Mary served it out. William grabbed for a supply of muffins, one for each hand, but she did not stop him or pass comment. Clarence likewise grabbed for a muffin. He was starving.

Mary had to apologize again. "I didn't mean to be this late. Office hold-ups and then I remembered I had to do an emergency shop run."

"Honest it's no problem." Clarence reached out to layer his muffin with jam, forgetting that he had requested marmite. No one touched the marmite.

Settled down Mary sat back, looking exhausted but determined to reenergize herself and be the proper host. She sipped her tea and watched Clarence as he struggled to coordinate cup and saucer around each other. On balance he was a mug man. Her son watched them both, saying nothing and having nothing to say – or at least nothing to say in public or to a parent.

Clarence felt her gaze slipping on and off him, like a lighthouse beacon. His intentions were nowhere to be seen or heard. His speech had simplified back to the basics and was in danger of collapsing into gibberish. He decided the best thing to do was to keep his mouth firmly shut.

Mary spoke on, just enough to keep things ticking over nicely. She was tired and her conversation did not come easily. "We were lucky with the weather."

"Yes I guess we were." Weather, thought Clarence. The bloody weather.

"It's nice to get a big thrill in life out of the little things, the simple things."

"Definitely."

Clarence cringed as he heard himself speak. The wooden reply irked enormously. He was usually above sort language. Worse still her son was counting his every word under his breath, weighing them perhaps for 'coolness'.

Mary treated herself to a muffin, while they were still hot, and turned on her son. Hard work ahead, but necessary. She spoke. He chewed on. Clarence tried not to watch them both as an item, as a display; but he failed. That aside he felt outnumbered.

"How was school today?"

William's face screwed up. Clarence had also heard it a thousand times before. Graciously William summoned up the same answer, and the strength to give it.

"Same as usual."

"Anything new? Interesting?"

William looked at his mother as if to say 'of course, goes without saying'. He said some of it. "Of course."

Then he retreated halfway into his shell, not liking the way that man Clarence was looking at him: too close for comfort.

Softly, with the patience and precision of a hospital consultant patrolling a private ward, Mary began to probe. "Like what?"

"I don't know."

"Mathematics?"

Irritated, William tried to shake his mother off. "I don't know. Probably."

Instinctively Clarence wanted to cut in and make a contribution. He managed to maintain his silence and impartiality. William made for his next muffin, desperate to be allowed to switch off, or better still switch onto something worth switching onto: something fast, loud, colourful, complicated. Not long after Clarence would follow him in a similar vein.

"Did you put the dirty kit in the washing machine?"

"Yes." William almost screamed, and the one word was spat out like a splinter of glass or a piece of rotten fruit.

Mary relaxed while Clarence continued in the opposite direction. She had one last question. "How many biscuits have you had tonight?"

William guessed, completely. "Two."

She got up and went into the kitchen, returning with a colourful, old-fashioned biscuit tin. It had belonged to her father. In unison Clarence and William watched her prize it open: William with a sense of reality distorted and in denial; Clarence with a sense of deja vu. His mother had always had a hang-up about too many biscuits he could now recall.

Mary inspected its contents. She was counting. Clarence held his breath. William began to visualize far away places and switching on his PC and beating the living daylights out of the opposition, probably a nerd.

Mary was not pleased. "Are you sure only two?"

William nearly choked on his latest muffin. He fought with himself to get out an answer and push her over with it. But deep down he knew it was not to be. It was always like this and always would be, day in, day out. Clarence meanwhile began to feel serious discomfort. But he could not leave. Like the boy with the biscuits he was stuck.

William began to count them. "Perhaps four then."

Mary closed the tin and suddenly looked worn out. "You know you'll only spoil your dinner. I keep telling you."

"I know." He didn't.

Clarence felt some old, familiar tension in the air and groaned inside. He wanted to be back home, in front of his telly, with a can, and preferably back to normal. If there was tension in the air mother and son were immune to it now: that's not to say accidents could happen. The fleeting glimpse of something unusual, out of place on her son, suddenly made Mary sit up and stiffen; alarm bells ringing; heart thumping; head leaping ahead towards new concerns.

"What's that?"

"What's what?"

"That green mark on your arm."

"It's a bruise," said Clarence, feeling a contribution – of any kind – was overdue.

"A bruise!" exclaimed Mary, a pitch up the scale. "How did you get a bruise William?"

William wriggled around within; becoming angry that he had been spotted, and that he was outnumbered. He did not give an answer.

"How did you get it William?" Her voice rang out sharp and focused. Even Clarence was put on alert.

William knew he was in trouble: she was using his name. He felt the last few years he had built up fall away. He kept trying to push away the truth, dissolve it. He tried to invent an alternative reality. He failed. The pictures and noise would not go away.

"William answer me."

The reply was docile when it came. "Nothing. I hit a desk."

Mary knew her son was lying. Even Clarence knew it. She stalled, realising she had a guest present, a very special guest, she choked on her next words. "You hit a desk."

William held his breath. Perhaps she, it and him would all go away and leave him alone, and with his spare time.

"That's what I said," said William tersely.

The words were blurted out. He was daring her to call him a liar. The rudeness in the voice even stung Clarence. And such a nice lady. Clarence felt another small contribution at this point was justified, necessary even; and its timing perfect.

"Probably just a little hassle with the competition. Fights break out all the time. They only last seconds." Words spoken, Clarence leaned back in his chair, suddenly feeling wasted but relaxed. He had actually said something worthwhile.

"That's right," said William. "It just happened over mid-morning break. The guy is an arse-hole. Thinks he knows everything when he just gets it off Google."

"See," said Clarence.

William gave him the shortest of glances, unwilling to recognise the word of support. The man Clarence was sticking his face into his business.

Mary was not pleased with the language used. "Don't call someone that. I've told you before."

William twisted and growled. Clarence saw he was looking for a fight and almost offered to give him one, to break him. Mary was feeling very tired.

"Look take your homework to your room and finish it off. I'll get food going. We can look at it later."

Relieved that he had been relieved, William squashed the remainder of his muffin into his mouth and swaggered off, pretending not to have a care in the world. His mother watched him go and tried to take notes. Clarence watched him go and hoped that that was the last of it; that that was the last he would see of him. He didn't particularly dislike the boy – he had seen them all before – it was just that he didn't need the hassle.

Mary shouted after William as he slammed shut his bedroom door. "And keep the noise down! We have a guest!"

Then she turned back on her guest. "I'm sorry I must get dinner going before it's too late."

Clarence held up his hands. "Don't mind me. I don't want to get in the way."

"Would you like to join us?"

Clarence made an immediate, unexpected decision. "Yes thanks."

With that Mary got on with the routine of a weekday evening meal. Even as she was making the offer she had planned it all out in her head. It involved cod in breadcrumbs. Clarence watched, impressed but nervously exposed as the lady raced around the kitchen and began to throw together the elements of a wholesome meal.

Mary, naturally shy but less so with this man, began to bottle up her frustration as nothing was said. The man just watched. The man who had expressly asked to drop by – and with urgency in his voice – now had nothing to say. She reached bursting, and had to let it out. She stopped in mid-flight.

"Was there something important you wanted to say?"

Clarence fell back, even though his feet did not actually move. Don't talk about football, he told himself. Don't talk about football scores or the weather. With that in mind he frantically searched for something to say while the woman kept looking at him, much like her son. Judging him she was, taking notes. This behaviour unnerved him even more and made it impossible for him to think, plan or execute any kind of message, announcement or tailored outburst. He had seen something good on TV but could not remember what it was. He fell back on the Simpsons. They were always good.

"Did you see the Simpsons?" he asked, with a limp wrist in his throat.

Mary looked puzzled. "Is that the cartoon thing?"

"That's right."

Mary came across flat. "No. My son watches it. Can't get enough of it. I've caught it a few times, in bits, but 'just don't get it' as my son keeps reminding me."

Now Clarence was really stuck. Then he remembered the really impressive programme. "Did you see the documentary about the rainforest? Amazing. All those trees, animals."

Clarence held himself in check, not wishing to use up what little ammunition he had left to defend himself with.

Mary looked blank and was apologetic again. "Sorry. I'm just so busy I don't have time for television these days."

To avoid the actual purpose of his visit Clarence tried one last thing.

"I watched a good cookery programme last night. Was quite surprised how easy it is to knock something good together." He made the point of sounding upbeat.

His innocence again revealed, Mary again smiled, conscious that tonight she was falling back on cod, mash and peas. From her there was a flicker of the connection again. Clarence just grinned like he was stupid, and held in there, all the while begging more and more to be allowed to go home. He wanted to watch some football or dirty late night TV.

Meanwhile for Mary, the thought of poor dear Clarence having come all this way and not being able to express himself - even in the most basic language – began to chew into her and hurt. She stopped everything she was doing and turned into him. She put softly a very direct, uncompromising statement.

"Look I think there's something you want to tell me. I'm a grown woman. I'm raising a child. I can handle it."

Clarence felt himself melting under her gaze. He was dissolving. Bits were falling off – important bits. His brain began to all choke up and he found it impossible to think or find words of any kind with which to negotiate his way out of an awkward piece of theatre. But finally he spoke, driven on by the simple need to state some kind of position, true or otherwise, accurate or otherwise.

"Look I'm not a nice guy."

He felt tears swelling. His eyes were beginning to fill with water and they scared him towards submission. But not quite. Ignore them, he decided. Ignore them. Perhaps they will go away.

Mary frowned, but was not taken aback, and did not feel the need to retreat in any way. She had come too far. Time to listen she told herself, reminding herself that this was not William as William blew up inside her brain demanding full attention.

"I'm a slob," confessed Clarence.

"I'm a slob sometimes," Mary added.

Clarence didn't like the reply. It was confusing things.

"I can't stand teaching." He nearly bit his lip, not knowing why he had let that cat out of the bag. It was probably because it was the only thing he had left in the bag which was not confusion or conjecture.

Mary turned his words over and over, getting use to their noise, engaging a reaction worthy of her high principles.

With the silence he received Clarence grew seriously scared. He shivered and almost began to shake. He retreated back to the chair he had adopted earlier and fell into it: too weak at the knees he was to stand it anymore.

Mary trailed him and stood over him.

"Did you like teaching once?" she asked.

Clarence looked up at her, overwhelmed by her question. To give her an honest answer was the right thing to do, and he was determined to do it. "Yes I think so. Yes I did."

"Well that's not so bad then," she said; and walked back into the kitchen, her first place of worship.

Clarence watched her go. He wanted to go with her but could not bring himself to raise himself out of the chair, weak at the knees or not. So he just sat there, wanting to yell or switch the TV on - a bit like William - until a part of his body demanded that he rush to the bathroom.

"Can I use the bathroom?" he shouted.

"Certainly. You don't have to ask now."

Funnily enough he knew exactly where to find it.

In there he found tiling which gave him a shock. After he did his business, and remembered to wash his hands, he inspected it. It was shoddy work, and had been started in the wrong places. The tiles did not go around the wall, they collided into its corners, badly. Some did not line up well, and what grouting had been done looked amateur. Clarence left the bathroom angry.

"Are you paying someone to do this?"

Mary stumbled as she was caught off guard and almost dropped something, something worth eating. "Sorry?"

"That tiling in the bathroom. Did you pay someone I mean are you paying someone to do that?"

"Yes," replied Mary weakly, realising that she had made a mistake and an error of judgement.

Clarence, calming down as he spoke, explained the bodge. As he spoke the urge to protect, and not to be screwed by the world-at-large, blossomed and inflated him with new purpose. He felt reinvigorated, reconditioned, almost ready to explode. Women in need had always struck him to the core, especially when it had been sex they needed. He demanded to know how much she had promised to pay. When he found out he immediately – without hesitation or calculation – offered to put it right. And right away, he explained, before the damp sets in. To avoid the pain of looming embarrassment he kept on talking.

"I've got so much spare time at the moment it will stop me going mad."

Impressed by the sincerity and grandeur of the gesture Mary thanked him. She didn't try to refuse him. The money saved would be useful. Looking like a man who had just stepped off a rugby pitch, Clarence excused himself a second time and revisited the bathroom, staring again in disbelief at the botch; then into the mirror, disbelieving what he had just said.

On his way out he vowed to go immediately home: that safe place. It was all becoming too much. He was no longer able to understand himself, no longer able to be sure that what he was was who he was.

He left the woman Mary baffled but forgiving. William would have extra fish to eat this night. He would gobble it up. In no uncertain terms she told Clarence to take care and to look after himself. Clarence grunted a vague acknowledgement.

All the way home the offer of help dominated his thoughts. He could not think. He could not banish it from his head. He had just gone and complicated things. He could not change his mind. He was an honourable man, he kept telling himself. He would do the honourable thing. He would borrow any tools off Dad - when he wasn't looking if necessary.

✢ ✢ ✢

Clarence sat in a mess of his own making. He had sat in a bathroom, in a mess all afternoon and he wanted out. Tiling sucked. He had to think about tiles in a way he didn't have to think about a pot of paint. And at times he had put his head down close to the toilet bowl. Mary had made a point of cleaning it thoroughly beforehand, and telling him so, but still it felt uncomfortable. Were he drunk he could stick his head down it no problem, but he wasn't. He was stone sober. And then there was the smell of tile adhesive. It smelt of used nappies. And it went right up his nose.

Each tile demanded his full attention and planning: those things Clarence did not want to give right now. Worse still he had to wrench them off the wall and scrap them down, and not always successfully. He had a rubbish bag full of broken pieces. Worse of all he was in the bathroom in the house of a woman he had no wish to pursue a friendship with.

The task of tiling did keep him busy, that he had to admit. Yet he was sure he could find other ways to fill his time if he tried hard enough. Still he could not work it out. He turned the scene over and over inside his head until it left a blister but still it made no sense. But it was the least of his troubles, the least of his worries, so he ploughed on. He scraped off and he scraped on. He positioned and pushed. He wiped and whistled. He measured and cut. He even cut his finger, as if to spite himself.

The music which streamed out of the radio stopped him going mad. The tunes and words, and the nostalgic they invoked were something to cling to, to digest. He sat sunk in the sounds with the radio close to hand. It could have been an indoor building site.

At first the act of refitting a tile had felt like a lifetime's achievement. Then after awhile it all blurred into one long continuous slog, with those still in their packaging pushing to sit beside the others on the wall. At one point he gave up. He was desperate for a smoke but held himself back. Smoking in her bathroom would not be acceptable. So he sat back and stared out of the window at the clear blue sky and the top of a tree. He studied the tree in detail, so avoiding a return to work on the building site. And as he did so he tried to sort out his memories: old and new; blunt and sharp; those based on hard reality and those the result of pure invention; but without success. They were thrown together in one vast shambles of a melange. Keep a grip, he kept telling himself. Keep a grip. It will blow over. And keep an eye on the clock. Always watch the time. Watch it like a hawk else it will slip through your fingers and bite you on the arse when you're not looking..

And then there was Fiona: lovely adorable sexy intelligent Fiona. He had to have her as his own. They were made for each other. He knew it to be so. He felt it in his heart. And they had been great in bed. Get better. Get back to school and shag her senseless he told himself. She would enjoy it. She would thank him for it. They would fall in love, he told himself. A cloud drifting across the sky cast its shadow and dulled the room. Tiling beckoned.

There was a noise downstairs. Someone was opening the front door. Clarence looked at his watch. It had to be that son of hers. Trouble. The door slammed shut and the rest of the house felt it. Clarence threw himself back into his work, wishing now to be seen to be busy; as if afraid that he might be accused of skiving, not pulling his weight. Clarence heard the boy moving around. Doors banged open and shut. Feet stomped up the staircase and in time back down. Clarence carried on cementing, furiously, wishing not to be discovered, wishing not to be approached. He didn't need the hassle of the headache which sooner or later came with contact. But it was bound to come. He could set his watch by it.

Footsteps came back up the stairs again, slowly this time. Clarence dismissed thoughts of Anthony Perkins carrying a knife and concentrated on the music instead. It was his lifeline to sanity. There was a light knock on the door. Clarence gripped a tile as he held his breath. Finally he spoke up.

"Hallo?"

A voice croaked. "I've got a mug of tea for you."

It was William's voice and it sounded raised, raw, and almost melodramatic.

A mug of tea: Clarence was surprised. "Thanks."

"The way you like it."

The way I like it? "Thanks."

Clarence waited for the door to open. It stayed shut. He was out of bounds.

"Aren't you going to bring it in then!"

The door slowly opened as William took his time. He had to watch the mug: the tea was in danger of spilling over. It had already done so on the way up. He stepped forward and Clarence reached out to take it. They made contact and the mug passed from hand to hand, like an act of settlement.

"Mum told me to do it," declared William in no uncertain terms. He had been forced to do it and wanted to set the record straight. Clarence was not bothered either way. He could do with a mug of tea.

William stared at the bathroom walls. This was not his bathroom. His familiar sight was missing and in its place was something unpalatable. He did not look happy and his expression was not lost on Clarence. Sod you, he thought.

Then William remembered something – not important to him but important nevertheless. "Mum told me to give you a biscuit – I mean to offer you a biscuit."

"Did she. That was very nice of her," replied Clarence, lacing his words with a splash of sarcasm.

William did not taste it. He stood on his mark, awaiting instructions.

"Yes I'll have one thanks. Two or three if they're going."

William squinted, trying to calculate if the man Clarence was pulling his leg, or just trying to be funny, or just being greedy.

"They're digestives," he explained.

"That's OK. I'll survive – and can I have a plaster."

"What do you want a plaster for?"

Clarence held up his finger. "To put over this."

William conceded to the request. He switched off and withdrew, and Clarence carried on, but this time unable to soak up the music. He turned off the radio – it was drowning him in noise – and sipped his tea while waiting for some biscuits to arrive. Surprisingly it tasted spot-on. The biscuits duly arrived, all three of them, delivered by a delivery boy who looked extremely fed up with his job. With them came a small plaster which Clarence wrapped around his finger. By now the plaster was not required.

Clarence crunched on his biscuits and William watched with typical attitude. He showed no sign of leaving. Clarence wished he would. They hung around each other: Clarence not bothering to speak; William not bothering to listen; and vice-versa. They both felt tired, wasted. Neither wanted to be there but Clarence had a job to do and William was drawn to sightsee. William began to pick his nose, furiously, and was glad to see that the man Clarence did not care. He sensed that the man had been recently hassled. The man looked worn out, just like himself; weak even, a lesser force.

Biscuits devoured and radio back on, Clarence pursued his course. He had thought to tell William to clear off but considered it inappropriate. It was not his house, not his turf. William stood with his hands parked in his trouser pockets and pretended to pay attention. He had drifted off and was now miles away, almost on a different planet.

"Bear with me it will come together," said Clarence.

William said nothing. He saw Clarence cut a tile with a weird looking ruler like device and wanted to have a go. "Can I do that?"

"You can do the next one."

William waited and this time really watched, and tried to kick the school day out of his head. But the unsavoury highlights remained, and were amplified; and they made him mad. When it was his turn to cut a tile he fluffed it.

"No worries," said Clarence, trying to calm the boy. "Here let me."

"I can do it!" snapped William. He hid the cutting tool behind his back and held his ground.

"No problem," replied Clarence. Not my tiles and not my bathroom, he thought, so not my problem.

William tried again but again failed. He threw the tool down and sat looking seriously angry with something - something not in the room.

"Don't worry about it. It's no big deal."

"I'm not."

"Well something's bugging you." If I know anything, thought Clarence, I know when something's bugging.

William kept his eyes down and Clarence ceased operations.

Clarence put what for him was the obvious question. "It's not girls is it?"

William twitched. When he thought of girls they gave him strange, sharp headaches, or the wish to flirt, show off. But no, it wasn't the girls.

"It takes ages to get use to them. I've been messed around plenty of times. Still trying to work them out." On certain subjects Clarence lived in a fantasy world.

William looked up from under his eyebrows. The man was in danger of making a fool of himself.

Clarence tried another approach. If he was going to be stuck with the kid then the kid had to lighten up. "Who's going to win the league, Man United or Chelsea?"

William didn't care and said so. "I don't care."

Fair enough, thought Clarence, you miserable sod. He tuned into another FM station for something more uplifting.

William woke up. "Do you have an Ipod?"

"What?"

"Do you have an Ipod – you know, plays file downloads."

"I know what they are. And no I don't have one." Clarence found himself having to justify himself. "Never needed one."

William sank back into snug isolation. He wanted an Ipod.

As one corner of his mind hugged an ipod the rest of it was seething with a potent mix of anger, resentment, rejection and worthlessness: all ingredients freshly picked that day. It soared and swooped, and spun on its point of origin; anchored in place but still out of control, fists flying. With each fist it banged on the window, and threatened the world it could not see but knew was looking in, and passing judgement. It fended off uncomfortable images, keeping them at arm's length. But still they invaded his preferred view of the world – a world in which he was king, protected, without care or cause.

He resented others not suffering as he did. He was angry at the lack of any defence - or any device for hurting back. He rejected the accusation that he could not handle 'it', that he was a mother's boy; as he did the challenge of denouncing friends and those other things close to his heart.

He felt worthless. He felt sat on. He felt wasted. He had no dignity to flaunt. He had been picked on. He had been pulled apart. And now he wanted to fight back. He was no coward. He was no clot.

William didn't want to be different. He wanted to be the same, even if it was boring. William didn't want to be the same. He wanted to be different: just slightly different; just enough to make a point, a gesture; just enough to have his own set of rules - rules which he could alter as and when it suited. William didn't like to shout but it was the only way to make himself heard. William didn't like to kick and punch, so he didn't. And he was paying the price.

William kicked the bin in the corner of the room. In hitting the wall it was stopped from totally spilling its beans. Clarence watched some of the crap escape and avoided contact with it. William expected him to say something but Clarence was disinterested in the outburst.

"A serious grievance dominates your thoughts. It has unleashed self-destructive energies. You are bursting to right some wrong."

"What do you know?"

"I know many things but I do not presume to know you. I can only offer you reflection and advice based upon observation."

"Meaning what?"

"I do not presume to comment without full engagement and analysis of the facts."

William found himself presented with a door to kick open, and the opportunity to make a fuss. Steam needed to be released. Confidence and certainty had to be reconstructed. An aging boy had to be allowed to live as a young man.

William called his bluff. "Tell me what you know then."

"I know you are in a state of denial, and a danger to yourself."

"Danger? What danger? How am I in danger?"

"You have not come to terms with some unwanted, indigestible facts; nor loose, intense emotions which drain your strength and cripple your capacity for self-determination and proper engagement with others. They cause conflict and draw you away from the regular task of coping with situations to come: situations both immediate and in the medium term."

William was slowly becoming hypnotised, and exhausted.

"I'm not feeling good," he said.

"You're feeling under the weather?"

"I'm feeling shit."

"Why are you feeling shit? Is there something out there so disgusting it reminds you of human faeces?"

"Human what?"

"Human excrement. Shit."

William looked into the water and decided to take the plunge, since where he was was not a place he wanted to be. "School was bad today."

"In what respect? Too much work?"

"No." William leaned against the door and it clicked shut.

"Too much homework?"

"No. Nothing to do with work."

"Relationships?"

William shot back up, back straight. "What?"

"Friendships gone astray? Broken down?"

With surprising ease William thought the nasty event over in his head. No, friendships did not come into it. "No. Nothing like that."

"Were you harassed, confronted by others?"

"Yes." William had to admit it.

"Did it involve intimidation?"

"Yes I suppose so." William had to think hard about the meaning of the word 'intimidation' but he got there in the end. He was finding it easy to think coherently again.

"And physical violence?"

"No, not really."

"You were outnumbered?"

"Yes."

"Were there demands?"

"Demands?"

"Did they want something from you, or a commitment to do something, perform some act?"

"No."

"So to conclude: you were bullied for no particular reason."

"Yes I suppose so."

"And not for the first time?"

"No."

"Which angers you even more. Being picked out like this for no apparent reason?"

"Yes." On the one hand William felt bombarded by the questions. On the other it felt good to let it all out – and to a near stranger, not to his mother. She was becoming too much baggage.

"Dealing with it is no easy thing when there's no logical basis for it starting in the first place."

William fell over the words as he tried to keep up. "No."

"But then that's the nature of bullying. It's often illogical, random in its choice of target, and without end objectives. So resolution is difficult. It just goes on and on. I can see why it would wear you down."

William shook his head in frustration. "Meaning what?"

"It can happen to anybody, and does. You were just in the wrong place at the wrong time, and continue to be so. Perhaps you are considered a threat to someone?"

"A threat? How can I be a threat?"

"Perhaps you are faster, taller, better looking. Perhaps you show better coordination during sporting activities. Perhaps you are more expressive in language, more articulate; simply more intelligent."

A big grin broke out across William's face. He liked the sound of all that.

Clarence folded his arms and gazed out of the window. "Question now is what to do about it."

"Yes what to do about it," echoed William.

"Confrontation may only excite them further and lead to physical harm, especially as you are outnumbered."

"Yes I am outnumbered."

Now William felt strangely detached, as if he was talking about somebody else's problem; as if he was in the war room, doing something important, and not at the front line.

"And it is impossible to concede to their demands as they have made none." Clarence looked back at William. "They have made no demands?"

"No demands."

Clarence returned to his view out of the window. It had not changed.

"I suggest bribery."

"Bribery?"

Clarence reached into his back pocket and squeezed out his wallet. It did not want to be moved. William licked his lips: quickly and without flourish, like a cat in a hurry. Clarence produced some large banknotes, the kind which rarely passed through William's hands.

"Go tell him you'll give him so much money each day if he'll be your best friend. Over time he will find it difficult, if not impossible, to be aggressive towards you as the two of you become familiar: especially if you confide in him your concerns, fears, hopes and dreams. Reciprocate. Help him with his homework. When the money runs out he'll find it almost impossible to revert back to his old ways. There will be too much shared history between you. You may even end up as true friends. If necessary I'll give you more money to extend. Human history has shown it's difficult for societies to hate and fear each other when they get to know each other at the individual level."

William was sceptical but agreed to the plan. The sight of so much cash nearly brought tears to his eyes. It was serious money. It could not be refused. He waited for Clarence to say something more but Clarence went quiet and returned to sticking tiles on the wall.

William quickly folded the money away and out of sight, afraid Clarence might change his mind and ask for it back. Clarence did not. Like an automaton he carried on tiling. Then as he stood up something hit William.

"Don't tell my mum about this, about what I said," he barked.

"I won't."

"Promise?"

"I promise."

William sank back, feeling better but still not perfect, still not fighting fit. Were he an athlete he would still be undergoing a course of physiotherapy, and popping the occasional pill. He bolted, back to his room, and Clarence was left alone to cut tiles as the wall went round a corner. With mathematical attention to detail he made each part fit, and minimized wastage. A feeling of accomplishment resurfaced. It filled his stomach.

Time meanwhile had leapt forward and Mary arrived home, home and dry. William ran downstairs to greet her as Clarence looked at his watch, in denial of the official time. There was another knock on the door. It was William again: this time he entered without waiting for permission. He was headstrong again, and comfortable in his lack of social engineering. He held out a small plate. On it were sandwiches: neatly cut and filled with tuna.

"I was told to give you these," he explained.

Clarence took the plate and lowered it onto the carpet. William was glad to be rid of it.

"Thank you."

Clarence began to eat them, wondering how she knew he liked tuna in bread. He was ravenous. William watched and empathized, if only crudely and fleetingly. The sandwiches were wolfed down in two minutes flat and William regretted not having taken one for himself first. Clarence handed back the empty plate in record time.

With no particular wish to be anywhere else William hung around, holding the plate like a well-read book. Clarence pushed half a tile into place then froze and looked up at his audience, suddenly with a dreamlike expression.

"I sense a longing, faint at times but firmly secured."

"A longing?"

"A long held wish for something. You have never let go of it from the day you recognised it as such. Sometimes it is at the forefront of your thoughts where it preoccupies you completely, if only for the briefest period of time. But during these times you feel crushed, and have to recover by whatever means possible. This usually occurs at night. At other times it makes a brief intrusion upon your consciousness and you promptly dismiss it; afraid it may yield implications you cannot handle; unable to admit to heart-felt want."

William glanced down and solidified: mind grabbing bits and pieces of what had been said and trying to string them together, to make them add up into something which made sense.

"You said I have a wish."

"Correct. A wish for something substantial."

William leapt at the chance to state his demand. "I want an Ipod."

Clarence peered into empty space and considered. "No it is something else."

"But I want an Ipod."

"That may be so but it is far more recent and of less significance."

William tried one more time, politely this time. "I would like an Ipod."

Clarence tossed the comment away. "No this involves people, one person: a particular kind of person; one required to fulfil a particular need in the physical world; one required to remove a vacuum in both your conscious and unconscious states."

William went silent, finding his sense of presence being methodically stripped away, leaving nothing with which to hide behind.

Clarence continued in the same vein, all thoughts of bathroom tiling pushed aside. "This person is a man: fit, clever; good at physical exercise, a good sportsman; excellent at playing games on the computer."

William felt a red hot poker pierce his brain. It hurt and set his thoughts alight. He fought them off with the single thought of his bedroom: that was the place he definitely had to be right now.

Clarence did not relent. "Though you deny it you need this person."

William had to leave the room. His head was about to crack open. His brains were about to spill out. He had to switch on his PC and lose himself. Homework could wait. He peeled himself off the wall and got out.

"I've got to go," he said, halfway out the door.

Clarence continued to tile, unsure when to quit for the day. When his stomach began to complain he decided to stop, and as he tidied up he was interrupted by another knock on the door. Mary popped her head in and produced a lame smile, one suffused with distant melancholy.

"Is everything alright?" she asked.

"Fine. Just clearing up."

Mary soaked up the change to her bathroom. "Yes that's much better."

"Good. Glad you like it." Clarence spoke in a hurry, wishing to get through the compliments and attention without fuss or bother.

"I must thank you again for all this. You must have spent all day doing it."

"Not all day. Just some of it. I started late."

Mary took in his face. It looked worse for wear, bearing the signs of weary capitulation. Clarence tried to look elsewhere, but all he had was the view out of the window, and that proved too boring.

"You do look very tired you know. Slow down won't you? Don't over do it for me. This can wait."

She wanted to reach out and take his hand but it was obvious that he was having none of it. She backed off, not wishing to corner him.

"Thanks but I'll be OK. Just under the weather."

"Are you getting a good night's sleep?"

"I think so."

"You think so?"

"Sometimes I wake up tired." Clarence wished he had answered with a simple 'yes'.

"Bad dreams can wear you out, or the stress of unfinished business: the kind you can't let go of."

Clarence grabbed at her gift of an explanation. "Yes that's what I keep telling myself."

Mary returned to the business of the day, not wishing to intrude further. "I'm preparing dinner. Would you like to join us?"

Clarence thought back to his original intentions. They were so far away, felt so weak; but he clung to them, determined to revitalize them. The thought of devouring a big hot plate of food felt good. But no, he had to get away. She was getting under his skin, even if for all the right reasons. Theatrically he examined his watch, and pretended to despair at the time.

"Sorry. I can't. Have to get on." The voice sounded fake.

Clarence caught the disappointment in her eyes, and it hurt. He did not wish to hurt. "But I will be back to finish it off. It will get finished. Promise. Including the grouting."

Mary smiled and tried to take it on the chin, reminding herself that she had no right to presume upon his time. But the sound of pleading prompted an enquiry.

"Did I say something wrong?"

"No of course not."

"I feel like I need to say sorry."

"You have nothing to say sorry for. I have to go. Sorry." Clarence had made his peace.

"Well take care."

"I will."

"And please try to get a good night's sleep."

"I will," replied Clarence, and he meant it: a fact which was not lost on him.

He left in hurry, at a polite speed, brushing aside William on his way out: glad to be out of the house and back on the street, yet at the same time registering regret for his hasty departure. He was leaving something good and wholesome behind.

On the way home he stopped off at an Indian restaurant and ordered a takeaway, drinking an Indian beer while he waited. At home he consumed the curry with a Guinness placed in his hand by Max. With nothing to say to each other the television quickly took over. It always had plenty to say.

Chapter Twelve

Log Entry

I attended a rally by a crowd of highly charged individuals intent on expressing collective opinion and rage by visual and vocal means: means complimented by physical co-exertion and mental hysteria. It was a protest, targeted at a state of affairs considered immoral and detrimental to the health and spiritual well-being of society at large.

The crowd gathered at a pre-determined time and place. As they gathered so their sense of expectation grew, and for some their sense of self-belief and purpose. Old friends were reunited. Thoughts shared were thoughts reinforced. Opinions suddenly mattered. Some were expecting change. Others were resigned to the opposite. Some demanded a repeat performance as soon as possible, as if unable to contain themselves between performances.

The protesters marched from point A to point B, and some back again. During this time some released a mix of resentment and anger, others resolve and delight. It was all directed ahead, or up at the sky, and in the course of time it became diluted by repetition. Large quantities of mental and physical energy directed at the whole world in general and a few specific individuals in particular. These individuals were not present despite having been invited. Their named were advertised on boards and formed the basis of many messages and slogans. More often than not they were the object of ridicule. It felt good to scream and shout and wave flags and placards about.

Some elements which made up the crowd demonstrated their feelings more towards each other than towards the intended audience, i.e. those who needed to be persuaded of the case for change.

For some the experience was therapeutic: just to be surrounded by friends and supportive, like-minded individuals rebuilt confidence and resolve, and belief in the righteousness of their position. They were lifted out of isolation and discrimination – if only temporarily – into the illusion of an immediate, universal consensus in which they represented the moral majority; or at least that was the feeling generated. Some were simply happy to be out with their friends, and looking forward to the eating and drinking which they were promised would follow.

Some were driven by personal grievance. If they were not heard they hurt. They refuse to change: the world must change. They are right. The rest of the world is wrong. Others took a position based upon analysis and contemplation of the facts: a purely intellectual process. The appropriate emotions were generated only after the intellectual position had been adopted.

A few just felt good getting involved. They believe it to be the right course of action, despite being unsure as to exactly what the wrong action was. They are no less sincere in their stated aims but are more vulnerable to dishonest manipulation.

Some had no wish to get involved but were drawn in by their partners: they dared not reveal this lest they be seen as weak, ineffectual and boring. Some regarded the whole affair as a social gathering, a party almost, a chance to make new friends, perhaps engage with a new sexual partner. They tended to be the better dressed individuals, and the least vocal.

Some revealed another side of their personality which was otherwise kept hidden, locked away. They exercised it to the full via intense agitation and outbursts bordering on the violent as circumstances allowed. Some were looking to start a fight. Afterwards they locked it away again and reverted to their earlier persona: temporarily satisfied even if they had changed nothing, persuaded no one.

Those strangers who stopped to observe were vastly outnumbered, and in most cases overwhelmed. They remained detached, uncommitted, in the main aloof. There were no converts. The occasion was recorded by the news media for immediate or later transmission and they seemed to be the only immediate audience. The point and purpose of the exercise was not so much in the detail but the overall impact of noise and scale.

At point B pre-designated guest speakers addressed the crowd. They were not challenged, hence their case was not proven to those who held opposing views. It appeared to merely reinforce the differences between participants and observers.

At the end the majority of protesters felt vindicated, reinvigorated, their beliefs reflecting the truth: they had been heard; they could no longer be ignored. When the crowd dispersed a sick, hollow feeling was left for some, with nothing immediately available to fill it. Even their original anger would have to be replenish as it had diminished in intensity.

⁜ ⁜ ⁜

Rally over, energy spent, point made, the crowd dissolved; some still fired up, some tired out, some resigned. Like many others John, George and Clarence sat at a table in an East End pub, exhausted, while Rebecca went to the bar to buy more drinks. She too was exhausted, but was determined to buy a round 'for the boys', to prove to herself that she could 'cut it'. She stood limp, hoping to be noticed by anyone behind the bar, and hoping to go home soon. She held on to her bit of space with dogged determination.

As they drank beer George watched John. John watched Rebecca. And Clarence watched the crowd. The crowd, thick and loud as any on a Saturday afternoon, was augmented by the addition of a group of five – a much smaller crowd but just as loud, and on average, thicker. They were dressed in the tribal colours of their football club; their raison d'etre, their passion, their fury and their grief. Females could not compete for such affections. Football fed them. It declared them present and correct. Everything else in life fed off them, and so caused offence. Three wore the latest colours. The remaining two had been left behind through lack of funds. Theirs had only lasted one season before being cast out by greedy accountants.

They laughed loudly at everything which entered the conversation, and jostled, and took the piss out of each other; and in Rebecca's view they stood too close for comfort. They intimidated, albeit accidentally and she dropped her purse. She looked down in horror, unable to bend her knees to reach down to retrieve it.

In an instant the youngest of the five – a youth with spots still chasing eighteen – jumped out of his circle, closed the gap and scooped it up. Despite being rough around the edges and rough in attitude he was a pretty young thing, acne aside. He smiled as he held it out to her. Rebecca snatched it back and dismissed his smile as moronic and misguided. Not the least put off, he stood waiting.

Rebecca tried to disguised her discomfort as she tried to ignore him. She failed in both and he basked in her evident discomfort. His smile transformed into an evil grin. She had had her chance. Rebecca held her nerve and reminded herself that she was in a very public, very crowded place.

The youth did not move away but continued with the torture. Rebecca threw him the dirtiest look and without warning fierce thoughts ignited in his mind like gunpowder. She was dressed like a lefty, a soft liberal. She wore her hair funny. She was probably a lesbian. The accusations sprang into his mind like hungry, feral cats. He thought that she thought that she was above him, and he was probably right; just as she was probably right.

But there was no plot: only his own inhibitions, his lack of confidence, his lack of definition, his untamed temper; and his refusal to relax back into a world that held no grudge against him. It never had. It just felt like it.

She was a threat, as he was a threat, and his only defence was attack. That was what he had learnt while growing up; that and nothing else, except perhaps to survive at any cost. Over the years the defence had served him well, but made him few true friends: only accomplices; only paper thin mates who would happily dump him for money, a bottle of whisky, or an endless supply of Big Macs. So now he was lonely most of the time, lonely enough to want to engage with people outside his normal circle - especially if they were female, young and pretty. In the final analysis it did not matter too much what they looked liked, what they stood for, or who they slept with just as long as they slept with him. He was not choosy. He was desperate. All she had to do was be nice to him, welcome him in: accept him and he would go away.

"Can I buy you a drink?" the youth asked. The question sounded hard as nails and the expected answer was yes.

"No," replied Rebecca, faint but firm, if a little rasping.

"Why not? I'm not good enough to buy you drinks?" The accusation in his scruffy voice disguised a deep, ancient hurt.

Rebecca had a diplomatic response ready. "I'm buying for my friends over there."

For protection she pointed at them, and saw that Clarence was fixed on them both; eyes glued, expression frozen, mind set thinking. This made her feel much better, stronger, cocky even. She had her protector.

"I'll buy you one later." He would allow her no way out.

"I won't be having anymore. This is my limit."

"What won't get pissed?"

For him cause and affect had no relationship. They did not connect. Things just happened or just had to said. There were no such things as conclusions, logical or otherwise, or simple statements of fact. Life was a series of jumbled knee-jerks, sudden revelations, broken promises and feeble excuses. There was only the rebound, the rebuttal, the denial; the jerk, the confrontation, the insinuation; the windup, the antagonism. They all suited his temperament and his means of entrapment – and here and now he was looking to entrap, for no other reason than the thrill of the chase and the taste of the catch.

"I've got no problem with getting drunk. But not this time of day, and not so far away from home." Her full explanation fell on deaf ears.

"You're not East End."

Rebecca took a chance. "Neither are you." And she was proved right. His team had played away today.

His face screwed up into a knot and his nostrils flared. He began to simmer. He was ten again and everybody around him, above him, was shouting abuse at him or each other such that he could not be heard. Feeling oppressed he wanted to give up the fight and return to the comfort zone of his mates but, trouble was, he fancied her. Given time he would make her fancy him. He put a couple of fingers on her arm and felt the soft fabric of her shirt, but could think of nothing to say. Trembling but still standing Rebecca shook him off.

"Don't do that. Please." She had remembered to say please.

"I wasn't doing anything." He spat as he spoke.

Saved by the attentions of a barman she placed her order while he stood aside, watching, lost for ideas and as ever lacking direction.

As Rebecca paid for the drinks Clarence joined her at her side, infiltrating the gap between her and her pursuer, much to her relief. Clarence turned on the youth and smiled, at once both friendly and overbearing. The youth did not back off: not knowing the meaning of intimidation he could not be intimidated.

"What are you looking at?" he snarled.

Clarence broke off from serious contemplation to answer. "I was looking at your shirt. A football club shirt? You support a particular football team?"

"Of course I do. You stupid or something?"

"It's not the same as those others behind you which I assume proclaim the same club?"

The youth kept Clarence firmly in his sights, suspicious at such an attempt to be friendly. "They've got the new ones. I'm still stuck on old."

Clarence offered to buy him a drink. Stung by the hand of friendship but tempted by the thought of a free beer the young man accepted and ended up holding a pint glass in each hand: one full; one half full. Having to balance them both limited his ability to move at speed.

Clarence continued to examine the football shirt. "How much would it cost to replace it?"

"Why?"

"It upsets you. It makes you feel excluded."

"No it doesn't."

"Yes it does."

"What if it does?"

"I'll give you some money towards replacing it."

Rebecca raised her eyebrows, then lowered them. She was impressed.

"You'll do what?"

Clarence repeated himself slowly. "I'll give you some money towards replacing it."

"I heard you the first time. What's the catch?"

"No catch."

"There's always a catch."

"No catch."

The youth looked upon the offer as if it was a haunch of beef left hung out to dry but possibly still edible despite the smell and the flies.

"Thirty quid," he lied.

Clarence reached for his wallet and produced a note. "Here's twenty."

The youth took it, snatching at it like Rebecca. He held it up to the light then held it tight, as if it were foreign money and he was stranded in a foreign country.

Next Clarence asked him what he was up to and where he was going in life. Did he have a dream to follow? The youth thought he was stark raving bonkers and told him to fuck off. For the record he had nothing to do and the entire day in which to do it. Dreams had nothing to do with it.

Clarence, reading the clear signal, obliged and turned back to Rebecca to check on her condition. She had been in two minds over whether to grab the drinks and return to the table or stand by him. She stood by him, as he stood by her. She was fine she lied and thanked him for his concern: it was visible and substantial.

"You're still shaking inside," he said.

"Am I?" She was. She hadn't noticed.

"Come on let's sit down."

Clarence took her by the hand and led her away. She was more than happy for him to do this. She felt an infatuation. She felt sexy. She felt like a woman again. The youth watched them both like a hawk, still clutching the money, still thinking her pretty and open to suggestion, no matter how crude. He was pretty he told himself. And without the spots, he was.

"When you've stopped shaking I'll let go."

"Will you?"

"Promise."

For Rebecca this was old-fashioned romance.

They sat down together. It would be two more minutes until Clarence let go. During this time Rebecca felt things could not be more right between them. John had to go and get the drinks.

As they drank more alcohol, George suffered: John was sitting next to him and doing his jolly best to ignore him. He put his hand on John's leg and squeezed to force a reaction but it was immediately pushed away. That was the only reaction he would get. His body and brain fused with alcohol meant that George was not going to give up so easily. They had been close once: they could be close again.

George attempted eye contact, all the while growing more and more alert to the fact that Clarence was watching him; just as the Rebecca woman was watching Clarence when Clarence wasn't watching. It was painful to watch – and they were all being watched by the youth now back amongst his own and talking football. When Clarence finally let go of Rebecca's hand the two struck up conversation based around Judy – she had been left alone all day. Clarence reassured her that Judy could cope. At this point George was determined to do likewise with John. Equilibrium had to be maintained. He put his arm around his ex-lover's shoulders and presumed innocence but before he could say something – anything - John got in first and pushed him off.

"Don't do that George." He sounded tired, aggrieved.

"Why not? I used to."

"But you don't now."

"It's only me."

"That's what I mean."

George turned red, unsure as to how far the insult was meant to sink beneath the skin, but sure now that past good times could no longer catch him up. Hurt, he got up from the table and made a theatrical exit. It was one of his best.

"I'm going home," he declared.

"Sit down," responded John.

"No," said George, and he stormed out.

"Oh Christ," exclaimed John, and he got up to follow, only for Clarence to immediately signal him to sit back down.

"Better I go and get him," he explained.

John agreed. He was too worn out to chase prima donnas.

As Clarence got up Rebecca began to worry for her man: the football fan had followed him out, convinced now that a faggot had tried to chat him up, buy sex off him. He had no idea what he would do but that was not the point – it never was.

George walked down the street, slowing as his legs were aching again. Clarence was catching him up quickly, as did the youth behind him: he travelled at the fastest speed; and always did, even when he had no reason to hurry, chase or flee.

Back inside Rebecca pushed John up out of his chair, demanding he warn Clarence of possible danger. John did as instructed, despite a lack of appetite for any sort of confrontation: after all it was Clarence they were talking about. He could look after himself.

As velocities collapsed the three men set on the same course nearly fell into each another, to form a singularity and a complete mix of intentions and reactions. George turned on Clarence, then on the spotty youth who was descending upon Clarence. The youth smelt fear in the fat man and revelled in it. Clarence, sensing someone behind him of a dubious nature, likewise turned.

The youth pulled the note from his pocket.

"What were you expecting to get for this you faggot!"

"Happiness."

The youth, blown wildly off course by the most unexpected reply, took one step back then two steps forward, fists clenched. Clarence wanted to engage in dialogue but had no idea as to where to start, knowing the man would not cooperate: consistency of thought was not his strong point Clarence had realised earlier.

Then John appeared and shouted after his friends, wanting to know if they were alright, if they needed help – not that he had any to give The youth turned on John, angry that another fagot was behind him and sticking his nose into his business. He was surrounded. Reasonable thoughts he discarded continuously, so any reaction was legitimate.

"Fuck off you. Tosser."

"I beg your pardon?"

John was perplexed by the stream of hate – and directed at him when he was the last and least to get involved. He began to shake at the knees. George was drunk enough to witness the scene as if from a distance, as if it was all being played out by actors on screen.

The youth shifted towards John and Clarence sensed violence ahead. He had to intervene else John would suffer pain and physical damage, which would not be a good thing. Swiftly he moved in close and tapped the youth on the shoulder. He swung around and waited for Clarence to speak.

Clarence did not speak. He had no intention of speaking. Words would fail: any rational attempt at peace making was doomed. The young brain was a tangled web with no way through. Instead he was gearing himself up for an explosion of physical energy: energy precisely targeted and executed for maximum psychological impact; and though he was loathed to do it, for maximum physical damage.

"Well?" asked the youth, as ever impatient with living in the 'now'.

Clarence swung his clenched fist through the air and punched him so hard on the nose that he crashed on to the pavement. Stunned by the force of the blow he just sat there and held his nose. It dripped blood and hurt like hell.

John nearly fainted and Clarence had to grab him by the waist and hold him upright while he recovered. George was immediately jealous. John felt electrified by the tough man's grip and didn't want him to let go. He had been right all along. He wanted Clarence to hug him and give him a big kiss of reassurance.

Punch delivered, Clarence apologized profusely and offered to pull his victim back up on to his feet. He even offered to attend to the wound and pay for damages. The wounded youth responded by kicking out. He almost hit Clarence on the shin but Clarence was too quick and dodged the bullet. He took that as a no thank you. At this point the shit really did hit George and he was scared shitless. He ran off to the underground station to catch a train home. Sod John, sod Clarence would be his final thoughts for the day.

As the youth shouted out for his mates, Rebecca ran up and pulled Clarence and John away. Clarence was persuaded to leave the scene immediately and quickly. John needed no persuading. As they walked away – at a brisk pace set by John and Rebecca - Clarence held each in his hands: Rebecca in his left, John in his right; unaware that he was bringing great pleasure and relief to them both, and in equal measure.

In a barely restrained rush the three of them followed George to the station where they reunited with him at the ticket barrier. Clarence apologized for his behaviour. George did not and went on his separate way. Rebecca squeezed Clarence around the waist, thinking him now to be the most wonderful man in the world. All he had to do before they got home was kiss her and her day would be perfect. Sensing this Clarence would do exactly as requested.

⊕ ⊕ ⊕

Fiona stood at the end of the room and waved him on. Clarence leapt out of bed and scratched his bum. He ran towards her, shouting her name from the roof top. She was in another room and he was all alone on the roof-top. He shouted out her name again. He heard a voice shout back. It could have been anyone. He heard lots of voices shout back. They could have been anyone else. He put his hands over his ears to cut out the noise and ran. He ran into another room. It was dark. He tried to turn the light on. There was no light switch. There was no light bulb. There was no light. He ran on, into the next room: just as dark, and equally devoid of light bulbs. He ran on, tripping over his teddy bear, on into another room. The rooms just kept on coming.

This room had two people in it. They sat at a table and ate dinner, calmly, matter-of-fact. They looked alike. Neither of them was Fiona. Clarence wanted Fiona. He tried to leave the room but there was no way out, just as there was no way in. He was trapped. A woman looked up and waved. A boy looked up and growled. Lots of boys looked up and hissed. Lots of girls looked around, positively bored senseless by all the boys acting like twits or just looking stupid – all except for the good-looking one. His name was Tim and he was always so much more damn good-looking. He was the only man amongst the boys.

He was pinned to the blackboard. His class threw paper aeroplanes at him; for no other reason except for laughs, for kicks. He was stuck out in front. He couldn't dodge, and cracks were appearing. Then they threw stones and that began to hurt. He tried to hug his teddy bear but it was nowhere to be seen. Someone had moved it again. Just like they moved other objects without his knowledge or permission.

He tried to say something intelligent, remarkable, useful but failed, completely. He gave up. He sounded too boring, even to himself. He chased after the taller boy who ran off across the playground. He couldn't catch up. The other boy was faster. As a favour he paused to let Clarence catch up. Clarence almost made it, but not quite. The other boy – the taller, better looking boy – was off again and Clarence was left behind. He shouted 'Tim!' but Tim didn't shout back. He was too busy making a stack full of money in the city, buying and selling gold like it was going out of fashion.

Tim offered Clarence his teddy bear but Clarence didn't want it now, at least not from him. Sam tried to hand it to him. He refused to take it. She kept trying. She kept waving it at him. She waved her knickers. He ran away: back into another dark room. This room had a bed and he was in his pyjamas. He crawled into bed. Mother had made him a mug of hot chocolate. He held it up, afraid to drop it. The mug had a crack. The contents tasted of chocolate. The mug was too hot. He put it down. It was gone: somebody had moved it.

Clarence grabbed his teddy bear and held on tight. His teddy bear felt good. His teddy bear had a nice big smile. His teddy bear never answered back. His teddy bear stuck by him, through thick and thin and everything else. His teddy bear never interrupted him; never broke his train of thought; never thought it was better than him. His teddy bear never demanded attention, flowers or chocolates. His teddy bear was always there on time, never late, never in a hurry. His teddy bear was just right.

Clarence rubbed his face hard into his teddy bear. It felt huge. It was a mountain of warm hairy flesh. It's heat flowed through him and relaxed, cooling his senses; tempting him to give up the struggle, make peace, focus in, kiss the teddy bear. He wrapped his free arm around his teddy bear and held on tight. His teddy bear now had a beard. He stroked it. His teddy bear had a beard. Funny that. His teddy bear had a beard. Teddy bears didn't have beards as a rule. His teddy bear had never had a beard. His teddy bear was a straight, no nonsense teddy bear. His teddy bear was a boy's own teddy bear.

A point of distraction, possibly displeasure, began to throb inside Clarence's head; on the outskirts of his brain proper, with the intensity of unrequited thought.

His teddy bear was furry and smelly. It had accumulated filth through the years. This teddy bear was hairy not furry – though only in places – and not smelly. This teddy bear was hot, slightly sweaty. It smelt a little, but in a nice way. It smelt of human flesh, and a little of soap. No matter.

Clarence tasted the salt. He stroked the beard. He stroked the beard. A beard. Human flesh. Hairy human flesh. A bolt of lightening struck his brain. His brain ceased to throb. It vibrated as its parts and points all sprang into action and did what it did best: processing all streams of input to make sense of the real world. It began to shake itself to pieces.

Clarence awoke, with a rocket up his backside, and a tingle down one side. His whole body was electrified, and raring to go. He opened one eye, and quickly followed it with the other. He did not like what he saw. He did not see what he liked. Instead he saw a man's body, attached to a man's beard. The head began to turn. He recognised the beard. The body began to heave. The monster began to stir.

Trembling and trying not to fall apart, electrified and trying not to electrocute himself, Clarence slid off the bed and onto the dirty, unwashed carpet. He was terrified. The monster had been disturbed. Backwards he inched his way away from the bed – his bed, the bastard was now sleeping in his bed – and negotiated his way around it; to make for the bedroom door without falling over; to run for the safety of the bathroom. He managed the task without falling over or fainting and on his way bumped into Max who also wanted to use the bathroom. His need was more traditional, yet no less severe. Max swore, apologized to his mother just in case she was listening, and veered off towards the kitchen.

Safe inside, Clarence locked the door. He looked around, desperate to know what to do next. He saw the bar of soap. He saw his flannel. He saw his toothbrush. He would brush his teeth, hard, like it was his last chance to get his teeth clean. He picked up the toothbrush and with it the crushed tube of toothpaste. Still shaking, he tried to lay down some paste on the toothbrush. As it came out of the tube it reminded him of grouting, which he didn't want to be reminded off. He managed to get a long thread of gleaming white paste onto the brush. It looked tasty. But before he could enjoy the fruits of his labour it fell off into the basin: his hand was shaking so much. For the first time he looked into the mirror. He did not like what he saw there, staring back as it did. It was a shock. It was someone else.

Soap – flannel – shower.

Those three things all united inside his brain and proposed a better place to go: a place to hide; a way to redress the indignity; a path back to some measure of dignity. He jumped under the shower. He had to have a hot shower, a really hot shower.

And he did. And it was hot. And he basked in the hot water. With the showerhead in charge he roamed all parts of his body: all surfaces; all backstreets; and especially all over his face. The hot water helped to fight off the headache which threatened to rise up and bite his head off. It had already bitten him on the bum. Then he scrubbed. And he really scrubbed. He scrubbed hard. He scrubbed and he scrubbed and he scrubbed, and he scrubbed to death all those parts which needed to be scrubbed: to hell and back he scrubbed. And while he scrubbed, with depression pressing and hysteria held in check, he tried not to think. To think would be to crumble, collapse. To think would be to cry. Hold out, hold on, he told himself. Hold out. Hold on.

The doorbell rang and Clarence froze, covered in soap suds, dripping like a big ineffectual drip. A voice croaked. It was that man John.

"I'm making coffee. Do you want one?"

Clarence reacted to the invitation as one would react to any invitation made by the least desirable, least interesting, least conducive; most dangerous, most disturbing, most excruciating, most unwelcomed person in one's life. He wanted to shout 'no, fuck off!' but didn't have the balls or gumption, or the nervous system to deliver such a passionate refusal. He dropped the soap instead. He winced. He gritted his teeth and held on for dear life.

"Is everything OK in there?" John sounded concerned.

Slowly, taking his time, Clarence bent down and reached for the soap. He had his back against the wall. He had nowhere to run to. He waited, on the edge of nervous collapse, but heard nothing more. He carried on scrubbing then washed himself down. Finally he was forced to step out of the shower and back onto dry land, and one step closer to the rest of the world.

He didn't have a towel. There was no towel in the bathroom: a forgivable oversight but one which left him stranded and shivering as the enormity of his mistake sank in. The shivering took on new meaning, a double purpose, as his body began to rot in the cold. He grabbed the one and only hand towel present and made it his shield to protect his engine parts and ward off the enemy. He banged his head against the door, twice, said 'why me?', and opened it slowly. He had a plan. He was saved by the plan which had crash-landed in his head in just the nick of time: John was in the kitchen – his kitchen – making coffee; ergo he could not also be in the bedroom. This insight struck Clarence with all the force and feel good factor of an unexpected pay rise set at twice the rate of inflation.

He headed out then nearly had a heart attack as, with only one hand on the job, he nearly dropped his only means of protection. He forced himself to think, calm down, and recovered his position. Grabbing the hand towel securely again with both hands he held it tight across his lap. It was his only defence. Hearing the right noises coming from the kitchen he crept back to the bedroom. Afraid to make any noise and give himself away, he squeezed in through the narrow gap created by the half-opened door. As he slowly eased it shut he turned and nearly dropped his pants. Instead he dropped his one defence. John was sitting in the chair tying up his shoelaces. He looked up and smiled.

"Is everything OK?"

Clarence collapsed to the floor, knotted himself up into a tiny ball of battered humanity and began to pray; whilst doing his best to ignore the painful reality of the world around him. He was dripping on the carpet, not that he cared.

"Are you alright?" asked John.

"Fine," croaked Clarence.

"You don't look it."

Clarence croaked a little more. "Fine. Just leave me alone."

"What are you doing down there?"

"Looking for something."

"Like what? Afraid to face me?"

"No. Me, afraid? I'm not afraid of anything."

"Well stop hiding from me then."

"I'm not hiding."

"Come up and face me proper then."

"Hand me a towel first – a big one – out of that drawer."

John complied; and cosy, pleasant thoughts of the night before slipped away into the void; to be replaced by those of deepening disquiet and encroaching mental fatigue. Bad Cop Clarence was in the room.

Better clad and holding on. Clarence rose up and stood erect, ready for the fall. John looked on, emotionally entangled but snatched from the warm recoil of a loving embrace.

"You were lovely last night," he announced, reminding all.

"Was I."

"You can be a great listener when you want to, a great comfort and joy."

"To the world."

"What?"

"A great comfort and joy to the world. Just like in the Christmas carol."

"Of course." John smiled and waited for events to unfold.

Clarence could not hold back the question any longer. He had to throw up. "So what did we do last night?"

"You don't remember?"

"No. Remind me."

"We talked about our day out together."

"Our day out? Where?"

"London. Central London. The rally – you don't remember any of this do you?"

"No. And glad of it."

John sank back into his chair, shoe laces forgotten. "That's a terrible thing to say."

"No it's not. It's the truth."

Clarence sat down on the bed. A wet patch spread across the bed. He was wetting the bed. Still he didn't care. He spotted his dressing gown. It was on the back of the chair – trapped behind John.

"Pass me that will you."

"Pass you what?"

"That, behind you. You're sitting on it."

John twisted round. "Oh this. Sorry."

He got up, handed it over - at a stretch - and sat back down again, aware that he had to keep his distance. Clarence slipped into it carefully, exposing as little as possible. The towel fell to the carpet. The dressing gown soaked up the remainder of the water. He felt like a wet rag. And still he didn't care.

"You said a rally. What rally?"

"The big rally. The really big one. We were all over the news."

"Big what?"

John rose to his feet and came closer, refusing to be dissuaded by the nervous twitch on Clarence's face. He sat down on the other end of the bed. Clarence took it as a challenge. He did not retreat. He held his ground. John with his clothes on no longer shocked – just the image of him naked.

"You're a complete blank again aren't you?"

"Yes complete. Tell me about the rally. Did I get arrested, in trouble?"

"No. We didn't get arrested."

Clarence missed the hint of relief in John's voice. "We?"

"You, me, George and your Rebecca friend."

"George? That guy at your place?"

"That's right. He's an old friend of mine. And you were very rude to him Clarence. Very rude. That was unforgivable." John avoided the word 'ex-lover'.

"Tell him I'm sorry."

"Do you really mean that?"

Clarence didn't. "I do. Tell him I'm just full of shit. It's what I talk."

John reached out. "Don't be so hard on yourself. You've got a problem. You know that. You must see him."

"You said my 'Rebecca friend' was there?"

"That's right."

"What was she doing there? You don't know her."

"You invited her along."

"Did I? Did I talk to her?"

"Of course. A lot. Just as you talked to the rest of us – and quite a few others I might add."

"Meaning?"

"Meaning nothing. As I said you just like to talk sometimes."

"And the rally was what? Gay rights?"

John drew in a deep breath and stood up. "Now you're being facetious."

"No I'm not. I'm being stupid. Tell me what was it?"

"G8. Anti-G8, anti-globalisation march."

The mention of 'G8' triggered some faint memories of George and crisps. Clarence drew a sigh of relief. "That's not so bad."

John passed no comment, though he wanted to. His heart was breaking in two again. He could only stitch it back together so many times.

"Do you remember anything about last night?"

"No." Clarence didn't and didn't want to.

"We sat on your sofa. We drank wine – I brought the wine on the way home, from your favourite off-licence. Afterwards you told me all about the nice girl behind the counter.

"Did I."

"You did."

John continued through lack of response. "We held each other tight. We watched a nature programme about penguins, in winter. It was lovely."

"Penguins." Clarence pictured penguins in his mind, so to avoid thinking about anything else. Penguins were safe territory. Penguins were cute.

"You were very romantic, very sensitive."

Clarence began to shake, which upset John. Now the devil lurking inside John wanted to make Clarence suffer, as John was suffering.

"You were my lover boy."

Clarence could take no more. He jumped up and ran for the bathroom.

John shouted after him. "We went to bed!"

Clarence tried not to hear him. He slammed the bathroom door shut and leant against it, to keep out demons, to keep sanity in check, to keep his balance. This time John banged on the door, this time not with an offer of coffee but an apology.

"I'm sorry Clarence. Please come out."

"No." Clarence was adamant. He would stay in there all day if necessary. He had all the time in the world and no place to spend it. So the bathroom was as good a place as any.

John begged. "Please come out."

"No. Go away."

"I promise to be nice."

"Fuck off."

Clarence held his breath and heard heavy footsteps stop on the other side of the door. It was Max. Now there were two of them.

John explained the situation. "He won't come out. You deal with it."

"Nothing to do with me mate." And with that Max passed on by, annoyed that he had missed his chance. He just wanted to have a piss.

John lost his temper. "Come out Clarence! Get help!"

"Fuck off!"

"This is the last time. Come out of there!"

"I said fuck off! So fuck off!"

"Well fuck you then!" And with that John did fuck off, and Clarence slid to the floor.

John headed towards the door, at double-speed, pushing past Max on his way: Max was on his way to answer it. Tim stood on the other side. He had rung the bell and was waiting to be received. He clutched a sports bag with a fancy racket protruding out of it. He was expecting to play squash that morning. The door flew open and Tim found himself staring into the red face of someone looking very hot and out of breath.

John looked down. "I haven't done my shoelaces up."

Without waiting for a response John did a u-turn and stormed back the way he had come – just as far as the nearest place he could sit down to do up his shoelaces, which was the sofa. That sofa had been a wonderful place the night before.

Tim was dissuaded from stepping inside so instead he stood like a lemon and waited for the next thing to happen. The next thing was the reappearance of John, still at speed, as if on speed.

"Can I get past please? I've got to fuck off." Tim was blocking his way out.

Tim shook himself free. "Sorry. Certainly." He stood aside and John flew past, and was gone.

The door remained open. Tim peered in, and looked beyond it, as if for signs of life. Max appeared, desperate to have that piss. He was seriously contemplating standing on a chair in the kitchen. Tim was not reassured but he struggled on.

"Can I come in? He's expecting me."

"Sure. No problem. I'll tell him you're here – but he still may not come out."

"Come out?"

"Of the bathroom. He's stuck in the bathroom."

"Has he had an accident?" asked Tim.

Max looked back at him as if looking at an idiot. He gave up and picked up the newspaper which had been dumped outside. Tim took a deep breath, took one step forward, then another; then carried on, all the way in.

Max knocked on the bathroom door. "Tim is here." No reply. He turned on Tim. "You talk to him." Then he left them to it.

Tim had no idea as to what the hell was going on, other than the fact that Clarence was refusing to come out of his bathroom. Was it Clarence's turn to have a breakdown? If so, Tim wondered, then when would it be his turn? Time was running out. He wasn't the lad in tight jeans he used to be – nor was his childless wife. He took his turn and knocked on the door.

"Clarence it's me. Tim."

Clarence had no problem speaking when he heard a friendly voice. "What do you want?"

"Are we playing squash?"

A long pause. "No."

"No?"

"Bad day. Sorry."

"Max says you won't come out."

"I will come out. In my own time."

"Well when's that then?"

Another long pause. "Any moment now."

"I'll be in the living room."

"OK you do that."

"Thanks."

In the living room Tim dropped his bag, sat down and waited; and while he waited he digested the first few pages of the Sunday newspaper which had been thrown on to the table. Being Sunday it had little in the way of fresh news to report. Old facts were churned over, spiced and diced; pulled apart and pushed together; refitted and reconnected. Yesterday's cooked meat was reheated and curried. It was good enough for Tim though as it took his mind off a most bizarre encounter.

Clarence appeared, looking like a man who had just mislaid his entire family fortune, or left his wife and kids in a motorway self-service restaurant and now had to go back and get them, and explain himself. He paced up and down the room in his damp dressing gown, arms folded tight, not wishing to stop for anyone, including himself. Tim watched awhile then, when he had finally had enough, cut in and forced Clarence to sit down. He almost threw him into the chair.

"Get a grip man!"

"On what?"

"What?"

"You said get a grip. Get a grip on what?"

Tim backed away from the source of madness.

"I don't know. Whatever it is you need to get a grip on."

"My life?"

"You tell me. I thought it was just blackouts."

"Just blackouts? Do you have any idea what these things are doing to me?"

Tim became defensive. "No. How could I. Is it bad?"

"Bad? Of course it's fucking bad."

Tim tried to make a joke of it. "As bad as that time you accused your sister of being a lesbian?"

"Worse."

"Worse than that time we were on that 18-30's and that button broke off and you had to spend the rest of the evening clutching your trousers like you had a hard on or stomach ache?"

"Yes worse."

Tim was still not convinced. "Well how worse then?"

Clarence looked his oldest friend in the eye just to make sure he could tell him anything, then looked down at the carpet. Tim could be patient for only so long, which was not very long.

"Well?"

Max slammed the bathroom door.

Clarence looked towards the door, then spoke in a whisper, afraid Max might hear. "I woke up in bed with a man."

Tim struggled to maintain a reality check. "You woke up in bed with a man. You, the guy who shagged two girls the same night on that trip to Corfu then shagged another one around lunchtime the next day?"

Clarence slipped down further in his chair and tried to avoid any further contribution to the conversation. He zipped himself up as the cat was already out of the bag.

"That guy who just left. The guy from the pub. It was him?"

"Yes."

"You've been seeing him?"

"Only once or twice."

Only once or twice, thought Tim. Well there's a thought. No different from the women then. "Do you fancy him?"

"No!" screamed Clarence. He almost jumped out of the chair, wishing to strangle a neck. "No," he whispered.

"Does he fancy you?"

Clarence ignored the question and instead gave Tim a dirty look of open disgust, and suspicion that his best friend was not taking his problem seriously.

"You know I've heard about this."

"About what? Having total blackouts and waking up with men in your bed?"

"No about midlife changes. We change they say. The male-female thing gets confused. It shifts, or something. Perhaps your blackouts are part of this."

"Tim what the fuck are you talking about? You're talking bollocks."

"Straight blokes sometimes go gay when they get older."

"I'm not old. And I'm not gay!"

"Well if you're not gay why are you sleeping around with men?" Tim was exasperated and becoming angry. In trying to be helpful he was quickly becoming pissed off with the lack of cooperation.

"I'm not. It was just a one-off."

"So it's not going to happen again?"

"No. Not if I can help it." Clarence kicked out at the table in front of him. The newspaper slipped off, dived, and divided. Its loose pages swept across the carpet. Someone would have to pick them up. In time it would be Max.

Tim decided time for a change of subject. "No squash then?"

"No. No squash. I'm too knackered."

"I bet you are."

Clarence kicked the table again. "Stop it Tim!"

"Sorry." Tim got up. "Come on let's go down the pub. If we can't exercise we can at least drink."

"Good idea."

They heard the toilet flush.

"Does Max want to join us?" asked Tim.

Clarence's response was immediate and firm. "No. Just us."

"Fair enough." Tim picked up his bag. "I'll just pop this back in the car."

"I'll put some shoes on, and clothes."

"And bring your wallet."

"And bring my wallet."

Clarence returned to his bedroom, dressed, and took one last long look at the bed before rejoining his best mate. It was now a dirty bed. He couldn't stomach sleeping in it again – at least not until he had washed the bedsheet. It had not been washed in ages and a wash was long overdue. It would have to be a hand job: no way it would squeeze into the washing machine.

Down the pub the pair found a table in the corner and claimed it as their own. There they sat, sometimes to watch the rest of the crowd, which was thin. For a time they were disconnected from each other. Clarence stared down into his glass. Tim alternated between his glass and Clarence: keeping a watch on both.

"Talk to me Clarence."

"What is there to talk about."

"These blackouts. Go and see someone. Will you go and see someone?"

"Yes."

"What you'll see someone? Someone who can help?"

"Yes."

Tim was surprised. The promise had come too easily. He had expected a fight.

"Can your GP help?"

"I've got the name of an expert."

"How come?"

"John recommended him."

"John? Who's John? Not the one who stormed out?" Tim tried not to choke as he spoke. The words tasted sour. They rose from his breath like stomach acid.

"Yes. But he's not my friend."

"Well whatever. Go and see the guy."

"I said I'll see him!"

Clarence pushed his glass towards his best mate. "Go get me another drink."

"Say please."

"Please."

Tim did as instructed and in time returned with two pints. "Say thank you."

"Thank you."

"Is it still going with that Fiona?"

"I don't know. I haven't seen her."

"She ignoring you?"

"I think so."

"Bad one. First Tracey and now this Fiona."

"That's about it."

"So you're not getting any then?"

"No. You are I take it?" Clarence raised the question in a sudden fit of jealousy.

"Me? Only just."

"Only just?"

"She's gone funny on me."

Clarence was suddenly interested in what his best mate had to say. Someone else's problem was exactly the tonic he needed right now. He swallowed a large liquid lump of beer.

"Gone funny on you? How d'you mean?"

"Doesn't hug me like she used to. I have to force it."

"Perhaps you squeeze too hard."

Tim went quiet and, copycat style, took a large swig of beer. He stared down at the wood grain pattern of the table top. "I think something's up. I think she's holding back on something."

"Holding back something?"

"Maybe just the baby thing." Tim looked up. "You know she doesn't want to have one – not now she says – as if she ever wanted one before."

"I know. She told me."

"She told you?"

"Just once. Just by mistake."

"Well don't tell her what I said today."

"I won't." Clarence felt the talk getting heavy so made an adjustment. "So you're still getting it then – if only just?"

"Yes but she doesn't put her life and soul into it. It's just a straightforward shag. I might as well make love to a sack of potatoes."

"Better than nothing I suppose. I'm sure she isn't seeing somebody."

Tim looked up sharply. His mate had spoken quickly, a little too ruefully.

"What do you mean?"

"Mean? What do you mean what do I mean? Just stated the obvious – or rather an answer to an obvious question."

Clarence was growing tired. He looked straight at his troublesome mate. "Look relax. I just meant she's just not like that. She wouldn't double-cross. You two have been together far too long for that. You're stuck with each other – I meant to say to each other, in a nice way."

"How do you know?"

"We go back a long way Tim. You get to know people." Clarence blocked further questions by slapping his mate lightly across the shoulders. The pair carried on drinking.

Clarence sat on his thoughts. Tim sat on his stool, replaying moments with Sam in his mind, trying to spot clues in her expression: the sound of her voice; the shove of her elbow; trying to trap evidence. Clarence did his best to hold them down. Tim did his best to spot any mistakes he may have made. Both failed.

For Clarence, one thought erupted unexpectedly and threw him into a fixation with guilt and the chaos which resulted. It was an old thought. It had been buried deep and covered over with the best of excuses. Time had done the rest, until now. He looked at Tim and began to sweat. Luckily Tim didn't look back – he may have thought it was to do with Sam. He was safe whereas Tim looked bad. He was the one with the big problem but Tim did look bad.

This one, old thought battered his head and set off a headache of massive proportions. Clarence tried to ignore it but it wouldn't go away. It was a guilt complex with a vengeance and it demanded resolution. Tim was clutching his pint. He was thinking of something hard. Clarence fingered his glass, guessing it had to be Sam. Shame if it all fell apart. Awful perhaps. His own thoughts he tried to drag back to the fore, but the big one was not having it. It refused to give ground.

Playing for time Clarence went to the bar and ordered two more pints. They were both consumed in haste. Both men were now committed to getting pissed. Tim began to talk about women again, but not about Sam, for which Clarence was grateful. Had Tim slagged her off he might have said something, something he might have regretted.

Regret. The sense of regret struck him down: the sense of regret that, if he hadn't said something before and if he didn't say something now, he might regret it for the rest of his life. He felt driven to confess. He couldn't stop himself. He became agitated, well beyond normal limits. Tim thought it had something to do with two men in a bed and tried to calm him down.

"Sleep on it. It will be OK in the morning. It was just a one-off, as you said."

"It's nothing to do with that." Clarence didn't want to be reminded.

"These blackouts? You're going to see this guy?"

"Yes I am – and it's not to do with that."

"What then?" Tim wanted Clarence to hurry up. He was feeling hungry and wanted food in his stomach - something greasy.

Before speaking Clarence wandered around the room, without ever actually leaving his chair. He was floating, on a sea of sewage. The only way out was to start swimming towards dry land. He set off, hoping it was in the right direction.

"You remember our last year at school."

"Sort of – doing A-Levels you mean?"

"Probably – yes A-Levels."

"And?"

"And you were after that girl Jackie."

"Jackie?" Tim put his head back and pushed his arms out, increasing the distance between him and his beer in doing so. He reeled it back in.

"Just about. Jackie? Always the one with the red lipstick to hand?"

"And the big boobs."

"Lovely things."

The memory of a beautiful pair of boobs cheered them both up a little.

Tim returned to the present. "And what about her?"

"I was after her as well."

For Clarence this was a partial admission of guilt: but there was more to come. For Tim it was an anticlimax.

"So? Everyone was after her. She was the best looking girl in town. She was fucking gorgeous."

Clarence felt a shiver of anticipation. A line of slugs was creeping down his back. An army of ants was crawling all over his face. But there was no turning back. He had said too much. He was at a loose end, the cruellest kind.

"I was in love with her. I was really in love with her."

"You didn't just fancy her then?"

"No it was more than that."

"So what exactly are you trying to tell me?"

Tim bit off a large measure of beer, now alerted to the fact that his old mate Clarence – one mixed up Clarence – had something serious to say.

"She really fancied you you know. You know that don't you?"

"No I didn't."

"But she thought you were seeing Tricia, for good."

"I was seeing Tricia – but nothing happened so I dumped her."

"I know. I was scared."

"Scared? Scared of what?"

"Scared I wouldn't be in there."

"Clarence I'm hungry. I want food. What is this about?"

"I lied."

"You always lie."

"I lied about you, my best friend."

"You lied to Jackie? What did you say?"

Clarence wanted to cry. It would make him feel better. "I said you had herpes."

"You said I had herpes?" Tim looked up at the ceiling. "You said I had herpes."

"Yes." The tears began to flow, just as Clarence had made peace with himself on the subject of double-crossing his best mate, his oldest best mate, the best one he had ever had.

Tim could not take it anymore and burst out laughing.

"Why are you laughing?"

"Why am I laughing? We were sixteen, seventeen, whatever. We were fucked up teenagers for Christ's sake. Does it matter now?"

"No I suppose not."

Tim slapped his mate on the back, hard. "So forget it. Lighten up."

"I still feel bad about it."

"Well for fuck's sake don't feel bad around me. I've got my own problems."

Another basement thought erupted, another one in possession of its own guilt complex. This one was smaller, less intense, but still present, still subverting his peace of mind when he had nothing better to think of.

"I also lied to Samantha."

"You also lied to Sam?" Suddenly Tim was fired up.

"You had just met. We were drunk. She was drunk. I was jealous."

Tim spoke in a hurry. "You lied. You said you lied. What did you lie about?"

Clarence swallowed before speaking in his lowest, lightest voice possible. It didn't help. "I told her you had a small willy."

"Thanks a lot."

Tim attacked his beer again, and pushed aside all thoughts of outrage and protest. Soon after he dumped them. After all they had all been drunk – so Clarence said. He couldn't remember so he guessed he had to have been drunk. He couldn't even remember the first time he had met Sam. Perhaps that was part of the problem now. He stared back at Clarence and saw him shrink with anticipation of something awful about to hit him.

"Don't worry. I forgive you. You were drunk. And obviously it didn't put her off."

"Sorry."

"Apology accepted – just don't do it again OK?"

"OK."

Later on, after they had talked football then the pros and cons of marriage to death, one of them made the mistake of raising the subject of work. Clarence talked about wanting to get out but having no idea where to go. Tim talked about never getting promoted and finding the job as boring as hell but as he was making tonnes of money so he put up with it. He'd stick with it and get out when he was fifty.

Clarence asked what he would do with all that spare time and no kids when he was fifty, at which point Tim sank into gloom. Clarence joined him, for totally different reasons and together they sank into their beers and joked about suicide, sex, and ladies' lingerie. They looked around the pub but there was no totty to stare at and declothe. It was nearly all blokes and a few older women – women their age which was no good.

Angry that his life was being fucked up by no fault of his own Clarence became agitated. He thought about school, then Fiona, then Ramsey; at which point he wanted to get up and hit the cretin even though he wasn't on the premises. Tim had to hold him down. Finally, concerned for public safety and his friend's well-being, Tim escorted him home. On the way Clarence began to cry and Tim had to hold him close, tight, and in the upright position.

Back at the flat Clarence crashed out on the sofa and demanded fried bacon, in a sandwich. Tim said stuff the bacon sandwich he wanted a proper fry-up. Clarence put on the TV and found the football. The world was now a slightly better place to live in.

Tim tried to fry and watch football at the same time. He was not successful. Clarence was falling asleep, which was good. He could do with a break and it meant more bacon for him.

The door bell rang. Clarence was roused but could not be bothered to get up. With no sign of the lodger Tim was left to answer it, which he did, though he was loathed to leave the pan or the football. It was a young woman.

"Who is it?" shouted Clarence.

"A woman!"

"Well invite her in stupid!" Clarence was now fully awake, and expectant.

Tim turned back to the woman. "Sorry about that. Would you like to come in?"

"Thank you I would."

She stepped in, followed by a cat.

"Sorry I don't know your name?"

"Rebecca."

"Clarence, it's Rebecca!"

As Rebecca entered the room Clarence pretended to doze off. Then Judy made her entrance and proceeded to make his life hell. Through narrow cracks he spied on her as she sniffed his trousers and threatened to jump up into his lap. Tim and Rebecca stood watching.

"He's not looking good," she noted.

"He's not feeling too well. Had a bad night," explained Tim, knowing full well that Clarence was playing a stunt.

"Who hasn't. Has he seen a doctor?"

"Oh nothing like that: just too much beer. Just needs some food inside him. You need some food inside you don't you Clarence!"

"I can hear perfectly well."

"See he's fine."

Rebecca sniffed, feeling excluded from some big joke. She smelt burning, as did Judy. "What's that burning smell?"

"Shit. My bacon. Our bacon."

"Here let me. He likes me to cook for him."

There was no stopping the woman and she charged into the kitchen where she took charge. Tim didn't try to stop her. A woman to cook for him while he was watching football? Just like home.

He called after her. "It's not just the bacon. It's everything. A full fry up!" He didn't know if she had heard him: a case of wait and see.

Clarence kicked the cat away and it chased after its mistress. Tim rejoined him on the sofa.

"So this is Rebecca, who cooks for you. What about Fiona?"

"I've no idea. I've no idea what's going on. As long as she just cooks, fine."

Clarence turned up the football to wash away his fears.

Rebecca stuck her head around the door. "The eggs, mushrooms and tomatoes. Is it all meant to be fried?"

"Yes please! And a slice of bread each if you please, fried – and whatever you're having!"

"I don't eat this kind of stuff."

"Suit yourself," said Clarence in a low voice.

Tim poked him with his elbow.

In time Rebecca returned with two plates of heart-warming hot food: hot and scrumptious and high on the toxicity scale. Tim pretended to nudge Clarence awake and Clarence pretended to be asleep again. As a joke it was wasted.

"Fried food will do you no good you know."

"I'll survive," said Clarence.

Rebecca surveyed the scene. "I'll get you some mats – though I don't know how you can eat off your laps like that."

"Practice."

Tim called after her. "Thanks for the food!"

"Yes thanks," added Clarence, abysmally.

"No problem!" Rebecca hadn't heard him, which was good for both of them.

She returned with mats and sat down. "Judy!"

Judy appeared and jumped up into her lap. There she sat purring, savouring the food and hoping to catch the cast-offs.

"How's the food?"

Rebecca had addressed herself to Clarence but it was Tim who answered.

Tim raised his plate. "Great. You managed to save the bacon."

Clarence winced. "Give it a rest for Christ's sake."

"Thank Rebecca for cooking you a nice lunch Clarence."

"No."

"Go on."

Clarence raised his plate. "Thanks." Then he turned on Tim. "Can we watch the football now? In peace?"

"Of course we can."

Rebecca watched Clarence eat. Eating out of his lap: it was a sight for sore eyes. A team scored a goal. Tim swung a fist and yelled 'yes'! Clarence barely reacted, conscious that he was being watched all the time by the woman in the corner, the woman with the bloody cat. The fried food did help matters though.

Rebecca did not stay quiet for long. "You said I could come over and talk, anytime."

"So talk."

Tim looked up. Clarence didn't. Rebecca stalled.

"He'll be better when he's got some food down him."

"Will he?" Now she was here she felt required to say something. Quickly she thought of something. "You said yesterday what was the point."

"The point off what?" One all and it was nearly half-time.

"Why waste all that energy marching and shouting. Why not just write to people, email them, persuade them. Network, you said. Why not network."

"Why not?" replied Clarence. It was all he could think of to say. Then a centre forward missed a goal two minutes before the half-time whistle and Clarence was disgusted, as was Tim.

"He should have had that."

"Would have set them up nicely."

Rebecca interrupted the play. "Because you need passion."

"You need what?"

"You need passion. You need to show it. Demonstrate it. You can't just win people over with logic. You have to protest."

"Do you. I'm very happy for you. Now can we watch the football?"

She gave up, grabbed her Judy, got up and make her exit. "I'll see you when I do Clarence."

"Sure."

"Thanks for the food," added Tim.

"That's quite alright. Just don't eat too much of that stuff it will send you to an early grave."

"We won't."

Get stuffed, thought Clarence.

"I'll see myself out. Bye Clarence. Come on Judy. Let him watch his football in peace."

"Ta," said Clarence under his breath.

"Nice to meet you, Tim?"

"That's right."

And on that note Rebecca left, in a rush. She needed to calm down. Tempted by fried bacon, Judy now demanded to be fed. She also needed to calm down.

✦ ✦ ✦

Log Entry

The point at which the emotional content of male friendship intensifies and transmutes into a passion for physical embrace and sexual desire is not easy to trap, nor the triggers which cause the transformation. Time does not appear to be a factor. My host has a close acquaintance of many years standing but there is never any hint of their friendship progressing beyond that point where it is now. There is a definite emotional bond – a bond which sometimes buckles under strain and requires repair – but never any suggestion of sexual desire by either side. On the other hand a very recent encounter with a male on my part has evolved immediately into an intimate relationship requiring sexual fulfilment on his part. It remains unfulfilled as I do not see it my place to permit such sexual engagement: nor do I see how it could be facilitated. It is not my body to experiment with; and to use it for a purpose for which it is obviously not intended would be an abuse of my position.

The male friend in question continues to exercise affection, despite the lack of reciprocation by my host. Denial is not necessarily a barrier. It can be an enticement.

The release of a guilt complex associated with a past misbehaviour appears to be very therapeutic for my host. Bearing in mind his current fragile state I may enable others as and when circumstances allow. There are a few still buried deep within his psyche and literally aching to explode.

With respect to males, the power of the television set, when displaying scenes of many other fit and healthy males engaged in some high profile sporting activity, is overwhelming. It is a magnet. It casts a spell, and it is a barrier: even an openly vulnerable female offering emotional engagement cannot breech it. The television set is master. It holds the position of supremacy every time.

The ability of the male to effortlessly crush the spirit of the female is astounding. Without even trying, my host reduced a female to the level of private distress and open hostility; such that she almost fled the scene, to inflict psychological damage upon herself, possibly even physical. This was a shame as I felt, on the evidence of previous encounters, that there was the opportunity for a greater degree of engagement between the two. I feel this situation needs rectifying. I will try to make amends on his behalf. Perhaps a gift accompanied by an apology: one which can make contact with her inner-most, most deeply held preoccupations.

The female in question is driven by her emotional demands more so than others – male or female. She will not let go of an emotional need until it is satisfied or made redundant by another – one which is stronger - and that often demands involvement by others in her concerns as and when it suits her. If she does not receive it, or the contribution is considered inadequate, she either retreats back into her shell or hits out. There is no compromise. There is no neutral position. There is no letting go.

✦ ✦ ✦

Log Entry

When I visited the female I accidentally interrupted one of her exercise routines: stretching out her limbs in every direction possible; and bending joints to almost breaking point. It was all performed very slowly she told me, intention being to exercise all body muscles, big and small. It made her feel good afterwards, she said. I apologized.

Her severe displeasure with my host's previous conduct was mitigated by the positive reaction her pet cat gave me: its enthusiasm for my appearance mattered and went someway towards my rehabilitation. I apologized vigorously for my host's behaviour and explained the reason why. This illumination she found funny and stimulating. When I proceeded to present her with a gift, the stimulation became outright excitement; especially when I explained that I had made the effort to match the gift to some aspect of her life, unfulfilled or unresolved, which was close to her heart.

The gift was a book: a book being a physical device which captures printed communication, be it words or pictures; in such a way that it can be conveniently held in the hand for viewing and mental absorption. I decided not to disclose that I had found the book by chance whilst inspecting my host's collection. To date my observations of the female mind suggested that this would not have been a good idea. The book was a handbook offering advice and suggestions on the subject of sexual intercourse: how to extract additional pleasure from what otherwise can become a very familiar, routine experience; and how to vary the manner of its execution. Its title simply referred to the joy of sex, which neatly summed up its scope and contents.

Her reaction was difficult to gauge as it was for the most part repressed and hidden from view. On the surface her response was muted and polite. She thanked me for the book and promised to read it sometime. The emphasize on the word 'sometime' leads me to believe that there are many other more important matters making demands upon her time; and therefore this will be low down on her list of priorities. No matter. It is the thought which counts.

Confusion set in when I also presented her cat with a gift, again one close to the heart of the recipient. It was a collection of small dead fish held in an oil-based solution, and sealed in an airtight metallic container. I enquired if between them they would be able to open it. She confidently replied yes, that would not be a problem. She said that she had encountered such objects many times before. I expressed my relief. Then she laughed, as if some kind of joke had been made.

I thanked her and made my exit, expressing my hope to see her again, perhaps to consume food together. She promised to consider it. (The consumption of food is a subject of importance both to her and my host, and may be instrumental in bringing them closer together. My interventions can them reduce and perhaps even stop completely.)

Chapter Thirteen

Clarence sat outside the office of the psychiatrist and watched the big white clock on the wall as he served time. He wanted to be anywhere else, even school. Sod's Law and his own suspicions of everything medical convinced him that he would suffer a blackout there and then. He held on to his chair but it was not to be. He would have to face this psychiatrist fellow, and with a hangover, which he did his best to conceal.

When she wasn't taking phone calls the receptionist lady behind the desk occasionally looked up from her appointments book and precious paperwork to check him out for signs of contamination. She had addressed him once, upon his arrival, and felt no need to follow it up. She ignored him. He ignored her.

The office door was wrenched open and a young, slim woman made a peculiar, fast exit. She did not look left or right as she rushed across the reception area towards the next door and the freedom beyond. As far as Clarence could tell she looked normal enough, though perhaps a bit too skinny for his liking. There was nothing worse than squeezing bone in bed. It was like sleeping with the dead.

That aside she had his sympathies. Clarence didn't like seeing doctors. They poked around. They asked too many questions. They stuck their fingers and noses into other peoples' parts. They made him feel ill. Just waiting to see this fellow made him feel physically ill. That said, it could have been the hangover still hanging on.

A crisp, commanding voice sprang out of the intercom and instructed the receptionist to send him in. This she did, with just three words: words articulated in a way which was devoid of all accent and warmth. It reminded Clarence of the headmaster's office. He complied, while making a point of saying nothing; not that she cared.

Pretending to read his latest case notes from the previous patient, the psychiatrist studied Clarence as he dragged his feet across the room and sat down. The man looked wasted, beyond repair. His act of open surveillance altered the body language of his subject: Clarence slid into the designated chair as if he had poohed in his pants and didn't want the person opposite to know about it.

The psychiatrist slipped his case notes into a pink cardboard folder and filed that away in a metal cabinet just within reach to his right. Such was the routine, he could do the whole action with just one hand, and almost without looking. Clarence was impressed but feared there was something similar with his name on it. The psychiatrist introduced himself – his name was Philips, and he was a doctor of Psychiatry – then introduced Clarence to himself, as if they were being monitored by some hidden third party. Philips immediately issued a legal disclaimer.

"I must make it clear from the start that you are not my patient. I won't be taking notes or starting a case file. Is that understood?"

"Perfectly." Not the headmaster's office, thought Clarence, the solicitor's.

"I'm not particularly keen on doing this but John begged me."

"He begged you?"

"That's right." Philips suddenly turned up the dial on the level of seriousness. "Is that a problem for you?" He sounded heavy.

Clarence dismissed the problem out of hand. "Me? No. He can beg as much as he likes."

"Can he. Tell me how are things between you and John?"

Clarence felt himself walking towards a trap. He side-stepped with a comfortable, bland answer; the kind he had heard a hundred times before.

"Same as ever. We have our ups and downs."

From that Philips took a lot.

Philips leaned back in his chair. It was designed to tilt and swivel and roll across the floor; and could be adjusted along three different lines. He had spotted it at a knock down price in a closing down sale of office and computer equipment. He also had one at home. "George still sees John I understand. How do you feel about that?"

Clarence sat up, back straight, slightly alarmed, but mainly mystified. He was suddenly much more awake.

"How do I feel about what?"

"About George still being important in John's life."

Philips began to twiddle the pen he was holding. It was something he always did about the second or third question in. Headmaster thought Clarence. Another bloody headmaster.

"Who gives a toss? I certainly don't."

"You don't give a toss. That's strong language isn't it?"

Clarence fought back. "Not in my book."

"Are you angry right now?"

"Angry? No. Impatient? Yes."

"Impatient? Why impatient?"

"Because we're talking about this guy John who I barely know, and a friend of his who I only met once, very briefly. I don't know what John's been telling you but let me make it quite clear that we are just acquaintances – not even proper friends."

Clarence came up for air. "Look are we here to talk about John – John and bloody George – or me?"

Philips backed down, sensing a change of tack was required. "Sorry. You're quite right. As I said this is not a proper first interview. I know John. He's a friend, so in that respect I struggle to be an impartial observer I'm afraid. I'm involved, which is why I cannot formally take you on as a patient of mine."

"Understood."

All that said, still Philips hung on. He could not completely let go. The discrepancy was too wide. "So you and John are barely friends?"

"Correct. Can we move on?"

"Of course." Philips looked over the top of his glasses: up at the ceiling which had just been repainted white by the overbearing but cheap brother of his receptionist; then across at Clarence, who looked like he was now looking for a fight. He had all the hallmarks of a full-time drunk.

"Tell me what's been going on then: in your own words and in your own time." Philips looked at his watch. "But be aware I've only got thirty minutes."

And you're not getting paid for it, thought Clarence. He folded his arms but otherwise stretched out, legs to the limit, as if about to be interviewed by the same policeman for the third time about the same thing when absolutely nothing had changed.

"Blackouts. I've been having these blackouts."

Philips immediately interrupted. "Have you seen your GP?"

Before answering Clarence looked away, at some big, brown chunky hardbacks stacked up on a bookshelf to the right of the psychiatrist. They were imposing, important looking, which was the reason why they had been placed there.

"Yes." The reply was slow in coming, and sounded chewed up. It was the vocal equivalent of old chewing gum.

"And what did he find?"

"Nothing." The follow-up came at lightening speed.

"Nothing? Have you had a brain scan?"

"Yes. At the hospital. Still nothing."

Philips scratched his nose unintentionally and it began to itch. He had to scratch it some more. Clarence did much the same.

"How long do they last these blackouts?"

"How long is a piece of string?"

"Meaning?"

"Minutes. Hours. At worse a whole day can go by – but that's extreme, and rare."

"A whole day?"

Clarence began to fidget. "That's right." 'And what's it to you', he wanted to add.

"And you remember nothing?"

"That's right."

"And the doctors have found nothing?"

"That's right. Found nothing. Sometimes it's not exactly a blackout."

"It's not? What is it then?"

"Hard to say. More like a kind of semi-trance, where I can see what I'm doing but I'm not in charge. It's like I'm watching from one side as another me is running things. At the time I want to do whatever it is I'm doing but I don't know why."

"'Another me' in charge? You must go back and see your GP and have him - or her - investigate this further."

"I will, asap."

"Are you suffering from excessive stress at work at the moment? You're a teacher I understand? Mixed comprehensive?"

"None at the moment. I'm off work."

"And before?"

"None. My girlfriend was a pain in the arse sometimes. But that's part of the deal with girlfriends isn't it?"

"So you had a girlfriend before you met John?"

Clarence glared back, feeling put on. "Yes I did. And I still do. Will you forget it about John. He's not my friend. I don't like the guy. I just met him – during one of these blackouts."

"You met John during one of these blackout episodes? I didn't know that. It's a strange kind of blackout."

"Well you do now. Now no more about John. Alright?" Clarence was becoming highly agitated. The chair was in danger of losing him.

Philips carefully laid down his pen at its usual place and spread his hands up and out as if to show he was hiding no cards, no wires. "Understood." He returned to script.

"So before these blackouts started to happen no problems with work, family -" Philips paused. "Or girlfriends?"

"No. It was simply work, play, TV, sports; and beer with my mates – and seeing my girlfriend of course for you know what."

"Of course."

Clarence caught something in the reply. "What? You don't believe I had – I have – a girlfriend?"

"Yes of course I believe you. Please calm down . . . Mr . . ."

"Kennan."

"Sorry. Mr Kennan." Philips looked up at the ceiling again - it was a lovely, outstanding white – and searched his mind for his backlog of standard screening questions.

"Memory problems?"

"Only with regard to the blackouts – total blackouts – otherwise fine. In fact never been better."

"And you're eating OK?"

"Like a dog."

"Do you drink a lot?"

"No I don't think so. I'm single and still young, just about, so like any guy in my position it's difficult not to drink."

"I see." Philips was a teetotaller so didn't agree with that sentiment. "Did you drink heavily last night?"

"Yes."

Philips was not surprised by the answer. "Why?"

"Why not? Had a bad day."

"Why was it bad?"

"Had a bit of a shock."

"Why what happened?"

Clarence considered his options and plumped for the safest. "I learnt my best friend's wife might be having an affair."

"And that was a deep shock for you?"

"Yes he's my best friend?"

"But she's not your wife? It's not your marriage. Surely deep concern is a more appropriate reaction in this day and age?"

"Sorry if I wasn't 'appropriate' enough."

Philips let it go. "Is there anything you do to excess?"

"No."

"Problems sleeping?"

"Not when I'm alone, no."

Philips was suddenly hooked. "Meaning what exactly?"

"Meaning nothing. It was just a joke."

The patient can make a joke of it, thought Philips. He can't take a joke, thought Clarence.

"And the relationship with this girlfriend is fine?"

Clarence side-stepped again. "Fine. Better than fine."

"What's her name by the way? Just out of interest."

Clarence had to pick and mix. "Fiona." His voice sounded limp: a fact which did not pass Philips by.

"Have you told her about your problems?"

"Yes."

Problems? thought Clarence. Surely problem?

"And her response was?"

"Very supportive," replied Clarence, convinced now that the psychiatrist had mutated into a policeman.

"You get on well with your parents? Sorry I'm assuming they are still alive. Is that the case?"

"They are and I do."

"How do you feel about them? Any favourites?"

"Favourites? What do you mean? Are we talking about food now?"

"Sorry: loose language. No I mean do you get on better perhaps with your mother rather than your father?"

"Neither."

"You get on with neither of them?"

Sternly Clarence made a correction. "No that's not what I said. I get on with them equally well – or equally not at all if I've done something wrong in their eyes."

Philips nodded and checked the time on the fat metal watch which was strapped around his fat wrist. He was rapidly becoming bored. He would cut it short he decided: after all he was doing this for free. He rushed on through the remains of his checklist.

"Ever felt put on? As if others are ganging up on you?"

"No."

"Have you ever felt abandoned? Do you feel abandoned after these blackouts?"

"No and no." Clarence was beginning to find his spirit and rhythm.

"Have you ever hurt yourself?"

"Only when playing football – or falling over drunk."

"No I mean on purpose: to spit yourself; to punish yourself."

Clarence stared back as if the man was mad. "No. Never. Why would I want to do a stupid thing like that? I'm not crazy."

"No of course you're not." Philips picked up his pen again and began to click it repeatedly. He did it purely for effect, having once seen it done in a really good movie. "One more question. When was the last time you got angry?"

Now Clarence looked up at the ceiling. Its brilliance was not wasted on him. He wished his could be like that: and it could if he bothered to paint it. He decided to paint it, sometime. Meanwhile a bolt of reflected sunlight smashed into his eyeballs and he had to look away, sharpish. Philips took the sharp reaction as a sign of anger at having been asked the question.

"Yesterday, early afternoon." Clarence was very clear in his mind about the time.

"And for what reason?"

For what reason Clarence was in no doubt. "A woman kept interrupting the football, and kept telling me I was eating crap food."

"Your girlfriend Fiona?"

"No another one."

"You have another girlfriend?"

"No of course not. Though I think she'd like to be."

"Interesting."

Clarence zeroed in on the psychiatrist. He wanted to know what was so fucking interesting - especially as he hadn't said anything remotely interesting. "Why interesting?"

Philips thought back to his conversations with John. "Oh nothing."

Then, looking tired, feeling lazy and ready to give up, he was suddenly disturbed. He sat up and in return Clarence suddenly felt very anxious, as if he was about to receive bad news.

"Just one last thing."

"What?"

"Has anybody else ever witnessed these blackouts?"

Clarence struggled with himself, wishing badly that he could say yes, but knowing that the answer was no and that for this question he had to tell the truth.

"No I can't honestly say they have – or if they have they haven't told me."

"Never? Not even a little?"

"No. Not even a little."

"I see."

"You see what?"

"Nothing. Calm down. I didn't mean anything by it." The clicking stopped: Philips put his pen down. It was nearing lunchtime. "Well I think that wraps it up."

"Wraps it up? So this is it is it?"

"I'm afraid so. As I said before you must follow this up with your doctor. Go see him again. He'll get you specialist help."

Clarence got up in a temper and a rush, almost kicking over the chair. "So you can't help me?"

"I'm afraid not. Not with just one interview. And as I said –"

"I know. I'm not your patient. You're just doing me favour."

"Exactly. Sorry."

"Thanks for nothing."

Like the woman before him Clarence bolted for the door, then before opening it stopped in his tracks and turned. For a moment Philips was alarmed: was the scene about to turn ugly?

"I notice you like to ask questions." Clarence was suddenly very calm, and came across as very confident.

Philips was slightly vexed. "It's my job: to ask questions."

"But it's more than that. You even like to be the one asking questions outside work, outside this room."

Philips became defensive. It was his turn to sit up. "I don't know what you mean."

"This set up - the office, the reception area - each is a shell. When you step inside each one you become more focused; more the centre of power and authority. Here your questions and advice carry more weight than out there, or at home. Your home is not a place you ever feel comfortable in."

"Sorry but I've no time for this. I don't know where it's coming from but it's all pure speculation." For someone who had just be subjected to pure speculation, Philips came across as someone stung by a harsh truth. Then he was struck by a thought.

"Hang on a second are you having one of your blackouts?"

"Yes, I suspect so."

"You suspect so. Tell me can you recall what we spoke about ten minutes ago?"

"Ten? Was it as long as ten?"

"Five then. Tell me what we spoke about five minutes ago."

Clarence thought hard. "Yes I believe so."

Philips waited. Nothing. He became irritated. "Well tell me then."

"You spoke about John and George, which made me impatient; and which reminded me of the Beatles. You've heard of the Beatles?"

"I think I have."

"They were a huge, world-wide musical phenomenon in –"

Philips cut him off. "Yes I have heard of them."

"Well, anyway, I denied any true friendship, which you found particularly interesting. You asked about my health – stress in particular – eating, drinking, sleeping habits. I said –"

Philips threw up his hands. "OK that's enough. You've made your point."

Clarence gave the psychiatrist an extended look of puzzlement, one which made Philips nervous again.

"What is it now?" He wanted to know.

"You seem to resent it when your patients are able to give you a full and coherent explanation about their behaviour in response to one of your questions."

"Do I?"

"Yes. We are back to the point about you using your profession status as a platform from which to exercise power and authority over others; others often less able to exert their natural confidence."

Philips squinted, as if being suddenly blinded by a burst of sunlight.

"I think that's enough."

"Sorry did I overstep the mark?"

Philips lied. "There is no mark to overstep. I've just run out of time." It was his ultimate fallback position.

"I detect an inferiority complex."

"Do you now."

"And the reason is your wife?"

Such was his training that Philips had to listen and take note. "Go on?"

"Does your wife work?"

"Yes."

"In what capacity?"

"She's a qualified doctor, a General Practitioner."

"And does this make you feel inferior?"

Philips shook himself free of his own routine. "OK that's enough. This has gone far enough."

"Sorry."

"Best you leave now."

But Clarence was not ready to leave just yet. "Tell me do you enjoy pulling minds apart?"

"There's no need for that. I'm just doing my job. I was asked to see you."

"No I really am interested. What drove you into such a profession? Human minds are difficult to penetrate, even when they are fragile. How do you do it?"

"Penetrate is perhaps over stating it. I examine and evaluate what comes out of it."

"And does that ever tire you out?"

"Tire me out? Why would it tire me out? I do an eight hour day like any other job."

"But all those barriers to fight your way through. All those self-imposed misconceptions you have to expose and strip away – and without causing further damage."

"It's what I'm trained to do."

Clarence had another question. "Tell me how fragile is the human mind?"

"Depends upon the human in question."

"Good answer."

"Thank you."

And still Clarence had more to say. "I can't help but notice that your approach appears mechanically driven, driven by routine checklists. You compartmentalize all answers and use those as your starting point for deeper exploration and analysis. Yet no matter how far you go, you will always shape your findings in relation to the nature of the original questions. Why not just let your patients talk and talk? Let them talk about something they feel strongly about then try to make sense of the output in its entirety?"

"Have you quite finished? Because I have."

"Now you're becoming defensive, agitated."

"That's because I get fed up with people who have an amateur understanding of the highly complex subject of psychiatry and want to lecture me – me a professional with many years training and practical experience behind him - on how to do his job." On the last word Philips ran out of breath, but not anger.

"I apologize. I never intended to tell you how to do your job."

"Apology accepted. Now go."

Clarence opened the door. "Why complicated?"

"What?"

"Surely there are only so many ways to elicit information about the human mind, and only so many varieties of basic mental illness?"

"Please. Just go." Philips was starting to beg.

Seeing the pain creeping across his host's face, Clarence left as instructed, receiving a dirty look from the receptionist on his way out. She seemed to have aged during the course of the interview.

✦　✦　✦

Log Entry

The human mind fascinates other humans; almost as much as sex, food, drugs and other wild animals. But though some try - some exceedingly hard it appears - they can never connect. It operates in isolation. At best one assumes a connection with one other: one other which also assumes the same connection. The result is the declaration and manifestation of a deep spiritual relationship: a relationship often accompanied by sexual interaction but not necessarily so. Sometimes the connection made is with the fictitious entity 'God'. It is assumed that he (rarely she or it) is always listening, and that the conscious mind is of deep concern to him.

These connections are very demanding. At their most extreme one expects the other to always be in the right position to receive and retain its output with understanding and without criticism; to always be supportive; to always react in the way desired for that particular moment; in some cases to be nothing less than subservient.

The human mind has a compulsion to share nearly all that it generates but is so inhibited that much of it remains trapped or suppressed. In the worse cases the invention of a god (or more likely the adoption of somebody else's god) or a collection of other supernatural forces may be its only relief.

The human mind plays tricks on itself (accidentally) and on others (usually on purpose, and for pleasure). Internal tricks are typically: the pretence of self-denial, happiness, realisation, rationalisation – in fact any positive state of mind it deems deficient in or missing; likewise the avoidance of emotional pain, rejection and deflation, awkward revelations and anti-climax, and any other negative state of mind. This way, for most of the time, the mind is able to maintain its defences and state of balance.

Sometimes, in extreme situations where there is no balance and has been none for an extended period of time, the mind simply explodes with a burst of energy which is directed into the physical; else collapses, silently. The remains, no matter how severely damaged or disconnected, are left to pick up the pieces (so to speak) and carry on performing basic functions as best they can. Even one simple malfunction, no matter how minor, is amplified with regard to the outside world; bringing the whole conscious being into disrepute and, more often than not, forced to defend its integrity and vitality for life.

The triggers for an explosion or collapse are varied. It may simply be a constant stream of excessive external pressure: the kind which cannot be absorbed and deconstructed; or dismissed and forgotten. It may be an unintentional reminder of, or an attack upon, something deeply buried and indigestible. Forced to the surface this aberration can cause total disruption to the state of balance. It may be something so alien that the human mind is unable to accommodate it, yet equally is unable to reject it: end result being the mind functions in a heightened, frenzied state of imbalance and slowly – or quickly - wears itself out, towards collapse.

With regard to the passage of time the human mind has a variable, love-hate relationship. Sometimes it moves at just the right pace required to absorb, translate, reflect and perhaps enjoy, else recover. At other times it flies by, without cause or reason; leaving nothing to hang on to. It has simply gone. Worse still it can slow to a tedious crawl: never catching up with the mind's agenda; always following in its footsteps; holding it back; suffocating it through a lack of co-operation.

The human mind constantly pushes on, into the future; wishing to let go of the past yet unable to do so. The past defines the present; and without the past there is no present; and without the present the mind becomes confused, unstable, unable to push on. Pushing is perhaps what the human mind does best.

Some human minds remain relaxed for much of the time. Others are easily excited and easily distracted. Others excite, unintentionally and without realising it. Others simply remain languid and unresponsive. They tend to survive the pressures of life intact and are rarely stretched beyond their capabilities. Likewise they rarely step outside their boundaries. Some are simply dysfunctional from the start and require special attention from whatever support services are available within the community. It appears that they do not always receive it.

The human mind loves to wander, to explore, to enter the realms of its own inventions; and it hates to have to come out. It does this best when the body is inactive, and at such times the mind is performing at its best. That said, it is possible for the mind to simultaneously both wander away from, and interact with, the physical world. It often does this when the physical world offers no stimulation and time is seen to drag. It can even happen in the presence of others, regardless of the degree of familiarity.

Fiction is the ultimate drug, the ultimate release, especially when it is audiovisual in nature. It provides a kaleidoscope of colour and emotional stimulation that the real world cannot match – at least not in one place or in one continuous passage of time. Fiction provides a sense of relief and escape from a reality which is sometimes brutal, demoralising. It is the ultimate drug as it has no limits and no negative, aftereffects – at least none which are immediately obvious. Most of all it gives the mind what it needs and demands: space and diversion, passion and persuasion. Without it the mind is potentially crippled. At its core the human mind requires an escape hole, a place of total freedom, a place to aspire to perfection. The human mind wants to fall in love with itself; and be loved, by itself.

The human mind lacks fixed boundaries, yet it requires them, and feels better if it thinks it has them in place. So it searches, often until it is worn out, or down. So it is never at peace with itself until it is too late to enjoy the fruits of its labour; or, on rare occasions, it finds a point of balance from which it never shifts, even when pushed. The anchor for this point of balance is often spiritual, and involves at least one god or supernatural force.

The human mind activity consumes the positive emotions emitted by others, and tries to use them for its own agenda and general welfare: adapting them; presenting them as self-made; reinventing them; usually unsuccessfully. These positive emotions could be passion (sexual, physical, intellectual), self-belief, aggression, relief, or contentment. To a lesser degree the opposite are also consumed: these it tries to dump, even more unsuccessfully. The end result is a permanent imbalance which can never be removed, but which can be contained within a greater framework of checks and balances.

The human mind is very good at coping with absolute, incontrovertible truths: those hard facts and mathematical models which officially describe their known physical universe. It likes things to add up, or at the very least not to be in conflict. It hates having to confront vagueness, or alternatives – especially when one alternative is considered to be more dangerous than another. Both distort and disturb the very fabric of certainty required by the mind to remain in charge. Some simply cannot cope.

The human mind is driven by appearance: it knows intuitively that it must always appear to be in command, at ease, above suspicion, beyond reproach; even when it is not. Appearances are difficult to maintain and so this deception is a heavy burden which must be carried throughout most of its life. Towards the end, when the end of life is in sight, it usually gives up; to be overwhelmed by a sense of total satisfaction. Death soon follows.

The human mind hates imperfections, and does its utmost to defeat them, deflect them or conceal them. Failing that it ignores them as best it can. Imperfections are typically: the sense of loss; feelings of inferiority; the inability to ignore anything which chooses to invade its space uninvited, and stay indefinitely.

The human mind operates at its best when it is focused on just one thing, and that one thing has the capacity to resolve uncertainty. The human mind hates uncertainty.

✦ ✦ ✦

Clarence did not drive straight home. There was a place he had to go first: the place where Fiona was hiding. He squeezed his car into a gap and freed himself from its confines. Immediately he felt better: he was standing in the street where she lived; in the same spot as before; and surrounded by much the same crowd of carefree cars. He looked at the curtains. The room was lit. She was in there somewhere, living life to the full and coping with it: getting things done; educating the uneducated; eating good, wholesome food; going out with friends; seeing family; and enjoying it all. In his mind he could see clearly the shape and texture of her hair. He saw her shake it. It shook him. He saw her eyes. They saw him, and he was taken prisoner again. He saw her lips move and he had to kiss them. He heard her voice and it commanded his respect. He saw her wrapped around her bed sheets and hugging a pillow, sleeping like only a baby could. He wanted to gather her up in his arms, and hold her tight, and say sorry, and beg forgiveness, and earn her respect; and never put her down. Naked, she was beautiful. Clothed, she was beautiful. Awake, she was wonderful. Asleep, she was wonderful. His thoughts tried to turn to sex and instant gratification but he dismissed them all. She deserved better. Another time perhaps.

He moved towards the door, heart pounding, head tearing itself apart as the wish to reveal himself was opposed in equal measure by the wish to hide. Each step cost the earth. Each step drained him of energy. Each step was back-breaking. He came within reach of the doorbell, whereupon he struggled to raise his arm and stretch out his hand. It weighed a ton, and more. He extended an index finger. Now he could press the doorbell, if he so chose. And if he pressed it it would bring her, his Fiona, to the door; and she would see him as he was, and for what he was; and she might not like what she saw. She might ask him questions. She might ask him in. She might send him on his way, greatly disappointed.

He wanted to press the doorbell but he held himself back. He wanted to ask for forgiveness, but he did not know what it was he had done wrong. He wanted her to see him at his best, but he knew he was at his worse. That, and the awful fact that he might never be at his best again proved to be decisive. He pulled back. He folded his index finger away in his pocket, turned, and walked off; feigning a stiff upper lip as he went. He did not see the curtain twitch.

He let go. He did not wish it but he let go. He thought of how it had all begun so well with Tracey, and how he had ended up taking her for granted. And though he was still confused by the final collapse, he feared exactly the same thing would repeat itself with Fiona. No, best remember the supreme moment, and capture it for prosperity. Fiona deserved better than that. She was the perfect woman. She deserved the perfect man.

Clarence drove home, flat as a pancake. Unable to face four walls he went for a long walk into town, winding his way through the shopping centre for the sake of distraction. He sought pleasure in the exchange of money for goods. He stared through shop windows at shoppers shopping and wanted to join in, to spend money, to intoxicate himself. He fingered his way through stacks of CD's in search of something eye-catching, something worth the effort of listening to, but found nothing of interest. He had reached the age where he could convince himself that he had heard it all before: every nuance of sound; every viable combination of words; every beat, rhythm, tempo; every combination of instruments and voices. He had his CD collection: no more did he need to buy CD's he decided. He left the shop empty-handed yet strangely satisfied, as if he had finally beaten some addiction, as if he had broken the first of many consumer chains.

He passed a bookshop. It was big and it was impressive. He had passed by it a hundred times before but had never stopped to look inside.

This time he stopped and peered in through the window, past the catchy window displays. Everywhere he saw mountains of books piled up on tables: big heavyweight hardbacks; small snappy paperbacks; and in between all other shapes and sizes. And then there were the books lining walls. He wanted to go in and search out the book which was just right for him, but felt he lacked the mental reserves with which to engage. And there was far too much choice. Deterred, he made his way home, setting a slow pace and demolishing a standard fare cheeseburger on his way; enjoying none of it except the distraction and its heat.

On his way home he shared the pavement with an on-coming tramp. They were acquainted. Wishing to avoid him Clarence made to cross to the other side of the road but the tramp beat him to it. Clarence felt insulted. The tramp felt relieved.

On his arrival home he was greeted with a shock, the kind which left him paralysed and pinned up against the wall with no way out, no bolt hole, no sense of reality; just a sense of unprovoked harassment. It had caught him on the hop, just as he was turning the key in the lock. And it had a voice, and that voice was that of a boy, a boy with a voice on the verge of breaking his balls. It was William, that William, and he was chewing cake. He held a piece in each hand: one was half eaten – the one which he was eating furiously. Alarmed, Clarence looked left and right and behind for sight of a Mary. There was no sighting. She was nowhere to be seen.

Still pinned against the wall, like a fly on sticky paper, Clarence tried to tackle the words which the boy had spoken – but not before forgetting what had been said.

He looked on blankly. "What did you say?"

William repeated himself. "I said Clarence can I come in?"

"You want to come in? Why do you want to come in? And what are you doing here?"

William kicked the ground, as was his habit. "I came to see you. You said I could come and see you anytime. I've been waiting ages."

"Why are you holding all that cake?"

"I'm eating it – oh that one's for you." William held out the untouched slice.

Clarence looked down at the cake. He only knew chocolate and it wasn't chocolate. "What is it? And where did you get it?"

"Carrot cake she said. She gave it to me."

"She? Who? Your mum?"

"No not her – the lady next door – over there." William pointed two doors down.

"Why did she give you cake?"

"For something to eat while I was waiting. I was hungry. I'm always hungry." William smiled, feeling proud that he had signed off with a joke.

"How long have you been waiting?"

"Half an hour?"

"You've been waiting here, half an hour, to see me?"

"Not here. At her place."

"Rebecca, the one with the cat?"

"That's right."

"Does your mum know you are here?"

"No."

"I'm calling her."

William jumped in. "She won't be home yet." Right now he had an answer for every eventuality.

Needing to resolve the puzzle, Clarence let the boy in, whereupon William began to stalk the living room, prowling for a place to settle, until Clarence made him stand on a spot while he went and poured himself a neat whisky. When he returned he found the boy still standing on his spot, eating cake like it was going out of fashion. He had started on the second piece. Clarence gave him a funny look, as if he had been delivered to the wrong address.

William, thinking he had been caught out, defended himself. "I assumed you didn't want it."

Clarence waved it away and collapsed gracefully into his sofa, careful not to spill his whisky. "Sure, go ahead." The loss of free cake was the least of his concerns.

William watched him fall, and his glass. "What's that?"

Clarence glanced down at his drink. "This? Whisky. My treat."

"Can I have some?"

"You? Certainly not."

William put on his special look, perfected over the years to make people feel bad about his situation, and spoke. "Can I have a beer then?"

It worked. Clarence was reminded of his first desperate, teenage requests for beer, and the subsequent subversive scavenging. "If there's lemonade to hand you can have it as a shandy – otherwise no."

William nodded, satisfied. He was in there.

Clarence checked out the kitchen: there was lemonade, still fizzy; so a beer shandy for the kid; and a beer for himself to wash down the whisky, or vice-versa.

Clarence handed William the glass with a strict condition attached. "If you ever tell your mum I'll kill you."

Again William nodded, this time not paying any attention, and wondering what it was like to get drunk. From everything he had seen and heard, it sounded too good to be true. Finally he was given permission to sit himself down. Clarence observed his movements across the expanse of carpet: an alien object had invaded his personal space. His thoughts began to float, back to his own youth. At any other time they would have been thoughts to savour. Now they simply highlighted his present predicament. Clarence shook them off and returned to his present surroundings, none refreshed.

"Did Rebecca say anything?"

William finished his cake. "Like what?" He needed specifics.

"Did she ask you anything?"

William licked his lips and fingers. "She asked me lots of things. Why?"

"Like what?"

"She asked me who I was."

"And you said what?"

William made it plain he thought it was a stupid question. "I told her I was William."

"You told her you were waiting to see me?"

"Sure. Why not?"

"Didn't she think it strange?"

William shrugged. "I don't know. I just told her you were doing up our bathroom – like you promised."

"You told her about your mum?"

"Of course. Why shouldn't I?"

Clarence let it go - the boy had a point - and continued drinking, as did William, doing his best to keep up. For awhile they drank together – the old bloke and the young bloke – until William could contain himself no more.

"My mum likes you you know."

Clarence could only stare down at the carpet. He had no response to such a charge so ignored it. It was an infantile outburst.

William had the upper hand and played it. "She's expecting you to call."

It was a neat lie but Clarence believed him, so adding to his misery. Then William spotted something peculiar on the shelves and pointed at it.

"What's that?"

"What's what?"

"All those?"

"That's my record collection. Vinyl."

"How do you play them?"

"On a turntable."

"Not like CD?"

"No, definitely not. They're analogue."

William looked bemused.

"You don't know what analogue is do you?" Clarence basked in the boy's ignorance.

"It's not digital then?"

Clarence looked up to the heavens to savour the moment. "God help us." Then it fell back down and struck him in the face. Was he really that old?

"Can we play one?"

"If you like."

Clarence rose up, as if lethargic, and made straight for the obvious choice. It was the right time for Dark Side Of The Moon. For his current state of despondency it was the perfect mate. Settled back in the folds of his sofa he stretched out, closed his eyes, and attached himself to the words and rhythm of the magic. William copied his moves but without result. It didn't take him too long to voice his disappointment.

"This is boring."

"Shout up and drink your beer."

"You said it was shandy."

"It's still got beer in it. Now shut up."

William did as directed and drank up.

Into the second track he got up and reconnoitred the room with military precision, looking for other surprises. He found one: Clarence also read Asimov. Clarence suddenly went back up in his estimation after the current relapse.

"Robots. The Robots are really good."

"Shut up." Clarence remained off limits.

"That's an old Walkman."

Clarence kept his eyes firmly closed. He would not be drawn. "Probably."

"I've seen those on Ebay. They only play old cassette tape."

"I know." Clarence kept hearing the word 'old' and didn't like it. Concentration gone, he gave up after the third track.

"Look what exactly are you doing here? Your mum doesn't know you're here. If you're here to ask me something in secret or demand some favour, then forget it. I'm not into playing those games."

His words were so strong, so uncompromising that William went rigid. But he wriggled free and fought back, knowing deep down he had to.

"Mum's waiting for you to phone to say you'll come round and finish the tiling."

"Well she can wait." Even as he spoke Clarence felt shamed: he opened his eyes. William was staring at him, like the arsehole he was.

'I'm not always an arsehole', Clarence wanted to say, but couldn't. So it was left to the jury to decide. Instead he said sorry.

"Sorry."

William moved quickly on. "When are you going to call her?"

Clarence sank the last trace of whisky. Now he had the beer to start on. "I don't know."

"You are going to phone her? You are going to finish it? She doesn't know how to."

"I don't know. I just don't know."

William pushed on, sensing his moment. "She wants you to phone her." He paused and swallowed hard. Something had stuck in his throat. "I want you to phone her."

Clarence looked up, slapped in the face by an emotional outburst from a most unexpected quarter. William made distance and kept his eyes down. He ended up flat against the window. Clarence didn't push for clarification.

"I'll think about it."

"You have to phone her."

"I said I'll think about it."

"You promised to finish the bathroom. It's a mess."

"I didn't leave it in a mess. I remember clearing up." The music began to give Clarence a headache. Pink Floyd had never given him a headache before. "I will. I will finish it."

"Promise?"

Clarence turned up the music to blot out the boy. "If that's it then, time you were off."

William didn't move from his spot by the window. He had one other thing, just as important, but more straightforward to deal with. It was just between him and the man Clarence. He delayed for ages before speaking, bemused by the strange music.

"I need more money."

"You need more money? What the hell are we talking about now?"

Pink Floyd added to the gravity of the moment by singing about money.

"I need more money to pay him off."

"Pay who off?" Clarence's head began to bulge. Things were all turning a bit too surreal.

"You know." William avoided the word.

"No I don't know. Pay who off?"

"Martin."

"And who is Martin?"

"Martin. The prat who's been picking on me."

"And you're paying him off?"

"Yes."

"Why don't you just punch the sod and send him on his way?"

"Because he's bigger than me – and you told me to pay him off."

"I told you to pay him off?"

"That's right."

William began to tire, experiencing the full effects of adult world-weariness for the first time. He felt he was sharing space and time with a blithering idiot. Now he was beginning to understand why adults so easily got fed up with the people around them.

Clarence thought and concluded, rapidly, that this boy was not making it up: considering his current state of mind it was just crazy enough to be true. Also if he gave the boy some money he would go away and leave him in peace. He found his wallet and handed over a tenner. William considered the cash value of the note in his hand and was not impressed. "Is that all?"

Clarence reconsidered. Fair point: ten pounds didn't go far these days. He placed another one on top. "That's your lot."

"Fair enough."

Clarence felt aggrieved. "A thank you would be nice."

"Thank you." William sounded like he didn't mean, when actually he did. He just struggled with gratitude - as he did with anything else which unconsciously involved submission. He pocketed the money: out of sight it was safe.

"Time you went home."

"I know."

William didn't move.

"Well off you go then." Clarence almost had to push him towards the door.

William got the hint. "Alright I'm going."

"Good."

At the door William stopped. "You will ring my mum?"

"I'll think about it."

"And finish the tiling?"

"I said I'll think about it."

"But you promised."

"No I didn't."

"You have to finish it. You can't just leave it like that. And she wants you to call her. I can tell."

Clarence withered under the constant, unremitting pressure of a boy's torturous repetition. "I'll call her when I'm better."

"Better? Better than what?"

"Better. As in feeling better?" Now it was William's turn to look stupid. "I'm under the weather right now. Tell her I'm under the weather right now – no don't tell her anything. Don't even tell her you were here. Understood?"

"Understood. But you will call her?" William refused to leave until he had a clear answer. He demanded nothing less than certainty, reinforced. Ambiguity had to be banished.

Clarence, strung out and strung up, finally answered yes. It felt like having a tooth pulled. "Yes."

William brightened up. "Thanks." And he meant it.

"You're welcome. Now go."

Obediently William went. Hit by a sudden afterthought Clarence stalled him.

"How are you getting home?"

"Buses. Two buses."

"Have you got enough money?"

William searched his pockets and added up. "Not really. Only if I include the twenty pounds you gave me."

"But that's to pay off that arsehole Martin."

"I know."

"Hang on." Clarence rushed back inside, to quickly reappear with a scruffy fiver. "Here this should more than cover it."

William's eyes lit up. "Thanks." He already had more than enough to get home.

Fleetingly Clarence thought about driving the boy home: but that would bring him to within close proximity of the person he was trying to avoid. In that respect another five pounds was the easier, cheaper option.

William arrived home feeling he had achieved something monumental, and with his secrets further amplified. His mother did not notice the difference: she was too busy being a busy mother. As for Martin, William had already told him to fuck off; and it had worked: Martin had fucked off.

Alone again, Clarence turned down the music and played the album from the beginning; but still he could not get back into it, even though it had once enthralled him, set him alight, chilled him out. Now it was just another piece of music, nothing more than nice. He thought back to the time he had spent loitering in the record store. Was there really nothing left out there?

Chapter Fourteen

Log Entry

I accepted another invitation on behalf of my host from the female neighbour who lives with the cat: he was in no fit state at the time of the offer to make a clear decision. He saw advantages and disadvantages in equal measure, and was suspicious of her motives – historically this has blighted their brief encounters. The quality and quantity of the food previously provided was good and he has need of a substantial intake of nourishment. With this in mind I asked if a piece of partially cooked meat would be available to consume. After a slight moment of disorientation (but not outright surprise it seemed) she agreed to consider it. When I pushed for clarification she quickly said yes, as if afraid I would change my mind. Reminding him of a previous promise, she also begged my host to join her at a formal gathering for the purpose of spiritual celebration and refreshment. It was held on a repetitive basis by a organisation which supported a particular representation of a god. Again I accepted on his behalf, guessing that an act of spiritual exploration may improve his general state of mind. It will be difficult but I will try to position myself such that he experiences the event directly and takes away substantial memories.

I enquired after her thoughts on gods. Were there gods? I asked. Yes, she replied. I asked how many had she identified. She hesitated before stating just the one. I thought perhaps she had been counting them up, but obviously not. I asked for the proof. She said proof was not a requirement: you simply believed. Does he, she or it exist outside your head? I asked. Yes, she replied, but not in the physical sense. This explanation appeared to suffice. Though it lacked little in substance it was the gateway to a vast, alternative world of high values, high expectations and incredible, unsurpassable rewards. It made it clear to me that humans cannot survive on logic alone, not within the confines of their physical world. They need to escape to somewhere better. For her this was a positive thing. For others it may not be so. In the worse case it may be a gateway to madness.

✦ ✦ ✦

Log Entry

When the time came for the appointment with her god there was strong negative, almost pathological reaction on his part. I had to take complete control. If I did let him resurface it was only for very short intervals, according to the nature and strength of prevailing conditions, and even then limiting the extent of his exposure.

The attendees seemed drawn by a magnet towards the entrance of the large, old imposing building. As they drew nearer a collective intent took over and individual behaviour was channelled towards it. As they entered voices were lowered. Most ceased talking all together. The human instinct to converse with others within earshot was suppressed: such conduct felt out of place.

Innocuous, unassuming dress sense appeared to be a prerequisite. The hats worn by some females were especially colourful and constructed from quality materials. Some reflected current fashions in headwear.

As we went through the large, wooden double doors the female friend gripped the hand of my host – he had no choice in the matter – and squeezed it, as if to reassure him that he was safe, that no harm would come to him in this place. He had no personal memories of such places. She may have been squeezing it for her own reassurance. Like a child she was eager to show him her secret world and the wonderful things contained within it. Her pulse began to quicken and her mind began to disregard its weighty, cumbersome baggage. (Though it would return, much like before; perhaps with a vengeance - again as before.) Strong currents of fear began stir within my host and it was hard work containing him.

The world inside was ostentatiously different from that outside. It was visually overwhelming. The intention was to deflect existing preoccupations, to relegate them to the far back of the mind; to grab attention and hold it for the duration of the meeting of minds. In here there was no room for uncertainty: those in charge did not express it; and if they were ever struck by it, they kept it hidden away. There was no deviation from an absolute, indisputable – and in their eyes indispensable – truth: a truth celebrated by elegant, majestic architecture and all manner of decoration and inscriptions laid down over many years. In here the mind was assaulted in the nicest possible way by the forceful invitation to let go of the old, latch on to the new, entertain the impossible; and embrace it all without reservation or regard for outcome. It seemed to be a tall order for simple creatures of flesh and blood who had, only relatively recently, distanced themselves from the very primitive instincts of survival in the wild.

In this place the pace of change had been slowed. It carried a heavy weight of history with distinction. It was a place which glorified the past and did not feel trapped by it. Rather the opposite: it was liberated.

The present day was held back, kept outside. It could not enter. If it did, the impact of the past would be diluted, perhaps even be shown to be disingenuous. It could not be allowed to infiltrate the building, nor for that matter the past which was held close to so many hearts and worshipped with such fanaticism. The future however was a completely different matter: it had no form; its function was still to be identified; its coming was to be celebrated as, according to some, it would deliver significant change.

The design and the materials used were directed towards imposing rules and structure. There was no room for chaos. The interior did not lend itself to comfort or relaxation in the physical sense. It took centre stage: those assembled within its walls were expected to show reverence and capitulate to whatever was on offer. This was not a place for fun or games, argument or secret agendas.

Its walls were high and thick, similar to those constructed in the distant past for the purposes of defence or suppression by armed forces. Complimenting these dimensions, the windows were tall and narrow: complex in construction they used natural sunlight to deliver pictures of colour to the onlooker. They illustrated stories or celebrated past events of religious importance. The floor was thick stone: hard and unforgiving if you fell over; not soft and yielding. Seating arrangements were designed as rows in order to maximise the use of space with regard to accommodating the crowd. The comfort factor had not be considered. Entrants were expected to line up in these rows in almost mathematical symmetry then, upon command, sit.

Seated, there was only one direction one was expected to look: that was ahead, towards the sheltered objects of high religious value and expression; and towards the elderly man who stood in front of them, to one side and on a raised platform; as if on guard; perhaps on the look out for thieves in the audience. These were valuable items in the commercial as well as the spiritual sense.

The elderly man was dressed in a style intended to differentiate him from the crowd and promote his authority. He took charge of proceedings from his platform. He set the whole agenda. There was no room for spiritual or philosophical deviation: what he said was what mattered; you could not disagree – at least not at that time and in that place. He did not have to focus attention but he did have to fill the vacuum. This he did with words, words intended to mesmerise and cajole, disturb and uplift.

The nature of his communication was intense. The building provided the perfect conditions in which to listen without distraction, so enhancing the message and feeling of taking in something profound. In many ways the actual words spoken contributed only in part to the overall effect. In any other place these words could have fallen flat, with resulting cynicism. His words demanded a reaction and were met with enthusiasm and respect. Much of it I suspect had been said on numerous previous occasions, perhaps with slight variations in language or accent. The participation was sometimes mechanized in parts and, being driven by a taskmaster, lacking true spontaneity.

The words were interwoven at predetermined times by invitations to sing. The singing was mostly enthusiastic, even if the quality was variable: it varied from poor and ineffectual to loud and inspired – even if it did wander away from the melody set by the male who laboured at a large musical instrument; and who for the most part looked into the distance, perhaps bored by his repetitive role. Some in the crowd seemed to come alive just for the singing. That was their only reason for being there: the extensive exercise of lungs and vocal chords.

Very soon all minds were focused, with deliberate intent and various degrees of admiration, on what he had to say; and just as importantly how he said it. He made them feel good. He looked good: some wanted to dress like him, act like him; be like him in the fullest sense of the word. A uniform pattern of conformance emerged, gathering strength as the feedback of visible endorsement took hold: those around you look happy, therefore you act happy; those around you appear reinvigorated, therefore you feel reinvigorated. A few were no longer happy with who they were and afterwards, as before, it would take them some time to regain their usual position of limited fulfilment. Here human endeavour is concentrated on closing the open-ended loophole which for some is the sense of existence in an ever changing present.

After some time spent sitting and watching the man in charge, and listening acutely to what he had to say (and he had a lot to say), parts of the body began to ache: specifically those in direct contact with the hard wooden seats and those which had been unable to stretch. When directed to stand, and sing, it was a welcomed relief for the vast majority of the audience.

As the elderly man spoke, so the female's thoughts raced towards a resolution of some longstanding unease, or longing, or character failure: but they never reached that point. As before something vital was missing.

There remained some gap between disaffection and complete harmonious accord within herself, and with the world beyond. As before the gap could not be closed. But as before she would not be deterred. Perhaps next time.

Upon entry and positioning her body for what was to come, I detected a sense of growing stimulation. I have encountered it before, in the lead up to the act of lovemaking. Like a child on the eve of some celebration where she was to be the centre of attention, and perhaps receive gifts, she stood tense in anticipation of some extraordinary encounter. As the event progressed and the words were delivered at greater speed and with greater passion, so she changed, physically as well as emotionally. The words became a challenge, a demand for outright, unconditional acceptance and the self-enforced denial of her position at the centre of her conscious being.

She grew anxious and she began to sweat, especially under the armpits and around the crotch area. The change was as much chemical as mental – as was the thrill of gaining admittance. (For some reason she had harboured the thought of being refused entry.) She tried to not look at the man in charge. She tried not to look at anybody. She tried to shut herself down - to disconnect from everything happening around her - and disclaim her identity; and lapse into a daydream, one where she could pretend all was well and good within herself.

I detected in her a sense of being besieged. She was under attack: the attack came from within and she split into two halves. One side was defending, and invoked a strong feeling of self-pity. The other was angry. It wanted to know what had gone wrong. Why this sudden collapse into a muddle of guilty embrace and anguished denial? It drowned her in self-loathing.

As the level of self-inflicted torture increased she finally responded with strength and managed to break free of her predicament. She took charge and pushed the whole agonizing, pulsating mess to one side. She forced herself to smile again, and with a blank sheet of paper taped firmly inside her head (metaphorically speaking) she was able to digest and savour the remaining proceedings without any sense of guilt: guilt over the fact that she did not, in fact, truly believe – at least not in the same thing that the old man in charge believed in. She wanted to believe as he did but could not.

The very concept of belief without proof she holds close to her heart as the ultimate aspiration. She feels required to believe in something, to raise herself up; and the constant battle wears her down at times. Her parents may have been responsible for this. I sense memories of a childhood subjected to a never-ending, concentrated stream of enforced education in facts and opinions across a wide spectrum of social and moral issues.

During this crisis she still took on board much of what was said with regard to the rights and wrongs of human behaviour and conduct towards others. This for her was not a point of contention in the intellectual or practical sense. I detected similar changes in a few others, though nowhere as extreme. An even smaller number were unaffected throughout. From start to finish they camouflaged their insensitivity and distance with the appropriate application of visual masking. For them it was a show: entertainment with good intentions, but little more. They seemed to be the ones most at ease with themselves.

At the end of his speech, and the accompanying musical interludes, the elderly man came down to mingle with the remains of his audience – some having departed in a hurry. My host was introduced to him but I did not allow him any participation. He was in rebellious mood, finding the atmosphere, the people and the celebrations too much to handle. I had to maintain the firm grip.

I enquired if these performances were physically as well as mentally demanding, and whether he could maintain his sense of spirituality indefinitely or did it have to be constantly revived or reinvented. Could he really raise the personal passion to the required level of inspiration on each occasion? And did his passion extend into other areas of his life? Areas such as food preparation and cooking, physical activity, artistic expression or sexual relationships. I did not receive much in the way of answers. I asked him if he ever become demoralised by the lack of hard, incontrovertible evidence for the existence of his god; and whether he had ever considered inventing his own set of moral principles and beliefs from first principles of conscious existence? He said no. I was led away quickly by the female.

✦ ✦ ✦

The light was fading. Clarence sat holding onto a bottle. He wanted to drink but was driven to ration himself. He stared at the bottle and the battle raged. He had survived the day on snacks and now he was paying the price. His stomach hurt but he was too tired to do anything about it. And anyway there was no food in the fridge – if there was it probably belonged to Max, and Max would be none too pleased if he stole it. His mind, for want of exercise, jumped on two words and their order of execution: eating and stealing; stealing and eating. If he stole it and didn't eat it he could give it back, feigning ignorance of his crime. But the food might be inedible, so it would had gone to waste. That would be two crimes. If he just ate it straight off the crime might remain undetected. If detected he could just apologize and say he had been desperately hungry.

Clarence went and looked in the fridge. There was some dodgy looking milk and a tub of stuff which celebrated the fact that it was not butter but something far more tasty and far more beneficial to health. There were two slices of salami left in their original packet. He had nothing left to put them on or in, so he popped them in his mouth, and they were gone. Short but sweet relief. There was one remaining item: a small tub of yoghurt. He opened it up and in under a minute scooped its contents into his mouth. From his stomach's point of view it made little difference.

Psychologically it added to his growing sense of depression – depression which time and time again he had managed to kick away. He was almost an expert now in how to lift oneself up when slipping down into big black holes. On this bleak early evening it really did refuse to go away. Thoughts of the workplace entered his head: he was not missing the place in the slightest. He was scared: perhaps they were not missing him. He thought of Ramsey, Pansy Ramsey. He missed the verbal knuckle fights with the buffoon. Having Ramsey around made him feel good: good as in superior. Ramsey's defects deflected attention from his own. Pansy Ramsey: cruel but fair comment. And yet the kids loved him. He got on well with them. He was one of them: never at ease with the world; trying to make sense of his place; trying to be 'one of the lads'; always trying hard to get it right – especially with females - and never knowing why – or when – he didn't. But Ramsey wasn't stupid. Just disorganised in the head perhaps. If he was a teacher how could he be stupid?

His thoughts moved swiftly on, and back, back to Fiona. He thought he had let go but he was fooling himself. Tracey he had let go of – history conveniently tweaked – and he had convinced himself that he didn't want her back. She had nothing to offer him. In his analysis he did not acknowledge the fact that she had decided to see the back of him for good. While he was clutching the still unopened bottle of beer and trying to fall in love, she was trying on a new dress and looking forward to a night out with the girls.

Fiona became a big broad poster inside his head. He stared up at it. She stared down. She was Big Sister. All of a sudden he could see her entire face in precise detail. The expression in her eyes tore him apart. He could even picture the colour and tint of her lipstick. He saw a few threads of hair sticking out of one ear – but nothing to worry about. His ability for visual recollection had never been so sharp. And things he really wanted to remember – those experiences which were true slices of his life – he could recall with bewildering clarity.

A tragic irony, he thought. Bits of my life are buried in a blur, or lost entirely, while the normal bits – he stumbled over the word 'normal' – stick out and shout back at me like a pop rock video with the volume turned up. He tried to carry on thinking about Fiona but Tracey had crept back into his thoughts. Yes, he could see clearly now. He had treated her like shit sometimes: demanding his own time as and when he wanted it – even when he didn't need it; expecting her to be around when he needed her; expecting her to 'fill in', 'make do', 'put up', and deal with the paperwork of life. He drew back. He was being too hard on himself. There had been good times. There had been great times in bed: at worse mediocre; but never bad. She understood the sexual power and medicinal properties of kinky underwear, and had treated him on many occasions; and he had shown his full appreciation. He had always paid for the drinks – or at least it felt like that - and had remembered to buy her chocolates, and other scrumptious items from time to time, and just in time. Yes all in all it had worked well for a while.

Thoughts moved on again, unwilling to sit still for too long in one place lest they discovered something unpleasant – an unpalatable truth perhaps. He thought about mums and dads, his mum and dad. Time to stop taking them for granted. They were getting on. They were getting old. He was getting old: therefore they were getting really old. He wanted to see them again. Take them out to dinner? Yes, good idea. Their choice. If they wanted a steakhouse so be it. Their choice. But when? He had to time it right. He had to get it right, when there was no possibility of another dodgy patch. He sat on the idea. He didn't throw it away, he just sat on it. It was a cushion for the soul. He didn't have many cushions. (As a rule he wasn't into cushions.)

He didn't know why but his thoughts gravitated towards an image of a large church, both inside and out; and people singing – and him singing - and looking joyful; and the Black And White Minstrels; and stuck up cows in silly hats who made their husbands turn up really early to ensure they got the best parking place. Eureka! Clarence thumped the carpet. (He had been sitting on the floor all this time.) Now he remembered.

Yes he had been to a church service that morning. Or perhaps he had just watched it on TV? Either way that explained it, just.

Guilt. It all disturbed his stock of gently stewing guilt, guilt which he had held firmly underfoot, buried below and out of sight. Now, warmed up and in liquid form, it was rising to the surface and threatening to boil over. He turned away. He refused to be threatened. He tried to completely turn off but that proved impossible.

He switched back to the poster. Fiona still stared down. Sam tried to muscle her way into view. He pushed her aside. She rattled him now and he didn't have a clue as to why. Now she and Tim were going through a bad patch he definitely wanted to keep a low profile. It might turn ugly. He continued to look up at Fiona. She fascinated him. Give me one more chance, he begged. I promise not to fuck it up. Just one more chance. But when? When would it be safe to take it? He bit his lip: he was about to make a fool of himself by crying. So let me cry, he declared. I've cried before. I cried as a kid. Didn't I? There's nothing to be ashamed about. Women cry all the time. Even grown men are allowed to cry. The best films had men crying, so cry.

Clarence began to cry. It was a slow beginning, a trickle. It had to be forced. And it was interrupted by the sound of the doorbell. Clarence swore. Fuck off! I don't want double-glazing. Stuff the survey: I don't want to enter a prize draw. I don't want my meters read: take my estimates or stuff it. I don't want to change suppliers. Relinquishing his hold on the bottle – it rolled across the carpet - he got up slowly, and on the way to the door forced himself to calm down. It was that Rebecca woman. Looking for that cat again?

Rebecca took in the face and with it one long deep breath. Clarence didn't care to speak but that didn't bother her anymore. He could be just as mad as her sometimes. She ploughed on. She had a heavy cart to pull. Clarence looked away. He could see her standing at his side in the church. He owed it to her to say something. He said hello.

"Hello."

Rebecca smiled. Clarence was back. Immediately she could tell he had forgotten.

"You've forgotten haven't you?"

Clarence scratched his head while he searched it. He had a vague recollection of a dinner invitation. He took a chance.

"No. I'm just not feeling very well. Totally under the weather. Thought I might have to go to bed early. I was going to tell you, honest."

Rebecca believed him and scanned his face as part of an impromptu medical examination. She was a CCTV camera. "Have you eaten today?"

"Sort of."

"Sort of?"

"Snacks."

"You've got to eat. We all do."

"I know."

"So come and eat."

"I'd rather not." For some reason the sight of mushy lentils sprang to mind.

Her heart was struck a blow and missed a beat. "But I got you a really lovely piece of steak. Top quality. The best bit the butcher said."

Clarence was sorely tempted. He was starving. She wanted to cook for him? Let her cook.

"I'm making a black pepper sauce to go with it."

"Medium rare?"

"However you like it. Steak has yet to be cooked."

Clarence was sold. "I'll be right over. Let me put some shoes on."

Happy again Rebecca left, in a hurry, to get back to her kitchen and her box of delights. Clarence slipped on his shoes, grabbed a bottle of wine – there was a question over ownership – and turned off all the lights on the way out – something he had never previously made a conscious effort to do.

Just as he put a foot out of the door he thoughts turned again to Fiona. This time she wasn't looking down from on high. In fact she was quite difficult to see. None the wiser he turned his thoughts back to food and the craving in his stomach for what was on offer: something juicy; something wholesome; something hot and with bite; something which tasted of meat. He shook himself free: he was confusing sexual appetite with the real thing.

At Rebecca's his entrance was greeted with something bordering on reverence – but she had a schedule and he was swept up and along, and deposited at the table, in the seat reserved for him. The table had a real spread: four lots of knives and forks; napkins; a jug of water; flowers. Flowers in a jar? And there were coloured candles. Christ, coloured candles! Clarence reined himself in and stuck his clear-cut agenda of food, food, food firmly to the inside of his head. Whatever her agenda was he did not want to know.

He remembered the cat and perhaps at the same time the cat had remembered him for she came into the room; jumped up on the facing chair; folded herself up into a position of what ostensible looked like preparation for meditation; and began to purr. Utter, glorious contentment was her state of being. Perhaps she knew there was steak on the menu thought Clarence. In his own way Clarence also began to purr.

Next door Rebecca was feeling in much the same mood, and struggling to dispel naughty thoughts and temptation. She had always had mixed emotions when it came to sex. Love it or hate it she had never been able to ignore it. It had always hung around, demanding a straight answer. Now, aided by a little push from Clarence, she had fallen off the fence, back to earth. The first few times had been a disaster. Then, much later, it had been a misery. Now she was determined to enjoy it.

She thought of Clarence sat next door. Until it was time to eat she had decided to leave him alone, give him space. She had learnt to read some of his quaint, quirky signals, so for the moment best leave him alone. Food would wake him up and wind him up. She saw the look of restrained resistance and concealed bewilderment on the vicar's face and wanted to laugh – but she did not allow herself to. Some things had to be taken seriously, and he was one of them.

Clarence offered to open the bottle of wine. Rebecca found him a corkscrew. He began to drink. She was determined to catch him up. Judy opened her eyes occasionally to check that he had not moved position, and that all was right in the world. Clarence watched Judy. He didn't know why he didn't like cats. He just didn't like them. Was he a dog person? He didn't think so. To avoid thinking about her in the kitchen he kept thinking over the same question. Why did he not like cats? He thought of litter trays and cat sick and Fawlty Towers. None of that was any reason to hate cats was it? Hate cats? Had he really taken it that far? He gave ground. No he didn't hate them. He just didn't like them. He searched for an answer. The cooking smelt good. Then, grudgingly, he admitted to himself that he had it. Cats demanded bonding, the emotional kind – or something like. And he didn't like the idea of an animal crawling around the house demanding he be emotional; and leaving fur everywhere. Girlfriends were bad enough, though they didn't need litter trays.

Rebecca appeared with a tray. On it she balanced two bowls of soup and two chunks of brown bread. The bread looked solid, home cooked. We've having starters, thought Clarence. When do I get to eat my steak was his follow on thought. She dished it out slowly, gracefully, and sat down opposite; gently pushing her lovely little cat away. She took a long sip of wine and said it tasted good. Clarence remembered to do the right thing and said 'cheers' and 'good health', even though he looked terrible, felt terrible; and the wine was cheap and nasty.

Like a couple of old timers they sipped on soup. It was thick and creamy, and bright orange. Clarence saw green bits floating in it.

"This is good."

"Thank you."

"What is it?"

"Cream of carrot soup."

"Just carrots?"

"Pretty much."

"Amazing." Clarence held back from mentioning the green bits.

"Thank you."

They continued to sip. Clarence took bigger and bigger sips and was soon gulping it down. Rebecca tried to get the ball rolling.

"How's work going?"

"I'm off work."

"Oh that's right." Rebecca trembled slightly. She had to start again. "Have you got any brothers or sisters?"

Clarence looked up. "Me? Just the one." He sprinkled more salt on to his liquidised, organic carrots. He had never been keen on soup but now he was converted. He would buy some packets he told himself. Stick a note on the fridge door when you get back, he added.

Rebecca waited for the rest of it. Nothing. He needed prompting. "Brother or sister?"

"Oh sorry. It's just that this is so good. Sister. I have a sister. She's two years younger than me. Always was. Always will be."

"So you always bossed her around!"

Clarence grinned. "Probably." He thought back. "No, definitely. I was probably a bastard." The thought that he probably still was, he stamped on.

"Though I bet there came that point when she started to boss you around?"

Clarence stopped swallowing soup. He thought back. The precise moment when Margaret had turned on him, to give as good as she got, came back as clear as daylight.

Margaret had been holed up in her bedroom with two of her best friends: both good looking, blooming girls, with wit and restlessness to match. He had lusted after one of them terribly. At times it had worn him out. They had been talking: probably about boys; perhaps about other girls not in their criminal circle. He had tried to gain entry. Sister had told him to clear off. He had said he wanted to give Jacqueline a present. Sister had said Jacqueline didn't want to see him – which was true but came across as a lie. He had said let Jacqueline speak for herself. Sister had said sod off. So he had forced his way in, past the girls trying to hold the door shut; and when he did his sister proceeded to humiliate him, exposing all his dirty habits and hang-ups, and more. He had left in a hurry. Later they had exchanged icy looks across the dining table and he had nearly stabbed his wretched sister. Mum and dad had been too busy to notice. Dad had been talking a lot while mum had been pretending to listen.

All this Clarence recounted to Rebecca with an air of implied confidentiality. She found it all very funny. For the first time in ages her flat sounded with raw laughter. Judy's ears stood up.

"I'm very jealous," she said as her giggles faded and her composure returned.

"Jealous? Why?"

"I was an only child." She admitted the fact as if a crime had been committed.

Clarence, in between his sudden lust for carrots, detected a announcement tinged with sadness and regret. He felt duty-bound to raise the tone and earn his dinner.

"You didn't miss much."

Rebecca jumped on his words. "What did I miss?"

Clarence didn't have a clue. "I don't know. But you still had fun?" he asked.

Rebecca looked at his bowl, taking it has a compliment that it had emptied so quickly. She got stuck into hers. She had to catch him up.

"I suppose so." As she spoke she put distance between herself and certain memories. She kept one step ahead of them. She could not let them catch up.

Clarence scraped up the last traces of soup left. "You had lots of friends though – or at least enough? That soup was lovely by the way."

"Thank you. Glad you enjoyed it. I haven't done it for a while. A good way to eat your vegetables."

"I'm now impressed by the humble carrot."

Rebecca raised her glass. "Cheers."

Clarence was inspired to raise his. "Cheers."

Judy watched, to see what would happen next. Her ears and eyes flickered around. It was as if she was taking notes.

"I think I had enough," said Rebecca.

"I can take some more."

"Sorry?"

Clarence explained. "Carrot soup? I could manage a refill."

"I was talking about childhood friends."

"Oh."

Rebecca forgave him. He was hard of hearing – she had noticed that in church.

"I think there's some left. I'll go and see."

Scooping up the empty bowls, she left Clarence to ponder, as did Judy who decided to chase after her food provider. Left alone, Clarence began to wonder what price he was expected to pay for his meal ticket. He strapped himself down in his chair and to his glass of wine - his wine so he could drink it as fast as he liked - and decided to hang on in there. Rebecca was only trying to be nice so he should do the same was his verdict.

"Sorry!" shouted Rebecca. "What little is left is all dried up."

"No worries!" Bring on the beef. Pepper sauce she had promised.

"Medium rare?" she shouted.

"Yes please!"

Like Judy next door Clarence licked his lips. She waited for some dish that would not arrive. Clarence waited, not knowing that he was a dish. Rebecca hurried in with a bowl of hot steaming vegetables dripping in cheese and a small bowl of thin, perfectly cooked chips.

"I did some chips for you especially. I normally avoid them."

"Thanks."

Clarence was starting to feel patronized – though he was still grateful and astonished by the fact that this woman was making so much effort. He hadn't sussed out her intentions yet but was he really worth it? He certainly didn't think so and he should know. Her sudden body movements accidentally blew out one of the candles and she looked disappointed. Clarence came to her rescue.

"Have you got any matches?"

He felt required to take an interest in even the smallest things now. He wanted his steak and chips and nothing could interfere. The soup had not reduced his hunger pains. He was still starving.

"Over there, top draw." Rebecca pointed and scurried back to her kitchen.

Clarence found the matches and relit the candle. He watched them both burn, the flame sending soot up to the ceiling; remembering Tracey and dreaming of Fiona. He remembered a night out with Tracey, Tim and Sam. Tim, drunk, had leaned across the table for some spurious reason and had brushed a candle, catching the edge of his hand in the flame and getting struck by falling wax. Both he and Sam had called Tim a twat. Tracey on the other hand had stood up for him. Clarence didn't know why he had suddenly remembered that, but he had, and in a way he was pleased. He could even remember what Tracey was wearing – and Sam for that matter.

Sam.

For some reason he did not want to think of Sam. He shied away. When Rebecca finally reappeared with his steak Clarence was in paradise. Judy brought up the rear, similarly in paradise - a cat's paradise - her sense of smell in overdrive and feeding her dreams. He saw no sauce on it, but was reassured it was on its way. What she had on her plate, he had absolutely no idea. It looked something like square pieces of barely cooked chicken, but he guessed it wasn't. Whatever it was it didn't look remotely appetising – which meant it probably was. Without waiting for permission Clarence helped himself to chips and vegetables. Then the sauce arrived and he really got stuck in. A piece of meat had never looked so good.

Rebecca watched him saw a piece off, stick it into his mouth, and chew, like a dog. The joy on his face stood out. She had not relished the visit to the butchers and she did not enjoy this spectacle. She saw blood, and the rest of the animal attached, and kicking. She would never understand it. That piece of meat had once been part of a living, breathing, conscious being, chewing away in some field. Far better to have grown crops. The field could have fed more people. It could have fed her. She looked down at her own dish. It was vaguely disappointing, boring, but oh so healthy. Judy stalked Clarence: up and down she prowled, looking for an opening; knowing she was missing out on the action.

"My parents got divorced," announced Rebecca out of the blue.

Clarence stopped chewing. He didn't need this.

"Mine didn't. Still happily married – as far as I know anyway."

Clarence started to chew again. Whatever was in the air he wouldn't be drawn. He just wanted his meat. Rebecca looked back down at her own food and prodded it with her fork, to encourage herself to get stuck in. Together, but apart, the two focused their attention on the food in front of them: one happy with what they had but not with what was to come, even though they had no idea what it would be; the other happy with neither. Judy continued to prowl. Twice she circled the table: tail up, head up, nose up; blood up.

Finishing well in front, and alerted by the extra knife and fork, Clarence sat back and waited for desert to come. He studied Rebecca as she ate. She barely used her knife. It was all portioned up with the edge of her fork then rolled on board before being ceremoniously loaded into her mouth. It all looked rather dainty, contrived. Tracey had never eaten like that. She knew how to eat. She had eaten like a man. Fiona he placed somewhere in between.

"What do you do?" he asked. The build up of silence had got to him. Judy rubbed against his leg.

"Work?" replied Rebecca.

"Work."

"I'm a graphic artist and illustrator – freelance."

"Oh that must be interesting."

"Not really. Was once but not anymore."

"What sort of things do you do, illustrate?" Clarence looked down at the blasted cat, then back at his plate. There was a lump of fat left. He picked up the plate and made a signal. "Can I?"

"Of course. It will be a treat for her. And nothing should ever be wasted."

How right you are, thought Clarence. Rebecca returned to the question while Clarence watched Judy get stuck in. He was glad – and proud – that he had made someone in the room happy.

"I do book covers, advertising, posters, calendars – in fact just about anything my agent can get his hands on these days."

Clarence caught her drift. "It doesn't sound like you're having fun anymore."

"No. No fun. Just like with you and the teaching, right?"

"Right."

Propped up by mutual despondency Rebecca picked up the plates and whisked them away. Judy hadn't finished and chased after her to reclaim her prize. She had earned it. It was hers by rights.

"Desert's coming," she shouted.

"Lovely! You know how to get to a man's heart!"

A plate hit the kitchen floor and Clarence held his breath. No outcry followed. He looked around the room. Nothing had changed. It was all heavy stuff. If he wasn't careful it could give him a headache. She was definitely interested in saving the planet. He was just interested in saving his sanity.

Rebecca returned with apple pie and custard. "I thought about just doing it with cream but then thought you might enjoy custard more. Just like your mum makes it."

"Yes custard's great. Love custard."

The special treatment began to work and Clarence began feeling happy, and without reservation. Consequences and pay-offs went by the by. Rebecca watched the man tuck into his pie and custard. Like a small boy he just lapped it up.

"I'll show you my watercolours afterwards."

"Great." Clarence didn't look from eating. "What of?"

"Flowers. All flower studies."

"Great." Great, he thought. Why did it always have to be flowers? Let's all look at pictures of flowers just in case we still don't know what they look like.

His lack of enthusiasm temporarily punctured her spirit and they both got back to the job of eating: spoon for spoon, mouthful for mouthful, they mirrored each other's movements, and perhaps even their ambitions. The only difference was that Clarence got more on his spoon and hence into his mouth. So again he finished first, and had to wait and watch Rebecca finish. But he was content now. His stomach was bursting with meat and vegetables, pastry, apple and custard; and he still had booze to down. He drank on. He was drinking at twice her rate.

Rebecca finished off her apple pie with a tinge of sadness. She had run out of dishes to feed him, which could mean his exit.

"When did you give up on the teaching?"

"Tricky one. Two or three years ago? It sort of crept up on me."

Rebecca nodded as she soaked up the information. "Same here," she lied.

"After awhile you feel so unappreciated you wonder why you bother. Most parents don't seem to be bothered about what their kids are up to."

A spasm of something approaching pain rolled over Rebecca's face. She remembered something he had said previously. "As you said, it's all become a routine, a lonely routine sometimes."

Clarence felt that was slightly overstating it. Then he was struck by a thought.

"For you though it must be something different? You work alone. It's always been like that. It's part of the job?"

Rebecca considered his question hard. It was a good question.

"Routine destroys creativity I suppose. I do much the same stuff over and over again. That's why I spend ages painting small flowers I suppose. Through a magnifying glass sometimes."

"You use a magnifying glass? That sounds like serious stuff."

"It is. Glad you think so."

Rebecca feasted on the compliment. It was the first real one she had been given all evening. She picked up the bowls and took them away. Clarence watched her go. He hated to admit it but the girl did have nice slim hips. She returned with a plate and a cheese knife and a small selection of cheeses. They would be sharing the knife. Judy followed her in, licking her lips and hoping for more rich pickings.

"Tell me about William and Mary. I'm interested."

Clarence was about to place a piece of Emmental in his mouth. He held off.

"You spoke to William?" Clarence feigned surprise.

"That's right. While I fed him. Couldn't help it."

Clarence forgave her. It was in the nature of women to get involved in the affairs of blokes. "I've been tiling her bathroom."

"Really? That's sweet of you."

Clarence heard himself falling into a familiar set pattern of frank denial and a plea for innocence when no charge had been brought. "There's nothing going on. I promise you."

"Relax. It's not a cross-examination."

Clarence tried to smile but the attempt ended up twisted, a miscarriage. "I was introduced to her through my sister. It was just a blind date that went nowhere."

Rebecca believed him, unreservedly. She could not see it in the man's nature to lie to her. He was an honest fellow and he was a typical Pisces. The fact that he was desperate to reassure her of his innocence sent her head and heart reeling.

"And her boy William seems drawn to you."

"Is he?" Clarence thought back. "Yes I suppose he is. Probably because he's got no dad." Clarence tried to laugh it off. "I keep giving him money." And failed.

"That's generous of you."

"It was a present. He doesn't get much."

In one of those rare moments Clarence looked his host Rebecca straight in the eye. "But like I said there's nothing in it. I'm just doing her this favour and then that's it. It's a one-off." He pushed a piece of cheese into his mouth, and chewed it over.

Rebecca did the same. "Does it scare you? Wives and children?"

As far as Rebecca was concerned she had asked a reasonable question. For Clarence it was scary. He grabbed a piece of stilton and sank his teeth into it, washing it down with wine.

"No. Why should it – they – scare me?"

"I don't know. Sometimes it does. It scares me."

"Not me," he lied.

"And it's so much hard work these days." Rebecca grabbed the remains of her Emmental.

"So much to think about. Too much information," added Clarence.

"And the fear of getting it wrong."

"It can scare you shitless."

"Something like that." He was right, she thought. It did scare her shitless. "Are you always going to stay a bachelor?"

"Who knows. I certainly don't. And you?"

"Me?" Rebecca seemed surprised that the question had been turned back on her. "Don't know either," she lied. "But I know I couldn't handle a traditional twenty-four hour, seven days a week marriage."

"Tell me about it."

So she did. She had it all mapped out.

"It would have to be a loose partnership. We come and go. I give him space. He gives it back in equal measure. We come together when we need each other. We let go when we're suffocating the other."

It had only been a rhetorical question but he had to give it to her: she did make a lot of sense. "And how about sex. Would there be the normal helping of sex?"

"Of course. Sex is important," she lied. A man had to have sex. She had come to terms with that fact. It was messy, and it often got in the way of greater things. But it was there to be enjoyed. So enjoy it, she told herself. But sex led to the children.

"Do you want children?" she asked.

"Do I want children?" Clarence looked up at a big picture of planet earth. "Do I want children?" The girl had set him thinking. Suddenly everything around him slowed, including her. Even the cat evaporated into a cloud of irrelevance.

He tried to weigh up the pros and cons, the benefits and costs. He thought about old age, and having someone to look after him at those key moments when he would feel naked and useless and scared. Did it scare him if there was no one? No. Not for now. Too far off. Was it a great part of the world to raise a child in? Not from where he was sitting. And what would they inherit? A fried planet and a mountain of waste. Hardly persuasive to giving a damn.

He thought again. He would have someone to look up into his eyes: showing respect; looking for answers to questions (some deep); giving him a purpose; giving him a hand; providing a distraction from all the crap in the world; making him laugh; making up a two-aside team on the football pitch. And then there would be the tantrums, the dirty nappies, the bed wetting, the screams for attention; things broken, things lost, things scratched – and all that even before the trauma of the teenage years.

He thought of teenagers, in particular those at his school. They were like a wall of bricks, impassable, impenetrable; but leaning dangerously; badly fitted together; a hazard, an accident waiting to happen. He had forgotten that once he had decided to sort them all out, turn them into something much better than he could ever be.

Teenagers. No, keep away from teenagers. Keep them in their cages, he joked, and throw them generous helpings of food on the hour, every hour. Only let them out if and when they have proved to the outside world that they have dumped the crap that they had invented beneath the bed sheets, in the school toilettes, on the street corners, late at night, or stolen off the web. But then he would get to teach him to drive, and help him find a place to live.

Clarence gave up. His brain had twisted up and run out of steam. He tried to throw a coin and commit to a simple yes/no answer, but couldn't. He finished off his glass of wine before replying to the question.

"Don't know." It was all he could say.

But Rebecca guessed there was a lot more behind those two words. Without asking, Rebecca refilled his glass and Clarence carried on drinking. They both gave up on the cheese. It suddenly looked very unappetising. Judy was the only one happy in the room now.

Clarence turned the question back on Rebecca. Give as good as you get. One rule for all. No exceptions. "And you?"

"And me?" Again she was struck, dumb this time.

She began to sink under the weight of her own conspiracies and imagination, into the mud the world – as she saw it – had dumped beneath her feet: always underfoot, no matter where she was standing. She saw blood, and a sharp surgeons knife. She saw her body distort. Something was growing inside it. It had no face, no personality. It wanted to escape – escape from her. She saw herself buckling under the weight of responsibility and a new lump of flesh getting bigger inside her everyday. She did not see herself as a woman, just another animal. She saw herself in labour, fighting to break free from someone small and weak who would immediately begin to cling, and demand milk from her body, on tap, at anytime and in any place. They started off as babies but soon became small children, then bigger children; and they would build their own private little worlds; and she would be left on the outside.

And she would immediately have to protect and nurture that little person day and night, day in, day out. And if she did any of it wrong – even just a little bit – the consequences could be catastrophic. She might drive him crazy, mess him up. He, or she, might end up hating her. He or she might end up thinking that she was the crazy one. But she might produce another Mozart, or a Picasso, or a Shakespeare; a Coward or a Cook. But then she might produce another Hitler, another Moors Murderer; or another Henry.T.Ford; or another politician; or just another suspicious looking character who hung around street corners.

The answer to her was as clear as the difference between night and day. It just took her a long time to get back to it. She had asked the question before and taken the same torturous journey to get to the answer – though the answer itself had changed back and forth over the years. The answer, when it was finally spoken, came as a relief. The question could be put away again for another time – though such times would become fewer as the future slowly, irrevocably moved the goalposts on.

"Me. I think not." She was sure not.

She jumped on another old chestnut. "And then there's old age. What do we do about old age."

"We can always die young."

Rebecca didn't see the joke: but then she hadn't been looking. "But are we still young?"

"True. I'm probably not. No, I'm sure I'm not." Clarence stared down at his glass and rattled its contents slightly with a gentle shake of his wrist.

"We don't really know what's it going to be like when we get there and nobody bothers to tell us."

Clarence tried to sound more upbeat. He wasn't ready to die just yet. "We'll just have to suck it and see."

"I must admit the thought of dying young does not appeal to me."

"I'm glad about that."

Exhausted by the turn in the conversation, they both lapsed back into a heavy, oppressive silence. Neither wanted to speak up, but each was willing to join in with whatever the other had to say; preferably something light and frothy, soft and sweet.

Rebecca was the first to find something. "You certainly gave the vicar hell."

Clarence stirred. "Did I?"

"It was a bit over the top wasn't it?"

"Was it?" From previous experience Clarence guessed it would have been. "Yes it probably was." He searched for a way out. "He probably deserved it."

Rebecca laughed, out loud, put her hand to her mouth and nearly spilt her wine with the other. Clarence was pleased he had made her laugh. He had forgotten the last time he had done such a thing. It felt good. She looked good.

"Did I say anything outrageous – other than to the vicar?"

"No, you were quiet all the time. You just looked nervous. And your singing was abysmal."

"My singing always is."

"You were very nervous throughout."

"Well it's not my normal place."

"What is your normal place?"

It was a hard question, and the annoying kind. Clarence looked around. He even looked down at the cat who never seemed to stray too far away from him. Clarence wanted to turn back the clock, travel backwards in time; back to the point when he had first cut into his piece of gorgeous blood soaked steak. Further back perhaps. Back to . . . back to where? He couldn't think where. The steak would have to suffice.

"My normal place is . . ." but he had no answer. He turned the tables again.

"What's your normal place?" He didn't think she would answer, but she did; and generously so. It was a generous helping of soul searching, and the uninhibited discharge of some of the clutter that made up the human condition.

"My normal place?" Rebecca patted her lap but Judy did not respond to the call. She turned to all the crap that had ever been invented and picked on the wholesome bits. "Up there, above the clouds."

She looked up at the ceiling. For some reason Clarence felt bound to do the same. Feeling foolish, he quickly looked back down, down at the cat who was staring up at him as if he had done something wrong. He hadn't, he felt sure of that – not yet anyway. Something inside advised him to say something upbeat. She might need the encouragement, else she might think he thought she was crazy.

"That sounds like a good place to be."

"It is. Better than the mess down here."

Clarence gave her that one. "But we're stuck down here."

"We don't have to be."

"Meaning?"

"Anything is possible. You just have to believe."

"Believe? Believe in what? C of E?"

"No something better than that."

"What exactly?"

"I don't know, at least not yet."

Clarence wanted to punch the table. "I believe in nothing."

"Why do you say that?"

"Surely the universe is more complicated than just one simple God idea can explain?"

"Agreed. There must be other life forms out there."

"True. I can't believe we're special. The physics is clear: throw together the right elements, light and heat, and bingo."

"And everything's interconnected."

"Possibly." Clarence's brain began to fuddle with muddle, and dissolve with discussion. "Not sure what you mean though." Neither did Rebecca.

She stopped herself, just in time to stop making a fool of herself. They were making contact: she didn't want to lose it. She wanted to move in closer, lean over, pop a piece of cheese in his mouth. Judy wanted more food. Clarence didn't know what he wanted. For now he was happy being nowhere, doing nothing, thinking nothing, saying nothing; and as for his wayward state of mind, sod it, let it do its worse. Perhaps he could take early retirement on medical grounds and spend a year or two wandering around the world's drink holes with a rucksack, mobile phone, and credit card. Find somewhere hot and exotic, with a beach. Get a job there. Suddenly he had a plan. How long it would last, only time would tell.

Unannounced, gloom descended on the two of them. They slowed, to fit in with the season. It was autumn. The music had slowed. Much had been talked about, but nothing had been said. There was much to say, but it would prove more and more difficult to say it. So why bother?

Judy was spoiling for attention. She stuck her claws into the carpet. The bigger stranger with the unusual smell was currently the stronger attraction. Judy licked her lips. She unwound her tail and wagged it, like a dog. She prepared to leap. She gauged the distance and decided her angle of attack. Her muscles tightened. They strained to be released, to do what they did best. She wanted to get closer to the top of the table, the place she could not see but could smell all too clearly. There was something up there. It was food. She might like it. She might not. She didn't know. The problem had to be addressed. She had to claim it.

Clarence made a movement. She saw her chance. She leapt. She landed, in his lap. She steadied herself. He almost doubled up in pain. He managed to regain his pose, just. Rebecca looked over the edge of the table, her initial thought being that perhaps there was more to this than reached the eye. Had he suffered a serous injury?

Judy looked around. The ground was soft, pliable, warm. She kneaded it. It felt good to the touch. She began to purr like a kitten. She switched to hunting mode. Her nose twitched as it sniffed and gathered up valuable information. Her eyes saw something promising. The smell did not particularly excite but on the other hand it did not dissuade. Food was food.

A hand came down on her neck. She was being stroked, roughly. It just didn't feel right. She made a line for the cheese but she was obstructed by the same hand, then another. She fought back, like a tiger. The two hands tried to contain her. She strained at the leash.

Rebecca came to her rescue. "It's OK let her have a piece."

Clarence let go and Judy lounged forward and grabbed her prize. She turned and scarpered. Clarence twisted and turned to avoid a misadventure. His hands went here and there, mainly there. He knocked over his glass of wine and was hit.

"Bother."

It was Rebecca's turn to jump up. "Don't worry I'll sort it out."

Clarence wasn't worried. He was just extremely bothered. Judy ran off, to chew on her catch, the jury still out as to whether it had all been worth it or not. Rebecca went and searched her kitchen cupboards for paper towels. She returned with a large handful. His glass had been approaching empty. She laid some flat out on the table to soak up the puddle. She sprinkled salt into the wound on the carpet. Something at the back of her mind told her that was the correct thing to do. Then she dabbed at the traces, not that there was much left to dab. It was disappearing fast.

"Here let me."

She tried to attend to Clarence, her special guest. She dabbed his trousers a few times before her hand was pushed away. She tried again. She wanted to fuss over him, show him she cared; reveal her caring side. It needed revealing. She wanted so much to be part of his scene now. And still he pushed her away. Wine stained trousers he could live with: it was the fussing over that took the biscuit. Left unchecked it could drive a man to madness.

"Just give it a rest will you." Along with the harsh words he gave her a brutal look.

This time she got the message, and crumpled back into her chair. Then she sat to attention, stooped forwards, hands clasped together and resting on her knees. She looked like an orphan, waiting for the day that would never come; her adoption. She looked like a hard-up angel: wishing to bring peace and harmony and goodwill to the world, but with no audience and no firepower. She looked like someone who needed to be cuddled and rubbed vigorously back into life.

Clarence was forced to admit to himself that he had said a terrible thing. He wanted to apologize, unreservedly: she had only been trying to help, nothing more. For want of something better to do he stood up, as if to smarten himself up, dress himself down. As spillages went he had suffered worse. He struggled to keep his balance: there was too much going on but not enough of the right stuff. Rebecca looked up at him.

"Please don't look at me like that."

"Sorry."

"And please don't say sorry. You haven't done anything wrong."

Unable to say sorry again, Rebecca was lost for words. She collapsed further. She was imploding, into a tight ball. The engine this time was her lack of self-belief. Clarence on other hand was falling to bits. He could see that she was deeply hurt by his words and the way he was acting. He didn't want to hurt her – or her cat.

Rebecca looked messed up. Clarence knew he was messed up. Their common denominator and mutual disintegration was a powerful aphrodisiac. But he was afraid to speak. He would only cause further trouble. He stood watching like someone hanging around at a car accident, waiting to give a statement, who wanted to be elsewhere.

"Afraid to show me kindness?" she asked.

Clarence went down on one knee, but didn't stop there, and ended up crouching, then kneeling as Rebecca put both hands up to his cheeks and drew him in close. He closed his eyes and tried to be somewhere else. He wanted to cry – but not in front of her. He wanted a woman's hands to gently run through his hair – but not hers. It was nothing personal. He just didn't want to get any closer. But get closer he did. His shadow of a aching, pale body needed a woman's body – even if only to cling to. He wanted to cry, but not here, not in this woman's place. She slipped down from her chair and joined him in the kneeling position. They were face to face, noses almost touching. Her hands moved down to his shoulders. She wanted to give him space to cry. He didn't want to cry. He wanted to make that quite clear, but didn't.

"Release the pain. Let the soul run free. Let it float up high into the sky. It's sunny up there. It's sunny down here. Every day is sunny. Even when it's raining it's sunny. Look for the sun."

As she recited her mantra she began to lose the plot. But no matter. Clarence was not really listening. His hands travelled up from the ground to find a place to rest which was delightful, erotic even. With his eyes held shut he had found her waistline. He squeezed. The girl in front of him did not object, the opposite in fact: she squirmed with pleasure, perhaps anticipation. She leant forward and rested her head on his shoulder. She wrapped her arms around his neck and held on for the performance to start and her nervous system to explode. This time it would be good she told herself. This time it would be good.

He kissed her around the neck and pushed her back, the way she had come. Now he was on automatic pilot, fully automatic. He did not need to think. He was not asked to think, or contemplate in any way about what was about to happen next. His body knew what to do and it badly needed to do it. It had been waiting ages, without complaint, and now it had the chance it was not going to miss it. It had to have sex; just as the rich had to have money, the poor had to have credit, the villain had to have his victim; the pope had to have his peace.

And sex it did have. She yielded. Her body was his to play with; to do his want, his worse or his best. She just begged to be given it back in one piece, and not bruised. Clarence pushed her over, to one side. He lifted her dress and exposed the centre of his delight. He pulled down the underwear – it was holding up proceedings – and did likewise. And for Rebecca it was all over in an instant. And during the brief moment of love-making Clarence did his best to remain completely detached. He hid his revulsion well.

Afterwards they both fell back, and apart. Clarence rolled over, and further away. Judy came up and began to sniff him. During the one extended moment Rebecca had thought of the book about sex only once, and in particular a few of the pictures. She had thought of it earlier in the evening, but to little affect.

Judy carried on sniffing. Clarence got up and apologized in his lowest voice possible and with the least number of words possible. He walked around the room at random, changing direction constantly, looking for a way out. He found it. It was the door. He said sorry and left. Rebecca wanted to tell him he had nothing to say sorry for, but never got the chance. She gathered up her furry baby and cuddled it. Judy did not complain. The watercolours never saw the light of day.

✢ ✢ ✢

Log Entry

Expectations of consuming a large serving of well cooked and well presented quality food can have much the same impact as those of sexual intercourse. The arrangement of the food and the equipment upon which it is delivered impacts expectation as much as texture, taste, smell and colour. Good food, like good human flesh, is highly stimulating. It enthuses and entices the brain with the promise of pleasure.

The female recognises the hold she has over the male when she is responsible for delivering food to his mouth. Sometimes she intentionally manipulates this position of importance for maximum advantage.

For this female the preparation and delivery of a substantial meal for my host was not considered a burdensome task but an honour, her duty even to place wholesome food inside his stomach; so ensuring that a feeling of satisfaction was created and extended for the longest period of time possible. No grand gesture or statement of gratitude was expected, and none was received. It's delivery produced a calming affect - perhaps even some bonding between the two - negating an otherwise tense encounter.

My host was highly charged by the arrival of meat in front of him: the impact on the cat was the same. They both salivated vigorously and both were eager to attack the food and digest it with haste. The cat was cruelly disappointed when she found herself excluded from the feast. This position was reversed when later she received the abandoned residue from my host who, despite his attitude towards the animal, took pity in her plight.

Like the cat my host loves to chew on meat. He becomes intoxicated with the taste, texture and colour of barely cooked flesh – especially when it still contains traces of blood. He takes simple delight in systematically dividing it up (to a rule possibly developed as a child) and slowly devouring it in parallel with the accompanying items, such that all are neatly disposed of at the same time.

For awhile all his thinking power was concentrated exclusively on the sole act of consumption. With regard to this, my host – perhaps males in general - regarded the female's style of approach and speed as a measure of her virility and dexterity, and ability to function like a man.

Eating a large volume food has a calming affect. It concentrates the mind and is sometimes a convenient subject for positive discussion. It can become an occasion in its own right and strengthen social links. When the pleasure of eating surfaces, the mind is able to concentrate on little else, and so it recharges. Large meals, constructed of many diverse elements, and eaten slowly for as long as possible, appear to be a simple, effective way to rest and recharge an overworked brain.

This particular meal provided a significant source of total mental stability and emotional support. Past family memories and values resurfaced to be considered for their worth and validity. It was an act of pure sentimentalization.

My host performed sex with the female, in his view badly. For her the performance was open to interpretation. He succumbed to what he saw as her invitation only because the biological urge was too strong to resist. Initially my host had felt driven to offer his body for sex as a way of repairing some hurt and insult he had caused. As he engaged to perform he switched to automatic: his body operated without the services or direction of the brain. Yet paradoxically he did not enjoy himself, and hated himself afterwards. Later, alone, when he thought back on his behaviour he was physically sick.

For his part the act of sex intercourse was brutally expressed and speedily executed. For her part it was a fearful, tearful encounter: one which required her to summon up all her reserves of strength and powers of commitment to see her through what for her was an ordeal. She did not enjoy it but saw it as her duty to gratify him.

The engagement was disconnected, out of rhythm: each to their own; each taking nothing away from the experience. The sex was physically punishing and copulation was reached in record time. Both sides were happy with this as both were in a hurry to move on. Neither participant enjoyed it yet each masked their lack of fulfilment well. The bonding was purely physical, a convenience of flesh. Each tried to remain emotionally detached but failed, and each was driven to feel repulsion: one much more so than the other.

As he made love my host thought of another female, and strove to lock her image firmly in his mind at all times. It was a source of comfort. The female present fed on the male's sense of misery, and amplified it needlessly. It did not make him feel better but more miserable that he had been reduced to this situation of physical intimacy.

The female tried to push aside her own anxieties and fears and rediscover the joy of lovemaking. She wanted to extinguish previous bad experiences. She did not succeed. These experiences continue to haunt.

The act of sexual intercourse left neither feeling satisfied. For her it was physical punishment and little more than temporary titillation, in parts, of her nervous system. For him it was a release of suppressed, accumulated nervous tension which afterwards left him only physically relaxed. Mentally he was still suffering. In many ways the whole exercise had been perfunctory.

There was relief when it was all over, that it was all over. Nothing was said afterwards of substance: just minimal politeness ensued when required. My host though did apologise: as if he had done something profoundly wrong and morally unacceptable, or without permission. He left quickly, saying sorry. The female was not given the chance to forgive him, correct him or reassure him. Each went their own way on a note of anticlimax. She was still hopeful that the liaison would develop and deepen into something profound and spiritual. He was bewildered as to what he had done. Even the cat sensed something unusual had happened and monitored events with heightened curiosity.

When it came to each other's perception of the other's intent there was the greatest of misunderstanding between the sexes. The female supposed that his moment of near emotional collapse had propelled him into her arms and made him gratefully take up the invitation of sex: where in fact he had simply failed to contain his body's fundamental need for sexual release. The male on the other hand had supposed that she, like any sexually active female, simply could not resist his body's prime condition (relatively speaking) and its capacity to perform sexually with distinction: where in fact she had fought, and overcome, her natural inclination to resist and decline such an offer.

The female regards sexual intercourse as a necessary evil, a path to greater emotional bonding, entrapment perhaps. Her memories of previous sexual encounters disturb her and are almost violent at times. The female is revolted by the thought of using her body for the purpose of reproduction. It is an aversion which dominates to extreme and induces severe, visually repellent images of her body suffering extreme disfigurement, contortions and biological invasion. This is fuelled by an over-anxious imagination. She has a particular dislike of blood, human or otherwise. Its colour and smell physically sickens her. Childbirth she sees as dangerous, unnatural; and she is overwhelmed by the weight of responsibility it triggers.

She feels an overwhelming need to always be in charge – total charge – of her destiny. Anything which can compromise this is perceived as a threat. This even goes as far as to suppress her mothering instinct and the normal mother-child relationship. Her aversion towards constructing a baby internally then raising it externally appears to centre purely on the fear of the unknown: not knowing how her body will transform,; nor what the final outcome will be in the far future when her child has fully matured into an adult specimen. She is highly sensitive to all possible outcomes, no matter how improbable or extreme. She even fears that she would be abandoned by the very life she had brought into the world and nurtured to maturity.

The female is horrified at times by the thought that she is constantly ageing, and there is doing she can do to stop it. The thought of her body deteriorating, losing its visual appeal and failing to perform terrifies. She pulls in many different directions at once: net result being zero movement and zero gain. This creates a permanent state of tension, and constant activity but without result; even when there is an attempt to progress an intention or further a current position. All parts of her conscious being connect, and connect well, yet in a way which results in an intensive, continuous state of self-absorption and tension with the exterior world. Anxiety dominates.

Chapter Fifteen

Clarence fought to remain in command of his senses. They were threatening to completely disengage and leave him stranded. He walked on, just about. His home was where he had left it. His life was as he had left it, just about to go down the plughole. There was dog shit ahead on the pavement: not the dry and discreet variety but the wet shitty kind, the kind dogs did to embarrass their owners. He slowed, steadied himself, steered to the right, and managed to avoid contact with it. It was a victory over one of life's hurdles but he was in no mood for celebration.

The afternoon pub crowd had been a disappointment. It had been too quiet, a touch depressing. It had lacked spark. So he had been forced to wander to eat up the hours. His time spent there had not been enhanced by the behaviour of the universal 'old geezer', resplendent in, and stereotyped by an old grey mac and flat cap. The old geezer had kept looking at him from the other end of the table – luckily a long one – at which Clarence had been sitting. It was the old geezer's usual place to sit. It was tradition. He had suddenly appeared alongside Clarence between blinks of an eye, then acted as if trying to revive a previous conversation. Clarence had sworn blind to himself that he had never spoken to the old man before. When he picked up his pint and moved away the old geezer had looked insulted, as if spurned by close family for being an embarrassment.

Clarence wanted nothing more than to fall sleep but while he was on his feet, staggering slightly down a street in full sight of the general public, he accepted that this was impossible. He staggered on, using the lines between the paving stones as his direction finder and map home. As he approached his home so he approached her home.

She.

Fearing She might be watching from behind her curtains, waiting for the chance to pounce and force-feed him, he broke into an ungainly, lopsided trot and raced past her windows. As he went he pleaded insanity. He arrived at his own front door unspotted and after fighting with the key in the lock dashed inside, to crash out on the sofa, and from there contemplate the void. It didn't come easily so instead he stared at the telly – and after awhile switched it on. There was nothing on worth watching but he did not switch it off. He could not bear to see it dead. He needed the stimulation of total strangers exercising their total banality, and the occasion advert to swear at.

The doorbell rang. Clarence ignored it: let Max answer it if he was in; else let it ring. Max was in and it was answered. Clarence heard voices. He shrank and sank further into relapse on hearing a familiar voice of youth: the boy William was at the door. He closed his eyes. It could be worse he told himself. It could have been John the Baptist. As Max encroached he pretended to be asleep, but to no avail: Max just leaned over him and shook him until he was seen to wake up.

"There's one of your schoolboys out there, wants to talk to you."

"Tell him I'm busy."

Max was not pleased with being a messenger boy, and having taken orders all day from a degenerate foreman he had no patience for more at home. "Why don't you tell him yourself?"

"I can't face him."

"You can't face him," repeated Max, bemused and the least bit sympathetic. But recognising the sad state of the man he decided to let it go. He threw his hands up. "Okay."

As he walked away Clarence perked up a little, thinking he was safe, but there was a commotion at the door and Max reappeared, this time more engaged yet ironically even more unwilling to get involved.

"He wants to know why he hasn't seen you, why you haven't been over to see them."

"Tell him I've been busy."

"Oh for pity's sake what is your problem. You go tell him." Without waiting for a response Max stormed off back to his room.

Buggered for choice Clarence pulled himself up onto his feet and ambled his way to the front door, deliberately taking his time and reminding himself not to get involved or show weakness. He was confronted by one bad tempered William, still in his school uniform. This reminded Clarence of school, which did William no favours.

"What do you want?" snapped Clarence.

Clarence tried to face the boy down but William simply stared back, giving like for like, measure for measure. He decided to state the obvious.

"You've been drinking," he said, meaning nothing by it. It was just a simple statement of fact.

"Thanks for that," replied Clarence between gritted teeth, having read everything possible into it and taken it as an insult. He leaned towards the piece of flesh and trouble, as if to swoop and sink his teeth into the neck for a kill. "So what do you want? What are you doing here?"

"I need a bit more money."

"A bit more money. You're always asking for a 'bit more money'."

William was happy to plead. "It's the last time I promise."

"To pay off this bully again."

"No it's for a present for my mum."

"Don't give me that. I'm not stupid."

William flared up. His face went red. His voice went for broke. "It is! It's her birthday next week. Friday!"

"Nice try but no."

"Just ten pounds will do it."

"No."

Giving up on a lost cause, William stared at the drunk standing before him. The drunk was swaying, threatening to fall over. "You mustn't let mum see you like that."

"I'll bear it in mind. Anyway what makes you think I'll going to see your mum."

Taken aback by the question, William gave Clarence a threatening look which only a thirteen year old boy with attitude could deliver. It usually worked well on other kids – and even on the odd adult - but on Clarence it was totally wasted. Clarence had received it many times before in the classroom. And anyway he was a grown-up. William was just a kid.

"You promised!"

"No I didn't."

"Will you come and see my mum?"

"No."

"You're making her miserable."

"Sorry but no." Clarence could not face the prospect of being in the company of someone so damn near perfect – and dare he admit it so sweet. The comparison would show him up in the worse possible light.

William had one last grudge to get off his chest. "You said you were going to finish the bathroom."

"No I said I would think about it."

"I'll tell mum."

"Tell her what? That you keep coming round here demanding money with menaces?"

"That you made me drink beer."

"Okay that's it. I've had enough. Go. Now."

William was not done yet. He took one step forward. Clarence took one step back. Dirty looks were exchanged. Clarence, fearing a scene, swung the door shut at speed to stop the invasion but did not complete the operation. Something stopped him. It could have been his conscience else his temporary lack of full body coordination. A small gap was left through which he could still survey the scene.

"Go home!" he shouted from behind his improvised barricade. William was now the Black Death.

William shouted back, sounding hurt. "I thought you'd like to know it's my mum's birthday!"

"Not really."

"You could buy her a present!"

"Why would I want to do that? And stop shouting."

William had it all mapped out. "So you could bring it over, give it to her. Surprise her."

"What makes you think I want to do any of those things?"

"You promised!"

That word again. The aggravation was beginning to seriously tire Clarence out. He was just waiting to fall over. He had to sit down.

"No I didn't. Stop saying that."

William had it all worked out: what to buy; where to buy it. "She needs a new toaster. It keeps burning the toast. Toast won't pop up properly. She likes her toast to pop up."

"This is fascinating stuff." The sarcasm was wasted.

William pushed his nose into the gap, like a dog wishing to have it scratched.

"I know where you can get the one she wants. I'll even get it for you. You could finish the bathroom while you're there – that's two birthday presents."

"Thanks. But no."

"But you have to give her something on her birthday!"

"No I don't. Now leave me alone!" They were both shouting again and Clarence hated it.

William could not incorporate that eventuality into his plan and his head locked up. To free himself up he had to dismiss it. "But you will come round sometime won't you? You know where we live."

Clarence wanted to shut the door completely but could not bring himself to follow through. Compelled to listen on to a list of demands which went round and around in a loop he instead feigned hard of hearing and hard of speaking. He lowered his voice, hoping to calm and perhaps even curtail the hopelessly circular conversation.

"As I said I need to think about it."

"I'll tell her you'll be coming."

"No! For Christ's sake don't do that!"

"Why not?"

"Because I may not! Listen to what I'm saying. I just don't know!" Clarence was on his last legs. He had to sit down, now. He had to switch off. It was the only way to stay alive.

"But you promised."

"Stop saying that word! I never promised!"

"But you did!" William was sure of his facts, even when he couldn't precisely remember them or make sense of them. In his mind he was always right, and would be for quite a few years to come.

"If I did - and I'm not saying I did – then it was a slip of the tongue. I can't commit just like that."

"Like what?"

Clarence gave up and cut short to cut his losses. "Go home. I'm shutting the door. Now."

Sticking to his promise he did exactly that and William, beached bruised and battered, left; anger burning in his eyes and throat. Clarence was left to lick the wounds in his head which had suddenly materialized. Loaded down with a bigger headache he fumbled his way back to his usual place in front of the telly. It continued to burn a hole through his damaged skull but still Clarence continued to stare at it, and decompose; until he was disturbed out of his mental semi-retirement by a phone call.

On the end of the telephone was Mary, sweet Mary. She sounded more than anxious: her voice was cracking and Clarence could hear her wiping a running nose. Then she blew it and Clarence cringed. That aside, she was a mother in distress and he was suddenly transformed into a lump of something soft, probably jelly, possibly blancmange. He held his breath, as if serious charges were about to be brought against him in front of the judge. Mary apologized profusely for disturbing him – Clarence said no bother – but had he seen her son. Had William called round?

Clarence felt his temples throbbing as if wishing - or threatening - to explode. He put his free hand up to his head and tried to consider his options, and if he had any. He never got that far: he just panicked and said the safest thing to say.

"No I'm sorry I haven't. But what makes you think he would come round here?"

"He had been talking about you that's all. I thought perhaps he had decided to make a visit. I'm worried. He's been tense, distant the last few days."

Clarence felt himself sliding into a deep hole of his own making and held back from further comment for fear of incriminating himself. But the lack of response only added to the suffering at both ends of the line. Sensing her pain he spoke up, wishing to calm her. He had been hooked.

"Look I'm sure it's nothing to worry about. When they're that age they go off and do things without thinking. He's probably with his mates: loitering down the shops or smoking cigarettes somewhere; all trying to act cool. Perhaps having a beer." He stopped himself there. Shit he wished he hadn't mentioned beer.

"But he hates shopping."

"They don't go down to the shops to shop. They just want to hang around." Then his tongue ran away and Clarence made his second Freudian slip. "Perhaps he's got money to spend."

"Money what money? We don't have any money."

"Well whatever."

Mary fell silent again and Clarence was pushed to act. Her heavy breathing was beginning to disturb him.

"Look remember I should know, I teach these kids. He's a teenager now, breaking free. They start doing this kind of stuff." Clarence tried to make a joke. "There's probably worse to come."

"Worse?"

"Just joking - look don't do anything yet. I'm coming right over."

"I couldn't ask that of you."

Clarence did his best to sound upbeat, masterful. "I'm not offering, I'm insisting."

"Thank you. Thank you very much that's very kind."

"It's the least I can do." Clarence heard himself sounding like a repentant sinner, but without justification, hence a charlatan. "Don't do anything stupid like calling the police."

"I won't."

"Promise?"

"I promise."

"I'm hanging up now."

"Okay."

Fired up with purpose, and strangely very aware of that fact, Clarence banged on his lodger's door.

Max yelled back, aggrieved. "What!"

"Can I ask a favour! Well beg!"

"There's no need to shout!" shouted Max. "There's only a door between us," he said in a more normal voice.

Clarence followed suit. "Sorry but it's an emergency."

There was a long pause then the thud of two feet hitting the floor. The door was snatched back and Max was revealed, dressed only in pyjama shorts.

"Sorry I didn't think you would be in bed so early."

"No matter," replied Max – though judging by his expression it did matter. "What sort of favour?"

"I need you to drive me somewhere."

"What? You want me to be your chauffer now?"

"I wouldn't normally ask but it's an emergency and I've been drinking." By the look on the man's face Clarence could see that Max had not make the link. No matter.

"What sort of emergency?"

"I need to see a woman."

"You need to do what?"

"I need to see a woman."

"What any old woman? A prostitute?"

"No. Don't be silly of course not."

Max glared back. He had been perfectly serious. "Is this something to do with the boy at the door?"

"That's right."

"So this is about that older woman with the boy you told me you wanted nothing to do with?"

"You got it – but it's not what you think – I just need to sort out a misunderstanding, sort of. The boy may do something stupid."

"Just like you."

"That's right. Just like me."

Max furrowed his eyebrows, scratched his crotch then his arse, and gave up trying to understand the logic of the situation. "Okay. Wait there. I need to put clothes on. As you can see." With that pronouncement he closed the door on Clarence.

"Don't be too long."

"Don't push your luck," retorted Max under his breath.

Clarence had been lucky: had he knocked five minutes later he would have caught Max with his hand in a delightful but compromising situation. Alternatively it could be argued that it was Max who had been lucky, for exactly the same reason.

Later, sitting in the car, Clarence stared out of the window as Max drove off. "Keep an eye out for that boy."

"Forget that. Remember I don't know where I'm going. You need to direct me."

"Don't worry I will. Just keep an eye out for that boy."

Max promised, and didn't.

"Shit!" exclaimed Clarence.

"What now?"

"Sorry. We should have turned right back there."

"Brilliant. So now what?" Max gripped the steering wheel even tighter and held on. The streets of London, crowded with rush hour traffic populated by tired and stressed out office workers, made him nervous.

"Drive on. We'll take a small detour. And mind him."

"Mind what?"

"That cyclist!"

"Shit!" Max swerved and just managed to avoid clipping him. "Why didn't you warn me!"

"I just did."

For all his trying Clarence never did catch sight of William and when they finally arrived at Mary's house both were suffering nervous exhaustion. Max slumped back in his seat while Clarence jumped out of the car and looked around. Now high on alert he was beginning to sober up. Max watched him and wondered if he was finally about to crack. The signs had been there awhile now. He had a nutter on his hands. Still all he had to do was last four more weeks and then he would be off: back to lovely Dublin and real Guinness; and real women with real hearts.

As the minutes dragged, twenty or more, Max grew impatient. He shouted out of the window. "Are we just going to sit here all night?"

Clarence waved him down. "Bear with me."

Time continued to drag and even Clarence began to question what he was doing. In frustration he slammed the back of his hand hard against the bonnet of the car. Doing that, he found to his surprise, hurt. Max meanwhile had become extremely pissed off. He sat with his eyes closed and the radio turned up loud. He was in the foulest mood and did not even have a cigarette to ease the strain on his brain. He wanted to be back in bed.

Suddenly Clarence convulsed into the full upright position and stood stiff to attention. William was speeding down the street towards him. His school rucksack dangled from one shoulder. He was in more than a hurry: he was in a race against the clock. The rucksack kept slipping down and William had to keep tugging it back up. When he saw Clarence he slowed, stopped, then loitered; looking from side to side as if for signs of a trap else an alternative route home. He sniffed, wiped his nose across the back of his hand and his hand down a trouser leg, then walked on, refusing to be intimidated. Clarence did look scary but he was almost home, almost safe back indoors. And it was late. Mother might hassle him. He pretended not to see Clarence until Clarence blocked his path and he was forced to react.

"William it's me."

"I know who you are. I'm not stupid. What are you doing here?"

"I need to see you, speak to you."

William saw Max sitting in the car. "What's he doing here?"

"He drove me here."

"Why?"

"Because I need to talk to you."

The answer didn't add up or go anywhere but no matter, William let that one go. He folded his arms. "Talk to me then – and quick, I've got to be indoors."

Now came the difficult bit, and Clarence was stuck for words. He had to persuade the boy to lie. He looked down at his shoes and also folded his arms. The two ended up facing each other almost like a skewed mirror image: one shorter than the other; one more confident than the other; one totally sober, one sobering up; one still with his future mapped out in his head; one still with his head intact; one heading for a fall; both insecure; both at times indiscreet.

Clarence spoke. "I want to apologize for what I said earlier, the way I treated you. It was unforgivable, unprofessional – no I don't mean unprofessional I just mean unforgivable."

His lack of sincerity drew forth a sneer and flat dismissal. William was old enough now to recognise something false. He gave no answer, no indication that what Clarence had just said had in anyway registered.

"Can we still be friends?"

"Friends? When were we ever friends?"

Clarence could not answer that one. Stumped, he fell back into negotiation mode: a skill he had practised on a regular basis in the classroom.

"Okay forget that. Stupid of me. Look the reason I'm here is that I need to ask a favour."

"A favour? Why should I do you a favour? You never do me any."

"Okay not a favour." Clarence had been brought swiftly to his knees. "How about a proposal instead. A deal?"

"A deal? What sort of deal? About what?"

Clarence chewed over his next words until all flavour and texture was removed.

"Look your mother rang me. She was worried. Didn't know were you were. I panicked and said I hadn't seen you."

"But you had. I called round. And you told me to clear off - not very nicely as I remember."

"I know. That's why I'm here."

"You lied, to my mum."

"I know. Unforgivable. But I wasn't thinking right. Haven't been myself recently."

"Is that why you stopped seeing us?"

Clarence jumped on the opportunity to excuse himself. "Yes. I haven't been well. I didn't want you or your mother to see me in such a state."

William was not convinced. Again it sounded false. He didn't know it but he had just been served a rank piece of opportune self-justification, and it smelt bad.

"What's this got to do with me? You lied. She won't like it you lied. But as you don't want to see her anymore why do you care?"

Clarence was thrown by the sharp and simple observation. Why did it matter to him? He had no answer. It simply did. So he told the truth. "It matters a lot."

"And what do you want me to do? Lie back? Lie to my mum?"

"Look tell her you didn't call round and I'll make it worth your while."

"Like what?"

"I'll give you the ten quid."

William sensed he had the upper hand. "That's not enough."

"Okay twenty."

"Let me see it. I want to see it."

Clarence reached down into his pockets, one by one, until he finally accepted the truth that he had no money about his person.

"Can't this wait?"

"No. I'm not going to lie for you unless I get paid now, in advance."

Management material, thought Clarence. He looked across at Max in the car. Max looked crashed out, asleep possibly, then again probably not as the radio was blasting away. Clarence walked up to a window and tapped; then tapped again, furiously this time. Max looked up and almost did his neck in as he twisted it around to face the music. Clarence was scowling down at him, over his shoulder.

"Turn the radio down!"

"Why?"

"Just turn it down! I don't want to shout! And I don't want you bringing us to attention! And it's my radio!"

Me bring us to attention, thought Max. That's a good one. At that point he was on the verge of turning the key and driving off, with or without Clarence; wishing in fact to leave him stranded. He turned down the radio, leaving Clarence temporarily satisfied.

"That's better. Can I borrow twenty pounds?"

"What for?"

"It's an emergency."

Another emergency.

Embittered and groaning under the weight and pain of compliance Max gave Clarence one of his twenty pound notes, along with a look of total disenchantment. He had just got the bundle of notes that day and was loathed to part with any of them yet: they just felt too good in the hand. Clarence did not bother to say thank you, just as he had not bothered to say please. He was after all just dealing with the lodger.

Max watched Crazy Clarence hand his note over to the boy and thought it strange. William looked at it, sniffed, folded it up and put it away safe in the zip pocket of his rucksack. So far so good was his verdict.

"And you'll finish the bathroom?"

"And that." Deep down, buried beneath layers of wasted thoughts and redundant speculation, Clarence had decided that he did in fact actually want to finish the tiling. He wanted to challenge himself, to prove to himself – and to her – that he was fit for purpose. He just hadn't come to terms with it yet.

"And you'll buy mum that birthday present?"

Clarence flared his nostrils and pursed his lips. Had they been the same age a fight might have broken out. William did not flinch.

"I'll finish the tiling. That's it. Else the deal's off. I walk away."

"Okay."

With old scores and new temporarily settled or set aside, each refocused on their own particular problem ahead. William knew he was very late home and lumbered with homework: he would be hassled. Clarence knew he had to put on a good act and fake it, and act more sober, less drunk. Without realising it the two became bound by the coming deception.

"Wait here a bit. Ten minutes. I need to go in first."

William sensed himself in a new adventure, which was a good thing. "Alright."

Clarence rang the doorbell and gulped continuously as he waited for the door to open. His stomach was churning over now, in competition with his head. Since stepping out of the car he had felt sick. William hid down low behind the car while Max, suspicious, tried to keep him in sight all the while trying to work out what the hell was going on. He wanted to drive home but he was stuck. He turned the radio back up, even though the music had turned sour.

When Mary opened the door and greeted him, Clarence immediately felt an age difference. Why this mattered to him he did not know. But he did care that it was so, almost with a sense of regret: as if things could be or could have been so much different, so much better; as if some indefinable opportunity had been or was about to be missed; as if a measure of useful, productive time had been or would be lost. The passage of Time was beginning to confuse him: his present was merging with his future. And the Mary who greeted him was quite a shock to behold: not the lovely lady he had come to expect but a tense mess reflecting a ravaged soul. Her eyes were wet, saturated. Her whole face was tense, breaking up and breaking down. This was someone he could relate to. He said hello in his softest voice and gratefully she ushered him inside: for her part Clarence looked tired out by her cause. Conscious of the great big lie looming he didn't want to say much, preferably nothing. He hovered and she hovered around him. She was very pleased to see him, and it was plain to see. Mary would fight to contain herself and Clarence would seek to disclaim himself. The less she succeeded, the more he would succeed.

Mary was the first to speak. (She thought she had a lot to say.) "He's not home yet."

"No? Well let's give it time." Clarence bit into his words. They were sticky, chewy, and stuck to his teeth.

"It's seven o'clock now. He needs to be fed. He needs to do his homework." Mary wiped her hands over each other, as if drying them out. The problem was logistical and well as emotional. "He's never this late – not without prior agreement, advance notice. This is very unlike him."

Half of him – the better half – wanted to take her hands in his. The other half refused permission, denouncing such a wish as self-destructive. "Let's wait another thirty minutes. Even then it's still not 8pm; 8pm is not late these days."

"It's late for him. Late for me."

"We don't want you to look a fool, or him for that matter. He's going to feel a right fool when he shows turns up and discovers his mum has called the police out. And if any of his mates find out he'll be a laughing stock."

Mary backed off, back into the living room. Clarence was expected to follow. She fell into a chair. Clarence picked another for himself, the one next to her, and followed suit. They were both looking very tired.

"But he's never acted like this before. He's always been the one for straight home. Gets the homework out of the way. Food. Then likes to go to his room."

Clarence turned to face her and spoke up. "Like I said he's growing up. Kids change. There always the first time. And this is his."

Mary looked straight at him, finally accepting that what he had to say contained a strong element of truth. For the required thirty minutes she would hold on. As she continued to look at him her eyes wandered around, and took in his general appearance. Clarence did not look good. In fact he looked terrible. A fresh, new expression of deep concern washed over her, along with another wave of vulnerability. Clarence, yielding to the combined power of mother and child, was driven this time to take her hand in his. He squeezed it. It squeezed him.

"It will all work out fine. Trust me. Remember I do teach – sometimes – so I know these kids."

"Yes you're a teacher. Still a good teacher?"

"I like to think so."

Another inner feud kicked off. Half of him wanted to hug her and squeeze her back into her comfort zone. The other half wanted to back away, run away even, knowing the whole was acting under false pretences, and therefore disgracefully. And on the backseat another elusive, undefined part of him, was bemused by the inner conflict and lack of a unified whole.

"When did you last eat?" asked Mary. Food was on her mind.

Clarence struggled to remember. "Must have been lunchtime. Some burger place?"

"You mustn't live on just burgers."

"I know I shouldn't – and I don't, I promise."

"Would you like to stay for a meal? I have to feed William."

"Sorry. I'd like to but there's someone waiting in the car."

"Someone?"

"My lodger. He drove me over."

Clarence replied in a flash, wishing to reassure her that this 'someone' was no female of consequence. Why he felt the need to do that he had absolutely no idea, but his wish to reassure her gathered strength. And did he really want to stay for food? Yes, he really did – and not just because it was free - but he was scared off: not by the small dangerous kid but by the great big lie. Mad Max was just a neat excuse to flee. (Reputation hopefully intact.)

"So you can't even stay for a cup of tea?"

"I don't think so."

"Would he like one – if he's stuck out there in the car?"

"I don't think so. No. Definitely not."

The words ran out and the conversation floundered, which Clarence did not want to happen. A previous conversation rang some bells and the blackouts bubbled to the surface of his mind. He just had to burst the bubble. He didn't want so many secrets inside his head – at least not those he had to keep from her. He took a deep breath and came clean, though heavily understating their frequency and impact. It was almost an aside.

Mary was nothing less than supportive. "Perhaps you're working yourself too hard. Overstretching the brain."

"It could be that." Clarence knew it wasn't.

"Look if you're feeling bad, just come round. Company often helps."

"Thank you. I'll bear that in mind. Problem is I don't know when it's going to happen. And then it's happened and it's all over."

"And the doctor's can't help?"

"The doctors?" Clarence threw in another lie. "No they know nothing."

"Forgive me for asking – "

"No go ahead."

"But have you discussed any of this with a specialist?"

"Yes, that I have."

"Was he any help?"

"No. No help."

They ran out of words again and they were stuck. They had something to share – something worth sharing – but they did not know what it was, or how to share it. On the face of it they were as different as different could be; yet somehow, somewhere, beyond the faces it made them much the same.

As an act of pure spontaneity he made a promise, an offer, wishing to redeem himself, raise himself up, be worthy of her friendship and goodwill, conveniently ignoring the fact that it was costing him nothing extra.

"Let me finish the tiling by the way. I must finish it."

Mary's eyes lit up. Her face lifted and she smiled. It was the first smile of relief that evening. "Could you? That would be lovely."

Clarence was struck dumb by the realisation that his minor demonstration of solidarity had made her happy on a massive scale. What for him had been an irritation had been hanging over her.

"You hassle me if I forget."

"Oh I couldn't do that."

"Yes you can. It's easy. Just hassle me."

They were still holding hands when the doorbell rang. Mary let go and jumped up, like a coil released from restraint. Clarence retreated back into his protective shell and stood up to stand guard – more pulled than pushed. He watched Mary run for the door and nervously clawed at his lips with his teeth. He heard a man's voice. It was Mad Max. He was not sure if this was a good or a bad thing.

"Is he causing you trouble?"

"Trouble? No?" Mary, greeted by the sight of an unshaven, rough looking man and not her precious boy, struggled to respond.

"I'm Max by the way."

"You must be the lodger."

"Yes I'm the lodger." Max had begun to detest the label. Even 'Irish Git' was beginning to sound like a compliment.

"Why would he be causing me trouble?" Mary was wound up: unusual for her.

"No reason." Max could give her a long list if he really wanted to.

Feeling slightly intimidated Mary waited for his next outburst.

"Is he there? Clarence? I've been waiting. I want to go home."

The request sounded almost childlike and it clicked Mary back on. "Sorry. Yes. Of course you have. Please do come in. I'll go and get him."

Max stepped inside and noticed the umbrella stand. He was fascinated. He didn't know such things existed: a particular place to store all your umbrellas, but then this was the heart of Old England – on hearing Mary speak he rushed to catch her up.

"Your friend is here," she said.

Max fell into the living room and saw Clarence as Clarence saw him. Max did not regard himself as a friend. As far as he was concerned being the lodger and being a friend had proved to be irreconcilable. He suddenly felt very Irish, and Clarence looked very English. Tough luck for Clarence. The two exchanged looks which said 'mind your place', 'be on best behaviour', 'don't drop me in it', 'keep your mouth well and truly shut'; 'don't tell me what to say', 'don't tell me what to do', 'I'm not just your fucking lodger', 'get off my back', 'you're an English git'; 'you're an Irish bastard'; 'you owe me twenty quid'; 'you owe me rent'.

Mary saw none of it. She wanted her son back, back in one piece, unharmed; just the same as he ever was; just the same as she ever was. She didn't want things to change. Standing there, Max felt stupid. Standing now, Clarence also felt stupid. Standing there, Mary felt duty bound to offer her guests tea.

Tea.

Tea would sort things out and hold back the troubles of the world. It was a troubled world which was why someone clever had invented tea: to be sipped slowly, so allowing the brain to meander and measure its next sane move and motion.

"Tea? Can I make you both a cup of tea?"

"I don't think so," said Clarence.

"That would be lovely," said Max in defiance.

"But we haven't the time," objected Clarence.

"Time for what? You weren't doing anything," retorted Max.

Mary sensed the room becoming smaller and the men getting larger but said nothing and minded her own business, which was far more important. And anyway would could she possibly say?

"Have you got a beer?" enquired Max, waking up to the possibilities.

"Beer?" Mary looked at him as if in defeat. "Sorry no beer."

"Tea will be fine then."

Clarence, displeased, threw him a heavily encoded look. Max threw it back.

"Yes a cup of tea would be lovely," added Clarence, determined not to be sidelined or appear noncommittal.

Mary hurried off to make her tea and the men were left to stand guard over each other. They both sat down, together; both placing their backsides on the seats of chairs at the same time; neither wishing to be first; neither wishing to be last.

"Did you lock the car?" asked Clarence.

"No. Why would I want to do that." The reply was harsh.

He didn't want to but Clarence let that one go unchallenged. Somewhere, out there, the boy William was waiting to burst onto the scene. Clarence had to prepare himself, build himself up, muster all reserves of mental energy for what might turn into a tricky, compromising situation; a nightmare even; at worse a one-way ticket to permanent rejection and shame. Shame?

Clarence could put up with a lot – or so he thought – but not the shame of Clarence the big time liar. He had made a deal. He just hoped William stuck to it. But then why wouldn't he? The boy wasn't stupid. Far from it, he was a clever, astute, manipulative little sod. He would go far. Management material. And the top-down world always had a need for management material, just as walls needed wallpaper to hide the cracks.

Like king lions the two men inspected and gauged the size of the other's mane. Like King Kong gorillas the two men judged the value of the silver running down the other's back. Alone together nothing more was said between them. It was all hanging in the air, waiting to fall like rain, sleet or snow. Four weeks, thought Clarence, I think he said only four more weeks. Four weeks, thought Max, I only have to stay another fucking four weeks.

Mary returned with a fully laden tray. On it was all she needed to distribute perfect cups of perfect tea, and biscuits.

"Why four cups?" asked Max.

"One for William."

"Whose William?"

"Mary's son," explained Clarence impatiently. "This is Mary."

"Oh yes sorry I'm Mary."

"Mary. Now that's a lovely name."

Clarence felt his lodger was now trespassing but what could he do? Act ungraciously? He jumped in. "He'll be back very soon. I promise you."

On hearing that Max gave Clarence the dirtiest look imaginable. Clarence pretended not to notice.

Mary sat down and crossed her legs. She was keen to make polite conversation. Max was keen to do likewise. Clarence was desperate to keep quiet, and for his lodger to do likewise: lest dangerous talk. Mary dispensed the tea and biscuits. Clarence took the tea and refused the biscuits, but then Max took two so Clarence took two.

"You lodge with Clarence?"

"That's right, for my sins."

"And mine."

Mary looked left and right and left again. "Have you come from Ireland?"

"That's right. Dublin."

"Not Northern Ireland then."

"No. Ireland. Dublin is in Ireland, the Republic of Ireland. Northern Ireland is Britain."

The sub-text passed over Mary's head. "Here to work?"

"That's right, building contract - electrics. Your London can't get enough Poles." Max turned to Clarence. "Why aren't you teaching your kids how to wire a fuse and plumb in a toilet?

"I don't know. Why don't I teach my kids that?" Clarence waited for the punch line but it never came.

Mary soldiered on. "Do you miss home?"

"Do indeed. Yes I do. But I'll be back soon so no matter."

"Do you miss your family?"

"Yes indeed. Mother. Father. Brothers. Sisters. Cousins. None of my own mind you. I'm not married."

"Nor am I," confessed Mary.

"Never you mind," Max told her.

Nor am I, Clarence wanted to say.

Max began to stir it. "So where is this William then?"

"I don't know. But he'll be back soon I'm sure."

"Is that so? Says who?"

"My friend Clarence here." Mary gave Clarence a smile. Max gave him another severe dirty look. It was two in a row but Clarence did not buckle. He had too much riding on concealing the truth.

"Does he now."

"Yes I do."

"Well that's good then. All well and good."

Max beamed. Clarence felt sick and the Irish charm only made it worse. Mary realised that she best intervene, though she did not feel equipped to do so. In the past she had always been dominated by men. It had never been the other way round. She searched around for a light-hearted remark and found one, off the television.

"Two men living in a flat together. Sounds just like that old comedy show. . ." Her voice died as she struggled to remember. With her eyes shut tight she tried to think of the name, and not of William. She wanted to bang her head against a wall. "Help me please. What was the name of that show?"

Clarence offered help, though he was equally stumped. "Martin Clunes. It had Martin Clunes in it. The big guy."

In the room two out of the three now banged their heads against a wall. The third skipped and jumped his way methodically through all the BBC comedy programmes he had ever watched, and quickly pinned it down.

"Men Behaving Badly. You mean Men Behaving Badly," Max announced triumphantly.

"That's it!" exclaimed Mary. "A bit rude in places but very funny. You are clever. Well done."

"Yes well done," said Clarence, purposely repeating the praise to lessen its affect. Kids, not adults, had taught him that one.

"And do you two behave badly?" Mary put the question as a joke when in fact she was very interested to know more about the domestic Clarence, and how he conducted himself in private.

Max laughed. "Oh yes very badly don't you know." He turned on Clarence. "Don't we Clarence?"

Clarence, crippled by the truth, was unable to respond. He could only stare back at his new tormentor. Mary's line of fire he did his best to avoid. Max stared back, waiting for a kick back. Clarence strained every mental muscle, pulled every mental sinew, kicked open every memory cell in an attempt to come up with something safe to say. Deflection appeared to be the best defence. Something at the back of his mind told him to deflate the situation with comedy, English comedy. Just deflate the gravity of the situation he heard himself say. It was good advice which he had never handed out before, to anyone.

"Yes we do. Like not always putting the top back on the toothpaste. My toothpaste. Toothpaste isn't expensive in this country."

Mary tried not to smirk, and failed. She tried not to laugh, and failed. Though she laughed only a little she felt guilt-ridden: this was not the right time for laughter. No way could she feel happy right now: if she did she would feel guilty for the rest of her life, and her child would never forgive her for her moment of weakness.

Max responded in kind. "Or not doing his fair share of the washing up."

Clarence could not argue with that one, so chose another target, not necessarily a good one. "Or nicking all the hot water to have a bath."

"I need a bath. I do a dirty job. Dirt sticks. Especially English dirt."

"What's wrong with a shower?"

"Nothing. Except your poxy little electric shower isn't strong enough. It turns the water works into needles – anyway who says I use all the hot water. Sometimes you're stuck in there for ages." Max turned on Mary. "And I don't know what he's up to in there sometimes."

Mary held on to herself tightly. A storm was definitely brewing. "Would anybody like another cup of tea?"

"No thank you."

"No thank you."

"Well do finish the biscuits. I can always get some more out."

"Thank you."

"Yes thank you," echoed Clarence, determined to match Max compliment for compliment, insult for insult.

Simultaneously they both grabbed at the remaining biscuits, whereupon Mary did as promised, knowing William – when he arrived home – would be hungry for food, any kind of food. Biscuits would reduce the risk of a foul mood developing. With Mary out of the room Clarence immediately tried to shore up his position and put Mad Max in his place. His situation was turning sticky. He spoke with a vengeance.

"Just cool it will you, shut it."

Max spoke with an acid tongue. "Meaning what exactly?"

"Don't say anything more about us."

"What have I said? Banter is banter. It's just a little banter or can't you take a joke anymore?"

"I can take a joke thank you very much. Just don't talk about us at home. And don't say anything about William."

"About William? I don't understand."

"Fine. Let's leave it that way."

Clarence fell silent as Mary re-entered the room. The biscuits were shaken out of their packet and onto the plate. Mary looked at them, as did Max and Clarence. Nobody took one. Now it didn't seem the right thing to do. So all three sat in perfect isolation, undisturbed, tempting no one. What tea remained in the pot was left to stew to oblivion and back. On this occasion Mary did not care.

"Are those all family?" asked Max.

"Don't touch those," said Clarence.

"I wasn't going to."

"Well don't."

"And if I was going to you couldn't stop me."

Max spotted another moving target. "Has he told you about his friend John?"

"No he hasn't."

Clarence butted in quick. "There's nothing to say."

Max butted back with relish. "Nothing to say? Are you sure about that Clarence?"

"Yes quite sure thank you." Clarence wanted to say 'fucking sure'.

"Well fancy that."

Mary was now very bemused and made no attempt to pretend otherwise. The men however no longer cared what impact they were making. The doorbell rang.

Eureka!

The doorbell rang and everything changed. Mary rushed towards the door again, faster this time. It had to be him. There was no other conceivable possibility. And it was him, her son, William: standing before her he looked very put out, and though she did not know it, put up. Mary grabbed him and drew him into her fold. She hugged him to death and almost squeezed him dry. He was down to his last drop of blood.

William struggled at first but soon gave up and caved in to whatever his mother had to do to make herself feel better about herself. It was a humiliating experience and he would not put up with it forever. There had to be a limit to this kind of behaviour: perhaps rationing if not a total ban on excessive female outbursts. Then she kissed him all over his head and ruffled his hair. His hair was her feathers. He pushed her away. He had taken more than enough for one evening. She pulled him back. For her it was a grave emotional moment: one of the deepest, most engaging, most draining. For him it was sheer agony.

"Where have you been? I've been so worried."

"Nowhere. Just seeing friends."

Mary pushed her son away slightly, while still holding on to him at the shoulders, like a dress in the shop she had pulled off the rack for inspection.

"Have you been smoking?"

William felt insulted. In reply he spoke his words precisely. "No I have not been smoking. Why would I want to be smoking. Smoking is bad for you. Every one knows that."

Max cut in. "Who told you that?"

Mary looked him in the eye, then her son; and believed him. "Why didn't you tell me you were going to be out so late? Why didn't you check with me first?"

William shrugged her question off. For 'check' she had meant 'ask permission'. He didn't want to keep asking permission. It was insulting. "I didn't think it was that important. Anyway I hadn't intended be so late home."

Then Mary remembered she had guests – guests she could not leave to burn and burrow into each other. "Come on in. We have guests so be on your best behaviour." William had come to hate that expression. "I'll make you a cup of tea."

"I don't want a cup of tea."

"No matter. Come on."

Resigned always to someone else's fate, William dumped his bag on the floor and followed his mother in, not that he had any choice in the matter: Mother still held a grip on him with one hand. He tried to proceed with decorum but was manhandled, almost dragged, all the way.

Clarence looked up. Max looked up. Clarence and William exchanged glances. Even William and Max exchanged glances. Nothing was being said but suddenly there was a lot going on in the room and plenty to be said. Mary, elsewhere, missed it all but was the first to speak.

"We've been worrying about you, Clarence and I."

"We have," said Clarence, trying his best to sound as if he meant it.

William gave Clarence one of his very special looks, and this time it hit home. Clarence took fright. Perhaps the deal was off. For Max the penny finally dropped. The dots pretty much joined up and he had a good idea that something big was going down, some big deception. It was really weird stuff and it could turn out to be fun.

William, though sorely tempted to say something, said nothing. Instead he reached out and grabbed two biscuits: one in each hand as was his way. They were shortbread. Beautiful. As he chewed and swallowed he thought about what to say to his mum. He could not remember ever having lied to her before on such a grand scale as this. It would take some getting use to as he may have to do it again – not that the act of lying was not something about which he held any strong views, moral or otherwise. He had lied before, to other kids, but he had never lied to his mother – at least not in living memory, which for him was not that long. This was definitely something different. Still, he persuaded himself, the reason for it was right, good and proper. It involved a birthday present for her so best keep his gob shut. He ignored Max totally and concentrated on Clarence and took some comfort from the fact that Clarence looked like a man less than sure of himself. Yes he had a hold over the man. The man was weak. He was showing weakness, just like a child, just like some of the kids at school.

Clarence did his best to avoid all eye contact with the boy, and likewise with Mad Max. He had only two places to look: down at the carpet or up at Mary. Max watched them both, intrigued. William waited for the questions to come: from his mother there were always more questions.

Mary lived up to expectation. "So what were you doing, you and these friends of yours?"

"Nothing."

"You must have been doing something. Where were you?"

"Just hanging around the shops."

Mary looked up at Clarence. He had been right all along.

"Were you and your friends causing trouble?"

"No! What trouble!" William was adamant.

"Which shops?"

"What?"

"Which shops did you hang around?"

"I don't know. The big ones. The ones in the shopping centre. The ones which stay open all the time."

"You didn't give offence to anybody?"

William picked at his words again, plucking them out of the bag one by one. "No I did not give offence to anybody. I was quiet and minded my own business."

"What were the others doing?"

"Others?"

"Your friends. You said you were with your friends."

William stumbled. "Oh them. I don't know. I was by myself."

"By yourself?"

William fell into a police cell. Even Clarence felt it. Max was impressed: the woman was doing a good job of cross-examination.

"I went off by myself. Okay?"

"Doing what?"

William grabbed at another biscuit before anyone else did. There were only two left. "Nothing."

"Doing nothing for so long? I don't believe you."

William nearly shouted out his secret to get his mother off his back. He just wanted to be fed so he could go to his room. Shit. He had homework stashed in the bag. He looked at Clarence and Clarence looked up from the carpet. Momentarily the two locked horns. Max watched them both. Mary missed it all. The exchange reflected deep reservoirs of nervousness on both sides. The end result was however in one sense positive: the deal held. And with regards to his sometimes obstructive, sometimes overbearing, always armour-plated mother, William gave up. Time for a change of tactics: play it for all it was worth; score as many goodwill points as he could; maximise the sympathy factor; show her he could be an angel sometimes, when it suited – enough to make her happy. He put his hands up in the air – literally - and surrendered, with half a shortbread held up like a cocked pistol. If so ordered he would be happy to lay it down. He wanted to eat real food now.

Clarence felt even more sick. The situation was slipping into dangerous waters. Was the boy going to spill the beans? If so would he get his money back? He turned his thoughts on to Fiona. Somehow, someway he had to make things right with Fiona – not that they were badly wrong, they could just be better, not stuck in neutral. And together they could go a lot further, reach a lot higher, get back into bed. The sex came flooding back into his aching head. It's potential cheered him up and its absence taunted him. Their time spent in bed together had been beautiful; better than Tracey, except perhaps at the beginning.

William suddenly spoke and Clarence was forced back into reality. It had not gone away. Max was having a wail of a time. This was just like back home when he and all his siblings were just kids, fighting off their parents, adults, and the world, in that order.

"I went in a big store."

"Whatever for?"

William looked hard at his mother for she presumed that big stores were just for women. "I was looking for something to buy. Okay?"

"Something to buy? What for? And what with?"

"I wanted to buy a present."

"A present? Who for?"

This time William looked hard at his mother, as if she had suddenly turned stupid. This was not his normal mum. She was acting like one of those silly girls. "For you. It's your birthday next week."

Mary forgot to breath. She had been well and truly flattened, and flattered. Her son was absolutely right. It was her birthday next week. Every year it came round, on the same day, yet she had forgotten all about it. Her face began to relax and radiate pleasure as the implications of what her son had just revealed sank in. He had just been thinking of her all along.

"Well done me boy!" Max could not resist passing comment.

Clarence kept his mouth firmly clamped. The deal as far as he could tell was still holding. William turned and grinned at the stranger. He was beginning to take to this other man. He wasn't so uptight as Clarence. He was more like a big kid, more like him less like Clarence. Clarence could never be a big kid – not that he considered himself still a big kid. He was bigger than that.

Mary began to settle. She was almost back to normal. "That's very kind of you, very . . . noble. But please tell me next time that you're going out and will be late home. I don't want to stop you I just need to know."

She sat down and watched the teapot even though it did nothing. Perhaps refill it? Perhaps start again? William felt fully vindicated, and soared to a new height of confidence peppered with arrogance. The wish to boast all his other triumphs suddenly surfaced. It was strong. There was no stopping it.

"And I got an Ipod at last," he announced with relish. "But only one of the cheaper ones," he added, as if to make it clear that he had been hard done by. He buried the fact that most of the money spent on that had been meant for her present. He would keep it secret until her dying day, and even then only share it with the four walls of her empty house. And still he would take it with him to the grave, along with much else accumulated along the way. He could never tell her. It would hurt her, and him.

"An Ipod? Aren't those things expensive?"

William, realising he had made a mistake, tried to limit the damage. "Not that expensive."

"Where did you get the money for something like that? You've got no money. We've got no money."

Right there and then Max wanted to give both mother and son money. Right there and then Clarence wanted to give the mother some money.

William was stuck. He licked all his teeth with his tongue. Though he was loathed to admit it they did need cleaning. He felt sweaty all over. He wanted to scratch his private parts, furiously. He wanted a big piece of chocolate, or a pile of crisps, bacon or prawn cocktail flavour. He got none of these things and had to answer the question. There was only one place he could go right now. He turned to Clarence. Clarence did some quick thinking: the quickest he had done in a long time. His brain was suddenly alive to danger.

"I gave it to him."

"You gave it to him?"

"He's a very generous man our Clarence." Max could not resist the gag.

Clarence brushed him aside. "He really wanted one – and he wanted to buy you a present. He couldn't do both."

"That's right. I couldn't do both."

Again the implications of this next revelation sank deep and Mary was left more happy, more content, more sure that all was right in the world. She gave Clarence the warmest, deepest smile possible and Clarence was loathed to accept it. He wanted to hang himself. Max also wanted to hang him. The exchange of money outside made a sort of sense but there had still been the earlier refusal back at the flat. He had heard it clearly. So things still did not add up. Yes there was some deception going on and this boy and this poor excuse of an Englishman were in it together.

"It was nothing, honest. Every cool kid has to have one these days. You got to have street cred, especially in the playground. Even the teachers have to have street cred."

Max could not resist another contribution, another to further wind up Clarence. "Don't sell yourself short me boy. That was a wonderful thing you did. Giving away your money like that. Makes me feel humble it does."

Clarence wanted to smack him but there was a lady and a boy in the room.

"My teacher's got no street cred: he's a dickhead," said William, bursting out.

"Don't say such a thing!"

Mary spoke harshly. William took cover. Max burst out laughing. And Clarence kept quiet. Fear of discovery, fear of being exposed as a first class liar and conman disabled all normal, spontaneous behaviour. Also it began to dawn on him that he wanted to throw up. He tried to hold himself together and concentrate on the problem to hand. It could send him crashing.

"And promise your mother you'll never do that again."

William protested. "Do what again?"

"Scare me like that."

"How am I suppose to know I'm scaring you when I'm doing something."

Max interjected, seeing the funny side of it still. "Phone or text her. Tell her what you're doing and ask if it's scaring her."

Clarence glared at him. William smirked then his face dropped when he was reminded that he didn't have a mobile – unlike most of his classmates.

"But I haven't got a mobile," he protested.

Max had the answer. "Clarence will buy you one for your birthday I'm sure. If you ask him nicely."

William turned on Clarence but Clarence was having none of it and kept his mouth shut. Mary suddenly felt a little deflated, as if she was failing in her duty to give her son everything he really needed to remain happy and fulfilled. It was true to say nowadays that mobile phones were part of that equation. Max saw her discomfort. Clarence did not, and Max knew it, which made him yet more angry with Clarence. So this was the woman or one of the women he fancied? Shame on you Mr Clarence Kennan.

The sickness in the pit of his stomach continued to expand: delicately Clarence repositioned himself in his chair in a desperate but in the end pointless attempt to satisfy his stomach. It would not be satisfied by minor adjustments. It was begging release and a return to normality, as was his brain. Both required a discharge. And still Max continued to bait.

"Talking about men behaving badly, we don't half drink a lot don't we Clarence."

Clarence could not believe what he was hearing. He swivelled in his chair and turned all his guns on Max. Max was now the source of danger, not small boys. Yes things had moved on.

"What?"

"Us. The lads. Drinking like there's no tomorrow."

"I don't know what you mean. I like a drink as much as the next person. Why shouldn't I have a drink."

"There's having a drink and then there's serious, continuous drinking."

Mary had no wish to hear any of this whereas William wanted to hear it all. Seeing adults lay into each other was always great fun.

Max turned to Mary. "Did you know he can really knock it back."

Mary was not surprised to hear that bit of news, but did not say so. She now regarded Clarence as an ally in life. She would stand by him. The man who was speaking was the lodger: he held no rights over Clarence. None of them could presume the moral high ground. Presumably this Max was Catholic. He should know better she thought. But then Max was not a usual Irish name.

Clarence made a suggestion. "I think it's time we left." He sounded fierce, and at the end of his tether.

William wanted to burst out laughing but managed to hold himself in check. He was old enough now to recognise those times when laughing was not on, despite the invitation; and this was one of them. He kept low and his mouth shut, hoping not to bring attention to himself.

"And he keeps falling asleep in front of the telly. And I have to turn it off."

"So do you."

"Even when it's not on."

"Well I must have turned it off then mustn't I?"

Mary came to his defence. "I've done that sometimes, fallen asleep in front of the telly."

"Scary sometimes. Sometimes he just stares into space."

Clarence had an answer for that one. "That's when I'm thinking hard. Something you wouldn't know about."

"Are you thinking hard when you're sleepwalking?"

This was a shock: Clarence didn't know he had been sleepwalking. He felt terribly, terribly sick inside. His stomach had something it wanted to share with him and say to him, loudly. Mary meanwhile now feared the worse. Time for William to go to his room, immediately: no arguments; no compromise; no deals. William saw no need for censorship and fought her tooth and nail all the way; and only gave up when she forced him up the stairs. She could not be dissuaded. He stormed upstairs, making a racket, adding to the bad feeling in the air. Mary didn't know what to do or say. Her home had never felt like this before. She felt her head begin to spin. Only Max – Mad Max – was left in high spirits.

"And Christ are his socks smelly. Takes them off in front of the telly."

Clarence fought back. "And your underwear is disgusting. Don't you have toilettes where you work? I don't want it lying there in my washing machine."

"My job is all physical. It gets like that. And anyway what am I suppose to do with it? You said I could use all the facilities when I took the room."

"Wash it by hand. Hand wash it."

"You must be joking."

"No I'm not. And don't whistle so much. It's irritating."

"So now you can't stand the whistling. Does your friend John whistle?"

Clarence held on to the arms of his chair, to hold himself back. This was twice now: John The Baptist was a forbidden subject. He wanted to hit Max the Mad Irishman and Max was more than happy for Clarence the Crazy Englishman to give it a go. He wouldn't have a clue what a real fight was all about. He was just a teacher, soft in the head and all that.

Clarence bypassed the mention of John and shifted to new ground. "And what do we know about you? Nothing except that you're from Dublin. How do we know you haven't got a criminal record for stealing cars or something? Knee-capping perhaps? And why can't you get a proper job in your own city?"

"There's no skeletons in my cupboard thank you very much. At least I don't lie to people. And bad jokes about knee-capping is in serious bad taste." Clarence had hit a sore point.

Clarence took stock. The man was right. He felt worse than sick. "Yes I'm sorry. That was wrong."

He sounded like he meant it, so Max was satisfied. The man looked very sick.

Mary finally intervened. "Gentleman please. For the love of God this has got to stop, now, right now. You're both acting worse than a couple of kids. Make up or get out. Right now."

Both men looked at her and blinked, equally bewildered.

"I mean it. Right now."

Clarence could contain himself no more. His stomach was about to rupture. "I'm sorry but I have to go to the bathroom."

"Off you go then. You know where it is."

Suddenly Mary was talking down to two children, two troublesome boys. She was back in her element. Clarence clambered upstairs, fighting a deadline, trying his best not to throw up on the way. He did not want to clean the carpet. He looked up. William was sitting at the top of the stairs and staring down at him like he was the king of the castle. Clarence asked him politely to move – to no affect – then asked him – ditto – then told him to get out of the way – still ditto – then pushed him aside – at which point William fell back at his touch, happy that he had made his point, point not exactly defined. He retreated back to his room, and stood behind his door, still watching and recording the event like some TV journalist reporting from a war zone. It was all great stuff, and he was the only one there to see it.

When he was sure Clarence was out of earshot Max shot him down again. "It's his own fault. He drinks too much on an empty stomach." Even then Max would not give it a rest. "And he never cleans up in the kitchen. I nearly always have to do the washing up. Not that he cooks much, but when he does he never cleans up afterwards. Leaves it all to me."

Nor did Clarence hear Mary tear into Max: had he, he would have been impressed. Instead he was left to gaze upon the not so wonderful state of the bathroom. Yes it was an eyesore: the unfinished tiling tore into his soul and the spaces begging to be filled stamped on the leftovers. He did his best to look away and headed straight for the toilet bowl. It was his prime consideration.

Meanwhile as Max took a thrashing William crept half way back down the stairs, enjoying every moment of it.

"He's a slob basically."

"You stop that now – Max isn't it? Right now. Or it's outside for you. I will not allow such behaviour in my house. It sets the worse example. You should know better. You should both know better."

Max froze on his spot. God Almighty his mother was in the room and speaking through this woman's mouth. (Shit, he just wanted to go home.) But she was right. She was always right. While Clarence sat on the edge of the bath and stared at the bowl, and considered its convenience, and felt truly sick – the sense of sickness having escalated with the reunion with the abandoned DIY – Max calmed down and apologized. Mary also calmed down and accepted the apology, then began to think about whether to cook a meal at this time of night. Perhaps just a sandwich or two: he could eat them while he did his homework. Mary knew he could get it out of the way at lightening speed when he wanted to. A good wholesome sandwich, homework done, send him to bed she concluded. Yes she had it all mapped out in her head now. It was not hard being a mother. It was only hard when she was not being a mother. This was her conclusion, time and time again.

Max sensing a weight on her mind, and that his time was done – or that he had done his time – made his exit. "Tell him I'm waiting in the car will you?"

"Certainly. Sorry if I spoke out of turn."

"Forget it. I deserved it."

And he meant that. And she knew he did. And he left, to camp out in the car and turn the radio back on, loud. Mary headed for the kitchen, having temporarily forgotten about Clarence and his current misfortune. She had an unmade sandwich in her head.

As Clarence leaned over the bowl it became a little black hole, leading somewhere extremely distasteful; and the little bit of junk food resting in his stomach decided, definitely, that it wanted to come up and see the world. And while Clarence thought of one little bit of food so Mary thought of another: a little bit of food to fill a sandwich; something healthy and filling and easy to prepare. She thought of cheese and tomato, and some slices of salami to entice her child into attacking it. The salami did not need to be cooked. She was sure she had some at the back of the fridge. Salami: such useful stuff she noted. Who invented it? The Germans? The Italians? The French? She didn't know. Google it, she told herself. Get William to google it. That was the way of things these days.

As the pieces of food came out of the fridge so much smaller pieces of what had once passed as food came out of Clarence's stomach. His aim was good (as always) and he did not miss his target. When his stomach settled back down he came up for air, pushed down on the toilet handle and watched the contents of his stomach get flushed away. A little was left behind floating, so he waited, and waited, and waited, and tried not to look as he waited until he could flush again. 'Guilty as charged', he admitted to himself as he pushed down the handle for a second time. Two flushes did the trick. There was no mess left to be seen, only the mess of his life. That was an uninitiated thought: the irony of which led him to put the toilet seat down; sit on it; and place his head in his hands and his elbows on his knees. He wished he could flush all the bad bits away.

His stomach was becoming compliant but his head was not. It had gone in the opposite direction. A whirlpool of pictures and sounds of people talking and shouting and whispering at him, about him, with him, through him, battered his brain. And in amongst it all there loomed the terrifying picture of John waking up alongside him, taunting him, torturing him, even tempting him; and just as his best mate turned up. It was too much, he had to kick it out. So he kicked, and managed to sweep it aside, back into the closet, back under the carpet. But for how long?

He wanted to cry, a little like a woman but mostly like a man. He wanted to confess, like a sinner, but could not pin down his sins. He had no one to believe in and no one to believe in him. He wanted to fall back in love with teaching youth but could not see the point anymore. He wanted to be with Fiona again – but that would mean not being with Mary, who he kept trying to avoid contact with. He wanted to hug his Mum and Dad at the same time but that would just embarrass them – and anyway Dad might fall over and hurt himself with the shock of close physical reunion. He wanted to get to like Des, find him interesting and please his sister; but that would never happen. Des would always remain a first class prat.

He was stuck, alone, and falling apart. There was less and less to hold on to to steady himself; and how much longer he could hold it together he simply did not know – or care to know. He had absolutely no clue. So take each minute, hour and day as they came, and expect the worse. Which was? Total mental breakdown? Or would he just blackout for good and never wake up. Perhaps it really was time now to see a real expert. But no: they would put him away. Then there was the question of money and the mortgage. How long would the sick pay last?

He had had a brain once, even if he had not always used it. It had earned him a decent living. On rare occasions it had even done some good. Now it was fragile, flimsy, near breaking point. And people all around him were causing confusion. Suddenly he remembered whose toilet seat he was sitting on, in whose bathroom, in whose house, and told himself to pull himself together; if only to get back home. He stood up, double-checked one last time that he was leaving the bathroom as he had found it, and opened the door to rejoin the outside world. He was met by William.

William was hanging on to his bedroom door, as if awoken to witness a public hanging for the first time: unsure whether to enjoy it, dismiss it, protest against it, report it; or just feel disgusted that such a thing was taking place on his patch in an almost, civilized society. He was clutching his new Ipod. It was still in its packaging as for now the antics of Clarence were proving to be far more interesting.

They exchanged frozen looks - both now use to such brazen eye contact. Not a single word passed between them. It was all said by the eyes, the lips and to a lesser extent the hands. Clarence looked at the picture of the Ipod printed on the cardboard box and concluded that he had been conned. No matter, he had done such things himself once. Good luck, he was forced to concede. The boy had balls, just as he had once. William looked down on him, with an open, definitely declared air of disgust. The man had been sick in his bathroom. He knew it. He knew Clarence knew he knew it. Likewise Clarence knew it (of course) and more importantly knew William knew it. Each knew the score, and the uneasy peace held. They were bound closer now. There were secrets to be kept, else mutual assured destruction was the name of the game; and Clarence did not want to go mad.

Softly, slowly, Clarence crept back downstairs; and softly, slowly William closed his bedroom door. He jumped onto his bed and ripped open the packaging. He just wanted to look at and touch his brand new Ipod – perhaps even work out how to use it before being forced to get stuck into homework. She never forgot when he had homework. And he was hungry: but she would take care of that: when it came to such things Mum was as regular as clockwork, come rain or shine, come hell or high water.

As Clarence approached the bottom of the stairs he slipped and fell back. His legs went wobbly then collapsed under his weight. Automatically his hands went out to stop the fall. Luck was on his side and reduced what could have been a serious injury to a nasty bump. As he straightened himself up he felt a sharp pain in his wrist. It was nothing like the pain he would suffer if William had seen him fall. He looked back. More luck: William was in his room. Luck: it felt good and he did his best to hang on to it. But luck had to fade.

Clarence re-entered the living room and was confused: it was empty. He found Mary busy in the kitchen, preparing sandwiches.

"Where's Max?" Clarence wanted to know where the enemy was hiding out.

"Waiting in the car."

Good, thought Clarence. He looked at her frenzied activity of food preparation. The slices of bread were thick. "Are you going to eat all that?"

"No silly. One is for William and one is for you."

"For me?"

"Yes. You said you hadn't eaten since lunchtime."

This was true and Clarence could not refuse. He was grateful, and humbled, and stunned by the fact that a) she had remembered when he had last eaten and b) she had wanted to do something about it. And it picked him up. He thanked her and like a starving dog watched the sandwiches come together, saliva on tap. He watched her because he knew she could not watch him. She ricocheted around the kitchen as if on skates and Clarence had to stand well back to avoid a collision. He wanted to say something special, but not too much – but even that he could not say. He wanted to hold her, just a noncontroversial part of her, but not too much and for not too long – but even that he could not do. He wanted to add her to his dreams – day as well as night – but feared the consequences of success. He wanted to start again, with her, from scratch; and at a time in the past when he was totally together and she was younger, less worn out, less a mother and more a woman – not that he was being fussy he lied: just a little nudge in the right direction was all he was asking. Words began to swell up inside him. And like the previous contents of his stomach they demanded to be released. He had to speak, and he had to speak first.

She was saying nothing. She was chopping and cutting and rearranging like a manic chef with the ultimate do or die deadline. He was all set but still he did not speak. He held back and watched his sandwich – the one he had adopted – take form.

Finally it was finished and Mary wrapped up in some strange kind of paper. With pride and joy she handed it over. Clarence never did say what he had hoped to say: instead he said something else, something much easier to roll off the tongue and into polite conversation.

"Thank you very much. I'm deeply honoured."

"Don't be silly. It's just a sandwich. Here just take it and eat it."

"Is that what you'll say to William?"

"Just about." Mary grinned. "Why?"

"Nothing." Clarence backed away and turned to leave the room, then stopped and turned to face her once again.

He still had a pile of things to say but no way of expressing himself beyond the ridiculous. There was one thing he could say though, to correct the situation somewhat, so he said it. Unfortunately he did not consider the full consequences of doing so.

"Will you say sorry to William for me. Give him my apologies."

"Apologies? Why give him your apologies? What have you done?"

Clarence was stuck, knowing he had just dropped himself in it big time. His stomach suddenly felt bad again and he was staring down the toilet bowl once more: that deep black hole of doom, despair and sick. He wished he had kept his mouth firmly shut, despite the wish to reset the record straight, put Mad Max in his place, and improve his standing in her eyes. It was too dangerous to talk. Had he blown it? Probably. It certainly felt like it. He had generated suspicion: he could hear it creeping out when she spoke. Would he dare to ever come back? Probably not. Would her son hate him for the rest of his life? Probably.

Best he leave now. Best he leave. Best he get out of her life and get her out of his. He withdrew to the front door, Mary chasing after him for answers; but all she got was a final farewell. As she slowly closed the door, wishing not to lose sight of him, their eyes met and locked for a brief moment in time, a moment which was extended by pure compulsion on both sides. The compulsion was based upon a mix of bliss and blackmail. This image of her he would take away and cradle through thick and thin; and it would trouble him. The image of him she would cherish and polish and hold close lest she dropped it. It deserved a place on her mantelpiece.

The drive home was dominated by a large, well-constructed, well-stocked sandwich. Clarence and Max had nothing to say to each other – not yet anyway – so the conversation that did take place concerned only directions home and turning the radio down. It was too loud and Clarence had to think. He asked Max to turn it down but Max ignored him. He had to do it himself.

Clarence did his best to enjoy his sandwich. The cold air had helped to revive him, and retune his stomach back to its normal rhythm. It was empty and it was hungry again. It was a great sandwich and Max could not help but repeatedly glance across as he tried to work out what was in it. It didn't take him long to spot cheese and tomato, and something green, probably lettuce. It took him a little longer to get to the salami – almost at the cost of an accident. The smell confirmed it. And he was jealous. He loved salami. The woman had made this big bastard a great fat sandwich but had not thought to offer him one. Max thought about eating it. Clarence thought about women and children. It disappeared fast.

Back home, car successfully parked in a very tight space, Max about to jump out and escape, Clarence finally broke his vow of silence. He had a lot to ask and a lot to say.

"What did you say about me while I was upstairs?"

"I told her you drank too much."

"Did you tell her I was an alcoholic?"

"Yes!"

The snarling began.

"You bastard!"

Clarence wanted to punch the git but was held back by his seat belt. Max wasn't wearing one so could have easily punched him in the face had he felt like doing so. And he did.

"No I didn't. So calm down."

Clarence didn't.

"But are you?"

"No I'm fucking not!"

"Fair enough. Just checking." Max changed the subject, seeing that the subject of drink was making Clarence extremely stressful, which meant he probably was an alcoholic. "So you threw up in her toilet then?"

"Yes."

"Did you clean it up?"

"Nothing to clean up: it was all under control."

"I bet it was."

"It was."

Clarence threw off the piss-take. "Look you listen here. You never talk about me like that in front of people again. You understand? You savvy? Not to her. Not to Fiona. Not to anybody I know. I demand it."

"Demand it? You demand it? You demand nothing of me sunshine. Go stick your demands up your arse and your head in an oven."

"You're my lodger. Go stick it up your arse."

Luckily for both, the snug confines of the car's seating arrangements held them apart. It remained all talk.

"I'm your lodger? So fucking what? Is this all because I'm Irish?"

"No. You're just my lodger."

Max shook his head in disbelief and stared first down at the dashboard then out of the driver's window. He decided to cut and run, back to his room.

"You've lost it. You've really lost it. Book yourself into a clinic mate, before it's too late and you do yourself some real harm."

"What's that suppose to mean?"

Max refused to look at him. He spoke out of the window. "You're going mental, really mental – you've gone mental." To make the point Max stabbed at his head with his index finger extended to its limit: at a temple to be precise; the assumed engine of all knowledge and understanding. "You're turning into a nutcase."

"And you're not helping things."

"Is that so? Well fuck you."

Though it hurt, Clarence allowed Max the last word. Bad talk done, Max grabbed the keys, jumped out of the car and flew indoors, slamming the door behind him. Clarence remained in the car and turned on the radio. Late night music: exactly what he needed right now. Stoically he let ten minutes pass, then another, then listened to the news on the hour; then finally pulled himself out of his seat and out of his car. Without the keys he could not lock it, which bothered him. He was a Londoner: he had to lock his car. He tried to go indoors but the door was shut and he had no key. And when he rang the doorbell? No reply. And when he banged on the door? Still no reply. And when he banged and banged and banged and swore and swore and swore? Still no fucking reply. No fucking reply at all. This bastard was a bastard. This lodger was a true git.

Clarence could not bring himself to scream and shout, and whispering seemed a pointless exercise so he sat down on the steps and spat into the nearest hedge. He looked across the road at a piece of well kept lawn: small but prized as so many were in his street. Green was always the colour. A cat caught his attention. It was that Judy. Stiffly she walked around in circles, as usual with attitude, then closed in on one particular patch of interest. She examined it closely, as if for signs of wear and tear, and sniffed it a few times, as if for its freshness factor. She looked around, as if to check that nobody was spying on her, filming her for eternal damnation on the Internet; then squatted over it. She concentrated, flexed the appropriate muscles and defecated, triumphantly, as if in a competition or celebrating the end of weeks of constipation. Job done, Judy didn't try to cover it up but just gave it one quick sniff of appreciation before she was off. She had disowned it already. She had no wish to hang around and be associated with a pile of shit.

When she saw Clarence she changed direction and headed towards him, not away; for some reason deciding that he was something worth investigating. As she crossed the road, looking neither left nor right nor left again, she ducked and swerved to avoid the stone that he threw at her: not that she had been in any real danger. His aim was that bad. She did however decide that her company was not welcomed and changed direction once again: back to her original course; and with barely an interruption to her flow or cruising speed. She could not have cared less. The man meant nothing to her. He was nothing more than a vague acquaintance who occasionally infiltrated her home and tried to ingratiate himself with those who lived there.

Clarence, satisfied that the cat had got his message but dissatisfied that he had missed, stared up at the night sky. There were few clouds but those that were stuck up there were illuminated by the light of the moon. It was almost a full moon. It was a perfect night for romance, for anybody else.

Clarence had to concede that the clouds looked captivating to the eye, especially around the edges. Their crinkly edges consisted of detail which broke down into more detail, which broke down into more detail; and so on, into infinity. There was a special word to describe such a thing Clarence reminded himself; some mathematical term describing infinite detail locked up within. Wishing to prove to himself that he could still cut it he racked the last remaining, active juices of his dying brain to find the word then rounded on himself for failing. That was now his problem he conceded: he didn't know anything worth knowing – or if he thought he knew something he didn't know if it was for certain. Or something like that. He wasn't certain anymore. He was entering the ultimate vacuum, the vacuum of the empty mind. Once in there he could never escape. Everything was falling away. Everything which was left was falling apart. Soon there would be nothing left, except possibly the most humdrum routines of domestic survival. People were deserting him - people had deserted him. Or he had deserted people. Those who were left he could not bear to make intimate contact with. His problem remained: it had not got any better; then again it had not got any worse. It just hung around and popped up from time to time, to poke him in the eye, to irritate him like a bad ulcer or a mother-in-law.

It was his big secret. But who had he told? Mary? Fiona? Perhaps in time he could learn to live with it: the total blackouts; the lack of self-control; the sometimes dysfunctional head and its vague sense of a split personality – or was that down to alcohol abuse? Clarence suddenly lit up, like a Christmas tree being plugged in. Perhaps that was it. He was – or had – developed a split personality. One half knew the other half was there. The other half didn't give a damn and just carried on doing whatever it felt like doing. Perhaps he ought to go back and see that psychiatrist fellow, properly this time. But that would mean paying him by the hour, and trying not to laugh as he spoke bollocks.

With nowhere else to take his thoughts, Clarence fell back into a languid stupor. He didn't know where to turn. All avenues were blocked, or mined. The doors which were open led to places he did not want to go. So he was stuck. He rang the doorbell and thumped the door one more time. But no change. The bastard truly was an absolute git. He thought of places to go. But he had no money, no cards, no mobile phone. He felt naked. He had transport but little petrol in the tank: that aside it did not occur to him to try and drive anywhere. He was drawn to consider the most obvious place to go: she would feed him, attend to him, smooth his brow, put him to bed or even take him to bed – but no, he simply could not face that. That would be the ultimate humiliation, being saved by her. There were limits.

He looked up at the sky again. It had not moved. It was still there. His decision was made. He began to cry. He lowered his head to look down at the ground again. That too was still there. Nothing had changed. Nothing was getting better. He was still stuck in the mud. He was still crying. He was getting cold. He was becoming very sleepy. He wanted that soft pillow. He wanted a soft, female voice to talk to him, to help him into bed. He wanted something hot to drink. He wanted a big fried breakfast to greet him in the morning: brought to him in bed after a long lie in, perhaps with a paper. But he did not want sex – at least not with her. He was not up to it right now and neither was she. To cheer himself up he consoled himself with the mental image of his fist flying into Mad Max's face; then dismissed that entirely, dissolving it with the truth of the situation and his own limits of acceptable behaviour. He stood up straight, ignoring the pain that had crept into his buttocks, wiped away the tears and marched vigorously towards Rebecca's front door. He was suddenly in a hurry to reach it and get inside, subject to permission of course.

Dressed in her nightgown and matching slippers Rebecca answered her front door. A tattered Clarence stood before her, doing his best to stay standing, upright and proper. He looked exhausted. He gulped. He was on guard. He folded his arms as if waiting for a reply to a controversial question even before he had spoken. Then Judy rushed forward from out of nowhere and knocked against Clarence as she dashed inside. Out of the three of them she exhibited the greatest physical energy, whether measured in relative or absolute terms.

Rebecca had gone to bed early to read her book or browse her newspaper supplements, to slowly leave the real world behind as she veered off into her own version of it: one which was bigger, blessed, more bountiful, less vindictive; one built more on belief and less on the laws of physics. That aside she was very pleased to see him, even if he did look terrible. The fact that he did look terrible gave her greater reason to be pleased to see him. She sensed straight away that he had come to her for help, and she was more than ready to help him, save him.

Though wary of what was to come she folded her arms and waited. When it came to Clarence she was patient. And it paid off. When Clarence finally spoke he chose his words carefully and articulated them slowly, deliberately; as if for maximum impact; as if to be sure in his own mind of exactly what he was saying and how he was saying it even as he said it, and how it was being received. He spoke without regret and without, it seemed, any injection of emotion, except perhaps for that which conveyed fatigue of the brain. To anybody else he would have come across as cold, uninterested, but not to Rebecca. For her it was the verbal equivalent of a diplomatic note.

"I am very sorry to bother you. Did I disturb you from sleep? You are dressed for the bedroom and bed."

"No I was just sitting up in bed, thinking and reading."

"It is said that a good night's sleep is very good for you. It allows the body to recuperate, rebuild, reconstruct cell structure."

"That's what I've heard." Immediately Rebecca felt a return to common ground. Clarence spoke her kind of truth.

"I am afraid I am at a bit of a loose end. I have a bit of a problem, a logistical one."

"Which is?"

"My lodger Max has locked me out of my flat and refuses to let me back in."

Clarence sounded calm, relaxed, and in the least bit angry. Rebecca was the complete opposite.

"Locked you out? Out of your own home! That's outrageous!"

"Well it is possible I deserved it. We did have an extended heated exchange. Things were said which perhaps were best left unsaid. And it went on for far longer than either of us had intended. Minor tensions transformed into major derogatory outbursts."

"Well even so. That's still extreme, still childish, and entirely unwarranted. He's not a child. He should be able to take it on the chin. I thought that's what all you men did: argued then made up like buddies over a pint."

"My thoughts almost exactly. But still that is irrelevant now: the fact is I am locked out which means I have no place to sleep tonight – at least no place which is dry, warm and sheltered from the weather. So I was hoping that you might be able to provide me with a place to sleep? Financial payment is no problem. A financial payment to mitigate the inconvenience?"

"Of course I can!" Rebecca unfolded her arms, intending to extend them; but stopped when Clarence made no similar gesture. She folded them away again, still wishing for a spontaneous, heartfelt embrace. There was more to come.

"I do not want to cause a fuss or create additional work for you."

"I assure you you're not causing a fuss." Rebecca was quite clear about that.

"And no additional work?"

"No. And even if you did it would not matter." And she was quite firm about that.

Judy reappeared at Rebecca's side, nosey, mildly interested in the unfolding event. She sat down and licked her lips - she had lapped up some water from her bowl - then some fur. She watched Clarence and he watched her. No words passed between them as Judy could not speak. Rebecca knelt down and briefly stroked her Judy across the head and down the back, as if to reassure her that everything was in order. Judy did not like that and rebelled. Clarence waited for her to rise up before speaking further.

"I am afraid I am at a low point right now. So I am not much fun to be around."

"And why is that exactly?" asked Rebecca.

"Exactly?" Clarence considered her enquiry. "Well I think it is due to a combination of factors: factors all acting together to multiply the problem; their destructive impact being almost exponential."

"Really?" It was all she could say. She was entranced by the man who could now so easily bowl her over just by opening his mouth.

"Really. It will not last though. It is a low, so things can only improve. It is just a question of when."

"Isn't that always the way."

Clarence thought her response slightly odd but refrained from investigating further. Rebecca leaned against her doorframe. Keen for further disclosures she forgot to invite him in so he was left to stand and explain himself like a naughty schoolboy or a wayward husband – other than an earful of verbal abuse bad boyfriends got away with it. Judy stood up and started to stalk the immediate vicinity, as if searching for something which threatened her jurisdiction.

"And what are these factors then? Do tell I'm fascinated – that's if you want to share this with me that is. I get the impression you do."

"Certainly. I have no problem with that. There is nothing to hide – not as far as I know. A little to feel ashamed about perhaps."

"Really? And what's that?"

"Moral confusion and compromise. I took an action on the pretence that it would be beneficial in the long run for all concerned, when in fact it was only good for me: objective being to maintain my reputation intact; to eliminate any suspicion of improper behaviour with a minor. These days more than ever communities are suspicious of men who ingratiate and endear themselves to children without their parents' permission – especially single, unattached men who are not engaged in a full sexual relationship with a female. Other factors are loneliness, a lack of self-confidence, a lack of purpose and direction, a lack of faith even, and the fear of complete mental collapse." Clarence counted up the score inside his head. "Yes I think that covers it."

It was a mouthful and Rebecca's head was beginning to ache as the words trundled in on the conveyor belt of verbal communication. And Clarence had just only got started. She guessed he had more to say. She began to feel the cold and took him in.

"Please come in. It's cold out here."

"Thank you."

Submissively Clarence followed her in while still talking. "Physically of course I have just burnt myself out: abusing my body with drugs and engaging in hostilities with the lodger has just worn me down. There's very little strength left. My body would like nothing more than to fall sleep right now."

"So would mine."

"Really?"

"Really."

Rebecca sat down on her sofa and signalled Clarence to do likewise. She turned towards him and waited for him to speak on. It was all enthralling stuff, what he said and the way he said it: just a little too heavy for her this time of night. It was more suited to talk over the dinner table with a glass of wine in the hand. Still, Clarence was as Clarence did, she reminded herself. And she would not have him any other way. It made him special, head and shoulders above the rest – not that there had ever been any others.

"My spiritual state is surprisingly strong, or to be precise stronger than it used to be. It just does not receive the support right now of the other parts of my body. It is feeling severely isolated, almost let down. Not that a body ever has an agreed internal contract defining peace and happiness or the rules on interconnectivity."

"Just like me," whispered Rebecca, hoping that he had heard.

Another odd comment, thought Clarence, but no matter.

"From the psychological perspective it all makes perfect sense."

"Does it?"

"But I could not share that with you."

"Why not? Please, why not? I'm Rebecca?"

"That would be divulging too much. It would leave no personal space between us which would distort our connection, perhaps dangerously. We could not engage as we do."

"Dangerously?"

"Wrong word: perhaps falsify it."

"Falsify it. I see."

Rebecca didn't but pretended that she did. The bottom line for her was that her Clarence was being totally open and honest and begging for her help and emotional support. She could not ask for more. She was in the ascendant. She took hold of his nearest hand and squeezed it in anticipation of something fantastic and near magical appearing on the horizon. Clarence winched. She had caused him pain and she was alarmed. She let go.

"What's the matter Clarence? What is it?"

"I sprained my wrist earlier. I had forgotten all about it."

Rebecca took hold of it a second time, but this time gently and cautiously, and examined it. She saw a big green bruise.

"You did more than that. What did you do with your hand? Were you in a fight with your lodger?"

"No fight. I smacked it against my car in a pointless act of frustration. Stupid of me I know. Soft flesh impacting hard metal is not a good idea, especially if it is your soft flesh."

"It certainly is not. Wait here, I'll go get my box."

Rebecca jumped up, accidentally exposing her breasts and not caring – in fact she was rather glad it had happened. She was determined to do whatever it took to make him better, even if her only contribution was to bandage a hand and kiss it better. She flew off, accidentally scaring Judy who jumped out of her way, miffed as she had just settled down. With Rebecca gone Judy prowled around the room, sometimes looking up at Clarence, sometimes not. She lived in a world which only occasionally overlapped with humans. Clarence waited patiently: his bruise was of not real concern to him. He watched Judy. Judy kept her distance and they remained poles apart.

Rebecca returned with her first aid box and did exactly as intended. She dabbed his bruised flesh with some slightly fiery ointment and stuck a patch on it. Then she kissed another part of the hand. Clarence sat still and said nothing until he was sure she had finished enjoying herself.

"I believe you are truly a most wonderful, generous woman. You could also be a wonderful, generous mother I think. You have that strong urge to give freely, without reckoning."

"Am I? Am I really?"

"I believe so - subject to confirmation of course."

"Subject to confirmation?" Rebecca laughed. It was a joke, she thought. "Of course. Thank you. Thank you very much. That was a very special compliment." An obvious question sprang up inside her head. "Are you hungry?"

"Hungry? No not hungry. I have just eaten something. And anyway if I was I would not want to put you to any trouble."

"You could never do that. You should know that by now."

"Really? There are no limits?"

Rebecca took a deep breath, held on to it a little, then exhaled. "No limits."

"That is encouraging."

"Is it - well let me at least make you a hot drink then."

"Yes that would be nice. I am thirsty I have to admit."

"Green tea then."

"Green tea it is." It was that colour green again. It kept popping up on the radar. Was his favourite colour green now? It had once been purple, after Deep Purple.

Rebecca rushed to make his tea, and with great impatience. She was blind now, blinded now by some twisted notion of something she defined as love. She simply wanted to serve him. When she returned she moved towards him slowly, like a nun on patrol. She was holding a full mug and was determined that he drank it all up.

Clarence looked down into the mug as it was handed to him. "It really is green."

"I know."

As he drank she offered him a bed for the night. He refused, insisting that the sofa would suffice. She in turn insisted. Again he refused.

"Come to bed," exclaimed Rebecca finally, now reduced to begging.

"No the sofa is quite adequate," replied Clarence, totally unaffected by her acute emotional outburst.

Exhausted, Rebecca gave up, but even as she started to deflate an idea jumped into her head. She had to put it to him. It would keep them close together.

"I've got a great idea."

"A great idea? That's unusual. What is that then?"

"Let's go for a picnic."

Clarence looked up at the ceiling. "Eating outside, at some scenic spot with views." It sounded like an outright dismissal.

"Don't you want to?"

"No on the contrary it sounds appealing to me."

"And I'll show you something special."

Clarence smiled. "Now you are playing with me. Something special?"

"A special place. A site where aliens have landed."

"Yes that is interesting. Evidence of an alien visit you say?"

"You believe it's possible?"

"Certainly. Can I leave it up to you to arrange?"

"Of course."

Rebecca was now all pumped up like a young girl drooling over the very first boy who had seriously caught her attention. She was astonished and ecstatic that he had accepted her — some would say controversial - announcement without batting an eyelid.

Clarence handed back the mug. "Sorry but I just cannot finish this. Too tired now. Too tired."

"No matter. Here lie down."

Clarence did as invited. Rebecca was determined to send him off to sleep. She would nurse him like a baby until he was deep asleep, just like a baby. She was determined to pass her latest test with flying colours, else there was little hope for her. She was pushing on, hard, towards her ultimate goal of the ultimate acceptance and the ultimate relationship – as defined by her. With Clarence she had set the bar very high: she could not, would not lower it.

As he faded away Clarence heard Rebecca in the distance, droning on about some picnic overlooking a field. He thought it was a dream, so paid no attention to it. It dissolved, to be replaced by other dreamy thoughts: thoughts about Mary, and Fiona; and to a lesser extent William; and to a far lesser extent Max.

As he drifted off he tried to hold on. He had questions to ask. Why was life so difficult for him and not for others? Why were the women in his life so difficult to sort out? He had not pulled them in, they had invaded. When would he get his life back? All 100% of it, undamaged, as it used to be? Far from perfect but as least intact and fully functional, should he ever choose to use all its functionality. And what about school? Dare he ever go back into the classroom? Had the little sods finally beaten him to the ground? Or was he now missing the place: the fights; the classroom stand-offs; the staff room fights and stand-offs; the spilling of subtle sarcasm in conversation with the Headmaster. He just didn't know.

And Fiona.

Fiona. Fiona pushed her way back onto centre stage. But even then she still had to share it with Mary. It was equal first billing.

```
-  Mary, the older one with the kid already
-  Fiona, the younger one with the kid or kids
to come who was great in bed
```

No matter. Two he could cope with he presumed, knowing no better. Somewhere he guessed Tracey was still having a drink; still sucking away on a cigarette like she wanted lung cancer; still having a laugh with her mates, perhaps at his expense. Jealous, he wished her an enormous bar bill, one which would hit her credit card like a cricket bat; which in turn could only be paid off by her stripping down to her underwear and dancing around on the bar counter before a crowd of drunken, jeering businessmen, preferably Chinese. Dreaming of underwear, Clarence began to dream of Tracey in her sexy black, silk kit, but it quickly wore him out and he moved on to other things.

Like sticking cheap ceramic bathroom tiles up in their allotted place, correctly and on time.

Like avoiding the carpet and kids when throwing up.

Like avoiding having to take in lodgers.

Like being kind to animals.

Like making up with sisters, and their husbands even if they were prats.

Like buying his mum and dad a slap up meal.

Like grabbing the chance to kiss the girl who sold him his booze.

Like making John The Baptist fall in love with a woman and marrying her – or just have sex with a woman and marry her – or just marry her. Like hoping never to set eyes on him again – at least not unless he was definitely married.

Like punching the Irish, then running away.

Like avoiding the Welsh, just to wind then up, then running away.

Like patronising the Scots, because they were expecting it, then running away.

Like thanking the Poles, and paying them in cash.

Like beating the French, and rubbing it in, and running away.

Like winding up the Germans, and again, and running away.

Like disowning the Americans, for good, and running away.

While he slept Judy wandered up and sniffed him. Then, discovering that parts of him were warm, jumped up to join him and immerse herself in his body heat. The two were like peas in a pod: one small and furry, one big and hairy; one with a big, battered brain, one with a small, sharp, highly charged brain; one barely able to walk on two legs with grace and balance; one able to walk and run on four, duck and dive, launch and leap off four, and without even having to catch her breath; one enjoying life to the full; one sick of life; both never sick of meat. One smelt and so did the other. One needed a bath. Both were too serious and needed to laugh more. One did not know how to laugh. One had forgotten how to laugh. Neither was in charge of their own destiny and neither knew this at this precise point in time.

Later, while he and Judy were curled up fast asleep, Rebecca sneaked back into the room to check up on him. She put a light duvet over him. Judy was purring. In her own way Rebecca too was purring. She stroked his hair. He began to snore but she forgave him. For her all was right in the world.

＋ ＋ ＋

Log Entry

The relationship between my host and his domestic male companion has suffered a fracture. It may be beyond repair. Though I have done my best to repress my host's frustrations with regard to the behaviour of the other male, sooner or later they had to be released. I could not contain them indefinitely without causing serious harm to his mental state. These two particular males, coinhabiting without the interaction or surveillance of females, formed a relationship which was finely balanced on a point: cooperation versus conflict; respect versus contempt; entrapment versus enticement. It was subject to unconscious but constant revaluation. The speed of the collapse however did take me by surprise.

Without warning the minor tensions and disagreements over lifestyle which had existed between the two suddenly erupted into major, open conflict; providing an excuse on both sides for a public, vitriolic display of aggression and criticism towards the other. The trigger appeared to be nothing more than a spurious attempt by my host to conceal truth by tight control of social dialogue.

Any bond of friendship I thought had existed up to now appears to have been superficial - almost invented for purposes of maintaining sanity in an environment where the defence (or acquisition) of personal space had to be compromised. The two males exhibited guarded familiarity and never true emotional intimacy. There was a lack of empathy with regard to day to day survival and in particular a lack of cooperation with regard to food preparation and consumption. Emotional problems were not revealed, except by accident. Some activities were always forbidden: in particular talking to one another while naked and discussing masturbation (but not sexual prowess).

Bonding did occur when the two simultaneously directed their natural aggression, sense of adventure, and the wish for freedom of thought at the rest of the world. However it appears that even a minor disagreement or misunderstanding can trigger a redirection: each on to the other. The affect of the feedback is exponential and the level of aggression generated can sometimes become physical. In such situations the presence of a female who has – or demands - respect from the male combatants is critical to the containment of such primitive urges.

At the height of the confrontation each participant anchored themselves to any feature of race, nationality or culture (real or invented) which highlighted a difference between them, and magnified it to maximise the emotional impact. Suddenly origin of birth was all important and a decisive factor in arguing cultural and social superiority. Each played by the same set of rules – rules which remained unstated throughout. Had the emotional aspects of this confrontation been removed the encounter could well have been classified as a game: nothing more than a game of fast thinking one-upmanship. But judging by the level of animosity generated it was definitely not a game: it was something far more serious – exactly what I cannot determine as the conflict was based upon little real substance. Upon reflection I suspect that a large proportion of the males who inhabit this little planet do not like to be considered like 'all the others', and so do their best to express individualism and independence at every opportunity (especially in front of those females who are significant to them in some way); especially when they suspect these attributes have been visibly eroded by getting too close to certain other kinds of males.

As I have discovered, two males coinhabiting and sharing the same environmental resources has its drawbacks. The battle for personal space fluctuates greatly between two extremes, rarely falling on middle ground. It is either protected with great passion, else shared with enthusiasm. The second condition is usually the result of two combined factors: celebration of a sporting event combined with drug-induced mental relaxation (usually in the form of alcohol). The consumption of alcohol in the home is often a ritualised affair involving both parties; and though no agenda is ever set, a sense of competition is immediately established.

The question is will this collapse pass just as quickly and without long term psychological damage? Or will it linger and fester for an extended period of time? To improve matters for my host I may try to engage in positive, intimate dialogue with the other male, as done on previous occasions with another. The offer of sexual favours may be one tactic worth pursuing as he is currently very sexually frustrated and needs an outlet.

With regard to the many discrete nation states which exist upon this planet the past, as recorded or reinvented, continues to interfere with the present and infiltrates the most neutral agenda. It locks the human mind and sends it down pathways it would not otherwise think of going. It demands reaction: usually proactive and defensive. In the worse cases it ejects reasoned thought.

The relationship between mother and child is in a permanent state of flux. At the beginning the connection is total but all one way: a new born baby has no perception of its mother's existence, nor for that matter any other human beings. It is only barely aware of its own existence. It is driven by a few simple needs: keep warm; eat when hungry; drink when thirsty; sleep as much as possible; do as little as possible to survive. At this time the typical mother's devotion towards the care and well-being of her new offspring is absolute and unreserved. It demands her constant attention and the mother, if she is to remain true to herself, must give it all, at any time, and without notice or gratitude.

As the baby grows so does its recognition of the mother's presence, along with the realisation that she is the main provider of food, security, comfort and even pleasure. The father, if present, may also provide some of these functions, but to a far lesser extent; and only after the baby's diet has become more sophisticated and no longer reliant purely upon its mother's milk. This it extracts, usually with haste and impatience from one of her two nipples. Her body produces it in two breasts (she never has more than two, but occasionally ends up with one or none); each featuring a nipple to provide for discharge upon demand. In the opinion of the baby this milk is never supplied fast enough to its mouth. For her newborn baby a mother's first and foremost duty is to provide, on tap and at any time of the day or night, this liquid food.

As a child begins to engage more with its immediate surroundings so the mother begins to formulate and exercise complex systems of care and control. When able to stand for extended periods of time the child usually develops the strong desire to walk then run anywhere and everywhere; and to make noises, some random, some structured towards communication and language learning. Some of these activities are reined in by the mother, else focused towards what she defines as a useful end: reason being to avoid danger and enforce convention. Sometimes its freedom of movement is curtailed, at other times encouraged, so confusing the child. This it does not find acceptable and confrontations result. The winner however is nearly always the mother. When the child is hungry it demands to be fed, and fed what it likes to taste and chew on. In response the mother demands it eats what she deems to be appropriate for a good diet. This creates yet more conflict and sometimes outright rebellion.

The mother wants her child to explore but not too much, and only in those places of her choosing. The mother wants the child to run but not too fast, and again only in places of her choosing. The mother wants the child to speak but not too loudly when she is in earshot. In short the mother wants her child to operate within fixed boundaries of behaviour as defined by her; and does her best to enforce this, either with inducements or threats. Unfortunately the moment the child recognises these boundaries it protests and does its best to cross them. As it grows and fully matures so the boundaries become more sophisticated, less obvious; and many of its spontaneous reactions with regards to close family may become internally suppressed.

The rebellion starts early in the child's life and continues, on and off, throughout much of it; sometimes right up to the point of the mother's eventual demise (assuming she dies first). Over time the rebellion can become more subtle, less public, more akin to psychological warfare. Grievances, real or imagined, can become so deeply engrained that they can never be entirely extinguished: at best only circumnavigated or ignored.

The mother wants always to love and be loved by her child, and on her terms. It takes the child a significant part of its life to realise this – understanding the nature of love in its general sense being the first step towards this. However even then it is not always prepared to reciprocate on her terms. This creates another conflict, again one which sometimes remains unresolved right up to the point of death of one of the parties.

The mother-child emotional link appears to be at its strongest when an element of danger and fear is introduced - on the mother's side, not on the child's. Her view of the universe nearly collapses into a single point of infinite uncertainty. As with a point of infinite mass it bends and distorts the psychological landscape such that all other thoughts and emotions are directed towards it, despite all attempts to do otherwise. The scale of the risks and potential ramifications of the situation become irrelevant. There is no release or solution save the child's safe reappearance: physical reconnection is the priority for her – at which point her outward demonstration of concern is not necessarily reciprocated by the child. She is expected to deal with it alone.

Accepting responsibilities is a difficult thing for a child to do (though no less difficult, relatively speaking, for a fully developed adult). Working to a set of rules which enforce when and where and what the child can do or should be doing provide the greatest challenge to date for both child and parent(s). It wants to rebel against them while the parent(s) must enforce them: sleep patterns and educational activities being of prime importance – and all for the child's welfare and ultimate benefit which the child rarely, if ever, appreciates. Confrontations can be extreme and the relationship can become very tense.

At the earliest opportunity parents wish to implant and impress upon their child a set of values and behaviour about which it has no reference point or understanding. Their actions are seen as restrictive, heavy-handed, sometimes unacceptable. The backlash can be passionate, fierce, especially when the child reaches the onset of puberty and high speed transformation into full physical maturity (mental maturity following much later).

The mind of a young, immature male can be strikingly incisive at times. My observations of the one familiar to my host has shown it to be highly charged and focused when opportunities for self-improvement are evident. It is able to lock in, observe and absorb the machinations of adults as they strive to progress a strategy or implement current tactics. When necessary it pushes aside all emotional baggage and distractions, and applies logical calculation. I have yet to see this practised at the same level of intensity (or success) in the mind of an equally immature female. From what I have gathered they appear to be more sensitive to, and encumbered by, both their own emotional state and that of others – especially when the two are entangled. One strength or the other may be the advantage in life here on this highly disorganised, highly emotional planet. Perhaps neither.

I suspect many young males – the most competitive, the most intelligent - watch the older males and learn quickly how to apply such things as deception and tactics to find or maximise an advantage. When they reach a certain age they must focus less on females in the family for such lessons in life. The adult males appear, on balance, to do it so much better.

Despite his attempts to clarify and simplify his problems the females who inhabit the mind of my host continue to disrupt and disorganise his thoughts. He is pulled in many different directions, often at the same time, net result being zero movement. Some he wants to engage with, at different levels of intimacy and respect. Others he wants to avoid. One, his mother, he just feels totally neutral towards. He wants to enjoy good, wholesome, uncommitted sex on a regular basis (between bouts of sleeping and eating); and he also hankers after a sensitive, fulfilling relationship in a domestic environment: one which is comforting, secure and family orientated with a sense of destiny and permanency. This is despite his wish not to become tied to the framework of duties, commitments and responsibilities which the typical family unit demands.

Two of the females can provide for some or all of these desires with varying degrees of emphasize. Another simply provides sex in the short term (though judging by his attitude not to any accomplished degree), and good food: otherwise she is just a source of irritation. He is stuck. He is unable to set his own criteria for what defines his ideal female. Hence confusion reigns.

Chapter Sixteen

Clarence fled the scene of his crime fearful but well-fed – even if it was between clenched teeth. He had made his excuses as he dipped and ducked, and was now on the run; defiant and having no wish to know why he had resurfaced in that living room. It wasn't that he particularly disliked her: it was just that he didn't much want to get to like her. Rebecca had stood back, with little choice but to let go. He was the hardest man to pin down, and this she accepted as a hard fact now. And as for his brutal honesty? That she respected. It was better than brutal dishonesty. Yes he definitely was a Pisces. Judy had watched him leave, monitoring his every move until he was definitely back out on the street and off her patch. The scraps of bacon he had left behind had left her barely able to contain herself. She counted her blessings. Bacon was back on the agenda.

As he stormed towards his own front door - determined to break it down if necessary - and pushed Rebecca from his mind so Sam fell into it. She was sitting in her car, contemplating something; perhaps how far she was from the kerb, perhaps her next MOT. She did not move. She looked weary, as if hung over from the weekly shopping, or too much overtime, or too little laughter.

Clarence suddenly acquired a funny feeling, like he had done something silly or stupid to her or with her in another splendid blackout. He kicked it aside, refusing to speculate or remind himself of the big black hole now permanently at his side, just waiting for him to topple in. To avoid detection he jumped into the nearest doorway. He didn't know why but he just felt it would be a good idea to lie low. He may have said something. He may have said nothing. She might be in a funny mood. She might just be knackered.

Still Sam did not move and Clarence began to scratch in all the tight places. He needed a shower. He wanted a shower. He wanted to scrub himself to death. He needed Max to open the door and let him in - in into his own fucking home. And still she stalled and still he scratched. Women were generally starting to piss him off now. He even felt Rebecca drooling down the back of his neck, and being far too accommodating: that thought sent a follow-on shiver. He was afraid to turn lest he see her – or her cocky cat – staring out between the curtains, taking feminine or feline measurements.

Still nothing happened. Still Sam sat still. His legs began to throb and he wanted to sit down. Finally she pulled herself out of the car and stood staring at his front door, clearly unsure of her next move. She leaned against the car door, as if struggling to identify some blessings to count. Clarence just wanted her to ring his doorbell then be off. And his prayers were answered: she finally picked herself up, strolled up to the door and rang. And it was a relief: for her; for him. The door swung open and there was Max, looking wary but certainly not in the least put out. Sam swallowed then spoke.

"Is Clarence up?"

"Up? He's not in."

"Oh."

"Can I take a message?"

"Do you know when he'll be in?"

Max shook her off. Sod any messages. "No idea."

At that point Clarence bounded forward from out of the suburban undergrowth. "Are you after me."

Max turned miserable. Sam turned.

"What are you doing up so early? You haven't got a dog."

"I like going out for really early morning walks. Isn't that right Max?"

"Don't know what you mean," replied Max. Then he was gone. He didn't want shit for breakfast.

Clarence shouted after him. "Thanks for opening the door Max!"

Sam was left confused. "Shall I come back another time?"

Clarence waved her down. "No come in. I could do with the company."

He stormed inside, as if chasing after Max. Sam followed gingerly, as if questioning her every step. He pointed to the sofa and she fell into it, on her usual side. He waited for her to speak. She did not speak. They were alone, and they had nothing to say to each other – at least not yet – not even about the weather, which was quite nice that morning. Clarence got up and did the usual, which was to offer coffee. Sam also did the usual, which was to accept; and together they sipped instant like it was a ritual. And still nothing was said. Clarence for his part was sure in his own mind that he had nothing to say. He suspected Sam was holding on to something, after all she had driven over to see him at this ludicrously early hour. Then it hit him.

"Hang on you're not at work. Shouldn't you be at work?"

"I'm off sick."

"You don't look sick."

"Well I am sick."

"Fair enough." Clarence decided it was best to shut up.

He watched Sam: she looked around the room as if conducting a search without the confidence of a warrant and without giving reason. She was looking vacant, pretty vacant. Word association struck with a vengeance and suddenly his head was full of Johnny Rotten, sex, and pistols at dawn. Other people's saliva also entered the equation. Which was not nice. He had the sudden urge to thump Max: it was throbbing and highlighted in red on his unconscious to-do list. But the woman in the room held him back – or at least that was his excuse. Max was bigger, fitter, stronger, less adverse to physical pain. Clarence felt driven to speak up as his coffee ran out. He stuck to the routine.

"Is the coffee okay?"

Sam looked down into her mug as if it was a big question.

"Coffee's fine," she concluded.

"That's good."

"Why?"

"Why what?"

"Nothing. Ignore me."

That was proving difficult. Still, Clarence gave it his best shot.

As if jolted Sam suddenly pointed accusingly: she had settled on an image of domestic obscenity. "What on earth is that?"

It was a plate.

On it were stuck shrivelled up, dried out, ubiquitous baked beans. The plate sat on a crusty, stale, tabloid newspaper. The newspaper was well past its best by date. It's front page screamed indignity and indiscretion. There was no calming it. It had to scream. And it demanded to be read. The pages were stained with the tomato juice else they had been bleeding. Once the words had resounded with some sense of worth. Now, only a few days later, they barely echoed with substance. And the reader had moved on, bored.

Clarence peered at the mess which stained the plate. "I think it's bake beans."

Sam stared at the baked beans as if they were laid out on a Petri dish.

"It's disgusting."

Clarence shrugged. He had heard it all before. "It's only bake beans."

And with that, as if with intended comic timing, Max walked in and made a point of picking up the plate. "I'll take this then shall I?"

He walked out without waiting for a reply. Clarence wanted to spit on him but threw him a reply instead. "Might as well."

Next he decided to ask the obvious. "How's Tim?"

"Tim?" Sam tensed up: she was suddenly alert. "Why what's he been saying?"

"Saying? Nothing? Tim's been saying nothing."

It was the right answer and together they collapsed back into silence, this time with added complications and dissatisfaction of a heavier kind. Sam looked around the room as if searching for a weakness. She latched on to a photograph of Tracey. She had seen it before and had never given it a second thought. This time she did and pointed at it by poking her finger demonstrably, decisively and precisely into the empty expanse of air which hung around in front of her.

"You've still got her picture."

Clarence followed the line of her outstretched index finger. Someone – it had to be Max – had moved the two plastic Kiss dolls he had placed in front of it. The face, grinning stupidly due to too much alcohol yet still vaguely sweet, triggered a rush of memories and emotions: some good, some bad; the rest mostly indifferent. The act of rejection pushed its way to the fore and he jumped up, bounded across the room, grabbed the photograph, and threw it at the wastepaper basket. His aim was near perfect and it crashed neatly in without hitting the sides. It landed on a layer of crumpled newspaper and avoided damage. Perhaps it was a Freudian Non-slip, or just good luck.

"About time to," said Sam. It was all she could say right now.

"No matter," lied Clarence. He sat back down, hard.

Taking more interest, Sam looked at his scruffy hair. It was stuck up and out in all directions, as if suffering from static, or extreme self-denial. She swore to herself that she could smell bacon fat on him – and cat? Could she smell cat? And was that cat fur? Cat was definitely in the air. She was confused. This was not her Clarence. 'Her Clarence': she could not remove the sticky label.

"Is that cat's fur on you?"

Clarence looked down in disgust at his clothes. She was right. He had been had by the cat.

"Where did it come from?"

"My neighbour."

"Your neighbour's got a cat?"

Clarence added distance. "Apparently."

"You don't like cats."

"I know." Clarence shifted uneasily, still struggling with the fact that he had woken up on the woman's sofa and had accepted her food, and her smiles; and her regrets. It was like she thought she owned him. Had he sold out?

For Sam a line of questioning opened up.

"Did this neighbour make you breakfast?"

"Yes."

"And why was that?"

"I had slept over at her place."

"At her place?"

"At her place," echoed Clarence. He glanced up, realising that Sam was acting strange; as if guarded, or guarding something. "I just woke up on her sofa. I must have slept over."

"You don't remember?"

"That's right."

Sam twisted her face to one side and drew back, as if being poked, or hit by the strong smell of sewage. Clarence proceeded to defend himself.

"I didn't ask her to."

"Didn't ask her to what?"

"Didn't ask her to feed me, look after me, fucking fawn all over me."

Sam was stirred with a stick of outrage.

"You should be grateful. You haven't got Tracey anymore to look after you."

"But she looks at me funny – she looks at me too much," complained Clarence.

"Perhaps she's lonely."

"Perhaps she is – but what's that got to do with me? I'm not a Good Samaritan."

"Or even a bad one."

"What?"

"Nothing." Sam cut to the chase and lashed out. "Did you have sex with her?"

She demanded to know.

Clarence rocked in his pants. He didn't want to give an answer and couldn't think why on earth she had asked such a question. If she had been any other female he would have told her to fuck off – though not exactly in those words. He didn't tell her to fuck off but nor did he answer.

Sam knew the answer and was not surprised. "So that counts for nothing?"

"What does?"

"That you had sex with her."

"Who said I had sex with her!"

"But you did have sex with her."

Clarence conceded the point. He didn't need the aggro. "Yes."

"And now she wants to be part of your life?"

"I don't know. I suppose so." He didn't care. He deflected fire. "Come on how is it with Tim?"

Sam flashed him a look of censure. The laid back delivery of the question was at odds with her circumstances. She looked down at her dress as a recent memory of her and Tim together flooded into her head. It nearly knocked her senseless. They were both sitting at the dining table: both exhausted and both partially crippled by a day spent in the office feigning enthusiasm and denying hardship. The TV was on in the background, delivering noise. They had not looked at each other. They had barely greeted each other upon arrival home. They were sharing a meal, which was good. But they had nothing to say to each other, which was bad. In desperation they had asked each other the same questions, which was fair enough; and without even thinking had given the same answers as the day before, which was definitely bad.

They had not touched. They had not kissed. Any passion for the presence of the other had been mislaid, worse still permanently lost. The voice of an angelic anchorman coming out of the screen was proving to be more interesting, more sympathetic, more persuasive for their attention. The face opposite merely hung in the air and bided its time. When Tim moved it was merely to pass the ketchup.

The air between them was heavy with fatigue. Neither was driven to start a conversation as both knew it had nowhere to go: it could not be sustained. It would hurt too much, like the death of a new born baby. It was the current state of their marriage. And at times it really hurt, like being burgled or beaten up.

"Are you okay?" Clarence spoke quietly this time.

Sam looked up, but gave no reply, content instead to gaze across the surface area of Clarence and take in his visible state of disrepair; and trying to care. She was flat, flat as a pancake; and without the taste, without the sugar.

"What do you think?"

Now Clarence was at a loss. He didn't need someone else going funny on him.

"You're looking a bit . . ." He paused, searching for a phrase which could not possibly invoke controversy. "Under the weather?"

He leant back, sucked in breath, and waited for the reaction. There was bound to be one. It was turning out to be that kind of day.

Clarence was no distance away but Sam dared not even reach out and touch him with even just one little finger: afraid she might touch him with a hand; afraid she might grab him with both hands; afraid she might reach out and fall on top of him; afraid she might kiss him; afraid she might fall back on a wave of anti-climax and ultimate disenchantment. No. He simply wasn't worth it now. He had devalued.

"I think we should just call it a mistake: put it down to experience as they say."

Clarence uncrossed his legs, having just crossed them tightly, and gripped his mug tightly. "Call what a mistake?"

He felt himself entering the twilight zone again: that part of his existence which was kept hidden from him, and usually nothing but a place of trouble.

"You don't think it was a mistake?"

Sam had him cornered. Clarence began to sweat – profusely under the armpits. He didn't know why but he had the awful feeling – and it was growing – that this was something big and important. And he had absolutely no idea what it was all about. He thought hard, as hard as he could, until his brain began to ache. He wanted to vomit. Then a fuse blew and he held up a hand – only after unwrapping it from around his mug with an act of extreme willpower.

"I don't know what 'it' is."

Sam swivelled her eyes around the room until they landed back on Clarence. Hot and bothered, her blood ran through her body in a torrent, bursting to find release. By simply sitting there, pretending to act cool under fire, he aggravated her predicament. It was insulting.

"Is this one of your blackouts?"

"I suppose it must be as I have absolutely no idea what the hell you are on about."

"That's very convenient for you."

"What do you mean?"

"You seduce me. We make love. And it's all just conveniently wiped."

Clarence was struck dumb. He stared at the woman who he had always taken for granted as a friend, an ally, a well-balanced woman solid to the core, and thought she had gone mad.

"Speak to me Clarence."

"Speak? I don't think so."

"You don't think so?" Sam stared him down, and consumed him; thinking him spineless, and a miserable sod for never having had the guts to face her after the event or even just talk about it, like it was important. She was not impressed.

"I mean I don't remember such a thing ever happening, none of it, honest."

"I don't believe you. You were far too with it, far too switched on. I knew it was you. A woman knows these things." Her blood was boiling. "You were there. Wide awake. Fully engaged. How could it have possibly been one of your fucking blackouts? This is just fucking insulting."

"I don't mean to insult you. I just don't fucking remember."

The word 'fucking' was back on the agenda.

"You don't make love while you're fucking sleepwalking."

Clarence fought back. "Says who?"

"I was with you all the way. You were you, wide awake. You didn't change. You didn't fall asleep."

The thought of sleeping with his best mate's wife was a thought too far. He could not entertain it because he could not contain it. He had to escape from it, to retain any vestige of dignity. The question 'what reason would she have to make it up' screamed for attention, so he ran around it. He had not slept with his best mate's wife. He had not slept with his best mate's wife. He had not slept with his best mate's wife. It became a mantra, his link to sanity. But he didn't actually deny it. He just couldn't remember – which for him meant the same thing, almost.

The doorbell rang and both looked up; both startled and for a moment caught off guard. Clarence was grateful for the interruption, grateful in the extreme. Max answered the door. His voice was answered by that of a female, speaking quietly, like a nurse talking to the wounded, or dead.

Clarence recognised it and began to sway discreetly in his chair. Sam watched him. He was not being that discreet. She was not after revenge as such but she did want to punch him in the face, hard.

Almost reduced to tiptoeing, Fiona entered the room, escorted by Max who was failing miserably to hide a big smirk. He looked first at Sam, then at Clarence, then for final theatrical effect at Fiona. Then he left them to it. Though bursting to laugh out loud he managed to hold himself in. It was tough though. Clarence wanted to punch him in the face, hard.

Fiona stopped in her tracks, conscious that she was being examined, judged, and was outnumbered. Clarence held his breath: afraid to speak, afraid to think; loathed to retire. Sam took it all in. She took in the colour of the woman's nail varnish and the cut of her dress, and was impressed. She sensed a woman already shell-shocked. Strange.

In turn Fiona took in the sight of two adults, red-faced and pumped up, and began to visibly crumble. She knew she had interrupted something – not illegal or immoral but not pleasant either. No one spoke. No one was ready to speak. The air was electrified, making breathing difficult for all.

Clarence just stared - less at her, more at her image. He smothered it with an emotional backlash: feelings of sudden resentment; feelings which had organised and surfaced without warning to leave him tongue-tied, unable to facilitate even a simple, mechanical 'hello'. She had stopped him in his tracks – not that he was going anywhere sunny - and she knew it. So she said nothing. She was feeling weak at the knees and wanted to sit down but adherence to convention meant she was forced to stand until permission was granted.

Clarence looked at her dress. He wasn't that impressed. He looked at her hair. She had done something to it. He couldn't tell what. Cut it shorter? Probably spent a fortune on it he thought – it was a child's thought, one born of petty spite and indifference. Fiona had finally condescended to pay him a visit - like she could make a difference, cheer him up; heal him. But he had to concede the point that she had put herself out. And grudgingly he did. Fiona managed to smile a little. Clarence did not smile back. The most he could manage was a frown of dissatisfaction. And Sam, awash with adrenalin – almost drowning in it - watched it all pass between them.

Finally when Clarence did speak his voice cracked, his throat dried up and he stumbled over his few words. Feeling stung he wanted to sting back, just enough to obtain redress, not to inflict any real lasting damage.

"So I merit a visit then."

Fiona, likewise stung, dredged up a reply. "I wanted to see how you were."

Clarence told a lie. "I'm fine."

Sam took secret minutes.

Despite her bruised, possibly fractured state of mind Fiona still held the capacity for logical analysis.

"Fine? How can you be fine? You've been off school all this time. We're all worried about you. Even Ramsey."

"Ramsey can fuck off."

"Language!" exclaimed Sam.

"Sorry. I meant to say go to hell."

Fiona continued. "Well whatever. We are all worried."

"Except the Head."

"Of course."

Her demonstration of concern cut away some of the ground beneath him. He went through the motions.

"How are you?" he asked, refusing to admit to himself that he did in fact care.

"Me? I'm the same. Same as ever." She really did want to sit down.

"Good. That's good."

Clarence eased back in his chair, like a gentleman with a pipe and time to kill after dinner. Then he remembered Sam was in the room and sat up. An uneasy feeling crawled up him and poked him in the eye. Somehow at the same time it fingered his arse. He shivered. The mad woman was looking at them both: spoiling for a fight. Like a dodgy doctor bearing a grudge she wanted to inject them both - the two broken lovebirds - with a dodgy needle then stand back, present her invoice, and watch death come slowly. Though that was possibly overstating it.

The space between them all suddenly felt very cramped, as if they had been forced to share a tent without warning, or preparation, or an ending in sight. And it was beginning to rain, heavily; and there was no gas in the cylinder; and no hot drink in the thermos flask; and the only toilet was a hole in the ground. And there was something big and smelly outside closing in fast. It had horns and it knew how to seriously eat and shit.

Clarence avoided Sam and instead stared down at those parts of Fiona which were exposed. Her thighs had suddenly caught his interest. Fiona tried to smile again but was defeated by both her own lack of energy and the other woman's open hostility. And still she was not allowed to sit down. Worse still she wanted to scratch her behind. It needed to be scratched.

Then Sam suddenly laughed out loud. "You don't fancy him do you?"

The sound of the laughter pierced the ears: it was out of place. It was like being heckled at one's own wedding, or divorce. It was almost a shriek.

Amongst the women knives were suddenly drawn and being sharpened. Fiona regained her composure – and energy – and shuffled about on her feet, rediscovering some fighting spirit and a boxer's impatience to get in the ring and knock down the loudmouthed upstart. But immediately she was stumped: she could not answer yes; she could not answer no; she could not be rude – or appear to be rude; and she had no place to go. She turned to Clarence for support but he had none to give. He didn't have a clue what to say or do: all he had was the growing feeling that he wanted to sneak away. But he wasn't sure, not yet anyway: something was holding him back, interfering, reinforcing his backbone. Against his better judgement he tried to hang in there and see it through.

Sam smothered her further, recognising a weak enemy.

"You don't say much do you?"

Now Fiona began to seriously flounder. She was under attack for the second time that day and she didn't have the strength to cope. Fiona taught kids in classrooms: most of the time with good grace and a steady nerve. Sam ran a City office with a rod of iron. She knew how to punch, swerve, and punch again, while at the same time kicking the coffee machine and pretending to lick her boss's arse.

Sam retargeted. "You prefer the quiet type do you Clarence?"

Clarence glowered. He could not believe this was his Sam of old, his Tim's Sam. She really was pissed off. He fought back, and said what she didn't want to hear.

"Yes I do actually."

"Well there's a surprise." Sam swung back on to Fiona who was doing her best not to appear intimidated. "He gets around you know. So don't expect him to hang around too long, show commitment or anything like that."

Clarence protested, as was expected. "I don't know what you're talking about."

Fiona whipped a handkerchief out of a pocket and rapidly wiped her nose, badly. The handkerchief was stuffed back into another pocket. Her hurt was now undisguised. Fiona no longer wanted to sit down. She wanted to leave. She wanted to get in her car and drive away, to some place nice. Perhaps see a girlfriend, or her mother, or go do some shopping. Likewise Clarence sniffed.

Sam remembered the photograph of Tracy and plucked it out of the wastepaper basket.

"She was one of them. I was another." Then for maximum affect she threw it to the floor.

On impact it received one long continuous crack across the glass. Clarence stared at it. Fiona stared at it. Sam folded her arms. She had used up her reserves of fire and savage wit. Now she could only sit back and await the backlash. But nothing transpired: Clarence continued to stare at his broken picture and Fiona had other ideas on her mind, like escaping.

The sound of a flushing toilet did nothing to distract the participants in the three-way stand off. It did however remind them that there was still a world outside: one populated by people, mainly normal people. It was at this point that Fiona actually decided to get out.

"I must go," she announced. And she did, suddenly, without waiting for reactions.

As Fiona went one way a suspicion came the other and attached itself to the inside of Clarence's head: a suspicion that he would not see her again outside school – worse still that he would not want to see her again, ever, and would change direction in the school corridors. Fiona had left the room, and somehow it didn't seem right. She had only just arrived. Clarence had wanted more. No longer scared, he turned to face Sam with a distinct air of gloom and no twist of lemon. He demanded recompense – at the very least a grovelling apology. He would get neither. His Fiona had left the room and this woman was to blame. And still he swore blind that he had never slept with her. He simply would have remembered such a thing - and he would not have done it with his best mate's woman. He had his limits. He had probably said something rude to her during a blackout – yes that was it.

Sam did not take the bait: avoiding him she locked on to the broken picture. Clarence followed suit. At first he was not keen to touch it – thinking of it and all it projected was hard enough. But it was a reminder of a part of his past which had been stable – if boring and predictable at times – and reasonably happy, and on the whole content. He stood up, paused for affect, leaned down and picked it up. He placed it back in its usual position and stood back to admire it, noting that the glass could be replaced. Sam stayed quiet, less than proud of what she had done, and rapidly deflating. She had known Clarence a long time: suddenly that counted for something and she knew it. She was starting to feel rather stupid.

Clarence sat back down saying nothing, happy to wait for Sam to say something, do something, or simply leave – much as Fiona had. These days women just tired him out – even the ones he liked or wanted to love. Women were like that. Why didn't someone – God or someone else equally important – sort it out, make things work better, design it all to fit. Sam twisted her lips, knowing that Clarence was waiting for her to speak and refusing to oblige. The last thing she would do now would be to make things easy for him, the bastard.

After a long delay Clarence finally spoke up. He sounded remarkably engaging and conciliatory. "You don't look at your best. Can I get you something?"

Caught off guard Sam said the first thing which came into her head.

"A glass of water. You can get me a glass of water."

"Certainly."

He's trying to out-polite me she thought, the bastard.

Clarence headed into the kitchen. There he found Max lurking, lounging, perhaps eavesdropping. Max broke out a broad smile as Clarence turned the tap. Clarence smiled back with total enthusiasm.

"You look happy," he said.

Max chuckled and went to his room, giving no reply or clue as to the joke.

Clarence returned to Sam, handed her a glass of water, and sat down to watch her take her medication. No thanks was expected and none was given. Sam did not want to be watched but had no choice in the matter. She suspected there was unfinished business.

"You are confused," said Clarence.

Sam lowered her glass.

"Am I now. And what makes you say that." She was dying to know, a little.

"Out of one isolated, spontaneous event you have built an emotional history - and hence a position – which demands recognition and some vague kind of moral justice – as if there has been an injustice. And all from the very person who is in no position to give it."

"And why can't he give it, Mister?" Sam hated being lectured to but was intrigued by the sudden onset of preposterous patronising. It was a bit of theatre. She put up with it at work only because she needed the pay rise each year, and a pay rise demanded a clean work sheet.

"Because he would be in exactly the same position as you." Clarence saw by the look on her face that he still had some convincing to do. "And remember one isolated act of sexual intercourse does not automatically lead to subsequent emotional engagement. This is nearly always true in the rest of the animal kingdom so should it not be at least occasionally true amongst humans – us humans?"

Sam's mouth had fallen half-open and her eyes had glazed over. She began to rock, ever so slightly. She began to breath in and out slowly, deeply, as if she had been anaesthetized in advance of major surgery. But still she was prepared to listen. She had made love to a man who was growing increasingly mad and detached from the real world: must be those famous blackouts. Suddenly Tim felt like the safer option. The suggestion 'stick by Tim' sprang up inside her head out of nowhere. She put it on the back burner. She would not throw it out. Throw out the bathwater first, with the baby.

"Cast your mind back. Did you not raise expectation? Did you not invite intimacy?"

"I was doing the iron – ironing Tim's fucking shirts."

"No you had finished the ironing. You were watching the television set and eating chocolate; determined to relax, loosen up, and detach yourself from circumstances which you felt were stifling you – which they probably were. And you had drunk alcohol: inhibitions were lowered."

"And you."

"Exactly. And me. I had little ability to control my basic instinct and urges. When you needed it you invited my attention, my warmth, my emotional support. And I gave it, unconditionally. And you took it, unconditionally. Sexual intercourse was offered on both sides and received enthusiastically on both sides. We discarded all inhibitions and came together totally – if only for a minute or two."

Sam wanted to butt in but her throat had seized up, and she had nothing coherent to say. She could only shout obscenities – had her throat been in working order.

Clarence felt good and continued.

"Was the sex not enjoyable? Did it not bring both mental and physical relief? Was it not something to be celebrated as an act of ultimate friendship and unity between two people who are more than just friends originally connected via a third party? Need it have negative ramifications? Can it not be filed away as a happy memory?"

Sam found her voice. "Fuck off. It's not as simple as that."

"Why not?"

"Because . . . because . . . oh I don't know." Sam twisted sideways in an attempt to bring relief to her buttocks which were beginning to ache. They needed a massage. She needed a massage. Clarence needed a smack on the head.

"You want me to give you something – almost like payment of a fine - but I have nothing to give. It's a need created inside your head as an easy way to resolve the dilemma of the situation. You have to resolve it, without contribution from me or from anybody else. It has nothing to do with the sex: the emotional fallout is a self-serving invention. Your real problem is with Tim, not me. That's why you turned to me. That's the reason why we made love. Now you're angry with me because I am not responding to form and because you cannot turn back to Tim. Why can't you face him? Guilt? As I said there's nothing to feel guilty about. So let go of me – let me go. Tim is your problem. As you are his problem."

Clarence waited for the next reaction. There was none so he decided to put the emphasis on reconciliation. "In time can we not be friends again? It would make things easier for both of us – and Tim."

Clarence looked Sam in the eye, demanding an answer right there and then. She declined to give one. Instead she sat impassive as she tried to hold back the weight of his words: with confidence they assaulted her senses and breached her walls. She developed cracks – to many. She wanted to fight back: hit him; or shit on him. She hated clever people. They really pissed her off and got all the better jobs at work.

"So you admit to it now."

"Yes."

"You tosser. Why are men all tossers?"

"Not true but I appreciate the reasons why you shape such an accusation in a question."

Sam wanted to jump up and go, and recover. She had been mixed up and turned into a muddle: but still she had a question left.

"How was the sex?"

"The sex?" Clarence looked up at his ceiling and thought back, hard. "If I'm to be honest with you I have to say disappointing. We performed in too much of a hurry to really get the most out of it. I rushed – I

· 417 ·

was rushed. It felt distasteful at the time when it should have been a celebration. I personally have experienced better. But I did release a lot of stress which was one good thing."

Sam turned red, in an instant. That was enough. She jumped up and steered towards the exit; stopped; turned; retraced her steps and slapped Clarence across the cheek, hard, really hard. Clarence nearly fell out of his chair. He had not been expecting it and it was quite a sensation. With that done Sam had nothing more to say or do and fled, slamming the front door behind her.

Clarence recovered his posture but sat disturbed and disjointed, and in a right pickle. Max peeked his head around the door and smiled, with a touch of cheekiness throw in for added effect – and good measure.

"Still got all those women problems then?"

"I'm afraid so. They are temperamental creatures. Intake of precise facts and logical argument does hurt them immensely sometimes."

"And you're not?"

Clarence looked puzzled. "Not what?"

"Temperamental."

Clarence looked at Max even more puzzled. "No. Certainly not."

"I see." To extend the fun Max threw in a suggestion. "Why don't you go after her. You're obviously attracted to her."

Clarence took it under consideration. "That's a good idea."

Max had to laugh again – which he did, with extra vigour as yet again he returned to his room. Work beckoned and he was late – late because he just couldn't tear himself away from all the fun.

Clarence replayed the whole incident with the women inside his head and decided he should go and see Fiona. Corrections and apologies were required. Seeing Sam was not an option. It would be a pointless exercise. He got up and hurried out of the room to seek a lady in distress.

✦ ✦ ✦

Clarence arrived at Fiona's flat wishing to rehabilitate himself and encountered a man standing over a stationary car, and looking displeased. The man was unhappy for a number of reasons, one being that the car refused to move. Its bonnet was up and he was gazing down at the mass of interconnecting parts which made up the engine, and more. It was a metal maze of cause and effect, not for the fainthearted. His hands were tucked away in his pockets, as if resting; and he was inactive, like the car. Clarence decided to approach. There was no sign of Fiona's car.

The man looked up and registered his arrival on to the scene with buoyant jubilation as if his transport problem was suddenly a problem shared. The jubilation evaporated when the man realised that Clarence was not the breakdown recovery man. It was replaced by a return to private suffering. That aside Clarence joined him in the meticulous but amateur examination of the machine's guts.

The man pulled his hands out of his pockets and folded his arms. He waited for Clarence to speak, just in case there was a chance he knew something about cars. Clarence did a visual inspection of those pieces he could see but without result.

"What do you think?" the man asked.

Clarence shrugged. "No idea."

"It's fuel-injected, which complicates things they say."

"Who says?"

"You know. The usual lot who say they know everything about cars."

"It does look complicated in there." The comment brought a glimmer of a smile to the man's face – the first in a long time and certainly the first that day – but no hope.

"Tell me about it."

"I wish I could."

"All I know is it's not the battery. The lights come on and it makes its usual whirring sound when I turn the key."

Clarence moved on. He had lost interest. "You look tired."

"I am tired. Shattered." The man glanced sideways, unsure of the direction the conversation was taking.

"When these things fail to perform they can really lower moral, and quickly – sometimes inducing major disenchantment."

"That's true. Never really thought of it like that before. I've been lucky with cars up to now. Can't remember the last time I broke down. Probably did as a student but can't remember. I must be overdue."

"They're integral to your lifestyle and you take them for granted. So when they're not there, not doing what you expect them to do, it's a major discomfort and interruption. You really feel it."

By way of public denouncement the man kicked a tyre. "And it's a pain in the arse." His agreement was heartfelt.

"Does it really hurt that much?"

The man grinned – again for the first time that day. "It certainly does."

"I'm not surprised. Expectations are set so high."

"How do you mean?"

"The marketing – especially that broadcast for television reception. The constant stream of advertising. The message is continuous and unrelenting. They distort the landscape to sell a fantasy. They sell it like poetry, like a romantic experience. They entice you away from your normal, rational standpoint with the promise of a perfect world which can only be acquired from the driver's seat of their particular make of vehicle. It's so removed from reality I'm surprised so many are taken in by it."

The man nodded, pretending to take it all in, and searched his thoughts in an attempt to contribute to the conversation. He came up with something, but not much. It was a statement of the obvious. "They must spend a fortune on them. They really want to sell you cars."

"And you bought one."

The man was thrown by the response. Was it a simple statement of fact or an accusation?

"And has it satisfied?"

"I think so." The man had to say yes, despite not having a clue.

"How?"

"How what?"

"How did it – how does it – satisfy?"

The man glanced down at the top of the engine, and the surrounding dirt and grease. It did not look inviting. "Gets me from A to B I suppose."

"Anything else?"

"Quickly? Fast? Yes very fast sometimes." The man took breath. "I can see what you're getting at. An extravagant waste of money I know: something smaller and cheaper would have done just as well. But I like the power, the acceleration: gets me out of trouble. And it looks good."

"When it's working."

"Yes when it's working." The man looked at his watch. That too offered mechanical attractions over and above foreseeable need: it told him what day it was. "Damn. I shouldn't still be here."

"You should be somewhere else?"

"Too right I should."

"The car has let you down."

"Like the women."

"Is that why you appear frustrated? Not just the car?"

"It's that obvious is it?"

"Yes I'm afraid so. Why is this then?"

The man pointed his thumb over his shoulder. "Her in there."

"Why that one in particular?"

"I don't know."

"You don't know?"

"I know. Sad isn't it."

"Not sad, more disfunctional perhaps."

The man turned sharply and shot Clarence with a funny look. He was getting too close for comfort. He was starting to sound like his doctor.

"Have you broken a connection?"

"That's one way to put it."

"That's a yes then?" Clarence had to drag it out of him.

"Yes that's a yes."

Now openly irritated, the man returned to staring down at his fucked up car. Where was the fucking breakdown van. He had paid his premium so give him his breakdown van.

"Does she regard it as broken?"

"She certainly does now."

"Her reasons may be entirely legitimate."

"What's that suppose to mean?" The man's heat was on the rise again, just as his car's had reached zero.

"Perhaps she has transferred her emotional needs to another man or woman."

The man was seriously stirred up. "Do you know something I don't?"

Clarence considered his reply. The truth invited danger. He decided a lie was in order: best all round. "Me? No." For effect he adopted a look of sweet and cheerful innocence.

The man, for now satisfied, returned to his broken machine. He was determined to outlast it. (Either that or he wanted his money back.) It was only three years old for Christ's Sake. He wanted the stranger to sod off, give him space; but the man just stood there, watching as if recording it all. And there was nothing he could do about it. It was a public street.

There was the sound of a car breaking and changing down gear. It grew louder. Its exhaust rattled. It came into full view. Both men focused on it and gave it their full attention: Fiona was behind the wheel, concentrating hard on slowing and manoeuvring it into a parking space. Only when she stepped out of the car did she catch sight of Clarence and Chris. Whereupon she forgot to lock to it.

The three stood in a triangle, a near perfect isosceles triangle with Fiona as the point furthest away from the other two. They were both studying her, like she was naked, or had confiscated their sweets and mobiles without reason. Her eyes settled on Clarence: she looked at him and he looked at her; and between them secret messages could have passed. Strangely although she kept her eyes on Clarence when Fiona spoke she spoke to her ex-boyfriend.

"Chris what are you still doing here?"

Chris spoke sounding bruised, hard done by. He threw her a dirty look of non-cooperation but when he spoke he spoke to Clarence. "I don't want to talk to her."

Fiona retorted. "You did earlier."

Clarence intervened. "I sense hostility here coming from both sides."

"You sense right," answered Chris curtly.

"So what are you still doing here?" asked Fiona a second time, determined to have her question answered by the man who up to now had been the cause of so many.

Chris decided to give instant satisfaction. "Waiting for someone who knows about cars to come and fix mine."

His cool wit had been one of the factors which had originally attracted Fiona. It was an untimely, uncomfortable reminder.

"Are you angry?" asked Clarence. A pointless question thought the others.

"Angry? Of course I'm fucking angry. My car won't start and it's not that old. It gets serviced every year. I spend a fortune on it."

Clarence added a clarification. "No I mean angry with this woman."

Fiona raised her eyebrows and fluttered her eyelashes. Chris slapped the side of his car. It no longer felt like his car. "Wouldn't you be?"

"I don't know. Would I?"

Chris became seriously aggravated. "What the fuck is that suppose to mean?"

"It means nothing. I'm just trying to understand."

"Poke your nose in more like."

"Possibly."

Chris gave Clarence a funny look, made space, then conceded a little. Why not let a little out? It would only embarrass her, not him.

"If truth be told I'm angry that she just did a cut and run."

Whipped up, Fiona piped up. "I didn't just cut and run as it happens."

Chris latched on to Fiona. "You could have fooled me."

"Did she?"

Chris swung back on to Clarence, slightly dizzy, and feeling surrounded. "Did she what?"

"Did she fool you?"

Chris twitched and leaned against a car door, as if needing to rest. "Yes I suppose she did."

Fiona drew in closer. She had to put her side of the story before it became too one-sided. Now Clarence was demanding answers. He had to be reassured. The triangle was now almost equilateral.

"I didn't intend to fool anyone. I just needed to get out."

Chris wanted to respond but Clarence got in first, much to his exasperation.

"Get out? Was this this 'space' you needed?"

"Yes you could say that."

Chris reared up, resting against a car door was no longer an option. He looked at them both, repeatedly, and tried to work something out – something close to the truth.

"You know her?"

"Yes I do. And she has been very good for me."

"Is this true?" One half of Chris wanted to grab the woman he had once made love to and shake the answer out of her, like it was all his. The other half managed to stop it happening.

Fiona had to vacuum up her thoughts. They were in turmoil. She had sprung a leak. She swallowed hard and tried to answer with composure. "That's not for me to say."

"Have you two been talking about me?"

Before Fiona could say no Clarence said yes. The cat was let out of the bag. It discovered broad daylight.

"Yes we have."

"Well thanks a lot."

"Don't get me wrong, it was nothing negative. Fiona did state some deficiencies in the relationship – or to be more specific your deficiencies – but it was nothing personally derogatory or vindictive; just an honest, almost impersonal statement of the failings in the relationship."

"Was it now. Tell me do you always stick your fucking nose into other people's business?" Chris was not won over.

Clarence was taken aback. "No. Certainly not. But in this case Fiona and I do share a history of intimacy."

Chris latched back on to Fiona, as he had done many times in the past when chasing up demands of comfort or compliance. This time he locked shut so tightly that the muscles in his neck began to pull. His body was protesting its innocence.

"Is this true?"

Fiona was driven to deny it. "No." She drew the word out and it sounded good, credible. Even as she spoke she was begging Clarence to please keep his mouth shut. He wasn't being clever. He was causing a calamity.

Clarence didn't get it. "No? But we had sexual intercourse?"

Fiona blushed and choked. "You must be mistaken Clarence."

"Don't be silly my dear. How could I make such a mistake? Of course we did. And you really enjoyed it." Then a thought struck him hard. A lie was required here. It would be a good thing.

"No. Sorry. Beg your pardon. You're quite right Fiona. For the record Chris we have never engaged in sex, not with each other that is." Clarence smiled broadly to emphasize his final, corrected position on the issue. "Out of interest have other relationships struggled? I assume there have been others? All with females?"

Chris had had enough. He couldn't take any more. The maniac was rubbing his face in his own humiliation and turning it into a comedy. He lost it - not that he had been holding it together that well. There was only one way to respond and it involved physical demonstration.

"Arsehole!" he declared and closed the gap – destroying the neat little triangle – and tried to punch Clarence squarely in the face.

Instead he just clipped his pain in the arse on the jaw, missing the lower lip by a whisker. The lip did not split and no blood was shed.

Chris was pleased: there would be a bruise to remember him by; enough to make his point. He would not be sued. Clarence fell back against the car then slid to the ground, stunned by the physical contact – rather theatrically thought Chris. He had barely touched him. The bastard was putting on a show for his girl, trying to make him look like the bad guy. That aside for split second he was afraid that Clarence would jump up and hit back, so he clenched both fists and held his breath for as long as possible. But he was safe. Clarence made no effort to retaliate and Chris was convinced that the man was a wimp – Fiona had slept with a wimp. She really was desperate. He gave her a look that left no room for misunderstanding then fell back as she closed in, arms raised, afraid that she might punch him back in lieu of everything that had gone before. She certainly carried the look of someone wishing to offload a major grievance – or it may have been the look of eternal damnation.

Clarence felt his face. It was still functioning, just very raw in one specific place: i.e. the point of contact. He expected the bruise to come along very soon: but no long lasting damage he concluded. He began to relax.

"So you can be very domineering just like she said. But she never said you had a propensity for violence."

"Normally I don't. Must have been something you said."

There was that cool wit again: it struck a chord within Fiona which she immediately dismissed in order to maintain her honour and rediscovered sense of loyalty.

Clarence agreed. "I concur."

"Do you. You 'concur'. That's good." Chris threw his next outburst at Fiona. She had lowered her arms. She looked less dangerous. "He's a tosser. You know that don't you." Chris was not in the least bit feeling apologetic. If anything he wanted to ramp things up.

Fiona had only one thing to say, and almost shouted it. "I think you better leave now Chris. You've caused enough trouble today."

"I'll leave after he leaves."

Clarence had no problem with that. "Very well I'll leave now."

Fiona was furious. Clarence had caved in. "What do you mean! You don't leave now Clarence!"

"No best I go. I'm causing a commotion."

"No you're not. He is."

Clarence struggled to his feet. Fiona helped him. Chris watched. On his way up Clarence secured leverage by grabbing a wing mirror. It snapped from its mounting to become a loose fitting hanging precariously and without purpose. The car was beginning to look like scrap. Chris was horrified and got extra mad again.

"Look what you've done you've broken it!"

Clarence looked on blankly. He had no defence. Fiona came to the rescue.

"It's your fault you hit him."

Clarence recovered his composure and carried out an inspection of the damage. "No I don't think so. Here let me. I think it's designed to just snap back into place."

"No don't touch it! You don't know how it works!"

"Very well." Clarence backed away. "I'll be on my way then."

"No please don't go!" Fiona was forced to beg – in front of her ex-, which made it ten times worse.

"I think it's best all round that I do. My presence here is causing a commotion – though I can see yours is as well – and yours."

Fiona was left hanging. Chris was left waiting for someone to fix his car, which meant time spent just hanging around. As Clarence drove off Fiona spat out her final judgement. "What is it with you? Why do you always mess it up for me?"

Then she raced indoors, slamming the door behind her. Chris pretended not to hear her and carried on hanging around, trying to look cool and in control. He looked at his watch: he would get a refund on his breakdown premium.

✦ ✦ ✦

Log Entry

I have reinstated the memory of a sexual encounter with one particular female: a companion of long standing. I had previously removed it for reasons of mental stability. However the last encounter with the female has left my host permanently exhausted by the uncertainty in his mind of actual events, and her accusations have struck deep. He has to work extra hard to hold himself together and this is a waste of energy. I have tried to diffuse the situation and the certainty he now enjoys may calm him.

I have lost contact with base - not entirely unexpected. Departure may be affected – probably require rescheduling. No option except to wait and see. I hope I am not stuck here. It is not such a pleasant place. They hurt each other, and appear to enjoy it. For no obvious tactical advantage or asset gain humans like to make physical contact with excessive force and without prior warning. It may be a way of expressing unhappiness – presumably caused by the other party - or protesting serious disagreement. The quantity of force released varies according to the scale and depth of the passion which fuels it: likewise the damage caused and the emotional fallout on all sides. The perpetrator is left in a serious muddle and even a touch disappointed if no sense of harm done results from his or her extreme action. Do humans have no other outlet which can bring satisfaction but not aggravate the situation?

It is not easy for two humans to totally and spontaneously disengage, intention being to terminate a relationship such that no trace of it remains in the present. Even if the relationship is considered to belong to the past it still manages to operate in the present, and perpetuates the emotional baggage: activity of the mainly negative, defensive variety. The bonds that bind them can be loosened but prove difficult to snap. The situation is made worse when the ongoing development of a new relationship intrudes.

On the whole humans have a basic, insatiable need to connect and feel connected: mainly with each other; sometimes with other animal types on their planet – instead of, or as a fallback position when no suitable human is available. A few are satisfied just to connect with an idea, a philosophy; a structured, well-documented, well-organised religion or movement; a current fashion; even a cultural icon – whether permanent or transitory, living or dead. But they are the exception.

The vast majority require a social and emotional connection, and optionally sexual intercourse: even if nothing of value is received in return. As part of this connection each participant will demand, sooner or later, that their definition of 'self' is respected along with everything they have to say which they consider important. With this in mind sometimes the 'one-way' relationship is considered a blessing. There is no risk of contradiction. It is harmony, one way. The institution of marriage and other definitions of partnership can provide for this with positive results on one side, negative results on the other.

✦ ✦ ✦

Many miles away in a rundown cottage standing proud on a prime piece of land an old woman sat rigid and to attention in her usual chair at her kitchen table; the table she had received on her wedding day and which bore the marks of a hundred thousand or more knife attacks upon vegetables and prime cuts of meat. She was chaotically dressed, like a dog's dinner. She stared out of her kitchen window – it had always been her favourite view – and waited, as if for something to make sense. She did not care to move. She did not count time. She knew the numbers inside out. Lassie sat to attention at her side, looking up; looking devoted, almost devout; also waiting, simply for anything to happen. A pot of tea stood on the table. A cup had been filled but not touched. She had forgotten to add her milk and sugar. Now the tea was stone cold. And still she waited, killing time with ease. It was a skill she had perfected over many decades of staying alive.

There was a noise at the front door but she was not disturbed. For his part Lassie twitched an ear and flexed his front paws. A key rattled in the lock and the door flew open, doorknob striking the wall in its usual spot. It was the daughter, charged up and charging in. She had convinced herself that she had much to do and little time to do it in. (Even when she had nothing to do she still felt like she had no time to do it in.) This gave her the excuse she needed to get in and get out quickly.

Like a south-westerly fuelled by the jet stream the daughter blew into the kitchen and dumped a bag of shopping down on the table. On her way she noted the cold cup of tea. Like her mother she was chaotically dressed, with extra emphasis on colour clash. Her husband – not poor or suffering, only awkward and easily agitated – was loathed to be caught in the same room with the both of them at the same time: the combined impact was too much to digest.

The daughter released her opening remark without enthusiasm for, or interest in the explanation. "You haven't drunk your tea."

No response, so she moved on. "Sorry I'm late."

Still nothing. She plucked the supermarket receipt out of the bag. "I got you what you wanted – wasn't sure how you were for milk so got you some." She glanced up and down the column of numbers and made a rough calculation, giving her mother the benefit of the doubt. "Call it a fiver."

Still nothing. But that didn't matter – and that didn't stop her.

"Had an awful day. Waited ages for the bloody washing machine man to turn up. Never did. So I was late picking the kids up. Got a dirty look. Some of those teachers are really stuck up." Enough said, the daughter felt the pot for heat and was disappointed.

Finally she caught her breath and caught up with the situation – or rather allowed it to catch her up. "Is everything OK? You haven't drunk your tea you know."

Lassie, sensing the start of some human 'happening', adjusted his position and began to whimper with expectation. His slobber dripped to the floor in a flood and he banged his tail against the floor tiles. And still the old woman remained locked tight. Resigned to her mother's folly the daughter began to unpack the shopping and distribute some of it around the kitchen. The milk and butter went in the fridge which, disturbed by a harsh intake of warm air, began to splutter and protest.

Oblivious to the commotion the old woman lifted a old wrinkled finger and pointed at the garden. Lassie sat up on his hind legs, extremely excited. His mistress was about to speak.

"What's down there?" she asked with pronounced curiosity and sudden impatience.

The daughter slammed the fridge door shut and looked up. "The end of the garden?"

"No beyond it."

"Your neighbour's garden?" The daughter rolled her eyes to Heaven and made a secret wish: please don't let her go funny on me now.

"Further."

"Further? You mean under the railway bridge?"

"Probably. What's three hundred yards beyond in a straight line?"

The daughter gave her mother her special look of moral fatigue – the one she had been giving her since the age of sixteen when she had first decided that she was superior. "Yes that would be under the bridge. You mean the allotments?"

The old woman began to lift herself out of her chair, bones creaking and cracking. Lassie was ecstatic: now something was happening, definitely. He didn't know what or where but they were definitely on the move.

"Take me there will you?"

"What right now?"

"Please."

The daughter looked from side to side, as if begging for exemption. There was none. She was the daughter.

"You want to visit your old allotment again?"

"Yes please."

"What on earth for? You gave that up years ago."

"I must see it again."

The daughter took measurements and decided it wasn't worth the hassle of a fight. Lassie began to walk around in circles, first one way then the other; ready to leap out and attack the landscape once the back door opened. The daughter looked at her watch. She had to concede that time was not an issue.

"Very well. Just as long as we make it quick." She wasn't in a hurry to be anywhere, she just wanted to make a point. It was the principle of the thing. She hated still being ordered around by her mother.

They stepped outside into the warm air of the afternoon sun and shuffled along slowly: the old woman holding on to her daughter's arm; the daughter holding on to her patience while holding up her mother; Lassie running around, to the left and to the right, ahead and behind, all fired up and ready to explode with coarse canine rage were the conditions right. He never would. It was all mouth and bark with him. Even a mildly agitated hedgehog could scare him off. When it came to the crunch Lassie was a dog of the indoor variety. He only ate food which came out of a can or a packet. His favourite position – feral or otherwise – was to be curled up in his basket. It was his favourite place once he had had a good piss, shit and walk.

As they shuffled along so the old woman would keep stopping to take in the detail: at which times the daughter would be forced to kill time by looking extremely put out. Not that it did any good. It never had. Failing that she resorted to task planning: planning the evening meal; planning the next load of the washing machine; planning when next to force her husband to act really sweet and gentle and loving; planning the next raid on the supermarket; planning morning coffee with the girls; planning a trip to the carwash; planning when to have some time to herself; but never planning the rest of her life. That just got swallowed up. One day it would spit her out. And when they did get there her mother said nothing, not even thanks. This put the daughter in a foul mood which she did nothing to disguise: quite the opposite, she played it for all its worth. It gave her strength.

"Okay so now we're here at last now what?"

She got no answer, which irritated, but there was nothing she could do about it. She was still her mother's daughter. Then the implication of something sinister, something final struck her and she had to rope in her disturbing thoughts even as they unravelled. This little demonstration had all the hallmarks of a 'last holiday' walk; that final farewell. The daughter looked at her mother. She didn't look like someone at death's door, or even someone contemplating her imminent demise. She looked fit and healthy – if slow. It was only her brain which was letting her down these days.

Two allotments down an old man leant a spade against a shed, looked across his rows of rising rampant runner beans, and waved. He had known the old woman from way back. They had once held long discussions about the state of their vegetables or the state of their children, often confusing the drift of the conversation in the process. Today the old woman ignored him. Instead she turned around and demanded to be taken straight home: back to her kitchen and her chair and her pot of tea. Lassie had no problem with that. He had urinated to heaven and back. Only the daughter exhibited resistance, and that was only because her mother had not said sodding 'please'. She was still treated like a child without rights and it rankled. Husband would suffer for it later.

Chapter Seventeen

Log Entry

Accepting her invitation to walk and dine in the open, wild countryside (reversing my host's earlier polite but immediate refusal), the female neighbour escorted me to a place where human interference with the surface of the planet was minimal. We travelled far in my host's car to reach this place, left the car in a designated area, then began a long walk. The route was circular, up and down. She advised.

On initial contact the damage to my host's face was a source of intrigue. My host dismissed it but I explained it to her as an unfortunate encounter with the domestic male companion – a misunderstanding over domestic arrangements – to avoid complications. Her reaction was to apply excessive attention and try to repair damaged tissue by applying constant but intermittent contact with her mouth. I had to stop this action abruptly when I detected overtones of a sexual nature. Without success I tried to explain that such an approach could not possibly provide a fast tract solution to tissue repair. Her reaction signalled some degree of disorientation.

In this place human beings are largely absent and little has been done to alter the land or manipulate the natural vegetation. There are few visible boundaries. Indigenous vegetation has invaded every available space, and in turn attracted many forms of life in large numbers – human beings excluded. It pushes up and out with vigour and a determination to survive. That said, later I did observe that in parts the land had been divided up by humans: allocated, manipulated and cultivated; presumably for the purpose of large scale food production - be it directly in the form of edible vegetation else indirectly via the rearing of animals for slaughter and consumption. Demarcation lines are evident in all directions: some are near straight; others follow the contours of the land. I suspect the need for all these boundaries is to define and declare the rights of land ownership, else chaos would ensue. Amongst all this random patches of wild growth have still been left to function according to natural biological and environmental cycles, without human interference.

Life here is rampant, chaotic, but not confused. All the vegetation and every distinct living creature knows exactly what it is doing within the context of its own particular construction, and exercises its routines of near automatic actions for the continuation of its life according to a predefined but undeclared set of rules: chasing, capturing and conserving resources; fighting if necessary for a place in the sun; consolidating and defending its territory; avoiding trouble and conflict where there is no gain to be had. Some – most – all - of these rules are exercised by humans. Most are in a mad dash as if their body clocks are winding down close to zero. I have witnessed this behaviour in humans.

Like the living creatures the vegetation here fights for space and resources to grow and reproduce. Some species grow big and tall and push aside all immediate competition until they are the dominant structure, so much so that they redefine the surrounding ground with regard to the general availability of sunlight and water moisture. Sometimes they create patches of near total and permanent darkness. Others, much smaller in size, multiple in abundance and by sheer weight of numbers come to dominate an area.

Nothing is wasted simply because there is no outlet except a return back into the land or the atmosphere; or into the mouths of those creatures who consume decaying matter. The death of one life is food for others, so extending their lives. However from the human perspective it is not correct to say that inanimate matter, organic or inorganic, always ends up in the right place, or in a state fit for their purposes of consumption and material gain. This can cause them much aggravation.

The female was in a hurry. The female was always in front, charging ahead. The female was always in a hurry. I could not move my host's body fast enough. It struggled to take in enough oxygen at the required rate. I could sense she resented having to stop and wait for me to catch up. We barely talked and soon the conversation died completely. In time she slowed and we plodded along in silence. It was as if she was hypnotised, or in a coma, or struck dumb. For extended periods I did not register in her mind. Being behind her much of the time I was out of view as well as out of mind.

Between them the land and the sky divide the view into two distinct halves: one half bursting with the energy, vitality and abundance of wild life; the other half a near sterile atmosphere, containing little except a few natural and unnatural gases, water vapour, and significant levels of human pollution. Yet that half, despite its emptiness, was an object of interest for the female. Constantly she referred to it: looking up as she pushed on, as if attempting to initiate a conversation or waiting for an answer to a long standing question. She looked up to the sky yet she did not look down at the dirt, the dust, the excrement and the human pollution. She filters out that which she prefers not to see, lest she feel hostility towards it.

The smallest land-based creatures on this planet which are visible to the human eye are present in vast numbers, mainly directly underfoot: topsoil being their natural habitat. Excluded from the interiors of human dwellings and those exterior places made artificial, they have compensated by massive population of the natural landscape.

The smaller the creature the more it appears to conduct its business in a frenzy, releasing a constant stream of energy as if about to be extinguished in the next instant; as if hanging on for dear life with still so much to do. I have noticed this state of mind in some humans, mainly females who are well into middle age and encumbered with family responsibilities.

I tried to avoid standing on these creatures and causing them harm whenever I caught sight of them. Sensing their presence like I can with humans and other complex forms of life is not possible: conscious mental activity is zero. The female found my behaviour odd but very amusing and I was happy that it gave her pleasure, but after awhile I had to stop. I found the continuous act of negotiating a non-destructive passage through all the micro-wildlife too exhausting for my host's body and it was clearly damaging his foot muscles and joints. My explanation for his behaviour was well-received: though she thought I was taking the principle of respect for the rights of all living creatures a touch too far.

We walked a long way. My host's legs and feet were not used to such extended exercise and physical deterioration soon set in. Damage was also caused to the skin by the strong sunlight. However I suppressed the signals of pain as I struggled to keep up, hampered as I was by my host's unfit body. It also had to carry a load on its back: a bag packed with food and water, and other items. The bag was not light nor was it comfortable to carry. Never once did she offer to carry it. I did consider mentioning this fact to see the response.

There was anal discharge everywhere. I presume from large herbivores judging by the shape, smell and consistency. I stepped in it once. After which I paid more attention to such risks.

To regulate its temperature my host's body excreted, via the porous surface of its skin, a mixture of chemicals dissolved in water. Over time this resulted in some measure of discomfort as clothing became soaked, having absorbed the constant discharge of sweat. There was also the smell, from both his body and hers. It was not pleasant: the smell of the female being more pronounced.

The female knew her way, which was fortunate as my host had no previous experience of the area or route. Her knowledge of the local terrain filled her with a sense of superiority which she laboured to externalize, advertise in some way. It created a feeling of frustration inside her head. I indulged her by feigning fear of losing our way and never finding the car again. I expressed myself in a manner which she found very funny, very 'sad'. (Her exact word.)

She was driven to make contact with some greater spiritual force, and again it was a struggle: not with her one god this time but with some alternative; one which encourages and orchestrates the natural rhythms of life upon the very active surface of this planet and within its extensive body of water. The female tells herself that this force pushes the trees up towards the sky to connect with it, along with the grass and flowers – with less emphasis on all other vegetation.

The thin atmosphere above and the solid layers of rock below do not figure in its mandate. They are of course an intrinsic part of the complete picture with regard to the geological and biological processes upon this planet, but they are not recognised in any spiritual or emotional sense by this female – despite the fact that, visually, the sky is a source of fascination for her. Like most other humans her mind is dominated by the immediate, visible surface of the planet and that which covers it. Add living, moving creatures to this picture and the sensation is intensified.

I noticed this when we passed by a cordoned off parcel of land clearly set aside for grazing by a specific type and breed of four-legged animal. These animals had insatiable appetites. They stood and nibbled and chewed as if ravenous, else sat and watched others do exactly the same; else they looked around as if on guard for signs of divergence from the norm – preferably anything interesting but not a threat.

They never stopped eating. It was as if they were determined, charged perhaps, to consume all the grass that was growing around them in such abundance. This instinct to consume food without pause for reflection or consideration for the consequences I have seen exhibited by some humans in commercial and communal eating establishments. For many humans the consumption of those solid and liquid substances classified as food - and therefore safe to eat - is considered the ultimate state of physical and mental harmony.

The female was keen to watch them and moved in close. This they were not happy with and they backed away, vocalising in no uncertain terms their displeasure and nervousness at what for them counted as uncalled-for harassment. The female was oblivious to this and continued to disrupt. The animals – a distinct, tightly-knit group - just wanted to be left alone to eat and wander, to shit and sit down, and to sleep at regular intervals. The emotional empathy she tried to generate and share with these grazing animals seemed to be truly at odds with the fact that humans happily kill them for consumption. She wanted to instil in each individual its own sense of identity – but one modelled upon various human elements, along human lines – not knowing that these creatures had already established their own identities: rudimentary by human standards but functional and expressive nevertheless, as demonstrated by their ability to recognise and interact with each other. And I noticed too that to look into their eyes was to feel an enigmatic sense of both recognition and surveillance. They acknowledged our presence and proclaimed theirs. For humans of an above average sensitivity such engagements must be a little disconcerting.

For the female this unrestricted, semi-wild expanse of land holds a special place in her heart. I do not know why and I sense neither does she. She reveres it for its disassociation from humanity – the lack of human interference - and its timeless, abstract quality of permanence. This is despite the fact that it is constantly changing, drifting; fragmenting, decomposing and reconstructing. She has endowed it with those properties more normally associated with a positive spiritual force or a distinct deity: one sympathetic towards the human condition; one able to heal or reengage a flagging human spirit; one able to loosen thoughts and stir up passion; one able to put into perspective the state of mind and being. And despite being nothing more than a vast stretch of land overseen by sky it never fails to deliver – simply because she makes it so, without ever recognising the fact that both cause and effect (including the wish for self-improvement and the pressure to change) emanate from deep inside her. There they reside deep in isolation, part of her yet beyond her recognition.

✦ ✦ ✦

Rebecca charged on ahead, always in front, always short of time; looking like she was late; but never out of breath, never lacking the stamina or the energy; never anything less than excited with anticipation. Clarence lagged behind, wishing to stop, gaze, admire and take in the scenery; but never able to, lest Rebecca left him stranded, lost. So he ran (kind of) to keep up, slowed, stopped for twenty seconds or so then repeated the cycle. He did not think to ask her to pause: he could see that she had an urgent need to get to some particular place as quickly as possible. Clarence did not want to interfere. The girl was having a good time.

So happy was she to be there and so beautiful, delicious was the view that she sometimes forgot to take it in. All detail was swept aside as she gorged herself on the big picture. So determined was she to be inspired by the great outdoors she aspired to nothing beyond a continuous eruption of emotional energy, one holding her on knife-edge.

When she reached her special spot she slumped down on the grass, waited for Clarence to catch up, then beckoned him to do likewise; hoping – demanding even - that it did for him what it did for her. He did as instructed, only slower, more delicately, for he had just sprained his ankle; and though it was only a minor injury he did not want to aggravate the situation. He was grateful for the break and allowed the bag to slip from his shoulders by loosening the straps. It had a picnic wrapped up inside it, carefully prepared by Rebecca, especially for him.

They had reached the top of a hill overlooking fields and woodland. Set back to back, the fields sliced up the countryside into discreet portions: portions of land to be processed, consumed and recycled but never reimbursed. Because it all appeared small Rebecca felt big, on top of the world, above average, better than the norm. And she wanted Clarence to feel the same, to take it all in, to breath it all in; to slowly breath it all out; and to feel God's hand in it all. And she wanted to share it with Clarence. So with that in mind she grabbed his hand and pulled him down to the ground beside her: down to the earth; down into the dirt where the bugs and worms played out their short, miserable, almost mechanical lives without any rhyme or reason except that they could, so they did. Some she accidentally squashed with the weight of her body but she was too big to notice and they were – had been – too small to protest.

Clarence winched as he folded himself up into some slightly comfortable sitting position and waited for her instructions: today Rebecca was definitely in charge. But he did not complain. Though he felt hot, sticky, and was aching in parts - positively painful around one ankle - he did not complain: that would be to spoil her moment, reduce her sense of inflated worth. He stuck with it, resolved to feast upon the view – which it had to be said was quite tremendous and well worth the hard ascent against gravity. Gravity: it could not be avoided.

Rebecca unpacked the food and drink and the limited cutlery, intending to feed and water her captive – hopefully captivated - man into romantic submission. Ants soon got wind of the bonanza and word was spread by chemical first class post to 'pile in'. Others – the solitary types - followed. Again and again Rebecca instructed her man to relax, chill out, take in the view, eat and drink, 'live a little'. She was talking at herself as much as she was talking at him. These things Clarence did as best he could, despite the physical hardships that distracted him: numb, aching buttocks; sunburn, sweat and stinging bites from creatures who had flown into him to snatch his blood. He could not fathom out why she had to keep repeating herself over and over again. Was it her current mantra? If so it was overextended.

"Isn't it beautiful?" she asked, demanding to hear the only one acceptable answer.

Clarence opened his eyes. The glare of the sun and creeping fatigue had forced them shut. "What?"

"The landscape silly – the sight of all this spread out in front of us. This is how it should be everywhere, always."

"Beautiful? No. It's wild and chaotic in some places, abused and remoulded in others by the hand of heavy machinery. Impressive? Certainly. Resilient? Within limits. Perpetual? Possibly."

"Oh Clarence!" exclaimed Rebecca. She slapped him across one thigh – light-heartedly but still with the strength to hurt.

Rebecca was seventeen again: he was a lot older. She wished for him to respond by rolling over, grabbing her, forcing himself on top, and kissing her passionately until he – or she – ran out of breath. Perhaps even ripping her knickers off and making love to her in a passionate, mad dash for spiritual union and sexual ecstasy. She wanted him to pin her down and push her apart with the thrust of his groin, then plunge in. She wanted to be hung out to dry; pressed and squeezed out of shape by the onslaught of savage, one-sided sex. A little devil inside her declared 'you are not just a human being you are also a piece of meat'.

He never did.

Clarence continued to concentrate on the view, as instructed: taking it all in, slowly, deliberately, piece by piece; as if locking it away in the attic of his mind to ensure none of it escaped. His deep concentration was evident and Rebecca was forced to respect it, though she was surprised that he could stare so long at the same bit of countryside. It was as though he had never stepped out into the great outdoors before. This she found hard to believe. He was ten years old again and on his first school outing – yes that was it. Her man Clarence was a small boy again. She would have to corrupt him she decided if she was going to enjoy any delights that afternoon.

A schoolgirl fantasy which still lingered – still rankled - was to make love outdoors, in the grass, to the man she loved and who loved her; with the danger of getting caught but not getting caught. She was almost there. Just a nudge and a wink would do the trick. She would start with a melting smile.

❖ ❖ ❖

Log Entry

I sense she is highly charged, engulfed in a temporary state of happiness, one of her own making. She has given this place extra special. Once it was the top of a hill, just like any other such geological feature. Now it is a place endowed with the properties of healing, and it radiates spiritual strength. The view from this high vantage point stimulates in her a fresh outlook: on this she can rebuild her fantasies and delusions which have been ground down by the constant routine of eating, sleeping, washing, working, wanting – the list goes on.

But it is just land: unenclosed, part wild, part tamed. It is earth and rock mixed in with rotting matter and water. It is awash with vegetation, dead and alive. Yet for all that she has instilled it with special worth and now turns to it for sustenance. She thinks it is making her happy when in reality she is making herself happy by self-stimulation, nothing else. In the same way she makes herself sad.

This uncomplicated, almost untouched piece of planet surface is how she wants it to be, always and everywhere. She wants to put a lock on time, freeze her own existence, and dispel her failings and hang-ups. She does not want to be anywhere else at any other time. And she wants my host to want the same, to feel the same, to be the same. She wants the two of them to be the only two humans in existence. She wants to start it all over again – it being the track record of the human race I suspect. And she wants to engage in fierce, intense lovemaking - right now, despite the lack of privacy and the uncomfortable ground. She wants. She wants. She wants. This female can be very tiring at times.

It must be noted that the actions of some creatures are not always benevolent: now we have stopped to rest and eat my host's body quickly attracts the attentions of small flying creatures. They attack the skin of my host: their key objective being the seizure and consumption of his blood. They pierce the skin to extract it, exchanging toxins in the process which inflame and irritate the skin. Others are out to sample the food we have

• 438 •

brought with us. Others it seems are just intent on being a nuisance. Have they nothing better to do?

She is looking constantly at my host, encouraging him to look back, to focus on her profile: the curves of her body; the spaces it both fills and leaves empty. She does not speak and does not want him to speak. She simply smiles a great deal and flicks her hair back and forth, from one resting place to another as if it needs constant distractions. She has allowed her short thin dress to ride up, so exposing her thighs in full. She requests that my host kiss her. I comply, punctually and precisely at the location indicated: her lips. Apparently dissatisfied she then asks him to kiss her again, in a different place: this time on the chest, almost between her breasts. Again I comply, having no wish to cause offence, but I do not linger. This appears to satisfy her for the present, but only just. She stretches out across the grass and crooks one leg to reveal her underwear. It is damp in places, having absorbed the sweat of the body. For no apparent reason she makes the sound of an exhausted human being: one wishing to fall asleep; else one suffering minor, internal pain. I sense no pain and no tiredness. The signals of an invitation to engage in sexual intercourse are clear. With her unspoken consent I am expected to look, enjoy, arouse the body and penetrate with the penis: the standard approach.

Sex is at the forefront of her mind. She is sexually arousing herself - perhaps for the benefit of my host as well as her own. He is expected to reciprocate, instantly. She shifts position such that her crotch (clothed) is fully visible and easily accessible. But I decline to take up the offer. Had my host been in full control I am sure he would have declined the invitation, perhaps even retreated to a respectable distance, disgusted by her attitude.

This refusal surprises her and she is left to wonder why. She closes the gap between her legs and looks away. Finally - a little afraid of the answer - she finds the courage to ask why: at which point I decide an answer of convenience is required rather than the absolute truth, which may offend. I tell her that this is not the time or place for such an intimate activity. She is satisfied with the answer and even impressed by the moral stance taken. It may have even reinforced her sense of romance.

All this time she has been clutching close to her heart a secret wish wrapped up inside an intention: to show me something which, in her mind, is stupendous, thought-provoking, mind-blowing even; and which will change my host's outlook on the world forever. She has worked hard to contain it but is eager now to give it free reign and take charge of proceedings.

She commands that we clear up quickly and get moving again. She is all fired up and in a hurry again. Just as I lift the bag on to my back she grabs my hand and pulls me along, fast. I suppress the pain emanating from my host's ankle. We are off to another special place.

⁕ ⁕ ⁕

The old woman watched her daughter fly around the kitchen. The daughter was in a rush and could not be slowed down by conventional means. Lassie watched the floor, disinterested.

Mother spoke. "Sit down. Take a break." It was a clear command.

"Can't. Need to get on."

"I can unload the washing machine. Sit down."

"What about your back?"

"It's fine for now."

The daughter glanced at her watch, wishing to avoid the boring chat. "I'm really pushed."

It had taken the daughter many years to master the knack of pretending to listen while others spoke – especially her husband – and now she was proficient. And she had every reason: her mum had the habit now of repeating much the same stuff from one visit to the next. The daughter just had to give out the same answers - sometimes in a slightly different order - and try not to look or sound bored.

"Sit down or I won't leave you my stamp collection."

The daughter was stumped: she could not tell if it was a joke. It didn't sound like a joke so she sat down as instructed. Her husband wanted that stamp collection. Mother poured out a second cup of tea and added milk and sugar to make it the way her daughter liked it.

"Have a cup of tea."

The daughter wanted coffee but couldn't be arsed. She said thanks instead.

"Why are you so busy these days? You never used to be."

"What?" The daughter lowered her cup. She had not yet drunk from it. "I've always been busy."

"Not when you were young."

"I wasn't married then." The daughter raised her cup up again.

"So it's your family. The husband and children. Why do you take it all on? Why do you try to do everything? Can't he do more? Teach

· 440 ·

the children self-sufficiency, how to clear up, organize themselves, cook food."

The daughter was not impressed by the advice. "What's brought all this on?"

"Concern for my daughter's health."

"I would be more concerned about yours." The daughter quickly corrected herself. "Sorry mum I didn't mean that. I'm fine mum. I'm fine."

Her mother had not taken offence. "You're stressed out, tired out all the time. You look more tired out than me."

"That's cos I am."

"Which is a bad state to be in. You must ease off."

Suddenly the daughter started to take the conversation seriously.

"I can't. If I don't look after things it will all fall apart. No one else can. Certainly not Keith. He's hopeless. And the kids aren't old enough yet to run even small parts of their lives. Give them a few more years then things should 'ease off' as you say – but you know all this. You raised me and Michael for Christ's sake. Anyway why all the sudden interest in the size of my to do list?"

"I need you to make some space."

"Space? What do you mean? Storage space?"

"No, space in time." The old woman pulled open one of the kitchen table drawers. Lassie looked up and wagged his tail.

"I need you to deliver this." She held out an envelope.

"You mean you want me to post it? No problem."

"No I don't want you to post it. It hasn't got a stamp on it."

"I know it hasn't got a stamp on it." The daughter felt a small scream developing at the back of her throat. She would do her best to hold it back and only let it out when she was back outside.

"I want you to deliver it to the man at the door – tomorrow."

"Tomorrow! That's my weekend. I don't understand. If it's important send it by registered post, next day delivery or whatever."

"No. It must only be you. One person. The one person being you, my daughter."

"How far?"

The old woman examined the address, as if for the first time. "Somewhere in the city of London."

"What!" The daughter stuck out her hand, almost into her mother's face, and shook it. "Here give it to me."

Grabbing the envelope she read the address, and was appalled. "This is South London. I'll have to go round the M25. It will take me hours – two possibly three if the traffic is bad. That's nearly a whole day!"

"I'm sorry but it must be done. I'll reimburse you for the travel costs – and the loss of your time."

"That's not the point." It was part of the point. "I have to find the time in the first place – and the energy."

"That's what I was talking about earlier."

"Just so you could ask me to hand deliver this . . . thing . . . with no name on it!"

The daughter waved the envelope in the air before handing it back.

"No. Not at all. It was a serious, heartfelt observation."

"What's in it that's so important?"

"I can't tell you."

"You can't tell your own daughter. You don't trust me."

"No it's not like that."

"You trust Michael."

"No more than I trust you."

"He helps you with all the important stuff. I just get to do the washing."

"I would ask him more but he's never around. Work takes him off all the time. You know that."

The daughter did know that and wished she didn't. From a position of ignorance she could criticize him. The daughter was stuck. She put her foot down in the mud.

"I don't want to."

"You must!"

"Get a delivery company to do it!"

"No you must!"

"But I don't want to!" She wanted to stamp her foot.

"Do this one small thing for me before I die. If you don't I'll cut you out of my will."

Now the daughter was really stuck. She wanted to bang her head against the table. Even more she wanted to bang her mum's head against the table. Her mother looked on, ferocious, quite animated, quite alive – which was unusual for her. She was deadly serious her daughter decided. The daughter began to simmer with rage. The daughter had ginger hair.

"Why do you always do this to me."

"Do what?"

"Make me do things I don't want to do."

"I don't, not now – except for this one thing which is extremely important to me. I haven't told you what to do for years."

"But you keep giving me advice, telling me how to do everything."

"Isn't that the job of every mother. You will do the same. Just give it time."

The daughter had no reply.

"So you'll take the letter?"

"I suppose so," mumbled the daughter, head down.

The old woman held out the envelope across the table for the second time. "Here you are then."

Head still down the daughter took receipt of it. "Thanks." She pushed back her chair, hoping it would topple over, and got up. "I have to get on."

"See you next time."

"Thanks."

"And drive carefully."

"I will." She wouldn't. She never did, despite the pleas from her husband. He did not have ginger hair.

✦ ✦ ✦

Log Entry

We have reached a point where we can look down on one particular field. It is a field like any other. In it has been planted – by mechanical means I suspect, judging by the regularity and consistency – a staple crop for commercial exploitation. The crop, having grown some height, and in the process of maturing prior to harvest, has been flattened in places to carve out distinct shapes: mainly circular and symmetrical in design; and, it has to be said, pleasing to the eye.

This is all it is yet it has transformed the female into a state of heightened, almost manic frenzy. She bubbles over with emotions and irrationality, and expects my host to react in the same way. She has deluded herself into accepting that she has witnessed something extraordinary, portentous, something alien: the only explanation for which demands a total re-evaluation of the state of the world and its place in the universe. She expects the same reaction and shift in mindset from my host. For her this would be the logical reaction.

As far as she is concerned (and others I suspect) there is only the one explanation for this phenomenon. It is evidence of the existence of extraterrestrial beings: they have visited this particular place and on leaving have left behind nothing except a signature in the landscape. She believes in this totally. No other explanation will suffice. She is totally convinced in her own mind that beings not indigenous to this planet have landed, here, in a place of no particular significance; then left, leaving no trace of their activities except the limited damage to vegetation. I conclude that she is mad, mentally unstable, and at risk of complete mental self-destruction – at the very least serious lapses of judgement during the course of her life. I must help in anyway I can.

✦ ✦ ✦

"You look happy."

Rebecca smiled. She looked happy.

"What are you thinking?"

"Why do you want to know?"

"I'm interested. I need to know you better. Understand what makes you tick."

"Thank you. That's lovely."

A compliment but no answer: Clarence had to repeat the question. "So what are you thinking?"

Rebecca answered in a lazy fashion, and with a lazy answer. "All sorts of things I suppose. And nothing."

"Are you happy?"

Struck by the directness of the question Rebecca could not answer. She turned back to the view.

Clarence was not deterred. "You seem afraid to answer."

The clouds drifted on and Rebecca was bathed in sunlight again. It gave her a warm feeling, both inside and out.

"Yes right now I am happy."

"But not always?"

"No. But what's wrong with that? Who is nowadays."

"I agree. No one." Clarence pushed on. "What is making you happy right now?"

"Right now?" Rebecca looked around. The answer was easy. "The land. The sky. The glory of nature. All doing its own thing, the way it was always intended." She stalled. "And you," she added quickly.

"Even the little events happening around us? At our feet? In the soil?"

Rebecca looked down. "Even that." She spoke proudly but with a hint of an apology.

· 444 ·

"I sense a very personal connection with this earth. You cling to it almost."

With alarm bells ringing inside her head she denied it – the word 'cling' for her represented an accusation, a deficiency. "I don't cling. It is what it is."

"But inside your head you are trying to make it so much more."

"Even if that's true what's wrong with that?"

"Nothing."

"Should we not celebrate Nature?"

"Certainly. But should we not be careful that we don't overstate it, try to turn it into something more, endow it with an existence beyond the physical and inanimate?"

Rebecca threw Clarence a funny look, and not for the first time: not sure whether he was still her friend, her lover or her ex-therapist. She shifted position to relieve the pressure on her backside. Then she fought back. Clarence followed suite.

"How can you overstate such a wonderful thing?"

"You can if you are looking for it to give you answers, put your mind at rest."

"You says I'm looking?"

"Are you?"

"Possibly."

"What are the questions? And are they so important?"

Rebecca tried to lessen the weight of the moment by shrugging and acting all nonchalant. "The same questions as everybody else's."

"Really?"

"What do you mean? 'Really'? You don't believe me?"

"Of course I believe you. But there are so many question. You must have some in particular?"

Rebecca looked trapped. She returned to soaking up the scenery. A small bird flew in close; landed; looked around; then flew off again. It had not been impressed with whatever it had seen or heard. They both watched it come and go.

Clarence spoke first. "Free of all baggage."

"What?"

"That bird: free of all baggage."

"Oh yes."

"That big tree over there. Must have been there for years, decades."

"Yes. Must have been."

"Does it live its life in the slow lane or do we live ours in the fast lane?"

"Good question." Rebecca, now impressed, wanted Clarence to hold her. As if reading her thoughts and deciding upon a compromise he took her hand.

"You say some funny things sometimes – don't get me wrong, great things. No one else could have thought of that. Just strange sometimes. Just strange. Better than being boring I suppose."

"Are we all not strange to some extent, from the viewpoint of another?"

Rebecca agreed, using silence to answer in the positive. Clarence was the first to speak again.

"You told me you were bullied at school?"

Rebecca almost jumped out of her skin but Clarence held on. He was not prepared to let go.

"What?"

"You told – "

"I heard you the first time. When did I tell you that?"

"After you had consumed some alcohol."

"What made you bring that up?"

"Sorry. I could not help it. I don't forget much. It was bugging me. I feel for you."

"You feel for me?" Rebecca looked up to the sky. It was still there, swallowing everything yet containing almost nothing. "You feel for me." She repeated the phrase almost in a whisper of content.

"Was it bad?"

"Was what bad?"

"The bullying?"

Rebecca twitched. Not wishing to answer made her nervous.

"It probably was at the time. Doesn't bother me much now though."

Clarence was satisfied that she was being honest and moved on. "I sense you really love this place – this 'non-place'."

"And you?"

"Me? I love it. It feeds the soul."

"That's good." Rebecca squeezed his hand, hard.

"Do you connect with your god in this place?"

"And everything else."

Clarence was not convinced. "Are you sure? Everything?"

Rebecca threw him another accusing look and threw his hand away. "There you go again: analysing me." Her blood was up. "Stop treating me like a child!"

Clarence sounded hurt. "I was doing no such thing. If it came across like that then I apologize, sincerely."

Rebecca looked into the grass, as if searching for mislaid treasure between the individual blades.

"Have I hurt you? I'm sorry if I hurt you."

"No you haven't hurt me. You just got me thinking that's all."

"Tell me what you are thinking. Share it with me. Please." Clarence was almost begging to be including.

"I was small. School holidays I think. Or maybe it was just the weekend."

Clarence passed her the bottle of water. Rebecca thanked him and took a sip.

"It was fabulous."

"What was?"

"I had found this bird's nest in a bush – must have fallen from the tree overhead. Yet it had landed okay, in the bush. There were two small chicks in it, chirping away loudly. I knew they were hungry, so hungry, and I was hungry. But I didn't leave them. I didn't let go. I had been playing on the common you see, before tea-time."

Rebecca paused for breath. The memory was expanding to take up all the available space inside her head.

Clarence nudged her on. "What happened?"

"I went and found some nice, juicy worms. I dug up some worms, out of the ground, the mucky ground. Normally I hated worms but I went and found some – for them – to eat. I knew they were hungry."

Rebecca paused again, looked down at her dress then continued, more mixed up child now, less a mangled adult.

"I watched them eat. They were ravenous. The worms were gone in seconds. I had never seen anything get eaten so fast. Even I had never been that fast. Where's the mother I wondered. Where's the mother?"

"What did you do next?"

"I went and got some more worms of course. They ate those up just as quick. Just gobbled them up."

"Any more worms after that?"

"Can't remember. I remember I was hungry. Probably had to go home for tea. Mother was always very strict about the time for tea. I went back the next day. Twice I think. Perhaps even more. Kept feeding them worms. But it was a struggle."

"Why a struggle?"

With that question Rebecca looked at Clarence as if he was stupid. "Finding the worms of course. They don't grow on trees." Then she grinned, convinced that she had made a very good joke. The happy face soon imploded though: she was thinking too hard.

Clarence squeezed her arm where it connected with her shoulder then left it sitting there. Grateful, Rebecca responded by placing hers on top.

"So what happened next? What happened to the chicks in the nest?"

"I made the mistake of telling others. I boasted."

"Others being friends?"

"Not particularly. Just other kids at school – or in the neighbourhood – or both. I can't remember."

"Why was it a mistake?"

"They made me show them the nest. Perhaps I wanted to show them the nest, show off. I can't remember."

"And then what?"

"I think they were impressed – but one wasn't. She was jealous. Yes that was it. The bitch was jealous, of me. Stupid girl." Rebecca broke contact with Clarence again, clutched her knees and began to rock a little. "As we walked away she flicked it. She wanted it to topple over – and it did the bitch."

Rebecca stalled. She had been interrupted by the arrival of tears. They were not welcomed. "The chicks fell out. I screamed and kicked her the stupid bitch. She kicked me back. The others just laughed."

"And then what?"

"I ran away. I should have stayed and helped them but I ran away. I should have picked them up, put them back in their nest but I ran away. They were small, defenceless – but just skin and bone, scrawny, not nice to look at you see. Now I think about it I don't think I had the nerve to touch them. And they looked too fragile to touch. I could have harmed them. They made an awful noise. I'll never forget the noise."

She had forgotten the noise. She only remembered that it had made an impact at the time. She tried to reinvent it, without success.

"I should have found them a home but I ran away."

"Did you ever go back?"

"Oh yes, but only days later. And then they were gone. The remains of the nest were still there but they were gone. I think it had been ripped to pieces. I hate to think what happened to them."

"So don't then."

"What?"

"Don't think about what happened to them. You were small, young, not in charge of events happening around you. So just let it go." Holding her full attention Clarence repeated himself, slowly. "Just let go. It is allowed you know." He had her full attention. "Is there anything else you would like to share with me?"

Rebecca thought of school and other girls in her year. Then she tried to totally block her own thoughts.

Clarence prompted her. "More badness in old school friends?"

"Yes," squeaked Rebecca. She could barely speak out.

"Over boys I guess?"

"Good guess. Yes over boys."

"Boyfriends I guess. Your first boyfriend?"

"I wouldn't have called him my boyfriend."

"But your first?"

"Yes." She sounded timid.

"Did you have sex with him?"

"Yes."

"More than once?"

"No."

"Did he desert you? Dump you for someone else?"

"Yes." The painful, affirmative answer trickled out.

"Did he ever say he loved you?"

"I think so." She had wanted to say yes, to condemn him further, but she could not honestly remember the facts.

"Did he dump you for a friend?"

Anger reared up and tried to throttle her. "Yes."

"A special friend? Your best friend at the time."

"Yes."

"That was cruel."

"Yes it was. Cruel."

"How did she react?"

"React? She told me – to my face – in front of our friends."

"Told you what?"

"That he didn't want to see me anymore. That he thought I was too grim. She boasted that she made him happy. He was going out with her now. She had always wanted him – always wanted what I wanted."

"You see that now?"

"Yes I see it now. She secretly hated the fact that he had fancied me first, over her. He had sex with me before he had sex with her."

"Are you sure?"

"Yes I'm sure." Suddenly she not grieving, she was boasting.

"Some people can be cruel. They can switch allegiance in an instant. Especially at that age. Rest assured not everyone is like that. They are a minority, just."

"Oh I know. I know." She didn't know.

"Some young men can be bastards when it comes to getting a woman to have sex with them. They will do anything, say anything to push the right buttons. And if they are lucky they catch her at that one time when she is of poor judgement, wanting to be loved. And some of them never give up that approach. And of those, a few will become lazy and take the most direct route: physical violence. Not that I'm suggesting he was ever that bad. Very unlikely."

"Oh I know. I know."

"I sense you are in a very troubled state right now. I'm sorry. I should not have taken you back there."

"No it's good to talk. And I can talk here, now, to you, now."

"Thank you. I take that as a compliment."

Clarence took her hand again and Rebecca leaned over, into him. She rested her head in his lap and closed her eyes. In the physical sense she was comfortable. Clarence was not.

"Let it all out. Here and now. It's a good place and a good time. We all build up - 'shit' I believe is the word to use - inside our heads over time. It's in the nature of what it is to be a thinking human being. We think a lot we humans. Sometimes too much. Yes?"

Though she had heard him quite clearly Rebecca barely registered his words. She was thinking of mother and father and her mother's sister.

"Tell me about your parents."

Rebecca spoke as if waking up but her eyes remained closed even though another cloud had planted its shadow across her face. "My parents? Mum and dad?"

"Or anybody else."

"I had an aunt."

"What was her name?"

"Aunty Jill."

"Did you like her, this aunty Jill?"

"Yes I did."

"Very much?"

"Very much."

Clarence did not hesitate when he put the next, key question. "More than your mother?"

"Yes." Rebecca almost choked on the word.

"And why was that?"

"I don't know." She knew.

"Not even a clue?"

Rebecca didn't need clues.

Clarence continued. "Was she a good mother?"

"I don't know." She knew. "No. But she tried to be." The last comment may have been an invention.

"What makes you say that?"

"I don't know. I could just tell. Some things you just know."

"So you turned to your aunt Jill?"

"Yes I suppose I did - she turned to me first though."

"And she was good to you, like a mother to you?"

"Yes."

"Only better?"

"Only better."

"Family, friends, lovers: there's no shame in feeling more affection for one over the other. It's all mixed up. There are no rules on rationing out your wish to love or be loved. Any connection made is a good connection, and one made like this is probably one of the best." Clarence paused to allow his statement to sink in before putting his next question. "Is your aunt dead?"

Rebecca, still wandering around the maze of his previous statement, had to catch up. "Yes."

"Are your parents dead?"

"No. Just divorced."

"May I say something?"

Rebecca sat up. "You've said so much so far why not continue."

"Thank you." Clarence was unsure if that passed as permission or a refusal. "Why do you strive to connect with this 'one god'? Are you so dissatisfied with the connections inside your own head? Is it such an uncomfortable place in there? Have you tried to rearrange things, put things in order, put things right?"

Rebecca looked around, unable to settle on the view.

"There is no logic to any of this. You know that don't you? Even the act of unconditional belief allows for a logical framework in which it – and you – can operate. Yet you say there is only this one god while at the same time trying to connect with some other 'great force of Nature' which powers the lives of all living creatures on this planet – presumably including your own? And this one god: you just keep him for yourself. You don't like sharing him. You even try to attach yourself to nothing more than a nice view or the colour of the sky. Does bright blue really do it for you?"

Clarence stalled, noting that his last comment was not being well received. It sounded too much like sarcasm. But he continued, applying more muscle.

"Before you start believing in forces outside your head I suggest you start to believe in those inside your head. Harness them. Use them to untangle yourself. Put the past in its correct place, out of harm's way, where it can't influence the present. If you must turn to it, turn to the good bits and enjoy them – that includes Aunty Jill. Let the bad bits fade away, die off."

Rebecca was lost for words. She was filled with indignation and anger, disbelief even; but most of all a new reality.

"And all this silly stuff about the stars and the moon setting human agendas, life choices and character profiles: dump it, else dump all the laws of physics. You have wasted too much time reading the wrong books when your thirst for knowledge could have been better directed elsewhere." Clarence thought of a phrase he may have heard once in a film or on television – or perhaps it was his own. "Straighten up and straighten out."

Rebecca wanted to slap him. The wish to resort to physical violence was a sign that she could not deny her situation or his appraisal. Clarence waited for the dusk to settle. Rebecca did the same, while refusing to look at him. They both sat in a dull trance; neither smiling, both thinking.

A big dog, pedigree, almost manicured, mud splattered but none the wiser, bounded on to the scene. He had big brown teeth, bad breath and a smelly arse but he was friendly and he wanted to make friends. On a bad day he could be a beast with a foul temper. Today was not one of those days.

The dog went for the female. He wanted to lick her face. She was having none of it. She pushed him off by the forehead but he also was having none of it. He tried again, not understanding the concept of not wishing to be friendly, not wanting to make friends. Rebecca pushed him off again, with greater force. This did make him back down. He stood back, to stare at her as if waiting for a change of heart. He drooled and gasped for air and his tongue was left hanging out as if for sale. He was trying to be friendly but all he had succeeded in doing was be annoying.

Like the dog, but at half his speed, an old woman came bounding up. Like the dog, but not as much, she was fit. Like the dog, but more so, she was gasping for air. Like the dog, but less so, she just wanted to be friendly. Unlike the dog she had more than enough friends to occupy her time. She wore clothes that didn't need care or attention. She lived in a small cottage which had for too many years lacked due care and attention. She had a dead husband. He no longer needed due care and attention – not that he had been getting it much in his final years. The dog, the chickens and the two cats got it all now.

"Don't worry he's only being friendly."

The old woman – the owner of many dogs to date - signalled and called her dog to her side. He responded in an instant, knowing who his friends were. The old woman – a retired school teacher and Archers fan - sized up the situation and read the expression on the young woman's face as vacant, lost, disgruntled: that plus the rest of her body language put her in a bad way, the old woman concluded. She turned her attention towards the young man. He looked stern, detached, almost smug – the 'too clever for your own good' type in her opinion. As was often her way the old woman put two and two together and made five; sometimes six. She drew up close to the female, almost touching her; ready to be touched, ready to offer a hand.

"Is everything all right my sweet?"

"Best leave her alone," said Clarence.

"You keep out of this young man!"

"I can't. I'm intimately involved."

The old woman turned up her nose, like she had been offered a bad cut of meat by her butcher, unable to respond. She turned her back on him and gave all her attention to the young lady in distress.

"Ignore him. Is everything all right?"

This time she got an answer, just not the one she wanted to hear.

"I'm fine. Now please take your stupid dog and leave us alone. He's annoying me."

With that the old woman almost reared up. She had been insulted – and her dog. But she knew there was nothing she could do except become embroiled in a senseless, pointless argument with a completely mad stranger. So she turned and marched off, at speed, with a slight tilt, her loyal dog at her side. In seconds she had wiped the incident from her mind. So had he.

Now dislodged from her deep and sudden onset of misery, Rebecca suddenly found herself able to put a question. She only had the one she wanted answered but it was complicated: was Clarence the enemy or a friend; was he a friend or her lover; was he her lover or her abuser? Would he stand by her or stand her up? Was he for real or was he a fraud, a trickster? She went straight for his jugular vein, having aimed for the heart but missed. The strength she put into the question would wear her out – despite the few actual words.

"Do you love me Clarence?"

The reply was spontaneous. Clarence shook his head without the slightest hesitation, nor even the slightest trace of regret.

"No."

It was the biggest slap in the face so far and it really hurt.

"I see."

Rebecca drew her follow-on conclusion in agony.

"I take it then you don't want to sleep with me. You don't find me attractive."

Clarence frowned. "That's not really relevant to the point. I don't want to have sex with you."

Rebecca gritted her teeth, jumped up and walked away; wishing to punch him as she passed him by at arm's length. There was nothing else to be said. The heartless bastard had made his position quite clear. She hear back the tears. She would not cry over him. She did not want to be seen to care. She made her way back to the car, tripping up and almost falling over on the way as she made no effort to look down at the ground in front of her.

Sensing his company was not welcomed now, Clarence limped on behind at a respectful distance, crippled by his sprained ankle. It really did hurt now. On the drive back she did not utter a single word. She just stared out of the window at the near scenery flying past and the distant land barely moving. Back in town, alongside other cars waiting at traffic lights of stuck in queues she would stare down at her knees instead. He would play with the radio.

✤ ✤ ✤

Log Entry

Still outdoors I asked the female what she was thinking. She was not sure. She took offence when I asked if she was happy and became defensive. She quickly felt exposed, vulnerable when I questioned her attempt to connect in some spiritual sense with the natural environment. I had to tread carefully. I proceeded to probe with caution, feigning ignorance at all times – in effect pretending to be human. I could not for one instant let her think that I had entered her mind, measured her emotions or engaged with her memories. (Though some were nothing more than echoes, sending out the same signal.) I did not want to scare her off by exposing her thoughts with absolute accuracy. I took charge the moment she found it impossible to hold back the truth. She released it grudgingly. Straight lying does not come easy to her. Self-deception does however. At times she would stare into my face, as if trying to decipher me, no matter how long it took.

We watched the movements of a small bird: they were sudden, intuitive, unconditioned. Unlike the female it was free of baggage. It used the passing of time to chase after life – it's own and others.

For a time we sat in silence and waited for nothing, for nothing to happen, for nothing to disturb us. We allowed time to pass doing nothing, going nowhere; changing nothing, letting nothing change us. For her it was a state of paradise, a refuge, an escape. Inside the brain time seemed to slow and not cause a fuss as it passed on through. This put her at ease so I dug deeper. This brought memories up to the surface and put them into sharper relief. I sensed pain, anger, and, interestingly, profound disillusionment. Disillusionment with what? School friends? She was surrounded. She refused to join in. She refused to be part of some silly game. She stood her ground. They called her names. One poked her with a finger. She was scared and she was angry at the same time but she did not run away. Finally they became bored and peeled off in ones and twos. The pack of tormentors dissolved in an instant and she was left to nurse her bruises, outer and inner – mainly inner. It will take a long time to forget – or rather convince herself that she has forgotten when in fact she has simply pushed her recollections back underground. Though forgetting their actual faces has already been accomplished. That was the

· 455 ·

easy part. In her memories they are all faceless. In fact I sense everybody in her memories of school are faceless, deserving of no recognition; dull, boring, non-descript. I suspect this reflects a generally harsh attitude she takes towards others, despite her loneliness and often recurring sense of vulnerability which disables her attempts to socialise.

She hates being treated like a child: any suspicion that this is so produces a flood of emotions which have nowhere to go. As an adult she is upset by the fact that her childhood still haunts her, despite her best efforts to cast it off.

More memories produced another girl inside her head, still no face but everything else: character and context were clearly defined. The other girl was a best friend, once. But no more. She is banished. This girl did or said something awful once and hurt her badly, without warning. I think it had something to do with a young but sexually mature male.

She jumped through time. She was small again, this time feeling very proud of herself, strong, smug, older and bigger than she was. When I asked what she was thinking she focused in on a big tree and bushes. She lowered a barrier and decided to share this episode in her life with me. Some of it she distorted: overlaying it with present embroidery. Reinvention of the self is definitely a trait unique to humans on this planet.

I pushed her on, gently, and physically reconnected whenever she would allow me. The more she thought the more she remembered, and the more it made her sad. An incident involving baby birds positively hurt. It made her want to scream and bang a table like a child – but there was no table in the vicinity. It stabbed her repeatedly, like it held a knife. At times she was on the verge of crying. She wanted to cry but somehow managed to hold off the tears. It was not because she did not want me to see her cry.

When I offered advice or gave instruction she looked at me, trying to decide if she should – or could – do as I suggested. In her mind she grabbed me and held on to my words while she tried to read me. At some point she divided herself, stood back so to speak, and began to analyse: a healthy sign I think – though I fear there was much bias and filtering of facts. She tried to do as I suggested, and was partially successful. The memory of the baby birds in distress receded: polluted by the present it was now not quite the memory it had been before. But the change was for the better. It was a positive shift.

Without prompting the female thought of school and other girls – bar one in particular whom she tried to exclude. She thought of a group of them holding together, doing things together, as one. Then she jumped: she was older. She saw herself and the other girl who kept intruding into her mind both thinking of boys, and sex. Another shift: she and the other girl were older still. Their bodies had fully matured and were fully functioning, and both were proud of that fact. She moved onto thinking of sex with a young man: an attractive young man and well sought after. She struggled to reassemble his face and then his entire body - naked. She could remember his hair. It was long and fair. It was gorgeous. She remembered him as being even more good-looking than he had been. She had allowed him to remove her clothing, finger her best underwear, finger her in her underwear. She had both wanted him and not wanted him to remove her knickers. She thought of him pulling down her knickers roughly. He hadn't: that was reinvention. She had pushed them away. She remembered quite clearly hoping that it would be good – this thing called sex. She remembered him fumbling around, trying to get it right and connect the pieces. And this time she forgave him. She remembered having to be patient. She remembered him forcing his way in. And she remembered it hurting. She had been shaken up and shaken around, almost violently. And it was all over and done with in less than two minutes. She remembered little else of that particular moment other than the fact that he left quickly without saying a word. He had been unable to speak. She remembered them never speaking about it and she remembered the gloom it created between them. There had been no celebration. She had wanted to try again, get it right second time, for his benefit – and make it last longer, for her sake. She never saw him again. That fact was burned into her brain and would always stand the test of time, as was the fact that she had given away her virginity so cheaply. She still considered herself truly stung: emotionally and physically, even spiritually. And because of that she remained crippled.

These memories threw up the other girl in her face. The face was clear. She could even remember the voice. She saw now that it had been a silly voice and hoped that it still was. She remembered seeing them together by chance, and being angry, and hiding. Ever since then she had regarded them as two worthless human beings, and sex as just sex, nothing more.

With the gates down other memories came flooding back, at which point she began to flounder, sink. She had no firm ground. I may have opened a can of worms.

At one point the female rested her head in the lap of my host. He was far from comfortable. I managed to suppress an erection of his penis. I encouraged her to continue, move on; give up some things and give up on others.

When I enquired about family – she had started to think about them - it was an aunt who was pushed into the foreground. She took the largest cut of the affections on offer. There was a grudge against the mother, for not being a good mother, perhaps for not wanting to be a mother- even worse I guess. Such thoughts made her feel numb inside. Others were too hot to handle. When things are seriously wrong a child spots it in its mother and a mother spots it in her child. Initially I had thought her parents were dead. She had thought of them as such.

Memories of her dear aunt almost put her in a trance as she drifted around her latest pile of reinvigorated memories. They had hung around for years, refusing to go away, settle; always demanding attention. And when they got it they made her sick. She saw her mother tucking her up in bed and trying to look as if she was enjoying the task – trying to turn it into a heart-warming, lasting experience. And she saw her father, standing further back, looking not happy but extremely dissatisfied. She had understood then that something was not right in the world. The world was not right: that conclusion stayed stuck to her in many different ways.

'Aunty Jill' came to the rescue: now, in the present as she had in the past. Back then 'Aunty Jill' had held her hand when it needed to be held and had squeezed it gently when it needed to be squeezed. My patient – if I can call her that - wanted her to squeeze it now. Immediately she pushed the wish away. She regarded it as a sign of weakness.

I sensed my comments were taken onboard and digested but the net impact was very small. She was too tangled up. At one point I decided to give her the mental equivalent of a 'smack in the face'. Gentle probing and prodding could achieve very little: at best nothing more than a minor adjustment in her outlook. I had some success. I managed to expose some rubbish inside her head which in time, when she is stronger, she may find the strength to shake off and banish. And she found it easier to think about her aunt. As for her mother, that still needs to be resolved, preferably rectified. But at least she is conscious of that fact.

And on and off throughout she was also thinking of her cat – no rather all cute little animals. Her cat made her feel positive about herself. What her cat thought about her I do not know. It guards its thoughts well sometimes.

Chapter Eighteen

That evening, her walk, picnic and biggest, latest fantasy all betrayed, Rebecca pushed up against her kitchen counter as if impatient to place an order for alcohol during Happy Hour. She gripped a tin opener with no immediate intention of exercising it. She was not happy. Her thoughts were locked up and she was locked in, unable to make all the parts of her life add up to the correct total, something close to 100%. Judy sat like a stiff at her side, head stretched up and out. She watched and she waited, without wishful thinking, only blind hope that her mistress would lower the usual bowl of food to the floor in the usual place.

Outside a rain drop fell from the sky and smashed into a paving stone, obliterating itself. In a fraction of a second it was followed by many more, and then hundreds more, and then thousands more, with millions more to come. And in no time it had started to rain with a vengeance. Rebecca did not care. She was elsewhere. Judy did not care. She wanted food to eat. Second to sleeping it was her favourite pursuit.

Rebecca stared down at the tin. It did not register. It was just a tin like any other: no bigger; no smaller; no more significant. Yet it held her attention. The rain rattled the windows as some tremendous event began to flex its muscle. The tin opener felt heavy, like the weight of responsibility, the start of a trial, or a long, insufferable, tedious task. She could not bring herself to open it. Judy could not make sense of the long delay. Where was her food? She licked her lips. Humans could be unreliable sometimes.

Rebecca closed her eyes and there was Aunty Jill. Aunty Jill did not see her. Rebecca saw Aunty Jill move towards her, lean over, smile, reach out and touch her hair, then stroke it for good measure. It felt good. Rebecca wanted to sit up and throw off the blanket; grab it, bite it, chew on its flavour and spit it out. The good feeling did not last: she had to watch Aunty Jill let go and take a step back, powerless to stop her. Then mother appeared, looking nervous, looking stretched; looking tired, worn out; looking almost wretched. Rebecca retreated back under the covers and peeked out, to gaze up at the faces of two sisters side by side. They looked much the same but they could not have been more different.

She looked away from the tin, and pushed them both aside. She saw breadcrumbs in a place she did not wish them to be but could not bring herself to exert the small effort required to sweep them up. She simply could not be bothered so instead she was forced to accommodate them, under protest. It was hard enough trying to find the energy to open the tin.

Clarence was locked up inside and she tried to avoid his voice. She tried not to register his words. She tried not to let him speak – how could he count himself as human when he had released such crushing statements? She tried not to remember all that he had said – said in his uniquely cold, calculating way. And in places she succeeded. Unfortunately she remembered all his key points, all the big words which had been harmonised to hurt. They could not be dislodged. These words kept repeating themselves. Like a sharp steel blade they cut into her. And the manner in which they had been delivered added to her anger, along with her failure to counter them. Even now she still could not produce a defence, only obstructions, delays, pretence: that further fuelled her anger, to such an extent that it wore her out just thinking about it.

She tried to make nonsense of them. She tried to stop them making sense. She tried to turn them into silly words not worth recognition. She failed on all accounts and her head throbbed with the pain of all their combined reasoning. She could not eject them. She could not argue back. She could not deceive herself with fakery, false hopes or fanciful fairy stories. She could not even sit down and cry. She had to open the tin else Judy might die and the sky might turn black. It was already dark grey and solid with thick threatening cloud: a severe weather warning by any other name (and any other means).

For relief Rebecca moved the tin opener to her left hand, this time holding it loosely. Her right hand relaxed. It was true: a change was as good as a rest. She was short-changed: she still saw Clarence; his face fixed in total concentration; his mission to talk talk talk and talk until she could no longer breath. She wanted to smack him. She smacked the kitchen counter instead, and it hurt like hell. But she refused to cry. Judy stood up on all fours, alerted. She could smell a rat.

Rebecca told herself to open the tin, open the tin, open the tin, and quickly wore herself out. She closed her eyes. Clarence was still there, talking at her, like she was a child in need of serious re-education and social realignment, like she had been picked off the street and didn't know how to hold a knife and fork. Five words in particular - precisely clipped and repeated by Clarence for maximum result - continued to provoke her: 'this is a typical response'. She thumped the breadboard with the tin opener and felt slightly better for it. Judy brushed up hard against her leg. She was also suffering. She was hungry.

"My Judy wants her dinner," declared Rebecca.

And those words were enough to shake her loose. Clarence was stashed away in the cupboard and the tin was cut open in a hurry. She dumped its contents into Judy's bowl and placed the bowl on the floor whereupon Judy rushed in, head down, eyes and jaws wide open. Arms folded, Rebecca found relief in the warm wave of achievement which rolled over her. For awhile she had something to feel good about.

Judy froze and sniffed the food. It didn't smell right. It didn't look right. It didn't have anything like the right shape. She decided not to taste it. Instead she touched it tentatively with a paw. It was baked beans: baked organic beans set in tomato sauce. Judy looked up at her mistress and meowed mournfully, baring her stained teeth. She did not get the joke. Rebecca looked down vaguely, as if not far off brain dead. At first she could not register the fuss or the facts. Judy continued to whine and then the penny dropped. Slowly, exhausted, Rebecca squatted down and picked up the bowl. She could see Clarence laughing at her mistake. Once she had wanted to plant her mouth in his face. Now she wanted to stick a fork in it, else smash it with a hammer: anything which would stop it talking sense or nonsense.

Evening, daytime lost, bones aching and body parts nearly busted, Clarence rolled over and refused to think about where his day had gone, or why. If his memory served him right – it didn't - he had marched around out in the middle of nowhere special, up and down, to the left and to the right. He could smell mud. He could smell shit. He could feel the hard bumps in the ground pushing pain up his backside. He could see that woman next door watching while he ate. He could feel the sun burning into him. He had chased after and had been chased after by that woman next door. He had been force-fed. Right now he didn't want to leave his bedroom. Right now he didn't want to get off his bed. It was his lifeboat. He was lost in a sea of big confusing blanks. And there was a storm brewing. It had begun to rain.

And if he wasn't being haunted by his own dreams he was being haunted – stalked perhaps - by her next door. He kept driving her from his thoughts and she kept coming back: to stare at him; to talk nonsense, or romance; to try to kiss him. Her taste still lingered in his mouth. He wanted to spit her out.

Wrapped up in his dressing gown Clarence stretched out across the bed, until cramp set in and he sat up, clutching his bad parts: clutching one clenched calf muscle; then one sprained ankle, to remind himself that it was sprained; then himself again, whilst willing all pain to pass. He fingered his face. Yes the bruise from the back of beyond was still there. Mad Max was the only suspect. Things were bad between them but had they really come to blows? Or to be more specific had Mad Max really clobbered him? Either way, best he be avoided – and stuff the extra money: no more lodgers. And then there was the sunburn across the back of his neck and forehead. All these things were painfully real, and really painful. His body, once his prized possession, if not always treated as such, was now truly knackered, just like his mind. He wanted to shout out to the world that it was not his fault, that he needed a break, that he was willing to change. But he knew the world was not listening, so shouting would be a waste of breath.

Something finally clicked, a safety valve perhaps: he could never make sense of it all so why the fuck bother? Just give it up, work around it. Best approach was to not care anymore. Clarence recycled that flow of thought a few times just to make sure it held. It did. So don't care anymore. Let everything be fine. Yes that was it: pretend everything is fine. Pretend hard enough, long enough, and keep pretending and everything is fine, will be fine. It works for small children so why shouldn't it work for him?

Everything is fine, Clarence told himself. Just don't go near Max and keep well away from that crazy woman next door, and her cat.

Speaking of Mad Max, he heard the man shuffle about between rooms. That was another good reason not to leave the safety of his bedroom. He was hungry but he didn't have the energy to make it to the kitchen – real reason was he was afraid he might bump into Max if he did, and worse still have to converse with the man. And still he could not shake off the woman next door. She kept trying to snog him, get him into bed even. It was a disgusting image. (In the past it had been acceptable for him to play that role. And one day he might take it up again.)

Hunger meanwhile reminded him of eating which reminded him of dinner which reminded him of eating out, of treating his parents tomorrow night. It was a crushing thought. No. No way. No way could he go through with that. He had to call it off. Cancel. Yes cancel. He reached out for his trusty mobile. It was parked in its usual place. Yes cancel. He switched it on and waited for confirmation of a connection to light up. It did, though the signal was weak. Yes cancel. It was the only logical option. Either that or jump off a high altitude bridge and don't look down.

He turned it off. Mum would be furious.

Rebecca apologised for her mistake and proceeded to scoop out the offending item of food into the kitchen bin. The sight of cold beans slithering and sinking slowly into the depths of the black bin liner did nothing to lift her spirits – the opposite in fact. Reaching into the cupboard her second choice of tin was correct and upon extracting its contents the familiar smell of cat food acted like an evil brew of smelling salts. The pleasure it brought to her Judy however was a joy which went some way to redress the balance. This instilled her with some measure of fighting spirit.

'Write him a letter and make him feel guilty, ashamed. Destroy him.' was the instruction that popped up inside her head. But her nerve failed her and she sat on it, preferring to watch her Judy feast instead. It did not give up. It bounced back, again and again; each time more seductive, more inviting, less intimidating; each time fuelling her ambition to give as good as she got.

Clarence reached out for his mobile again and again switched it on. Again he got a connection, and this time a strong signal. Cancel. Tough luck mum. Slowly and methodically he tapped out each digit and observed the number expand on the display screen – a sequence of digits which, when completed would dial his parents' home phone. Mother would be furious, or disappointed: probably both. He never completed the call. Two digits before the end he bottled out, switched off the mobile, put it back in its place and rolled over on his bed to face the wallpaper. He liked the wallpaper in his bedroom. It consisted of vertical stripes: thick green alternating with thin cream. They were separated by a very thin band of faint gold, slightly undulating and of variable thickness. If he stared at it long enough the pattern could be quite hypnotic, entrancing. He stared at it long and hard. It wasn't. It was just wallpaper. Cancel dinner. He held on to the thought, afraid it might escape. Cancel dinner. Don't stay too long on the phone. Get in and get out quick. Just like the SAS. Don't hang around for the chat. Say your piece then say you have to rush out or something.

Judy sat back and licked her lips, having just scraped the bowl clean with her crusty tongue. Job well done. Hugging a familiar routine for comfort Rebecca proceeded to dish out milk in the usual saucer. She went to the fridge, only to be disappointed in one sense, grateful in another.

There was no milk but there was an open bottle of Chardonnay which needed to be finished off. It was the perfect excuse. She filled a mug – to fill a glass would have inferred a celebration - and began to sip, swearing that this would be her first and last 'glass' of wine.

To combat the heavy rain she switched on the radio. The voice of a gruff, outraged woman boomed out. She boasted a thick North Yorkshire accent and she was furious with the behaviour of her friend's teenage son. According to the script the two women would have a major fallout and their husbands would be left to clear up the mess – and avoid being seen together doing business in the pub.

"He's a good for nothing scoundrel. I'd give him a good beating across the backside if I had my way. That's what I would do. Give him a good beating across the backside. Bring him down a peg or two."

Her friend took exception. "I'll have a word with him," she lied.

"So do something about it!"

The outburst of fiction was enough to provoke Rebecca into action. She did do something about it. She sat herself down at her table and produced a pad of lined paper and, after some searching, her trusty old fountain pen. It had been with her since art college. (She still believed in the benefits of fountain pens and fresh ink. For her they were a reminder of better times past, when quality counted for something.)

The blank page was a challenge and though Rebecca was willing to take it up, try as she might she could not find the words. They were not forthcoming. Lacking focus, she consumed more wine – sips having long since been superseded – until, frustrated, she threw the pen across the room. Instantly she was up and out of her chair to retrieve it, praying that no damage had been done. Luck was on her side: no ink had stained the carpet and the nib was undamaged. No, luck was not on her side: the pen had ink in it but the nib had seized up. For use as a writing implement it was completely useless. She resorted to the humble plastic biro.

To avoid having to listen to the argument raging inside his head Clarence switched on the radio. The farmer's wife switched off the engine and stepped down out of the landrover cabin and into thick mud. She wasn't bothered. She had a big pair of wellies on. They were permanently covered in mud. She saw her son at the far end of the farmyard looking shifty, looking like he wanted to get away fast. She waved him over.

"Jack you get your arse over here right now!"

Her voice made both the chickens and Jack jump. The landrover rolled back a few centimetres before getting a grip. She had not put the handbrake on. Jack weaselled towards her, taking as much time as he could. His mum lit up a cigarette while she waited for the bad news to arrive within smacking distance. She had decided not to be too hard on him. Just one smack.

Finally Clarence drove himself to make the call, either that or go mad. He tapped out the required number again, this time completing it, and watched the phone do its thing. With symbols flashing and signal strong, his sense of apprehension rose. He hoped beyond hope that Dad would get to the phone first. Dad rarely did these days: Mum was in charge of everything and these days quicker on her feet. Clarence held the mobile some distance away from his ear, relatively speaking. It was mum on the phone, and it had flashed up his name.

"Clarence is that you?"

Clarence reminded himself that he didn't care anymore and jumped in, head first.

"Yes it is. It's me."

"I've heard nothing from you for ages."

"Are you sure about that?"

"Of course I'm sure." She wasn't and shrugged aside the uncertainty. She had no room for such states of mind. The standard fitness questions rolled off her tongue.

"How are you keeping?"

"Could not be better."

"Are you eating properly?"

"Eating well enough."

"Are you sleeping properly?"

"When I don't get disturbed, yes."

Mother noticed that his voice sounded unusually flat and monotone. But then he was calling her on his mobile.

"You don't sound good."

"I sound fine."

"Have you been drinking?"

"No. I have not been drinking." Clarence highlighted each word of his denial for extra clarity.

His voice could not have sounded more unconvincing but it convinced her. And anyway she was too busy being delighted at having received a phone call from her son. She got phone calls from her loyal, loving daughter all the time, but from her son? No, those were special occasions.

"Looking forward to seeing you tomorrow."

"That's why I called."

"Why? What do you mean?"

Clarence gritted his teeth and reminded himself that he did not care.

"I'm afraid I'm going to have to cancel."

"Cancel? No. Impossible! It's tomorrow!"

"No I'm sorry but I must. I, I insist." He squeezed his mobile tightly, to death, as if willing it to fall apart under the strain; wishing for the connection to be broken. It wasn't. She was still there.

"Why? Why must we cancel? I am so much looking forward to seeing you: you, my only son."

"I'm just a bit under the weather right now." Clarence sounded feint. His voice sounded cracked. There was no crackle on the line.

"But you just said things were fine. Couldn't be better. That's what you said. Couldn't be better. I heard you."

Mum was demanding a full explanation and she would not let go until she got one. If necessary she would draw blood. Clarence knew that and still he didn't care. That said, he would do his best to give her one without divulging any secrets. After all she was his mum and that gave her certain rights, like the right to demand – unlike Dad: he was now a congenial best mate, most of the time.

"I'm just very tired. I've been out all day. Just got home and I am extremely knackered. Excuse my language."

Mother was far from sold the line. "But surely you'll be back to normal, rested, by tomorrow night? And hungry? A nice big meal will do you the power of good."

Clarence held his nerve. "I don't think so."

"You don't think so?"

"I don't think so." Clarence felt himself beginning to drain away, like melting ice-cream, or a bad joke.

Mother played the fury card. "You know you just can't do this to your mother. I'm your mother."

"No you're absolutely right. I can't." But he did, despite his stuttering voice and faltering conviction in the belief that he was doing the right thing.

"So am I going to see you tomorrow?" She sounded more upbeat, thinking she had won.

Clarence recovered. Something in his head had kicked in. "No you're not."

She hadn't so she played the disappointment card, her last remaining card.

"Well I'm very disappointed, very disappointed, heartbroken in fact."

Clarence felt obliged to apologize. "I'm sorry, very sorry."

"And so you should be."

"And so I am." Although he had won Clarence felt crushed. This did not feel like victory, more like defeat.

Requiring refreshment his mother moved on. "Your birthday's coming round again soon. What would you like me to get you this year?"

"I don't want anything."

"You don't want anything? What do you mean you don't want anything? You must want something."

Metaphorically speaking Clarence stood up again. "Well I don't. I don't want anything. I don't need anything."

"Don't be stroppy."

"I'm not being stroppy. I'm stating a fact." Clarence wanted to get angry now but he couldn't. Something was getting in the way and preventing him. He could only get frustrated.

"Well you're being difficult then." Mother had an idea. "I know I'll buy you a proper coffee making machine!"

"Why would I want something like that? I drink instant."

"Exactly. That's why you need one and I want to buy you one. That way you can serve us proper coffee."

"Thanks." Clarence looked to his wallpaper for inspiration. "Look can I go now?"

"Why what the rush? We haven't spoken in ages."

"No rush. I just need to go. As I said I'm very tired right now. It's been a long hard day."

"Why don't you let me organise a little birthday party for you? Nothing big and complicated just family and a few of your friends? And Tracey of course. Speaking of which how is Tracey?"

"She's fine."

Mother noted the lack of sparkle in his voice – and he had not referred to her by name: always a bad sign.

"When did you last see each other?"

"Can't remember."

"You can't remember?"

"No I can't remember. It's been a long time."

She was hanging off his every word, even those he repeated. "Well go and see her. Buy her some flowers."

"Tricky. Things are not great between us."

"Have you had a row?"

"Yes you could say that."

"Shame. I liked Tracey."

"She's not dead."

"She's got spunk."

"And spit."

Mother decided to bypass that comment. It didn't sound quite right. "Go see her. Make it up."

"I'll think about it."

"No don't think about it. Do it."

"I'll think about it."

"Girls like Tracey don't come along that often."

"They certainly don't."

"So promise me you'll go and see her?"

"For the last time Mum I'll think about it."

Mum finally took the point. "That's good. And what about the party?"

"No thanks."

The limp, languid reply did not dissuade her. "I could invite your uncle Ted, and your cousins. You haven't seen them in ages."

"No."

"What do you mean no?"

"I mean no. No thank you. I'm not in the mood." Each time he refused his mother something, said no, Clarence felt his willpower diluting, his lifespan shortening.

"But you haven't seen them for over a year – nor have I come to think of it. Probably two if my memory serves me right." Like her son her memory did not serve her right. It was only fourteen months. "It's about time we all got together."

"Honest I have no wish to see my cousins, especially on my birthday." Not caring, Clarence went for the full confession. It was well overdue and now was the perfect time to let it loose and send it packing. "We never get on."

"That's a terrible thing to say."

"No it isn't. And even if it was, sometimes the truth is terrible." This felt good he told himself.

Thrown off course, Mother shifted to firmer ground. "How is the teaching going?"

She was talking too much: Clarence wanted to scratch his balls. They had begun to itch. One was stuck to the side of his inner thigh. Body sweat was the adhesive. Gentle he pushed his finger in and prised apart the two surfaces which had become stuck together. One was hairy, almost prickly. The other was almost smooth by comparison. He began to scratch his balls, and when finished he started on his nostrils with equal relish.

"I don't know. No idea."

"Don't know? What do you mean you don't know?"

"I've been off work. Sick leave."

"Still off sick? I thought that was just one day? Just one day? One of those 'sickies' as you call them. You never told me it was serious!" She almost flew off the handle.

"What's there to tell? I was sick. Or rather I am sick."

"Sick. How are you sick? Have you been working too hard?"

Clarence grabbed the suggestion and pulled it in close to his heart. "Yes that's it. I've been working too hard. Needed time off and my Head kindly gave it to me. He's a great bloke my Head when he wants to be."

"Well you mustn't work yourself so hard."

"I'll try not to. But it's difficult. I just love my job so much."

"That's no reason to let things get out of control."

"No you're quite right. I mustn't let things get out of control."

"Well make sure you have a good rest."

"I will."

"Promise?"

"Promise. Can I go now?" Clarence was sure now he was in danger of passing out. His mother was siphoning off all his emotional energy. Physically, there was little left to be extracted.

"Your father's got a terrible cold."

"That's a shame."

"It's not funny. Not at his age."

"I wasn't being funny."

"Well it sounded like it." And it did.

"I really do have to go now."

She wasn't having it. "Don't hang up."

Confronted by a clear command he didn't. She was still very much in charge.

"Father's brought himself a new drill. The type without a plug. You don't have to plug it in."

"A cordless drill."

"I think so. He doesn't have to plug it in, get out the extension lead."

"He can't plug it in. It doesn't have a lead and plug. It's cordless. You recharge it."

"Well whatever."

"Please can I go now?"

"No, one more thing."

"What now."

"How often are they collecting your rubbish?"

"What?"

"How often are the council collecting your rubbish?"

"I don't know."

"You don't know? You must know. Weekly?"

"Yes weekly."

"Well now they're only going to collect mine once a fortnight."

"That is sad news." Clarence was back on track: he didn't care about; and on the particular issue of rubbish collection he couldn't care less.

"Not for another three months though."

"Not sad news yet then."

"No I suppose not. But it attracts rats they say."

Clarence had never cared for rats. "Please please can I go now? I really must go. I really must."

She had worn him out, good and proper. He barely had the strength to hold the mobile up to his ear. It wasn't heavy and it was mainly made of plastic but it felt like a ton of lead. And while it was on it was costing him a small fortune.

"When are you going to call me, see me, your mother?"

A mother had her son by the balls. Clarence knew it would hurt to break free was prepared to suffer the pain. It would be short term pain for the long term good, like the dentist's needle or the hairdresser's bleak conversation.

"I don't know. I'm going now. Bye."

He lowered his lead weight and pressed the red button, and she was disconnected, gone. She could be too much sometimes. She had taken years off him. He had to get them back. Also disconnected himself, Clarence wanted to throw his mobile across the room but something

· 470 ·

stopped him. Instead he pushed it under his pillow - logic being out of sight was out of mind - rolled over and stared up at the wallpaper. It was still there, green stripes climbing up his wall and grabbing all the attention. This time it felt like it was staring back down at him. In time he would doze off, for awhile without a care in the world, just casual defiance. At least that was the plan.

Rebecca stared down at the empty lines on the page, clicking her pen as if to maintain a beat. She was unable to compose – else afraid to express herself. Judy wandered into the room, purring, and leapt up into her lap. There she proceeded to make herself comfortable at Rebecca's expense. With her front paws she kneaded her human cushion and persuaded her human to stroke her. With the stroking the purring reached a new level of intensity. Judy was ready to explode.

Rebecca emptied her mug and kissed the top of Judy's head in gratitude. She had found her hook. She had her way in. She wrote down the date. Then immediately she scribbled it out. There would be no date. She did not want to slip into the mode of formal, precise correspondence. No. No date.

She could not bear to write the words 'Dear Clarence' but she could think of no other way to get going. With an unsteady hand she wrote down the two contentious words – two words loaded with the assumption that she still had some positive feelings towards the man, that manic man. That hurt.

'Dear Clarence' she wrote.

It mocked her. It gave him dignity through recognition. It was too much. Rebecca lifted herself up out of her chair, casting Judy aside like a terrible toddler who refused to stop clinging. For Judy that hurt.

Both stalked the room: one like any bad tempered big cat; the other like any bad tempered, elderly nun who was in danger of losing her faith, and knew it. With nowhere to go Rebecca was forced to sit back down. Furiously she scribbled over the words until they were obliterated. The act of vandalism made her feel better, but at a price: she was stuck again and her head was knotted up by an evil headache. Her head was threatening to crack open. She was unable to communicate with the very man to whom she had once turned for complete stewardship and security of her soul.

She wrote down the word 'Clarence' but that was still to give the bastard the dignity he did not deserve. Frustrated, she deleted this word with just two strokes of the pen and went to the next line. The obvious change of heart was appropriate and worth preserving.

She had to find something to say. She had to construct some spirited defence. She had to document his crimes. There was no avoiding this. She was not in a court of law but she felt surrounded by a panel of judges: all staring down at her and each taking notes; all waiting to pronounce her a weak and willing victim. She had to turn the situation around. Judy prowled the room as if for prey, knowing something was up. She created her own suspense, and revelled in it.

Rebecca saw his face again: so calm, so collected; so assured and confident in its message – a message designed to smash her into pieces, atomise her, leave her bleeding, reject her love. The words 'this is a typical response' stuck in her gut. And he never blinked. He had so much to say he didn't have time to blink. That made her angry too – angry that he was so confident that he had no need to blink like any other normal person.

And he had not tried to kiss her once. That had crushed her. She had wanted him to make love to her, explode inside her, and he had declined the offer. And that made her furious. Her body was not good enough for him. He thought himself better than her – the best even – and he did not desire to bond with her. She ran her fingers through her hair and tried to imagine it untangled, smooth and shiny like the stuff that got blown around on catwalks, like the stuff that was worth stroking.

She wanted to drink more wine but the mug had been emptied. She refilled it, telling herself not to drink so fast: make it last; slow down. The morning had gone so make the evening last. In an instant she contradicted herself and took a large swig. A voice on the radio – a man this time – shouted 'Get those pigs in mate! Get those flaming pigs in!' It was followed by the sound of noisy pigs.

Rebecca hurried back to her seat. She had her first word and was afraid to drop it. She wrote it down in capital letters and underlined it.

PIG!

It looked promising.

I simply cannot make sense of you. Has this all been one big game for you? Am I really such a joke? Do you take pleasure demolishing another human being? I cannot begin to describe the way I feel about you right now.

She proceeded to do just that – even if in a rather convoluted, twisted fashion, and with a slow start. She sat back to admire her work. She had her next line already waiting in her head.

You think you know it all.

The throbbing in her head began to tear into her. She sank more wine. There was no stopping her.

You can't treat me like this. I deserve better. I'm not your plaything, your experiment, your piece of cheap entertainment.

She began to shake. Judy jumped up into her lap again but was pushed off even before she had made a proper landed. Judy became dispirited, which for a domestic well-fed cat was a rare condition.

You don't love me. You don't love anybody. You only love yourself. You're incapable of love. You haven't got a clue about anything important. Who are you to judge me? Who are you to judge anybody? Is your life so perfect? I don't think so.

She sank more wine. Now it flushed away down her throat to do both its worse and its best at the same time.

You think you know everything and you don't even know how to smile – even on the brightest sunniest day of the year. You don't know how to kiss, how to make a woman happy.

The image of her first deadly 'boyfriend' rode roughshod into her head. Once he had smiled. Once he had smothered her with his heavy snogging. Now he was gone. Now she visualised him on his knees, cleaning out toilettes in some office block in the dead of night, barely making ends meet. Now she saw him trapped behind a supermarket till or a cramped desk in the City: a caged animal, stripped of all dignity and subject to constant scrutiny and evaluation. Now she saw him fat, overweight, unhappily married; smoking himself to death and avoiding his wife as she avoided him.

She tried to sink more wine but the mug was empty again. Dismissing her bitter thoughts she jumped up and made for the fridge – for the last time she told herself – telling herself on the way 'no more wine! no more wine! no more wine!' Judy followed, tail up in the air, sniffing the action. Quickly overtaking she took point and headed straight for her food bowl, hoping it would be refilled. She would be disappointed.

Opening the fridge – motor bursting into life as the cold air escaped – Rebecca told herself to drink no more wine, not one drop. She paid no attention and grabbed the bottle by the throat, crashing more wine into her mug. Then she plodded back to her unfinished business, on the way trying her best not to cry. Love was now hate. Pleasure was now pain. Virtue was now vice. Ready or not, an identity crisis was about to come crashing in, and with it the danger of a total, naked collapse. The hole in her stomach, the rip in her heart and the backlash in her head could not be repaired by words, neat expressions or dismissal of the truth. Judy rejoined her and like always sat down at her side, staring up and waiting for instructions. Rebecca tore into her drink and examined her handiwork. Her words, disfigured by haste, sprang back at her. They stank now but she could not turn up her nose. She was part of the smell.

Up one moment them down the next she shouted at Judy for not helping, for not empathising, for gawking at her as if all was right in the world; then she begged forgiveness and the chance to cuddle. But Judy was having none of it. There was something wrong, both in her mistress and in the air. The whole place felt electric. She retreated into a corner under the table, refusing to come out. The rainfall was now severe.

Rebecca fumbled around inside her head, fending off the enemy, snatching up his words and flinging them back in his face. But they were not mud and they did not stick. Instead they struck her down again on the rebound. Repetition did not dilute their force and they did not suffer from competition. Repeatedly she rubbed her free hand across her breasts in an attempt to relieve the pain which seem to erupt at times from her nipples. For her this time of the month was not a good time to be wound up.

As she tried to connect up the right words with which to counterattack, so she found herself turning on herself, the old enemy. She was the easier target. And the expressions she constructed she was driven to dismiss for fear of exposure: those which did make it to paper she obliterated. But they hung on inside her head, to agitate and aggravate her injuries. Not wishing to be the victim she stepped outside of herself. And some returned to see the light of day.

You always let me down. You must try harder. Try harder. You're in the wrong place now, and living a lie. Admit it. You've got it all wrong. So what are you going to do about it? Why do you bother? Why do you bother with anything? No one else bothers. No one else gives a damn. So let them all go to hell.

Rebecca wanted to throw up. Later she would throw up, and Judy would be distinctly unimpressed by the smell of the human sick which had been discharged from the stomach at speed.

When she ran out of space and turned over she laid down her pen. The next blank sheet of paper was too much to fill. She could not go on. She pulled her work from the pad, screwed it up and threw it at the wastepaper basket. It missed and Judy chased it across the room, battering it from side to side with her claws. It was fair game.

Clarence awoke abruptly, from a dream that didn't feel like it belonged to him. His bloody phone was ringing next door. Why the hell didn't Max answer it. Reason was Max had popped out to get milk from the garage, and possibly a sandwich if he could find one still edible, and with which he was prepared to engage his digestion system.

Clarence made a slow, sluggish move to get out of bed and onto his feet – onto his sprained ankle which he didn't much care to do. Then the phone stopped ringing so he collapsed back into his original, preferred position and back into his infatuation with his beautiful green striped wallpaper. It made him happy. Nothing else did right now.

Just as he began to settle and slip back into his altered state so the phone rang again. He buried his head further into the pillow and squeezed the pillow around it, like it was in danger of splitting open. No. Let her stew. She may be his mother but let her stew. He didn't care. And still it rang. And still the bastard didn't answer it. He rolled over and felt his sunburn across the back of his neck. If he touched it it would hurt like hell. He touched it. It hurt like hell. And still he didn't care. But it was his mother, a woman like no other. And she was determined to speak to him. He was stuffed, and suffocating. He dredged himself up and moved a bit faster on his feet this time: less the slug, more the terrified snail being chased by something that wanted to devour it.

Under fire he trooped into the living room, first taking a deep breath and dismissing whimsical but stupid thoughts: like wishing to be held in quarantine, in his own room, in a private hospital; like wishing to be slightly dead, if 'slightly dead' was a possible state of being. This time he got to the phone before she hung up. The rain was bad.

"Clarence, it's your dad."

Clarence relaxed a little. Dad sounded calm, sane. It was the voice of reason, but one accompanied by the sound of sniffing. Things were beginning to look up.

"I know it is."

"You've upset your mother you know. She doesn't like it. You're not playing by the rules."

"I know I'm not."

"So dinner's off I take it?"

"Afraid so."

"That's a shame."

"Yes."

Dad sniffed. "But can't you please at least just come round and see her? And while you're at it see me too?"

Clarence closed his eyes and reminded himself that he didn't care. (He needed convincing again.)

"I'm really knackered Dad."

"I'm also knackered, all the time these days. But I still make the effort. She's really worried about you. You must come and see her. Put her mind at rest. And give me some peace. Come round for lunch, tomorrow. It won't cost you a penny that way."

"Dad it's not about the pennies, or the pounds. I'm just so knackered right now."

"But you'll be okay tomorrow surely? After a good night's sleep? Mother will cook you a nice big lunch. She still loves to cook for her children."

"But I'm just so knackered."

"You don't have to stay long. Just do a flying visit. I promise not to let her wear you out."

Clarence conceded a little ground. There was that: saves having to cook; moreover saves having to wash up. All he had to do while he was there was keep his gob firmly zipped up.

"You must give her some space. We both know what she can be like sometimes but she's only worried about you. She can't let go of you. I know you're all grown up now –"

"Grown up. I certainly am that."

"But you're still her baby and she can't just let go of that fact. And right now she's very concerned for you, especially as you're off sick – you've been off sick for ages now I hear?"

"I have."

"So will you come round?" Dad sniffed.

"I just don't feel like it right now. Haven't got the energy. I'm exhausted."

"Why are you exhausted?"

"Been traipsing around the countryside, up and down hills, bumping into trees."

"What on earth for? And shouldn't you be tucked up in bed if you're off sick?"

"I was until the phone rang."

"So tell me why the countryside?"

"No idea. To see real trees and fields and enjoy a lovely view I suppose – oh and if my memory serves me right to feast on a picnic, just like they do in the movies."

"You can't remember if you had a picnic?"

"I can, just about, only vaguely."

"When did you do all this?"

"Today. If my memory serves me correctly."

"Stop saying that. You're starting to scare me." Dad became desperate. "Look you must come round and see us tomorrow. Please. Just do it for me. I promise we won't give you a bad time." His last swing of the axe struck a weak point in the armour, but it still bounced off.

"I'll think about it."

"I begging you please. I'm begging my own son. I've never had to do that before."

"There's always a first time."

"And stop that right now."

"Stop what?"

"That sarcasm. Mother may not notice it but I do, every time. It's not nice and it's beneath you."

"Sorry." Clarence meant what he said. He was sorry. Upsetting his dad was one of his few remaining no-no's.

Dad sniffed. "So please will you come round?"

"Only if you promise not to mention my bad memory to her. She'll only crawl all over me, all worried."

"Okay I promise. And you promise to come and see us?"

The last switch was thrown in his head, the one which made all the difference. And like a man not in love, standing exhausted at his own wedding ceremony and trying to withstand a nasty hangover, Clarence spoke softly and made his grave promise.

"Yes I promise."

"Good. I'm glad that's settled."

"I'm not." Clarence wanted to throw the switch back.

"There you go again. Stop it."

"Stop what? I wasn't being sarcastic I was stating a fact." Clarence swore his father was starting to sound like his mother. Time to cut the conversation.

"Well stop it, whatever it is. And we'll see you tomorrow?"

"For the last time yes."

"That's good then."

"Maybe." Now Clarence was being sarcastic. "Can I go now?"

"And things are not going too well with Tracey?"

"No they are not." Clarence waited for the next sniff. It was due about now.

On cue Dad sniffed. "Well no matter. I wish you luck. They are the hardest things to get your head around sometimes."

"What are?"

"Women. The mortgage, kids and the job I could handle, but the women just wore me out."

Clarence had to cut him off before he got going again about his childhood spent surrounded by women: sisters and his own mother.

"Thanks Dad. I'll bear it in mind."

"And you definitely don't want a party this year?"

"Definitely not."

"Fair enough. But surely a present? Let me buy you a present – from both of us of course."

Clarence relented. He needed one less skirmish to fight: just concentrate on the main battle. "Okay just a present then. Just something small. Don't go spending too much money."

"Don't worry I won't."

The joke was fully appreciated and it galvanised Clarence. He threw another log onto the fire – a fire which up to now he had been trying to extinguish.

"How's your terrible cold? You keep sniffing."

"You're being sarcastic again."

Clarence was piqued. "No I'm not. Mum said you had a terrible cold."

"Well rest assured I don't. It's just a normal cold. It will be gone soon."

"And how's your lovely new drill?"

"I don't know. I haven't had a need to use it yet. It's still in its packaging."

"So why did you buy it?"

"Saw it going cheap in a sale. The current one is so clapped out it won't last - and this one doesn't need the extension lead out."

"Fair enough."

"You can have the old one if you want."

"No thanks. If I need a hole drilled I'll just ask you to come round and do it."

"Fair enough."

"So you are coming round then?"

"For the last time. Yes."

"Good. Just checking."

"Now leave me alone. I have a DVD to get through."

"Understood. Bye, and take care."

"I will. Bye." Clarence put his phone down first. His dad held on to his, just in case his son wanted to say something more, and sniffed.

Breathing a huge sigh of relief that this conversation had not been as bad as the first, Clarence began the slow journey back to his bedroom, back to his lifeboat, pillow and wallpaper. Progress was poor. He was hampered by major indecision: having lied about the DVD he now felt compelled to make amends and watch one. Leaning against the living room door he fumbled about inside his head for a suitable choice. At which point the front door opened and Max stepped inside, clutching a carton of milk and a big BLT sandwich, feeling happy – then not so happy when he saw his landlord, Crazy Clarence, on the prowl. He held back. He had to find another place to stay, and fast. Electric cable had to be laid, and fast. And women had to be laid, and fast. Then back to his lovely Ireland – no cable or women to be laid but better Guinness and better conversation.

Clarence gave up on the DVD idea and restarted his journey back to his room. He had too much fiction already inside his head. He didn't need more of it. He registered Max but avoided eye contact and the two slipped around each other like opposite ends of a magnet. Even so Clarence was driven to speak up: there was a hint of a smirk on the face of his lodger.

"I know what you think of me."

"I'm not saying anything."

With nowhere to go but wishing to be elsewhere Rebecca took to exploring the length and breath of her flat, perusing and rediscovering all the objects which littered her living space. Once they had consumed her attention, energies and finances over the years for no other reason except that they were there to be consumed. Most of it now stood for nothing more than pointless decoration: now out of date and out of fashion; without purpose except to remind her of her extravagant, almost delusional ambitions to make the world a better place. She felt the compulsion to chuck out all the clutter and start afresh. But she held off and the trash remained in place, surreptitiously stealing her living space for no return.

She returned to the living room and stepped up to a large poster depicting part of the Brazilian rainforest, one bearing the scars of intensive deforestation. It had hung there for years – for how long she had forgotten – and now it had faded, with regard to both the colour of the print and the strength of its message. It had ceased to make any emotional impact. It wanted her to save the rainforest. These days she just wanted to save herself.

Once it had inspired her, stimulated her. Now it annoyed her. It was a constant reminder that she was in fact powerless to change or influence any situation, deflect any danger, set any moral standard. She pulled it down and ripped it up into small pieces. The act of destruction energized her and she looked around the room for other obsolete items to rip up, break up, or smash up. For now there were none. She gathered up the pieces and stuffed them proudly into the wastepaper basket, catching sight of her discarded letter of protest just as a thunderclap struck. Judy panicked and darted around the room, making 90 and 180 degree turns as she sought better cover. She ended up back under the table, in the corner up against the wall. There she sat screwed up tight, unsure if the worse of it was over.

Rebecca gave her no comfort. She stared into the pile of scrap paper she had created with a growing feeling of regret. It was a cop-out. She was angry with him and she wanted him to know it. She retrieved her piece of paper, smoothed it out and rewrote it, neatly; editing as she went to remove those bits which had nothing to say about him and everything to say about her. This time the words did not hurt half as much. Furthermore a little devil popped up inside her, inviting her, enticing her to write her worst and scare the living daylights out of the nasty, two-timing monster who had tried to devour her. Enjoy watching him crumble under the onslaught. It was a good idea so on she went. The pen, clutched tightly in her hand this time, she kept firmly pressed against the paper, its tip almost piercing through the paper. She pushed out each word with short strokes, chiselling as she went. But she did not remain composed for long and soon lapsed back into scribbling at speed, and on the way fell back into confession.

Exhausted again, she laid down her pen again, telling herself that it was not finished. There was plenty more to say - once she had recovered her strength. For now she was willing to hug Judy but Judy was not having any of it. Judy was still recovering from her own near collision with a nervous breakdown. And still it rained cats and dogs.

There was a thunderclap and it made the phone ring, and it made Clarence swear to high heaven and leap out of bed. This was getting to be impossible. 'For the last time' constituted a key part of the swearing. He rushed to snatch it up. The phone refused to lie down and die.

"Yes," he almost shouted.

"It's me." The words transmitted an air of grievance.

Things were not looking up. It was his sister. The moment she opened her mouth Clarence could tell that she was spoiling for a fight. He told himself he was ready for it. Ready or not he was ready. Let her do her worse.

"And what do you want?"

Clarence made no attempt to sound welcoming, the opposite in fact. It was quite plain he could not wait to be rid of her. Margaret was stung but not deterred. The black sheep of the family had to be spoken to, just as wasps had to be crushed and flies had to be squatted; and difficult husbands had to be contained, sometimes coaxed.

"I rang to check up on how you are."

The statement sounded contrived and right now Clarence didn't believe in coincidence.

"You've been talking to mum haven't you?"

Margaret made no bones about it. "Okay what if I have. I can still check to see how you are."

"I'm fine." Clarence lied gracefully. Anything to get rid of sister.

"Explain what is going on."

"Nothing is going on."

"Something is going on."

"Your mistake."

"Mother says you won't go and see her. Mother's very upset."

"I guess she would be."

"So what are you going to do about it?"

"Absolutely nothing."

"What! Why won't you go and see her?"

"I will."

"You will what?"

"I will go and see her – for lunch – tomorrow."

"Well that was easy."

"No it wasn't. I had already promised Dad I would go round tomorrow."

"Oh." Margaret was nearly thrown from her high saddle. "Well just you make sure you do that then."

"Yes sir."

Her route blocked, Margaret immediately jumped into another subject. It was a technique she had picked up from her mother.

"You can't go on like this."

"Like what?"

"Like . . . I don't know. Just stop being sick and get back to school."

"I'll stop as soon as I can - when I feel like it. Anything else?"

"I take it you haven't got it back together with Tracey?"

"No."

"And have no intention to?"

"No."

"I thought not."

"And why's that exactly?"

"You're seeing Mary now."

"Who said I was seeing her?"

"She did."

Clarence was stumped. One all at half-time. No injury time yet.

"Well . . . I don't know about that."

"Well you sort yourself out soon. You're confusing her."

"Thanks for the advice."

"No problem."

"Your ability to deliver it on tap, in a continuous stream almost, never ceases to amaze me."

"Good. And so it should. I'll take that as a compliment."

"It wasn't meant to be one."

"I'm sure it was."

"Trust me. It wasn't."

Two one to Clarence.

Despite the brotherly battering still Margaret would not let go. "Aren't you going to ask me how are things with Mary?"

"No why should I?"

"Because you should."

Clarence surrendered the moment and responded as requested, though now back to sounding as flat as a pancake.

"And how are things with Mary?"

"The poor woman is confused. She wants to know when – if – she'll see you again." Margaret waited. No response. "Well?"

"I don't know. I'm also confused. Tell her to hang in there."

"Hang in there? I don't think I can tell her that."

She dug her nails in and Clarence felt it.

"Well tell her something. I can't right now."

Clarence could hear air being expelled from his sister's nostrils at high speed. It was not a pleasurable sound.

"You amaze me sometimes." Likewise her remark was not meant to be taken as a compliment, and nor was it.

"I amaze myself sometimes."

And still his sister had more. "And what's all this I'm hearing about you not finishing her tiling?"

"What about it?"

"Get your act together Clarence. Get your act together. Just because you're off work sick is no excuse."

Two all.

"Sounds like a good excuse to me.

Three two to Clarence.

"Right, that's enough dear brother. I'm going now."

"Good. I think you've overstayed your welcome."

"I think I better go before I say something I regret."

"Likewise."

"And you'll be there tomorrow?"

"Yes. How many times do I have to say it. YES."

"Well you make sure you turn up."

"I will."

"And you make sure you stay on your best behaviour. Don't be rude."

Clarence could see her wagging her finger. He wanted to bite if off.

"Anything else?"

Margaret thought for a moment while Clarence began to rock the phone back and forth, impatient that the traffic lights had not changed and he was still stuck.

"And don't say anything to Mum or Dad you might regret afterwards."

"Anything else?" Clarence noted, with almost devilish glee, that she had not included herself in the list.

"And don't come round to our place unless invited. I don't want you upsetting Desmond."

That was a fair point, and a request he was more than happy to comply with.

"Anything else?"

"I don't think so."

Suddenly Clarence had something else. "You're not going to be there are you?"

"No. Rest assured I'm not."

Four two to Clarence. Still no injury time.

Margaret wanted to squeeze her brother's testicles. Once, when they were a lot younger and even more antagonistic towards each other, she had made such an attempt. But he had stopped her just in time. She had been nine so had not realised the full implications of her attempted assault.

Had his sister said yes it would have been the perfect excuse for Clarence to change his mind, on grounds of health and safety. But she hadn't, so he didn't. He would go round there he promised himself, say little of substance – preferably nothing – stuff his face and get out quick; perhaps to South America, or Cornwall.

"Goodbye then. And give my regards to Des."

"I don't think so."

"Fair enough then."

Five two to Clarence. Final whistle. No injury time.

"Goodbye." And with that Margaret slammed her phone down sharpish, this time seriously stung.

Clarence was over the moon. Sister was gone. That last bit had felt good. It was all becoming hysterical. He had got rid of her in style. He executed a hysterical laugh. Rock on. Max almost jumped out of his skin and nearly pissed himself. He was about to visit the bathroom to have a pee. He held back, waiting instead to see what Crazy Clarence did next.

Clarence drifted back to his room, avoiding the straight line, even slower this time - so slow that he was in danger of going backwards. From the safety of the kitchen – though what exactly was safe about the kitchen was not clear – Max watched him get stuck between rooms, as if unsure where he truly wanted to end up. And still clutching his precious carton of milk, Max waited for the kettle to boil. Crazy Clarence looked dead, else dangerous, else dangerously close to death. (And they say the Irish are mad.) It was like watching the walking dead lose their way.

Finally Clarence reignited, kicked open his bedroom door, stormed in, and slammed it shut behind him. He fell back onto his bed, with such velocity and such ferocity that he almost bounced off it, like it was a trampoline and he was a big kid, acting crazy. Seeing the coast was clear Max put down his milk and headed for the bathroom. He had to have that piss. The kettle reached boiling point and switched itself off. The mobile phone tucked under the pillow followed suit as best it could - in the only way it could - and switched to standby. Later Max would switch off, but not Clarence.

He stared at the wallpaper, now with the added load of Tracey being back in his thoughts. Perhaps, he wondered. He admonished himself. No you're clutching at straws, and for what purpose a few straws?

He wanted a bath but could not bring himself to run it.

He wanted a bacon sandwich but could not be arsed to fry the bacon.

He wanted to dial up a curry but could not remember the number, and was not prepared to go hunting for it.

He wanted a cigarette but he had none in the house. He had thrown his last packet away and he could not bring himself to ask Max for a fag.

He wanted to strap up his ankle but could not drag himself across the floor to the chest of drawers where there were bandages mixed in somewhere with his socks, underpants and handkerchiefs.

He wanted the cramp to go away but it didn't.

He wanted his duvet dry-cleaned. It smelt rank again.

He wanted to feel great but knew he was in trouble.

He wanted to settle old scores but was lost for ideas, and didn't know who to settle them with.

He wanted to punch Mad Max in the face but knew that would be suicide.

He wanted to give up teaching but did not know what else he could do, if anything.

He wanted a shag but he was alone in the room.

He wanted a wank but didn't feel the time was right.

Fall asleep now, Clarence told himself. Keep staring at the wallpaper and give it all up; and you might, you might just manage to drift off, back into dreamland – a dangerous place these days but no more dangerous than reality. And funnily enough he did exactly that.

And he dreamed of jumping up and down on a cat. And he dreamed of flying saucers – the shiny ones made from tin which had flow in during the 1950's. And he dreamed of sheep. And he began to count them, even though he was already asleep and dreaming, of sheep. And he dreamed of treading in someone else's shit. And he dreamed of making love to lots of women, next-door neighbour included. And he dreamed of being punched in the face by one of them.

✧ ✧ ✧

Log Entry

Mother-child communication is intense when there is a conflict of interest or expectation. The language used is sometimes heavily loaded with emotional blackmail. And there is an obvious imbalance of respect. The mother drains her child's resources of energy as a result of inflicting general discomfort and perhaps even a sudden feeling of inferiority. This is probably not intentional but it is routine. The child has no choice except to give, and to defer judgement on the situation. It cannot resist. The feeling of inadequacy may fester long after contact is broken.

It is a state of affairs which kicks off in childhood, when the child is old enough to register it's mother's impact upon self-esteem and self-determination. It later intensifies, amplifies and becomes entrenched as a modus operandi when the child is able to gauge such interactions – collisions even - as one-sided. This usually happens long after puberty when the child considers itself fully mature, and can remain in place for the rest of its life.

Within the same context, father-son communication is a different matter. It is built upon a sense of equality, real or not, and a shared sense of justification – justification on both sides that the particular communication is necessary – along with the recognition that resolution is the aim. Words are exchanged with a sense of ease, even where there is a conflict, and open, direct negotiation is considered to be an acceptable approach. It could be considered more efficient. Emotional outbursts are curtailed, else wrapped up tight inside packets of discourse: be they demands or disclaimers; invitations, interference or insistence.

Chapter Nineteen

After a few false starts the old woman managed to tie up her shoe laces. After one false start she evacuated her easy chair, entered the kitchen, and tugged hard on the backdoor until it gave way. She stepped out into the sun as if on the lookout for gold, or chasing paradise. With a stern expression and without regard for her physical condition she set off, shuffling along. Always loyal, Lassie went with her. She ignored the delights of her garden and headed straight for the garden gate. Over time its hinges had suffered but it could still be opened, at a pinch, by most old ladies. She was one of those old ladies. It opened and she was out, with Lassie racing ahead when he was not racing back to start the race again. Then on to the railway bridge, then under it, and beyond. By the time she reached the allotments she had to sit down to catch her breath – all of it. Luck was with her: she found a weathered old chair, or rather the remains of one. It was a shadow of a chair: it had no top half and most of its varnish had peeled off. It was dirty, but not so dirty that it could not be sat on. It still functioned as a chair, and in that sense it could still be classed as 'standing proud'. Lassie made circles then stopped to take a pee.

The old woman took in the sights, in particular the short thin strip of land she had once cultivated. In return for her devotion it had given her joy through achievement. And it had been her medicine with regards to counteracting the sometimes torturous impact of the never-ending passage of time, and the hours which had to be consumed, hungry or not. It was like having to chew your way through a mountain of pasta, from the bottom up and from within, with no end in sight and with its full weight bearing down.

Beyond the runner beans the head of an old man popped up. He saw her and swung his watering can up into the air, once, in a basic, simple gesture of recognition. It was that old man. Today she did not ignore him. She waved back, once, with a clean sweep of the arm. Simplicity was the communication protocol. He came towards her, zigzag fashion, his route being roundabout, his speed not much quicker than hers. As the gap closed a spark jumped between their faces and smiles flickered. He said hello but did not address her by name. He had forgotten it. She sensed this so did the same. She knew his name was Peter. Time was short these days: he brushed past extended introductions involving state of health and instead went straight for points of interest.

"I take it that was your daughter I saw?"

"That was."

"Do you want your cup of tea? I've still got your mug."

"Yes please. Is it clean?"

"I'll make it clean. Follow me."

She struggled to get up and struggled to keep up. He did not offer a hand up and he did not adjust his speed down. But she made it: into the spare deckchair he kept for guests. It needed a good scrub. He brewed up using his portable gas stove and planted a mug of tea in her hand. He couldn't remember her name but he remembered she took milk and sugar, and he forgot to take the teabag out. He lowered himself down into his own deckchair and together they surveyed the scene: tea and no talking, that was the rule.

It had barely changed. Everything was growing as it should be: right colour, right shape, right height; right place and right time. (The definition of 'right place' had changed over the years from 'here' to 'there', from 'over there' to 'over here'.) Everything was growing with distinction and strength - and due to the old man's dogged efforts, few enemies. It was proving to be an exceptionally good year. This year he had beaten back the slugs after a long bitter campaign involving salt and bad homemade beer as the main tactical weapons. This year no blight had hit his tomatoes. He had nothing to say: from his point of view everything was back to normal after a three year gap.

"Has it been a good year for gardening?"

"Every year's a good year for gardening."

"Those beans are just running away this year."

"Well they are runner beans. I've got a few left in the freezer from last year. Want some?"

"I expect so." The old woman looked down into her mug. "Yes I'm sure I will. Yes please."

"Remind me nearer the time."

She didn't think to ask him what time.

The old man looked down at the dog. It now registered as a threat. "You've still got that dog."

"Lassie."

"Stupid name for a Scots terrier."

"He likes it. And he's a Scottish terrier."

"But shouldn't he be a collie?"

"He doesn't want to be."

"Fair enough. Just don't let him do it in my soil."

"I won't." She beckoned Lassie to calm down and sit down at her side. "Three years. Who would have believed it."

"Believe what?"

"Three years. How time flies. Feels like only yesterday."

"Not for me. Each year has its place. What's three years?"

"And do they take their toll?"

"What, years? Only if I let them. And I don't."

"And you have your allotment."

"And that."

"Are you still seeing your boys?"

"Roger on and off. Tom only once a year."

"That's a shame."

"Not at all. He's gone to New Zealand. He's very happy over there. Best decision he ever made. Now Roger wants to go as well."

"How is your wife?"

"She's dead."

"Oh I'm sorry."

"Don't be. She went off happy. She had been in a lot of pain and she felt useless. She hated being useless. We cremated her. That night I dragged the boys down the pub and demanded we got pissed. They didn't take to the idea at first but soon came round to it after a few pints of toasting her memory. Then Tom buggered off to New Zealand." Bored of retelling his same old story the old man shut up.

The old woman decided to give a little back.

"Michael's doing well for himself. Hires out farm machinery and workers to go with them. Yvonne is happily married – I think – and raising her family like there's no tomorrow, and not much of today for that matter."

That was enough information for the old man. He sat on his thoughts. She followed suit. He focused on the jobs to be done tomorrow. She did the same. For both of them 'tomorrow' was the only unit of time that mattered now: for him, as many tomorrows as possible; for her, tomorrow in particular. Thoughts crumbled and fell to pieces when the mobile went off in her jacket pocket.

"You've got one of those things."

"Yes my daughter makes me carry it whenever I go out. Usually I forget to turn it on."

"You didn't this time."

"No. Excuse me."

It was the daughter shouting into her phone that she had made it to the M25 junction but was now stuck in heavy traffic which was barely moving probably due to the road works and the redirected lanes and the fact that it was Saturday. And it was dammed hot and she hoped this hard work and sacrifice was being fully appreciated back there. Her mother reassured her that it was. The daughter promised to give further updates and abruptly ended the call, returning to Radio Two and her bottle of warm mineral water. The Mondeo in front suddenly moved ten feet as if in a hurry. The daughter did likewise, as did the guy behind. They were all impatient to move their lives on. They were all in a hurry. With total freedom of choice they had all chosen to go the way of the M25. The guy behind could claim back his petrol and lunch on expenses. The other two were not so lucky.

✛ ✛ ✛

Clarence stood transfixed and inert, zombie-like outside his parents' front door, nose almost touching and almost out of joint as he contemplated some form of substitute death and how to achieve it. On the journey over his support for the idea of family contact had collapsed but the more he had tried to turn back the more he had pushed on. Now he was here and his last line of defence, the closed door, was about to be cast aside. Unwilling to be restrained, his better half shook off the other half and poked the doorbell in the eye, just once. He heard the sound of footsteps come thundering towards him, racing like a fire engine towards the reported fire. The door was thrown open. It was his mother of course. He was late. She was going loopy. He had no defence.

She did not like what she saw: in particular the mark on his face, the fading traces of a bruise. When asked, Clarence explained it away as an unfortunate encounter with a large, shoulder-high branch of a tree while out exploring. She accepted this and moved on: grabbing him, hugging him; checking him over and pulling him inside into her own comfort zone. It was a large comfort zone: the size of a semi-detached. Clarence floated in on a whim and put up no resistance. Resistance was useless - though he drew the line when she tried to check behind his ears.

Dad was lingering inside, uncertain of his part in the unfolding drama and not keen to make enquiries. Upon his release Dad also checked his son up and down his length and breath: more going through the motions as he looked for signs of anything amiss. He found nothing except a truly vacant look. He put it down to fatigue. He had seen it before, usually after binge drinking the night before.

Mother thanked her son for making the effort and asked how he was keeping. Clarence said that he was fine. She asked about the sunburn. Did it hurt? Clarence said it was fine. She looked at the bruise, more closely this time. It was on its way down but she guessed it must have started off nasty. She asked if that too hurt and Clarence reassured her that it was fine. Each time he spoke he was deflating his situation and containing hers. He was slowly and systematically strangling to death the small talk Mum insisted on deploying. He was not being cruel, only perfunctory.

Mother raced on. "I nearly rang. It was getting so late I thought perhaps you were not turning up."

"I did think about it."

"Oh."

"Sprained ankle," explained Clarence, quickly letting himself off the hook. "I sprained it yesterday but it's bandaged up now so I can walk on it, with difficulty."

"Your walk in the woods?" asked Dad.

"That's right."

Mum looked down and took his word for it. (There was nothing to see of course.)

"Oh. Well, thank you for coming. It is appreciated."

Clarence jumped a beat. "Is lunch ready now?" He did not want to stand around like a lemon.

"Yes, more than ready. I've had it on hold."

With that announcement he headed for the dining room, scuppering his mother's plan for a nice long cosy chat. Forced to participate, she watched him move gingerly across the carpet and sit himself down in his usual place. Despite his injury he had moved at speed. It was rapidly becoming apparent to her that her son had no wish to hang about. To be fair he did look exhausted so she decided to let him be and instead concentrate on fulfilling her side of the bargain: to get good food inside him, and lots of it. Send him home well-fed. She returned to the kitchen leaving Dad wondering which way to turn: kitchen or living room; wife or son. He decided to keep watch – stand guard even - and stood at the dining table opposite his son. He was on the lookout for signs of animation. He even tried – repeatedly - to sponsor a conversation. He failed each time as his son showed a distinct lack of cooperation or interest in any subject raised, including even premier league football. To keep himself occupied he opened a bottle of wine, then wished he hadn't when Clarence refused a glass. No one else would be drinking it. He wanted to return to his shed.

Lunch progressed much like a well-managed, low-key funeral service: little was said of an upbeat nature and a sense of deferential gloom hung over proceedings; but no crisis, no tears, no outbursts of faked anguish. Mother served up chicken soup and was pleased to witness her son demolish two servings at speed. He may have had nothing to say but he had not lost his appetite. He may have looked worn out but he could still find the energy to attack with nothing more than a spoon. This brought some measure of comfort. Her appetite returned. (Dad's had never gone away.) Now she just had to get him talking: coerce him into light conversation then perhaps heavy.

Dad, now convinced that Clarence was just in one of his moods, detached himself from events and glided back into his preferred agenda for the weekend. This included extended amounts of time spent hiding out in the shed, pottering about, paying attention to detail, reorganising; else looking things up in books; else watching television; at worse taking his wife down to the shops then waiting in the car while on the lookout for traffic wardens and those determined to sponge down his windscreen for that inflated fee.

Things seemed to pick up when Mother served her son what she considered to be his favourite dish: homemade beef burger and chips; accompanied by a quality side salad, one bursting with complexity and creativity. It was there to keep balance, stop the slippage, negate the fast food factor; to set her mind at rest by reassuring her that she had not let standards slip.

One by one – sometimes two or three – Clarence loaded up his fork with chips, stabbing each one like he was in possession of a death warrant. Then things warmed up: not only did a smile break out across his face but he started to talk about the weather as he cut into his burger and dug around in the salad bowl for the juicy bits - the bits worth pursuing but buried under lettuce. He even asked Mum if she was going to receive a council reduction for the change to a fortnightly collection. His brain appeared to have switched back on. She put it down to plenty of meat.

Then things took a turn for the worse: his sister turned up, uninvited yet acting like she was on time.

Once she was through the door Margaret bounded on in to where she thought the action was. Mother tried to keep up. Dad was pleased to see her, Clarence definitely not. She said yes to salad and the spare burger which Mum had been holding back as seconds for her Clarence, but declined the chips. She sat opposite her brother and monitored his behaviour. She did not comment on his condition, only the salad, which she said was good, worth repeating. She did not say it was brilliant. With two woman in the room the pickled talk picked up. Interest in Clarence was put to one side, but not for long.

With her daughter by her side, reinforcing her position as unelected head of the household, Mother proceeded to dig into her son and prise open details of his current domestic regime. She did not have to be a locksmith, only an extremely patient, results orientated social worker. He had nothing to hide, only a lack of interest in her concern for his welfare and disregard, possibly disdain, for the fact that anything so unimportant to him could be important to her. He was bluntly dismissive until Margaret stepped in and forced him to cooperate. Dad, bored by now and unable to shore up his son's position, left the room to get fresh air: let them do their worse, Clarence could take care of himself.

When Mother enquired about his eating habits she was not impressed. Dissatisfied by the description of his domestic arrangements – or rather the lack of them – she volunteered to visit regularly, to clean up and cook. The free offer did not go down well with Margaret. Normally she would have protested, exploded even, but today she forced herself to keep her mouth shut – except when her brother's mouth needed to be forced open. When, for some strange reason, Mother asked if Tracey cooked for him that was when Margaret opened her mouth wide and spilt the beans.

Mother was indignant. "Why didn't you say something yesterday?"

"I didn't want you to be concerned," Clarence replied, disingenuously. Real reason was he couldn't be bothered. Now he was bothered: sister was beginning to seriously bother him.

"So is there any chance of you two making things up?"

"I don't think so."

Clarence looked up at his sister, a piece of burger dangling from the end of his fork, fat dribbling from its interior. On a large scale it would not have been a pretty sight.

"Correction: I'm sure. Definitely not." He sounded exhausted tired but very sure of himself.

"That is a shame," said Mother. She definitely felt for him.

"Yes it is," added his sister for effect. She did not.

"No believe me it's not."

"Well is there anything else I should know?" asked Mother abruptly, never happy to be the last to receive news.

The question was knee-jerk and Clarence was under no obligation to answer. His sister decided to answer on his behalf.

"He's been off sick because he's been having these blackouts."

Margaret braced herself for a backlash, possibly a denial, but neither was forthcoming. Clarence remained strangely subdued, in control. This lack of hostilities, the refusal to come out fighting, wound her up. Adrenalin was her drug, far more than alcohol. Meanwhile Mum bore down on him. And still he was unflinching.

"Why didn't you tell me this before?"

"Because I didn't want you to worry." Clarence was telling the truth this time.

"How many? How much?"

It didn't last. He went back to lying again, seesawing, refusing to be made to feel guilty. He was determined to hang on to his secrets.

"Not that many. Not that much." He locked onto his sister, head on, as if challenging her to a duel, challenging her to contradict him. She declined.

"And before you ask: I did see somebody. He found nothing. It was just a passing phase."

"So it's all over now? These blackout things have stopped?"

"Yes."

"Well that's some good news I suppose." Relieved, Mother got up and picked up two plates: destination dishwasher. She could not conceive of her children ever telling her a barefaced lie. They watched her go with equal interest. Alone together, both had something to say. Margaret got her oar into deep water first.

"You're lying."

"Says who?"

"Says me. You should be ashamed of yourself."

"Your favourite expression. I'm only ashamed of one thing."

"And what's that?"

"That I've hung on to guilt for so long – worse still the trivial kind."

Margaret was rattled. She sat up. Her brother was not talking proper, like normal. "What are you blabbering on about?"

Having put the question, she was not sure now she wanted to hear the answer, especially as Mum had just walked back into the room to pick up the remaining plates. She had to feed her dishwasher.

"Guilt: that thing which distracts us, holds us back, soaks up energy better spent in other pursuits, like making amends. Guilt: that thing which simply creates a dilemma with a long torturous lifespan. Guilt: that thing which can break us."

"Give it a rest brother."

Mother was more conciliatory. "Clarence are you feeling alright?"

"I'm feeling fine Mum, never better."

She picked up the remaining plates, stacking one on top of the other, and then the salad bowl. She was ready to go.

Clarence turned on his sister again. Something bad was brewing and she felt it coming her way.

"Margaret, I owe you an apology."

Before she could react or he could elaborate, Dad wandered back in. Seeing the clear up in progress he made the obvious suggestion. As was his way he did not help in the clear up itself.

"Shall I put the coffee on?"

Clarence was the first to sign up. "Yes please that would be good." He turned back to his sister. "As I said I owe you an apology."

"Why? Why do you think you owe me an apology?" Whatever it was she didn't want an apology, at least not on his terms.

"Oh but I do. I should have made it years ago."

"If this is about me marrying Desmond I don't want to know. You've made your position quite clear."

"No it's not about you and him."

"Good." In her mind it wasn't good: 'good' meant there was more to come, which was bad.

"I broke a promise."

"You broke a promise?"

"To you."

"And you want to make an apology?"

"I do. I need to get it off my mind."

Margaret pushed her chair back as she pushed the confession forward. "And what was this promise you broke?"

"Are you sure you really want to know?"

"I really want to know. I'm fascinated," she said, sounding just like him. Now she really was rattled: she didn't want to know but now she had to know.

"I promised not to reveal your secret about that fling you had at university with that other girl. It was during your first year. Remember?"

Margaret turned deathly pale. Her muscles tensed up and her body fat hardened into stone. She gripped the armrests, squeezed, and held on for dear life. She didn't answer. She dare not answer. She could not answer. She simply looked on, gawping and wondering if her brother had gone stark raving mad. She concluded he had. He was mental.

"Alice was her name if I remember correctly. She was an English student. A nice girl but lonely, insecure. And you were a bit mixed up then. Remember? Surely you remember?"

"Yes I remember. Thank you for reminding me." The words crawled out as if from under a stone and Margaret glared back, making it quite obvious that she wanted him dead, strung up.

Clarence did not get the message. He carried on smiling, at ease with himself, as if he had done her a big favour, one which was well overdue.

"I told Tim – my friend Tim – and probably a few others. My only excuse is that I was drunk at the time – no not an excuse, just an explanation of how it happened. A loose tongue. I have no excuse. It was inexcusable."

"I need to put the dishwasher on," said Mother quietly, before hurrying out of the room. The dishwasher was barely stacked and would not be switched on for ages yet.

She brushed past Dad on the way out. He re-entered the room with a tray loaded up with everything required to drink a cup of coffee except the coffee itself. He steadied himself, having only just avoided a collision. The coffee had yet to come.

Clarence continued. "I was very immature at the time – we both were I believe – and I think it was done in a fit of jealousy: jealousy that you were getting all the action, lots of erotic sex and I wasn't. When men think of two women making love it sometimes sends them crazy. Nothing personal."

Dad, alarmed and wishing to retain neutrality, left the room to get the coffee. In the kitchen he was filled in on the facts. From then on Mum and Dad could not help but listen in on their children's latest collision come blow-up.

Margaret stood up, almost falling over in the process. If looks could kill Clarence should not have still been drawing breath.

"You bastard."

She did not shout – although she dearly wanted to – not wishing to be overheard. She did not even speak loudly. It was closer to a condemning whisper – but still it was overheard. Dad – his hearing better than his wife's - hurried back in, suspecting a peacekeeper was needed. Somehow the coffee did not seem important right now.

"Okay calm down both of you."

"I am calm Dad," announced Clarence. "But she's not."

"Fuck off Clarence."

"See what I mean."

"Language please."

"If I want to say fuck off I will say fuck off. I'm not a child."

"No one said you were."

There was no holding her back.

"Secrets? I'll give you secrets you little shit. Do you remember the time we had to share that tent and I had to put up with you masturbating inside your sleeping bag like I didn't matter, like I wasn't there? You were so stupid back then you didn't think I would notice. You still are stupid – even if you do teach."

Clarence had an answer to that and gave it, calmly, dispassionately. "I wasn't stupid. I knew you would notice but I was just desperate. You are at that age when you don't have a girlfriend."

Dad, outnumbered, called for reinforcements. "Sheila! I think you should get in here fast!"

Clarence remained steady, unnaturally calm in what was turning into an extremely tense family confrontation. His coolness under fire added to his sister's fury.

"Your outburst by the way was not driven by guilt. It was a grievance, aired. The two are completely different. You should not confuse the two."

"Confused? I'm not confused." The words tumbled out of her mouth but order was maintained.

"I didn't say you were. I just said the two –"

"I heard you the first time."

"I'm confused," said Mother. "Why all this now?"

Clarence explained. "Why not? The sooner the better? Isn't that what we all say?"

Margaret of course did not agree. "Is it. Is it really."

"If you have any other grievances, probably best you vent them now, while I'm in the mood."

"Grievances. I'll give you grievances."

Margaret threw herself back into her chair and tried to conjure some up. She knew she had lots stuffed away somewhere but could not think straight now. They were difficult things to unpack and rekindle. She delayed.

"Any chance of that coffee Dad?"

"Coffee? Yes of course. I'll get it right now."

Dad threw his wife a look of bemusement bordering on resignation and left the room. They were both suddenly thirty years younger and had two teenage brats laying into each other. This time around the energy and skills to cope were sadly lacking.

"You read my private diary and scribbled rubbish – your stupid comments - in it."

"Again I apologize for that, wholeheartedly."

His sister didn't want more apologies. She wanted a fight. "Stop saying that!"

"My only excuse is that I was bitter. You always put me down, belittled me in front of your girlfriends."

"That's because you deserved it."

Clarence thought back. He had no problem with that. "Yes come to think of it you're probably right. Anyway that's the reason why I did what I did."

"And my friends saw it."

"Again I apologize."

"Stop saying that! Stop apologizing!"

"Sorry."

The coffee cut in and as it was served all collapsed into silence. After a long heavy pause Mother decided to be the first to speak again.

"Jim why don't you show Clarence your new drill?"

"I don't think he's interested in my new drill right now."

"That's right I'm not." Clarence wanted to pick up where he had left off. "That was another grievance aired. Do you feel better for it?"

"No." Margaret sounded miserable.

"Odd. How about guilt? Is there any guilt you would like to purge from your system?"

Mother interrupted. "Oh Clarence please. This is all too much. Leave your sister alone. Let's all settle down please. Drink your coffee."

"I've finished mine."

"Well have another one."

"One's enough."

Margaret saw he still had more to say and wanted to duck.

"You resented me doing better at school and university?"

She avoided the question. "Possibly."

"And that continued into resenting the fact I took up a proper profession?"

"Yes – no. I decided to raise a family. Something you seem incapable of doing. Much more important, and much tougher – and by the way you hate teaching."

"True, on both accounts, but that's now, not then." Clarence studied his sister's face hard, until it began to hurt both him and her. But it didn't crack. It held firm. "Nothing else?"

"No. Definitely not."

"How about the time I caught you stealing coins, small change, out of Mother's purse?"

"What?"

"I promised never to say anything but it's probably best it's brought up now and put behind us. So we can move on as they say."

Margaret turned to her mother for help. "I was very young at the time. I was very young, honest."

"I'm sure you were dear. It doesn't matter now. We are all guilty of things like that. I'm sure I must have done the same when I was your age."

Clarence was interested. "Really?"

Caught out and feeling vulnerable, Mother began to back-pedal. "Well I'm not sure for definite. Who knows."

"You do. The incident is buried away in your head somewhere, by design or by accident. You just need to search it out and link up to it."

"Do I. Do I really." Now Mother began to sound like her daughter.

Margaret suddenly felt she had an ally, and having no intention of finishing her coffee she stood up again, this time to take her leave. She was worn out, shattered, feeling sat on from a great height.

"I have to go."

No one tried to stop her. After she said goodbye to Dad she was led – nursed almost - to the door by Mum.

"I'll pop round later."

"No not today thanks. Some other time."

Clarence was not given the opportunity to say goodbye.

"Was all that really necessary?" asked Dad.

"I think so. I feel much better for it."

"I don't think she does."

"She will, in time."

"You think so?"

Clarence began to shrink. "Perhaps not."

"Any other surprises?"

"I don't think so."

At that point Mum stuck her head around the door and pointed a finger. It was aimed at her son, though her husband felt a little of it also – for no other reason than he had fathered the child.

"You. You go and apologize to her immediately."

"Yes Mum."

Under instruction Clarence left, immediately, but having no wish to chase after his sister. It was a dog's dinner.

Clarence dithered under duress until he saw his sister drive off and skive off then headed off in the opposite direction, trying hard to control his speed; his dodgy ankle a constant reminder that he was damaged goods. Tracey attached herself to the inside of his head, this time like a limpet mine. Previously she had been slapped there like a used post-it note. Either way she was polluting his conscious being, except this time she could not be removed, no matter how hard he tried to scrape her off and chuck her out.

It was not a bad thing. The lack of physical, social – human even - contact between them suddenly felt refreshing and suggested new opportunities, like a glass of ice – just ice – no mixer, no cocktail, no alcohol of any kind – just ice cold ice, slowly melting, slowly thawing into romantic slush. Clarence was moved and felt himself in a rush but he resisted. It could have been a trick. His life was full of tricks these days: he just didn't trust it anymore.

Driving felt good, isolated and protected inside his car. No one and nothing could touch him, question him, tell him what to do – except perhaps the traffic lights, and lorries, and large vans, and those with the right of way. And against his better judgement he had a destination, a point to aim for. But he was in no rush to get there, the opposite in fact: at the very least he wanted to take his time; perhaps even abort and head off elsewhere, anywhere except home. He needed time to gather up some words: words which roughly speaking, and roughly spoken, would give voice to some rough thoughts – thoughts of reconciliation. Driven, he drove on. He was on his way.

And on his way he slowed, and even stopped once to ask himself what the hell he thought he was doing. What was he chasing? Fairy tales for grown-ups? What the hell he thought could he possibly achieve beyond making a fool of himself? Yes, he had second thoughts, and third thoughts, and fourth thoughts even. But he returned, full cycle, to the first and drove on, overriding the protesting ankle. It had done enough driving today.

He arrived at the familiar address still with no words or sense of what he wanted to say, only that it had to be said: not too quickly, not too lightly, not without feeling; and it must not be faked, or sound faked or contrived even if it was; and it had to impress, it had to convince, it had to convey a sense of regret. It had to invite. Yes, that was it above all else thought Clarence: an invitation to make up. Easy. But hard. Still, he was up for it.

When he got within striking distance of her front door things proved to be not so simple. He became scared and lacking in strength. He began to shiver. He had no sense of feeling in his mouth: talking would be a tough task. On the plus side no bad memories of her came flooding back. In fact no memories of her came back. She was a blank. He tried to question his intention, his quest, but was overruled. He had to make contact, contact of the third going on thirtieth kind. She was a blank piece of old parchment. He could start again and write all over her.

He drew in a deep breath, released it with flair, and took the dive. When the door opened he took a step back: the she-wolf had appeared, without the sheep's clothing. Tracey thought the same, and did the same. Both thought the other was about to pounce. She held an extra long large fork and a pair of oven gloves in defensive formation, attack imminent. They were her sword and shield. She waited for something to be said, for words to leave his mouth; as he did. The only difference between them at this point was the fact that he had less expectation that he would speak first, or make sense. And still she was required to wait, eyes locked on the trouble ahead. Clarence was stuck. He had been locked out.

Tracey gave up. "Say something then. I haven't got all day."

"Have you got a moment?"

"No. Speak anyway."

Clarence began to speak: he would start out badly; not improve; and end up pretty awful. For starters he grabbed at a well-worn phrase, lunged, and pulled back.

"How are you?"

"How am I? None of your business."

The enquiry had not been well received. This was not going to be easy. Clarence considered his options: try to keep talking; or get out now. He wanted to get out now but again overruled himself as physically he was in no danger – though that was a large sharp fork which demanded to be stuck somewhere.

"I thought I'd drive over."

"Obviously."

This was going to be hard. Clarence noticed that there was good, stirring music in the background: possibly Led Zeppelin. This girl of his had always gone silly over Led Zeppelin. He wanted to listen to it, as did she but with him gone.

"I thought I'd say hello."

"Say it then."

"Hello." That was easy.

Clarence waited. Tracey did not bite. She was being difficult. She was exhibiting a mood of extreme impatience, denial and possibly even malice. Sod her, he thought, I'm off. But he did not leave. He overruled himself again.

"It's been a while."

Tracey visibly stiffened. This was turning silly – not tragic or sad but silly.

"Look if you've got something to say just say it quick. I haven't got all day. I've got food on the boil and a roast in the oven and I'm really not interested in anything you've got to say." She did not mince the words.

The word 'food' gave Clarence a handle, something to grab on to.

"What are you having?"

"None of your business."

"Fair enough."

Clarence knew for sure now he was only wasting his time but still he did not leave: too early to quit, show her some gumption. He thought back to when he had just been driving along, with some sense of objective, with a challenge, with some idea of why he had decided to call on her. A previous thought suddenly hit him, and just in the nick of time: an invitation to make up, put the past behind them, start afresh as if reborn.

Yes that felt good: an invitation to make up. He was on the verge of forcing a turnabout and storming off, at speed, ego in tatters. Now he would hang in there a little longer. The woman still looked good, even when trying to look bad. Yes that was Led Zeppelin.

Nervously Tracey began to fiddle with her oven gloves: screwing them up as best she could in one hand then reversing the process until they were left hanging back at square one. She was killing time and she wanted it dead. Clarence was killing time and killing himself at the same time. She was willing to help. She wanted to help.

"Clarence talk or go. It's your choice."

Clarence found some words, enough to start the ball rolling, uphill. "I came over, came over to see how you were keeping, to see how you . . . how are you keeping? I came over to see you, check you were fine, good, feeling good. You look good . . . you always looked good . . . me, not so good . . . things not so good . . ." Clarence broke off. He had run himself down, as had her silence.

"And?"

"And . . . don't know . . . thought perhaps we could talk."

"Thought perhaps we could talk. No I don't think."

"No . . . no I didn't think so either. But I have got something to say. I think . . . yes I think I have something to say."

Tracey could not take her eyes off the idiot standing before her. "Say it then. And be quick about it."

Clarence wanted to sit down. He wanted to sit down at the back of his class. He wanted to sit down in his car. He wanted to sit down in his car, turn on the radio, start the engine and drive off. But again he was overruled and continued to take the punishment he himself was dispensing. Tracey did not need to serve it up.

Realising he was fighting to save face, the makings of a speech reared up inside, out of nowhere. It was nothing more than a rough draft. It had no structure, no punch, no clear message; and it would never be typed up.

"We had some good times. In the beginning yes we had some good times. Yes. Yes I know we did. Didn't we? I don't remember them but how could it have been otherwise? Else how could we have stuck together so long? We had ups and downs as they say. Yes we had those, those ups and downs. But we had plenty of good times. Didn't we? We laughed didn't we? Didn't we?"

Tracey wanted so much to laugh. She could not take any of this drivel – his drivel - seriously. She kept her face fixed on the right side of patience, patronage and pity and pretended to show interest. Not far below the surface hysteria was building and bubbling up. Led Zeppelin raised the tempo and Clarence, gaining confidence through her silence, began his pitch for equality.

"I appreciate I'm not the easiest person to hang out with but are you? Is anybody?" Clarence paused, hoping for a considered reaction to what he considered to be a profound question. He was to be disappointed.

"I am."

"You used to keep me waiting, waiting around in shops. I offered to cook. You didn't like my cooking. You said I couldn't cook."

"You can't cook."

Suddenly a value was opened, a tap was turned and it all came flooding out. At last Clarence found the guts to stand up to her, to talk back.

"If I was even five minutes late you complained. But it was okay for you to be late. And you were more often late than me. I had good reasons to be late. I don't remember you having any."

Snoring: Clarence had always wanted to complain about her snoring. Now the time felt right. It may be his only time to set the record straight.

"You know we both snored. You used to hassle me for snoring but we both snored."

Tracey did not wish to know this. Turn away now, she thought. But that would be to feed her sudden onset of guilt. She was starting to loathe what was being said against her. She twiddled her fork. She had nothing to say in her defence. She couldn't be bothered. Tracey saw her ex- rapidly diminishing in statue, rapidly shredding years and retreating in age back to infancy. Let him go.

"You crunched my bumper and headlight once. You never paid for any of it, and I lost my no claims bonus. The excess was two hundred quid."

"I said sorry."

"Too late now. You never said sorry when you lost my remote."

Tracey didn't bother to say sorry again. She wasn't even convinced she was the one who had lost it.

"And why did you keep leaving the milk out? Even in high summer? Even I didn't do that."

That one he had invented. She had only left the milk out a total of three times and only twice had it gone off.

"And then there was my phone bill."

"What about your bloody phone bill?"

"It went up while we were going out. You kept using my phone."

"Oh come on!"

Clarence wanted to calm down. Clarence didn't want to calm down. Tracey wanted Clarence to calm down. Calm down Clarence, she thought.

"And the worse thing was you never took care of my things. Remember those tape recordings I lent you? My special compilation of all their single releases – unique, fucking unique. On chrome tape they were, perfect, fucking perfect. When I finally got them back they sounded shit, fucking shit." Clarence had rediscovered the joy of fucking everything. "Shit. Those tapes were fucking irreplaceable. You can't put all that material together anymore. You even mangled one of them. You never looked after them despite your so called 'promise' that you would. I could have sold them on Ebay for a fortune, a fucking fortune."

Clarence wanted to cry now. Tracey thought he was getting well out of hand. Was he going to cry? Now her guilt had surfaced. A lump grew in her throat. Best stick to not saying anything, she decided. It was the safest bet.

"And I never got back my Rubik's Cube or that Pink Floyd book. I bet you've lost them now."

Exhausted, having let it all out, Clarence now wanted to pull some of it back in. He searched for some humility, and found it.

"Look. I fell in love with you once. I didn't always stay in love – I fell out – I fell back in. It was like potholes in the road of . . . of life? You know what I mean?"

Tracey didn't. She wanted to return to her roast, and stab it, repeatedly, until it bled.

"Sometimes I took you for granted I know – and I didn't take your work seriously I know – and I avoided your parents I know – not that you were much different – but I tried. I did try. Honest. And they avoided me."

Tracey had digested too much too quickly. She felt sick. She wanted to close the door on him and escape back indoors. He wasn't just deranged he was dangerous.

Humility put to one side, Clarence carried on. "And on holiday you always had to be in the shower first. Afraid to miss out on the hot water.

Speaking of that holiday – you know the one I mean - you made no effort to have a good time."

"What was there to enjoy?"

"You flirted."

"I flirted? You flirted!" Shut up Tracey told herself. Shut up. Don't get involved in this. "You drunk too much."

"Well, whatever. Sorry about that. I wasn't myself. I was drunk a lot. Though to be fair you didn't exactly help. Enthusiasm was lacking as they say." Clarence rediscovered some metal mettle. "You must take some blame for that. It was a waste of precious time. You have to admit that."

Tracey did not have to admit anything. And she knew it. Instead Tracey had to laugh, and so she did, with gusto as she let it all out. The wave demolished Clarence. It swept him up and dumped him upside down. Afterwards, tears of joy in her eyes, she felt much better for it. There was none of him left inside. All the toxic waste was gone. He was now just a joke.

Though he was still standing Clarence felt like he had just toppled over. Now was definitely the time to cut his losses and go, get out: not a moment's delay – except perhaps an angry outburst of typically male proportions, except that today he had nothing in the way of energy reserves to do it justice. It was little more than an indignant growl of deep displeasure and raw resentment.

"Well sod you if you're not going to take this seriously."

"So now it's suddenly 'sod me' is it? For not taking 'this' seriously? For not taking you seriously more like. You little shit."

Clarence wanted to turn and flounce off the film set, pretending he had won the argument, or at least got a draw. But he was obstructed by an ego which demanded he get in the last shot, stand up to her and show her he could not be intimidated even if he was. Tracey had always been a tough cookie. It was one of the qualities which had first attracted him to her. She had always been good for a fist-fight - figuratively speaking. Then things went from bad to worse.

Her sister suddenly appeared, looming up and sticking her head over the parapet of her sister's shoulders. She could also be as hard as nails, and today she was. Detached from the situation but conscious of it, she had no problem doing her sister's dirty work. She was a hammer and she had to fall. She hit the nail on the head.

"Clear off Clarence. She doesn't want you round here. She doesn't ever want to see you again. Am I right?"

"That's right." Tracey spoke boldly.

"Come on Trace I'm starving."

Tracey complied and slammed the door shut in the face of the man whose name she could now find it easy to forget. And just as easily the guilt over her own failings evaporated in an instant. She was home and dry. She was the totally innocent party.

Unusually for Clarence the recovery was near instantaneous. He marched back to the safety of his car, not so much feeling insulted as feeling relieved of his burden. He was lighter on his feet. His stride had increased. As he fell into his seat he tried to bounce off it. When he drove off it was without direction or due care and attention. A passing cyclist swore loudly and questioned his parentage. But he didn't care. He knew he didn't want to go home – that would mean hiding out in his bedroom until dark. He felt for his mobile. Phone someone. Phone someone safe. Have a chat. Phone Tim, his best mate, and chat like best mates do. Tim was his best mate – even if he had slept with his wife once. Only once? The fact that he couldn't remember beyond the once didn't mean a thing these days. Just don't mention her.

Clarence and Tim made contact, both glad to hear the other's voice. Clarence was very glad to hear Tim's voice even if it was a surly grunt; and in return Tim was extra glad to hear it was Clarence even if he did sound pensive, evasive. Yet neither advertised the fact, lest it be seen as a sign of male weakness; and neither wished to sound inferior to the other. To each, the other sounded off key, like they needed cheering up. Neither obliged. Neither provided cheer. Though both were currently stuck in the middle of a drama come trauma it was all matter of fact.

"What are you doing?"

"Nothing much."

"Bored then?"

"Yeah bored."

"I'm bored. Why don't you come over. There's footy on the TV. We can be bored together." Tim did his best to sound charitable rather than begging, and succeeded.

Clarence was not taken with the offer. Tim meant Sam. Sam was a reminder of an uncomfortable truth – an inconvenient truth to coin a popular phrase currently in circulation. Sam was guilt and shame. No Sam meant no guilt, no shame. Right now no to Sam meant no to Tim.

"Hello? Can you hear me?" Tim wanted an answer. Tim wanted to hear the word 'yes'.

"Yes I can hear you."

"So are you coming over?"

Clarence played for a delay. "Not sure."

Tim heard a car moving fast. "Where are you? Are you at home?"

"In my car. Outside Tracey's."

"Good for you. Come on over and tell me all about it."

"I don't think so."

"Well come on over and don't tell me all about it. Drink beer and watch football instead."

"I don't think so."

"What do you mean you don't think so? Why not?" Tim was reduced to begging.

"I don't want to impose." Like any ice cream left to rot in a hot car Clarence felt himself abandoned, and melting fast.

"You don't want to impose? What the fuck are you talking about?"

"I don't know." Without moving Clarence had done a u-turn. He wanted to be left alone. The call had become a bad mistake.

"Look bury Tracey. Don't let her bury you. Buy some beers. Bring the beers round here. I'll order up pizza, our usual. We have a night in without any women and get pissed. You sleep over. Easy."

"A night in without any women?"

"No women. Just us, beer, pizza and TV, perhaps a DVD. Sam's going out."

"Going out? For how long?"

"All night, staying over with a friend she said." Tim's voice slowed. It was tinged with hurt. "I think she's out to get pissed like me. Why?"

"Nothing. Just us then. Just us two blokes."

Tim began to tire of the fine analysis and reiterations. "Yes just us. Just two blokes as you say – and beer – bring those beers."

Clarence's voice lifted. "Okay I'll be over."

"So you're happy to come over now?" Tim was struck by the change in attitude.

"Yes I'm happy."

"Now that Sam's not going to be here?"

"Not necessarily."

Tim was not the most sensitive man in the world but he had known his best mate Clarence a long time and could tell when he was being defensive, or lying through his teeth. That last reply was total bollocks. It didn't ring true. Why, Tim had absolutely no idea.

Clarence did a recce. "How is she anyway?"

"Sam? Not at her best – but don't tell her I said that."

"I won't. Not at her best? What do you mean not at her best?"

"I don't know. Does it matter? What's it to you anyway?"

For Tim, Clarence's interest in his wife was being to sound unhealthy.

"Nothing. Sorry." Clarence had one more question, pretty much a repeat. "She's out you say?"

"She's going out yes. Do you want to speak to her first? She's still here if you're quick."

"No. No need for that."

Clarence hadn't answered quick enough: he cringed, and pinched himself with the tips of four spare fingers when he heard Tim shout the same question to Sam somewhere upstairs. He did not hear the reply. He did not need to. Sam did not come to the phone.

"See you soon then."

"Cheers."

Clarence switched off his mobile and wound down the window. He needed fresh air like he needed to stick his head under a cold shower. Tim parked his phone slowly, burdened by a sudden outbreak of rampant speculation, the result of intense cerebral activity. Such a thing rarely occurred inside Tim outside office hours. Something did not feel quite right, and he had heard it clearly in the voice of his best mate. Clarence turned the key; started the engine; turned on the radio; changed channel; changed channel again, and again; then finally drove off, deciding not to drive straight over. Give the woman plenty of time to get out of his way.

Clarence went via his adopted off-licence. He wanted to see that girl, see she was still serving, see she was alright, see if she would say something nice to him. His prayer was answered: she was there, and surprisingly she said something nice to him, almost as if she was pleased to see him still alive. As always she made him feel ten years younger. As always he made her feel twenty years older. It cheered him up no end and gave him the fuel to get himself over to his best mate's place with a wishful, wistful yet still positive attitude. A smart, fresh looking girl behind a counter selling beer and taking cash or credit card could do wonders for the male spirit. Clarence left the off-licence with a strong urge to give her lots of money. As a compromise he told her to keep the change.

'Wonderful', she thought. This will change my life.

In anticipation of better times ahead Clarence stood before his next door, this time more cheerful: behind it was not family, was not an ex-, but his best mate. The cheerfulness evaporated when the door opened. Tim, his best mate Tim, looked like he had just come out of a fight, or was gearing up for one. Clarence suddenly had second thoughts. The moment was fleeting: Tim was now smiling, though with difficulty. Clarence did not know this. He saw a smile boosted by the desire to disarm the guest. By Tim's standards it was over the top, more 'in your face'.

Clarence held out his pack of beers, his entrance fee. Tim, his best mate Tim, appeared to be more pleased to see them than him. They drew forth some honest affection and Clarence was momentarily sidelined as Tim took command of the pack, smile gone. Then he was hustled inside and made to sit in front of the telly. Clarence assumed his best mate was in a rush to get back to the match. Yet this did not square. Clarence sensed – remarkably for him as Tim was giving nothing away – that his best mate was watching his movements, not those of the players on the pitch, not the ball about to suffer a goal kick. Suddenly the spur of the moment visit was beginning to feel like not a great idea, more like a bad idea, perhaps a very bad idea – despite the fact he had removed all risk of a dangerous collision with a troublesome member of the opposite sex. But today had been full of bad ideas and troublesome members of the opposite sex, so with that in mind Clarence began to sink into a fatalistic mood. In all this time the two 'best mates' had exchanged words only once:-

'Hi. Got the beers.' and 'Hi. Quick, in you come. Sit there.'

The two 'best mates' - one seated, one standing - began to drink beer from their bottles: one trying to get into a good mood; one trying to stay in a good mood. Who was who was impossible to say. With beer and big screen footy to draw their attention both were content to not talk, but both felt required to do exactly that. Best mates had to talk: it was part of the agreement. Tim tried first. It was his house.

"How's your head?"

"Fine."

"Did you see somebody?"

"Yeap."

"And?"

"He said fine." Clarence would not be drawn on a subject he constantly fought to forget.

Then during a short spell of ignominious stoppage Clarence felt required to have a go.

"How are you?"

"Same as ever."

"And Sam?" Clarence felt duty-bound to ask after her.

Tim threw a wobbly. It was one he had been saving up shortly after putting the phone down. "No need to ask me. You can ask her yourself."

His timing and delivery were perfect. He shot Clarence with a loaded look, across the bow and out of the blue. He was fishing for a certain reaction; and he found it, clearly written across his best mate's face. It was the look of badly disguised, barely suppressed alarm. Clarence had twisted up. His throat dried up and his eyes darted around the room. For Tim things were suddenly beginning to add up. He dreaded calculating the final answer. The moment Clarence opened his mouth he virtually condemned himself.

"What do you mean, I can ask her? She's not here?"

Tim turned towards the door and yelled out loudly to ensure his voice carried to the top of the house. "Sam! Have you got a mo!"

"But you said, you said she had gone out? Sam's out?" Clarence stumbled over his words.

"I said she was going out."

Tim noticed there was a lot of froth in the bottle his best mate was holding. It threatened to spill over.

"Don't, don't let me hold her up." Clarence sounded pathetic.

"I'm sure you won't. Sam come on!"

Sam shouted back. "I'm coming!" And with that she came thundering down the stairs.

Sam was advancing, on all fronts, and the stair carpet could not dampen the steady thump thump thump of her shoes. She came hurtling into the living room, clutching handbag and dressed for some occasion, not for Tim. On seeing Clarence she skidded to a halt, and like him looked very uncomfortable, unseated, unmasked almost.

"Oh it's you," she snarled, accidentally.

The response from Clarence was weak. "Hi."

Tim took everything in. It was like being in the office: watching two screens for all signs of movement, and any hidden messages. In his world of trades and trade-offs, 2 and 2 sooner or later added up to 4. They may pass through 3.91 or 4.05 but sooner or later they settled on 4.

Nothing was going on but everything was happening. Nothing was being said because it had already been said. Two people in the room were tightly joined against their will and neither of them was Tim. And Tim knew it. Both wife and best mate had gone red in the face. His best mate was in danger of spilling his beer. His wife was clutching her handbag and in danger of spinning out of control.

A triangle briefly existed. Along all its lines ran back and forth pulses of bad or broken thoughts. Those belonging to Clarence were the most broken. Those belonging to Sam were bad, worse than the other two. Those belonging to Tim had yet to catch up with the others, but they were gaining in strength. No one in the triangle moved to break out of it. They were all locked into position, held on the spot.

Sam could not bear to look at Clarence, nor Tim. She looked at her fingernails instead, feigning disappointment with her nail varnish. Clarence went back to staring at the football. Tim was forced to join him. He had nowhere else to look. It was Sam who broke the deadlock.

"Well?" she was pushed to ask.

"Well what?"

"Why the delay?"

"Thought you might like to see Clarence before you left."

No comment.

"Can I go out now? I'm late."

"Yes my sweet of course you can. Have a nice time dear."

Sam threw her husband a dirty look, turned and left fuming with the thought that there was trickery afoot. She pretended to be late.

When on form Tim had the knack of taking the smallest clue, the smallest piece of detail, and using it to make a fortune. It was what he was paid to do, and when on form he did it extremely well. Today he was about to make a fortune. Then he would have to spend it.

"Well she was in a good mood."

Clarence pretended to be locked into the game and unable to look away. Tim was back to watching him. He had almost counted up to 4.

"And not particularly glad to see you."

"What are you talking about. You're missing the football." There was no football not worth missing.

For now Tim didn't give a shit about the football. "How's it been since Tracey dumped you? Seeing anybody? Shagging anybody?"

Clarence knew he had to get out. His best mate was asking him complicated questions about his love life: nothing to do with football; nothing to do with pizza. He pretended to be totally hung up on the ball and the way it was being blindly bounced around in mid-field. The mid-field was in chaos. He answered as if totally uninterested in even anything he himself had to say.

"Seeing no one at the moment. Shagging no one. I'm taking a rest from all that. Leave of absence as they say."

"No sex? Christ that must be hard."

Clarence was caught between a rock and a hard place, but he was aggressively on the defence and thought he could hold out if he simply did not think and instead just concentrated on watching a load of super fit, bruising blokes kick a ball around for a shit load of money. But it was not to be. He began to think and he began to sweat. The guilt factor, that X factor, was looming up inside, trying to break free and inflict damage on its way. It was getting out of control. He could not rein it in. It had a life of its own and it wanted to live. The more he tried not to think of it the more he thought of it, and the more it crept up on him. It was like that huge pile of the most revolting, steaming dog shit he had once encountered and nearly skidded in. Despite not trying to, he could still see it clearly, still steaming – and the worms it entertained – and it made him sick beyond belief. It had to go, along with the guilt. But how? And go where? Confess and ask forgiveness? No, don't be bloody stupid! He had already fallen out with his best mate's wife. He didn't want to fall out with his best mate. She wasn't worth it. With everything else falling apart he could not afford to fall out with his best mate. Elsewhere, Clarence's alternative, quick-fire analysis was also completely flawed (but just as convenient): he had already fallen out with his best mate but his best mate had not yet told him about it. So delay the pain for as long as possible: stay mates for as long as possible. Finish half the beers. He had paid for them.

While two sides battled for control of his guilt complex, a third, smaller, unknown and barely established force sent him a completely different message: one far more radical; one far more emotional; one far more of a challenge and far more risky. It was simple but striking: stuff them all, each and every one of them; let it all hang out and blow the consequences; let them all go; chuck it all overboard and start all over again, from scratch, and get it right next time. It was a life plan extraordinaire, and not one for the feint-hearted.

Clarence felt himself being over-ruled again. Yet again he was failing to stay in charge, set his own agenda. This definitely was one of his worse days – as bad as the day before, if that was possible. The guilt had to be set free, he argued else it would bring the house down. 'Bugger off!' he retorted. 'Confess!' was the demand. 'Confess nothing, say nothing!' was the order. Just find the quickest exit out of here. And still his best mate would not give it up.

"So not getting a shag anywhere? From anyone? Not even that friend of yours John? It is John isn't it?"

"John can go fuck off. He's no friend of mine. I haven't seen him since . . . well you know what." Clarence put up a defence shield. "There was the woman next door. My dodgy neighbour. But it was a bad move, a one-off. We never got on."

"The one that comes round and cooks for you?"

"That's the one. Mad as a hatter."

'Mad as a hatter', thought Tim. I see. "So still on the prowl?"

"Could be. There's a friend of my sister. She's nice."

Clarence jumped up, hating himself for producing that last, flippant comment. He had just devalued something good in his life. Enough was enough. Make that exit.

"Look, sorry mate but I have to go."

"Why the rush?"

"No rush. Just got to get back. I'm fucking exhausted. Had a run in with my sister today, and another with Tracey."

"And with Sam?"

"What?"

"Nothing. Ignore me. You seeing her again?"

"What do you mean?" Clarence fired up.

"Tracey. You seeing Tracey again?"

"Tracey? No fucking way. She chewed me up."

"Fair enough. Tracey's out of it then. Nothing else I need to know?"

Clarence froze, then restarted, having won the argument within to say nothing, confess nothing.

"I'll let myself out."

"Fair enough." Tim had had enough for one day. He was also fucking exhausted.

Clarence left angry: angry that Tim – hopefully still his best mate - had not cheered him up; angry that he might be exposed as a dirty rotten, double-crossing scoundrel, and not a best mate.

Now it was Tim's turn to lock himself into the game of football. Alone now, he really was interested in the result. Clarence had scarpered and the first goal of the match had been scored and Tim was left with seven beers to down all by himself: a positive result at half-time.

Clarence rushed off, rushed home, rushed in, and ran into Max. Max, embedded in the sofa in the place where Clarence usually sat, looked up from his newspaper and gave him his special tired look, the one he kept just for Clarence.

"You're popular with the ladies today." Max did not want to talk but it had to be said.

Clarence was stunned senseless. How could his lodger possibly know. How could he possibly know? Was he psychic?

"Meaning?"

"Meaning two ladies have called on you today, in quick succession, both in a hurry. Both fucking manic as far as I could see. One of them was your neighbour." Max stared Clarence into the ground. "What have you been doing? She looked really pissed off."

"She's pissed off? I'm pissed off. I'm really pissed off." Clarence took a breath and asked the obvious. "So what did they want?"

"They didn't want anything. They just wanted me to give you these."

Max reached out and picked up two envelopes lying by his side: one brown, one white; one opened, one sealed; one addressed to Clarence, one not. Clarence reached out and snatched them up; unhappy that Mad Max was meddling in his affairs; unhappy that he had to speak to him; unhappy that soon he would lose the rent money.

"One of them's been opened."

Max was not bothered. "I know. She told me to open it, read it. Thought I was you."

"Who did?"

"Some lady I've never seen before. She was in a real hurry. Gone just like that." Max clicked his fingers for added effect. "I didn't have a chance to ask her what was going on. Not that she wanted to talk. She made it sound really urgent so I read it."

"What does it say?"

"Don't ask me. Bloody read it yourself." Max returned to his newspaper and shook it back into shape, searching not for news but for something on TV to watch.

Clarence unfolded the piece of paper. He did not recognise the handwriting. It was an urgent precise instruction to be at a certain place – a place he had never heard of – by a certain time, 'tomorrow', for 'the journey home'. There was an apology for 'losing contact' and it was signed 'a colleague'. As with Max, it was all total bollocks to him. He scrunched it up with its envelope into a ball and threw the ball across the room, out of sight and out of mind.

"That was total bollocks."

Max made no comment. He did not want to be drawn further into the weird world of Crazy Clarence. He dug in, hiding out in the pages of his tabloid, inspecting the shape of tits. These days anything to do with Crazy Clarence gave him a headache.

Clarence examined the other envelope. This one was more intriguing, possibly more dangerous, and hence more inviting. It was addressed to him, and clearly signed 'Rebecca'. He shivered. He did not want to read it. But something stopped him from discarding it there and then like the other. Not wishing to appear troubled or timid in front of Max he made a special effort to sound nonchalant, like he was in charge of events.

"I'll read this one later."

"A love letter?"

"I don't think so."

Clarence retreated to his bedroom. Max reached for the remote, forced to watch English league football to kill time. There was no rugby.

Back on his bed - his favourite most secure place on the planet right now - Clarence consigned himself to bitter isolation, for now and forever: going outside and facing the world, meeting people, speaking to them, trying to engage in normal social activities just seemed to make his situation worse. And he didn't have any beer to keep him company. Tim had stolen his beer. He wanted to get drunk but could not face stepping outside again. And no way was he going to get down on all fours and go crawling to his lodger, to beg for a bottle from the stash he knew the guy always kept in his room. And he was stuck with this unopened envelope.

It would not go away. It was stuck to the palm of his hand. It would not let him put it down, discard it, let go. It demanded to be read, if only once, and its demand was going to be met. He swivelled around on his backside, unable to settle, unable to get comfortable, wishing to scratch here there and everywhere. He wanted to undress, slip into bed, turn off the light and go to sleep – no matter how long it took to fall asleep. But it was far too early for that. Then amongst all the gloom, doom and despair which permeated - flooded nearly - his mental landscape, there was the flowering of one positive thought. Perhaps it was a letter saying that she didn't want to see him anymore, that she didn't want to have anything to do with him; saying that their one brief moment of intimacy, their one brief liaison, was one big mistake and they must both rewind the clock back to the way things had been: mutual disregard laced with a basic level of common courtesy, or something like that.

It was something like that, only worse.

As Clarence read the letter, and read into it, and read on, riveted, so the world turned upside down, again. Things could not get any worse he had kept telling himself. And now they had done just that, as if out of spite. The stupid woman next door – the woman with the stupid cat – was going to kill herself and she was blaming it all on him. This was not a tragedy. This was farce. She was not the tragedy, he was he complained. He was the one with the problems, not her.

No. He was not having it. No way was he going to be stuck with this one. Stuff her. He had no stock of sympathy. If she wanted to go kill herself then so be it. Good luck to her. She didn't need his permission. Just don't create a fuss or leave a mess. He had only slept with her once, and that was during a moment of weakness. That was no crime. He had never made any promises, never lied to her, never suggested that it was anything more than a bit of convenient sex – convenient for both sides.

Just as he thought he was home and dry again he began to drown in panic again. What if they blamed him? What if the police, her family, the authorities held him responsible for not trying to stop her, for not calling 999? Would he go to jail? But then how would they know? He had the letter. No one else knew of it. But they were clever that lot: they would make enquiries. They would speak to him, and Max. Max would say she had called. May would say she had handed over a letter addressed to him. Max would say she looked 'manic' – was that the word he used? Manic? Max would drop him in it. Checkmate: he would have no way out.

Clarence stuck his head between his hands and bent forward to rest on his knees. He stared down at the carpet pattern and compared it with the wallpaper still at the back of his mind. Kill Max. Kill Max and dump the body, burn the body. He began to sob. He was going mad. Correction. He had gone mad. There was no way he could kill Mad Max. The man would just beat the shit out of him.

Max looked up from his paper. Now he had a beer in his hand and beans on toast on his mind. Crazy Clarence was hovering at the door and staring down at him. He looked calm enough, in control, but still he gave Max the creeps. To provide comfort Max swallowed a large amount of Guinness. Clarence took to smiling, as if content to watch Max quench his thirst.

Max snapped. "Are you going to say something or what? Or just stand there?"

The outburst was enough to wake Clarence up. He apologized.

"Sorry. Didn't mean to stare. I know it's rude. Just popping out for a moment. May be some time."

Max wanted to ask 'why are you telling me all this, as if I give a damn?' but decided to give it a miss, best not get involved. The man was, without doubt, a full-time nutter. He returned to his drinking, reading, and TV viewing. Soon he would be out of here. Clarence stuck to his word and popped out, to pop up elsewhere.

✦ ✦ ✦

Log Entry

I tried to initiate a reconciliation between my host and a female with whom he had once had a relationship. They engaged in sex on a regular basis. And judging by one particular hoard of closely guarded memories, both had always found such couplings worthwhile, eventful, exhilarating and inspiring. Though I am not sure this was actually the case. He was still harbouring positive thoughts towards her despite the sudden termination of the relationship. (He does not harbour them now.) It was to no avail. The moment I left him to his own devices he returned to ways which were self-destructive in respect of this issue. Their once intense sexual relationship now appears to carry no weight, and had no bearing on anything the two had to say to each other.

Guilt is a strange creature. It is not complex. It takes up no space yet it has enormous substance. It does not need to be regularly fed with new experiences or even recirculated memories. It is self-sustaining. It can survive on nothing except the original trigger. It does not need to be continually in the forefront of conscious thought. It can be 'tucked away' for years, yet when 'reremembered' (awful word) it has lost none of its original impact. Perhaps its strength lies in the fact that it makes its host beholding to another in a most fundamental way; and humans hate being beholding to one another, even if they declare they are 'in love' with that other person. (I mean 'in love' in its broadest sense: non-physical, sex free love between family members and friends as well as between sexual partners.)

Though much can hang off it with regards to cause, it appears to be nothing more than a point in the mind, a point of pain: a point brought into existence by accident or design; a point difficult to extinguish. It is a point of permanence: self-sustaining; sometimes self-adjusting (according to the imagination and fantasies of the host); rarely self-correcting. It can drift so may not stick to the truth of the original cause. It is permanently off-balance, inherently unstable, threatening when active, distant when inactive. Yet it never collapses, never fades.

It comes into existence in a flash, between two moments of conscious thought. And it is gone in the same timeframe.

Some points of guilt create nothing more than irritation, simply because they are there. Others are the cause of great stress and worry over a very long period: behind those resides a complex structure of cause and effect, timescales and intransigence, fact and fiction. The wish to eject it, extinguish it, expunge it is sometimes constant, sometimes intermittent; sometimes self-perpetuating, sometimes triggered by external forces. Whatever the mechanism it is always accompanied by risk assessment, an activity driven almost by pure logic, even if the cause for guilt is highly illogical, highly emotional. These two activities create a sea-saw, bipolar stream of constant re-evaluation and reverberation which drains the human mind and reduces its capacity to concentrate on other matters of concern.

Fallout from its public exposure, the act of externalising it, can vary widely in severity and scope: a direct reflection sometimes of the original cause. In some cases the fear of massive, detrimental fallout and new discomforts, e.g. public shaming and rejection, destroys any chance of release and resolution. The guilt continues to thrive, and feed the fear which hangs over it.

Sometimes guilt is regarded as shared within a closed loop of two-way 'cause and crime' between two humans. In which case its release is all the more harder, problematic, perhaps impossible. For that would mean two-way close communication to enable joint recognition, agreement on original causes, and forgiveness on both sides in equal measure. If the victim is a third party then agreement would also have to be reached with regards to who contributed what to the 'crime'. Group guilt extrapolates these problems and makes them insurmountable. The recorded historical facts of human activity demonstrate that guilt on this level is never totally extinguished.

Guilt can be transient, ephemeral. It can come into existence on a spurious thought and vanish again, across a moment of time so brief as to make it worthless, as to make its host question why it happened. Yet the guilt was there and it impinged, if only for an instant, so giving it legitimacy and authority. It can even return.

Guilt traps just as much as it is trapped. In this sense its power extends beyond most other states of mind. Love, hate, fear, aggression, remorse, jealousy, etc: none of these seem to trap their own consciousness or sub-consciousness quite like guilt. Guilt is as much a container as it is a point and an obstacle. It collects together to hide from view an assortment of many unwelcomed, unpalatable, potentially harmful facts, feelings and opinions.

The cause for the onset of guilt appears to be identifiable in the majority of cases. If it is not then it is usually illogical, and carries no weight. In that case it rarely lasts: it is transient, perhaps even the result of self-indulgence – the need to feel or be seen to feel totally human in all aspects.

Guilt directly imposed, from an external source, without obvious rational cause or justification is the perhaps the most irritating come agonising to deal with. It simply cannot be accommodated. It cannot be buried, sidelined. It is the ultimate insult. Even if it is resolved it can still leave a grievance – which in itself is an irritant.

Guilt, when active, does have one redeeming feature. It keeps the brain alive, ticking over, sometimes at a furious pace. It does not allow it to fall asleep – even during that period defined by humans as sleep.

Guilt is often accompanied by secrets. A secret is a strange phenomena. It is nothing more than knowledge of a single fact or a collection of related facts. It can lie dormant, undisturbed and harmless, indefinitely until brought to the conscious foreground. There, it takes on added importance and weight, and its capacity to disturb increases tenfold, one hundred fold even. The acceleration can be exponential in the right conditions. It has the power to cause serious disruption, suffering or retaliation if brought into the public domain – more so if it is a secret shared and maintained by prior agreement. I have yet to see their release generate the opposite: positive feelings of relief.

A secret shared – even when its continuous containment is a problem for both parties – remains a problem when it is released without prior agreement, even if its public exposure is of no consequence. Secrets released within the family unit, between members, create negative feelings at an intense level; perhaps because loyalty is expected as the norm in all circumstances and for all time.

Some secrets are connected to guilt. Others are not. Some carry great significance. Others are trivial by comparison and cannot be justified: they should simply have never come into existence. Some are created by accident, in private. Some are planned, hatched, between parties.

Chapter Twenty

Rebecca perched on the corner of her bed in the corner of her room at a corner in her life and stared down at her miserable black shoelaces until they ceased to draw her attention. After that she had nowhere to look. She was cornered: afraid to reach out; afraid to touch anything; afraid to object; afraid to shout. She had wrapped herself up in a blanket for concealment and for the immediate future did not consider coming out alive. She had done with running around inside her head, chasing or being chased, picking up or dropping dangerous thoughts; having to fight causes. All she had found there were monuments to the living and the dead. She wanted to be rescued - she demanded it as a right. She had grappled with herself, alone, without help, but had wasted her breath. Alone in her room there was no room for debate. She had boxed herself in, with no way out: too polite to complain, too timid to shout.

She had wanted something to connect with, something worth the fee.

She had wanted to join with Nature. She had wanted to climb its tree.

She had wanted to start a gang. She had wanted to court the boy next door.

She had wanted to beat him at conkers. She had wanted to throw him across the floor.

She had wanted to teach him a lesson or two. She had wanted to smash his favourite toy.

She had wanted to recite a poem. She had wanted to sing a song.

She had wanted to play in a band. She wanted to right a wrong.

She had wanted to be wonderful with a stranger and invite him home for tea.

She had wanted to connect with the next generation and balance one across her knee.

She had wanted someone to talk to but not that someone to talk back.

She had wanted to drink herself silly, get drunk – like a skunk - until she crashed.

She had wanted to smoke herself well out of joint and crawl from the party, smashed.

She had wanted to put on lipstick, to purse her lips like sexy.

She had wanted to shake her hips and dance to the rhythm of Roxy.

She had wanted to better her looks.

She had wanted to read clever books, and she had.

She had wanted to hang on, hold out, dig in; not give in, not crack up, not commit a crime, not mess things up. She had wanted to reduce her torment to zero, if necessary at the cost of others. Her deepest pain had been cut to ribbons. Her highest distinction had fallen from grace. She could make no further contribution. She could not fit her face.

She wanted her innocence back, this time around to do it harm, not wear it as a charm.

She wanted something to hold on to, but for nothing to persist.

There was nothing left she had control of, so why bother to resist.

She wanted to vanish and leave no trace. She wanted to apply make up to conceal her face.

They had sold her pleasure. They had sold her vice. They had sold her naughty. They had sold her nice. But now she did not buy it. Now she did not care. She wanted to leave it all behind she declared. She would not lift a finger. She would leave it all to rot. She would not stoop. She would not stop. (She made that her one remaining aspiration, her final ambition, to be protected.)

Rebecca was weighed down by the rock which had lodged inside her head. It could not be moved by the combined strength of all her discarded dreams, loose thoughts or entrenched imagination. It had squashed her flat. She managed not to scream as she held her head and begged to be rescued. She had no place to land so she was forced to keep on flying, around in circles. She had no place now for sound charades so she hugged the silence and made it her new companion. She took all that silence had to offer and made it her own, adding to its weight with the zeal of someone who was more than comfortable with the notion of death. Finally she hung it around her neck and wore it proudly as the latest fashion accessory or torn war decoration. It would be the constant reminder of the gravity of her situation.

Rebecca had her rock. It kept her company now. She had no place for pointless pursuits. She had her rock. She had no cause to complain. She had her rock. She had no wish to receive, no need to deceive. She had her rock. She had no reason to resort to reunion. She had no reason to revert to type. She had no need to insinuate. She had no need to snipe. She had her rock. She would not be pushed. She would not be pulled. She would not be punished. She would not be cruel. She had her rock. She would not falter. She would not crash. She had her rock.

She had no energy left to argue her case, to raise a defence, to take offence. She had no energy left to hope for the best, to expect the worse, to keep abreast. She had her limitations now. She could not make herself a cup of tea. She could not tie a piece of string. She could not lift her heavy head. She did not hear the telephone ring. She could not impress. She had no feelings left to depress. She counted the seconds as she spent them, as they counted her: one by one then one by one again; then back to one. She no longer cared for the minutes, the hours, the days or the years. Now she regarded them as overrated, diseased. Only the seconds retained resonance.

She contested her scrap with religion. She insisted she was broke. She did not want to dress for the occasion. She did not want to put flowers in her hair. She did not want to fall from her nursery chair. She did not want to cause distress. She did not want to cause a fuss.

Rebecca, shivering out of context despite the blanket keeping her warm, convinced herself that she had reached the end of the line. She had no plans. She had no rock.

It was not all sadness: she looked forward to the termination of time and its destructive, draining progression through the caverns and loopholes of her mind. With the energy and economy of a mouse in winter she pulled herself off the bed and moved out; to move slowly but at steady speed around the space which over the years she had come to make her home, her most special place. As she went she looked at everything and she took in almost nothing. She touched here and there but she sensed nothing.

And the loneliness that led was the loneliness that followed.

And the fury that had surfaced was the fury that was spent.

And the sickness that was summoned was the signal that was sent.

And the ego that had choked was the ego that was swallowed.

If an object was out of place she moved it back into position. She straightened it up. She corrected the fault. She wanted everything to be tidy, a good advertisement for good contact; and she made it so. Objects she could dominate. Objects she could throw around. Objects she could break. Objects she could replace. Objects she could know. Objects knew their place.

She realigned the photographs which guarded her bed then, being honest with herself, admitted she had no further use for them there. They had always been just for show, and now there was no show. She scooped them up and laid them face down, whereupon for the first time in ages she felt like she had done something right: and to look down at them without face value made her feel superior. It was another fickle moment.

Tidiness and the wish for consistency took a grip: she began to turn things off and put things away. From room to room she went, unplugging as she herself was being unplugged. She switched off the hot water boiler – no further need for hot water. She disconnected the phone – no need to make a call, to wish to take a call. She turned off the gas: better safe than sorry. She yanked plugs from their sockets with a force and a fury which almost produced whiplash and a sprained wrist. She paused in front of the television and stared at the empty screen, at the picture of make-believe heaven which was not there. It had once filled her time. Now she had no time for it. It was overrated. It was all hot air. She unplugged it and moved on.

She rediscovered some old artwork. It had been filed away for a rainy day. Today was that day. Her agent had rejected it, twice, despite the pleas for mercy. She examined it and now agreed it was poor. She tore it up and threw it away, thinking no more of it. It was gone.

She went through her books one by one: some were a source of comfort; some were a waste of space; some still sparkled; some still tempted; some still held secrets; some should never have entered her home. She picked up the one entitled 'The Joy Of Sex' and threw it across the room. It landed behind the armchair, out of sight. Judy nearly jumped out of her skin. She decided not to investigate the disturbance.

The exercise in hectic housekeeping did not take long but when it was done Rebecca had to sit down, exhausted, rock still making her head swell and feel like it was going to topple over. She thought hard, seeking other tasks to occupy her mind and eat up her time; lest her mind dissolve into a stream of bubbles and froth. While she had it she had all the time in the world, and she wanted to be seen to be spending it wisely: right up to the last moment; right up to that very last moment. She wanted to be in charge, driving events, managing her world around her, enforcing her stamp: right up to the last moment; right up to that very last moment. Right up to the very last moment, the very last moment before that special moment, she was determined to prove her sanity, by doing all the things sane people did towards the end of the day: like doing the washing up; like putting out the rubbish; like gathering up the dirty laundry and putting it out of sight.

Yes there was the washing up to do. It had to be done. If she left it a stink would arise. Now was not the time to let a stink enter her life. She would not let a stink be her epitaph. She gathered up the dirty dishes, knives and forks and deposited them all in the kitchen sink: for a change dropping them from a great height to make a great noise. She forced home the plug and turned on the hot tap, and waited the usual age it took for the cold water to turn hot. Tonight she was more than patient. It could take all the time in the world. She would wait, for as long as it took. And when it arrived it was well-received and she was well-rehearsed; and she applied herself to the task with no sense of haste but instead the motion of neat, steady decontamination; as if what she was going to leave behind would be measured, marked and held up to public scrutiny. She would leave her place clean, beyond reproach, a shining example to good living. She did the job well.

Tired out, Rebecca dried up. Washed up, she crashed out, to rise again ten minutes later, whereupon her dirty underwear caught her eye. It was not a pretty sight. She snapped it up and flung it soundly into the laundry basket, then followed it up with anything else which was remotely dirty and deserving of a wash. She did not want her dirty laundry to be aired in public.

Rebecca looked down. Judy was staring up at her, saying nothing like she always did, but meaning something. That unknown something sparked a suggestion and Rebecca decided to serve her cat food, lots of cat food. Let none go to waste. Judy must never starve. There were five tins in the cupboard and she opened each one as if it would be Judy's last – or her first. She scooped and dumped the contents of each tin on to its own plate and laid all five plates down on the kitchen floor in a neat, straight line. As the plates began to arrive (from Heaven) Judy jumped in and got stuck in: she began to polish off the first as it hit the floor; then straight into the second with pause. The third she gave up on halfway through. There was only so much a cat could take. It left her extremely disappointed: food was meant to be eaten. That was the way of things. Bloated, Judy belched loudly.

Rebecca found herself standing in judgement in front of her dressing mirror. She wanted to play the part – and to be seen to be playing the part. It was time to discard her clothes, her uniform. This she did slowly, methodically. Sensing crushing solitude and a little stage fright she measured herself; she took readings. She hoped she looked sexy. She wanted to feel sexy. She wanted others to crave her sex, not declare her ugly. She did not want to be so thin. She wanted it to be more than skin and bone, waste and wasteland. She did not want to be so worn out. She did not want to feel so used up. Shivering again, she covered herself up with her bathrobe and moved on to the bathroom, the discarded clothes having been added to the laundry basket. She had to keep stepping over Judy who kept crossing her path in the act of keeping up but not moving ahead.

The bathroom was the place to be now. There she could relax in a hot bath. There she could sink beneath the water – entirely if she had no wish to breathe. She ran the hot tap and watched the steam rise. She ran the cold tap and adjusted the balance, and she waited; and she waited; and she waited, not daring to consider her options or revise her estimate. The dripping sink tap caught her attention, possibly for the last time. She watched a drop gather body and take shape, then lose its will to grip and plummet; to smash itself to pieces. It was as if it had never existed. Then she watched the whole process repeat itself. She was glad. She did not have to bother herself about getting the tap fixed - not that the last plumber had not been nice. He had not spoken English the way she did but he had been nice, and more than willing to please.

When her hot bath was ready Rebecca entered the kitchen again, for the last time she boasted; to spy the clock on the wall for the last time; to lay down a saucer of milk for the last time; to pick out the sharpest knife from the drawer, for the last time. She choose one and checked its edge for sharpness. She was not impressed. She could do better. She threw it back and picked out a smaller one. It was not polished silver, but it could have been. It was what she called her trusty cheese knife – in truth not a cheese knife but she used it for cheese. She pretended it was a lethal dagger, deserving to be drawn in battle. She wanted to hold it like Hamlet but she did not know how to.

She took her knife back to the bathroom, sat down, and ran her fingers through the water, testing the temperature as she tested herself. She threw in her plastic yellow duck and told herself to wait. She did not have to rush she told herself. She would not be rushed. She would not be pushed. She would do this her way in her own time, of her own violation and of her own persuasion. She heard Judy make painful noises at the door: scratching; pleading for physical contact. To avoid confusion on both sides Rebecca locked the door: to keep Judy out, beyond reach; to keep herself in, and focused on the job ahead with the tool in hand. Judy was no longer Judy. Judy was just some cat and she would have to get used to that fact.

Rebecca stared down at the knife. She stared at the blade of the knife. She stared at the serrated edge of the blade of the knife. It had a powerful presence but it made no sense. It gave no message. She became angry: it was reminding her of cheap cheddar cheese, in a big fat lump, at a time when she didn't want to be thinking such a silly thing. She turned the knife over and over: first in one hand then in the other; as if checking it was still sharp, still up to the job; looking at it sometimes joyfully, sometimes with cool hatred, sometimes with disengaged astonishment - sometimes not, sometimes just as its slave. She lightly touched its edge, to check that it was still dangerous. It was. She only had to give it the green light. On the other hand she only had to make a wish and everything would be alright – or if not alright then at least better.

Rebecca stared at the bath. She stared at the body of hot water in the bath. She stared at the final wisps of steam which rose from the hot water in the bath. It still made no sense. And then, with perfect timing, just as she was about to slip out of her bathrobe and into hot water the doorbell rang, and rang, and rang again; and it kept on ringing as if it was angry with her, as if she owed it an explanation.

Rebecca knew who it had to be – if there was any justice left in the world. She fancied dropping her bathrobe to the floor and answering the door naked; to see the reaction on his face; to see him squirm; to put him into shock; to put him in the dock where he belonged. She dropped her robe then, as she moved towards the front door, her old enemy inhibition got the better of her and she scrabbled back into it - but this time holding it loose about her body as a final protest.

Under this protest Rebecca answered the door. It was Clarence of course. She expected no less, no worse. He looked very happy with himself, very cheerful, annoyingly confident, smug; and not short of a word or two. She let go and let her bathrobe fall open but he acted like he had not noticed, like nothing had happened. His broad grin unnerved her and she backed away, sensing ridicule when she was expecting trouble. Like a big sickly, sticky, overcooked, overglazed Sunday afternoon pudding it drove her away and brought a nasty sensation to the pit of her already fragile stomach. She had no taste for him now. She was starting to feel sick. One large smile produced one large frown. One woman lost at sea produced one man about town with time on his hands: one taking the brunt; one committing a stunt; both putting up a front.

Now Rebecca did not like the silence – he had infected it – and she was forced to speak. "So have you come to gloat?"

"Gloat? Why on earth would I want to do a thing like that? I have no desire to see you come to harm. Such a thing would be monstrous of me, inhuman."

As an attempt towards reconciliation his response was a complete failure. Rebecca became angry – so much so that she broke her own record. The pompous clown was not taking her seriously in the slightest. To him she was just one big joke. She wanted to wipe the smile off his face with a hard slap - no a hard scratch from her fingernails. She bit her lower lip for entertaining such an unworthy, base thought.

Clarence spoke on. "You look very upset. You are very upset."

"Of course I'm upset. Why wouldn't I be upset. I'm only human."

"Yes that is true."

To reinforce the point Rebecca gripped her knife as if about to attack with it; as if intending to slice something off, something close to him personally. Clarence tried to calm her.

"Now you are just being silly. I don't believe you truly want to cause me physical harm. Just as you don't want to cause yourself harm."

"Perhaps I do. You don't know what I really think, what I really want."

Clarence did not answer, concluding he had said enough. He looked down. Judy the cat was at his feet, pushing against him, demanding to be stroked. (She was getting nothing from her mistress.) Clarence obliged appropriately and Judy took to his charms with energy and excitement. Rebecca was not so impressed. And she felt left out.

"You keep your hands off my Judy."

Clarence straightened up quickly, not wishing to inflame an already fragile situation. "Sorry."

Judy skulked off, back to her cat food, rediscovering a taste for it. Rejection combined with boredom had given her renewed appetite.

"You always want to hurt me."

Clarence looked perplexed. "I never want to hurt you. I have never wanted to hurt you. Let me be quite clear about this: I have never intentionally meant to hurt you. I promise you that from now on I will do my utmost to ensure that I never hurt you."

Rebecca felt her flesh crawl and a fresh, new type of alien headache coming on. "You're all words."

"But surely words are all there are?" Clarence looked down at the knife for the first time. "You are gripping that knife very tightly, in a very agitated fashion." He considered the sharpness of its blade. "Here, give it to me as you may cause yourself some harm with it unintentionally."

"No." Rebecca was adamant and held her ground. She would not be told what to do by this man. "Perhaps I want to cause myself harm with it, 'unintentionally'."

Clarence smiled, warmly, even though the smile was not received as such. "No I don't think so. You are just letting emotional hysteria get the better of you. There is a time and a place for human instinct to take charge and there is a time and a place for it to not. For all your deficiencies you are a rational person most of the time Rebecca. Now is the time to apply rationality."

"Oh is it. Is it really."

"Yes it is."

"Well why don't you piss off – I say that rationally mind you."

Clarence was not insulted. "I am more than happy to 'piss off' as you say once you hand over that knife."

Rebecca looked down at her knife. Suddenly it was now a very powerful weapon. She had her next answer.

"No. If I don't intend to hurt myself then what's the danger in me holding a knife, a nice sharp knife? I may wish to cut up some cheese."

Clarence stalled and considered her point. "Good point. Keep it. I have no wish to create a new conflict between us."

He looked her up and down as if for the last time. Rebecca felt him taking measurements, acting superior, and she hated him for it.

"Why are you doing this to yourself? There are many other, more imaginative ways to protest a grievance." Clarence put his question with renewed vigour and purpose.

Caught on the hop Rebecca played the ignorance card. Let him suffer. She would not play his game.

"Doing what to myself?"

"Punishing yourself. Tearing yourself apart. Trying to split yourself down the middle, psychologically speaking. You know it can do you no good."

Rebecca nearly screamed back. "Who the hell are you to analyse me, tell me what I should or shouldn't do – what is or isn't good for me!"

"You misunderstand me. I am not telling you what to do or what not to do. I am just asking, out of interest. I appreciate you don't want my help right now. And I respect that, wholeheartedly."

Rebecca had to wrestle to dam a surge of tears in the making. They were not tears of grief or sorry, or even fury; just tears of total bewilderment with another human soul: the kind that trod on other souls.

"You are setting up conflicts inside your head then feeding off them: in some strange way to make yourself feel better. It is all unnecessary you know. Why not just accept from me a fully comprehensive, unequivocal, truly honest apology for all misunderstandings, discourtesies, insults – unintentional I might add – or emotional distance. You are capable of far more constructive activities. You have great potential."

Clarence stopped speaking and raised his eyebrows for a moment, just like an actor on stage or in film. It was intended for effect. "There is always a future and it is always undefined: so reinvent it as and when required. Forget the past. Pack it away. Bury it. This is such an exciting world. So much creation and chaos, diversity and dreams."

Rebecca felt a sulk coming on. She did not want a compliment right now, especially not from him. "What do you mean?"

"I don't know. You will have to find that out for yourself."

That was not the answer Rebecca wanted to hear and she shook him off. Clarence had overstayed his welcome.

"Why don't you take your intellectual, analytical bullshit and piss off!"

"Why do you continue to be so aggressive? Surely the moment has passed?"

"Because it makes me feel good!"

Clarence paused again to consider her latest explosion of raw energized sentiment.

"Fair enough." He turned to go.

"Where are you going?"

"Back home."

"Why?"

"I am not wanted here."

Rebecca was stuck for something to say. As always the ball – the truth – was in his court. She watched him walk away, casually. The bastard really meant it. She lurched forward, as if to chase after him but then held herself in check after just one step. She wanted to both shout abuse at him and shout to make him stop and turn and think again. She stopped herself from doing either, vowing not to shout after any man again; and turned, at speed, intending to slam the door on the world. But she never got that far: she tripped over her own doorstep. As she fell she held on to her dignity. She did not cry out. She did not cry.

She felt her ankle. Suddenly everything had changed: now she was gripped by the fear of a sprained ankle; and she had dropped her knife. She glanced over her shoulder: at lightning speed Clarence was by her side, but his help she violently rejected out of hand. Instead she snatched up her knife, perhaps this time more for protection. Now, finally, she was losing the battle with the tears in her eyes.

Clarence remained calm, distant, barely involved. "You look in need of help."

"Looks are not everything. I don't need your help."

"Have you sprained an ankle?"

"What if I have. What do you care."

Clarence took that as an indirect 'yes' and put a hand under her elbow, offering to help when she was ready to lift herself back up onto her feet. Rebecca got wind of this and elbowed him firmly in the stomach. Clarence fell back and Rebecca felt the desire to celebrate: to celebrate his pain, perhaps his humiliation; and to celebrate her extended misfortune. In that instance all thoughts of Clarence and the state of her body were swept aside by the greater thought that she had a hot bath waiting. She looked at Clarence with contempt. He was looking at her, politely; patiently waiting for her to speak or make the next move. Rebecca did not know why but she felt like she owed him an explanation for sending him packing.

"My bath will be getting cold."

When she tried to move her worse fears were confirmed: she had sprained her ankle. Her tears began to flow but the worse tears had yet to come.

"Bugger. Bugger bugger bugger. I've bloody sprained it." A part of her wanted to play to the gallery, despite audience hostility.

Clarence moved in close a second time. "Here let me help you. I sprained my ankle recently. They can be a serious nuisance, especially if you employ them too soon after the time of the injury."

He put out his hands, offering support and encouragement. "Do not bear your bodyweight down on it. Rest on the other foot. Let that bear the brunt."

"I know. I know. You don't need to tell me. I'm not stupid."

This time, despite the voice of frustration, Rebecca's body language suggested that she was willing to receive him. But Clarence found out he was wrong: when he placed both hands on her she shoved him off, hard.

"Apologies. I did not mean to intrude."

"Just don't touch me."

"I will not touch you. I promise."

Now the tears which spilt out across her face could be seen by everyone and anyone, for conclusions to be drawn. It was a potential flood and Rebecca wanted to cry her heart out. But still she held the worse of them back. She was determined not to let him - the man who had devoured her - see her cry.

Judy appeared, to see what the commotion was, sniffing for clues and licking her lips after gorging on more top class cat food until it had begun to hurt. She could no longer walk properly; and as for mice she had no chance in the world of ever catching one of those right now, not even if they were blind.

Rebecca ignored her and hobbled on towards the bathroom and her hot bath, wishing to forget about all other living creatures within the immediate vicinity. As she hobbled, Clarence maintained a respectable distance, and did it respectfully: not saying a word, just waiting to be spoken to or shouted at – like every small boy waiting for the big woman to speak to him (and perhaps give him a piece of cake).

Finally Rebecca made it to the bath and ended up sitting on its ledge, there to take stock of her miserable, confounding situation. She turned and looked up over her shoulder to check that Clarence was still there. She knew he had been following her. She stared. He stared back, saying nothing, keeping all opinions and advice to himself. He did not wish to offend or inflame the fragile, emotionally charged situation by entering into a monologue about ways to improve the human condition. Right now the woman had an overriding, near psychotic wish to wallow in isolation.

Finally Rebecca could not contain her situation and began to cry. The tears were now a flood and she felt disgusted with herself. She did not want to be seen sobbing but now she lacked the willpower and physical strength to shout him away, out of her home. She wanted him off her planet.

Clarence spoke up. "Why have you begun to cry?"

Rebecca nearly choked on his fatuous words and answered sarcastically. "What do you mean why have I begun to cry?"

"I really want to know. Please do tell me."

Rebecca looked up, this time eyeballing the man still in her life with her teeth clenched, as if he had just stolen her job and trashed her intended career, and all dreams which went with it. Then she relaxed a little when he spoke again, again in his soft voice, the one he seemed to keep for special occasions – like when she wanted to kill herself.

"Please tell me why you are crying. I really want to know."

His concern for her seemed to be genuine: Rebecca could not dismiss that; and deep down she did not want to. She wanted to hug it. She wanted to answer him. She wanted to tell – perhaps kiss and tell. She badly wanted to let rip. Temporarily she put aside her own misfortune. She badly wanted to put the smart arse in his place. She stared up at him wide-eyed, the knife now held in a strong grip again, though she was not conscious of the fact.

"You're insufferable. That's the only way to describe you. You treated me like dirt. You don't give a damn about me, about anybody."

"I apologize. For all of these things."

Her memory was fired up and she fired it down upon Clarence.

"When you first arrived I baked you that lovely cake. It was a welcoming present. You just said it was OK – and that was under pressure. You only spoke to me when you were drunk. You're an animal sometimes."

"Are not all human beings animals?"

"There you go again, trying to be smart."

"I am just trying to be precise."

"You threw a stone at my Judy. You thought no one was looking but I saw you. I saw you. I saw you throw that stone at Judy."

"There was no excuse for that. I apologize – perhaps she was attempting to defecate in an unacceptable place? Perhaps I only intended to frighten her off? I cannot recall the incident. Whatever the circumstances you have my apologies."

"You played some stupid ballgame in the street with your mates. All of you drunk. All loud. That game cricket I suppose. Didn't think for one moment you might be disturbing everybody else's peace and quiet."

"Again I apologize."

"And then you threw up – didn't clean it up, just went indoors!"

"It had begun to rain as I remember, and hard. Soon there would have been nothing – or at least very little - to clean up. That aside it was still disgraceful behaviour on my part: thoughtless and anti-social. Again I apologize."

"Stop saying I apologize all the time!"

"I am sorry."

"The way you spoke to that lady in the street. It was so rude, disgraceful. You called her a desperate housewife."

"What can I say?" (Clarence was at a loss for words because he had been barred from giving an apology.)

"You could say sorry."

"Sorry."

"Say it like you mean it."

"Sorry. I am truly sorry." It sounded authentic, and pathetic.

Rebecca had run out of steam and had nothing left to punch. He had shown no emotion, put up no fight. He had simply caved in, leaving her nowhere to go. Rebecca looked down at her shiny plastic duck. It was floating. It still had its silly smile. She leaned over to flick it, and as a result she nearly fell in. Clarence grabbed her by the hand and pulled her back upright, back to safety. Rebecca held on to his long after it was necessary: flesh against flesh had its appeal; sweat intermingling was a temptation. Then she let go, judging it to be an act of weakness on her part.

Rebecca felt getting hotter. She felt even more flushed. She felt herself overheating. The rush of blood to her head had opened up the floodgates. It was a free-for-all but now she was all by herself. Her grip on the knife had weakened. It nearly slipped from her grasp.

"Why don't you ever call me beautiful, sexy!" She threw her bathrobe open and back over one shoulder as she spoke.

Clarence had a clear view of her breasts – not ample but adequate – and her pubic hair. All black and curly it was. But as usual Rebecca got no charged response, no hint that he was in anyway engaged or shocked or disturbed, or even just feeling slightly uncomfortable.

"I will do it now if it will please you."

"Too late!"

"For my lack of timing I am sorry."

Rebecca covered herself back up – barely - head still hurting from all the blood, heart now bleeding again, figuratively speaking. She wanted romance. All he had to offer was ridicule and rejection.

Rebecca looked down at her mighty duck. Unlike her it was unsinkable. "I know. You think I'm pathetic don't you."

"No I do not think that. I have never thought that. And apologies if I have ever given that impression. Sorry I said that word apologies. You are sick of that word now."

"It doesn't matter." She sounded tired.

"You have much to say. Why not just say it? I will be listening, with all interest, and no preconceptions."

Rebecca swept the water and watched her plastic duck bob up and down. She remembered the baths her mother used to give her, then those Aunty Jill used to give her. They were in conflict. This was despite the fact that the details were vague, perhaps reinvented. She had imposed her bias and now it could not be removed.

"When Aunty Jill did it I felt good."

"Is that a bad thing?"

"I set sister against sister."

"Are you sure about that? How could a child exert such influence upon two adults. Is that not to overestimate your abilities?"

"I liked her more than my mother."

"And who is to say that is a crime?"

Rebecca glanced up at Clarence to check he was being serious, not pulling her leg. Satisfied, she returned to her yellow plastic, most mighty duck. It had travelled down to the far end of the bath, as if to escape the conversation, and observation.

"She was not a very good mother my mother."

"Being 'a good mother' is a difficult thing. It is not an innate, guaranteed skill. Your mother had to take a chance when she decided to give birth to you. Feel sorry for her yes, but do not condemn her – just as you must not condemn yourself."

"I told her to get out of my life once."

"How old were you when you said that?"

"I don't know. In my teens. Sixteen? Eighteen?" Rebecca swept the water again, testing the temperature.

"Well that is a difficult age for anyone, especially when it comes to parent-child relationships. You were acting no worse than - no different from - many others of your age. I think you can forgive yourself for that outburst – and any similar which may have occurred. I feel sure she would have put it into context."

"And then they got divorced."

"That certainly was not your fault: they fell in love then out of love. The strength of their relationship and its ability to survive the passage of time was their responsibility, not yours. It was a totally private affair. And it commenced before you were born."

"You've got an answer for everything haven't you."

"Not necessarily. Only when the answer is obvious, or can be calculated from basic principles."

"And what about this crazy, immoral world we live in. Have you got a neat little answer for that?"

"That was not a question. You just made a statement – more an opinion if I may say so."

Clarence leaned against the wall and folded his arms. Rebecca thought – feared - he was contemplating a speech. She wanted to get in first.

"In some parts of Africa they stand like sticks – barely able to stand – walking miles each day just to get fresh water. Over here some of us can't move for body fat. Explain that!"

Clarence shook his head. "I cannot. There is no denying it is an imbalance – moral, economic, nutritional, however you wish to define it."

"I define it as obscene!"

"As you wish."

"Over here we're eating chemicals."

"I take it you are referring to industrial methods of food production?"

"Yes I am."

"Can you not reverse the trend?"

"Me? No of course not. Not by myself."

"No of course not. Not by yourself."

Rebecca threw him a sharp dark look. The man was playing with her again.

"I refuse to eat those chickens."

Clarence nodded: in her view giving her the respect she had earned – and craved.

"They're all squashed together like mice. It's criminal."

"Like mice?"

"You know what I mean."

Rebecca smashed the water with her hand, as if wanting to sink her duck.

"They bullied me at school for speaking my mind, for standing out."

"I thought you said that did not bother you anymore?"

"It doesn't, sometimes. Sometimes it does." She smashed the water again. Her hot bath was cooling down.

"Well they were young and brutal, perhaps stupid, whereas you were young and sensitive, perhaps clever. An unfortunate combination. Let it go. It is in the past, where it belongs. Do not let it drag down the present. Do not carry it into the future. It is a pointless burden."

"And what's so good about the present? I'm useless."

"You are not useless. How can you be useless if you got this far? Your own home. Your own business?"

"I was hopeless at making friends."

"Well start now."

"Even my boyfriends were useless."

"Surely just the one? And the fault was his not yours. It seems like she was a friend you could have done without."

"I was humiliated."

"That is understandable. You have a right to feel angry, misused, but not useless."

"I am useless! Stop telling me I'm not useless!" To make her point Rebecca struck the side of the bath with the end of her knife. Suddenly it was back in her hand with a vengeance.

"Very well."

"I'm a sad joke. I can't even kill myself."

"And who can?"

Rebecca looked up and snarled. "I can!"

"No you cannot."

She gripped the knife tightly. "Watch me!"

Clarence was not moved, or impressed. He tried a different approach. "Killing yourself is nothing to be proud of."

"Yes it is. And I want to be proud!"

"You want to be proud of yourself?"

"Yes!"

Clarence went silent and just stared at her, barely concealed within her bathrobe within her bathroom: face flushed; temper rising towards explosion; one hand shaking, the other tightly gripping a device which could cause great damage if used to full effect.

"Stop staring at me like that, like I'm inhuman."

"Excuse me. I did not mean to stare like that – or like anything."

Clarence tried to look away but it proved difficult. Finally he settled on the plastic duck. Rebecca felt abandoned – every gesture she now amplified.

"You don't believe me do you."

"Believe you?"

"That I can kill myself."

"Of course I do not believe you. You cannot do such a thing."

"Just watch me then!"

"I would rather not."

Rebecca ripped back her cuff and exposed her wrist. "Look at this then! See this!"

Clarence kept his eye on the plastic duck. As a totally inconsequential, near pointless object it had its uses. "No thank you. I am having no part of this."

Rebecca held the blade over her wrist. "Look where the knife is!"

"I have a good idea where the knife is."

The moment was frozen. Her ego had sucked up all her strength and left her hanging by a loose thread, just waiting to snap. And while her pounding, panic driven, heartbeat kept her alive her head was ready and willing to die. Rebecca held her breath as she waited for a reaction. There was none. Clarence did not attempt to intervene. He did not even look at her. As instructed he continued to look away and not stare.

"I'll do it you know."

"Go on then, proceed if that is your true wish."

"I will."

"Then do so. You need no signal from me – and certainly not my permission or approval."

Rebecca touched her skin with the blade. It was a shock and she began to shake. Clarence decided now was the time to step in and stop the charade. Gently he loosened her grip and extracted the knife from hand, being careful not to drop it in the bath. Secretly Rebecca was glad to see it go. She was breathing again, but still shaking.

"I think this hot bath would do you good."

"Yes," replied Rebecca modestly, and in a low, barely audible whisper.

"Here, stand up, let me help you out of this."

Rebecca, ready to comply, stood up; but only just. She was weak at the knees and would have collapsed had Clarence not held her up. This time she did not object to him making physical contact. Feeling his arms wrapped around her waist injected her with much needed and much welcomed vitality and reality.

Clarence helped her disrobe then, with her bathrobe laid neatly over one arm, helped her into her bath. He was acting the true gentleman. And it was appreciated. She was acting the true child. And it was admired.

"Is it still hot?"

"Just about."

"Here. Let me add some more hot water."

Clarence turned the tap and as more hot water piled in so Rebecca sat like a child: watching her lovely yellow plastic duck bob up and down and smiling, always smiling. For the moment Yellow was her favourite colour again. She leaned back, bent her knees, and slipped further beneath the water. And the heat swallowed her up. It consumed her, and left her too weak, too vacant, feeling too sublime to find cause for complaint. And as long as Clarence did not speak she did not mind him standing guard over her – she assumed he was standing guard over her. She even permitted herself to indulge in the fantasy that he was her protector again. Then he spoke and the illusion was shattered.

"You have been thinking about death recently, even to the extent of abruptly terminating your own life. And the idea does not terrify you?"

Rebecca, startled, sat up; creating a surge which rolled away from her, hit the end of the bath, then rolled back, to smack her in the midriff. The duck nearly drowned. It was saved only by the fact that it was plastic and full of air.

Rebecca turned defensive. "Of course it terrifies me."

"I saw no evidence of that."

"Perhaps you were looking in the wrong place."

"I was looking in the right place, the only place. And all I detected was demoralisation, then anger and hostility."

"I wonder why that was."

"I beg your pardon?"

"Nothing." Rebecca reached out for her duck and snatched it up, lest anybody else steal it from her.

"Death by your own hand. Does it not terrify you, scare you, at the very least unsettle you? Consider it: no more opportunity to participate in this world, embrace it – this world you obviously care so much about."

"Yes it does terrify me." Now she meant it. "Now can we change the subject please. I'd rather not talk about it thank you very much."

"Why did you contemplate such an extreme measure?"

"I said I'd rather not talk about it."

"Sorry. Please forgive me."

"I forgive you."

Rebecca played with her duck and Clarence continued to stand and keep watch; with an intensity which quickly made her feel ill at ease.

"Why do you give that toy so much attention?"

"Because I like to."

"No other reason? It cannot be reciprocated. And it is not another living creature like your cat."

"No other reason."

"I see."

"Really? I don't think so. And please you don't have to stand over me like that. I'm alright now."

"Are you sure?"

"I'm sure, quite sure."

Clarence suddenly jerked and turned his head. "What was that?"

"What was what?"

"That noise? Your cat? I think it came from your cat."

"I didn't hear anything."

"I'll go and check."

Rebecca slipped back down into the water, as far as she could go and still breathe, letting the water cover her up as much as possible. It was a neat, convenient way in which to escape the world. And she wanted to escape. She needed to relax. She wanted to dissolve.

Clarence rushed from the room, but not for long: in ten seconds flat he was back to break some news. Rebecca raised herself back up he was back, took one look at his face and almost wished she was dead.

"Your cat has just regurgitated a large quantity of partially digested food across your kitchen floor. It is not a pleasant sight. And it is accompanied by a foul smell, quite revolting. But then you would expect that."

Rebecca did her best to push the unsavoury news from her mind. There were other things she wished to mull over. She did some vague calculation in her head then spoke, politely, in earnest.

"As you came round today will you come round tomorrow?"

Clarence shook his head. "I am sorry but I cannot. Tomorrow I will be extremely busy."

"Extremely busy." Rebecca squeezed her duck tightly until it deformed and deflated under the pressure. But still it smiled. "What about the day after tomorrow then?"

"I cannot make any promises. You may never see me again."

Rebecca went red (again) and punched the water with her hand clenched into a solid fist. She created a big splash. She was back to square one, back to being the fool, back to feeling abandoned.

"Get out! Get out now! And don't ever come back!"

"Certainly." Clarence did not object to her very clear, very forthright order and left, at once. On his way out he stopped at the front door to shout back one last message. "Remember there is that mess to clear up!"

"How could I forget!"

"Well it is possible! You do have other matters weighing on your mind right now!"

"I said go away!"

As she shouted Rebecca pulled the plug and felt the escaping water suck on her toes. It was trying to suck her away, down into a hole.

"Understood!"

She heard the door shut. She watched her hot bath disappear. She would have to get out and go clean up an ugly mess. This was not the way she had envisaged the end to her evening. Anything was better than this. In one sense Judy had let her down. In another she had saved her.

✤ ✤ ✤

Log Entry

Time to go. First I had to try and help a female out of her troubles – assuming she was willing to accept my help. Even now I am not sure if my help was accepted. She had threatened to take her own life: though I did not sense that she was committed to carrying out the act. I may have been a contributory factor to her predicament.

Her connection with death was abstract. She simply wanted to detach herself from her own existence. She did not consider the consequences of her action, were she to follow it through. In particular she did not leave any instructions for cleanup and disposal of the body. The decomposing body would have produced a stench. The thought of her dead body lying undetected, decomposing did not alarm her, only the act of violence required to achieve this end. It was the one obstacle, not the thought of death itself. Throughout the episode that remained remote, abstract.

When the actual moment arrived she detached herself from the act of decision making and waited for some other agent – not my host – to make the decision for her. In this time she never thought about union with her god. He did not enter her thoughts. At this point I intervened, successfully.

Her interest in death may have been the result of wanting to disconnect from all other human contact: the emotional burden had become too much to support. She felt them to be too judgemental, too hurtful, too uncaring – some more than others. To countenance such an extreme action of self-destruction the human brain has to be misfiring, perhaps permanently dysfunctional; as to consider taking one's own life conflicts with every natural survival instinct. Every life form I have encountered prefers life over death and does everything possible to maintain that state.

Chapter Twenty One

The telephone rang and it rang and it rang. It was early morning and nobody would answer it – not Max, not Clarence. It carried on ringing, refusing to be dismissed, until finally Max, cursing and against his better judgment, dragged himself out of bed to answer it. There was always the possibility – albeit a very small one – that it was for him. It wasn't of course. It was for Crazy Clarence.

"Clarence! Get out here!"

Nothing – as Max explained to the man on the end of the line. The man sounded extremely pissed off when Max explained that Clarence was unlikely to come to the phone. The man begged him to try. It was important, extremely important. Max went and banged on the bedroom door, demanding that Clarence get out of bed and take the call.

"I know you're awake! I know you can hear me! It's your mate Tim."

"What does he want?" croaked Clarence, sounding scared, which he was.

"He wants to talk to you. What d'you think."

"What about?"

"I don't know – and I don't care – but he sounded pissed off about something."

Silence. Max waited for a reply but all he got was silence.

"Well are you coming out?"

"No. Tell him no. Tell him I'm not well."

"You tell him – though I suspect he already knows."

"No."

"Tosser." Max plodded back to the phone and passed on the message.

Tim did not take it well and slammed the phone down, after swearing at Max, the innocent party.

"Tosser," said Max, just before the line went dead.

He crawled back into bed, in a bad temper and unable to get back to sleep. This made the bang on the door forty minutes later less of a disruption and more of an inconvenience. He knew he was the one who would have to answer it.

It was Tim of course, looking like he had just fallen out of bed, looking like he was looking for a fight, looking like he had a bone to pick; looking like he would not take no for an answer; looking like shit. Judging by appearances he and Max had much in common – mostly Clarence.

"Where is he?"

"Where d'you think this time of day."

"In his bedroom?"

"Well done."

"I want to speak to him. Can I come in?"

"Be my guest. I'm not going to stop you."

Tim hesitated, momentarily thrown by the unexpected act of invitation and cooperation. This was all too easy. Then he stepped inside, gingerly, as if it was the first time he had ever stepped inside this particular place. He caught his breath then marched up to the bedroom door of his best mate, paused to frame his opening address, then banged on the door. No reply. He banged on it again. Still no reply.

"I know you're in there. Come out. I want to speak to you – I demand to speak to you. I think you know what about."

Still no reply.

"If you don't come out I'll come in there and drag you out."

Still no reply but this time there was the sound of movement. An animal was stirring: shuffling about in its cage, adjusting its nest; hoping the bigger animal which wanted to kill it and eat it would get bored and go away.

"I mean it. You know I can do it. Remember the last time you really pissed me off like this."

The door was pulled open just enough to create a narrow gap through which Clarence could peer. He had only his underpants on, and he wore a quaint, superfluous smile – in full recognition that a smile was not required and would not be appreciated.

"I'm changing." Clarence spoke with a limp.

He looked sad, sunk, and he too looked like shit. He had not slept a wink and it showed, from the top of his chin to the top of his hair. From Tim's perspective he looked like any guilty, once decent, once trustworthy, man should look: collapsing under the weight of his own guilt. The instinct to feel sorry for his best mate reared up. Tim stamped on it. Instead he grabbed his best mate by the collar, kicked the door back, and whipped him out, like a fish out of water or a roast out of the oven. He wanted to barbecue him over hot coals.

"Why? You're my best mate – were I should say."

Clarence had no answer, except the pat one. He played it for pity.

"I have been going through this bad patch. I have not been myself. You know that. I think the same can be said for your wife."

"Sod that. That doesn't give you the excuse to sleep with my wife – you, my best mate, or so I believe."

"I am still your best mate."

Tim rammed his ex-best mate against the wall and banged his head. Clarence wanted to pass out, but held on.

"And I'm Father Xmas."

"It won't happen again. I can promise that with absolute certainty. Such things like this only happen once. After which the ground shifts. The model of the relationships involved is changed - sometimes for the better – and new rules of engagement apply. The universe is different."

"Too right it won't. I suspected she was sleeping with someone but I didn't it was you."

"You seem to suggest this has been a continuous, repetitive course of action. It only happened once. Did she not tell you that? Or is it that you do not wish to believe her? Will you believe me? Will you believe both of us?"

"Okay so it was only the once. And that makes it OK does it? Less of a crime?"

"No of course not. Just not so bad? There is more to good and bad than Boolean logic surely? For the rules of moral engagement to work and be practicable there has to be more than zeros and ones, plus versus minus. Otherwise all human interaction comes to a halt very quickly."

"Shut up. I don't want to hear this crap."

To shut him up Tim really wanted to punch him but Max was looking on, as if ready to step in and pull them apart. He couldn't have been more wrong. Max was just enjoying himself. Entertainment like this didn't come along every day, and rarely was it alcohol free.

"Don't I at least get an apology?"

"Yes I of course you do. I can do that and I want to do that. And I can give you some money. Let me give you some money. Everybody likes to receive money. Especially those who do not have enough."

"Money? I don't want your money."

"Understood."

"Just give me that apology."

Clarence sucked in air, filled his lungs, gulped, and spoke, with a heavy heart – just like he had seen it happen in an old black and white film about a man chasing after a woman for love – a woman who could run faster than him, metaphorically speaking.

"I apologize."

"Say it like you mean it."

"I apologize. I do. I apologize. Wholeheartedly. Without reservation or excuse. Without any thought for the repercussions."

As he spoke Clarence sounded wasted: so much so that Tim had to let him go. He was also spent. They both hung there, waiting for the other to make the next move.

Max, sensing that he had seen everything worth seeing, slid back into his room, determined to go back to sleep; refusing to be interrupted anymore; refusing to take anymore calls or open any more doors or get involved in other people's lives in this neck of the woods. He wanted out - as did Clarence – as did Tim – as did Sam.

Clarence repeated his apology twice as Tim walked away then shut his bedroom door on the big wide world: perhaps to seek solitude and escape from suicidal women and angry mates; or perhaps just to continue dressing. No matter how hard he tried he could not get an image of Rebecca, naked and in a bath, out of his head.

In return Tim shouted 'fuck off' on his way out. Each additional apology reduced the impact of the first once. Each additional apology sounded more and more like empty rhetoric, even a crafty piss-take. Tim didn't want to believe that. He still wanted to believe in Clarence, his best mate. They had shared too much. They had too much to lose. Somehow he would square the triangle. Somehow he would make the circle round again, all bumps and cracks removed. Somehow he would win his wife's heart back again. They also had too much to lose.

Back outside in the sun Tim bumped into a familiar fraught face coming the other way in a hurry. It was the troublemaker John, that 'non-acquaintance' Clarence always did his best to avoid, but this time without a beard. Tim was struck dumb, and so immobile that he made no effort to move aside. He could not move aside. He was stuck to the spot. John, irked, was forced to ask permission to pass. The request passed Tim by: or to be more precise it could not enter his head and register.

"I will ask you one more time. Will you move aside please."

Tim woke up. "What are you doing here?"

Taken aback by the ferocity of the question, John decided not to cooperate.

"I came to see Clarence obviously but what business is it of yours?"

"None. But no. You can't see him. He doesn't want to see you."

"Are you going to get out of my way? I may be a poof to you but I can still punch." John looked like he meant it.

Tim began to lose his nerve. Things were slipping out of control.

"Look I know he doesn't want to see you right now – not any time I think. It's nothing personal. He just doesn't want to see anyone right now."

John began to wind up for a serious confrontation. If it came to the crunch he would not hesitate to push this irritating stupid little man aside.

"Clarence is expecting me. He needs my help."

"He needs your help?"

"That's right. He needs me."

"I don't think so. He's still in bed."

Tim suddenly remembered Clarence decked out in his underpants. He did not want to think about it. He certainly did not want to speculate.

"Still in bed?" John looked at his watch. "Well let's see."

He looked back up at Tim.

"Can I get past please? This is the last time I'm going to ask nicely. I can do it you know. I can get physical. Just ask George."

Tim's mood began to swing towards a new place of safety. The thought 'sod it what do I care' entered his mind.

Tim backed off, and to one side.

"He's all yours."

Now he didn't want to leave. This was suddenly becoming all too interesting.

John moved on, reached the front door then stopped.

"The front door's open?"

"As you said he's expecting you."

John tapped lightly on the front door and spoke softly, afraid to disturb.

"Clarence?" Then he repeated himself loudly. "Clarence!"

He turned to Tim for clues but Tim gave none. He did however give permission to proceed with a neat baseline stroke of his arm. John ignored the taunt. He pushed the door further open but did not step inside. It was another man's castle.

"Clarence! It's me, John! Here as promised! And on time! Well almost!"

With that Clarence burst on to the scene. He was dressed. He looked happy, full of joy. He looked like he was ready to go somewhere right away. He looked at his watch. This man John was very good at keeping to a schedule. Tim could not believe the change in him – despite the fact that he still looked like shit. But then state of mind counted for a lot – most things in fact.

"Only ten minutes late. Excellent!"

John threw Tim a thoroughly female, thoroughly maligned look of 'I told you so'. Tim had to just stand there and take it on the chin. He was outnumbered.

John put a question. "Can I use the loo before we go?"

"Certainly. Help yourself."

Both Tim and Clarence listened as John took a long drawn out, overdue piss. The heavy flow of urine smashing into the toilet bowl could be heard throughout the flat. Max turned over in his bed and swore. He did not want to listen to this. When he heard the toilet flush he finally resolved to get up, get dressed and go out, anywhere – preferably somewhere that sold alcohol this early on in the day.

As he waited Clarence calmed down and took on a look of total deadly seriousness. He looked racked – the result of fighting his own fatigue. He was clutching his ropey old road atlas. It was rolled up in his hand like an article of war, or a field-marshal's baton. It had served him well over the years. Tim noticed it but made no comment. All he could do was watch. He was in no fit state to get involved.

Then John appeared, looking relieved, then looking worried when the true physical state of Clarence sank in. John wanted to take his hand and check his pulse but Clarence brushed him aside.

"We must leave right now. No time to hang around."

"Understood. Have you got all you need?"

"I don't need anything except this map."

Clarence turned to Tim who had taken a few steps back.

"I'll see you again, soon Tim I'm sure. And when I do I will be better, back to my old self. I promise. But for now I have to leave you."

"So you won't be shagging my wife then?"

Clarence looked at Tim, completely puzzled.

"No. Definitely not. It was a lapse of judgement, a momentary act of weakness. As I said before conditions have changed. It cannot happen again. Rest assured: your wife would simply not allow it to happen again – not with me not with anyone, male or female."

"Thank you. That's reassuring."

Fuck him, thought Tim. And fuck you, he thought as he threw John one last look. John was trying not to grin, but not trying that hard.

"John shall we go?"

"I'm ready when you are. I are ready for this?"

"I am so let us proceed."

John offered his hand and Clarence took it; and both faced Tim down, both puzzled as to why he was still hanging around.

"Where are you two going?"

Clarence answered him. "On a trip. Into the countryside. To see someone important. I have a very important appointment to keep."

"And what's he got to do with this?" Fist clenched, Tim poked his thumb at John.

John jumped in. He felt an immediate need right now to justify his presence to this terse little sod who was upsetting his day of cause and adventure.

"I'm in charge of the driving while Clarence navigates. He's a nervous driving. He doesn't like driving. And it's a long way."

"And where is this place?"

"Somewhere in Norfolk – sorry Clarence should I have told him that?"

Clarence smiled, badly. "I have no secrets to keep."

He looked at his watch – time keeping was now very important to him - and prodded John playfully.

"Come on we have to go."

He squeezed John's hand and the two headed off towards John's car but they did not rush. Clarence looked fragile, unsettled. Tim watched them both, then followed – but keeping his distance. It was like watching patient and nurse. Clarence was walking tentatively, carefully – so carefully that John notice and make a comment.

"Just my ankle. It is still tender after an injury. Nothing for you to worry about."

John did worry. On a day like this worrying came easy.

"Who are you seeing?" asked Tim.

"Someone you don't know."

"How long are you going for? I mean when will you be back?"

"Hopefully today."

"What are you seeing them about?"

"Sorry, that is private."

As John unlocked the passenger door Clarence squeezed him around the waist.

"I do appreciate your help today."

John went red but said nothing. Tim was gob smacked and beginning to go slightly berserk. With John's help - not actually needed - Clarence manoeuvred himself into his seat.

"In you go."

"Thank you."

John then ran round to the driver's side and jumped in. On his way he threw Tim a final look of possession and power over loss and hopelessness.

Settled, Clarence gestured towards Tim to come to his side. Tim responded and caught him up.

"Tim I see you are worrying. Do not worry. I should be fine. If all goes well I will be back to my previous self."

"And if not?"

"Well then things will stay the same for a little while longer."

Clarence lowered his voice.

"Tim, one last thing. I have given you my most sincere apologies for my behaviour with regards to your wife. Can I ask you to pass them on to your wife? I created unnecessary complications."

"Okay. But why don't you do that yourself?"

"I might, but it is unlikely. We will have to wait and see."

Clarence pulled his door shut. "Come on John time we got to get moving."

As John started the engine a thought struck Tim and he almost stuck his face to the glass.

"Hey you're no nervous driver!"

Clarence waved back.

"You can't let him take you away!"

"Yes I can!"

"Will you call me!"

"Cannot promise you anything!"

Tim watched them drive away, like Bonnie and Clyde, Gilbert and Sullivan, and was left with a sick feeling in the pit of his stomach; like he had been left holding the baby while its parents shot off to the shops, leaving no instructions, no disposable nappies. Clarence had attained a new level of weirdness. He had fled the scene with the one man he had sworn he was scared of. Clarence did not swear slightly: Tim knew that. Unless of course – no, thought Tim, that makes no sense.

Fighting off that loopy ludicrous thought Tim retreated back into the flat, slumped down into a chair and did his best to chill out after the two-way grilling. Perhaps he had been too hard on his old mate – no, the bastard had slept with his wife. On the other hand it could be argued that his wife had slept with his best mate. Perhaps she had seduced him. In that respect call it evens.

Tim jumped up. No he wasn't having any of it. He couldn't let that man have him, take charge. He had to go after his mate. They shared too much precious history. They had a connection which had survived through good times and bad. He could not walk away from this one. He banged on the lodger's door.

"Do you know where he's gone!"

Max rolled over. "Who!"

"Who do you think!"

"Not a clue."

Damn it, thought Max. Sod it. His head rolled. Sod it, just get it over and done with.

"Yes I have. It's all in the letter she gave him yesterday!"

"Where's the letter!"

"No fucking idea! Now leave me alone!"

Tim entered Clarence's bedroom to begin his search - it was the obvious place to start. There he was surprised to see that Clarence still held on to his teddy bear. Tim remembered they had used it once as an indoor football. The room was the usual tip and more than usual it smelt disgusting. Immediately he spotted some badly folded sheets of writing paper by the side of the bed. They were crumpled, curling and crushed and were held down by two two pound coins. It was as if they had demanded payment – and had received it.

Tim sat down and rushed to read all there was to read. He spilt the money and a coin rolled under the bed. One letter made for interesting reading, but was scary. The other made for boring reading, but was relevant. One left him hopeful. The other left him fearful. One left him interested. The other left him distressed. One invited questions. The other had no answers. One implored him. The other dismissed him. Both consumed him. Both were written by women: one had to see him urgently; the other threatened to kill herself. This was the man who had slept with his wife and had now fled the scene with another man; and not just any other man. Try as he might, Tim could not make any of the pieces add up.

Tim was left feeling knackered and numb in the head; with nowhere to go; with nowhere to take the story, with no place to fall back on. He could not get out. He knew he had to go get his friend and get whatever it was that needed sorted sorted. As he threw himself out flat across the bed to draw breath and expel gathering demons so the doorbell rang. He froze. Next door Max rolled over and buried his head in the sand. It was followed by a tap on the door, then the sound of a slender female voice.

"Clarence? Are you there?"

Tim's initial reaction was to remain motionless, to not make a noise, to not get eaten. He could not explain why. It just felt like the right thing to do. The voice grew closer, stronger, more concerned.

"Clarence? It's me Fiona."

Tim sat up, electrified: the bedroom door was being pushed back slowly; just enough for Fiona to poke her head around it, and inspect.

"He's not here. He's gone."

"Who are you?"

"Tim. I know you. You're that Fiona he's been on about. You're one of his women."

"Thank you."

She looked around the room and was not impressed, Then she saw the teddy bear but was not amused.

"You said he's not here. Do you know where he is?"

"Not exactly, but I know where he'll be – and even when."

Fiona frowned as she tried to get to grips with the information.

"Sorry I don't understand."

"He's headed off to see someone, about something important. Urgent it is. It's all very serious, all very secret, all so fucking weird."

"I need to see him. I need to know he's alright."

"Same here."

Tim kicked the teddy bear across the room. Fiona watched it fly a little then land a lot.

"Have you tried calling him on his mobile?"

"No. Good idea."

Tim got up then wrestled with a problem.

"Mine's in the car."

"Here, use mine."

Fiona pulled hers out of her handbag and Tim made the call. They both jumped when another mobile woke up and made a singsong racket under the bed. Tim felt compelled to crack a joke, to try and lighten things up.

"He hasn't got his mobile with him then."

The joke fell flat and Tim fell back down on the bed to consider his earlier commitment. Now it felt even more urgent that he chase after his mate.

"I'm going after him. I don't know what's wrong. I don't know what's right. I think he's snapped. Acting weird. Just run off with a man I thought up to now he couldn't stand to be within three feet off."

"He sounded strange last night."

"What do you mean?"

"He rang me."

"And?"

Fiona made a pitch.

"Can I come with you? Let me come with you. Please. He rang me last night. He sounded odd, very queer, fatalistic almost."

"And?"

Fiona let fly.

"He said he may not see me again. He said he was sorry for any complications he may have caused. Said there may be another woman in his life but he wasn't sure. Said he was only trying to be honest with me."

"That was gracious of him. Always the gentleman our Clarence."

Fiona detected a sour note. "What do you mean?"

"Nothing."

"So can I come with you?" Fiona could only just hang on.

"Sure. If you feel that strongly about it. Do you mind doing some of the driving?"

"No."

"One of us will need to map read."

"I've got that satellite thingy in my car. I'm not very good with maps."

"Sat Nav?"

"That's it."

"We'll take yours then?"

Fiona nodded emphatically. She didn't like driving other people's cars.

"I'll still bring my map along – just in case. I don't trust those things."

"It's been fine up to now."

"But we're talking Norfolk – middle of nowhere."

"You know best."

"Let's go then – do you need to use the loo first?"

"No."

"Let's go then."

And they did. And Max never knew it. And Tim felt he had just poked his wife in the eye. He did not ring his wife. He was not talking to her and she was not talking to him. It would be a long time before he would be missed. It would be a long day.

✦ ✦ ✦

Log Entry

To acquire the help of my companion I had to fake key facts and manipulate his emotional involvement to ensure concern for, and commitment towards my welfare. I had to do this. I cannot complete this long journey without help. This method of manipulation is a device humans use regularly and I have to admit it does have its uses. I did not go so far as to offer sexual intercourse as this may compromise my host.

We are now moving at great speed and we are engulfed by the noise of a great many combustion engines. I have noticed a distinct change in the behaviour and attitude of my pilot, a male companion. He is concentrating hard on the task of piloting his machine, though there is much else going on inside his head. He has become very subdued and has reversed his wish to engage in conversation. He is even questioning his own judgement and current role. Conversation between us has almost collapsed.

I suspect this is primarily due to my repeated refusal to divulge any further information about the female we are going to see – despite his constant pressure. He is keen to know more about this female. What is her name, her profession? What are her qualifications? And of course what exactly is my ailment? Secondary to this is my deep interest in this peculiar world, especially that created by human beings for their own particular needs and gratification. Hence I have little time for him. He resents this. He feels he is being shut out. These sentiments are bottled up inside his head and as a result his head is beginning to hurt.

My companion enquired about my host's visit to his friend: an expert (relatively speaking) in mind examination and analysis. I explained that the man performed no analysis of any worth and presented no results. I sensed my companion did not believe me.

All that aside, he is piloting well and maintaining good speed along this multi-lane channel which has been designed specifically for use by cars and other machines designed to provide fast, comfortable movement across land. Judging by the large number of machines which pack every lane, it is a very popular route. In places their density is so high that individual units appear to coalesce into one amorphous moving mass. We are all speeding towards something, or away from something.

High speed movement in these machines soon becomes hypnotic. Interior conditions are too comfortable. They make the human body lazy. All movement is strictly channelled along lanes precisely constructed to cut a route across land with an almost mathematical elegance. I presume sacrifices were made to allow this to be. As these lanes are congested with the heavy traffic of humans on the move, the irony is it is the land and the life on it which is isolated.

Enclosed within this machine creates a sense of disconnection from the world around me. I am travelling away from it. I am travelling towards it. In the distance it remains unchanged. Up close it is unrecognisable. It has become a piece of fiction. I believe this world is starting to affect me. Must leave soon, before I become too involved and non-objective.

Only forward movement is permitted, and to maintain constant flow a minimum speed is strictly enforced. You do not stop unless compelled to. If you suddenly reduce your speed you disrupt the flow around you and suffer criticism from those directly affected. Some of it can be very severe, brutal even. Thereafter you are held in low regard.

At times these machines are packed together, as if for company or safety, with little space separating them even when the speeds are high. Yet the level of concentration varies quite significantly between pilots. Some barely register what is happening around them and apply only minimum effort with respect to monitoring their situation. They let their thoughts wander, to the point that they concentrate on anything but the task of piloting. They are distracted by others things: work, domestic and relationship issues; the in-built entertainment technology; their passengers; the behaviour of other pilots. At the other end of the scale some minds are intensely focused: they concentrate wholly on the act of safe, considerate piloting. Some have completely worn themselves out. They struggle to remain alert.

In general most pilots appear to be in a state of denial or a near trance. All wish to arrive somewhere sooner rather than later. All are in a hurry. Yet despite moving at speeds far in excess of what they can achieve through natural means, few display signs of contentment. A lack of gratitude appears to be the norm.

A minority are in far more of a hurry than the rest: they travel at speeds far exceeding the average. They expect their machines to perform as directed and trust them to provide protection at all times. Their actions towards those hindering their progress are aggressive and reckless. Circumstances must be exceptional for them to be exhibiting such behaviour.

Some pilots are extremely capable when it comes to performing multiple mental tasks in parallel. They steer and adjust speed and process feedback received from surrounding conditions while simultaneously engaging in two-way conversation and related thoughts through the use of mobile communication devices. Some even push themselves further and engage with other passengers. Where there are small young humans on board most pilots do their best to ignore them, or are ignored.

Most pilots expect other pilots around them to behave in a certain way. They do not always conform and this is a cause for conflict, even if only within the mind of the single individual. It can lead to an angry exchange of hand and facial signals: signals designed to express unhappiness, criticism, dismay or dismissal.

Some pilots need to submerge themselves in a continuous stream of loud sounds, usually rhythmic and repetitive with language thrown in: a form of human entertainment designed to please and placate, or provoke. This behaviour is a reaction to the audible intrusion of the surrounding environment, and/or to alleviate the effects of boredom.

I caught sight of a male and a female who had parked their car on spare space adjacent to the lanes. I presume their machine, a car, was not functioning according to specification and they had been forced to stop. The male looked very unhappy with the state of his machine and, judging by the way she directed her frustration at him, the female regarded the problem as his fault. I sensed they felt isolated, abandoned and excluded from all other humans on the move. They were outsiders now and it hurt. Strange, as (I assume) this machine failure was not their fault. My pilot did not give them a second glance.

With regard to manufacturer, size and quality machine build has an impact on the minds of pilots and passengers. The bigger the machine, the greater its power, the more sophisticated its operating parts, so the greater the sense of superiority and isolation.

Pilots – custodians perhaps – of very large powerful machines designed to transport huge quantities of matter over very long distances are the most isolated: physically as well as psychologically. The height of their control cabins is much greater than the norm for all other machines. At this height the pilots literally do look down at the crowd around them. Some big machines are designed to transport large numbers of human beings in comfort – presumably with their agreement.

The relationship of these 'super pilots' with each other and with the environment around them is different from that of other drivers (for whom it is almost non-existent). There is a sense of brotherhood and bonding. There is a higher degree of aspiration and determination with regards to time and motion, deadlines and delays, and even fuel consumption. But sometimes in conflict with all this is a lack of concentration and low levels of physical energy: the result I suspect of lack of sleep; or perhaps too much sexual activity combined with too little food consumption.

Suddenly, without warning, my pilot had to decrease his speed in an instant, and almost stop. He became very alarmed then dismayed by the nature and size of the delay ahead. We became part of a slow moving queue. Other queues moved at similar speeds on either side of us. Humans around us reacted in much the same way. Being caught up in a queue changed everything, for everyone. Anguish was released on a major scale. Stress levels rose. My pilot made various negative, judgmental comments while I said nothing – though I was extremely aware of the amount of time being consumed for negligible progress.

The dynamics of the queues was interesting: they moved at slightly different speeds; and nearly always in waves, or surges, hardly ever at a constant rate. The difference in queue movement was such that some pilots aspired to take advantage of the relative shifts and promote their position. They did this by carefully observing the movements of other machines and slipping – jumping almost - into any gap which opened up in a faster moving queue. It paid small dividends but at a great cost in mental energy expended. Also the reaction of the watching crowd was not positive, so there was a sense of social exclusion.

This delay continued for a long time, until we reached a point where two queues had to merge into one. It was here that we discovered the cause of the disruption. Two machines had collided – one into the back of the other I presume – and now neither could function. Their pilots stood in heartfelt discussion with uniformed officials responsible for managing and resolving such incidents. Like their machines the pilots and passengers looked broken. In this respect the relationship between humans and their machines borders on the spiritual. They were the sole object of interest for passing drivers, then immediately dismissed as two queues became three again and normal travelling conditions returned. Gratitude – in a fleeting but intense burst - was felt by all those affected, including us. I had lost time but a contingency remains.

In time we left the high speed channel and returned to the slower, more traditional model of one or two lanes: irregular in design and disrupted by connecting junctions and pedestrian traffic controls. This put greater demands on the task of piloting. On the plus side we were rewarded with superior views of the open countryside, which in turn generated fresh interest during the journey – at least it did for me. The intensified irregular motion did however affect the body of my host. In particular his digestive system began to suffer. It left him feeling uncomfortable, feint and nauseous. The wish, then the urge, to eject food matter back out through the mouth grew in strength. I contained it, suppressed it, until we had some legitimate reason to stop.

Stop we did, at a fuel depot, when my pilot saw the need to refuel and stretch his limbs, especially his two legs. He had been sitting in the same position for a long time and it was not to his liking. I saw this as a golden opportunity for my host's body to relieve itself of its digestive burden and recover its balance and composure.

While my pilot pumped fuel into his machine's storage tank my host's body ejected a small quantity of semi-processed food matter at high speed. My pilot was not impressed but did want to come to my aid. However he was committed first to completing his current task: a financial transaction was required. Instead I was approached by a young male who took great interest in my state of health. There were no sexual overtones. It was purely a manifestation of concern. I discovered he was also a making a journey. At his request I allowed him to join us. He needed transport and human company I suspect. This was against my pilot's wishes, though he made no public protest. I had to persuade him to introduce himself.

✦ ✦ ✦

John showed no interest so Clarence did all the talking, which he was more than happy to do. He put his heart and soul into making their guest feel at home, to the point of exhaustion on both sides. Clarence twisted round in his seat as far as was possible and made the hitchhiker the centre of attention. It was like a small kid eager to sit with the big kid: to get to know him; to earn his respect and confidence. This, the young man would grow to hate – but his hate could not be released, not if he wanted to hang on to his free rise. And he knew that. So it would be a case of staring out of the window and pretending to be interested in all the stuff on the outside. The car was small and it gave its occupants no space, no relief from the infringement of others; and it stung them with the imposition of a fake intimacy. The signs were right there at the beginning: Clarence had to extract the man's name like a bad tooth.

"So your name is Terence."

"Yes it still is."

"Are you comfortable? You do not look comfortable." Clarence felt Terence was not completely at ease with himself.

"Yeah. Thanks. Whatever," replied Terence, unsettled by the attention.

"Do you always sit like that?"

"Like what?"

"Tensed up."

Terence turned back to the window, tension level pushed up another notch, guard up against a danger not yet defined.

"Whatever."

"Do you travel a lot?"

"On and off."

"Do you have your own means of transport?"

"No. Don't need it and can't afford it. Rely on others. You know the score."

"Like us," quipped John.

"Like you."

"So where are you going today?"

"Here and there. All over the place. You know what it's like."

"No I don't. You must be going somewhere specific. Else why ask me where we are going?"

"Swaffham. I'm heading to some place near Swaffham." Now give it a rest man, thought Terence, before I smash your face in.

Clarence studied the open pages in his road atlas.

"We can get you most of the way. Why Swaffham?"

Terence turned his attention to the back of John's neck and thought of a female friend, without her clothes on. She was not his girlfriend but he dearly wanted to have sex with her, again and again and again. Her current boyfriend was a wanker, a first degree tosser. Seeing her naked inside his head was easy: he had once passed her a towel as she stepped out of the shower, all wet and delicious and flaunting her naked body. She knew the score. She was playing the market.

Clarence brought him back down to earth with a hard landing.

"Is it for sex?"

"What!" Terence shifted position and nearly sprained his neck as he did a twist and shout.

John banged the back of his head against the headrest and clenched his teeth. The car jolted as he accidentally pushed down hard on the accelerator. Clarence realised his mistake.

"Sorry. I thought perhaps you were pursuing a romantic liaison."

"Well I'm not." So fuck off.

"There must be some reason. Work? Pleasure? Home?"

"Home? I don't have a home." Terence answered proudly but with a pinch of regret.

"No home? How do you survive?"

"I live on the move. Stay with friends. I'm a free spirit."

"A free spirit?"

Clarence did not sense a free spirit, more a mass of tangled up compulsions and irreconcilable conflicts.

Terence returned to his desolate window view with an increased determination not to look elsewhere, especially at that face. John took a reading in the rear view mirror. In his judgement this was a poor excuse for a free spirit. Standards had dropped. And the radioactive hairstyle was scary. Why the pink and orange lines? Was it to attract the opposite sex? Perhaps I am getting old, thought John. Where are you George when I need you? All that aside he did find the shambolic dress sense rather sexy.

Clarence did not give up. "Work or pleasure then?"

Terence wanted to bang his head against the window.

"Pleasure I suppose. Or work. Could be work. Bit of both."

"That must give you a great feeling."

"Why?"

"Working for the sheer pleasure of it as opposed to financial gain. Finding pleasure in work. A rare condition these days judging by the evidence."

"Yeah right whatever."

"What sort of work? And what sort of pleasure?"

Terence threw his head back as if making an appeal to the gods.

"Is there a point to any of this?"

"Just interested. Other people's lives interest me."

John glanced sideways with a sense of war torn deja vu.

Terence's head began to buzz: he was suddenly presented with the excuse to lecture, to boast, to impress these sad elders of the community. He did not regard them as belonging to his world. The age gap kept them out and kept his spirit safe from corruption, 'free' in his book. Hence all the alcohol, the joints and the regular sex to relieve the strain and monotony of so much liberty and independence. He took the plunge, pulling his dirty rancid, ransacked rucksack closer in as if for protection or for easier access to its contents. Perhaps he was going to pull out his bible or a bar of chocolate, or a bottle of whisky.

"I protest."

"You protest?"

"You protest?" echoed John, now cautiously interested in this glamorous declaration.

"You protest about what?" asked Clarence.

"About what? Where have you been man?"

"Sorry I don't understand."

"It's all bad. It's all shit! The planet's gone to shit! We have to protest!"

Suddenly Terence was very animated, and very sincere. This pleased Clarence. He had hit upon a truth.

"So you are protesting. About lots of things?"

"Of course."

"All at once?"

"No don't be stupid. Not all at once. One at a time."

"Are you protesting today?"

"Yes."

"Protesting alone?"

"No, with mates. We're meeting up. Together we make an army to be reckoned with."

"You fight battles?"

"Yeah. But peacefully. We keep it peaceful. We don't give them an excuse to arrest us."

"And this brings you pleasure? You did say it was work and pleasure?"

Terence frowned and tried to avoid making eye contact with the face bearing down on him. Staring out of window provided no escape. His natural tendency towards outright aggression – always in the name of protest - began to gather strength. It had started the moment he had made the discovery that upsetting people brought him pleasure: starting with his smaller sister; then moving on to his parents; then moving on to anyone in a position of authority; and then, logically, on to the 'system' – one might say all the result of natural career progression.

"It's not a matter of doing it for pleasure. It has to be done."

"So it is just work then?"

"Suppose so if you put it like that."

"What other way is there to put it?"

Terence shot the driver a look in the mirror, urging him to shut the other tosser up. Their eyes briefly locked, exchanging both distrust and problem recognition in equal measure.

"It's something I have to do. It's my duty."

"Because?"

"Because I say so." Back to the window and much the same view.

Appreciative that his guest was now in a state of high vexation Clarence went quiet for a few minutes before putting his next question. He fiddled with the radio until John told him to stop.

"Can I ask what is it you protesting about today?"

Oh fuck, thought Terence, give it a rest man.

"Animal welfare."

John spoke up, impressed. "Good for you."

Clarence wanted clarification.

"All animals? Including humans?"

"No of course not. Just those used in research – fucking pointless research just to produce another drug or beauty cream. It's a fucking disgrace."

"That I do agree with." John wanted to clap but the steering wheel came first. "It's outrageous."

"Exactly." Terence, boxed in, was glad he had an ally. He was no longer outnumbered.

Now John had a question.

"How will you make your protest?"

"Usual way. Stand outside the gates with banners. Make a fucking loud noise. Annoy the owners. Embarrass the workers. Play cat and mouse with the security guards. And grab it all on camera for the web."

Clarence suddenly had a thought.

"But today is Sunday? Does this establishment open on a Sunday?"

"We're doing all that tomorrow. Today we just meet up, have a party, get pissed, get stoned. Blow our brains out of the water."

John jumped in again. "Hence the pleasure."

"If you like. Play today. Work tomorrow."

"And then what?"

"We wait for the news to pick it up then piss off – job done."

"Very commendable. Very effective." John sounded scathing.

"Meaning what exactly?"

"Meaning what happens after it makes the news. Nothing. It's just an event to titillate the audience, fill the schedules."

"Says who?"

"Says me. 'Job done' you said. That's not the job that's just an incident, an event, and a self-indulgent one I might add."

Terence had a new enemy. He was forced to look to Clarence for support.

"Is he always like this?"

"Like what?"

"So fucking morally superior?"

"No. Just sometimes. Right now he is suffering from stress and resentment."

"Thank you for sharing that Clarence. As usual your honest candid comments never cease to impress me."

Clarence took note of the underlying hostility and Terence shifted position, needing to stretch his legs and scratch his reproductive organs. They had not recently been washed. As John continued his attack Terence felt both threatened and threatening. He was back to his normal self.

"I've done all the things you're doing now – in much the same way – and it didn't make a damn bit of difference. You have to get organised. You have to hit hard with a number so large that it really does makes a permanent imprint on history – remember London, Iraq? Were you there?"

"Of course I was," lied Terence. In fact he had been crashed out on a beach in Ibiza, dehydrated, head hurting, heart and soul abandoned.

"And you persuade with clear logical argument: continuously, patiently; for however long it takes. You persist until your audience – be it one individual or a crowd - starts to crack; starts to open up and let you in, their preconceptions and positions now up for negotiation."

"That doesn't sound like fun."

"Fun? So you're looking for fun in all this? Not hard work?" John's blood was up.

Without realising it Terence was collapsing back into juvenile rebellion and self-absorption.

"Why not? What's the point if it's not fucking fun?" Fuck him. Fuck them.

"What's the point?"

John had to come up for air. His hands nearly slipped off the wheel. Terence tried to hide behind his rucksack.

"Do you work for a living?"

"What's that suppose to mean."

"Simple enough question."

"Mind your own business."

"You don't work then? You don't pay taxes? You don't contribute to society you just take from it."

"I protest."

"You protest. That's all you do is it?"

"Yes. And proud of it."

Clarence noted that the atmosphere was turning nasty.

Confounded by the lack of common ground and immaturity John disengaged and returned to his sole activity of navigating his way along unknown roads. Terence hoped for a respite but Clarence still had room for more: more to give, more to take.

"Why the embellishments on your skin and the dyed hair?"

"Cos that's the way I like it. Got a problem with that?"

Clarence had no problem with that. Nor for that matter did John the more he thought about it.

"You used the word 'duty' but I sense no such thing. There is only the moment, the positive feeling you get from participating in a emotionally highly charged group event. There is nothing before. There is nothing after. You fear banality, repetition. You fear the day you will want to settle down. You fear falling in love and becoming restricted by its demands. You fear having to settle down to raise a family."

Terence's response was to shut out the noise, hug his rucksack and pretend he was far away, somewhere where they served booze. John came to his rescue.

"Leave him alone Clarence. We've still got a long way to go."

"You have no permanent place of residence?"

"You mean my own place? No. Like I said no home."

"Does that bother you?"

"No."

"The sense of drifting and the lack of roots does not depress you?"

"Look give over will you. I'm not answering anymore fucking questions."

"Good for you," said John.

Clarence got the message and returned to his normal sitting position whereupon Terence stuck a finger up as a final gesture of ill will. John caught it in the mirror, and though he could not condone it he had to concede it was justified.

The journey continued in silence: a comfortable cushion for two out of three; a wasted opportunity for the other one, but so be it. It was to be interrupted only once, by a spider, a big fat but fit spider. Merrily it scrambled up Terence's hairy arm, having vacated his rucksack. Terence watched it for a minute then raised his arm, hoping for a result.

"Look what I've just found."

He directed his remark at the driver and struck gold. John almost went into permanent spasm. Clarence had to take charge of the wheel.

"Steady on. It's just a fellow living creature."

"What's that doing in here!"

Terence had an answer. "Hitchhiking?"

"Get it out!"

"How do I do that?"

"Out the window!"

Terence opened the window and was hit in the face by a blast of air. He tried to flick the spider out but the wind blew it back in. It hit the floor but landed undamaged, without even feeling dizzy. In fact it was still in a perfect state of health which, when compared with the other occupants of the car, placed it in a unique position.

"Is it gone?"

"No. Now it's down there somewhere."

"Shit!"

On that note John suddenly signalled, slammed on the brakes and pulled over, all in under five seconds. The driver behind was forced to break suddenly and veer sideways. He swore at the driver in front but never for one second entertained the thought that he had been contributed to his own near accident.

"Why are we stopping?" asked Clarence.

"I'm not driving on with that thing in the car."

And with that declaration of his human rights John was out of the car, arms folded, waiting for someone to sort things out. Terence didn't give a damn so it was left to Clarence to search the car. John observed the operation with a look on his face that suggested Clarence was looking for something far more dangerous, something like bowel cancel. Finally he found the innocent little culprit and snatched it up. With a delicate touch he deposited it on the ground and watched it hurry away, a free spirit again. Then Terence stood on it.

"There you are it's dead."

Clarence was not impressed. "There was no need for that."

John didn't care but took Clarence's side just to put the arsehole down a peg.

"You could have let it go but no you had to stamp on it like a big bully."

"You don't like spiders."

"I don't like them up close. Which is not the same thing. Any moron can work that one out."

Clarence sensing serious aggression surfacing on both sides took command and herded the other two back into the car. But even when they were on the move again he was not happy: he had lost another ten minutes. Also John was not happy: he had been made to look silly and he was still stuck with this arsehole. Despite the free ride, Terence was also not happy: he had to stick with the company of two middle-aged tossers.

✦ ✦ ✦

Tim stared down at his order of all day breakfast. It did not look appetising but it did remind him of Sam and better times, especially in the kitchen. Her fry-ups were the real McCoy. When they slipped down his throat he was in heaven, and ready for sex. Still it was cheap and he was hungry.

Fiona spoke. "Are you going to eat that? It's getting cold."

"I don't know."

"You said you were starving and as you've paid for it you might as well eat it."

"I suppose so." Persuaded by clear logical argument Tim got stuck in.

Fiona watched him nibble, chew, suck and crunch then finally swallow as she in turn injected herself with pieces of chocolate laced croissant; each piece precisely bitten off. It was her way to cheer herself up.

"You look downcast. Are you really that worried about him?"

"Yes – and no."

Fiona blinked and suspended her injections of dark chocolate and sweet pastry. A piece of croissant was held in limbo inches from her mouth. It was torture.

"Meaning?"

"I'm also worried about you."

"Well it's appreciated but you really don't need to worry about me. I'm quite capable of looking after myself."

"I think I do."

With a touch of inspired melodrama Tim pulled the suicide note from his right pocket with his right hand. His left hand held his fork: it had an important function to perform. Intentionally the other letter was stored in his left pocket. He felt they should be kept apart. He handed over the note, head down as he speared the remains of his sausage and forced it into his mouth. As sausages went it was shit. But right now he was starving.

As Tim chewed he observed Fiona read and bleed over every word. Fiona forgot about her remaining croissant. It was a spent force and would remain undisturbed on the plate. If he looked carefully he could make out a slight nod of the head. It was rhythmic, as if Fiona was reciting a prayer or signalling her sympathy for everything the poor girl had to say. Stony face, hand slightly trembling, she handed it back.

"Don't tell me she went through with it."

"I don't know."

"You don't know! You mean you didn't check!"

Tim dropped his fork and sat up, upright and uptight.

"I don't know where she lives. She must be alright though else he wouldn't have been so cheerful. He didn't say a thing about it. If she had topped herself wouldn't he be helping police with enquiries? I know Clarence – I've known him most of my life. Despite his faults he couldn't ignore something like that. That's not Clarence."

"That's not good enough. If that's the case the poor woman needs help. I'll speak to him. I want to see her and I want to hear his side of the story."

With that she put the subject to one side, but not to sleep, and watched Tim scramble through his remaining egg before speaking again.

"Was he always like this?"

"Like what?"

"I don't know." Fiona stretched her thoughts. "All over the place. Coming from different directions."

"No not Clarence. He was never the buzzing type, far too lazy for that. I'm sure it's all down to those blackouts. It's bound to have unhinged him."

"No more blackouts and he'll be back to his old self?

"I suppose so. But I'm no doctor."

"And what is his old self?"

Tim wiped up the last of the yolk with his remaining lump of bread, trying to choose his thoughts carefully, and do Clarence a favour. It was a struggle to come up with something positive and he had to fight off the subject of 'sex with other people's wives'.

"He was – is - one of the lads. We both like a drink out with the boys."

Tim paused for a reaction but got none. He was expected to continue until told to stop.

"Gives our women a break. He's just an average guy."

Fiona recalled their intimate moments together. Clarence was not average.

"No he's more than that."

Tim stared down at the large lump of grizzle he had found earlier. It spoke volumes. You get what you pay for.

"He was always straightforward with Tracey. She was always straightforward with him. At least that's how we saw it. You know about Tracey?"

Fiona nodded.

"It seemed to work well until they suddenly split up a couple of weeks ago, right after their holiday. She dumped him without warning."

"He told me they split."

"Well, whatever."

"Teaching. Tell me about Clarence the teacher."

"Clarence the teacher? I don't know. You must know that better than me?"

"Try your best." It was an order.

Tim looked down at his empty coffee cup.

"Can I get a refill? I must have more coffee to keep going."

"Of course. You don't need to ask me."

Tim got up, taking his plate with him. He wanted to see the back of it. The grizzle was beginning to haunt him.

"Get me another orange juice while you're at it."

Tim flagged her request with a raised hand and as he stood at the counter he continued his struggle to find something positive, exciting even, to say about his old mate Clarence.

"Cheer up it may never happen," said the lady behind the counter as she served up his order. "First coffee top up is free but not the juice. Want to settle up now or leave the tab open?"

"Settle up."

Tim produced his card; stuck it into the reader; watched the instructions flash up; bashed in his pin number and whipped out the card back out. Fumbling he put it back in its place in his wallet. The lady gave him a receipt – but no smile - which he stuffed away in his back trouser pocket. Slowly he returned to his table, taking care not to spill the drinks. He still hadn't come up with anything to say so he made it up as he went along.

"He was enthusiastic in the early days. He was out for the kill. Then I suppose like any job it just became a monotonous routine. Still he hasn't been sacked so he must be doing something right."

By accident Tim was talking about himself: and when he realised it he stopped speaking and considered, looking glum in the process. Fiona did not push for further information.

The two finished their drinks and got back on the road; reverting to their earlier contract of silent self-possession. It was the hallmark feature of virtually their entire journey and it suited them both down to the ground. Things had changed though: Tim was beginning to feel more like the chauffeur to the lady in charge.

✢ ✢ ✢

John saw his chance: a large restaurant tempting the tired travelling public with special deals and a mouth-watering menu. He broke the truce of silence and made his demand.

"I have to stop."

"Stop? Why?"

"Clarence I have to eat. I have to piss."

"So do I," said Terence.

Outnumbered, Clarence did not contest the vote. They pulled into the car park. They all went for a piss. Only Clarence used an urinal: the other two preferred total privacy. Only two of them washed their hands. Terence was the first to grab a seat and the menu. With attitude he ordered the most expensive steak available. So he's not a vegetarian then, thought John as he continued to gather evidence.

Terence shifted uneasily as he ate and leaned over his food to such an extent that it looked like he was trying to stop it being taken away. He finished off his meal well ahead of the others. Even when not starving Terence had long perfected the art of eating in a hurry: as if on the run; as if some nerd at school was about to snatch it away. He sprang up – mumbling something about having to go 'for a dump' – and hurried off, rucksack held in a tight grip. Clarence had his mouth full so could not comment. John, suspicious, swallowed quickly and threw out a question at Terence while he was still in earshot.

"Why are you taking your bag with you!"

"Medication!"

Terence was never seen again and his hosts were left to foot the bill. I told you so, thought John. Must have been something I said, thought Clarence. John refused to pay half the bill. Clarence reassured him that he had nothing to pay. It was his treat. It was his day out.

They drove on, now definitely not on speaking terms. Then Clarence nodded off and John reduced his speed along with his sense of urgency. Fortunately the road atlas sat open in Clarence's lap at the right page. For convenience John adjusted its orientation by about fifty degrees, taking great care not to make physical contact with the man's crotch or thigh. And the more John thought about it the more he was glad that Clarence was asleep. It was the only way he could cope with Bad Cop Clarence right now. Just get him to the doctor, get him sorted, and bring him home in one piece.

They were entering dangerous times. John also felt sleepy – his brain had lost out to his stomach in the battle for blood. Fortunately on the first occasion when he was in danger of nodding off Clarence awoke, as if jolted by a bad dream or a bang on the head. He looked around. He didn't recognise the car. He didn't recognise the landscape. He did recognise the driver but this brought no comfort.

"What the fuck is going on this time. And why is it always you."

John wanted to smack him. But of course that was impractical. Instead he was forced to remind himself that Good Cop Bad Cop Clarence was back. Which of course was the reason for the trip. Without waiting for a reply Clarence went back to sleep and John tried to cheer himself up with the thought that he was doing a great humanitarian deed.

✤ ✤ ✤

John knew he was in trouble. He was lost in the middle of nowhere, alone, with only the heads of identical cows sticking up above the hedgerow to keep him company. He looked across at Clarence. Clarence was fast asleep like a baby. Let trouble sleep. He didn't need the aggravation. And until he found a road sign that made sense what use was a map reader, especially this one. So on he drove, along twisting country lanes, panicking when forced to choose between left and right. And all the time the same thought kept coming back: where had all the other cars gone?

As if let off the lease he increased his speed whenever he hit a long straight section of road, then forgot to decrease it again in equal measure. He needed speed. Unfortunately country lanes had a habit, born of historical accident or geographical necessity, of suddenly changing direction without warning. Such was the case when John went racing up an incline, shifting down to third to maintain speed, and fantasizing that he was being filmed by Top Gear. It was here that his luck ran out.

As he came over the top he slammed on the brakes and did a right turn – and he would have got away for it except for the mud: mud, that commodity the countryside produced in abundance but could never sell on the open market. He slid sideways and slammed into the trunk of a large oak tree. The front left wing and passenger door took the impact. It left him shaking like a leaf. He almost wet himself. He looked across at Clarence. Clarence stirred and woke up slowly, as if from hibernation. He scratched his groin and focused on the fact that they were not moving.

"We are not moving?"

"Of course we are not moving."

"Why?"

"Why? Are you mad! Look out of your window!"

Clarence did as instructed and made an assessment of the situation.

"Because you have collided with a tree. Apologies. Now I understand."

"Well done. Nothing gets past you."

John turned off the engine and clutched his no claims discount to his heart to try and stop it evaporating into thin air. He fought back the tears. He did not want Clarence to see him cry. He put his hands up to his head to hold it in place, afraid it might fall off its mounting, unhinged as it was.

"I deserve better than this."

"I take it the only damage is to my side of the car?"

"Correct."

"How did it happen?"

"I wasn't concentrating."

"Perhaps you were driving too fast for the surface conditions?"

"Well yes perhaps I was."

John, struggling to breath normally, restarted the engine and drove forward a few yards before stopping and turning it off again.

"Can you open your door?"

Clarence yanked on the door handle and pushed against the door with all the force he could muster.

"No."

"Marvellous. Bloody marvellous. It just gets better and better."

"What does?"

"Never you mind."

John got out. Finding it difficult to stand steady he held on to the door.

"You'll have to crawl out my side."

Clarence undid his seatbelt and clambered across, at one point banging his knee against the radio and CD player. John winched. They were his favourite objects inside the car. And today, more than any other day, the radio had helped him stay sane.

"Ouch!"

"What?"

"My ankle."

Sod your flaming ankle, John wanted to say.

Together they inspected the damage. It was not a pretty sight. In an instant a very expensive object, engineered to represent grace, beauty and mechanical perfection, had been transformed into something ugly, repulsive and disfunctional. Anyone who drove it now would be classed as second class, a tramp on wheels – not only by other drivers but also by pedestrians.

"Can you get it fixed?"

"Of course I can get it fixed but it's going to cost. There's my excess and I'll lose my no claims."

"Well let's be thankful it can still be driven."

Clarence tugged at John's shirt.

"Come on let's get going."

John did not budge so Clarence tried again. This time he was elbowed off.

"Stop doing that."

"Come on we cannot afford to waste time."

"I can."

"And what is that suppose to mean?"

"Nothing."

"Well come on then."

"No."

"No?"

"I'm not driving." John folded his arms.

"Very well I will drive."

Problem solved, Clarence was off like a shot and into the driver's seat while John continued to gaze, depressed, at his trashed little car. It was an injustice – despite the fact it was he who had been driving too fast. He wanted to be back in bed with a hot water bottle - even though it was summer – and he wanted George to sit by his side and hold his hand and for a change just listen to what he had to say. Clarence honked the horn and cut short John's brief escape into fantasy.

"Come on John time is short. We cannot hang around!"

John throw him his best dirty look then found the perfect excuse to delay, to wind him up, to make him hurt.

"Wait a minute. I must pick up the broken plastic. It's an eyesore and a danger to other motorists."

"Well hurry up then!"

John had no intention of hurrying up. As he walked back towards the accident spot he threw Clarence a second look: it was just as dirty as the first.

"You know you could help me. That way we save time."

The penny dropped.

"Good point."

Like a shot Clarence was back out of the car. He dashed past John and began scooping up the debris like a man possessed. The small splinters ended up inside his trouser pockets. The big bits he handed over to John. John was more than happy with this arrangement. He didn't have to do a thing: he just stood there; studying Clarence; looking for signs of bipolar brain disorder or simple schizophrenia – not that he presumed to be an expert. The rubbish he received he deposited in an old plastic bag he found in the boot.

When at last they did resume their journey Clarence asked John to take charge of map reading. At this point, from the safety of a back seat, John admitted that they were lost. Since the crash he had honestly forgotten all about it. Clarence did not take it well, which for John was some small measure of moral redress.

"So you cannot say where we are?"

"That's what being lost normally means."

Clarence banged the dashboard with a fist but did not swear. He looked up at the sky and the clouds which hung there in the balance. Home was a long long way away.

For John it was a moment of pleasure. He just wished he had caught it on his mobile so he could replay it to Clarence – in his face - whenever Clarence was being too sanctimonious, too superior, too cocky, or just too much in control of himself. He had to be brought back down to earth.

"I cannot afford to be late!"

"I cannot afford to smash up my car if that's any consolation."

Clarence looked around, as if searching for the right way out of his problem.

"I'm sure they'll understand. They won't turn you away having come all this way. They want your money remember."

"Who wants my money?"

"These doctors of course."

"It is not exactly like that."

"Well what exactly is it like then? You won't fucking well tell me!"

"I have to be on time, for an exact time."

John folded his arms as he folded himself up tight and began to sulk. He was in danger of meltdown.

"Bollocks." On this trip John had rediscovered the joy of unrestrained cursing.

Clarence held up his hands.

"So what do I do?"

"Drive on until you hit a sign that's worth anything – or someone who can give directions. Just don't hit them."

"Why would I do that?"

"I don't know. For the pleasure of inflicting human suffering?"

Clarence stared at his disenchanted friend in the mirror, trying to make sense of a totally illogical statement. Then, making no progress, he dropped the matter and drove off, fast, until John demanded that he reduce his speed to thirty: either that or Clarence couldn't drive his car. Clarence did not argue, conscious of the fact that John was suffering from a state of acute stress and had lapsed into mood swings of an aggressive-defensive nature. Hamstrung, he drove along at speeds which would have embarrassed even the driver of a Morris Minor.

After some time spent simultaneously watching road and clock Clarence spoke.

"This hurts."

"What hurts?"

"My ankle hurts."

"Tough."

Clarence took that as a clear signal that John was unsympathetic to his cause.

At a crossroads he passed three men digging a long trench, seemingly from nowhere to nowhere. He reversed at speed, stopped and jumped out. The three men stopped digging, straightened up and rested on the handles of their trench spades; each vaguely intrigued by the commotion or just glad to have a break from their backbreaking routine. One of them took the time out to roll a cigarette. Another copied him. The remaining man took a piss in the grass after winning the fight with an uncooperative trouser zip.

The three men didn't like digging for a living but they put up with it if they were digging together. They all hated being stuck indoors: outdoors was their natural habitat. If they had to go indoors it was to eat, watch TV, get shit-faced, have sex, fall asleep. Only one of them was married so for him sex came on a regular basis, though at a price: his wife never made much effort to join in.

The three men swore at each other, no holds barred. They swore at everybody else: family; friends; complete strangers; even the man who was handing out their wages on any one particular day, but only when he couldn't hear them. Sometimes they meant it. Sometimes they didn't. It was hard to tell the difference.

They had been born local. They had always lived locally. They placed their thoughts within local boundaries; consuming only local facts; treating everything else as so far away as to be irrelevant or fabricated. And what gave them a headache they kicked out at the first opportunity. The only exception was sports: football to be precise. Football had no boundaries and football had results. They soaked it up at the local, national and international level. Because it had nothing to say only something to see it did not give them headaches like the news on TV.

They hated having to think beyond the obvious. The one who was married left most of that to his wife, not that she claimed to be much of an expert. In turn the other two left it to him to do it for them, despite his lack of qualifications. What they lacked in mental exercise they made up for with physical; and somehow it worked out right.

They stabbed at their food in the same way that they stabbed at their lives, caring little about what they hit. They took baths, not showers. They often purchased one newspaper between the three of them - the one with the biggest tits on the front page – but rarely read beyond the first four pages. They were picky about their beer and cider. Cold beer was sent back.

They were employed by the local council when not working on the farms. They stuck by each other – unless they got seriously pissed, in which case they might well lay into each other if no one else was available. They complained about the cost of gas and electricity, the price of beer and petrol, car tax, council tax, the TV license, their pay (much of it undeclared) and the hours they worked. They rarely complained about the weather.

They tackled their work with pride: for them leaving their mark on a landscape which their forefathers had tended was a privilege, a noble cause. It made them feel tall, indispensable. And when they were not digging holes or filling them in, or laying pipes for the council they were fixing roofs, sheds, laying patios or working on farms: planting or harvesting; shovelling shit or cutting back the undergrowth. And though they didn't know it they had in fact secured a reasonable degree of happiness, enough to see them through life. The only cloud which blighted their landscape was the lack of a pension. But then that fact barely impinged upon their consciousness and judging by the rate at which they abused their bodies with alcohol, cigarettes and self-enforced hard labour they were unlikely to make it much past seventy.

The first man, the unelected leader, exhaled and pointed his cigarette at the car.

"Had an accident?"

"Yes. Can you help me I have no idea where I am."

The three men laughed. Clarence smiled and tried to understand the joke.

"Why are you limping like that?"

"I sprained my ankle recently."

"And why is he sitting in the back of the car all miserable like that?"

"He is upset."

"Did you thump him?"

"No he is my friend. I would never hit a friend." Clarence turned towards the car. "John come and say hello!"

He got no reply. The men laughed again, longer and louder this time. Clarence smiled again. This time the joke made sense.

"He is shy sometimes."

"So what are you doing in our neck of the woods. You're not from round here."

"Correct. We come from London, its south suburbs to be precise." Clarence noted their glazed expressions. "London is south of here, the capital of this country?"

"We know where the fuck London is."

"Apologies. No slight intended. We are trying to get to the village of Kirsten Green? But as I said we are lost."

The leader raised his spade and rammed it back down into the ground, then returned to leaning on it. At the same time John got out of the car, afraid he was being talked about. Self-consciously he strolled up stood alongside Clarence, not charmed by what he saw. He did not hide his discomfort.

"So you two are just friends then on a day out?" The leader loved to wind it up and hear it play.

"Yes we are. Just friends as you say. There is no sexual activity in the relation. We are on a day out but - "

Clarence never got to finish his sentence. John punched him squarely in the ribs and he fell down on to one knee, as if about to be knighted. All three men were now pissing themselves.

"That hurt!"

"It was meant to."

"No matter mate. Everything shags everything else round here." The leader turned to one of his mates. "Your uncle was a bit of a bum boy wasn't he?"

"That's what mum says."

John could not let that remark pass and made his feelings quite clear.

"Why don't you piss off!"

He had raised his voice with clarity and conviction. It was a fatal mistake: up there with Stalingrad, the Partition of India, the Poll Tax, the invasion of Iraq, and Rambo IV.

The smiles on the men's faces collapsed, to be replaced by sour grapes and open hostility. They tensed up, ready to fight. One spat, then another.

The leader began to swing his spade back and forth like a makeshift pendulum.

Clarence stood up.

"As I said we are trying to get to the placed called Kirsten Green. Can you set us on the right track? We really would appreciate it."

The leader spoke in a low sullen voice. "I'm sure you would."

He looked around at the possibilities. He had four to choose from. He pointed with his spade.

"That way. Go that way. You'll pick up the signs for it."

"When?"

The man wiped the back of his hand across his dripping nose then rubbed it at speed. It needed a good rubbing.

"Ten minutes?"

"Thank you. Come on John back to the car."

Clarence tried to take John's hand but was pushed off.

"I can make my own way back thank you very much. And don't talk to me like that. I'm not your dog."

Clarence led the way back to the car, keeping his mouth shut. Reluctantly John followed.

Like a pack of wolves on the prowl the three men watched the two misfits get back into their car, fiddle with their seatbelts, fiddle with the radio, and then drive off. It was a complete transformation. When the strangers had first appeared they had acted more like farmyard pigs: heads down, scratching out a living in the dirt.

After fifteen minutes without any hint that things had improved, Clarence began to panic. John had to keep telling him to hold down his speed - and whose car it was. As they passed an assortment of parked vehicles in a lay-by – camper vans, caravans and old cars which had seen better days – Clarence slowed right down. He managed to park just before he ran out of lay-by. A mixed crowd of all ages were congregating around two large plastic picnic tables; each with its own massive umbrella; each laid out with a serious spread of drink and food.

Some, the oldest, were sitting in plastic chairs. The youngest were off the lease: running around, letting off steam and finding fun in the middle of nowhere. Somewhere a baby could be heard complaining, then likewise its mother. It could have been a party if it wasn't for the stern, alert expressions on the faces of the adults.

Clarence clambered out and dashed as best he could back down the entire length of the lay-by to reach the crowd. Pain was no barrier. As he did so a boy went in the opposite direction, having spotted a business opportunity. When he arrived Clarence was heaving and panting and looking grim. The crowd stopped talking and laid their eyes on him, soaking up the signals and taking measurements. He looked like someone on the run, someone barely holding it together. This was a man in distress.

The boy tapped on John's window. "A fiver to wash your car?"

"No thanks."

The boy turned to go.

"No hang on. Yes give it a wash."

John could not pass up the chance to infuriate Clarence further. He was beginning to view this as their last ever day together and with that in mind he wanted to redress the balance of hurt and hardship. The boy ran off thrilled, to quickly procure bucket and sponge, and nick some water without permission.

When Clarence finally spoke up he sounded like a man on his last legs, a man who had hit rock bottom, who had lost his way in life – which he had. He had tears in his eyes and his nose ran like a torrent of abuse.

"I am sorry to interrupt your gathering but I am desperate to reach Kirsten Green, the village of Kirsten Green, as fast as possible. Without the risk of overstatement I can say it is a matter of life and death."

One of those seated, an old man, spoke. "A matter of life and death you say? Whose life and whose death?"

Clarence turned his guns on him. Others drew back. Some took up guard position.

"My life. My death."

The old man was impressed by the answer and look up at another, younger man; possibly his son.

"He's heading away from it isn't he?"

"He is that. No matter. You might as well carry on as you are until you hit the dual carriageway. Join it heading away from Norwich. It will be signposted when you need to come off. Off the bypass you'll head straight into it no mistake."

"It's got two good pubs if I remember right. One right in the village. One outside."

"Thank you. Thank you both ever so much. You cannot begin to appreciate just what that piece of information means to me."

"I think we've got a pretty good idea."

"That we have. On your way now while you still have breath."

An old woman, also seated, felt her duty to offer Clarence a cup of tea.

"Have a cup of tea first my love. You need to calm yourself. You're about to blow all your fuses."

"I don't think he's got time for tea darling. The poor man's in a rush. Life or death he said."

"Sorry but the gentleman's right. I would love to sit and talk but time is dangerously tight. I would have been there an hour ago if I had had my way."

"Never mind. You have a safe trip now."

"Who had his way then?" asked the son.

Clarence pointed back at the car. "Him in the car."

The son moved away from the table to bring the car into view.

"Jamie's cleaning your car."

"You might as well have that cup of tea then – and invite your friend over."

"What! Excuse me. I must go."

Clarence stumbled back to the car and accosted the boy.

"What's going on?"

Jamie stabbed the air with his dripping sponge.

"He told me to wash his car."

Clarence banged on the window.

"John why did you tell him to wash the car!"

"Because I wanted to have my car cleaned."

"There is no time for this. Surely you know that by now."

"Sorry. I forgot."

"Well we must leave right now. I know what I have to do. Hey you. Stop doing that!"

"But I haven't finished." Jamie was narked.

"No matter."

Clarence got back into the driving seat and started the engine. Quick as a flash the boy jumped in front of the car.

"Where's my money!"

John opened his door and waved him over.

"Here you are. Take this." He handed over a ten pound note. "Keep the change."

Jamie snatched it up and held it up to the light, suspicious of the fact that he had been handed twice the fee. But the note looked okay.

"Thanks mate."

He ran off back to the family, stuffing the note away in one of his pockets. Later he would transfer it into his secret savings account located deep inside his mattress.

Clarence drove on, again flipping between the road in front and the minutes clicking over on the clock. He could not believe that travel across country could be subject to so much delay, distress and complications. And his friend John was not helping.

✤ ✤ ✤

Tim drew up alongside three men sitting by the side of the road. They were smoking, gorging on well stuff sandwiches and pork pies, and taking swigs of water from metal bottles. They looked knackered. Tim turned the music right down to a whisper and leaned out of the window.

"Sorry to bother you guys during lunch but we're trying to find our fucking way to a place called Kirsten Green?"

The men broke off lunch and looked up. One of them had just bitten off part of his sandwich but he made no attempt to chew. None of them was willing to speak.

Tim got the message and pulled out his wallet.

"I'll give you ten – no twenty quid." He held one out.

Fiona leaned forward to see what was happening.

The nearest man jumped up, reached out and grabbed it. "Cheers."

He pointed in the opposite direction to which the car was facing.

"Back the way you came. First left. Get on to the main road heading towards Norwich. Off at the next junction. It's marked all the way then. Couldn't be easier."

"Appreciate it."

"No problem. You want directions to anywhere else?"

"No not today."

"No problem." The man sat back down. He had his pork pie to finish off.

Tim did not hang around. He did a high speed three point turn and sped off. The recipient of the note waved it at the other two.

"Easy fucking money."

"You're getting in the first two rounds tonight," said one.

"If any more pass through shall we take it in turns?" said the other.

✤ ✤ ✤

The directions had been precise and unambiguous. The moment Clarence saw the village green with the pub on one side and the church on

· 581 ·

the other he became a man even more possessed. He knew exactly where to go. He raced recklessly down the narrow backstreets and screeched to a halt outside a whitewashed cottage – upsetting a cat which jumped off the lap of an old lady asleep in her armchair who in turn awoke and dropped her buttered scone on the carpet. He leapt out, not pausing to explain his actions to John, not bothering to include him in his plans. John eased himself out more slowly. This place was no medical centre.

Clarence banged on the door and an old lady answered it. She had a small black, dog by her side. She had long hair. He had long hair. She looked displeased yet they shook hands in a firm, businesslike fashion and escorted each other back inside. Not one word was exchanged. John was left alone to hang around outside. Dumped, he felt a bit of a lemon, a pumpkin even. He took it as a personal insult – along with the growing conviction that he had been severely screwed. He walked around to the damaged side of the car and kicked the crumpled door panel. It felt good but not as good as kicking Clarence.

An elderly gentleman doffed his cap as he past by. As was his habit he was out enjoying the sun.

"Afternoon."

"Afternoon." John sounded dreadful, like a man who had misplaced his winning lottery ticket.

The elderly gentleman had a word of advice. "I would get that fixed."

"Good idea. Thanks for pointing that out."

The old man passed on by without a break in his rhythm. He did not hear the reply as he was deaf in one ear.

John, stuck, got back into his car – this time back behind the wheel – and turned on the radio. With the seat tilted right back he tried to reclined and relax, arms folded tightly again in protest at the injustice. He stared up through the sunroof and considered his options. Right now he couldn't think of one. Clarence still held power over him. There he tried to kill time, cushioned and motionless, exhausted and disinterested in the world around him.

Ten minutes later John was disturbed by the sound of a loud car horn. He looked in the mirror. There was a car edging up his backside. Some woman was pulling faces at him and gesturing. He had parked in her place. John told her to fuck off under his breath and turned the music up. It was Fingal's Cave and it was stirring stuff – not that John needed any more stirring.

Without warning the woman, irate and slightly barking mad, was at his window and looming over him like a mad mother superior. She rapped on the window until finally he was forced to lower it and acknowledge her presence.

"Who are you!" she shouted.

John noted the ginger hair. Over time he was beginning to see a pattern.

"There's no need to shout."

She lowered her voice. "Well who are you."

"I'm the driver, the dogsbody."

John was expecting a backlash and was surprised when none came: the answer made perfect sense to her.

"Where's your friend!"

The woman was back to shouting again. Shouting was her natural level for communication with strangers or across distances of more than five feet.

"He ran off inside with some old woman and a silly little dog."

"That old woman is my mother. And that silly little dog is extremely intelligent I'll have you know."

"Is it?"

"It is. And you stay in your car."

John raised his eyebrows and looked away. He had no intention of getting out. Now leave me alone, he thought. I'm not the enemy.

He watched the crazy woman produce a key, fumble around with it inside the lock, then finally manage to break in. She shot inside. John closed his eyes and returned to Fingal's Cave. When it ended he was cursed by a string of adverts, all trying to sound endearing, on his side: one wanted to sell him car insurance; one offered to purchase his endowment policy; one offered him a weekend getaway break on the cheap. It was at this point that John was saved by the sound of another car drawing up, this time alongside. He looked across and recognised the driver. He was faintly amused and somehow not surprised to see him. This was no normal day.

Tim wound down his window as John turned down the music and wound down his.

"John!"

"Tim."

"Where's Clarence?"

John pointed. "In there."

"Doing what?"

"No idea. Might be having tea and a cream cake for all I know. I'm just the driver."

Fiona leant forward and gave John a long hard look, forcing him to look away and feel stupid. Tim got out and walked up to the door. He bit his lip. Open doors confused him. He stalled. It was thrown back by the daughter, now very much in a state of panic.

"Who are you?"

"Tim, a friend of Clarence. Can I see him?"

"No."

"Why not."

"Because he's not here."

"Well where is he then? I have to find him."

"Don't know. If I knew that I wouldn't be here wasting my time talking to you would I."

"Let me help you find him."

"No. Now go away and leave me alone." She slammed the door shut in his face.

Stuck for choice Tim turned back to John.

"Can you tell me what this is all about?"

"No idea. He told me this trip was about seeing some doctor, some specialist about his problem. Instead we turned here, at some old woman's house. He buggered off. I haven't seen him since. And I don't think I want to see him again."

Tim, feeling useless, went and shared what little information he had with Fiona. She told him to move the car: he was blocking the road. He parked it in front of John, so blocking him in instead. Fiona looked around at all the doors and windows along the street. The windows were too small and the doors were too close together for her liking.

Alone inside the cottage, with no clue as to what to do, the daughter peeked out through the net curtains at the crowd which was encamped outside. This quiet backwater had never seen so many cars lined up at any one time. This would not please the neighbours. She decided to give it ten minutes them call the police. And tell them what? That her dippy old mum had invited some complete stranger over and gone off for a walk with him and had not been seen since for ten minutes? She crumbled under the weight of the absurdity of the situation and had to sit down. She felt a flush coming on. Grudgingly she came to the conclusion that a problem shared might be a problem halved. She dragged herself back outside. Shouting at the top of her voice she grabbed the attention of the crowd, along with some of the residents in the other cottages. Tim and Fiona got out of their car. John stayed put in his. All were in agreement that she did not need to shout.

"So you all know him. He's your friend right?"

Tim gave an affirmative nod. Fiona studied the woman with the ginger hair. John kept his head down.

"So how come he knows my mum? And why does she want to see him?"

Fiona closed in on her, in an attempt to be friendly.

"Honest, we have absolutely no idea. We were hoping you could shed some light on this."

"Well we're truly stuffed then."

"But please don't worry. He's a thoroughly decent chap. He's the gentle type, sensitive. And he's a teacher. We teach at the same school. I'm sure your mother is in no danger of any kind."

The daughter screwed up her face. "And you can guarantee that can you?"

Fiona stumbled when she should have held firm.

"Well no, not one hundred percent. But in the short time I've known him it would be completely out of character."

"In the short time you've known him."

John, feeling abused, was keen to contest her assessment but bottled out and wound up his window. The daughter turned to go back inside, only slightly reassured by this fresh disclosure.

Fiona had one more thing to say and said it quickly.

"Please can I use your loo."

"No this is not my house," replied the daughter as she shut the door to cut out the crap which had invaded her life.

She sat down in the kitchen, to fume and gestate. But she had no plan. She was grid locked. She had no next move. She saw an open box of cornflakes. In her opinion it was sitting there so smug, so superior, so unaffected. She picked it up and threw it across the room: this was her act of protest against her mother. Deep down she hoped that this act of vandalism would make her mum instantly reappear to berate her.

It worked.

The back door opened and Lassie bounded in. He skidded across the cornflakes then chased them around the floor for fun. He was followed by her mum and a man she had never seen before. Startled, the daughter shot up out of her chair. Her mother looked down at all the cornflakes but said nothing. Lassie stopped chasing them and began to eat them. He lapped them up. The man gave the daughter a broad smile. She glared back as if he had just passed judgement on her tits.

The old woman sat down, legs creaking.

"Make us a pot of tea will you dear. I'm gasping."

"Who's that."

"He's our guest."

"He looks terrible."

"I feel great."

"He's not the man I gave the letter to."

"Well obviously you gave it to the wrong person. Fortunately that mistake was of no consequence."

Clarence felt able to speak at last.

"Yes thank you for bringing me that letter. It was a long way you had to come."

"Piss off."

"Understood."

"Please don't be like that dear."

"I'll be like I sodding well want to be. Do you know what you've put me through?"

"I think you're overreacting to the situation. Put the kettle on and let's all have a nice cup of tea."

Clarence had a question.

"Is all this food on the floor meant for the dog?"

"No. Fortunately though he's doing an excellent job of clearing it all up."

The old woman looked up at her daughter: she was standing in a defensive position, waiting to be told off. Old habits die hard.

"Come on dear get the kettle on. I need that cup of tea and we haven't got all day."

"I'll do it," said Clarence.

His attempt to intervene was enough to spur the daughter into action.

"No you won't. Don't you touch anything. I'll do it."

Under orders and under duress the daughter scrunched her way back and forth across the kitchen, grinding cornflakes into crumbs and her teeth into the ground. Lassie licked up the crumbs in between visits to his bowl of water. When at last they were all seated and sipping tea, the daughter punched the air with the obvious question. It was directly purely at her mother.

"So where have you been?"

"We went to the allotments."

"What?"

"I wanted to show him my allotment."

"He came all this way to see your old allotment?"

Clarence chipped in.

"It is true. I did want to see her allotment. I was impressed. All that edible vegetation grown solely for human consumption."

The daughter ignored him.

"I don't believe you. That's just too daft. As usual you're hiding things from me."

"Well that's not the only thing he's come to see. I also want to show him my local public house – whose name now I am struggling to recall."

With that the old woman threw Clarence a look of barely suppressed panic. With a small discreet movement of the hand Clarence signalled her to stay calm and in control.

"Tell me dear what is the name of the one outside the village. It was your favourite when you were growing up here."

"The Lamb Inn - is he going now?"

"Soon dear. He will be gone soon. And everything will be back to normal."

"Why do you want to go there anyway?"

"To have a drink of course."

"I'm coming with you then."

This announcement did not go down well and mother and daughter faced each other across the kitchen table in stony silence. Mother was thinking. Daughter was watching her think, steeling herself for trouble. Clarence watched them both. Lassie watched all three of them. He had had enough of cornflakes.

Mother spoke. "Very well. But can you go and get me a local map of the area. It will be somewhere in the front room amongst my books."

"Very well - but don't move - and watch him."

The daughter pointed at Clarence, afraid he might jump up and run off with the family silver. Even as she left one room and entered another something at the back of her mind told her that this did not add up. Even if mum had forgotten where to find the pub she knew where it was. So why the need for a map? She was right to question: Clarence had already closed the kitchen door and jammed a chair up against the doorknob.

The old woman looked at her clock on the kitchen wall and became agitated.

"Come on we must go. We'll take her car."

"Is your host's memory reliable?"

"I think so. She went there many times over many decades. You drive. This body is too old. Reaction times are poor."

They left by the back door again and made for the garden gate – Clarence hobbling and having to hold on to the old woman for support. Lassie went with them, as usual refusing to be left behind. Stealthily they made their way up the path which ran alongside the cottage, working hard to avoid the nettles – during which time the daughter was rattling the kitchen door and swearing furiously. Finally she gave up and went for help. Acting rough she picked on Tim and pulled him indoors. Fiona followed, uninvited, desperate to use the loo. And still John stayed put, now slipping in and out of sleep as exhaustion began to take its toll.

Unnoticed, Clarence commandeered the daughter's car and helped the old woman in. John caught a flash of him as he drove past. Clarence waved but John was past caring.

Tim reappeared, the daughter by his side. They looked around, like coppers on the beat, like bodyguards who had mislaid their president.

"Someone's stolen my car!" screamed the daughter.

John wound down his window again.

"I think Clarence drove off in it. I think your mother was in the car," he explained. He was barely able to keep up with events.

"Why didn't you tell us!"

"I just did! It's only just happened!"

The daughter grabbed Tim's arm and did not let go.

"I know where they're going. Come on. I want my mum back."

Tim held firm. "We're not leaving without Fiona."

The daughter span round on her heels and shouted into the cottage. Her voice travelled its entire length and breath.

"Come on woman! It doesn't take all day to have a piss!"

To disassociate himself from her outburst Tim slipped back into Fiona's car and started the engine. The daughter fell down beside him. There was a long extended pause as they waited for Fiona. The daughter tapped her fingernails across the dashboard and began to fiddle with the buttons on the radio. Tim had to stop her.

"Don't touch that you'll mess it up."

She stopped playing with the radio and switched her attention to the compartment box: opening it and peering inside as if looking for something; then closing it as if disappointed by what she had found in there.

John watched them, glad now that he was being totally ignored. He wanted to get out, have a good stretch, perhaps find somewhere proper to lie down. He switched off the radio and toyed with the idea of sneaking inside, to use the loo and crash out on the couch – in that order.

Finally Fiona did appear, apologizing profusely for causing a delay as she took a back seat, miffed that the other woman had presumed to take her place in the front. When they were gone John did sneak inside to use the loo, banging his head on a ceiling beam as he made his way upstairs – only to discover it was a wasted journey. The loo was downstairs. After the restorative, satisfying act of urinating at high speed until his bladder was empty John found a couch and fell asleep on it – having first tripped over a rug and then knocked over a wooden chair.

❖ ❖ ❖

Final Log Entry

My final interview was with a young man I encountered on route to my prearranged departure point. It was a difficult exchange as he did not welcome the attention. He is still in competition with both himself and those around him. His self-confidence has a fragile base so he has reinforced it with an agenda (mainly political) designed to magnify his presence and importance in society. This agenda is second hand, borrowed, in bits. It does not derive from his own fundamental beliefs or observations but rather it has been constructed from pieces, at random, according to perceived popular trends which appeal to his age group. Moreover these pieces have been chosen for convenience, for their ready-made, prescriptive actions. They do not fit into any obvious moral framework.

Proactively engaging in this agenda allows him to fulfil both his social and emotional needs. The only drawback appears to be his inability to perform any constructive analysis of an issue from first principles. Any analysis he does perform is handicapped by his own cultural bias or the blind application of unreliable evidence and misinformation. This paralysis of the mind however does not hinder him in his day-to-day activities. Engagement at the superficial level is all that is required. He has no wish to think deeply, about anything. His only one real problem – and one he recognizes when under the stimulation of drugs – is his inability to revise his agenda and move on, evolve.

He wants to be different because he is afraid to be the same. He wants to stand out because he is afraid he will go unnoticed. He makes a noise because he cannot bear to live in silence. I suspect he has never been held in deep affection and therefore is afraid to manifest the same: the consequences are unknown to him; and because of his inborn lack of confidence he is not prepared to take the risk.

All that aside he has the potential to make a serious contribution to solving the problems which exist within his society. If only he could learn the art of self-introspection and dismantle all those comfort zones he has constructed to protect himself, to save himself from having to think to hard about the world in which he lives.

I have to admit that during my journey I became extremely worried that I would miss my connection and be marooned here for an extended length of time until another pickup could be arranged. My worries escalated to such a level of intensity – it became a state of fear – that my host's body engaged completely with my own state of mind – against my instructions – and reacted according to form. This is an alarming development as I have always maintained tight control over my host's physical functions when in control. I think it is time to leave. I am not sure if I wish to return.

I am very pleased - elated - to have made contact with my colleague: he has come to my aid and rearranged my departure. I know he has his own very busy schedule so this has been at some cost to his own research. For this I am extremely grateful. He owed me no favours. Luckily he had the foresight to arrange for a backup plan as I arrived too late to rendezvous with the first departure point. It was only by the smallest measure of time – a few Earth minutes – but late is late. We are now approaching that second departure point, on schedule, and so this is my final log.

❖ ❖ ❖

Try as he might Tim could not catch up. Try as she might the daughter could not make him drive any faster. Try as she might Fiona could not get a look in. They were cut down to size by a slow moving tractor: they joined the queue of traffic which had formed behind it. Unwittingly the tractor driver had set two speeds and two moods: his speed, comfortably average; their speed, painfully slow; his mood happy; their mood miserable. When he finally threw out a hand signal and turned off into a field all hell broke loose.

Just as things were looking up Tim next got trapped behind two horses being ridden at a gentle trot by two teenage girls. The daughter slapped him down for getting too close. Like the tractor the horse riders did not know, or care, what was happening behind them. Unlike the tractor driver they regarded their speed as dismally slow. Unlike the tractor driver their mood was one of detached boredom. They wanted to gallop off – or at least canter - but were stuck with the less glamorous job of guiding their horses between fields, to fresh pasture. When Tim was let loose again the daughter reigned him in.

"No need to rush now. We're almost there." The daughter sounded downbeat. She had run out of spit.

And she was right of course: seconds later the sign for the pub car park came into view. Tim dropped his speed and Fiona, sitting behind in the middle, leant forward and grabbed on to the top of each front seat. She was afraid she was missing out on all the action.

Tim swung into the car park, crunching the gravel. It was busy. Some of the evening regulars had decided to start early, so overlapping with the lunchtime lot. It was that time of year and that kind of weather and that time of day.

After much manoeuvring Tim did manage to park the car: the women jumped out before he had the handbrake on. The daughter found hers hidden round a corner at the other end of the car park. It had broken the cardinal rule: it had crossed the line into an adjacent bay. Without any exchange of words Fiona and the daughter rushed into the pub. Tim followed on behind. He wanted to but did not rush up to the bar.

The placed was packed and its construction included lots of nooks and crannies and waist high interior walls designed to shield those sitting at tables: picking out two faces would be no trivial exercise. The two women got stuck in. The daughter was looking for two faces. Fiona was looking for one. Tim, feeling redundant, hung around at the bar, wishing he had the balls to buy a pint.

Outside meanwhile customers were enjoying the spectacle of an old woman and a young man struggling to walk down to the riverbank. The old woman was staggering under the weight of the young man who was holding on to her and hobbling. They both acted like they were drunk. And they had a small black dog with them who was darting back and forth and making circles in the long grass. A young mother pulled her pram closer in, not wishing for it to cause an accident, or be hit. It was extra wide: it contain her twins. One man whistled.

"Yes! Go on you can do it!" shouted another.

His wife thumped him on the arm.

When the two reached the edge of the water they collapsed on to a bench, taking up the last remaining spaces. Those who had been watching cheered and raised their glasses. Those already sitting there did their best to ignore them and carry on talking: this proved difficult as they had lost the thread of their conversation.

At the same time their pursuers stepped out into the beer garden. The daughter spotted her mum and pointed.

"There. There they are down there!"

Without waiting she ran towards her mum. Heads turned. Tim and Fiona followed at a more discreet pace, wishing not to draw attention to themselves.

The daughter found her mum head down, eyes closed, holding hands with that man. It was if she was holding on for dear life. And there was a look of contentment on her face. Lassie sat by her side, head raised, waiting for orders. He wagged his tail to welcome back the daughter. The daughter, bemused, reached out and touched her mother on the cheek. She was fast asleep. Tim and Fiona caught her up. Fiona took Clarence's hand in hers. Tim did not want to touch.

And still neither of them woke up. They were in a deep sleep and they looked happy. The daughter wanted to slap her mother awake. Tim wanted to do likewise to Clarence. Fiona was transfixed by his sweet, cute little face and marvelled at the expression of total contentment. It was totally at odds with the day's hectic events. Interesting times, she thought. I'm living in interesting times.

Strange, thought Tim. He's not snoring.

"What do we do?" asked the daughter.

"Get a drink?" replied Tim. "I really could do with a drink."

Fiona was not impressed and threw him a heavy-handed look of displeasure.

"That's not such a bad idea," replied the daughter. "Go get me one. Mine's a draught cider."

"Fiona?"

Fiona caved in. "I'll have a tonic water then, with ice. A large one."

Even before she had finished her sentence Tim was gone and the two women were left to stand guard.

"Is this normal behaviour for your mother?"

"No."

"They look so happy."

"At our expense."

"What do we do? Try and shake them awake?"

"No. My mum wouldn't like that. It might spook her."

"So we watch and wait?"

"Looks like it."

The daughter looked around for somewhere to sit. The others who sat around the table had no intention of making space. They were intrigued. This was all good stuff and saved them the effort of having to make light conversation. Twenty yards away by a wall which was leaning dangerously she caught sight of a load of red plastic chairs stacked up next to a couple of matching tables. She went and grabbed three off the top, lugging them back with them hooked over one arm. Fiona helped her unstack them and together they sat down, to watch and to wait for a response, and their drinks.

The drinks took ages coming. The bar was packed. People were ordering food as well as drinks in abundance. Everybody was out that day. The weather demanded it be so. Tim had to grin and bear it as he bore down on the bar staff as they in turn charged up and down the length of the bar. Even in this part of the world some of them had foreign accents. It made Tim feel at home in a funny sort of way.

When he arrived back nothing had changed – except of course that now everyone was seated. He handed out the drinks and sat down to join in the watch. And in all this time Lassie never lost faith. He just looked on: always loyal; always thinking the best of the situation, never entertaining the worse. His tongue hung out and his mouth dripped saliva.

One man on the other side of the bench was driven to speak. He wanted to join in the action, even if nothing was happening.

"Were those two out on the razzle last night?"

The daughter cut him down before he got out of hand.

"Never you mind. It's none of your business."

That plus the ginger hair was enough to put him back in his place. His girlfriend carried on reading her magazine, not wishing to be associated with him at this point in time. For her the interest had worn off. His mate and his mate's girlfriend had likewise lost interest.

And then it finally happened: without warning; without reason; without any trigger. Simultaneously both the old woman and Clarence opened their eyes and began to blink in the sunlight. The old woman was struck by the face of her daughter up close and drilling down into her. It was both reassuring and disconcerting at the same time. She didn't know where to turn or what to say. Suddenly she realised she was holding a young man's sweaty hand. Immediately she let go, almost flinging it away. The feeling was mutual.

"Yvonne!"

"Mummy!"

Clarence had a similar wake up call: except for him it was two faces and double the impact.

The old woman saw the river beyond. She knew exactly where she was. She looked down and there was her Lassie looking back up at her, a look of blind obedience in his eyes. She wanted to reach down, pick him up, hug him, and bury her face in him. But he was too far away. Lassie wagged his tail and barked. He knew his turn would come.

"What are we doing here?"

"I've no idea. I just followed you here. You ran off with this man."

The old woman glanced sideways and did not like what she saw. This man was alien to her. Clarence did not notice the slight. He was struggling with his own demons.

"Tim. Fiona." Clarence saw the drinks. "Tim, get me a drink."

"No problem."

Tim got up. He was in need of a refill.

Warily the old woman looked around at the strange faces who were making her the centre of attention: that she did not like. She felt she was being diluted.

"Yvonne take me home. I want to go home. Go home right now."

"Yes mummy."

The old woman tried to lift herself up. It was a struggle. Her joints had seized up: the hurt of the hard wooden bench had come home to roost.

"Careful mum. Take it easy."

"Don't tell me to take it easy. Just take me home. I want to go home."

"We are. We're going home right now. Just take your time. You've had a stressful day. I've had a stressful day."

"Who are these people? I don't know any of them."

"Never you mind about them. They'll go away. We just bumped into them."

Slightly reassured, the old woman allowed herself to be lifted up by her daughter and escorted back to the car. As she walked away clutching her mother the daughter threw Clarence and Fiona one last cutting remark. Lassie ran ahead. Somehow he knew they were going home.

"You lot. You keep away from us. We don't ever want to see you again."

Both were happy with that. Cheeks flushed and trembling Fiona struggled to smile to signify compliance. Clarence ignored everything that was going on. He stared out across the river as memories of a long torturous time spent in a car with that bloke John flooded back. It really rattled him. Why could he never escape from that bloke John. He began to deflate as slowly, and methodically, he found it easy to recall events in his life which up to now had been shut away.

This cannot be invention, he thought. I'm remembering it. This was real. It's filling in all the blanks. I can even smell it. How can I remember a smell? That wasn't me talking was it? I don't talk like that. Perhaps I used to in front of the class when I had to impress but not now.

The fragments of his past were being reconnected up with those which had gone missing, to create once again one continuous stream of consciousness. The gaps in time were being squeezed out of existence. His life, in all its entirety was coming back together again, in a neat logical fashion. His mouth fell open as for the first time he remembered things he had said to Fiona. Then he felt miserable: seeing no way he could repeat such a performance; and not knowing if he wanted to. To add to that he felt physically shattered.

Fiona, seeing his pain, stood up and leaned over him. Using her stomach as a pillow she hugged him to her heart and planted a kiss, then another, on the top of his head. The young woman sitting at the far end of the table watched in wonder. She could have been taking notes. At this point in her life she could not see herself doing that for any man.

It warmed Clarence up by ten degrees or more. He took great pleasure from the attention but dared not show it. He wanted more of the same: a repeat performance, without the curtain ever coming down. And he would have got it had it not been for Tim reappearing with a pint of beer in each hand and a smug look on his face.

"Drink this Clarence. Then let's go home."

"Thanks mate."

"So what happened."

"I don't know."

"Well what the hell are you doing here? What are we doing here?"

"I don't know. That old woman wanted me to pay her a visit. So I did. I don't know why. But I feel better though. I just want to go home and go to sleep."

Tim was far from satisfied.

"After all you've put me through that's the best you can come up with?"

"Stop it with the questions Tim. He's in no fit state. He's completely shattered."

Clarence looked up at Fiona with a hangdog expression: she was rapidly becoming his guardian angel. He wanted to squeeze her waist and push his face deep into her stomach.

"Fair enough. Let's have a drink and then let's go. I would like to get home before dark."

Tim's next comment was aimed directly at Clarence.

"I want to see my wife. I hope she still wants to see me."

Clarence got the message and stared down at his feet, and the long grass which was being crushed underfoot. It was the trigger for the return of another lost memory: the walk in the countryside with that unhinged Rebecca. Try as he might he could not dismiss it. He could not devalue the experience. He had to admit it: he had enjoyed it. It had been an adventure, a bit of fun; despite the injury; despite her crazy stories.

"Of course she wants to see you Tim. Trust me. I know I'm right on that one."

"I hope so."

Fiona did not presume to ask what they were talking about but instead renewed her efforts to finish her drink. Likewise Clarence sipped on his beer and turned his attention on to the stretch of river. He made it his task to measure the speed of the moving water. Tim did his best to appreciate the scenery: but in his book grass was grass and water was water – nothing to make a fuss about.

"I drove out here with John right?"

"That's right."

"So where is he?"

"Back at the cottage."

"And I came to see this old lady?"

"Apparently."

Clarence gave up trying to work it out.

"Fuck it I want to go home." He drained his glass. "Come on Tim drink up. I want to go home."

Tim followed suit. Fiona did not attempt to finish hers.

"How did you two get here?"

"We came in my car," she explained.

"I want to go with you."

"You take it easy. I'm happy to drive," said Tim.

"No. I want to go home with Fiona. Just me and Fiona. You go with John. He won't make it home by himself."

Tim sniffed. "Well if that's the way you want it."

"He's right," said Fiona. "That way we all share the driving."

Tim was struck by a thought.

"Shit. We better get back there quick then."

Clarence, with the most vested interest, would have been up and out of his seat like a shot had it not been for the curse of the wooden bench. A pain shot up his backside.

"Ouch!"

"Careful."

"My bum. It's gone to sleep."

Clarence sat on his hands and tried to massage his buttocks free of the cramp.

"You always were a tight arse."

"Piss off Tim."

Now Tim knew things were getting back to normal.

Once Clarence could move again the three of them made their way back to the cottage, to see John standing outside. He was remonstrating with the daughter while her mother stood in the doorway wielding a big metal poker. The women were on the attack and John was fighting his corner and throwing a tantrum. He looked wasted.

Tim went to his rescue: he broke up the standoff by putting a hand on John's shoulder and gently leading him away from the frontline. The daughter went back indoors. The old woman shut the door, bolted it, and put the chain lock on.

"Come on John. Let me drive you home."

That might have been enough to put John some way back onto the path of recovery but then he saw Clarence and began to cry.

"He owes me the big apology! He lied to me!"

"And you'll get it, later. Like you he's in no fit state to do anything right now. So let me drive you home. We've got a long way to go and we're all knackered."

"Will he pay for my car?"

"I'm sure he will."

Tim was prepared to say anything that would get John into the car.

"You promise?"

"I promise."

It was enough. John got into the back of his car.

"I get to choose the music."

"Whatever you want. It's your car."

Loose end tied up, the four of them headed off home.

They arrived home late, exhausted. Each prayed never to have to go through another day like that. John slept most of the way back so Tim ended up doing all the driving. When Tim got home Sam gave the poor man a cup of tea and a sandwich as a thank you for returning her husband safely. She asked him to stay for dinner but John declined. He just wanted to go straight home and get into bed.

Clarence had much the same wish: except that he allowed Fiona to put him to bed; to cuddle him; to kiss him better; to put a glass of water by his side. She even picked up all his clothes which were scattered across the floor and stacked them up in a neat pile. And he loved every moment of it. She made herself a cup of coffee to see herself home and sat on the edge of the bed, sipping from her cup as she nursed him asleep. And he was in heaven. If he hadn't been so tired he would have attempted to chat her up, seduce her, make mad passionate love to her. When he finally nodded off she tucked him up, turned off all the lights and went home. In all this time Max was nowhere to be seen.

Chapter Twenty Two

The doorbell rang and made Clarence jump: off the bed and on to his feet, despite the fact he had been waiting for it to ring. He was expecting her. On his way to let her in he tried not to rush. He straightened up his clothes and tried to better arrange his hair and tried to not act too keen, appear too eager, give anything away. He only straightened up his clothes. He opened the door and smiled, like an idiot. Fiona smiled back, like a nurse.

"You look happy."

"I feel happy."

"Did you sleep well?"

"Like a log. Didn't wake up until gone noon."

Clarence carried on smiling, as did Fiona – but to a lesser degree – until she came to the conclusion that unless she took the initiative they would remain stuck there, smiling at each other until their faces wore out.

"Are you going to let me in?"

"Sorry of course."

Clarence stood back and Fiona took up the challenge. She had tidied her hair and was not acting too keen, too eager; and she had nothing to give away. She sat down on the sofa as directed whereupon Clarence hovered over her, waiting for her to start a conversation. This she did.

"You're feeling much better then?"

"Definitely."

"What makes you so sure?"

"Nothing is missing now. It's all come back. It's all in here." Clarence tapped his head. "And everything is sharper. The more I remember the more detail I discover. The more I look the more I see. I see you trying to measure me up."

In her defence Fiona crossed her legs and tried to laugh.

"I'm not measuring you. I just want to check up on how you are."

"Don't worry about it. It's not a criticism. It's a perfectly natural human action. I would expect nothing else."

Fiona blinked, twice, and let it pass.

"So how do you explain yesterday?"

"Yesterday?"

Clarence stuck his hands firmly into his trouser pockets, deep down, as far as they would go, and looked down at his sneakers as if to check they were still wrapped around his feet. They were.

"No idea. It just had to be done. It was like a release – for me and that woman. I had to go see that woman - she asked me to visit her you know."

"I know. I saw the letter."

"I felt better afterwards, much better. Reborn even!" Suddenly his eyes lit up. "Perhaps she's a witch!"

"I don't think so." Fiona was quite sure about that.

"No."

Clarence fell down next to her. He couldn't stand standing any longer while Fiona was sitting there, waiting to be sat next to. The momentum of his body weight delivered a small earthquake which shook her all over.

"Enough about me. I'm better. I feel better. Take my word for it. Time will prove me right."

"Your word is good enough for me right now."

"Thank you. Saying that means a lot to me." Clarence felt himself going all wobbly so quickly he changed the subject. "I rang the Head today."

"You rang the Head?"

"I'm seeing him tomorrow. Should be back on Wednesday."

"That's good. I'm pleased for you. I am. With you around perhaps Fairchild will get off my back."

"Has Ramsey been bothering you?"

"Only in the sense he keeps trying to impress me, be nice to me – it's embarrassing. He's asked me out twice. I haven't got the guts to tell him straight to his face that I don't fancy him. I pretended I was busy."

Suddenly Clarence began to scrutinize, and turned the screw on the conversation. It became tight.

"Why is that so difficult?"

Fiona caught the change of mood. The tables had turned: Clarence was checking her out. For now she could only repeat the question.

"Why is that so difficult?"

"You had the same difficulty with your ex- I think. Though this is nothing like on the same scale. Fundamentally though it is the same problem."

Fiona was hooked. Her other Clarence had returned: the one who never failed to truly excite her; the one who could jump right inside her head and still make her feel comfortable.

"You hate to hurt people's feelings? Even when you have a perfect, legitimate reason to do so? Even when it's in everybody's interest?"

Fiona could only smile, grin and bear it. But that aside his conjecture made her feel good. Clarence was back on top form. And it sounded like the truth. And that she could live with.

"A quality to be admired. Never lose it." Clarence crossed his legs. "I wish I could act the same."

And then he crossed his arms. He was tightening up, reigning in, creating distance; with all the conviction of a man who knew he was far from perfect. Fiona saw it, and was not prepared to let it happen. She put out a hand, demanding he reciprocate. He did. And they held hands.

"I think you are being too hard on yourself. And remember I did finally dump Chris so I can hurt feelings when I want to. He's gone now by the way, completely gone."

Her last remark carried the most weight but did not steer the conversation on to a new course. Clarence was still stuck on the old.

"I don't think so."

"You don't think so what?"

"I don't think I'm being too hard on myself. Not if you knew me half as well as I do."

"Meaning?"

"I'm lazy, a slob. I hate my job but haven't got the guts to do anything about it. And I don't understand women."

Fiona squeezed his hand. "That's rubbish. I can't accept that – certainly not the last one. You do understand women. You understand me."

Clarence was genuinely surprised. "Do I?"

"I think so. When you make the effort."

"When I make the effort."

Clarence considered her testimony and tried to chuckle but little came of it. "I'll try to make the effort more often then."

Clarence threw his head back. "Enough of me. I'm boring. I want to talk about you."

This time he did the squeezing. "How is it going at school. Are you settled in?"

"I think so. The routine is there now. I'm in a rhythm."

"The right rhythm? Not my rhythm I hope."

"Your rhythm?"

"Mind switched off, or on automatic. Watching the clock. Biting off the next fifteen minutes and forcing myself to swallow. Asking the same questions. Getting the same answers – or nothing. Marking the same scores. And all that despite the changing faces."

Fiona looked down, downcast and downbeat. "No. None of that. I enjoy teaching. My rhythm is . . ."

Fiona frowned. She was stuck so Clarence searched her face for clues.

"Is one of flowing contentment?"

Fiona lit up. "Beautifully put. And you say you don't understand women. You understand me!"

And now it was Clarence's turn to light up. He pulled her in close. She pulled him in close. He leaned over her. She leaned back. He put his free arm around her. She wrapped her free arm around his neck. They kissed. It was heaven. She leant back further. He leaned over her more, until he was almost on top of her. Suddenly sex and its execution was on the agenda.

Suddenly Fiona froze. "Is Max here!"

"No he's gone, for good. He left me a note saying thank you and goodbye – and he left me a bit of rent money."

Fiona loosened up again and Clarence kicked off again, his engine powered by pure lust. Then Fiona froze again and Clarence misfired on all cylinders.

"What? We're alone."

"I want to meet this Rebecca. That's the other reason why I came over today. I want to meet your friend Rebecca. She is your friend?"

Clarence disentangled himself and Fiona was able to breath easy again.

"Please, not her. She gives me nothing but grief."

"But hang on Clarence surely you gave her some grief? Grief of the highest order?"

Clarence looked puzzled, caught out.

"Tim showed me her letter."

"Ah."

"She is alright I take it. No harm done?"

"Yes she's fine – if fine is the right word. It was a false alarm."

"But what drove her to write such things?"

"I don't know."

But he did know and the look of torture which broke out across his face made it quite plain to Fiona that he did know.

"No. I do know."

Fiona took his hand again. "Tell me."

"It's simple really. I was too honest with her."

"Too honest?"

"She was all tangled up. She needed sorting out. I tried to untangle her, deconstruct her. And in the process I may have accidentally crushed her spirit, demolished her, cut her up into bits rather than carefully unpicking. I was direct rather than delicate. Also she had a crush on me: a misunderstanding which I had to correct. The truth hurt."

"Why did she have a crush on you?"

"I slept with her – just one once. It was a big mistake I assure you. It happened in a moment of weakness. I had drunk alcohol. I was feeling lonely, left out – by you – and I let my guard down. I'm only human – as we all are."

Clarence squeezed Fiona's hand again, as if to check it was still there.

"Can you forgive me? As I said I wasn't seeing you. I was feeling lonely."

Fiona found it easy to forgive him. She had to forgive him. He was absolutely right. He was only human. She had turned her back, if only briefly. She almost went so far as to take the blame but then reminded herself that no one was to blame. Such things just happened. It was her turn to squeeze.

"Of course. We're all only human."

Forgiveness requested and received, the two sank into silence and Clarence thought he was home and dry. He thought about the bedroom, and his bed, and making love in it, to Fiona. He made to lean over her again; to initiate a cuddle; to pick up where he had left off; but was stopped in his tracks by Rebecca.

"I still want to meet her. Check she's coping."

"Coping?"

"With life."

Clarence broke off physical contact. "I'm not sure she'll want to see me."

"Try your best."

"Try my best?" Clarence felt the words penetrate deep, far deeper than he would ever have imagined possible. After all they were only just words.

"Yes. You're right. I must try my best."

Without warning he uncoiled, sprang up, and headed for the door at extreme speed.

"Wait here. Don't move."

"I won't."

"Make yourself a cup of tea, or coffee."

Fiona heard the front door open. "I will."

The shouting began.

"Have a biscuit, or two!"

"I will!"

"And don't worry!"

"I won't!"

Fiona heard the front door close. She sat back, to wait. She felt full. Clarence was her man.

✦ ✦ ✦

Rebecca opened the door slowly, almost tripping over Judy who as usual was wrapping up around her ankles. She nearly closed it again when she saw who it was. Had she tried she would have failed as Clarence was holding his hand against the door. He was out of breath. She would soon be out of breath.

"So. You decided to see me again. How nice."

"Please don't send me away. I need to speak to you. Just a quick word."

"A word? What word? Is that all I'm worth? One word?"

"I was being rhetorical. Nobody on this planet is worth just one word. Please hear me out. I just want to say I really am truly truly sorry about all the things I have ever said to you. I never meant to leave you so distressed. I'm just too blunt sometimes. I say what I think should be said at the time without considering the consequences, without considering alternatives, without considering just saying nothing. I truly am sorry. I'm an idiot. But I am trying to change – I will change. I promise. I will change. If we can be friends you'll see the difference over time. I'm sure of it."

Rebecca stood back – nearly treading on her Judy – opened the door fully and allowed him to step inside to finish his speech. She did not want such things to be said in the street.

"You nearly broke me. I'm still mending."

"It was not my intention. I was just trying to throw some truth your way – truth as I saw it. Which of course I had no right to do. Truth is

• 604 •

yours to define, to protect, to live." Clarence came up for air. "Can we be friends?"

"I don't know. I'm not sure I can handle you."

"I have the same problem – but I'll change. I'm changing now. I've already changed a little. Just standing here and talking to you like this is changing me. I can feel it within me."

"You sound so sure. What makes you so sure?"

"Don't take my word for it. Ask Fiona."

"Fiona?"

"My friend." Clarence gulped down his next shot of air. "She's my girlfriend now."

"She's your girlfriend?"

"That's why I said what I said. I had been dishonest with you. It was a mistake. It should never have happened. She wasn't exactly my girlfriend at the time but I should have shown more patience, and waited, and not caved in to human weakness."

Rebecca waved to shut him up. "Why the book?"

"Why the book?"

Clarence thought back hard, but had to make something up. Or was it true? He couldn't tell.

"The book, yes. I thought – mistakenly now – that the book, following the sex, would help relax you, loosen you up. But it was a stupid mistake, a grand imposition. I can see that now. It was a totally stupid act, an idiotic act."

Clarence paused, breathed out, and dropped his voice to a whisper.

"I'm ashamed of myself. You're a far better person than me. After all you've been through you have a perfect right to be fragile, to contemplate, to avoid. So don't take any notice of what idiots like me say. I don't know anything."

Clarence held out a hand.

"So can we be friends? I really want us to be friends. Because sex is not getting in the way friends can do a lot together. Far more than lovers."

Clarence gulped again. And Rebecca could see that he wanted to cry. And that made her want to cry. There was no fighting his avalanche of words. Only Judy was left feeling cheerful. She meowed. Something was in the air.

At a stroke the slate was wiped clean of poor past performances and the clock was reset. There was hard work ahead.

"Promise you'll be nice to me?"

"I promise."

"And we can go walking together?"

"Definitely. I'd like that."

"This Fiona won't mind?"

"She won't mind. Perhaps she can come with us if that's alright by you?"

"Of course she can." Rebecca drew her conclusion, like a five year old clutching a crayon. "Okay we can be friends then."

Clarence breathed a big sigh of relief. "Thank you."

Then he remembered Fiona sitting all by herself, perhaps sipping a cup of tea and nibbling a stale old biscuit. He arrested Rebecca's hand.

"Come on. I want you to meet Fiona right now. So we can all be friends starting today, starting right now."

Rebecca was happy for her hand to be arrested. She was happy for him to lead the way. She was swept off her feet. Cheerfully, job done, bridges rebuilt, Clarence led the way until he was stopped by the sight of William loitering outside his front door, wondering whether to ring the bell or not. He was loitering without intent.

Clarence allowed Rebecca's hand to slip from his grasp. Rebecca almost walked into him. She spoke first.

"I know him."

"So do I."

"I know you do."

Together they watched the boy until the boy spotted them at which point both pretended to have just caught sight of him. William knew it was all fake but didn't care. That was the way adults acted to keep reinventing themselves. Clarence was forced to interact. He walked up to William and said hello - 'hello' being the obvious thing to say.

"Hello."

"Hello."

"What is it this time?"

The question could not be answered, at least not so directly and not so immediately. William gnawed at his lower lip with his upper teeth and pretended to consider, to act cool. He could only consider and contest his confusion.

"Is there something you want to tell me?"

William had something to say but wasn't sure exactly what it was or if he wanted to say it now. Nothing was right right now. Clarence sensed the stalemate. Best back off, give space, he thought.

"Look, wait here a mo. I'll be right back."

Clarence wanted to dash back indoors. He had only left Fiona alone for a few minutes – ten at the most – but it felt like a few hours. He could not leave her alone that long. She might die. He might die. He had to dash back indoors and save her from the crushing conveyor belt of moving time. This he did, and he found her exactly where he had left her. She was sipping a glass of water. No biscuit. No protest. Fiona looked up and smiled.

"Just wanted to check you were okay."

Fiona didn't get it. "Of course I'm okay. Why wouldn't I be?"

"Don't know. Just me being silly I suppose." Clarence looked at the glass of water. "Is water all you need? I've got tea or coffee."

"Water's all I need."

"Sure?"

"Sure."

The answer satisfied and as Clarence thought about his next move so Rebecca walked in, casually, as if she owned the place. Without warning and without waiting for permission she exchanged quick fire introductions with Fiona.

"Hello."

"Hello."

"He says his mother is not 'acting right'. 'Something is wrong with her.' His words, not mine. He wants you to see her. I think he blames you."

"Understood. I'll take him home now."

Clarence looked around, searching. He was searching for his ubiquitous mobile.

"Where's my mobile?" It was not to be seen. "Must be in my bedroom."

On his way out of the room Clarence stopped and did an about turn.

"Oh by the way. Fiona this is Rebecca. Rebecca this is Fiona."

They both said hello again, this time solely for his benefit.

"Hello."

"Hello."

The exchange made Clarence feel better, as if he was in charge of events. He found his mobile and then went on to link up with his keys and wallet.

"Can I leave you two alone together? I won't be long. I'll be straight back. Promise."

"We'll be fine," said Fiona.

"Don't worry about me," added Rebecca.

Clarence had no intention of worrying about her – in his mind that part was over – but did not say so: sometimes best to hold the truth back. He looked around the room, afraid he had forgotten something, afraid he would lose something; then left, abruptly, without saying another word. Speed and silence: together they provided the least painful method of self-extraction. Let the women sort themselves out, he heard himself say inside his head. They didn't need him – at least not right now, he pretended.

Back outside in the fading sunlight he found William where he had left him: still looking like he had been suddenly transplanted in time and space against his will; still looking like he had been logged off against his will. Funny, thought Clarence, that's how I used to feel up to yesterday afternoon. He scooped the child up and dumped him in his car for the ride home.

On the way home William found it easier to speak. Perhaps it was the fact that he was caught in motion, on the move. Perhaps it was because the music playing was shaking him up, shaking him loose. Perhaps it was because he could not be overheard. Perhaps it was because Clarence looked like he was listening. Clarence was listening: he was listening to the radio but was more than willing to switch to William when William was ready to speak. When the end of a track was reached Clarence threw a pebble into the pond.

"How are things at home? Everything alright? Everything the same?" It was a rock.

William stared out of the window. She would be home now and wondering where he was. She would have started making dinner. He was in trouble.

"Same as what?"

"Same as it always was."

"Not the same."

"Different then. In what way different?"

Clarence was made to wait while William looked for differences. They got through half the next track and a bit of DJ waffle before William spoke.

"She doesn't make the food with fun anymore."

"Anything else?"

"She doesn't chase me over homework."

"Are you doing all your homework?"

William was insulted and made his feelings plain. "Yes. Why wouldn't I be?"

For Clarence that was water off a duck's back.

"Well it sounds like she doesn't need to chase over homework."

"That's not the point."

Privately Clarence agreed. That wasn't the point.

"And when I tell about what went on at school she only pretends to listen. I can tell she's not interested." William had got going. "She acts tired all the time. She acts like my grandmother."

William fell silent. He had said enough. Let others pick it up and sort it out. It wasn't his job.

Clarence kept note inside his head and the rest of the journey was spent in silence – except for when Clarence swore at another motorist and William told him off for swearing – except for when William caught Clarence using his mobile at the traffic lights.

"But I was calling your mother."

"That's no excuse."

On reaching home William was up and out and off before Clarence could register the fact or engage the handbrake. He was unsure whether to get out himself or try and stay hidden, incognito. Drive home? Wait? He decided to wait: the news on the hour would keep him company; and to leave so soon would be like running away from something. He watched William search his pockets for his key – not necessary: the door opened all by itself. William was not surprised to see his mother. Mary was not surprised to see her son. She looked at him, intently, and took measurements. He did not look at her. He pocketed his key and waited; and when he saw his chance he rushed inside, to disappear upstairs and into his bedroom, and from there into a world of his own making.

Mary looked across at Clarence and the two engaged. He got out of his car and approached, with respect and with caution. He didn't why – he had no reason – but he felt unable to speak. Luckily Mary spoke first. And as luck would have it she did not put a question, just a statement requiring not even a comment.

"I'm sorry about this. Has William been bothering you?"

In a change of heart Clarence wanted to answer. He wanted to talk. He wanted to talk about anything.

"It's no bother. Honest." It was not enough: Clarence felt compelled to say more. "Your son can pop round anytime he likes."

As the last word dribbled from his mouth Clarence felt himself being struck dumb by his own words – words which had sounded noble as they were spoken but now just sounded stupid, which in turn reflected badly on him. Mary smiled and saw that he was being too hard on himself.

"If you're in no rush I can make you a cup of tea."

She sounded tired. Talking was tiring her out.

"I'm in no rush."

Mary turned and led the way and Clarence followed. A cup of tea was not on his mind. Nothing was. He was temporarily lost. On her way to the kitchen Mary paused at the foot of the stairs and shouted, with substance but without style.

"William would you like a cup of tea!"

William flatly refused. "No!"

She carried on to the kitchen, not caring, with Clarence always one step behind and starting to care.

In the kitchen food was out and about. It had been released, for cooking, for consumption. Mary was in the middle of preparing dinner for two, as she had always done, ad infinitum. It was routine: sometimes heavy; sometimes light; sometimes nasty; sometimes nice. Today, like yesterday, and much like the day before, it had started off heavy, and had become heavier. Her son had thrown her schedule only a little but it was enough, enough to transform a straightforward, proven piece of work into a complicated piece of hard work.

Like Judy Clarence knew immediately there was something in the air. It had no substance. It had no smell. But it had gravity and it was not nice. He bided his time and watched Mary, the dispossessed mother and housewife, struggle to make a pot of tea while trying to pick up where she had left off thirty minutes earlier. Clarence decided not to change his mind and decline the offer. He could see that Mary was determined to make tea, both for herself and for her guest. Mary was not to be messed with: she would make tea, for herself and for her guest. Meanwhile some fishfingers sat hidden beneath the grill in the oven, slightly cooked; once warmed up but now cold again.

Once the hot water was in the pot and she had stirred the tea leaves into submission Mary put the grill back on. And then there were the greens and the peas and the real mash potato she was determined to make by mashing real potatoes, the way her mother did it. The potatoes were sitting in a pot of lukewarm water. It had been boiling away once. Mary turned the gas ring back on again, full. In between attending to her pot of tea and her guest she began working on slicing up her greens: removing all the bits both she and her son did not like and did not want to see, taste or swallow. That was the greenery rule.

Clarence sat motionless in his designated place, in his self-imposed state, wondering whether to offer a helping hand while at the same time reminding himself that he would very likely be more of a hindrance than a help, a distraction for her. He watched Mary suddenly jumped over to the door and shout, impressed by her speed and manoeuvrability. The woman could move when she wanted to. And she could shout. She reminded him of his mother: in her younger days his mother could shout.

"William dinner will be ready in ten minutes!"

Mary got no reply, which was quite normal.

Tea made and poured and secured on saucers, and the matter of milk and sugar sorted, Mary finally allowed herself the luxury of sitting down next to Clarence, to allow herself – and him – to speak, to make polite conversation. Unfortunately she did not have much to say at that point in time, which was a shame as recently she had had lots to say, just no one to say it to.

"Is the tea good?"

"The tea if fine. No perfect." Clarence manage to stop himself saying the tea was beautiful.

Mary fell silent. She had run out of words, even simple little easy ones which made up small talk so effortlessly. Clarence took over.

"What's for dinner?"

"Fishfingers. Tuesday is always fishfingers."

"But it's Monday?"

Clarence felt uneasy about correcting her. She might take it the wrong way. She might fly off the handle. She didn't. He was overreacting.

"Sorry. Monday is fishfingers."

Clarence smiled at her cup of tea. It seemed to be the safest place to plant his smile. She pushed her cup and saucer away. It was as if she no longer wished to be associated with the contents, despite all the hard work she had put into making it. But she continued to stare at it. For his part Clarence took a sip of tea. It really did taste good.

"I'm feeling a lot better by the way."

Mary looked up. She looked relieved: one less thing to worry about, possibly.

"Really?"

"A lot better. I'm one hundred percent certain the blackouts have gone, for good, vanished. They won't come back. Never. That's a promise. And I can remember lots of things which had just disappeared from my memory, from my consciousness."

"Hence the blackouts."

"Hence the blackouts. The blackouts are being plugged."

"And it's all gone you think?"

"Think? I know. It's all gone. I feel one hundred and ten percent."

For Mary, Clarence was not prepared to be anything less than totally positive. For some strange reason he felt that was what she needed from him right now.

"I'm glad. I really am glad for you." Mary spoke in earnest. "Honest I really am glad for you."

Clarence was confused. He didn't expect her to be any other way.

"I know you are."

"Good. That's good."

He left it there and she looked around the kitchen, stopping to stare here and there. Things needed doing, attending to. Things needed synchronising. Things needed washing up, cutting up, getting out, putting back, cooked, served up.

"Will you excuse me why I get on?"

"Of course. You go ahead. Don't mind me."

Mary stopped suddenly; slowed herself right down; thought of her question; built up her courage; and put the question.

"Would you care to join us for dinner?"

His response was automatic. "Sorry I can't. I've got my own guests waiting for me back home."

Clarence didn't think about his answer. He didn't want to think about it. That would prove too difficult.

"No matter." It did matter.

Mary tried to concentrate on cooking dinner but now everything was proving more difficult – even more difficult since William had fled upstairs and Clarence had come indoors for a cup of tea. Things had been difficult before then, just as they had been the day before and the day before that and the day before that and so on – or at least that was how it felt. Should I offer him a biscuit? she thought. Should I offer him a biscuit? Is he expecting a biscuit with his cup of tea? Does he prefer to drink out of a mug? I can't remember, she admitted to herself.

"Would you like a biscuit with that mug – sorry I mean cup of tea?"

"A biscuit? A biscuit would be lovely. I never bother with biscuits at home." Clarence quickly did a correction. "But a biscuit would be lovely."

"I'll get you a biscuit."

Mary fought hard to think hard to remember where the biscuit tin was located. She was determined to put a biscuit into the hands of her guest Clarence. He was a special guest. She remembered! And darted across the kitchen floor to the cupboard in question. The biscuit tin was not there. That fact struck her hard.

"The biscuit tin isn't there."

Clarence cringed. "It's no problem. I don't need a biscuit."

Mary wasn't having it. "It's alright I know where it is. Hang on a moment."

She left the room and Clarence was left to ponder the importance of tea and biscuits in everyday life. He was not stranded up a mountain with no hope of rescue, freezing to death while drinking his last cup of tea and saying what a privilege it had been . . . No a biscuit was not that important right now. Something is wrong here, thought Clarence. Something is wrong. So what do I do about it? What do I do about it? He had no answer. He was interrupted by the sound of Mary shouting from the foot of the stairs.

"William have you got the biscuit tin!"

No reply.

Mary repeated herself. "William I said have you got the biscuit tin!"

Still no reply.

This she was not prepared to tolerate.

Clarence heard her march – no storm, like a storm trooper – up the stairs. Then he heard her bang on a door. After that he lost track. His attention was drawn to the peeled and chopped potatoes. They were boiling away like mad in their pot and they were falling apart. They had his sympathies but not his help. He did not want to get involved. Trying to help around her kitchen – with or without the woman's permission – was now well outside his comfort zone he had concluded. Stay safe: keep it simple. Stay simple: keep safe.

Clarence just made out the sound of Mary speaking, in a raised voice, in a way which for him was alien, a new experience, and totally discomforting: Mary sounded angry, harassed, impatient, at odds with something – presumably her son. He didn't like it: Mary had lost her temper; Mary was losing it. Clarence got up: but with nowhere or no one to turn to he was forced to sit down again.

Like a grand army Mary came marching back down the stairs. Clarence got up again as she entered the room. Mary was holding a tin. It was labelled biscuits. It was the infamous biscuit tin. It had witnessed many battles, many wars; and it had the dents to prove it.

Mary ripped off its lid and held it out. "Here have a biscuit."

"Thank you."

Clarence grabbed at the nearest one and dunked it straight into his tea without first checking whether it was suited for dunking. Luck was on his side: it was. He sat back down and bit into his soggy biscuit. Mary copied him: she took a biscuit, any biscuit, and dunked it. Clarence now felt himself stranded on top of a mountain, against his will; freezing and sipping his last cup of tea while others had buggered off without him. He decided to make a helpful suggestion.

"I think your potatoes are more than done."

Mary jumped up. "Oh Jesus!"

She turned off the gas ring and she got on. "Greens. I still have to do the greens."

She got stuck into her greens – nothing less than fresh greens. Some still needed cutting up. Then she stopped again.

"Excuse me."

"Sure."

Clarence watched her, spellbound, as she stormed out of the kitchen again: then listened, still spellbound, as she shouted out from the foot of the stairs again.

"William are you coming down! Dinner in five minutes!"

Clarence was starting to see the pattern. Mary marched upstairs again – it kept her fit - and boldly Clarence helped himself to another biscuit. He felt it to be the honourable thing to do. This one he did not dunk. He bit on it slowly and felt it snap roughly in two between his teeth. Bachelor heaven, he thought. Perhaps there was a bachelor heaven.

When Mary reappeared – looking more flustered, more aggravated, more overdue, more overworked, more underpaid, less appreciated, less enamoured with her current job role and position – Clarence stood up again, this time almost to attention, as if awaiting detention. He was not relaxed. Mary had not been relaxed for ages.

"I'm sorry about this. I can't get him out of his room."

"Don't apologize." Clarence was suddenly hit by an awful thought. Is it me?

"Would it be better if I left? Does he want me to leave?"

"No certainly not."

She might be lying, thought Clarence. She might by lying.

"It's not a problem honest." Clarence held out his cup. "Look I've almost finished my cup of tea – and I've had a biscuit. I won't feel insulted if you want me to go. Just tell me to go if I'm the problem."

"No no certainly not. You're not the problem. I want you to be here. I like the company."

That said, Mary stopped in her tracks, feeling extremely embarrassed, like she had let everything out of the bag, like she had let her hair down and thrown it about – and even giggled. Clarence also stopped in his tracks, unsure how to respond: but only because he was fully aware of how she was feeling straight after her outburst. And secretly he was proud: proud that he was in tune. He didn't know what was going on but he knew he was in tune. And that made him feel good.

Mary returned to slicing up her remaining big green leaf. When it was done she banged the kitchen counter with the butt of her knife handle.

"About time! Greens ready for microwave."

Clarence wasn't sure whether to join in the celebration. Perhaps clap? In the end he decided on passing a simple aside.

"Well done. What's next?"

Mary looked around, almost hopelessly. "Peas. Frozen peas. I need to get some peas out."

"In the fridge?"

"No in the freezer."

"Sorry of course."

Clarence felt required to explain himself, lest she think him stupid.

"I only have an icebox at home. No fridge freezer."

Mary was not listening. She went for her peas like a big cat goes for the kill. She grabbed them and began ripping open the packet as she crossed the floor, intentions not yet known. She just felt she had to cross the kitchen floor. She needed somewhere to go: keep on moving; keep busy; don't stop for fear of not restarting. It was an approach which had served her well and which worked most of the time. But not today.

Mary spun round. "Blast I forgot the fishfingers."

She rushed forward to turn on the grill and in doing so spilt frozen peas across the floor: lots of peas; about one third of the packet. Frozen, they could travel far and wide. And they did.

Clarence watched them roll and scatter. Had it been him at home he would have sworn loudly and kicked something then perhaps, if it was a particularly bad day, have given up and grabbed a beer from the fridge. Today, in this place, he contained himself: and he was highly conscious of the fact that he could do that without difficulty.

"Oh hell!" screamed Mary.

She threw her hands up into the air, on her way letting the rogue packet fall on to the kitchen counter. She had given up on peas. No peas for William tonight. Greens or nothing. Fishfingers or nothing.

Clarence did not like it now when she swore. He looked at the potatoes sitting steaming in the pan. It was now drained of water but still he felt they should not just be left sitting there. 'Mashed potato' she had said. He decided not to mention it. Frozen peas were the problem right now.

"Here let me help you pick these up."

"No certainly not. You are my guest. This is my job."

"No I insist. This is nobody's job."

Clarence crouched down and started picking up peas. Mary began to kneel then changed her mind and sat down instead. She had slowed. She had stopped. All she could do was watch Clarence pick up peas. He wasn't very good at it and soon his legs and back were aching and he was in obvious trouble – and one hand was full of unpleasant peas: weighed down it was by a clutch of cold peas; some still frozen, others thawing in the heat of the palm of his hand. Mary had to stop him. She could not take it anymore. She waved one hand.

"No stop there Clarence. Stop there. Forget about the peas. You've done enough. I'll sweep them aside with the broom, into a corner, then deal with them later."

Relieved that he had been relieved of his duties, Clarence collapsed back into his chair. It was his chair now and it felt good, like home. The poisoned peas he dropped into his cup. He was rid of them. He rubbed his knee joints – slightly playing it up to maximise the sympathy vote from the woman in the audience. Mary was not smiling. Clarence felt the air turning heavy again. Thunder might strike. Time to say something humorous, he thought.

"Dangerous things peas. A real headache sometimes. Especially the frozen ones."

Mary took no notice, which disappointed him. She was just staring at the potatoes waiting to be mashed up. There was a blank look on her face begging for mercy. It was the look – or rather the 'non-look', the 'negative look' – of total dejection. Clarence knew he had to come to her aid.

"Let me mash those potatoes for you. I want to mash your potatoes."

Mary shook her head and spoke softly. "No."

Clarence stood up, trying to look defiant, in charge.

"But I like mashing potatoes." As a kid, and thereafter, he had always preferred chips.

But Mary was not having it. "No. It's my job. Sometimes it's William's job. If the homework is finished."

Before he could reply Mary jumped up again and went to the door. Not being at the foot of the stairs she shouted, louder.

"William are you doing homework?"

"Yes!"

He may have been lying but Mary really didn't care. She had just felt required to put the question. She sat back down again and switched off again. Like any mobile phone she could automatically switch back into low energy, sleep mode after making a loud, shrill noise in the cause of human communication. Clarence also sat down. When Mary was sitting down he felt like a prat standing up. He waited for the silence to settle in then decided to break it, on his terms.

"Forgive me for speaking out of turn but I think there is something wrong."

Clarence tiptoed through the tulips.

"There is something wrong isn't there?"

He could see by the movements on Mary's face – all small and subtle but he caught them all and saw them for what they were – that she wanted to let go of something: that something was hurting her, dragging her down, and making her a drag in the eyes of her one single, most beloved child.

He wanted to take hold of her, but dare not.

She wanted to tell him everything, anything, but could not.

They both stared down at the peas on the floor, and by the door.

In the main they were still frozen.

He wanted her to divulge but did not want to intrude.

She wanted to spill her guts but did not want to indulge.

In the main they were still frozen.

Clarence decided to start again.

"What would you like for your birthday? I would like to buy you something for your birthday."

Mary glanced across at him, as if totally baffled by a new concept. Perhaps she was. In turn Clarence was also baffled. Had he spoken badly, out of turn? Or perhaps there was a simpler explanation.

"It is your birthday on Friday, right?"

Mary nodded and drew in breath. It was as if he had reminded her of some enormous, overdue task ahead: like the next clothes wash; or top to bottom hoovering; or taking the car in for its annual service and MOT; or anything except her next birthday.

Reassured that he had got his facts right, Clarence pushed on.

"I would like to get you something. It would make me feel good all over."

"I don't need anything."

"You must need something. Everyone needs something."

"Well if I do I can't think of it right now."

Clarence persisted. "Well when you do you let me know. It doesn't matter if Friday's come and gone. I want to buy you something."

Clarence went for the heavy impact in the hope of stirring Mary up.

"I demand it. I demand the right to buy you a birthday present."

Mary did not respond. She did not stir. She was already stirred up inside but not on the subject of birthday presents, and especially not on the subject of her birthday. For years now another birthday in her life meant another year had slipped by, which meant one year less ahead, which meant one year less in which to break out and do . . . she didn't know what. That was where the trail went cold. She shivered. The thoughts were cold, too cold.

Clarence leaned over and took her hand. He did it automatically. He did not have to think about it. He was not nervous even though the stakes were high

- far higher than they had ever been with Tracey
- far higher than they could ever be with Fiona
- and in a different but less dangerous way, higher than they might be with Rebecca were he ever to accidentally hold her hand again.

Through his hand she held on to him.

"Is William causing you problems?"

Clarence did know a bit about teenage kids. He had to reign in the wild animals for a living. They could be terrors: tearaways; tempestuous; temporarily tearful, rarely timid; taking everything, giving nothing. They could be rogue traders: trading emotions as they fed on frenzy; trading insults and ingratitude behind one's back. They were all round trouble.

Mary dismissed that suggestion immediately. "No."

A long pause followed. Clarence kept his head down and waited. He knew something was coming over that universal hill which separated two or more souls.

"It's just me."

"It's just you? Why what have you done?"

Mary jerked her head as if an accusation had been made, as if out of the blue she had been arrested.

"Me? I've done nothing."

Accusation denied and discounted, Mary deflated again and looked back down at the peas. They were beginning to thaw. And then things began to slip out.

"That's all I do. Nothing. Just the same old thing over and over again."

"I don't understand." Clarence did understand but wanted her to talk on and talk it out.

"Same things."

"What same things?"

"Work. Commute. Feed William. Tidy the house. Feed William. Get up. Go to bed. Do the washing. Do the ironing. Try to help William with his homework."

Mary stalled. Her list had dried up. "That sort of thing."

Clarence squeezed her hand: it was as much an act of pleasure for him as it was for her.

"That's nothing. That's a lot. That's tonnes more than I could ever manage."

Mary gave him a queer look.

Oh God, thought Clarence, she thinks I'm patronising her. She wasn't but he was taking no chances.

"That wasn't meant to sound patronising."

"I know it wasn't. You would never do that to me."

"I . . ." Clarence stumbled. "I just wanted to remind you – all of us – just how much you carry on your shoulders. It's bound to get you down from time to time."

Clarence felt good about what he had just said. He felt good about himself. He was talking total sense. Mary had yet to catch him up. She was the one suffering turmoil. It would take more than a straight statement of facts to recover her, to make her well and fighting fit again.

"That's easy for you to say."

"I know it is. But that's not the point."

"No. I'm sorry. It's not. Sorry I didn't mean to have a go at you."

This time Clarence shook her hand and half her arm into submission.

"Have a go at me if it makes you feel better. That's what I'm here for silly."

The action, the motion of joined up limbs, managed to extract a smile from her.

"It's not just the workload, the schedule, the nine to five. It's the pretence."

"The pretence? What pretence?"

"William. I must always be my best, look my best for William. I must always be in charge, for William. I must always be ready, for William."

Mary wanted to bury her face into Clarence and cry it out.

"William is my son, my only son."

Clarence bit on the inside of his cheek, trying hard to think of something to say next which would be classed as worthy, enlightening, noble and above all useful. He was now setting his sights high, towards the heavens. Mary deserved no less.

As Clarence did not immediately reply and the silence returned so Mary began to panic: she had said too much; she had let too much out of her bag; he thought she was a sad washed up old has-been. She was wrong of course on all accounts. But to make things worse Clarence let go of her hand, stood up, and leaned against the kitchen table; folding his arms in the process. When he finally spoke it was because he had something important to say. He stared down. She looked up. Clarence was now her lifeline, her lifeboat. But he was not her man.

"Look William is what, fourteen?"

"Thirteen."

"Right. William is thirteen."

Clarence paused. He had lost his rhythm. Then William came storming downstairs. Gravity was on his side. Like approaching thunder he was heard by all. Clarence kept his mouth shut. Mary waited for the storm to arrive. William stormed in. He wanted orange juice – in the carton or in a glass, he didn't care – or a coke. Clarence stopped him in his tracks. Clarence was teacher again.

"Just give us a moment please will you William?"

William froze then began to twist round towards his mother. Too stunned to object he looked at his mother, looking for help or guidance. The expression on her face made it clear that she was not in dispute with Clarence – Clarence the intruder – nor his firm instruction. William wanted her to say something. She didn't. So he gave Clarence one long hard look, turned around, and ran off back upstairs. The staircase took a real hammering, as did his opinion of that Clarence.

Clarence started again. "William is thirteen. Right?"

"Right."

"He's at that age when he can take a lot more than what your giving him."

"You mean housework?"

"No I don't mean housework or cooking or washing up – though there's no harm done if you want to share some of that."

It was now the turn of Clarence to focus on the peas. Those peas had to be picked up or swept out of sight before they drove him mad.

"I mean . . ." Clarence had lost his position again. He had to go back slightly.

"William is at the age when he can share a lot more grown up problems and hassles and hardships; the stuff you try to bury. Share a bit with him. Get it off your chest. Tell him when your tired and need to be left alone in peace and quiet. Tell him he needs to be more in charge of himself. Yes and start teaching him to cook things, even if it's just simple things. Perhaps even tell him he has to look after his own room from now on. Tell him you can't do it all by yourself. You need a break. You've earned a break."

He had finished speaking: Clarence was pleased with himself. It was a big leap and Mary would need time to take it all in, to accept a shift in the universe, to adjust. Mary jumped up.

"Fishfingers! My fishfingers are burning!"

She jumped over to the oven, threw on an oven glove and whipped out the tray. They had just started to burn but beyond the black they were still edible. Clarence also jumped into gear and the conversation evaporated. They were back to cooking dinner. This time Clarence was determined to do something useful and make a contribution.

"I'll mash the potatoes. You stick your greens in the microwave. You put butter over your mash yes?"

"Yes."

"Butter's in the fridge?"

"No on the counter over there." Mary pointed.

"Where's the thingy to mash with?"

"In that draw."

Mary put the tray back in the oven: the grill was now off and the open door meant they would stay warm but not cook further. Clarence mashed his potatoes like they were the most important potatoes in the world and Mary attended to greens and everything else which went into putting a decent meal on the table in front of her son. She made one last visit to the foot of the stairs, to shout the obvious one last time.

"William! Food! Now! Homework can wait!"

"Coming!" When it came to the bottom line William knew the score.

Back in the kitchen Mary turned back on Clarence.

"Please stay for dinner with us? Please?"

Clarence struggled with his answer. It was 'no'. He didn't want to say no but he had no choice. He held on. It was almost destroying him on the spot.

"I wish I could but I have to say no. I've got people waiting for me. They're expecting me." Carefully he avoided the use of the word 'women'.

Mary gave up. "I understand. You go."

"But I'll come back and finish that tiling a.s.a.p."

"No need. I've got someone in. He doesn't speak very good English but a friend recommended him."

"Let me pay half then."

Mary stepped back. "No I couldn't take your money."

Clarence stepped forward and closed the distance which had opened up.

"Yes you can. Take it. I demand it. It's a birthday present."

Mary backed down. She did not want to get into a fight – certainly not with Clarence of all people.

"Okay then. Thank you. That's very kind of you. But I can afford it you know. I don't need charity."

Clarence wanted to thump the table. Instead he came over all insistent and strong.

"It's not charity. I want to have the pleasure of giving you a present and this is the way I want to do it. Handing over money is not very imaginative but in these circumstances I think it's fine, just right, spot on even. It nicely wraps things up."

Mary threw up her hands. "Okay I accept. Thank you."

"Thank you. Now I must go."

Clarence was loathed to go. It was a drag. He wanted to stay and eat fishfingers around the table with the best of them. But he had to go. He dragged himself away, out the kitchen door, to the front door; all by himself as Mary could not leave the kitchen. (And secretly she could not face seeing him off: she might come over all tearful and she didn't want to be seen like that.) At the door, about to drag himself back outside, Clarence took a peep up the stairs. Mary was right. Life was a drag sometimes. He caught William flying out of his room and down the stairs. William slammed on the brakes: that Clarence was in his way.

Clarence had a simple question. "You okay?"

"Yeah."

"Sure?"

"Yeah."

"Okay. See you."

"See you."

Clarence closed the door behind him. It was a drag. William went after his fishfingers. They were a drag.

Clarence didn't want to walk to his car. It was a drag. He walked to his car. Clarence didn't want to get in his car. It was a drag. Clarence got in his car. Clarence sat and stared at the mobile phone on the dashboard. It was a drag. He looked down. There a small white dice sitting in the tray along with dirt, fluff and some screwed up credit card receipts. Clarence felt he had more to say. Clarence felt Mary had more to say. It was a drag.

Clarence looked up at the mobile phone. It was still a drag. He picked it up, along with the dice and got out of the car, pretending to himself that he needed to get a better signal. (He hadn't turned it on yet.) The car was still a drag. He stood gripping his mobile and stared at the front door. It was closed now: which was a drag. But then Fiona was waiting for him. But then Rebecca might still be there: which was a drag. He wanted to make love to Fiona. He wanted to eat fishfingers with Mary, even with William if he had to. It was all a drag.

With his spare hand he fingered his dice and rolled it around in between his thumb and the end of his fingers, like it was a diamond or a gold coin. His spare was not so spare. While rolling dice he nearly dropped his mobile. It was a drag.

He stopped playing games with the dice and looked at it for the last time. It had six sides, one to six: which was a drag. He corrected himself. It had two sides, even and odd: which was perfect. He threw it high up into the air and watched to see where it would land.

Printed in the United Kingdom by
Lightning Source UK Ltd., Milton Keynes
138616UK00001B/291/P